ANDERSON UNIVERSITY
D0914631

le MAISTRE ARGENTIER du ROY
JEAN de VILLAGE
JACQVES COEVR

PS 3505 .062 M66 1947
Costain, Thomas Bertram
Moneyman

THE MONEYMAN

BOOKS BY

THOMAS B. COSTAIN

The Moneyman

The Black Rose

Ride with Me

For My Great Folly

Joshua: A Study in Leadership

(in collaboration with Rogers MacVeagh)

THE MONEYMAN

THOMAS B. COSTAIN

GARDEN CITY, N. Y.
DOUBLEDAY & COMPANY, INC.
1947

PRINTED IN THE UNITED STATES
AT
H. WOLFF, NEW YORK

To

NELSON DOUBLEDAY

INTRODUCTION

STORIES speak for themselves and so an author's preface is, in most cases, superfluous. When the setting is historical, however, there are certain explanations which become necessary. It must be made clear to the reader where history ends and the work of the romancer begins and also which of the characters are real and which fictitious. With this as my excuse, I wish to point out that the story of Jacques Coeur, the Moneyman (L'Argentier) of Charles the Seventh of France; as set down in the pages which follow, adheres to the record as closely as possible. Some liberties have been taken in the matter of time sequences and, because the chronicles of the day are both scanty and full of gaps, it has been necessary to draw on the imagination for some of the details with which the bare skeleton of known facts has been fleshed and clothed.

It is surprising how little has been written about some phases of the career of the great Moneyman. Monstrelet and his fellow scribes of the day went to great pains to set down the activities of unimportant knights and to tell of the daily lives of dull kings and stupid princes but they seem to have been lightly concerned with the spectacular career of Jacques Coeur. There would be little known about his trial were it not for the happy discoveries of C. Joseph Jacques, as given in his *Un Scandale judiciaire au moyen âge*. Even with the explanation M. Jacques supplies of the parts played by Robert de Poitevin and Ferrand de Cordule, it has been necessary to reconstruct the scene and to invent more tangible and believable evidence.

Those who approach the past with reverence for the traditions of chivalry will perhaps object to the part I have given that great paladin, Jacques de Lalain. He devoted himself exclusively to challenge encounters with other knights (like the barnstorming prizefighters of the present day) but he did not fight the Sire d'Arlay, for the very good reason that the Sire d'Arlay had no existence in fact. I conceived the duel as necessary to point up the absurdity and the unfairness of the chivalrous practices of the day. As Jacques de Lalain was the recognized champion and, as a close study of his career had convinced me he would have behaved in exactly this way in the given circumstances, I cast him in the role of the bully who refused to fight for France but was ready to fight on any other pretext.

I have striven to give a faithful picture of Agnes Sorel, that lovely and unfortunate lady, and of Charles the Well Served. Robert de Poitevin lived and played his courageous part as described in the drama of the trial, as did Jeanne de Vendôme and Guillaume Gouffier, the villains of the piece. As Valerie Maret and D'Arlay and the Comte and Comtesse de Burey are fictitious characters, it follows that the train of events in which they are depicted as playing parts has been invented to supply a note of lightness and romance in what might otherwise be a grim story.

THOMAS B. COSTAIN

BOOK ONE

Chapter I

I

THE ROYAL STANDARD of France waved above the towers of the Louvre. It was an unusual sight, for the King bore Paris no love and seldom came there. The citizens, as might be expected, were making a carnival of it and the streets were filled with banners and pennons, and there were peep shows and Mysteries, and trading booths at every corner. They were having a good time and a profitable one (being shrewd enough to charge well for supplying the needs of the court) and yet they were viewing the proceedings with tongue in cheek. They knew, these burghers of the wise and worldly old town, that the gallants who rode or strutted through the streets, their noses high in the air and their cold eyes unconscious of the rabble, had lost to the English all the great battles of the Hundred Years' War and would lose more if allowed their own way; and so sometimes above the creaking of leather and the stomping of horses and the shrillness of the silver trumpets could be heard jeers and catcalls and the bitter invective in which the Parisian excels.

Jacques Coeur could see the standard from the window of the white-plastered room which he used, when in Paris, for the direction of his many activities. He had been at work since five in the morning. Visitors had passed in and out in a seemingly endless procession and he had talked with them all, briefly and decisively, dismissing each one with a peremptory wave of the hand when convinced the purpose of the call had been accomplished. He had read mountainous piles of letters and documents, he had scrutinized lists, and had issued so many orders that all over the busy establishment his people were in the throes of carrying them out. He had exhausted completely the patience of his servant Nicolas.

He got to his feet and went to the window where he gazed through a break in the clustered rooftops at the turreted splendor of the Louvre. "Charles the Well-Served," he said in a half-audible tone. "You are well named, I think, my amiable but irresolute liege lord! I wonder what names they will have for you when the history of these days is written? . . . I wonder what will be written about Jacques Coeur?"

Seen from the rear he could not have been mistaken for anything save what he was, a prosperous and middle-aged man. When he turned about it was a different story, for then his eyes captured the attention and made everything else about him seem trivial and misleading. They were extraordinary eyes, large and gray and very much alive. They smiled, laughed, lighted up, sparkled, burned, smoldered, suffered, exploded into vivid dramatization of every mood. They never lacked animation for a moment. His voice, which was of an eager timbre, had something of the same quality. It could not be denied that he inclined to the theatrical in his gestures, but the lift and play of his fine white hands did no more than keep pace with his constant and quick change of expression.

A closer view made it clear that he dressed with rather particular care. His tunic was laced tight with cords of silver thread and there were pearls in the tufting of his sleeves. His hose fitted him well and his shoes were of the finest leather; although, being intended for active use, they lacked the extravagant upward curl at the toe.

"I think, Nicolas," he said to his servant, "we may assume that we have given this place a thorough shaking, like medicine in a bottle. The other half of our day begins. I shall now wait on the King. A cloak, my ever-smiling Nicolas."

Nicolas, as a matter of fact, had rarely been known to smile. If his outward appearance could be accepted as an indication of what went on inside him, he lived in a state of bilious discontent. His eyes moved with painful slowness in yellow sockets and the corners of his mouth drooped. He was a Norman, with a head shaped like a pear and a jowl the color of a ripe plum.

This gloomy apparition produced a heavy cloak which was richly lined with miniver, and held it out for his master.

"Must you go to court today?" he asked. "You've done a full day's work already, my lord. My head buzzes with all the orders I've had."

"I am expected, Nicolas. And when the King expects, the subject obeys; particularly if he happens to be the Moneyman."

"Truly I have a fool for a master," muttered Nicolas. "He will work himself to death. And then I will have no master and I will starve."

Jacques Coeur looked at the bottle-bellied figure beside him and smiled cheerfully. "You could live for a long time on what you've stored under your belt," he said. Then he felt the weight of the proffered cloak and frowned doubtfuliy. "Is it cold enough out to wear this?"

"Would I bring it to you, master, if I didn't think you needed it?"

"That is true," admitted the merchant. "I should know by this time that in such matters your judgment is better than mine."

"In matters of your comfort and well-being I am always right," admitted the servant. "And you, master, are always wrong."

"I wouldn't have said my record was quite as blank as that," demurred Coeur. "You will allow, perhaps, that in concerns of a rather more general nature I display somewhat better judgment. Well, Nicolas the Omnipotent, lead the way. We shall walk today."

They descended by a stone staircase and emerged on the street through wide bronze gates. The air was brisk and Coeur realized at once that his servant's selection of a cloak had been a wise one. He wrapped it more closely about him and stepped out at such a swift gait that Nicolas had to go at a jog trot to keep on his heels.

"Master, master!" protested the servant. "Won't the King's affairs wait a few minutes longer? Do you want to wear yourself out? After all, you're not a young man any more."

The merchant's good nature was not proof against this suggestion. "I may not be young," he said, with a sharp glance back over his shoulder, "but I'm still as strong as I was in my twenties. You needn't shake your head, Nicolas. You are ten years behind me in age and yet compared with me you're doddering into senility. I can still outwork, outthink, and outwalk any man I know."

"You can outclaim anyone, master," puffed the servant.

It was at once clear that the people of Paris did not include the King's Moneyman in the veiled hostility they felt for the rest of the court. Coeur and his servant were followed by a company of admiring men and boys like the tail of a comet. Cordial greetings reached them from the doors of taverns and the windows of houses, "It's the Moneyman!" "Brava, good Jacques!" and "Jaquet the Fox is our friend." Coeur returned these salutations with readiness and good humor. It was apparent that he enjoyed the attention paid him and so Nicolas stepped closer to grumble at his shoulder, "They would gape just as wide if it was the hangman passing, master."

When they reached the stone-lined ditch which surrounded the Louvre, Coeur stopped abruptly. "Nicolas," he demanded, "has any word been received yet from the Sire d'Arlay?"

"Wouldn't I have told you if it had?"

Coeur would have realized, had he ever stopped to consider the matter, that his cross-grained attendant seldom or never gave him a direct answer.

More often than not Nicolas countered with a question of his own, as in this instance. But the Moneyman was too concerned with the question itself to give any thought to the nature of the response.

"This day," he said to himself, "may go down in history. It's unfortunate I've had no reports from Robin d'Arlay. I'm sure what he has learned would have enabled me to put additional ribbing on the familiar carcass of my arguments."

The armed guard at the entrance to the palace smiled and motioned the Moneyman to enter. Jacques Coeur, his fur-lined cloak flapping about his well-shaped legs, made his way briskly through crowded halls to the foot of the Great Staircase. Here a chamberlain in green-and-white livery gave him an obsequious, "A fine day, my lord Coeur."

"Where shall I find the King?"

The chamberlain motioned up the staircase with a splayed thumb. "The ladies and gentlemen of the court are with the Queen, my lord Coeur. The King is expected to join them any moment now."

The Moneyman paused. "Tell me, Guyot, in what mood shall I find the King? Is there any hint of a twinkle in the royal eye today? Does my dread lord walk easily and with something of an air of expectancy?"

"It is my opinion the King does not feel well today. He walks slowly. He was silent all morning, according to report. No one has seen him smile."

A clatter of conversation fell on Coeur's ears as he entered the Great Chamber. The court had already settled down to its new preoccupation of the moment, the playing of *cards* with painted slips of stiff cardboard. The ladies and gentlemen were so engrossed in what they were doing that not a single pair of eyes was raised at his entrance. "Painted monkeys!" he thought. "Wasting all their time with their foolish games and wagers." Then, as usual, he began to think in terms of trade. "I must get an artist to paint a new set of cards, and copy them on the best of paper. They must be very special and costly. I might as well make a profit out of this."

He was careful to pause by the silk alms bag attached to the wall and to drop in a gold coin. Ordinarily the eyes of Queen Marie fixed themselves on each newcomer to make sure that this unwritten rule of the court was observed. Today, however, she was too occupied with her game to notice, and, as a result, the sound his contribution made suggested it had found little company in the alms bag.

The Queen was seated at the head of the room and Coeur knew she was playing *Glic* because her opponents were two in number. One was a young woman with a vivacious manner and a pretty dark face under a heart-shaped hennin, the other an enormous man in disorderly gray. Many other games of Glic were being played at small tables scattered over the floor but a good part of the company seemed to prefer watching the royal contest, standing in a silent and respectful circle.

The Queen was so absorbed that the Moneyman realized it would be unwise to interrupt her to pay his respects. Her overlarge nose, which robbed her otherwise pleasant face of any claim to beauty, showed a tendency to twitch, a sure sign that she was in a disturbed mood. Her well-rounded bosom was laced low in a dark green robe with broad bands of ermine sweeping in generous curves to the tips of her shoulders. The folds of her sleeves were so long that they sometimes touched the floor and so gave her much trouble in the handling of her cards. He heard her say in a distressed voice, "I am having *such* bad fortune today." The large man answered in a rumbling undertone, "In the game of Glic, liege lady, good luck can be compelled by a proper playing of the cards one holds."

Coeur found his way to a bench by the wall under a new tapestry representing in lurid realism the Seven Virtues and the Seven Vices. It had an occupant already, a soldier with a sword buckled to his belt and a look of distaste for his surroundings on his thin, leathery face.

"Dunois," said Coeur in a whisper, watching the attractive brunette who played with the Queen, "does it seem to you that Mademoiselle de Maignelais is pressing rather hard in her effort to usurp her cousin's place?"

"She's a pert minx," said the old soldier. "The lovely Agnes progressed to the King's notice through the favor of the Queen but I doubt if the method can be followed a second time."

"We mustn't feel too secure about it. The Queen is reconciled to Agnes Sorel. But it may be she thinks Agnes has been her rival long enough."

Dunois shook his head. "You and I have every reason to know how fickle our royal master can be; but in this matter his constancy verges on the miraculous. There's something about the fair Agnes which holds him on the tightest leading string. Will he ever be content with the raven locks of this little cousin on the pillow which has known the golden loveliness of Agnes Sorel?"

Coeur had fallen into somber speculation. "Agnes isn't well," he said. "Have you noticed how pale she is? She confesses to a malady of the spirit as well as of the body. I'm concerned about it, Dunois, deeply concerned."

The old soldier looked at his companion with a certain slyness of expression. "That I believe," he said.

An interruption was caused at this point by the entrance of the King. The voice of the single attendant who had preceded him was lost in the buzz of animated talk and it was several moments before the fact of the royal presence was generally recognized. Then there was a hurried clatter of heels as the ladies and gentlemen rose and made their bows.

"He looks his usual melancholy self," muttered Dunois.

Charles the Seventh stood for a moment in the entrance to the Great Chamber. His bow to the company was a perfunctory one and clearly a matter of habit. He sighed abstractedly and bowed again before beginning his progress through the room.

There were times when he looked every inch a king but this was not one of them, for he had donned his favorite short jacket of green which exposed his legs. The royal legs were not good. They were short and skimpy and bowed, and there was no denying that an unexpected lumpiness around the knees compromised seriously the dignity a wise monarch should always strive to maintain.

When he reached the Queen's table, he bowed moodily. "I have no wish to interrupt your—your new afternoon diversion, Madame," he said.

"We play only to fill the time until you honor us with your presence, liege lord," declared Marie of France.

"It is very clear, Madame, that you find this matching of wits most diverting. Under the circumstances"—the King seemed to suffer from sudden uneasiness and was careful to avoid her eyes—"you will be content that my stay must be unusually brief today. Matters of state demand my attention immediately. I must ask you to allow me the attendance of" —his glance strayed about the room—"of Gouffier, Chabannes, Dunois, Coeur. Questions of the utmost urgency demand our attention in my own chambers."

The Queen found it hard to conceal her chagrin. Drawing a linen kerchief from the broad gold-mesh belt at her waist, she dabbed at the end of her long nose. To forestall any open remonstrance, the King rose to his feet.

"My most profound regrets, Madame," he said. "I trust you will spend a pleasant afternoon."

2

The four men named fell into line behind him, Jacques Coeur bringing up the rear. All maintained a proper decorum as they left the room although each of them knew he was playing his part in an open farce. Even their selection had been a matter of routine, for they had been called out in this order many times before. Without a word being said, they passed through the screens and on to the landing of the Great Staircase. Instead of ascending to the apartments of the King on the floor above, they turned of one accord and proceeded down a long passage which ended at another staircase.

An iron door clanged to behind them. They began to descend in single file, as the steps radiating out from the ornate newel were not wide enough to permit them to walk two abreast. It was a curiously designed staircase, with a separate ascending tier; and the soffits were so low and carefully placed that it was impossible on either tier to see anyone going the other way. Coeur had often thought of this arrangement as a perfect reflection of the prevailing state of mind at the court—sly, secretive, suspicious, constricting.

Guillaume Gouffier, who preceded Coeur in the line, turned his head and grinned back at the Moneyman. His nose was so long that the act of smiling made his mouth curl up closely around its vulpine tip.

"A most convenient stair for—for the purpose," he whispered.

Reaching the ground floor, they proceeded down a flag-tiled passage. A guard was standing at the end and, at the first glimpse of them, he scuttled out of sight. The door at which he had been stationed was of oak, ornamented elaborately with a spreading branch of the surelle tree. Here the King halted and bowed to his followers.

The door opened immediately. They caught a glimpse of a well-lighted room and a tall *prie-dieu* with crimson tapestried panels. The King vanished within and the door closed after him with a speed which suggested a surreptitious intent.

Before it closed, however, they heard a pleasant feminine voice say in a tone of mock despair: "My lord, my lord! That very short jacket again!"

"The fair Agnes," declared Gouffier, "has never admired the royal legs."

The state ministers turned in a body into a small room on the other side of the passage. It had, apparently, been prepared for them; there were four chairs, a table with a flagon of red wine and a triangular slab of green-veined cheese, a fire on the hearth.

"How long," asked Dunois, as they seated themselves, "have we played our inglorious parts in such mummeries as this?"

"Too long," answered Gouffier. He stifled a yawn and glanced covertly at Jacques Coeur. "Could it be construed as faintly treasonable if one voiced the opinion that it grows tiresome?"

"No one has been deceived from the start," grumbled the old soldier. "All France knows that the King pays afternoon visits to the Lady Agnes.

Too many know of the way he tries to cover his movements, and they laugh at him for his pains."

"And at us no doubt." Gouffier gave another sly look at the Moneyman. "One of us should convince the King that no purpose is served by going through these discreet motions. I lack the finesse for it myself. You, perhaps, Jacques Coeur?"

"The deception," said Coeur shortly, "is not of the King's will. It's the Lady Agnes herself who insists that a veil be kept drawn. You're all aware that she's of a pious turn and refuses an open avowal of——"

"Of her adultery," said Gouffier, when the Moneyman hesitated to use the word. He had cut himself a slice of the cheese and was consuming it with voracious bites. "We would be well advised, the four of us, to learn this game of Glic. I fear, my lords, a distaste for your faces will grow in me if I have to suffer them much longer in idleness."

"I had a distaste for your face," said Dunois bluntly, "long before the curtain went up on this far-from-sacred play."

Gouffier turned and scowled at him over the cheese. "It's a prerogative of military greatness to speak one's mind openly," he said. "But you may not always find it wise, my doughty Bastard, to abuse the privilege."

The soldier glanced at him and then at Chabannes, who was sprawling morosely in his chair. "We are two against two," he said, "and it's becoming increasingly hard for us to sit down together in peace. The Moneyman and I desire an immediate resumption of the war. You are in favor of continuing the present policy of inactivity. It would be idle for us to attempt any further persuasion. Your minds, I regret to say, cannot be swayed into a more patriotic way of thinking. It would be easier for us to sit here and blink at each other in the silence of mutual dislike; but, sirs, we might as well recognize that the issue must soon be resolved and so speak with complete frankness."

"If it's frankness you want," cried Gouffier, "I'm ready to say that I consider you nothing but an animated sword hand, Bastard of Orléans! Your views should carry no weight as they are dictated by self-interest, a desire to display your leadership again in action. As for the Moneyman, I say again what I have spoken openly on many occasions. We have come to a sorry pass when common men are raised to posts of responsibility in the state. If I had my way, Jaquet the Fox would be shorn of all his honors and herded back to where he belongs, the fashioning of furs for the wives of town burghers."

Jacques Coeur gripped the arms of his chair. He wanted to spring at the throat of the smirking state minister but was restrained by force of habit.

He had never had any illusions as to the esteem in which he was held at court. Although he had been ennobled by royal decree, the aristocracy had never accepted him as one of them, and never would. It had been necessary to accept their rebuffs as part of the price of his rapid elevation. Outwardly he had remained impervious to the hostility of the court but inside he still suffered as much from each new proof of contempt as he had at the beginning. Trying to be philosophic about it, he had said to himself that his tormentors were men of narrow mind and that what they said and did was of no real concern; but there was no longer any concealing from himself that this constant bludgeoning of his pride was having its effect. The floodgates had been dammed so long that it might prove impossible to let them swing open. He did not want to become completely stultified.

He remained silent for several moments and then addressed himself to Dunois. "As you know, I have never sought honors at court. I serve the King at his own suggestion and command. When I can no longer be of service to him, I shall be happy to devote myself entirely to the control of my own affairs. In the meantime I can't be a good servant if I quarrel with those about him, even though I hold them in contempt."

Dunois nodded somberly. "Moneyman, I think you allow us to see that you have a strong stomach."

"My stomach," said Coeur, "threatens to rebel."

Silence settled on the room. The two courtiers devoted themselves to the flagon of wine and tossed an occasional word between them. The eyes of Dunois became fixed on the window and it was clear his thoughts had wandered to a more congenial plane. Perhaps he was dreaming of the days when he and the Maid had routed the invaders before Orléans. Jacques Coeur got to his feet and paced up and down, his arms folded on his chest. The comment of the old soldier rankled in his mind. "Is that what all men think, that I will swallow any insult?" he asked himself again and again. "Would it be better if I fought them with their own weapons?"

"As for the issue between us," said Gouffier suddenly, "I find that I have much to say."

"Ha!" cried Dunois, emerging instantly from his reverie. "Out with it then!"

An hour passed in bitter argument. They went over and over the old familiar ground, the two courtiers advancing the specious reasons with which the peace party bolstered their desire for a continuation of the treaty with the English invaders. Coeur took no part in it, the turmoil inside himself making any participation in the debate impossible.

He was on the point of announcing that a press of duties would compel his departure without waiting for the royal sanction when the sound of a door opening and closing reached their ears from across the hall. A moment later the King appeared in the doorway.

"I see you are at each other's throats again, gentlemen," he said. "Must this dispute go on forever? I confess that I weary of the sound of it." After a moment, he added in contrite tones: "I have been delayed. Please believe that I feel a deep regret at keeping you here so long. I fear it's too late now for a full discussion of the matters I had intended to propound for your advice and so I suggest we postpone our talk until tomorrow. There's still time for a turn in the gardens before supper."

3

In his capacity of comptroller of the royal purse, Coeur had a small room in the tower overlooking the Rue Beauvais. It was an inconvenient location, being far removed from the rest of the household offices, and as a consequence the officials who attended him there brought sulky looks with them as well as their accounts. He spent two busy hours after leaving the King, checking over lists of supplies and issuing instructions to a long succession of chamberlains, valets, almoners, even cooks. It was trying work, for these minor servants took their cue from the nobility and treated him with condescension under the thinnest veneer of respect.

It was dark by the time he was through, and the wall hangings were rippling with the night drafts which found their way through the mullioned windows. He realized that the court supper was now over. That he had missed it was of no importance, for he lacked the intense interest in food which most men seemed to share. Perhaps, he reflected, it was just as well he had lost the chance to partake of the rich viands served by the royal cook; on the occasion of his last talk with the court physician he had been advised to watch his weight.

Free of all interruptions at last, he set himself to the task of writing letters. His pen moved rapidly and incisively. He never hesitated for a word.

When they were finished and sealed with an embossed ♡ and the motto underneath *A Vaillants Coeurs Rien Impossible,*[1] he began to undress without bothering to summon Nicolas. "I've had enough of his grumbling for one day," he said to himself. His movements now were

[1]To valiant hearts nothing is impossible.

slow and unwilling. It might have been construed from this that he felt he was laying aside with his clothes the responsibilities and the stimulating activities which filled his days, and that he regretted the necessity.

He was about to step naked into bed when there was a knock at the door. Ensconcing himself between the sheets, he called, "Come in." The only unlocked door perhaps in the Louvre opened at his summons to admit a minor court official.

"Your attendance is required, my lord Coeur."

"Is it the King?"

The official hesitated and then said, "Yes, my lord Coeur."

The Moneyman sprang out of bed with alacrity. He seemed glad to dress again and thus to resume the duties and the importance of his waking hours. It took no more than three minutes to complete his toilet.

The route by which he was conducted supplied the Moneyman with the reason for the officer's hesitation. They were not going to the apartments of the King. They proceeded to the ground floor and went out into the courtyard where the night guards had already been placed and were stamping their feet to keep warm. Jacques Coeur knew from the sounds which reached his ears that the chains were being drawn across all the streets leading to the palace.

After reaching the far end of the court they proceeded along a covered passage. This ended in three doors grouped darkly together. Opening one with a key, the official led the way up a short flight of stairs to a square apartment where the gloom of the outside was left behind suddenly and completely. There were a score of lighted candles and a cheerful fire crackling on the hearth and bundles of bittersweet and evergreens in pots and vases; a pleasant room and most distinctly feminine. Jacques Coeur did not need the surelle device which appeared in all the decorations and in the embroideries to tell him where he was. "We walked three times as far as was necessary to get here," he thought. "The King will take an even more roundabout way. And when he arrives tongues will be clacking all over the palace and everyone will know where he is!"

His reflections were cut short by the arrival of the lady to whom the apartment belonged. She paused in the doorway with a nod and a smile for the visitor. Their eyes met and held; and, if anyone else had been in the room, it would have been apparent that a look of understanding had passed between them.

"Is it to be tonight, then, my dear Lady Agnes?" asked Coeur.

"Yes, my old friend, it's to be tonight."

It is impossible to convey in words the full effect of Agnes Sorel's great charm. Her loveliness was owing only in part to the gold of her hair, the vibrant blue of her eye, the delicacy of her features. It was in equal degree a matter of spirit. Hers was a fine and high spirit, in which vivacity, sweetness, and resolution were combined. Jacques Coeur, who understood her better perhaps than anyone, found himself instantly under the spell of it, as he did on every occasion they met. At the same time he noted, with a catch of his breath, that there were deep violet shadows under her eyes and more than a hint of weariness in her manner and bearing. He asked himself, "Must Time be so unsparing that even the beauty of Agnes Sorel suffers from its passing?"

She was dressed rather simply in blue velvet with a veil of ivory lace about her shoulders. With the courage which only a conviction of beauty can give, she had disregarded the stern dictate of fashion by which women wore hennins on their heads at all hours of the day; instead she kept her hair uncovered and piled high on her head in a profusion of curls. A prayer book in a gold case was suspended by a thin chain from her wrist.

She walked slowly into the room and it became apparent at once that her gown did not depend for effect on its simplicity. There was artfulness in the cut of it, particularly in the way the waistline fell to a V in front. There was art also in the slit of the skirt at one side, extending almost to the knee and allowing glimpses of a froth of lace on the under kirtle; this, however, the sole concession to the craze of the moment for elaboration and embellishment.

"I arranged it so you would arrive first," she said. "There is a matter to be discussed before the King comes."

Coeur was still concerned about her appearance of ill-health. He frowned and said, "You are tired, I fear."

"Yes, a little tired." Then she nodded her head slowly as though unwilling to be anything but entirely honest. "It's more than that, my kind Jacques. I haven't felt at all well of late. I am beginning to fail—in health as well as in looks."

"But you have never looked more lovely, my Lady Agnes!"

"Must you play the courtier with me? I can be honest enough with myself to believe what my mirror tells me. There are hollows in my cheeks and these great shadows under my eyes. I found three gray hairs this morning, and I tore them out as fiercely as a pious churchman casting out a sinful thought!"

"You are still so beautiful that you could do me another great favor. A new silk has reached us from the East, a rich variety stiffened with other material which makes it rustle with every movement. If you would condescend to wear a gown made of it, there would immediately be a great demand for the stuff."

Agnes Sorel rose to the bait with a look of eager interest. "A skirt that rustles as you walk? That would be quite enticing and very, very feminine. I will be glad to use some of this new material. We have introduced many new things between us, haven't we? And I don't believe anyone has ever suspected."

"What Agnes Sorel wears today, every woman in France wants tomorrow," said Coeur.

She began to speak in a low and hurried tone. "Old friend, it pleases me to hear you say I'm still fair to look at. God grant I never see the day when I'm too old and faded to find favor with men or"—she smiled wanly—"to start a new fad in dress. I think I never shall, for I must tell you that—that matters are serious with me. I suffer continually from a weakness in the limbs. It's no longer easy to rise in the mornings and I have no desire to walk or ride or dance. I've always been active and so I'm sure that—that I haven't much longer to live."

She drew closer and her voice dropped to a whisper. "I'm going to tell you a secret, Jacques Coeur, because it leads to something you may have to do soon. It was through the influence of the Queen's mother that I won the favor of the King. Do you find that hard to believe? I'm sure you must. And yet it's true. Yolande, with all her great goodness of heart and her fine understanding, established a rival for her own daughter."

"I don't find it hard to believe," said Coeur. "I understood the Queen's mother well enough to know the reasons she had."

"The old lady was very wise," whispered Agnes Sorel. "She knew the weak side of the King, that he would always have a mistress. She preferred to select one who would cause Queen Marie the least distress and who would help to keep His King's Grace from listening to the wrong advice. She chose me."

"And what a wise selection it has proven to be!"

"Thank you. . . . It hasn't been easy and I'm happy you think I have justified the choice." After a pause she went on in the same hurried tone: "She counseled me at every step. She urged me to use my influence in the matter of the ministers he kept around him. You, Jacques Coeur, she preferred to all others. Did you know that? Ah, what fine things she said about you; she was so sure that all would be well with France if the King continued to listen to you. Yes, she was very wise. It was a great loss for France when that wonderful old lady died."

"It was a great thing for France when Agnes Sorel was born." The

Moneyman nodded. "I knew Yolande was at your shoulder all the time. You have been an apt pupil, Agnes."

"I know what she would say if she were alive today. She would say, 'My child, you must face the truth. Time is taking its toll and you must be ready to step down.' Yes, she would say that, even though she knew it might hurt me very much. I thought it all over last night and made up my mind to speak to you, to tell you that we have work to do between us. We must be ready to have someone else to—to continue what I have done. It wasn't easy, Jacques Coeur, to reach that conclusion; I am proud, I like to stand first, I like to have power. But I made up my mind to it; and last night in my dreams Yolande came to me and smiled—such a wise, sweet smile—as though she knew and was pleased with me."

"No one can ever take your place!" exclaimed the Moneyman. "The King's devotion is as complete as ever. It will be time enough to think of such things when he shows signs of wavering—if he ever does."

She shook her head positively. "I'm the only one in a position to judge. I'm growing old. Jacques Coeur, Jacques Coeur, I am nearly forty!"

"Years do not count when they prove as kind as they have to you."

"*Your* devotion will never lessen, I am sure, and there is much consolation in that." She shook her head and pronounced two of the most bitter of all words, "My successor—yes, my successor must be carefully chosen. We must be as wise as Yolande would have been. I think the selection must rest with you. I might not have the grace to be sufficiently detached in my judgment. Yes, I must be wise enough to entrust this to you and to abide by what you may decide. My friend, I have only one piece of advice to give. You must be ready—when the inevitable need arises."

"That you have the courage to say this to me," declared Coeur, "is even more remarkable than the wisdom of Yolande."

"The Queen has always known, I think. It's even possible that the old lady told her. She liked me very much at first and she has always been as tolerant as possible under such circumstances. What a strange situation for the three of us to face, Yolande and the Queen and me! It seems to me that the Queen will prove sympathetic when the time comes." She leaned closer to him and he was acutely conscious of the slow lift of the lids which enabled him to look full into her unusual blue eyes. "Now that I've summoned the courage to say this, I feel a great sense of relief. It's as though a burden had been removed from my shoulders—and added to the heavy ones you carry yourself."

"A heavier burden than everything else combined, dearest lady. The most unwelcome one I've ever assumed."

She continued to look at him intently. "You have always liked me, I think, Jacques Coeur."

"Yes," he answered slowly, "I have always liked you."

4

Charles of France entered the room a moment later. His chin was sunk in the collar of a long fur robe as though he desired not to be recognized, and the quick glance he cast about the room was both apprehensive and sulky. He made it clear at once that he had not expected to find his Moneyman there. *"You?"* he said. "Now what is the reason for this?"

"I asked you to come, sire," began Agnes Sorel, looking at the monarch with an air of supplication, "because we desired a chance to waken your great generosity. Ah, if you will only give that generous instinct full rein! There is a gift I hope you will grant soon. Not for me, sire—for the people of France!"

Charles shifted uneasily. "I should have known it!" he exclaimed. "Another lecture, my Agnes? Out with it, then! What can I do for France beyond what I have done already?"

The lady looked at Jacques Coeur as though seeking his support. When she failed to find the right words to continue with her plea, the latter took it on himself to reply.

"I think, sire, I know the nature of the gift she asks. Permit me to point out that the English are still in Rouen."

The King frowned with sudden impatience. "Is another war the boon you crave?"

"Sire," said Agnes, "the people of France will know no rest, no happiness, as long as the invaders hold a square inch of our soil. There is war now, even though undeclared. Part of your people groan under foreign rule. The rest are at the mercy of the Free Companies. It's not war we seek, sire, it's peace, the peace that can be won for the unhappy people of France only by a final effort to drive the English out."

"The time is ripe," declared Coeur. "The English are torn by dissensions at home and their garrisons are small. This is the golden opportunity to end a century of fighting. I, a man of peace, do not need to point this out, for no one can see the truth more clearly than you, sire."

"Am I to have no peace, in God's Holy Name?" cried the King. "You are always girding at me, Jacques Coeur, you and Dunois and De Brézé. And now you, my Agnes, to whom I have always looked for consolation after the cares of the day. Twenty years of war I have had already. By St. Denis, is it not enough?"

"There can be no peace, sire, as long as the English stay at Rouen," said Coeur.

Agnes Sorel slipped forward from her stool and rested on her knees beside the royal chair.

"My liege lord," she whispered, "when I was a child it was foretold of me that I would live to be honored by the love of the greatest king and captain of his day. Make it come true, sire! Finish the work you have begun so well!"

Charles drew his hand away from hers. "It's easy to talk of war. I grant you the English garrisons are small. But what if they pour their armies across the Sleeve again? Would we suffer another Crécy, another Azincourt?"

"Has my liege lord talked with Jean Bureau?" asked Coeur.

"The bombard fellow? Yes, I have listened to him. I have heard him spin his fables about the big guns he can mount against the walls of Normandy. That is still a dream, Moneyman, but the arrows of the English archers are a reality. They have cut the chivalry of France to pieces in all the great battles of the past. We still have nothing to match them."

"Sire," Coeur exclaimed, "the winning of the war will not depend on the chivalry of France. That must sound like the rankest of heresy but I have no hesitation in saying it. I know that it's true. The men whose fathers lost us Azincourt and whose grandfathers died so helplessly at Crécy have learned nothing from the disasters of the past. They still think and talk of war as it was fought a hundred years ago. If the issue lay with them, they would die just as surely and in the same kind of defeat. But, sire, the English have not learned anything new either. They still depend on the longbow, thinking it the supreme weapon. They have no cannon like the powerful bombards of Jean Bureau. An Englishman named Walter FitzRauf, whose ancestor of the same name went to Cathay two hundred years ago and brought back word of the cannon of the Far East, was in Rouen this summer. Rumors of what he had to say have reached our ears. He was begging the English leaders to turn their attention to the use of gunpowder and not to depend any longer on archery. They laughed at him. The English beat us in the first campaigns because they had a weapon we did not understand. Today things are reversed. We have a new weapon and the English are refusing to recognize its possibilities. We can beat them easily, sire, and almost bloodlessly."

The King listened to this impassioned plea with a frown of suspicion. "You speak so glibly, my good Moneyman," he said, "that I suspect you have rehearsed all this in advance."

Coeur smiled. "That is true, sire. The issue is of such importance that I gave careful thought to what I should say. I would be a poor advocate if I left it to the promptings of the moment."

Charles frowned again. "Talk, all talk," he muttered. "How can I be sure there is truth in all this cant about our great cannon? I can't risk a defeat."

"My great king and captain can't be defeated!" cried Agnes Sorel.

The King began to stalk about the room. The long cloak he was wearing made him seem more kingly than he had appeared in the green jacket of the afternoon. His face reflected the gloomy doubts which filled his mind. After a turn or two, he paused before a crucifix on the wall and fell into silence.

Agnes Sorel watched him for several moments before she turned to Coeur. "Have we made any progress tonight?" she asked in a whisper. "Do you think he listened to us in a more receptive mood? I thought so, but it may have been my fancy."

Coeur also had been studying the bent back of their royal master. After a moment he gave an affirmative nod. "I think so," he replied. "I've learned to read the kingly moods and it seemed to me he was on the point of giving in. He's slow at making up his mind, as you know, but in a very few minutes you may find, my most gallant lady, that your efforts haven't been in vain."

Her eyes lost their tired look. She leaned forward and touched his arm. "If you are right," she whispered, "I'll be well content. Even if what I suspect about this weakness of mine should prove to be true."

The Moneyman nodded slowly and, perhaps, reluctantly. "If needs be, I have another inducement to offer him. There's a great risk I can take to tip the scales. I've been turning it over in my mind, realizing all it might mean. After what you have just said, my sweet Agnes, I would be a coward if I hesitated any longer."

Jacques Coeur had the best of reasons, nevertheless, for hesitation.

His was the type of mind which sees far beyond the range of vision of the ordinary man. Starting as a furrier in his native city of Bourges, he had sensed the chance to revolutionize the whole face of trade by a new type of shop, one in which goods of every description would be offered for sale. The next step in his program was even more radical, the duplication of his first department store in all the major cities of France. He now had twenty-four; two in Paris, two in Tours where the court was located most of the time, four in Lyons, six in Bourges, four in Montpellier, and single shops scattered all over the face of the country. They were not, as he phrased it himself, "small holes in a wall behind a single pair of shutters." They were towering houses, stuffed with every kind of article which entered into the lives of people. They had made him enormously wealthy.

Back of these extraordinary moves was a basic discovery which had come to him early and had dictated each step he had taken. Combination! He had seen that trade could be made the most powerful force in the civilized world if it were no longer confined to the individual efforts of small men. He had realized that there must be a multiplying of interests, of manufacture, of shipping and selling. One of his first steps had been to establish a fleet of his own ships to bring goods from the East. Now he was building factories all over France for the manufacture of cloth, shoes, hats, gloves, armor. He was buying mines.

It was not solely the desire for power and wealth which had urged him on. The thought was firmly lodged in his mind that this was how things should be. The world was full of natural riches which men had not found the means to use. Commerce must be bound together, taking in the whole world if necessary, so that goods could be brought from all the far corners of the earth and then sold at prices which all people could pay. He had said on many occasions, "I want the wife of the artisan to wear silks like the fine lady of the court and the poorest tinker to have spices in his wine."

He was the earliest and the greatest of merchant princes. He was a monarch, presiding with infinite skill and almost incredible foresight over an empire of trade.

The inducement he had in mind to make the King would put this great empire in jeopardy.

The King faced about and walked back across the room. He still wore a frown but there was less uncertainty about the glance he gave them.

"Granted that all you've said is true," he began, "there is still a great difficulty we haven't yet mentioned. One to which I fail to find any answer. Money, Jacques Coeur. I don't need to remind you of the empty state of the treasury. How could we pay the cost of another war?"

The Moneyman said to himself: "Now it is your turn, Jacques Coeur, to make a sacrifice for France. You must throw everything into the scales—your fortune, your future, the great enterprises you have created. You may lose everything you possess. You may see your dream of a different world dissolve back into the mists of the past. Is it worth it? Have you the courage to take this step?"

"Money," sighed the King. "Always that same dire problem."

Coeur said deliberately, "We will pay the cost of the war with the fruits of peace, sire."

"But armies cannot be paid with promises. My soldiers cannot be equipped and fed on the hopes of a prosperous future. Where can we raise the funds? At what figure do you estimate the cost of this war you demand of me?"

"Two hundred thousand *écus,* sire."

The King looked startled, as though the figure exceeded even his worst fears. "I might as well reach for the moon as try to raise that stupendous sum!" he exclaimed. "I can't put fresh taxes on my people. They are overburdened now. What rash scheme is in your mind? To raise the salt gabelle? More land tailles; a heavier tax on hearths? Would you bring me to the danger of another revolt?"

Coeur found that all his hesitation had left him. "Liege lord, I will undertake to raise the necessary funds myself."

King and merchant faced each other in a tense silence for several moments. The monarch's expression had changed. His eyes had lighted up for the first time since the debate began.

"But how?" he demanded finally. "In your capacity as a minister of the Crown?"

Coeur shook his head. "Not as your minister, sire. As Jacques Coeur, a private individual. I am a rich man and I have extensive credit against which I can borrow if necessary."

"If we win, I could repay you. If we lose——" The King paused and shook his head. "Do you realize what that would mean? Are you prepared to stake everything on this—this great gamble?"

There was no trace of hesitation, of uncertainty, or of fear, in the answer of the Moneyman. "Do you think I value my fortune, the future of my enterprises, except for the use they can be now? I know the risk and I give it not a single thought. *Sire, what I have is yours!*"

Chapter II

I

IT WAS DREARY COUNTRY through which Pregent Kennedy had been riding all day, and the company of a fat priest on a broad-backed roan had done little to alleviate the monotony. The churchman had attached himself to the Scot for greater safety. The *écorcheurs* had been raiding freely hereabouts and as a result travelers rode in continual peril. The Free Companies had not only burned villages and castles but had wantonly destroyed everything, even the signposts at crossroads.

In no part of France was it more apparent that the country had been at war for a hundred years. All normal life had ceased and it was a rare and startling thing to see a human face peering out from the walls of a ruined house or a cow straying disconsolately in a blackened field. Even the roads seemed to have taken on the fears of the few travelers who ventured out on them. They did not march straight ahead nor strut with confidence; instead they were like dim rakes in a bewitched forest, and seemed to slink, to hesitate at crossings, to gaze uncertainly ahead before making a turn on lagging legs. The sun had lost the power to shine with warmth and good cheer (or so it seemed), and the only birds seen above the fields and the woods flapped ominously on black wings. A continuous wind blew from somewhere high up in the hills. Men met with suspicion in this desolation and parted in haste; and anyone who lacked food in his saddlebags rode on an empty belly.

The two companions had reached a crossroad and the priest fell silent for the first time that day as his eyes lighted on a long train approaching from the north. A nobleman of high degree and great wealth was on the move. Many knights were in attendance, their armor clanking as they rode, and there were squires and men-at-arms and almoners and lackeys without number in the cavalcade. In the center was a carriage of the type ladies used in following the hunt, being open on one side. This afforded a full view of a middle-aged woman wearing a hennin of majestic white plumes under which her face looked ailing and severe. In the lead was a young lady on a gaily-bedecked palfrey; the daughter of the house, without a doubt, for a page rode on one side of her and a priest on the other, and there was arrogance even in the way she held a hawk on her wrist. She was a plump young beauty with a curling plume in her high hat, a habit of peacock-blue velvet, and ruffles of ivory lace at her neck and wrists. The glossy tip of a red leather shoe showed briefly beneath her skirt.

The priest began to speculate aloud as to who they were. Had good King René of Sicily been on a visit to his sister and brother-in-law of France? Was it the rich Comte de Foix or, perchance, the great Comte de St. Pol? Or, rather, was it Havart, the esquire-carver of the King, who because of his office always appeared in azure velvet?

Pregent Kennedy paid no attention. Flicking the ends of his tartan around his long and somewhat stringy neck, he gazed instead down the side road along which a curious equipage was approaching. He slipped a hand out of its steel gauntlet to give a twist to the ends of his graying mustache and allowed an amused grin to spread over his long and usually severe face. "Now what," he asked himself, "can this be?"

The carriage was of the type known as a *chare* but with eccentricities all its own. The seat was perched precariously high on shafts which swayed so much with each turn of the wheels that the driver seemed in constant danger. It was drawn by a pair of ambling mules, and the clear treble voice of the girl at the reins could be heard urging them on to greater efforts. "Come, Olivier. We'll never reach an inn at this rate. Annette, Annette! Less of sloth, I beg of you!" Her anxiety was natural, for it could now be seen that she was alone.

"Here," said the Scot, to his companion, "we have two young persons of the gentler persuasion who present certain points of contrast. I can see that you're all agog over the damoiselle in velvet. I concede that she has her points. But, good Father Imbert, permit me to voice a preference for the brave little pea-chick who is closer to Heaven up there on that absurd Ark of the Covenant than some of us can ever hope to get."

The forest lined the roads so tightly at this point that the girl guided her weary mules to the center of the crossing before she had any inkling of the approach of the lordly train. Most unfortunately one of the wheels became wedged in a deep rut. The conveyance stopped. Realizing now the gravity of her offense, the driver urged her team on frantically but failed to rouse the lethargic mules to the effort needed to extricate the imprisoned wheel. The young lady at the head of the cavalcade was compelled to rein in.

"What is this?" demanded the latter in a petulant voice. "What impudence in the creature to drive directly in front of us! Eduard, see that she moves on at once."

The page, to whom this order had been directed, saw no way of obeying it. "The wheel is stuck, my lady," he pointed out. "We'll have to wait until it can be dragged clear."

"Then get down and shove, lazy one!" cried the damoiselle in a sudden gust of anger. "Down, all of you! Get this unsightly thing out of our way!" Then her mood veered and she began to laugh. "What is it, in God's Good Name? Is it a new kind of scarecrow and is the girl a part of it? Stir the creature up, Eduard. Perhaps she's out of a circus and has trained monkeys under that filthy blanket."

The page answered eagerly, "If that's what you want, mistress, just watch me!" He dismounted and began to belabor the nearest of the mules with the shaft of a pennon. The animal strained at its harness but still failed to get the chare into motion. The boy redoubled his efforts.

"Stop! You'll do him an injury!" cried the girl from the seat above.

The boy grinned. "I want to do this stubborn old mule an injury," he said.

One of the men-at-arms came up at this point with a pike in his hands. "Watch *me!*" he declared. He drove the pike into the haunch of the mule and the animal gave a loud scream of pain. It lunged forward frantically, carrying its mate with it and causing the wheels of the chare to grind and churn. The ramshackle vehicle shook violently and then began to move. The man-at-arms followed up his success by smacking the wounded hindquarters of the mule with the butt end of the pike. The frightened team broke into a run, dragging the carriage over a brash of stones at the side of the road. The seat rocked like the top of a tree in a windstorm and the girl had to hang on with both hands to avoid being pitched out.

Most of the members of the noble train had hurried forward to watch this comic spectacle. The men doubled up with amusement. The women jeered and laughed. Even the daughter of the house unbent and joined in the merriment, and the priest laughed so hard that he had to wipe his eyes on the end of his sleeve.

Kennedy turned his horse with the intention of overtaking the runaway team and bringing it to a halt. He was too late, however. There was a sharp turn in the road and the frightened mules rounded it at such speed that the chare was thrown against the bank. One wheel was torn off and went spinning and bouncing down the road like a child's hoop. The carriage collapsed with a sound of snapping shafts and splintering wood.

Kennedy saw a black cat, which had been curled up unnoticed on the seat beside its mistress, leap into the air and achieve a claw-hold on the trunk of a tree. The girl was less fortunate, being thrown from her high perch to the road. She rolled over twice before coming to a stop. The Scot dismounted and ran to her assistance.

She accepted the aid of his arm in getting to her feet. The hood of her cheap chammer cloak had fallen back, revealing a head of fair hair which shimmered in the late afternoon sun like harvest grain. Kennedy said to himself, "I would like to see her in the clothes of the other one."

Her cloak, which had been old and worn to begin with, had sustained some rents in the fall and she was covered with dust from head to foot.

Her hands had been scraped and there was a small cut on her forehead. It was with great difficulty that she was restraining herself from breaking into tears, and he thought at first this was from the pain of her injuries. He realized when she spoke that it was because of anger.

"The beasts, the cruel beasts!" she exclaimed. She rubbed at the dirt on her face with one sleeve. Then, seeing that the damoiselle was still watching with an amused air, she burst out with, "I would like to scratch her eyes out!"

She wheeled about and began to walk back to the intersection of the two roads. Kennedy took hold of her sleeve to restrain her. "Take heed, my child," he said. "It will be unwise to say anything to them. They will think nothing of beating you as they did your mule or even riding you down. I won't be able to protect you against all of them, and yet nonetheless I am a shrewd and doughty fighter—one of the best in all France, I'll have you know."

She shook off his hand and continued to walk forward with a determined air. He gave up and contented himself with muttering a proverb, "He who chases folly, soon catches it."

The girl halted a few yards from the daughter of the house. As the Scot had remarked, they presented a striking contrast: the aristocrat in her velvet and gold, so disdainful and yet so lovely with her lustrous black hair and bright black eyes, the other in her brownish cloak with its lack of fit and its ugly bell-shaped sleeves and yet quite as lovely because of the gold of her hair and the intense blue of her eyes. For several moments they regarded each other in a silent and growing antagonism, each conscious and resentful of the beauty of the other.

"You couldn't have known what you were doing!" said the girl on the ground. "No one, not even you, could be so cruel and callous!"

"If you say another word or delay us any longer," said the other, "I shall have my servants tie you to a tree and whip you soundly as you deserve."

"My carriage is broken." The voice of the one in the ugly cloak became choked with emotion. She was silent for several moments while she strove to control her feelings. "Under what you called that filthy blanket is the body of my father. He died last night. I was seeking a place where he could be buried." She crossed herself passionately. "And now what am I to do?"

A sudden silence fell on the group. The squires and men-at-arms gaped at the bereaved girl in a discomfort which manifested itself in a sheepishness of mien and in embarrassed scraping of feet in the dust of the road.

Even the daughter of the house seemed nonplused for a moment. Then she tossed her head impatiently and called an order to the almoner.

"Father Ambrose! Give her some money. Enough to pay for repairs and the burial of her father. And now all of you get to your places! We've lost more time already than we can afford."

The almoner produced a small gold coin and walked over to the slim figure in the chammer cloak. He placed it in her hand with a hurried, "*Benedicte,* daughter," and then resumed his place in the train. The girl stood without moving for several moments, looking at the coin on her palm. When she raised her head her cheeks were flushed and her eyes were flashing angrily.

"It's true that I'm entitled to compensation for the breaking of the chare," she said clearly. "But this has been given as charity. I will have you know"—she was staring up straight into the eyes of the daughter of the house—"that I can't accept anything at your hands. Here!" She tossed the coin in the direction of the servants. "Divide it among you. My hand would sicken and wither if I held it any longer!"

"It's clear you don't know your place!" cried the girl on horseback. "You presume too much. I lack patience for such impudence as this!" Her anger getting the better of her, she blazed into invectives. "Guttersnipe! Baseborn creature! You shall be well whipped for this!"

"Patience isn't the only thing you lack! I'm not afraid to tell you to your face that you lack decency and fairness!"

"Enough of this! Eduard, Bertrand, Jules! Get this dirty waif out of my sight! If you spare your whips on her back, I'll not be sparing in my punishment of you."

Before the order could be obeyed, one of the knights at the rear of the cavalcade rode forward and said, "One moment, if you please, Lady Alys."

There was an alien suggestion about him; for, having the hint of a stoop in his shoulders, he seemed almost scholarly, a quality which all good knights fiercely scorned. His hair and eyes were dark and his features tended to length and even gauntness. He was dressed with great richness and taste: a fine feather in his hat, a fur-lined cloak, hose which fitted his legs with the skinlike exactitude which fashion demanded. This, however, was in the way of secondary impressions. The first glance given this cavalier was always for his sword which was exceptionally long and with a jeweled handle in the manner of the East—an aggressive, even a truculent sword in an age when men carried weapons for constant use, and consequently out of keeping with the appearance of this sober knight of thirty years or so.

"Lady Alys," he said, reining in beside her with a diffident air, "I confess to finding your instructions hasty and not well advised. Permit me to say that your father, if he were here, would regard himself as in the wrong in this matter. His sole concern would be to make amends."

"I've tried to make amends, Sire d'Arlay!" cried the girl. "My offer has been spurned, as you've seen. She has dared to answer me back and that's something I can't allow!"

"I find myself in an awkward position," said the knight, regarding the offended beauty with some hesitation. "I've ridden in your train for two days and so consider myself as a guest. In spite of that I must say that I can't permit you or your servants to molest this unfortunate child."

The girl turned in her saddle. "You joined us for the protection we could afford you, Sire d'Arlay! It's a poor return to interfere in matters which don't concern you at all! My mother is ill and I'm sure she will join with me in demanding that you spare us your company further." Her eyes flashed angrily in his direction. "It will be pleasanter riding without you. There will be no taint of trade on the air!"

"You refer, no doubt, to my connection with Jacques Coeur. Is it possible you don't know how your father acquired his new lands in Beaune?" Then the frown on his face gave place to a smile. When this happened the suggestion of melancholy, which the serious expression of his eyes gave his face, vanished completely. "I know you well enough, Lady Alys, to be certain you don't mean the things you say when you're in a temper. Nonetheless I propose to delay my departure long enough to make sure that you don't indulge it any further."

The intervention of the knight had caused the servants to remain in their places. They now waited uneasily to see what course their mistress would take. To their obvious relief, she decided not to force the issue. Turning her horse's head back into the north, she called out an order for the cavalcade to proceed.

After watching the long train pass, the Sire d'Arlay looked at his servant who had stationed himself with discretion behind his master. "Helion," he said, "we've changed sides, it seems. What do you think of this new company with whom we find ourselves?"

The servant sniffed contemptuously. "A mangy crew," he said.

D'Arlay smiled. "I sometimes think, Helion, that you're more conscious of my rank than I am myself. I detect in you a tendency to look down that long nose of yours at people."

"I'm the servant of Robinet de Burey, the Sire d'Arlay. Isn't that just reason for pride? I was at Montagne-Noire when you were born, master.

I've been in your service ever since you fell heir to the domain of Arlay. Who serves you has no regard for the rabble."

"What's your opinion of this tall soldier? The one with all the colors of the rainbow at his neck?"

"A tug-mutton, that one."

"A Scot? I believe you're right. What think you of the churchman?"

"A hedge-priest. He carries a knife in his sleeve."

"And the girl?"

Helion's air became less confident. "As for the girl, master," he said, "I can't make up my mind about her at all."

"You and I are in the same case there, my Helion. I haven't been able to make up my mind about her either."

2

Pregent Kennedy and the girl were standing beside the wrecked chare. He gave reluctant consideration to the shape under the blanket which was stretched on the floor of the conveyance.

"Was it the truth you told them?" he asked.

"Yes, my lord. My father died last night. It was very sudden. He was in great pain and I could do nothing to bring him relief. I tried to find help but there wasn't anyone, it seemed, within miles of us. And so I—I had to sit beside him and watch him die."

"I can see, my lass, that you've been taking it hard." Then he added in a grumbling tone, "You must be well left if you can refuse gold in such a lavish manner."

"I have no more than will pay for a single night at an inn."

Kennedy surveyed her downheld face with an air that verged on horror. "What madness is this? Is your mind buzzing with waxwings that you could do such a thing? It was sinful pride, my lass, that made you do it!"

"There are the mules to be sold. They will be of no further use now that the carriage is ruined." Her face took on an expression of the deepest grief. "It will distress me sorely to part with them. They've been such faithful friends!" She walked over to the one which had suffered at the hands of the man-at-arms and put an arm around his neck. "My poor fellow! My patient old Olivier! How sad to be born a mule and have a master who keeps you on the road every day. And now you're old and they've hurt you badly and yet I must sell you to some stranger!" She was on the point of tears. "I'll never forgive myself, my good Olivier!"

Kennedy had been giving the team a critical appraisal, examining their teeth and running his hands over their haunches. "They'll be ready for the crows in another year," he commented. "Still, you're in luck, minikin. Anything that travels on four legs is so much in demand that you may get a good price for these hobbling ghosts."

"Will there be enough to pay for a decent funeral and for masses to be said?" asked the girl anxiously. "I loved him but—but, my lord, he will need the masses, and many of them. He was a drinking man and there was little piety in him even when he was sober."

"Aye. There will be enough—if we can find any way of getting him the burial. There may even be a few pence over for you. I'm a rare hand at a bargain and you will be wise to trust the selling of the mules to me."

"If you'll be so very kind, it will be a great load off my mind. I'm a very poor hand at a bargain."

The Sire d'Arlay had dismounted in the meantime. He walked over to them, studying the Scot first and then turning his attention to the girl. He stopped abruptly and it was apparent that he had experienced a surprise. "I've seen her before," he said to himself. Then he realized it was not that. She resembled someone he knew. There was a sense of shock about his discovery of the resemblance because he was sure that in some way it would prove of great importance to him. And yet everything was vague in his mind and he had no idea at all of whom she reminded him.

"May I inquire your name, Mademoiselle?"

"It is Valerie Maret." There was no trace of the pride she had shown in her encounter with the other girl. She kept her eyes lowered. "It was kind of you, my lord, to interfere in my behalf."

D'Arlay said to himself, "Her voice is low and rather beautiful. Where could she have learned to speak in such a way?" Aloud he asked, "And where do you come from?"

"We had no home, my lord. My father, who is dead, was Damian Maret, an actor in Mysteries. We lived on the road."

Kennedy had raised the blanket for a look at the dead man. He dropped it back into place and said to the girl: "He has a noble head, my lass. I would have judged him an expounder of the Holy Word or even a philosopher rather than an actor in wicked and heathenish nonsense."

Valerie Maret lost her diffidence at once. "You are wrong!" she declared. "The Mysteries are not wicked. They do much good."

"I've seen many and I agree with you," said D'Arlay, addressing the girl.

"My father was a very fine actor, my lord," said the girl proudly. "But it was a great tragedy for him! His legs were short and crooked and so he had to play the villains or sometimes, even, comedy parts! The best they ever gave him was Judas, and sometimes he was Malice, and once Envy."

A desire to justify the Mysteries, aroused in her by Kennedy's criticism, led her on to boasting of her father's ability. "Ah, you should have seen him as Judas! And as Simon Magus. He learned to do magic tricks and sleight-of-hand to play Simon, and everyone agreed he was the greatest Simon since Anton Fresche, who was a German and had been a magician himself once. Ah, my lords, he longed so much to play the Part—Christ in the Resurrection. But how could he with such bandy legs? I think it was because of this he drank so much."

D'Arlay was still musing over the contrast between her way of speaking and the station of life in which she had been born. "She chooses her words like a lady of birth," he said to himself, "and not like the daughter of a common strolling player. Can there be a real mystery here? One in which she's playing a part?"

He had been watching her with intense concentration. Everything about her added to the effect of familiarity she created—her eyes, her hair, every play of expression. And yet the answer still eluded him. He would think he had it and then the clue would be lost. It would slip away from his mind like a firefly through the clutching fingers of a child.

It was with growing surprise that he noted details of her appearance. She had a fine brow, wide and white and intelligent. Her nose was straight and without any of the coarseness of line found in the peasant type. At first he had set her down as pretty but now he realized she was the possessor of real beauty.

Seeking for an explanation, he began to ask questions. "Were you born in Anjou?"

She shook her head. "No, my lord. I was born in Berri. At least it has always been so believed."

He grasped at this hint of obscurity in her past. "Surely your parents were not in any doubt?"

Her diffidence had reasserted itself and she seemed distressed at the necessity of answering. "It—it's a long story, my lord, and one which wouldn't interest you."

He said to himself, "This isn't the time to press her on that point. I'll find out about it later." Aloud he asked another question. "You've traveled about the country a great deal?"

"All my life we've been on the road. I've seen all of France save—you will smile at this, my lord—all save Paris itself!" Her eyes suddenly began to glow. "I have seen where the Maid was born. I stood there for hours and almost I was persuaded that the Voices were beginning to speak to me! Once, when Father had no part, I had him take me where she led our armies. Someday, when our King wakens up from his long slumbers and drives the Godons[1] out of France, I shall go to Rouen and offer a prayer on the spot where she died!"

"I think," said D'Arlay thoughtfully, "that it may be possible to go to Rouen soon now." He hesitated, as though uncertain of the wisdom of giving an explanation for this belief. "I also have been in every part of France during the past six months. I went to test the feeling of the country about the question of war. I found this: The people want war, they want it so badly that the King will have to yield."

"I pray God you are right, my lord. And that another Maid will come to lead the armies of France!"

"That," said D'Arlay dryly, "may not be necessary."

A pause ensued and then D'Arlay turned to the Scot to ask, "What is your name?"

"I am Pregent Kennedy." Apparently the Scot was surprised that the name evoked no sign of recognition for he frowned and added, "It must be that I am less well known than I thought."

"Unjustly, perhaps, I am unaware of the claims you have to fame, Monsieur Pregent Kennedy."

"I know more of bombards than any man in the world. Will it mean anything to you if I say I commanded a battery of the guns against the heathen Turk? I'm on my way now to see Jacques Coeur. *He* will know all about me and will see to it that I'm given a command when we fight the English again."

"I've heard Jacques Coeur speak of you. Will you forgive my lack of memory, Sir Scot?"

"My father fought at Azincourt as so many of my brave countrymen did," went on Kennedy, with a bitterly assertive pride, "and he died there with a Sassenach arrow in his throat. I have fought your battles for thirty years myself, Sir Knight, and little reward I've had." He looked up at the sky and shook his head. "There's a mizzle coming on from the tinge of things. We'll spend a damp night, I am thinking. . . . My mother was French but I'll have you know I was born at Maybole in Ayrshire. May she rest in peace, my sweet lady mother dead these many years, but she did me an ill turn by naming me after her own father. It fits ill with the fine Scottish name I bear though I swear I have done enough to lend distinction to the combination. I," he added grandly, "am a Kennedy of Cassilis."

[1]Godon was a term of contempt applied to the English invaders. It was first used by Jeanne d'Arc.

"I presume it's a distinction of some importance."

"Aye," said the Scot. "It's important in Scotland. And," with a scowl, "wherever *I* happen to be."

There was a pause and then D'Arlay asked, with an air of deliberation, "You have ridden with the Free Companies?"

The Scot looked at him sharply. "It is true," he said, after a moment. "I'm a soldier and I must live. I had my own band for a time. And," with rising emphasis, "I was doing handsomely. I always see to it that in anything I do there's a profit for myself, even though no more than a souldie, as you might say. Can you quarrel with that, Sire d'Arlay?"

"I quarrel bitterly with the right of any man to prey on innocent and defenseless people. Since the truce was signed with the English, the Free Companies have bled France white."

"The Free Companies are made up largely of Frenchmen," said the Scot. "What excuse can you offer for that, Sire d'Arlay?"

"I offer no excuse. Unfortunately it's true. Perhaps one hundred years of fighting has turned us into savages." With an air which terminated the discussion, D'Arlay turned to the priest. "Where do you hail from?"

He looked closely at the churchman while waiting his reply, noting the multitude of purple lines which gave his face an odd resemblance to a map of the world. At close range it was possible to read in Father Imbert an amiability and trustworthiness not apparent on first inspection.

"I am from Provence," answered the priest. "I carry papers to Paris."

"And now," said the Scot, in an impatient tone, "if your curiosity concerning us has been satisfied, may I inquire as to the prospects for supper? The lass has nothing in the carriage save a stone jug of wine which I suspect is thin and sour, and a loaf of bread of questionable age. The priest and I fed well at noon in expectation of locating an inn before nightfall. As a result our saddlebags are empty."

"What have we left, Helion?" asked D'Arlay.

The servant answered grudgingly. "Enough for all, master. There is the better part of a roast capon and some scraps of other meat. And there is meal and bread."

"We shall do famously," declared the Scot, with an expression of relief.

The girl spoke up in a hesitant tone. "I am a very good cook, my lords. If we can have a fire made, it will take little time to prepare a warm meal —if my lord is ready to trust the food to me."

"With the best will in the world, Mademoiselle. Helion has had much experience in the building of fires since we took to the road and will have a good blaze for you when it's needed. The rest of us had best use the interval in pitching tents against the prospect of rain which you've already noted, my brave captain of Free Companions."

Valerie Maret said to herself when she saw the variety of supplies which Helion produced for her use, "How wonderful it must be to have things like these!" Then she added hastily, "Since I have boasted of my skill, I must do my very best." She studied the supplies and decided to make a dish called a mawmenny which was a popular one with all who could afford it. Accordingly she poured oil and wine into a pan and dropped in sparing quantities of herbs and porret and the thinnest possible slice of garlic. This she stirred over the fire until the ingredients became crisp and brown. She then poured in the meal, whipping it furiously with a spoon as she did so. The cooked flesh of the capon was added, and it was not until the last moment that she stirred in the sliced dates and dried mulberries which give a mawmenny its full perfection of flavoring.

At exactly the right moment the pan was removed from the coals and placed on the ground between the three men (Helion remaining in the background) who had seated themselves in an impatient semicircle. When she made no move to join them, D'Arlay looked up inquiringly at the young cook. "The food will have no flavor if we lack your presence, Mademoiselle," he said.

She shook her head quickly. "It wouldn't be right, my lord. Always my father ate first, and then my mother and I sat down. It's a custom on the road."

"A custom, then, which we must break tonight." D'Arlay moved to one side to make room for her. "Sit here with me. I shall see to it, moreover, that you are served first."

He was unable to fulfill his promise, however, for Pregent Kennedy had already dipped a spoon in the savory dish. The Scot nodded his head with approval as the first mouthful vanished down his throat. "A toothsome dish," he said, smacking his lips. "In Scotland we call this a Bouce Jane. We cook it plain without all these knickknacks and kicksey-winseys. The wholesome food of Scotland," he went on defensively, "is what makes the strong backs and arms of the Scots, and the strong heads. These same strong arms will drive the English into the Channel for you when the chance comes." Sensing that this boast had roused resentment in the others, he added: "What I mean is this: The knights of France won't win the war, if war there is."

D'Arlay commented with some unwillingness, "I agree with that."

"It will be the cannon, the bombards. And many Scots, being shrewd and farsighted, will be serving as bombardiers."

Nothing more was said for several minutes. The men were all hungry and were applying themselves to the food with the good will which is the cook's accolade. D'Arlay was aware, as he consumed his share, that the girl had not started to eat. "It's not strange that you abstain from food," he said to her. "But it won't be wise to give yourself entirely to your grief. Come! Dismiss these gloomy thoughts and dip a spoon into the dish before these ravening wolves have scraped it clean."

"I have no appetite, my lord." She obeyed him, however, and began to eat, slowly and sparingly.

There was still no rain although the threat of it remained. Not a star was to be seen. Bats circled about them and swooped through the area of light on swiftly weaving wings. A belated wheatear fluttered by and vanished, and then returned to hover about uncertainly, uttering its startled "Chat! Chat!" before finally taking itself back into the gloom. An owl hooted continuously from somewhere close at hand.

Watching the girl with the interest which he had felt from the instant he detected the resemblance, D'Arlay saw that she was progressing mentally through a cycle of moods. At first she held her head down and was obsessed quite clearly with her grief, for she sighed and lost all concern with food. She passed from this stage into one where her eyes showed signs of agitation and her fingers gathered together tightly. He was convinced that she was thinking of the clash with the Lady Alys and he said to himself, "There's nothing passive about her; she has her share of fighting spirit." Gradually she became less tense. She relaxed into a spirit of reflection, her hands lying limply in her lap, her eyes fixed on the darkness which had closed in about them.

"What thoughts are in your mind," he asked, "which take you so far away from us?"

She flushed. "I would be ashamed to tell you, my lord. It was—it was something most trivial. You would have a very poor opinion of me if you knew."

The rest of the company were still eating with avidity and paying no attention. The chomp of Helion's jaws could be heard from the spot he had selected for himself which was not close enough to the fire to constitute lack of respect but not far enough away to lose him all benefit of the warmth. D'Arlay leaned closer to her.

"Tell me," he urged.

She still hesitated. "Truly, my lord, it's a matter for great shame that I—I can think at a time like this about"—she looked up at him and her face took on a deep flush—"about the beauty of the velvet dress the lady was wearing!"

He smiled. "I rode for two days in her company and I can't tell you now what color it was. Was it a very pretty habit?"

"Oh, it passes description! It was of a color one seldom sees, I'm sure the most lovely blue in the world." Now that she had begun to talk, the words came tumbling out. "And did you notice the lace at her neck and wrists? But of course you didn't, since you were not in an observant mood. Never have I dreamed of such beauty! And the plume in her hat! I longed to feel the softness of it in my hands. Her shoes——" She stopped suddenly and with a hurried motion of her arm draped her skirt over her own shoes in fear that he might look at them. She was too late. He had already observed, with a feeling of compassion, that they were old and broken and most meanly clobbered. He had noticed also that her hose, the one article of apparel in which all women, old or young, high or low, took the most meticulous interest, were cheap and covered with patches.

"And do you think clothes so very important, then?" he asked.

She hesitated and sighed. "I think they are most important when you lack everything you would like to have. I've made my own clothes since my mother died, six years ago. But I've little gift with the needle, my lord, as you must have noticed."

"You need good clothes less than anyone I've ever seen. You're so attractive, in fact, that I've been wondering about you. You must have found admirers wherever you went—to the extent even that it became a danger."

"Tinkers and barbers and ale-drawers in taverns." She was speaking in a lighter tone. "Yes, I've had admirers but they've been of the lowest degree. No girl traveling about as we've done could escape that kind of attention."

"Has it been difficult for you?"

"No-o-o." Her manner had now shown a definite change. For the moment she had forgotten her grief and distress. She even indulged in a smile as she started on an explanation. "I had ways of avoiding it. When we had money and could stay at an inn—it wasn't often, my lord, and so it was always a great event—I would usually do something like this when we went in."

She straightened up and said, "Observe!" The corners of her mouth drew down and something strange happened to the shape of her eyebrows. It was hard to believe and yet there was no gainsaying that she had succeeded in giving herself an air of slyness and ill-nature. Then it vanished, and she laughed with satisfied pride. "You can believe now, my lord, that they would take one look at me and that would be all. But sometimes, when there were many men about, and it seemed wise to be more thorough, I would pull my hood down over my forehead and make myself look like this."

This time she managed to create a suggestion of broadness about her face. Her eyes had a hard glint in them. She had become common, a drab, a vixen, and yet at the same time something of a goose-cap as well; and so completely lacking in attraction that no man would have given her a second's attention.

"That one always accomplished its purpose," she said. Her face had changed back to its normal lines. "My father said I would have been a fine actor if I had been born a man. He even said I might in time be as good as he was; and that, my lord, is the highest praise an actor ever gives."

Pregent Kennedy flicked the ends of his tartan lightly across his lips and sat back from the dish. He glanced about the circle of faces, barely perceptible now in the dark of evening.

"We have a problem to discuss," he said. "What's to be done about the body?"

It had become apparent to all of them that Father Imbert possessed no more than a limited share of understanding. He looked up now and said: "There must be a burial. But where? And when?"

"Here," answered the Scot. "And now."

"Do you want to know how far we are from a church?" asked the priest. "I will answer as best I can: I don't know."

Kennedy turned to D'Arlay. "Are you familiar with these parts, my lord?"

D'Arlay answered with a negative shake of the head.

"And you, child?"

Valerie responded in a low voice from which she strove to keep any hint of the emotion she was feeling, "I know little of this part."

"Then," said the Scot, "the burial must be here. It's fortunate we have Father Imbert to conduct the service."

The girl was distressed. She looked at Kennedy, her eyes full of supplication, and then turned in the direction of D'Arlay. "Please, my lords! Surely there is something else to be done!"

Kennedy proceeded to explain that none of them had time to waste in reaching their destinations. She could see for herself that the chare could not be used again. What other way, then, was there? "After all," he added, "your father will have an easier resting place than soldiers who fall in battle."

There was a long and uncomfortable pause. "I understand the difficulties," said Valerie finally. "You've all been so kind that I don't want to cause more trouble. And yet I—I can't reconcile myself to this."

D'Arlay asked, "Is your reluctance because he would be buried without a coffin?"

The girl nodded her head. "Yes, my lord. He wouldn't have any rest." She was on the point of tears and it was apparent that she found it hard to continue. "He suffered for many years from an ache in his bones. Many times he said to me, 'Never bury me in damp ground.' He said that all he asked of a grave was that it be wide and dry. Sometimes he laughed when he said it but I knew that he meant it." She turned her head toward the sky. "It will rain before morning, my lords, and the ground will be soaked."

D'Arlay indulged in some speculations. "I have a little skill with tools," he said finally. "If you're prepared to let me use what's left of the chare, I could make a coffin of the wood."

Valerie said to him eagerly, "If you will do that for him, I will say a prayer for you every day as long as I live!"

"It will take me a long time and I'll need all the help you can give me." D'Arlay rose to his feet and called to his servant: "Helion! My ax!"

3

For two hours D'Arlay and the girl struggled with the task. The others had shown some inclination at first to assist but had given it up early. They were now asleep, stretched out on the ground with their feet turned toward the fire. Valerie had worked hard, keeping the fire going as well as undertaking the demolition of the chare (a task which caused her infinite regret, having always taken a pride in the family possession of a vehicle), and carrying the wood to D'Arlay.

"I have less skill than I thought," said the latter. "This is taking me a much longer time than it should."

Her face acquired at once a look of remorse. "I am shamed to be the cause of so much trouble, my lord."

D'Arlay laughed. "To be honest, I'm enjoying myself in spite of all the difficulties. I may say with just pride that I'm accomplishing quite a feat here. If it had been my good fortune to be born a carpenter, I might have been a success. Instead, I'm a landowner and a knight, and a sorry failure at both."

"I'm sure you are not, my lord."

"The only thing to my credit is that I've acquired a certain skill with that." He nodded in the direction of his sword which he had deposited on the ground. The blade shone in the light from the coals. "And skill with the sword is little considered. A knight should have a mastery of the lance, the battle-ax, and the morning star,[2] but the sword is counted a womanish weapon. I predict that someday it will be considered the only fit weapon for a gentleman. . . . Also I had the good fortune to fall in with the great Jacques Coeur and to become a friend, and, in a sense, a partner of his. That I've prospered is due entirely to the partiality of the Moneyman." He wiped his brow and flexed the muscles of his arms gratefully. "It would be wise for both of us to have a rest now and a drop of wine. Carpentering is thirsty work."

"You must be very tired," said D'Arlay, as they sat beside the fire, their thirst satisfied. "All the menial part of the work has fallen to your share." He paused and then made an abrupt demand. "Let me see your hands."

She held them out for his inspection. They were small and well shaped, the fingers slender and tapering. Although the palms were calloused and the skin rough and chapped, it was clear they were not the hands of a peasant girl. "Nor," he said to himself as he examined them, "the hands of the daughter of a strolling player. There's a story here and I must get to the bottom of it."

"You've had a great deal of work to do," he said aloud.

"Since he took so ill I've had everything—caring for the mules and making fires and setting up the tent." She held her hands in front of her and studied them ruefully. "That isn't hard to see, is it? They are hard and ugly."

"So far from ugly that I'm beginning to wonder." He turned about on the ground to face her squarely. "You said there was some doubt as to where you were born. Do you care to explain what you meant?"

Valerie hesitated. "We never told anyone," she said finally. "But now they're both dead and it's my secret—to tell if I wish. I didn't know about it myself until I was ten years old and then my mother—Madame Maret—told me." She looked up at him and added impulsively: "I'm sorely tempted to tell you, my lord. You are so kind."

He waited for her to make up her mind.

"It's this, my lord. I wasn't their daughter. They found me."

D'Arlay was not surprised. The long war, complicated by the operations of the écorcheurs who harried the countryside during the recurrent truces, had resulted in countless cases of a similar nature. Every army movement,

[2]A mace. So called because it was oftenest used in surprise attacks at daybreak when it was handy to bash out the brains of sleeping opponents.

every raid for plunder, left smoking ruins and charred fields and the bodies of victims without number. Parents were killed and the children left, to find homes where they might or die of starvation. All records had been destroyed and it was generally an impossibility to trace the missing. It was said that in the areas over which the contending armies had fought back and forth for so many generations there were few children who could be certain of their parentage.

"I thought so," said D'Arlay. "And I'm quite sure your real parents were from a higher station in life than the—the couple who raised you. I'm still amazed at the way you speak, for it's impossible you can have had any education."

"I've already told you that Monsieur Maret was a great actor," said the girl, with a trace of pride. "He often said that the only thing he could do for me was to teach me to speak properly. He began as far back as I can remember. He would recite lines from the Mysteries and have me repeat them after him. Sometimes he would read from the *Imitatio Christi*.[8] I had some education, you see—in listening to him and asking questions."

"Did he teach you to read yourself?"

She shook her head regretfully. "No, my lord. When I grew old enough there always seemed to be too much to do. My mother, Madame Maret, was an invalid."

"I can understand now why you have such a fine voice. But the rest can be explained in one way only. You have beauty, Mademoiselle, and of a kind which proves you come of good stock. Will you tell me under what circumstances you were found?"

Now that she had broken the ice, the girl was willing, nay, eager, to talk.

"I wish I had more to tell. They, Monsieur and Madame Maret, found themselves in a village which had been raided and burned. Some of the houses were still blazing, and so they knew the écorcheurs couldn't be far off. They were going to drive on quickly—and then they heard the cry of a child. Madame Maret insisted they must do something. She went to look and found me in a basket just inside the entrance to the church. A woman had gone there for sanctuary, taking me with her. But it had been of no use. The robbers had killed her. They had even stripped the church of all its vestments. I must have been hungry, for I was crying loudly."

"And you believe the murdered woman was your mother?"

[8]A book published in parts over a period of years which was widely read because of its inspirational power. The handwritten copies were so eagerly sought that it was, in fact, the first best seller.

Valerie hesitated before answering. "Madame Maret did not think so. The sheet in which I was wrapped was not of dowlas but of the very finest linen."

"Was the woman a peasant?"

"It seemed so. Madame Maret said she was plainly dressed and that her hands were large and rough. She was young and of a heavy build."

"She was being paid as a wet nurse. Everything points to that."

"We always believed so. But now there's no way of finding out anything more. They, the Marets, went back to the village six months later to make inquiries. It was still deserted and so they learned nothing."

"And they didn't go back a second time?"

The girl shook her head. "No, my lord. It's my belief they didn't want to find out anything after I began to grow up. They thought of me as their own child. Monsieur Maret was very angry when he found I had been told. I could hear them quarreling about it after they thought I had gone to sleep. She said to him that he had been willing enough once to get a reward for returning me but he said that was at first. He had changed his mind."

D'Arlay remained silent for several moments, turning over what he had heard. "Is that all you know?" he asked finally.

"Madame Maret didn't have time to notice anything more. The roof of the church was blazing and so she picked up the basket and left at once. She saw that the woman was swarthy and that blood was running from a wound on her face. I curled my hand around her thumb while she carried me to the chare. And that's all."

"You know the name of the village?"

When she told him the name, he shook his head to indicate that he had never heard of it. "The chance of learning anything more as late as this," he said, "seems very small. But I think you should make every effort to see if you can discover your real identity."

She responded in an eager voice: "I intend to when the chance comes. I dream about it all the time. I'm sure in my own mind that the poor woman who was killed was not my mother. Who could my real mother have been? Is she still alive? If so, does she have any suspicion that I'm living also? Would she claim me if she knew?"

"There's one way in which I might help you. You remind me of someone I know."

"Who is it, my lord?"

"I don't know. All evening I've been trying to remember but I haven't succeeded."

"And you think it might lead to finding out who I am?" She was looking up at him with the most intense and eager interest. "Could it be a relative? A sister? My mother, even?"

He gave his head a shake of warning. "It won't be wise to build any hopes or expectations on it. The closest resemblances can be accidental. There's a man in Paris who looks so much like me that we might be thought twins. I went to see him once—and once only. He was a dull and timorous fellow who sniffled all the time. I felt irked that such a weak-spirited clod should walk the earth in the same guise as I."

"But——" She was far from content to leave the matter there. "Is there nothing to be done? I have a conviction, my lord, that I would learn who I am if you *could* remember."

"It will come to me soon, I'm certain." He got to his feet with some difficulty. The energy he had expended in unaccustomed toil had stiffened the muscles of his back and arms. "All I can do for you now, Mademoiselle, is to finish arrangements for the burying of the only one who might have been of assistance in getting at the truth. Do you feel equal to further effort tonight?"

Valerie rose promptly. "Of course, my lord."

An hour later he drove in the last nail. He thought, "I must contrive to give some small note of grace to this crude and clumsy thing," and began to carve a Latin text on the lid. He had succeeded as far as *Nil nisi bonum* when he glanced at his companion who was standing close by him to watch. He read both absorption and gratitude on her face.

"What does it mean?" she asked.

"I'm a poor scholar, but if my memory and my spelling are not at fault, it will mean, when I am through, something to this effect, *Think only good of the dead*. Do you approve of my choice?"

"Oh yes, my lord! I'm sure he would be grateful too, and proud, if he could see it."

Spurred on by this praise, D'Arlay said, "I'll try to carve some roses, and perhaps an angel with spread wings, when I finish the text."

He didn't go right back to work, however. The flicker of light across her face again stirred his desire to solve the matter of the resemblance. He said, "Stand over here where I can see you better." Dropping the ax, he placed a hand on each of her shoulders and proceeded to study her face with complete absorption.

He now perceived things about her which had escaped him before. Her fairness was of the kind which comes from the effect of the sun. It was as though its rays had become imprisoned in her skin and hair; and so she had none of the fragile and flowerlike prettiness of gold and pink and white but displayed instead a molten quality, the vitality and radiance of the sun itself. He could not be sure of the color of her eyes. They were, he thought, blue, a very light blue. But it was apparent also that there was a tawny quality about them as well. He realized that the distinctive quality of her looks came from her eyes.

"A most unusual kind of loveliness," he thought. "It should be easy to remember who it reminds me of. And yet it still eludes me."

Then, without knowing why he had stopped or when, he was thinking no longer of that point. He had been completely carried away. He was conscious only of the curious charm of the face turned up to his. Her eyes (how could he have believed that another pair like them existed?) held him in such subjection, such thrall, that he had forgotten everything else.

"What has come over me?" he asked himself. "Have I fallen under a spell?"

He felt an almost uncontrollable impulse to draw her into his arms. He said to himself, "I'm afraid that I'm falling in love," and this thought helped him to resist the temptation. He dropped his hands from her shoulders and stepped back. It would not do for him to fall in love. There were the best of reasons why it would not do.

He said to Valerie, "I must finish the carving," but to himself he was saying, "As soon as we've buried this poor actor fellow in the morning, I must be on my way."

Chapter III

I

THE glove was up! It was suspended over the gates of the city as a sign that a fair was being held. For the time it remained there, ordinary affairs would be forgotten. In the daytime people would trade in the booths set up along the streets and in the evenings there would be feasting and drinking and dancing, and merrymaking in general.

Valerie experienced a nostalgic feeling as soon as she came in through the gates. Fairs had always been the high spots in her not-too-gay existence. They had meant parts for Damian Maret and money once more in the family purse and, perhaps, a new dress for her or a hat or, at the very least, some ribbons. When she saw that a stage was being erected on the main square, with a block and tackle for the Ascension and a curtain on rings, she said to herself, "If poor Father were alive he might be picked at last to play the Part and he would be stamping up and down this very minute rehearsing his lines or he would be shouting to me to know if I had unpacked his costumes and wigs." She sighed, however, when the realization came to her that Damian Maret more likely would be in one of the taverns, drinking in advance to the success he hoped to achieve.

The errand which brought her here was in no sense a festive one. After the burial service and the departure thereafter of the Sire d'Arlay (she had been sorry to see him go and had wondered why such haste was necessary), she had known that the time had come to strike out on her own. Pregent Kennedy, who had sold the mules for a good figure, had given her sound advice. There was only one course open to her, he had pointed out: she must get married, and to a middle-aged husband, one with plenty of gold in the chest he would use for the headboard of his bed, and the capacity, which only an elderly spouse would have, of appreciating her good looks. As the best chance of finding such a husband was to go where the most men were to be found, she must accompany him to Paris. If the right kind of husband did not put in an appearance, there was always the certainty that a place of some kind could be found for her in one of the many establishments conducted by Jacques Coeur. The Scot's purpose in going to Paris was to see Jaquet the Fox and, of course, a word from him would suffice.

Valerie didn't want to go to Paris. Damian Maret had been afraid of the city. Perhaps he had heard so much of the greatness of the actors that he had secretly lacked the courage for such competition; perhaps he dreaded the poverty which would be his lot there. At any rate, although he talked loudly and overmuch of invading Paris and setting it agog with the splendor of his talents, he had always found some reason at the last moment for not going. His fears had been communicated to Valerie. She thought of the city on the Seine as a great walled prison. She had heard more of the bodies swinging in chains at Montfaucon than of the beneficent shadow of Notre Dame. Furthermore, she had lived all her life on the edge of destitution and one thing she had learned was that rosy hopes and expectations such as the Scot was holding out could easily be blasted. She had thought of a plan of her own which would be surer and safer. Accordingly she had listened respectfully to Kennedy's arguments and then she had quietly packed up and disappeared.

She was carrying a bundle of clothes in one hand and a basket in the other as she made her way through the crowded town. She kept her eyes wide open and was the first to jump to one side and flatten herself against the wall when a party on horseback came galloping at top speed down the narrow cobbled street. A murmur of curses rose around her as the knights disappeared and she saw nothing but faces black with hate. This was not new to her. Those who travel the roads and know the people of the spittal-houses and the slums learn all about their hates and fears.

She saw a tall blond youth in a shining hauberk and with a bill on his shoulder come striding through the crowd, whistling with easy confidence. The people made way, knowing him to be English from the leopards on his scarf. They would not have been so ready to respect the truce had they known the air he was whistling was the campaign song of the days of the great English victories, "Sir Robert Knowles All France Controls." Valerie looked at him in fear and wonder and took pains to make sure that he had nothing in the way of a tail. Most of the people of France, who knew the invaders by reputation only, were sure that the term applied to them of *Longues-Coues* was a literal description.

She stopped beside a friendly looking citizen in the flat cap of a vintner to ask, "Can you tell me, Monsieur, where the Giglet fair is being held?"

The man motioned over his shoulder. "In the yard of the next inn back, minikin," he said. Then he noticed the bundle and basket. "If you're thinking of offering yourself, you'll have to hurry. It's nearly over. They tell me the *Petit Gaste* is still to be suited. Take a hint and don't sign with him."

The innyard was crowded still and there was much chattering and laughing going on. The blue flag had been hoisted on a low platform and the clerk sitting under it was striving to inject a lively note into the proceedings by a continuous monologue.

"The Giglet fair is open!" he intoned. "Want you good servants, Messires and ladies? We have a number here for your inspection and questioning. Look them over well, you who are here because of your needs and not for gaping-seed. The men are strong and the women are diligent and neat. Look at them, Messires, standing there in youthful innocence and confusion at being forced to parade themselves in public.

Never have we offered a better lot than you see before you today. Come up and make your selections!"

"The same lot, year after year," complained a merchant. He glared up at the clerk. "They're misfits, and well you know it. You know how poor they are when the Petit Gaste can't find one to suit him. They're doddypolls, these, or they're lazy, or dishonest."

The candidates were standing on benches along each side of the yard, the men on one and the girls on the other. If they were covered with confusion or filled with youthful innocence, there was nothing on the surface to indicate it. Rather, they seemed to be enjoying themselves on this, their one day to strut in public, and were exchanging badinage of a heavy-handed variety with the spectators. Each wore a placard with a number lettered on it.

The spectators clearly were of the opinion that the matter in hand was part of the entertainment of the fair. There was a continual offering of witticisms. "Jacques," shouted one, "you'll have the Petit Gaste as your master if you don't find another soon. He'll cure you of sitting around on your fat blind-cheeks." Another raised a laugh by suggesting: "Flip up your skirts, Margot, and let them see your fat calves; that will get you hired if anything will."

Valerie's confidence in her plan had received a severe shock by this time. She looked about her and wondered if she could go on with it. The prospective masters, walking up and down the line and inspecting the candidates with a callous air, seemed to her as poor a lot as the candidates themselves. She had to fight down a wild desire to turn and leave while there was time.

A young man whose garb proclaimed him a mercer at this point tossed a coin in the direction of the girl Margot. To catch it would be to accept engagement. Margot did not lose a moment in reaching up and plucking it from the air. After biting it, with an impudent flash of eye for his benefit, she raised her outer skirt and dropped the coin into the pocket of the scarlet kirtle she wore underneath. Then she followed the custom of the fair by removing her placard and handing it to the clerk.

The latter went into brisk action. "Good Master Bellay," he said, "you've hired yourself a servant. It's affirmed that she's in good health, has no trace of contagion about her, and that she's not with child. If it should happen that a child *is* born at any time within nine months, it will not be your responsibility. After that—he, he!—it will be a different matter. If you find it necessary to beat her, it must be with a stick no thicker than your thumb and it must be limited to ten strokes. You will provide her with one warm dress of woolen material, a sleeping shift, two pairs of hose, and a cap. She will have four ounces of soap for the six months. You will pay her one denier a day."

"Agreed," said the mercer.

In accordance with custom, the girl said, "I accept you as my master for six months, and I promise obedience, and I will do every task set me with willing spirit."

Valerie had succeeded in edging up close to the platform. She now plucked nervously at the sleeve of the official in charge and said, "I desire to offer myself as a servant, Master Clerk."

The clerk was busying himself with a paper and did not look up. "Very well," he said. "I've no time to question you now but it can be done later. Get yourself up on the bench and, if you want a good master, smile." Then he chanced to look at her and his mouth gaped open with surprise. "St. Christophe! It won't be necessary for you to smile, my girl. You may get too good a master if you do."

He handed her a placard with the number sixteen, uttering a feeble joke, "Your age, no doubt, my little one." Valerie pinned it on the front of her cloak. Then she mounted to an empty section of the bench.

The appearance of a new candidate so late in the fair created something of a stir. The would-be employers moved forward with one accord to look her over. Painfully aware of the avid eyes which roved over her from head to foot, she clenched her hands and her lips in an effort to hold her feelings in control. She looked fixedly at the top of the innyard gates where a flimsy girouette jerked about in the wind.

As soon as she entered she had noticed a man of unusual size who was prowling about and grunting and snuffling and muttering to himself. Now she became acutely conscious of him for he had shouldered his way to the front rank and was staring at her like a tomcat at a caged bird. His exertions had brought out large globules of perspiration on his round face, making him look like a wax statue which was starting to melt.

Someone safely in the rear shouted: "How do you like her, Red Fins?" (An allusion to the custom butchers had of painting the fins of stale fish to make them seem fresh.) "Are you suited now?"

The unpleasant apparition began to speak in a high-pitched voice, addressing the company at large. "You say the Petit Gaste is hard to suit. Well, I'm suited now. This little chick is mine. I'll have you all notice that I'm the first to put in a claim."

This evoked an instant chorus of protest. "Wait, she suits me!" cried one man. "I want her myself," from another. A stern-looking woman, with the mustache which marks the approach of the late forties, at the most favorable reckoning, said, "It will be for the girl to decide."

The large man shoved his competitors back with an outward sweep of both arms. He scowled about him ferociously. "Any one of you who moves an inch closer will feel the weight of my hand," he announced. He looked up at Valerie (his head was almost level with hers as it was) with mounting approval. "I spoke first. But everyone knows that I'm a decent man and a fair one. You will all have a chance, even though I could knock your heads together and cave in your ribs and tweeze off your ears with one twist of my fingers!" He brushed his damp forehead with a grimy forearm. "We'll draw for her, my good fellow townsmen. Could anything be fairer than that? Here, Alain-All-Alone, a broom!"

When the inn servant had obeyed the command by producing the remnants of a broom, the giant pulled out a dozen straws of different lengths. He glanced about him until his eyes lighted on a shrinking little individual at the edge of the crowd. "You, Godenotte, come here!"

"Not me, Gaste! Please, not me!"

"Come here!" roared the big man, in a sudden fury. "Didn't you hear me right? Come at once or I'll tear out your teeth and use them to curry my mules!"

The small man came forward so slowly that the butcher reached out impatiently and yanked him the rest of the way. "All I want you to do, Calf-Lolly, is hold the straws. Here! Double your puny fist over them so that only the ends show. Now we'll see who's to be the lucky man."

Godenotte did as he was bade. One of the claimants, with more boldness than the rest, came forward with outstretched fist. Little Gaste stared at him for a moment in amazement and then cuffed his hand aside roughly.

"What! You would take first draw when I am giving you this chance out of the goodness of my heart? I shall have first draw myself."

The giant gripped the wrist of Godenotte so tightly that the fingers curled up under the pressure, revealing the lengths of the straws. Gaste examined them carefully before making his selection.

"And, now, the rest of you."

Afraid to cross him, each one of the claimants went through the farce of drawing a straw. Then the lengths were compared and the Petit Gaste was declared the winner. He looked about him with increased bellicosity.

"Are you all satisfied?" he demanded. "Was it a fair draw?"

Those nearest him, and thus the most exposed to danger, nodded at once and said, "Yes, it was fair."

He had hoped, apparently, to meet with some dissent. He looked now at those who stood in the rear and picked on one of them, a young fellow with a weak chin. "You haven't opened your mouth, Olim," he exclaimed. Stalking over, he proceeded to shake the victim with a pistonlike movement of his muscular arms. "Are you content, Olim? Are you, Olim? Say that you are, hulverhead, or I'll wrench your giblets loose!" He gave the young man a final shake and then sent him sprawling with a shove.

"Olim is content," he said, grinning about him.

The butcher turned then to look at the girl he could now claim as a servant without any hint of opposition. A blank look came over his face. The section of bench she had occupied was empty.

Valerie, watching the proceedings with feelings which can readily be imagined, had realized that she would have no chance to find employment unless she were prepared to accept the Petit Gaste as her master and this, needless to state, was a prospect she could not face. Taking advantage of the fact that the attention of everyone was focused on the drawing, she had discarded her placard and climbed down from the bench. When the triumphant butcher turned to claim her, she was already on her way to the entrance of the courtyard.

The Petit Gaste caught a glimpse of her and started in pursuit. Valerie fell into a panic when she realized this. She began to run in blind haste, saying to herself, "It was madness to come here!" Wheeling suddenly to escape his outstretched paw, she ran into the side of the platform. It collapsed with a loud crash and she caught a glimpse of the clerk's heels high in the air as he went over with it. A sound of breaking crockery made it evident that a jug of wine which had been on the platform had come to grief.

2

As usual a court had been set up to settle any disputes which might arise during the time the fair lasted. It was called Pied Poudre (in England, where they followed the same plan, the name was corrupted to Pie Powder) and it was quite literally a court of Dusty Feet, being conducted by merchants who had come from great distances. The judge was a trader in silks from Marseilles, an elderly man with a shrewd and kindly face.

The judge smiled as he said to the group assembled in front of him, "But it's clear, Messires, that it was an accident."

"A costly accident for me," whined the clerk of the Giglet fair who appeared as the complainant.

"The girl was frightened," went on the old judge. "She did not want to be claimed by the Petit Gaste, which is easy to understand. That she overturned the platform was unfortunate, I grant you, but there was no intent in it."

"I've suffered heavy losses," declared the clerk. "Item, a valuable jug, broken. Item, a gallon of good wine, spilled. Item, a rent in my cloak, suffered in the fall. Must I, the victim of the mishap, assume this threefold loss?"

The judge asked with a twinkle in his eye, "Have you considered claiming damages from the Petit Gaste?"

"No!" answered the complainant hastily.

"I didn't deem it likely. The Petit Gaste might display a slight tendency to violence under such circumstances. I hinted earlier to the one officer this court possesses for the carrying out of its decisions that it might be necessary to collect from that—that amiable citizen. I was informed he would rather lose his post than make any such attempt. In any event, the legal claim on the worthy, if somewhat hasty, butcher is a slight one." He reached out for a paper the clerk was clutching in his hand. "You have the amounts there? Let me have it."

"Thirty-four deniers," he announced after studying it. He glanced down at Valerie who was standing in front of him with a forlorn look on her face. "It seems, my child, that you have created a loss amounting to that sum. Are you in a position to pay it?"

"No, my lord judge," she answered in a frightened tone of voice.

"Have you anything to offer by way of compensation? Can you pay a part of it?"

"I have no more than two deniers, my lord judge."

The judge looked about him. "I am reluctant to send this child to prison——" he began.

Valerie caught her breath. She was under no illusions as to what a term in prison would mean. She would be thrown into one large cell with other prisoners (in the smaller towns the sexes were not separated) and there she would stay until her time was up, subsisting on the foulest food and exposed to every kind of disease. She knew that when poor people went to prison they were seldom the same afterward. She looked up with frantic appeal into the gentle face of the old judge.

He was continuing: "—or to order that she work long enough to pay the amount of the damages, inasmuch as that would mean entering the service of that kindly citizen who supplies the needs of the community in the matter of flesh and fowl. May I suggest that all present, including myself, make a donation and that the amount thus raised be accepted by you, Monsieur Clerk, as payment in full?"

The silence which followed this suggestion was a conclusive answer. The judge sighed. "I had hoped to strike a spark of generosity in your hearts, Messires," he said. "Having failed in that, I am under the necessity of——"

A voice spoke up from the rear of the courtroom. "I'll pay for her."

Valerie turned eagerly. The voice had a familiar ring to it and she was infinitely relieved to find that it belonged to Pregent Kennedy. The Scot came forward slowly, casting her a side glance as he passed which said as plain as words, "Now do you see how foolish you have been and what I am compelled to pay for your folly?"

"I know this girl," he said to the court. "I'm prepared to make a money settlement rather than see her sent to prison. But first I must cast an eye over the items on the bill of damages."

"Naturally," said the judge, handing over the paper.

"It's clear," declared the Scot, flourishing the paper after a quick survey of what it contained, "that the claimant has been guided by the promptings of hopes and, even, cupidity, rather than a sense of honesty and justice in fixing his estimates. What! Can it be that the wine which was spilled was costly Cyprus or Tokay? Did it come from the slopes of Lebanon and did flakes of gold float in its clear amber? Was the jug itself a chalice fit for the lips of a princess or a holy saint that he sets this absurd value on it? Monsieur Judge, I am a good whittler and this statement of claims will be like a willow wand in my hands."

Valerie felt a sudden weakness in her knees and, with a nod to the judge to beseech his permission, she walked to a bench at the side of the room where she seated herself. She watched the proceedings from there with a sense of relief so great that the leathery face of the Scot became to her like that of a guardian angel filled with wisdom and benevolence. She heard him brushing aside the passionate protestations of the clerk with a coldness of logic which reduced the claim to shreds.

"Seventeen deniers!" announced the judge, after an agreement had finally been reached. "This worthy soldier of an allied nation has been generous enough to pay that amount and so I am happy to declare the incident closed. May I add that I hope the Giglet fair will conclude with the Petit Gaste still unsuited."

Pregent Kennedy was honest enough to disclaim any undue credit when he escorted Valerie to the street. "I've a liking for you, minikin," he said. "But I'm compelled to tell you that it might have taken more than that to involve me in such a disastrous transaction as this. I am never prodigal with my"—he was compelled to fall back on his native tongue for the right word—"with my *siller*. There are other reasons for this seeming madness on my part. The Sire d'Arlay, who has a share of the wealth the Moneyman has created, left a sum in my hands to be used in just such an emergency. Further, I confess, minikin, that I was not as fast asleep that night as I appeared and so I heard what you were telling him about the mystery of your birth." When Valerie looked startled, he went on in a reassuring tone: "Your secret is safe with me. Nay, I think you lucky that I know. Let me help you, my child, and I'll dig out the truth for you like a dog with a long-buried bone."

"I'll be most happy to have your aid," said Valerie.

The Scot nodded his head. "I'm an honest man and I want you to understand at the outset that I am not actuated solely by generous instincts. I'm not above taking advantage of this to add to the weight of my purse. There must always be a souldie for me in everything I do." He looked at his companion with a dry smile. "Do you think you can unravel the secret if you sell yourself into service with butchers and the like? Nay, child, you must be prepared for bolder courses than that. Come with me to Paris and we will make a start on things from there."

"I'm ready to go," answered Valerie humbly.

Chapter IV

I

THERE was a small section cut off by a low oak screen from the rest of the white-plastered room. Here, on benches against the wall, visitors waited the convenience of Jacques Coeur. The screen was not high enough to prevent them from seeing the great merchant himself as he sat behind his desk, and so the period of waiting served a double purpose. The visitors achieved a proper appreciation of the demands on his time before they were summoned inside; and, when he so desired, he could look them over and give them a quick appraisal in advance.

"Who are out there today?" Coeur asked Nicolas, not raising his eyes from the papers in front of him.

"A dowsy lot," answered the servant. "Gerhart the fuller. He wants to wheedle you about the debt he owes you. I hope you heat his ears for him. A priest from the University; he'll be begging for something. A pilgrim who says he's just back from the Holy Land and has a splinter of the Cross to sell. A fakir, that one."

"Tell Gerhart to come back another day. I'll see the priest as soon as I can. Send the pilgrim away. Who else?"

"A soldier who calls himself Pregent Kennedy. He talks with a foreign twist. *Ecossais,* I think."

"Pregent Kennedy?" Coeur repeated the name thoughtfully. "I've heard of this Scot. He's been in the East, in Constantinople. He handled the bombards in a campaign against the Turks. I'll talk to him, Nicolas. Who else?"

"A girl."

"A girl? Well, go on. What does she want?"

Nicolas was smiling wisely. "I don't know what she wants, master."

"If she's here to beg, give her something from the alms bag and send her away."

"In that case you had better have the Lombardy banker up. He's waiting your convenience below."

"Why didn't you say so at first? Filling my ears with talk about this catch of small sprate when the big fish is waiting!"

Before departing to obey the order, Nicolas said in an aggrieved tone, "You know I always save the best for the last."

On the other side of the railing Valerie was watching the great man with fascinated interest. At the same time she was uncomfortably conscious of the close scrutiny of the other visitors and was careful to keep her feet hidden under the skirt of her cloak, not wanting anyone to see how dilapidated her shoes had become. She had placed a small wicker basket on the floor beside her.

Pregent Kennedy leaned toward her and whispered, "What is there about Jaquet the Fox which interests you so much?"

"His eyes," she answered in a low tone. "I'm sure he can see right through me. And yet they're so kind and understanding. I think he must be a wonderful man."

"Wonderful?" The Scot peered across the screen at the Moneyman with a dry smile on his long features. "Aye, he's wonderful—in his own way. Hard, acquisitive, sharp. His mind's as nimble as a ropedancer."

Nicolas entered, escorting a weazened old man in a plain gray gown which swept the floor as he walked. The arms of the newcomer were folded under his chin as though to provide a rest for his palsied head.

"A banker, I'll swear, from the looks of him," whispered the Scot. "Now watch how quickly that old frame of bones will be allowed to see the great Jacques Coeur."

"I've thought it over," said the banker, when he had seated himself across the table from the Moneyman. "Ten of the estates I must have, Jacques Coeur. The list is here. I have put Beaucaire at the head. Beaucaire I must have most certainly."

Coeur looked at the little man with a bitter frown. "I have thirty-two estates in which most of my profits have been sunk," he said. "And you, leech from Lombardy, are demanding ten of them as security for this miserable little loan you're making me. The lands you demand would repay the loan three times over. Are you forgetting I must make other loans and that all my creditors have to be satisfied?"

"You call this loan a small one?" quavered the old man. "It is so considerable I must scrape the bottom of my coffers to find the money. And, bear in mind, it's for the making of war. If the Engloys beat you again, and well they may, for they are a rude and fierce race, they will take every acre you own, Jacques Coeur! How, then, would poor Guiseppi of Lombardy get back his forty thousand écus? Would your Engloy masters pay him? Na, na! It would be a total loss. The return must be heavy, and the security good, to make this terrible risk worth while."

"The return," said Coeur, with a wry smile, "*is* heavy. Thirty per cent interest!"

The Italian, who looked as though he had been living in a steam bath and had been reduced thereby to the human limits of desiccation, piped up sharply: "I would demand of the King of France forty per centum for such a loan. You may know by the difference, Jacques Coeur, how well I think of you." He plucked at his beard with hands so thin they seemed all nails and veins. "As to Beaucaire, it's far enough south to be out of the reach of the Engloys. Yes, yes, I must have Beaucaire."

"If the people of Paris knew what you were demanding of me, they would stone you to death in the streets."

The veil which had obscured the rheumy orbs of the ancient banker suddenly cleared. Coeur found himself looking into the most predatory pair of eyes he had ever encountered. They were ageless eyes and as much out of place in that shrunken body as a beating heart in a scarecrow. "Have a care to yourself, Jacques Coeur," shrilled the moneylender. "They are more likely to stone *you*. The common people do not like rich men. When they hear that Jaquet the Fox is paying the whole cost of the war himself, they will want to know where he got the money for it. They will say that it came out of *their* pockets. They say now that he is so rich he has his horses shod with silver shoes. They gaze after him with envy in their hearts." He paused and nodded his head several times. "You are a generous man and a brave one, Jacques Coeur. You may win them their freedom—and be stoned as your sole reward!"

Coeur had never doubted that he stood well with the common people, never doubted that they looked with pride at what he, who had been one of them, had accomplished. "Old age is robbing him of his wits," he said to himself. "His avarice has addled him."

And yet there was a prophetic ring to the words which nettled him with a first stirring of fear. He got to his feet and began to pace about in an effort to regain his self-confidence.

"Guiseppi of Lombardy," he said finally. "I am not modest. I know myself for a man of infinite resource. If these loans I am now compelled to make should recoil like one of Jean Bureau's bombards and bring ruin to my enterprises, I have enough inventiveness here"—touching his forehead with his hand—"to build a new and better structure on the ruins. I'm afraid of nothing. I'm not afraid of the English. I can snap my fingers at all who yap at my heels.

"I've made up my mind about the terms I'm prepared to accept on this loan," he went on. "Banker, I won't give you Beaucaire as security. I won't give you all the others you have demanded. Five you shall have and no more; and I myself shall have the selection of them. Those are *my* terms. *Aut cape aut relinque.*" [1]

"I must have time," whined the Lombard. "I can't risk my moneys without due thought. My good lord Coeur, I must give the matter the deepest consideration."

"Take a week," said Coeur. "Go back to the Grand Pont and think it over well. I'll see you here one week from today. Wars can't wait for moneylenders."

"Wars," declared the old man, recovering some shreds of his arrogance, "can't be fought without moneylenders."

[1]Take it or leave it.

"You're wrong, banker. This one can be fought without moneylenders. But not without Jacques Coeur."

The banker shuffled from the room, muttering to himself, and Jacques Coeur returned to the papers heaped on his desk. He went through them with the utmost speed, recording his findings with a decisive "Yes" or "No" on the margins and scrawling at the bottom of each his bold "De ♡."

Nicolas returned. "Robert de Poitevin is here," he said. "Because he's the King's physician, should he stamp in here as though he owned us body and soul?"

The Moneyman's face had taken on a grave expression. "I'm afraid he's the bearer of ill tidings. Well, bring him in, Nicolas."

A sound of scratching could be heard from the other side of the screen. Coeur frowned and demanded, "What's that?"

"A cat, master. The girl has it in a basket."

"Is she still here? I thought I told you to send her away. I've considered sending *you* away a thousand times, my gome. This time I may do it."

Nicolas was not disturbed. "You needn't buy any flutes[2] from me today, master. You need me and full well you know it."

Coeur raised his hands in a gesture of resignation. "In the name of all the saints! Bring the physician in!"

2

Robert de Poitevin was a small man who looked the world squarely in the eye and feared nothing. He was not afraid of contracting the diseases and mischiefs he encountered every day and so had never adopted any of the devices his fellow physicians used. He did not wear a tunic steeped in chemicals nor did he fill his ears and nostrils with rue or carry a clove of garlic under his tongue. Instead he dressed in a plain gray habit, and the only sign by which he could be identified was a small caduceus embroidered on his collar.

He walked in briskly and seated himself beside the Moneyman's chair without indulging in any form of salutation. "Jacques Coeur," he said, pointing at him with a forefinger, "Agnes Sorel is going to present the King with another child."

The Moneyman was both shocked and disturbed. "But, my good Robert, she's in very bad health! Can she hope to survive childbirth when she's already in such a weakened condition?"

[2]In Paris jargon of the day, pick a quarrel.

The physician answered in gloomy tones: "I'm not pleased, you may be sure."

"Have you told the King?"

Robert de Poitevin nodded. "An hour ago. His King's Grace was disposed to regard the news with pride at first. When I made it clear to him that the unfortunate lady was in no condition to stand the ordeal, he became very angry with me, as I knew he would. Our liege lord doesn't like to face unpleasant facts. He told me that he wasn't satisfied with my unsupported opinion. . . . Well, I shall have to call them in, Olivier de Bousse from the University, that great blowhard, that maker of empty phrases, and the rest of them. We'll have the consultation he demands and they will sit around solemnly for hours, talking in Latin texts and making it abundantly clear that they know nothing at all. And then they will say to our liege lord that his servant, Robert de Poitevin, has been hasty in his opinion, that they in their joint wisdom do not agree with him entirely. They will say that the Lady Agnes is undoubtedly quite ill but that, on the other hand, she is still a young woman and God's ways are inscrutable and why should any mortal take it on himself to know what is in the heavenly mind. Sometimes, my lord Coeur, I am ashamed of my calling! We pretend to know so much and in reality we know so very little! Consider the matter of poisons——"

"Come, my good Robert! If you get launched on that subject, you'll talk for hours. Frankly, I can't allow you that much time today. My hours are filled—and the news you have brought me will weigh so heavily that I can't hope to accomplish much."

The two men stared at each other in an unhappy silence for several moments. Then Coeur said, "Tell me the truth, Master Robert. Is there any hope for her?"

The physician shook his head slowly and sadly. "Jacques Coeur," he said, "Agnes Sorel is going to die!"

Nicolas watched his master from the other side of the room with a worried frown. It was unusual for Jacques Coeur to remain impassive for such a long time; the news he had received from the physician had been disturbing, quite clearly. When he fell into a mood of absorption like this it was better to leave him alone, and so it was with reluctance that the servant crossed the floor again. He said, "Master, he's here."

The Moneyman roused himself with some difficulty. "Who is here?"

"Would I disturb you again for anything short of a summons from the King? Or because the Sire d'Arlay has returned at last?"

"Robin has arrived?" There was a note of relief in the voice of the Moneyman. "I am glad to hear it. Bring him up, Nicolas, bring him up!"

3

That there was a bond of mutual esteem between the two men was apparent when D'Arlay entered. Coeur met him halfway across the room with both arms outstretched. He wrapped them around the newcomer and gave him an affectionate hug.

"How, Robin!" he cried. "I'm delighted to see you. You're as brown, my gadling, as though you had returned from another journey to the East with Jean de Village."

"I have much to tell you," declared D'Arlay, settling himself down in the chair the physician had vacated.

For an hour they talked. They discussed the results of the tour D'Arlay had made, his meeting with Coeur factors in the course of his travels (Coeur knew them all so well that he could have quoted the profits of each for any given year), the news from the East which the last ships in at Montpellier had brought, the presents that D'Arlay had picked up, particularly for Isabeau (Coeur's scowl was evidence that he did not approve the bringing of presents for Isabeau), and the state of the country generally.

They had not exhausted their interest by any means when a trumpet sounded in the street. Coeur sprang eagerly to his feet.

"The convoy from the south has arrived," he said. "You must see this, Robin. There has been a procession through the town so the people could gape at the marvelous things we shall have for sale."

He motioned D'Arlay to follow him. Donning his customary *houve,* a curious type of headpiece which closely resembled in shape an oriental turban, Coeur led the way out to the open gallery which overlooked the inner courtyard on all four sides at a height of about fifteen feet. It was a narrow and picturesque passage with elaborately carved stone pillars. They took up their station beside one of these. The merchant, all eagerness now, leaned over the stone railing.

The trumpet sounded again, a high, shrill note. A company of heralds rode into the courtyard, three abreast. They were astride fine black steeds and wore tabards of crimson with the Coeur device of heart and shell in gold thread and the familiar motto in bold letters, *A Vaillants Coeurs Rien Impossible*. Men in eastern costume followed, leading camels by their nose cords. The camels, clearly, were for display only; they carried no burdens save maidens in white who sat high up on the red leather saddles, and they swayed and minced along and raised their muzzles in demanding bleats. Above their veils the eyes of the riders sparkled with a lively sense of the part they were playing.

"The East, the magic East!" said Coeur, turning around to nod and smile at his companion. "It's the home of mystery. You never know what to expect. And it's the same with the goods which reach me from there. They are always a treasure trove of surprise. Who knows but what we may find in one of the bundles a tiara which once graced the brow of the Queen of Sheba or a lamp from which a dread genie may be released."

A train of jugglers followed, tossing knives of polished steel in the air, and after them a body of musicians who struck up a curious refrain on instruments of the East.

"How this takes me back!" sighed Coeur. "That music gets in your blood. How clearly I remember my first visit to Damascus. They thought ill of Frenchmen then and every night we were herded to prison and locked up. They treated us like pariah dogs. But I soon changed all that. They found they could trust Jacques Coeur, that he was the one to trade with first, instead of the wily merchants from Venice and Genoa. Today, as you know, my ships have the freedom of eastern waters and my captains get the cream of the trade."

The van of the procession, which was devoted exclusively to entertainment, had now unwound itself and taken station at one end of the courtyard. The musicians continued to play as the pack mules ambled in, loaded with bundles in red, green, and white canvas.

"It's hard for me to wait until the unpacking begins," said Coeur, shifting his feet as though he also found it hard to stand still. He stopped suddenly, his eyes fixed on the spectators below who had been forced to crowd back against the walls. He reached out one hand and touched D'Arlay on the shoulder. "Robin, do you see that girl?"

"I see a score of girls. Which one do you mean?"

"The one near the foot of the east tourelle. See, she has on a long gray cloak and a hood. It's extraordinary, Robin, quite extraordinary!"

D'Arlay looked in the direction indicated. The crowd, made up for the most part of customers who had been in the shop when the procession arrived, was so thick that he could not identify the girl in question. Certainly he saw nothing to account for the excitement which had taken hold of his companion.

"She looks like——" Coeur broke off and slammed a fist down on the top of the stone railing. "She's gone! Come with me, Robin. I mustn't let her get away. I must find her at once."

D'Arlay followed at his heels, wondering what had come over him. Coeur was so excited that he began to run as soon as they turned in from the gallery. He raced down a short stretch of hall, beckoning D'Arlay to do the same, and then footed it pell-mell up a narrow flight of stairs. This brought them to a door with a cresset burning rather fitfully above it. "I hope we're in time!" he muttered, opening the latch with an eager hand.

They found themselves in an unlighted corridor, so narrow that they could touch the wall on each side and so low that they had to bend over as they walked. There were apertures in the walls at regular intervals through which shafts of light appeared. Coeur peered ahead of him and shouted, "Antoine!"

"Yes?" answered a voice from somewhere in the gloom ahead of them.

"Sound the *Coquille!* Quick! The Coquille!"

They heard hurried footsteps and an instant later a bell tolled out. It was so loud and urgent that D'Arlay had no doubt it could be heard in all parts of the vast establishment.

"Now all the doors will be closed and guarded," explained Coeur, with a note of satisfaction in his voice. "No one will be able to leave. I think, Robin, we are in time."

"What is all this about?" demanded D'Arlay impatiently. "Why is it so important not to let this girl get away?"

The Moneyman motioned down the corridor. "This is a way I've found to prevent the theft of goods exposed for sale. The corridor runs all around the building and overlooks the sections where the most valuable articles are shown. I keep four men here as long as the shop is open. They watch what goes on below through the slits in the wall. Nothing which happens escapes them. If a customer takes a fancy to something beyond the reach of his purse, or hers, my man sees and pulls one of the ropes. The bell sounds, the doors are closed and they are not opened again until the guilty one has been located. The matter is always resolved to the great discomfort of the thief."

"A most ingenious arrangement."

Coeur led the way back through the door and closed it after them. "There are two ropes for the use of each watcher," he said, with an air of conscious pride. "The second is to warn of fire. They are in all parts of the building as well, each attached to the one bell. The theft bell is called the Coquille and the other the Incendie. They have different sounds and so there is no mistaking the reason for the signal in each case. I planned this method myself."

"This girl, I judge, is a thief."

Coeur laughed. "No, Robin, the girl isn't a thief. Do you think me so concerned over the loss of some paltry gewgaw that I would go to all this trouble myself? It happens that the Coquille is serving me in a matter which may be of the utmost importance."

"Explain it, then, in God's good name!"

"I prefer to leave the explanation," said Coeur, leading the way back to his own apartment, "until you can see the girl at close hand. It may be I've been deceived. I shall wait to see what you think."

4

Valerie followed Nicolas into the presence of Coeur and his companion. She was frightened, not knowing the reason for the brusque way she had been singled out, and she kept her eyes lowered. The reed basket was clutched tightly in both hands. When the servant urged her forward, her sense of alarm grew. She plucked nervously at his sleeve.

"Monsieur," she whispered, "what have I done that's so very wrong?"

"You needn't be afraid, Mademoiselle. The master means you no harm."

He found it necessary, in spite of this reassurance, to take her by the elbow and compel her reluctant steps forward. They halted in front of the table.

"Is this the one, master?" asked Nicolas.

The Moneyman took a glance at the downcast face of the girl and nodded triumphantly. "Yes, my argus-eyed Nicolas, this is the one," he said.

He got to his feet. Placing himself in front of the girl, he studied her face with care. Then he ejaculated a hearty, "Remarkable!" and seizing both her hands, patted them together exuberantly. "I was not mistaken!" he cried. "It's even closer than I thought. Remarkable, indeed! My child, who are you?"

D'Arlay had been so astonished when Valerie entered the room that he had brushed a hand across his eyes to make sure he was not being deceived. When he had left after the solemn ceremony of burying Damian Maret, there had been no talk of her coming to Paris. He had heard no discussion, in fact, of her plans. In leaving he had entrusted a sum to the Scot which he knew would suffice to cover her needs until such time as she became settled in some new niche in life. He had not expected to see her again.

Standing before the Moneyman in her badly tattered cloak, looking frightened and thoroughly bewildered, she had much the same effect on him as she had when, in the light from the campfire, he had placed his hands on her shoulders and drawn her close to him. He had known then that he was perilously close to falling in love. Now, he realized, he was walking even closer to the edge; one blind step would carry him over. "Was it fated that she should come here? That I should see her again?" he asked himself. It had required an accident to bring them together. If Jacques Coeur's eye had not happened to pick her out, she would have vanished immediately and been swallowed up forever in the great city.

"Her name is Valerie Maret," he said, stepping forward.

The girl looked up quickly and a smile of great relief lighted up her face. "I don't know why I have been brought here, my lord," she said. "I've done no wrong. Perhaps you will tell them that I'm honest and make them let me go."

It was Jacques Coeur's turn to be astonished. His eyes darted back and forth from one to the other. "You know her?"

"Yes," answered D'Arlay. "An accident brought us together one evening not so long ago in a desolate part of the country. I don't know what purpose you have in summoning her here but I'm sure she can't have done anything wrong."

Jacques Coeur's face became grave. He put into words the thought which had flashed through D'Arlay's mind a few moments before. "I can see the hand of fate in this. Why else should she have come, and today of all days? There can be no doubt about it. Everything fits into a curious pattern, even the refusal of this fellow of mine to obey the orders I gave him. A divine hand guided her to this spot, I swear."

D'Arlay smiled at Valerie as though to say, "I don't know what he means any more than you do but you mustn't let it disturb you."

"My child, what have you in that basket?" asked the Moneyman.

"A cat, my lord."

"And that's the final proof!" cried Coeur. "By St. Martin of Tours, I know it was not mere accident which brought her to my attention. Even the cat did its best to waken me. How unreceptive I was! I was determined not to see her. . . . Most fortunately it had been willed otherwise."

"Perhaps," said D'Arlay, "you will now condescend to tell us what you mean."

"Look at her!" exclaimed Coeur. "Surely you can see what I see."

"I've been aware from the first that Mademoiselle Maret resembles someone I have seen but so far I haven't been able to tell who it is."

"Think, Robin!" Coeur planted himself in front of his friend and stared into his eyes as though striving in that way to set his mind in the right direction. "Think back. Back many years. Back to the first time we met, you and I. You will recall the occasion well."

A light flooded D'Arlay's mind. He threw back his head and laughed triumphantly. "Of course!" he cried. "I see it now. How could I have been so very dense?" Then his mood sobered. "It's hard to believe and yet the resemblance is quite unmistakable."

Chapter V

I

D'ARLAY'S THOUGHTS had gone back to the saddest day in his life.

He was seventeen years old and Isabeau was marrying his brother. He walked in the procession, dressed most handsomely in ceremonious white, even to his shoes, which curled to a point in front like whitecaps on a rolling tide. His heart was heavy as he paced up the aisle and he kept saying to himself with an almost frantic insistence: "This is all a terrible dream. It can't be true! She was to marry me, not Regnault. Something will happen to put a stop to this, because it's wrong and unthinkable that she should wed anyone but me!" He hoped that a specter from his brother's unsavory past would rise up somewhere in the dark recesses of the cathedral to call a halt. He more than half believed that the all-seeing and wise God would send down a thunderbolt to prevent such an unseemly plighting of vows.

But nothing of the kind happened. In an unhappy daze he heard the solemn words of the bishop, the rise and fall of the choir chants.

"If a stop is to be put to it," he thought, "I must do it myself!"

He was standing, with no knowledge of having risen to his feet. There was a rustle of sound about him, faces staring up at him, amused and unfriendly faces, elbows nudging, whispers of surprise. He opened his mouth to say that the ceremony must not go on but no sound issued forth. A parched sensation in his throat made it impossible for him to speak, despite the torrent of protest which filled him. After a moment he brushed a hand across his forehead and it came away damp with perspiration.

He crushed his way out to the aisle, realizing that he had made a sorry spectacle of himself and unable, as a result, to sustain the amused scrutiny of all those peering faces. He began to walk down the aisle, arms held stiffly at his sides, his eyes fixed straight ahead.

"I'm a fool!" he said to himself. "A stupid, blundering fool! Everyone is laughing at me. Isabeau will hear about it and then she will laugh at me too."

Sometime later he found himself in the cathedral entrance. The ceremony was over. The sun was high, the sky a joyous blue, the talk of the people who crowded the steps loud and animated. This was all wrong, he knew. How could they chatter and laugh as though nothing had happened? For that matter, how could the sun think it worth while to shine so brightly in the face of this catastrophe?

A hand fell on his shoulder and he looked up into a friendly face under a most curious kind of hat. He roused himself sufficiently from his state of dejection to realize that the stranger was a walking example of everything that was unconventional. The newcomer's eyes proclaimed his moods openly instead of peering stealthily from behind an evasive curtain. He had a manner free of the stilted niceties of the court, a laugh which had the courage to be a real laugh, a jauntiness in the matter of dress which also required courage in this day of rigid adherence to set fashions.

"Is it possible," asked the stranger, regarding him with frank curiosity, "that you are the young brother of the bridegroom? I've nothing to say against my good gossip Regnault, who amuses me in spite of everything; but truly, my boy, the difference between you is remarkable enough to make one doubt the relationship."

"I am Robinet de Burey."

"I'm told you are of a bookish turn," went on the stranger. "That is surprising, and admirable, in itself; for the minds of all aspirants to knightly honors of your age do not seem to me to rise much above an interest in birds' eggs." The keen eyes under the strange hat studied him closely. "You look pale, my boy. Are you not feeling well?"

"I'm quite well, Monsieur."

"My name," said the man, "is Jacques Coeur. You have heard of me, no doubt."

Everyone had heard of the King's fabulous Moneyman, the furrier of Bourges who had risen to such wealth and power. Despite the lacerated state of his feelings, young D'Arlay looked at his companion with a certain amount of interest, liking him at once and sensing in him a genuine warmth and friendliness.

"I'm of an interfering turn," said the Moneyman, "and you may resent what I'm going to say to you, Robinet de Burey. It happens that I have acquaintances in Anjou who have told me about—well, about you and your brother and the fair lady who has just pledged her vows to him and thereby acquired what she wanted most, an ancient title. Come, you need not look at me as though I had committed sacrilege and wounded you mortally in so doing. I've been guilty of no more than putting into words what you know inside yourself to be the full truth, my boy. My desire to help you is my excuse for this frankness of speech." He threw an arm around D'Arlay's shoulders and began to lead him down the steps. "It seems like the blackest of tragedies at this moment. Life has become a dreary affair, the future as dark as the plume in the hat of the brave Bastard of Orléans. But time is a great thing, my boy. It can cure almost any ill in its slow but very sure way. I can look back to a tragedy in my own life which was not entirely unlike yours; and there is now even a certain sweetness in my memory of it."

Not knowing how to answer this unexpected and uninvited confidence, D'Arlay said nothing. After a moment the Moneyman went on. "There are no limits to my capacity for interference," he declared, with a broad smile. "We are complete strangers and yet I'm going to be bold enough to propose a cure. You must go away. You must allow yourself time to become accustomed to what has happened."

D'Arlay found himself in instant agreement. This was the solution! He must get away, far away, where he could see nothing of Isabeau and Regnault and the friends they had in common. He was sure he could no longer maintain the pretense of indifference which he had assumed the instant Isabeau told him of her decision. This, clearly, was the course he must follow: to go away and, if necessary, to stay away forever.

"I think you're right, Monsieur Coeur," he said.

"I'm a busybody—but I'm many other things," declared Jacques Coeur. "I am, for instance, a shipowner. Perhaps you know I have some ships engaged in the eastern trade. Tomorrow my stout Jean de Village leaves for the south and he will take out my finest vessel from Montpellier on the run to Alexandria. Would you care to go with him? Egypt is a land of wonder. The whisper of dead centuries reaches your ears the instant you sight the roadstead. And you will have a chance to go on to the Holy Land and even up to Damascus."

D'Arlay made up his mind on the instant. He had always wanted to go to sea; the East had worked on his imagination like a magnet. He would take this chance so generously and gratuitously offered him, and if he never saw Isabeau again, it would be all for the best.

"You are so kind I can find no words to thank you," he said to the Moneyman. "I accept your offer, Monsieur Coeur! I accept it gladly."

"I thought you would. I was so sure of it that I risked a rebuff in coming to you like this. You'll soon get over this present mood of yours, I give you my word on that. The keen winds of the Inner Sea will sweep all the cobwebs of regret from your mind, my boy. Well, come to see me tonight. I'll have Jean de Village there to greet you. He's a famously fine fellow, this Jean of mine, and you will become the best of friends in less time than it takes me to sell a bolt of camelot cloth to a buxom housewife."

They had reached the street. D'Arlay glanced at his companion and suddenly found himself determined to assert a new manliness of sentiment over what had happened.

"I hate my brother!" he said. "And as for his wife, I shall never see her again as long as I live."

The Moneyman halted beside a carriage in the street with four mettlesome white horses. A lady sat inside and, as they stopped, she leaned out and smiled at Jacques Coeur. She was so beautiful that D'Arlay looked at her with an almost incredulous wonder. This being his first visit to Tours, he had few acquaintances among the people of the court and he found himself considering who she could be. That point was resolved at once by the Moneyman.

"Lady Agnes," he said, moving closer to the carriage and bowing low, "I'm happy to see that you've recovered so soon from your indisposition. May I present a new friend of mine? This is Robinet de Burey, Sire d'Arlay. My boy, this is the Lady Agnes Sorel who is, I am sure you already agree, the most lovely lady in all the world."

So this was Agnes Sorel, the mistress of the King! D'Arlay had heard the stories about her which circulated over France and even reached the secluded corner of Anjou where he had lived all his life, stories of her great qualities of heart as well as of her unusual beauty. Reports of royal mistresses were generally edged with malice and dislike but Agnes Sorel was so kindly regarded that many people were disposed to put some stock in the suggestion that she was not actually the mistress of Charles of

France, that their relationship had been kept on a platonic plane. Even those who pointed to the existence of her three pretty young daughters and balked at the sacrilege in assuming that immaculate conceptions could have occurred in a royal court, were still willing to concede that her influence over the monarch was a beneficent one.

The boy bowed to her, finding himself somewhat discomfited by the frankness of interest with which she was regarding him. The reports he had heard of her had not been exaggerated in the slightest degree. She had a beauty which excited as well as pleased the senses. His attention went first to her eyes, which were a light blue, a most unusual blue, and then to her mouth. It was so vividly red that it suggested passion and yet, on closer inspection, he could see that it was gentle and highly sensitive.

"I've heard of the Sire d'Arlay," said Agnes Sorel, in a pleasantly low-pitched voice.

"He has made up his mind to sail East on one of my ships," announced Jacques Coeur, giving his companion an encouraging thump on the back. "We are men of quick decision, this young friend of mine and I; we thought of the plan no more than a minute ago and it was settled between us quicker than you could lirp a finger. He leaves tomorrow with Jean de Village and will sail at once from Montpellier."

Agnes Sorel smiled and nodded her head. "What an excellent idea," she said. "I'm sure, Sire d'Arlay, you'll find your journey most stimulating. It will be"—she looked at him with so much sympathy and understanding that he knew she had heard his story also—"it will be a great adventure for you. And the very best thing—under the circumstances."

"He will come back loaded with wealth," declared Coeur. "With precious stones and wonderful fabrics and spices and perfumes. Perhaps he will bring back also—who can tell?—a beautiful eastern princess as his bride."

D'Arlay had never seen Agnes Sorel again and so it was not to be wondered at that the resemblance borne her by this little waif had eluded him for so long.

2

"And now you know," said Jacques Coeur.

"And now I know."

The Moneyman, whose eyes were sparkling with excitement, took her hand again and gave it a reassuring pat. "My child," he said, "you must forgive us. We are talking in riddles. You must be patient until—until tomorrow, perhaps."

"Yes, my lord." It was clear from her tone that she was more puzzled than ever.

"One of two things will happen," went on the Moneyman. "I may say to you that a certain dream in which I had indulged myself has dissolved and that I won't have any use for you after all. If it turns out that way, there will be a little present for you to compensate for the strange way in which we've used you. On the other hand, I may have something quite different to say to you. In the meantime . . ." Coeur frowned as he pondered the question of what was to be done with her immediately. Then he gave a satisfied nod. "My factor lives with his family at the top of this building. There will be a room for you there, and a bed, and plenty of food. Later, I hope, it will be necessary to make permanent arrangements." He called to his servant, "Nicolas, I'm entrusting Mademoiselle Maret to you."

Valerie, now thoroughly bewildered, turned her eyes in D'Arlay's direction. Reading the question in them, he said, "I'm almost as much in the dark as you are, but I assure you, Mademoiselle, that you need have no fears."

"This way, Mademoiselle," said Nicolas importantly.

When they were alone, Coeur began to address D'Arlay in excited tones. "What a remarkable thing! The Lady Agnes is the acknowledged Queen of Beauty, she's without a peer in this or any age. And yet here is a girl with no advantages, who comes of peasant stock, if one may judge from the clothes she wears——"

"Her father was a strolling player named Damian Maret."

Coeur nodded his head with satisfaction. "That explains her voice. It puzzled me, for it shows definite traces of culture. Well, here is the daughter of a cheap cullion who's sufficiently like the Fair Agnes to be a full blood sister—or a daughter. It's hard to believe but we've seen the evidence with our own eyes."

"I saw the Lady Agnes once only and so I'm not the best judge. But it does seem to me that the resemblance is quite astonishing."

Coeur sat down in his chair and swung one parti-colored knee over the other. He began to enumerate the points of resemblance. "They are identical in coloring," he said. "There's the same blue of eye and the same yellow of hair. The girl even has some of the same characteristics. She looks at you with a slow raising of the lids just as the Lady Agnes does. She has the same way of lifting a hand to gesture." He swung around in his chair to face his companion. "And now, my gossip Robin, what can you tell me about her? Under what circumstances did you meet this extraordinary child?"

D'Arlay did not answer at once. He had no way of knowing why Coeur was taking such an interest in Valerie. He felt himself on the defensive. He was still amazed also at the unexpected depth of the feeling he had experienced when he saw her escorted into the room. He had realized then, from the exultant jump his heart had given, that he had been wanting to see her again, that he had been regretting his unceremonious leavetaking.

Reluctantly he began to tell of his meeting with her. He intended to make the recital a brief one but Jacques Coeur would not permit that. The Moneyman asked innumerable questions and was not satisfied until he had extracted a detailed report of the occurrence.

"Do you believe these people were her real parents?" asked Coeur at the finish.

D'Arlay hesitated. "No," he said finally. He pondered the question of how much more he should tell, his fingers busy with the pleated drapery of the roundlet he had removed from his head on entering. Finally he decided to repeat the whole story.

Jacques Coeur's face lighted up as he listened, and at the finish he nodded his head with the most intense satisfaction. "Of course!" he cried. "There's the best of blood in her. She's no child of the people, this small one, no get of a strolling player. The mark of quality is stamped all over her!" He paused for several moments and then burst out with, "How very fortunate this is!"

"Fortunate? Why do you say that? I don't understand why you are taking so much interest in her, Jacques."

The mood of the Moneyman underwent a quick change. "There's something I must tell you," he declared. "The King's physician came to see me no more than an hour ago. He told me that Agnes Sorel has a short time only to live."

"I'm sorry to hear such news."

After a long silence Coeur began to speak in a low tone. "It will be a great tragedy. Usually I take the optimistic view of things. I always expect that matters will come out right. But in this I find myself fearing the worst. I'm sure the outcome will be a sad one for—for her friends. And for France, D'Arlay, for France above all else."

"I still don't understand you."

"This is a strange King we have. I don't need to tell you that. We both know he has certain fine qualities and I confess to a deep affection for him. But"—Coeur shook his head solemnly—"his unguided choice of advisers has always been bad. If Agnes is not there to speak the right words in the royal ear, things will go wrong.

"I've no illusions about my own position," he went on. "I've slept in the royal bed and, for the moment, the King seems to have every confidence in me. But, Robin, my tenure in reality hangs on a single thread—a frail one and of the finest gold. If it breaks——" He paused. "I have more enemies than you know. The court is packed with them, whispering, running to the King with every malicious bit of gossip they can pick up or invent. The King lacks constancy. He did not bestir himself to save the Maid. Would he do more for me?"

After another minute of silent thought the Moneyman began to speak in a brisker tone. "The King will mourn Agnes deeply but he will soon take another mistress. Her vixen of a cousin is angling already for the succession. If that happened—— Robin, has it ever occurred to you that I should have a candidate to offer?"

D'Arlay was so startled that he made no effort to reply.

"Have you noticed that the preferences of most men run to certain types? More often than not a second wife is much like the first one. No man has ever been more deeply enamored of a woman than the King of Agnes Sorel. She has suited him completely." He paused for a moment. "The most likely candidate would be one who resembled Agnes closely. Now you will understand, my good Robin, why I took an interest in this girl as soon as I set eyes on her."

D'Arlay sprang to his feet. "This is unheard of!" he cried. "It's absurd! You can't be serious about it!"

"I'm completely serious about it. Before I make any move, of course, I must convince myself that the child has character and courage as well as the physical likeness."

If D'Arlay needed any further proof of how he felt about Valerie, he had it now. "I can't yet believe," he said, "that you are in earnest. It's an idea of the moment. You'll brush it aside after giving it more thought."

Coeur looked up in surprise at the feeling he had detected in D'Arlay's voice. "Is it possible that you take a personal interest in her?"

D'Arlay indulged in serious thought before answering. "I like her. Perhaps it was because of the circumstances under which I met her but certainly I feel protective toward her."

Coeur spread out his hands in a questioning gesture. "Why are you so emphatic about it?"

"Surely there are better ways of meeting the situation—if it ever arises. Is the favor of the King worth saving at such a price?"

Coeur laid a hand on the other's arm. "It's not favor for myself which concerns me. You are honorable and patriotic, Robin. Will you acknowledge me to be the same?"

"You've given convincing proofs of your patriotism. And I know you to be the most honorable of men."

An even greater gravity manifested itself on the face of the Moneyman. "It's regrettable that sometimes you must do things as a minister of the state which you wouldn't do as a man. When a certain step, which may be harmful for individuals, is best for the state of the nation, there can be no holding back. I have to do many things, Robin, which gall me bitterly. I don't need to tell you that there can be no recovery or prosperity for France, no happiness for her people, until the invaders are driven out. The King must be held in line! It's not only necessary to finish the war but to provide our sick and bleeding country with strong leadership through the first years of peace. Can we allow personal feelings to sway us in this all-important matter?"

"That much I grant you——"

"Listen to me! When Agnes Sorel dies, the King will fall under the spell of Antoinette de Maignelais—unless his fancy is directed elsewhere. The succession so far is in her hands—her selfish, grasping, cruel hands. She's committed to the other party, to men who will use her influence with the King to get power and wealth for themselves." He remained silent for several moments and then burst out with, "That must not happen!"

D'Arlay did not answer. His mind was occupied with the reflections natural to one who, realizing himself in love, is faced with a danger to the object of his devotion. The Moneyman went on by asking him a question.

"You see dishonor in the course I propose?"

"I shrink from the thought of it, Jacques!"

"Have you been blaming Agnes Sorel all these years?"

D'Arlay shook his head with some reluctance. "I must acknowledge that I've always had the deepest respect for her."

"Then it's clear that you are not being consistent. I'm prepared to strive for the salvation of France by any means whatever rather than to stand aside in scrupulous delicacy and see my country suffer. In matters of state the result justifies the means. I firmly believe it was fate brought this girl here. Why otherwise should a seemingly perfect instrument be delivered into my hands at this moment?"

"But the girl herself——"

"The girl may not have the capacity or the will for the part. That is still to be determined. And, of course, there's always the probability that she'll refuse to try."

"When anyone has lived the kind of life she has," declared D'Arlay, after a moment of uneasy reflection, "they can't be blamed if they accept such a chance."

Coeur regarded him steadily for the moment. "The aristocrat in you prompted that," he said. Then he asked a question, "Could France have been united under Charles if there had been no Jeanne d'Arc?"

D'Arlay frowned in a puzzled way. "Certainly. It was Dunois who commanded the army and saved Orléans."

"And is that view generally held in court circles and among the nobility?"

"Yes. You know it is."

Coeur leaned forward and began to speak in a tone of the greatest earnestness. "It's different with the people of France. They hold the Maid in the deepest reverence. They speak her name in whispers. She is the saviour of the country, a heroine, a saint, the one figure in history above reproach or blame. Someday all of France will come to see her in that light. Even the nobility, unlikely though that may seem now. Someday, perhaps, the whole world."

"We seem to be talking at cross-purposes."

"I've been leading up to this: if the girl accepts the proposal I may make her, it will be because of the inspiration of the Maid, because she also wants to serve her country. She won't see it as a chance to improve her lot."

"I had no intent to speak ill of her. On the contrary, I—I have a fondness for her. But I still believe the idea an impossible one. How could you hope to fit her for the part? And, if you succeeded, would the King stoop so low?"

"The King's infatuation for the original is so great that I'm sure he would be happy with a copy. We mustn't overlook the possibility that she has good blood, derived perhaps from the Sorels. Failing that, I can provide a pedigree for her while she's being made over. A pleasant little fiction can be arranged to cover the point."

"Are you prepared to go to such lengths as that? Kings don't enjoy being duped."

"If the King found her to his liking, he would be eager himself to supply the lack of a fitting pedigree. But why balk at obstacles we may never meet? I promise you one thing: any scheme I commit myself to will be so carefully prepared that it will stand the most hostile scrutiny."

D'Arlay tossed both arms in the air with a gesture of resignation. "What more can I say? Will it avail anything to point out that changing her into a lady will be a task possible only to someone who knows the ways of the court? Can you find such a person? Do you dare let another into such a dangerous secret?"

"As to that, I have a plan in my mind already."

D'Arlay said nothing more. After a few moments of silence the Moneyman leaned over and placed a hand on his companion's shoulder. His manner and the tone of his voice when he spoke seemed to beg for understanding. "Do you think I'm happy about this? My good gossip Robin, you must know this Jacques Coeur well enough to realize that he has no more liking for the plan than you have. The need to find a substitute for the Lady Agnes—— Robin, it's like a sword thrust in my heart. I still nurse a slender hope that the physician's report will prove wrong. But until such time as we know for certain, we must prepare for the worst. We must be ready to play for a big stake, the biggest stake of all —the saving of France!"

A still longer silence ensued. D'Arlay could not say, "I love her and so you must give up this scheme." He could not say it for a number of reasons. Time might prove that his interest in her had been temporary; but even if it were certain that his devotion would never lessen, he still could not say it. Only matrimonial intentions would give him the right to interfere further, and marriage was out of the question.

Both men were relieved when Nicolas came in with candles. As he placed one on the table beside his master, he asked in a grumbling tone, "What am I to do about the Scot?"

Coeur looked across the low oak screen. The anteroom was empty. "He seems to have lost patience and gone."

"He has lost patience, master, but he hasn't gone. He wasn't able to find his way back here. I heard he was making a disturbance in the Spicerie but by the time I got there he had wandered on to the Horsegear. I found him at last in Mortars, Pestles, and Pots. He demands two things, master: to see you at once and to know what has happened to the girl."

"I'll talk to him now."

When the servant had left, D'Arlay said in an urgent tone, "I strongly advise that the Scot be kept in ignorance of this rash plan."

Coeur laughed easily. "I've no intention of telling him anything. Beyond my promise to obtain a command for him with the guns, he'll have to be content with a few friendly words and perhaps a small purse of gold."

This assurance did not entirely allay D'Arlay's fears. "Did you know he had his own band of Free Companions?"

"I'm not surprised."

D'Arlay frowned uneasily. "He seems to be acting as her guardian and I'm not sure you can satisfy him as easily as that. Much as I shrink from what you have in mind, I don't want to see any trouble come of it. It might be wise if I took him along with me. I have plenty of room and Helion has a leg of lamb on the fire and a roast train[1] big enough for three. I suggest this because it will be necessary to keep an eye on the fellow."

"An excellent idea. I'll talk to him for a few minutes and then turn him over to you." The Moneyman looked up at a huge clock on the wall over his head. It was marked off into the twenty-four hours and the hand was hovering over the fifteenth. "I should have been at the Louvre long before this. A full day's work awaits me there."

Chapter VI

I

D'ARLAY did not regard Paris with the eyes of his king. He loved the city. He loved it so much that he forgot the things weighing on his mind as he and the Scot made their way toward his house in the Rue Grenier sur L'Eau. He nodded his head at the tangle of spires against the skyline. "It's unfortunate," he said, "that there has never been a poet capable of interpreting the spirit of Paris."

"I'm not a poet but I can do that for you. And in a very few words. The spirit of Paris is made up of bombast and insolence. Not to mention thievery."

"That comes in poor grace from the mouth of an alien," said D'Arlay angrily.

"I have fought and bled for France and yet in this city dirty little

[1]A batter of flour and wine flavored with ginger and sugar and baked about the meats.

urchins shout 'Tug-mutton!' after me. When I stop at an inn, I am underfed and overcharged. Women take one look at the tartan around my neck and turn away."

"Paris," declared D'Arlay, in resentment of these criticisms, "is so fine a city that even the smell of its streets, which is most peculiarly rank and penetrating, is like incense in my nostrils. The spirit of Paris is made up of wisdom, sparkle, irreverence, abandon, fortitude, and rebellion."

Kennedy was not to be put down. "All kindliness has gizzened out of Paris like water from a cask in the sun."

They came shortly thereafter to a spot in the town where an inn, towering high above its sign which bore the name *La Galimafrée,* faced on the dilapidated sheds of a market. The space between was filled with men staring up at a balcony on the front of the tavern, which, at the moment, was empty.

There was a great deal of loud talk going on. "It's said," one of the watchers was remarking as they drew abreast, "that he took his battle-ax and sliced the flesh from the ribs of Don Guzman as evenly as a butcher cutting chops." A dissenting voice said, "But he's a Burgundian." That brought a quick answer. "And can't we, as Frenchmen, be proud of a Burgundian?"

Drawing on the resources of his own tongue, Kennedy demanded to know what all this *curfuffle* was about.

"I think," answered D'Arlay, "it has to do with the great Jacques de Lalain."

There was a stir at this moment, occasioned by the opening of the door at the back of the balcony. A tall knight sauntered out and waved a careless hand to the crowd assembled below.

"There he is, the greatest champion in the world," said D'Arlay. "I met him once and it was like talking to a battle-ax equipped with a small brain and a huge pride. He spends all his time traveling about and seeking new opponents to kill or maim." He turned to his companion. "Jacques Coeur said a very true thing once, that all knights-errant are like cruel small boys who have never grown up."

Jacques de Lalain was a powerful young animal, both tall enough and broad enough to make the squire, who had followed him out on the balcony, seem small by comparison. He was dressed in white from head to foot, with enormous tufted sleeves and an ermine cloak tossed over one shoulder with an affectation of carelessness. A nose like the beak of a parrot arched out from between eyes of an opaque blue. His hair was dark and straight, falling full-bottomed to his shoulders.

He advanced to the railing and looked about him with a smile of amused pride. "Ha, scum of Paris!" he called. "You've come to see Jacques de Lalain. Well, look at me closely. You will never see me again. You will never see me in the lists, canaille of Paris. Your brave knights have prudently abstained from taking up the cartel of defiance I sent on in advance." He stared about him with mounting arrogance. "I am the greatest fighter in all Christendom! I can defeat any knight born of woman with any weapon invented by man! Take one last look at me, starved and sniveling worm bait, for I shall never come back."

D'Arlay swore bitterly under his breath when the great champion withdrew out of sight. The crowd was already scattering, well pleased, apparently, at the insulting reference to the chivalry of France. He motioned the Scot to follow him and was vigorously plowing his way to the side of the street when he heard his name called from the door of the inn. He stopped and looked back.

"The Sire d'Arlay! The Sire d'Arlay!"

"Who wants me?"

The squire responsible for the summons came out through the crowd. "My master," he said, "is sitting down to supper and begs the honor of your company."

D'Arlay asked in a tone of surprise, "Did your master see me from up there?"

"An eagle," said the squire with an intolerable air of pride, "can spot its prey in the air at a distance of a thousand feet. Is there reason for surprise when Jacques de Lalain recognizes the Sire d'Arlay at a mere twenty yards?"

"Convey my respects to your master and say that the Sire d'Arlay regrets his inability to accept. I have a friend who accompanies me to my own house for supper."

"My master said the bidding included the Scot if needs be."

Kennedy grinned. "He can pick out a tartan at twenty yards also, it seems."

The two recipients of the invitation looked questioningly at each other. D'Arlay whispered, "It might be interesting to watch the ravening boar of Burgundy at his feeding."

"Aye," said the Scot. "I wouldn't be above making my boasts that I had broken bread into the gravy with Jacques de Lalain."

D'Arlay turned to the squire. "Our thanks, then, to your master and say we'll join him as soon as we have washed and set our clothing in order. Warn him that by comparison with his own grandeur of raiment his guests will seem like plucked crows."

The squire belched indifferently. "They always do, my lord."

2

Jacques de Lalain received them in a room back of the balcony in which a table had already been spread for supper. He had dismissed his followers with the exception of one servant and was sprawled out in a chair, his massive white-clad legs spread wide for comfort. He got slowly and reluctantly to his feet.

"Robinet de Burey, Sire d'Arlay," he said with a stiff bow. "I'm happy to see you again. And this is the Scot? His name does not matter. This is most fortunate, as now I needn't sup in solitude."

"It's fortunate indeed, my Lord de Lalain," said D'Arlay, bowing in turn. He scrutinized his host's face closely, saying to himself, "There is something noble about him and yet his is the cruelest face I've ever seen."

The supper which the servant proceeded to serve had been chosen with discrimination. There was a loined sole, the very best of all fish, served with a white sauce in which the appetizing tang of porret predominated. This was followed by an unlaced mallard, and then the main dish appeared, a roast kid with flutings of ribbon around the tail. At the finish there arrived a rich *hastelet* of figs, raisins, and dates, cooked together and served with a gilding of egg yolks. D'Arlay watched this procession of noble dishes with inward pride. "I would like to tell him," he thought, "that only in Paris, and certainly never in his native Burgundy, could a meal like this be served."

Their host monopolized the conversation, speaking in a voice which seemed surprisingly thin to issue from a frame of such huge proportions. He confined himself to his own exploits, the antagonists he had worsted in single combat, the plans he had for future jousts. Once only did he deviate from this saga of self-glorification. Pausing to look his guest over, he remarked on the lack of resemblance between D'Arlay and his elder brother who had been at the French court when De Lalain had last visited there.

"The Comte is a mally old gossip," he said. "He made me laugh at some of his jibes—an indulgence I seldom allow myself. His lovely Lady Isabeau"—the opaque eyes turned back questingly to D'Arlay—"reminded me of a fair creature—Spanish, as it happens—whose favor I carried on my lance when I fought Don Guzman in Castile a few months agone. But before I beguile your ears with the details of that pleasant little affair,

I must pray tribute to the fair Comtesse. I consider her far more lovely actually than my little Spanish spark. She approaches the years when the flower of beauty begins to crisp on the stem but . . . Well, Sire d'Arlay, I confess to a liking for the tang of maturity."

"My fair sister-in-law," said D'Arlay, speaking in a carefully casual tone, "is most charming."

"Your good opinion of her was made known to me. You are not married, Sire d'Arlay?"

"No. I have no wife."

"Nor I." The Burgundian indulged in one of his admittedly rare laughs. "But for a different reason, I think."

D'Arlay felt a wave of resentment rising in him. He said to himself, "There's insolence in every word he utters." His distaste grew as he observed the exaggerated manners of his host: the ceremonious elevation of the goblet to a level with his closed eyes whenever he took a sip of wine as though drinking a silent pledge; the fastidious manipulation of spoon and knife; the regal gesture for silence before he began to speak.

"As I said out there, there are no champions in France who dare meet me," proclaimed De Lalain, going back to the topic which interested him most. "Now I must go to Scotland, to England, perhaps even to Italy, to find opponents worthy of me."

"The knights of France," said D'Arlay, "disregarded your challenge on the order of the King."

Jacques de Lalain snorted. "A brave lot of toy knights to hide behind a royal proclamation."

D'Arlay found his dislike growing every moment. When he spoke, however, it was in a casual tone. "The King is striving to prevent dueling as he will need every loyal subject with him when he renews the war." He replaced his wine goblet and looked at his host. "Why not fight with the knights of France instead of against them? You are a Burgundian, of course, and your duke may not share in the campaign. But the English are hard and shrewd fighters and we'll need all the strength we can muster. If Jacques de Lalain rode under the lilies of France, it would stimulate our men to greater exertion."

With a delicate gesture the Burgundian crushed *pimpernel aromatisante* into his goblet and then motioned to the servingman to fill it with wine. He took a deep sip before answering.

"I've no intention of serving with the French Army," he said.

There was a moment of silence and then D'Arlay said, "I confess that this is a surprise to me."

"Your feeling in the matter is of no importance. But if you want the reason, I'll strive to make you understand."

"I," said D'Arlay, "shall strive to follow your reasoning."

The knight-errant drew his ermine cloak around both his shoulders. The fire on the hearth was dying down and a chill had settled on the room. He motioned the servant to leave.

"I disapprove of the use of cannon," said De Lalain. "It's said you plan to make much use of these fire-spitting tubes called bombards. It's a sorry thing that war will no longer be an honorable meeting between brave knights with Almighty God as the arbiter." He turned his pale and expressionless eyes on his guest. "I can't fight for a country which resorts to black magic."

"The bombards," said D'Arlay quietly, "will be our answer to the magic of the English longbow."

The Burgundian brushed this aside. "I may tell you that my sympathies are with France. The English have been overlong on this side of the Channel and the time is ripe to drive them back to their own barbarous island. But I swear to you," he cried with sudden vehemence, "I would rather see you lose every battle than win by any means save by the might of the chivalry of France!"

D'Arlay stirred impatiently in his chair. "We can't drive the English from Normandy by losing battles," he said.

"You are of noble blood, Sire d'Arlay, and it should not be necessary for me to explain what I mean. The result of a battle is not the important thing. All that counts is the way it is fought. I hold firmly to the belief, as all good knights should, that God awards the victory to the side which strives most bravely and in accordance with the Code of Chivalry."

D'Arlay was finding it increasingly hard to hold his feelings in check. "It's that kind of thinking," he said, "which has cost France a hundred years of defeat and suffering."

"I'm a bombardier of some note," declared Kennedy, speaking for the first time since the supper had started, "and I tell you now, Sir Knight, that the guns will clear a way to the Channel with the greatest ease."

Jacques de Lalain did not deign to look at the Scot. "You're not a knight and my invitation to join us did not include the privilege of taking part in our talk." He turned to D'Arlay with a shrug of his padded shoulders. "I've no intention of disputing with you the principles of honorable warfare." He frowned and twirled his goblet as though reluctant to proceed with what he had to say. "I had a purpose in asking you to sup with me tonight. Your brother told me you were associated in some obscure manner with this greedy merchant who has put a spell on your king. I've heard also that your Jacques Coeur is the one who is urging the use of bombards. I must ask you to do something for me, to go to the Fox with a message." He shoved his goblet aside with a movement which indicated distaste for this necessity "I have a cousin, Alain de Kersai. He has taken the vows of knighthood and is a goodly enough lad, though not capable physically of winning much glory for himself. I had intended making a place for him in the company I'll take with me to Scotland or on such other travels as I may decide upon." He paused and regarded D'Arlay with a frown which carried a suggestion of incredulity. "You'll find what I must now tell you hard to believe. Alain has refused! The little fool is set on serving with the bombards. I have talked to him, I have reasoned with him, I have even made threats. He remains obdurate. I'm asking you, therefore, to say to Jacques Coeur that he must not allow Alain to join. He must help me in saving the boy from this great disgrace."

"It's no disgrace," said D'Arlay. He was keeping his eyes fixed on the table in front of him. "If we win the war, it will be by the use of the cannon you affect to despise. Your cousin could find no better way to serve."

"I've tried to consider Alain's youth and not judge him too harshly. His place is with me. Serving cannon is fit only for common men, blacksmiths and such."

"I'm thinking of serving under Jean Bureau myself," said D'Arlay.

The Burgundian settled back in his chair with a laugh. "I see now I made a mistake in thinking you might act as my advocate. My first impression of you was unfavorable, Sire d'Arlay. I should have realized that one who associates with the Fox would have no spark of knightly honor in him. Well, I must go to Jacques Coeur. Or I may take my case to the King himself. I shall demand that the boy be sent home." The face of the Burgundian suddenly became white with passion. "I've an affection for Alain, but I tell you, Sire d'Arlay, I would rather see him dead, and by my own hand if need be, than consorting with common men and—and noblemen who forget the obligations of their class."

"You would get no satisfaction from the King."

"I am sure," declared the Burgundian, "that the King of France would think twice before refusing a reasonable request from me. I am Jacques de Lalain, the greatest champion in all Christendom. My wishes are not to be disregarded."

It was no longer possible for D'Arlay to contain himself. "You are Jacques de Lalain, the greatest champion in Christendom!" he cried.

"True. But you are also a fool, a blind and stupid fool! It's the duty of all patriotic men to see that our country is no longer shackled by such folly as you are preaching!"

Jacques de Lalain shoved back his chair and rose slowly to his feet. He rested his powerful hands on the edge of the table and stared down at his companion with the eagerness of a tomcat when an unwary mouse ventures out within reach of his claws.

"Robinet de Burey, Sire d'Arlay!" he said. "You have insulted me, grossly and wantonly. You're no fit opponent for me but the words you have spoken can be answered in one way only. I demand satisfaction."

"Satisfaction shall be yours."

The Burgundian looked at him in a kind of wonder, as though he had expected some effort to seek an escape by qualification of what had been said. D'Arlay had risen in his turn. Now that his first wave of anger had passed, he realized he had placed his life in jeopardy. "What chance will you have against this butcher?" he said to himself. "He will cut you to pieces with the greatest ease."

"I can fight only with men whose family lines show nobility for at least four generations on each side," said the Burgundian, willing perhaps to find a flaw in the D'Arlay genealogy.

"The De Burey family goes back more generations than most noble knights can count," answered D'Arlay. "My mother, as you may know, was Amalie de Mailly. Can you match that?"

The two men stared at each other for several moments in silence. Then an enraged flush took possession of the Burgundian's face and he gripped the handle of his sword. His anger was so great, in fact, that his enormous sleeves gave the impression of being puffed out by it.

"I was willing to give you a chance to withdraw," he said, with a snort. "You've disregarded it and now the issue between us can only be settled on the field of honor."

"I suggest we take our seats again," said D'Arlay, suddenly conscious of the fact that his legs were trembling. "We can at least make our arrangements in comfort. Now, I propose that first of all we explore the provisions of the Code of Chivalry bearing on this situation."

"The provisions," declared De Lalain, seating himself and raising his wineglass to take a long draught, "are explicit and to the point."

"They're not as simple as you seem to believe. As it happens, I know the Code as well as you do. Permit me to point out that the intent of the Code is to provide as much equality as possible where opponents are of unequal prowess. You, the greatest knight in Christendom, will concede that an inequality exists between us. That consideration will enter into the choice of weapons."

"The offended party has the choice of weapons. I am the offended party."

"On the contrary, it was you who provoked the quarrel between us."

The Burgundian raised an impatient hand. "Spare me your arguments. I'm not a lawyer. I fight with good and honorable steel and not with crafty words. You insulted me to my face as this fellow will attest. The choice rests with me."

D'Arlay realized that his life depended on the resolving of this point. "The giving of offense," he said, "is not always a matter of words spoken. The real incitement to a quarrel may consist in an overt act, a hostile look, even in a state of mind. You, Jacques de Lalain, have given mortal offense to me. From the moment I entered this room you showed contempt in every word you spoke. There was a rancid pride in the very curl of your nostril. The views you expressed were an insult to every man of French birth."

"The fact remains you spoke the words."

"If we cannot agree, what course do you propose? To carry the issue to a Court of Honor?"

The Burgundian snorted again. "If necessary."

"Then," said D'Arlay, "let us consider some other words which have been spoken this evening. You openly scoffed at the bravery and prowess of the knights of France. What would be the ruling of a Court of Honor on these open taunts?"

The quickness with which the Burgundian turned to look at his table companion was proof that his complacency had received a jolt.

"I spoke in general terms."

"That makes it worse. You reflected on the courage of the whole knightly body. Give a thought to the consequences before you take the decision outside this room."

Jacques de Lalain squirmed in his chair like a sulky schoolboy thwarted in some pet desire. It was several moments before he broke the silence. "What weapon would you select?"

D'Arlay answered quickly, "My sword."

The Burgundian broke into a loud and confident laugh. "The sword?" he cried. "Don't you realize I am the best swordsman in all the world?"

"My own sword," amended D'Arlay. "You would fight with one of the same weight, length, and shape."

The exuberance of De Lalain's mood subsided slightly. He said sharply, "Let me see it, if you please."

D'Arlay detached the weapon from his belt and laid it on the table. His opponent got to his feet and picked it up, touching an exploring finger to the point before hefting it with expert intentness.

"It's a curious one," he said. "Where did you get it?"

"This type of sword comes from the East originally. This particular blade reached me from Spain."

"I've never seen one quite like it," grumbled De Lalain. "It has a womanish blade but the point is keen."

"It will be used without armor of any kind."

"Ha, there would be conditions! I might have expected it. I can see that a shrewd thrust, or perchance a lucky one, would drive the point clear through a man's body." He gave D'Arlay a suspicious glance. "There is method in your suggestion. This begins to smack of trickery and I care little for the smell of it."

"The advantage would still rest with you. You have asserted your supremacy in the use of all weapons."

"I've never before held a sword such as this in my hand."

The Burgundian gave a quick cut at the air to test the balance of the blade. Then he raised the hilt and squinted at the tiny inscription in Arabic. It undoubtedly would have added to his misgivings had he been able to decipher the words.

> Inalienably bequeathed by Alassir-al-Asmeed. May hostile hand that touches this steel wither and rot at the wrist.

"It may be you have a special skill in the use of this tricky blade," he said, after a moment.

D'Arlay nodded. "I have skill with it," he said. "It's the only weapon I use."

"I won't be fluddered into the choice of it!" The Burgundian threw the sword back on the table. "I find I've no will to fight you like a mincing master of arms."

"Then," said D'Arlay, "we must leave the matter to a Court of Honor."

De Lalain scowled. "I give you this as my last word: Leave the selection to chance; toss a coin in the air and abide by the result."

It was D'Arlay's turn to hesitate. An urgent thought hammered in his mind, "If you lose, you will surely die!" He said aloud, "It's only with the sword that we could fight with any reasonable degree of equality."

The Burgundian refused to move from the stand he had taken. He repeated stubbornly, "Let it rest on the toss of a coin."

Kennedy, who had been turning back and forth from one to the other and breathing hard with excitement, plucked at D'Arlay's sleeve and whispered in his ear, "By St. Andrew, you'll sign your own death warrant if you give in to this butcher!"

D'Arlay whispered back, "He will proclaim me a coward if I dispute the point any longer. I was rash enough to get myself into this quarrel and now I must face the consequences."

There was a moment of silence and then D'Arlay said loudly: "In God's name, let it be as you demand! Toss the coin!"

De Lalain drew a piece of gold from his purse and held it up. "An English noble of Harry Fift'. A great king and an honorable fighter. I claim the side with the King's head, D'Arlay. You may have the other with the Cross and arches trefoil. Is it agreed?"

"Agreed."

"I'm not content with a mere toss of the coin," declared the greatest knight in Christendom. "There are fingers nimble enough to throw this noble clear to the ceiling and still control the way it will fall. You consort with tricky company, D'Arlay, so I insist on doing it the Burgundian way. I'll spin the coin in the air and you'll catch it in a flute glass of good red Burgundian wine. You hand it to me and I turn it upside down. Then we shall see what the god of chance has decided."

"Agreed."

D'Arlay rose to his feet, resting his weight against the table. His whole body was trembling. The Burgundian, his face shining with excitement, gave the coin a preliminary toss, catching it on his wrist. He looked at the exposed face. "The King!" he cried exultantly. "There's an augury to give you pause! Come, D'Arlay, the goblet. Is your hand steady enough to hold it without spilling the wine?"

He threw the noble high into the air. D'Arlay, clutching the goblet in both hands, caught the spinning yellow disk in the wine. It required an effort of will to keep his hands steady as he handed it over to his opponent. The Burgundian turned it upside down on the table and the spilled wine spread out over the cloth in a widening stain.

"Lift it, lift it, my doughty antagonist!" cried De Lalain, almost dancing in his eagerness. "Which will we find staring up at us, the King or the Cross? The King, I swear; and, if it is, you will die miserably under the blows of my battle-ax. Come, are you afraid to look?"

D'Arlay reached out a hand and raised the goblet. He did not venture a look at the yellow noble resting on the red stain and his first intimation of the result came from the silence of his opponent and an exultant laugh from Pregent Kennedy.

"The Cross!" said De Lalain, in an angry voice. "By the Moine Bourru, it's the Cross!"

D'Arlay looked then. An intense relief flooded over him. "Never have I seen a more gratifying pattern inscribed on minted gold!" he said to himself. "An arched molding and a Cross potent. God has decreed I am to have a fair chance."

"I claim a delay," said the Burgundian sulkily. "I must have time to find another plaything like this and to train myself in the use of it. You'll have that much longer to live, D'Arlay." He scowled. "You will hear from me when I'm ready."

"Agreed," said D'Arlay.

"And now," said D'Arlay, when he and his companion found themselves again in the street, "we shall seek the comfort and security of the Rue Grenier sur L'Eau. I confess to a weariness both of mind and body."

The Scot snorted indignantly. "There will be no rest for you for another hour at least." He laid a commanding hand on D'Arlay's shoulder. "I know an arms master here in Paris, one Gaspard Soullaine, who has the best hand with the sword I've ever seen in action. You will be in need of his services, my lord, if you're to get yourself into proper condition to meet this great bully and braggart."

"I'm sure," said D'Arlay stiffly, "that I could teach your arms master some things about the use of the sword."

"When Jacques de Lalain summons you to battle," said the Scot earnestly, "he will have acquired so much skill with this piece of lath that he will be as hard to resist as a blustering wind from the north. Come! Gaspard's place is a half hour's walk from here. We must see him tonight and engage his services."

Chapter VII

I

VALERIE went to bed in such a confused state of mind that the only impression she got of her bedroom was of its terrifying grandeur. She roused next morning when the first light of dawn came through the windows. Wide awake at once, she was gratefully conscious of the softness of the bed on which she lay. She gave a low exclamation of wonder over the coverlet which was embroidered in blue and gold with a most curious device: the heart and shell which, as she learned later, was the Coeur insigne. The bed was an enormous one with a canopy above, and immediately under the canopy a shelf for books, and attached to the shelf a bag filled with aromatic herbs. There was a candlestick on a table and it was at least two feet high and as big around as her wrist.

She lay perfectly still for several minutes, thinking of what had happened the day before and wondering what plans were hatching in the mind of the owner of this huge stone building. "What a strange man!" she said to herself. "His eyes seem to burn. I know he's kind in spite of all his sharpness and the way he hurries. How I wish I knew what he has in mind to do with me!" She was certain of one thing: that all this mystery had to do with the problem of her parentage. Jacques Coeur had known at first glance who she resembled and had assisted the Sire d'Arlay to the same knowledge. What else could it mean?

"Today," she said aloud, sitting up in bed and nodding her head emphatically, "I shall learn who I am."

Her thoughts went from there to the Sire d'Arlay and became firmly anchored. This second encounter with him had confirmed the impressions she had carried away from the first. He was not handsome and he had none of the airs and affected manners she associated with highest gentility, but in spite of that she had no doubt at all that he was a great gentleman. He was showing himself just as kind as he had during that long evening when they labored together at the fashioning of the coffin and she had confided to him so much about herself. She thought, with a surge of pride, "He likes me!" It was gratifying and exciting to know that he liked her even though she had made no serious effort to define for herself how she felt about him.

Her thoughts came back to the beauty and wonder of this room. She studied the *prie-dieu* against one wall. It was tall and had panels of red needlepoint. There was a bench piled up luxuriantly with velvet cushions, a carved chest with massive bronze hinges, a crucifix with so much compassion depicted on the face that her own eyes filled with tears. She measured the width of the bed with an incredulous eye and decided that as many as five people could sleep in it. "How fine to have it all to oneself and be able to stretch right out!" She had always been cramped as to sleeping space, in the Maret tent and in malodorous rooms in taverns. In fact, there had been for her something mean and furtive about slumber, a need to dress and undress hurriedly and under a certain constant inspection.

She threw back the covers and set herself to test the width by rolling across the bed. She accomplished six revolutions safely but the seventh projected her over the side. She landed on the floor with a loud thump.

She was on the point of raising herself, rather ruefully, when her eyes fixed themselves on a pair of shoes beside a chair. They were unbelievably lovely. The leather was soft and of a shade of green which suggested spring and the first foliage on the trees. The tops were turned back to reveal an inside lining of soft white material. The greatest glory of these amazing shoes, however, was the presence of a bow of yellow velvet on the instep of each.

She lay still and looked at them, not fully trusting the evidence of her eyes. Something was wrong! She had put her clothes the night before on this particular chair and had deposited her own shoes beside it, thinking at the time how out of place they looked. What had happened?

Slowly she raised her eyes, finding further food for surprise at each stage of the elevation. The chair was covered with clothes, but not the old and somewhat bedraggled objects she had left there before getting into bed. All her own clothing was gone and in its stead was a complete new outfit!

She sprang to her feet. She was shivering now, as much from excitement as the fact that, according to custom, she had slept naked.

"They must be for me!" she cried, in an ecstatic tone. She lifted with reverent fingers the tunic which was silk and of the same soft green as the shoes. "How lovely! These things are fine enough for a lady to wear."

She hesitated over donning the clothes, but another glance about the room convinced her that it was a case of taking this new outfit or not dressing at all. There were no signs of the worn garments she had discarded the night before.

First she picked up a linen kirtle which was intended for use next to the skin. It was quite plain but so cool that she shivered with delight at the first touch of it. The tunic came next and it fitted her perfectly, with a high waist and a rather daringly low bodice and tight sleeves diapered with gold at the wrists. She found, somewhat to her surprise, that it emitted a rustling sound with every move she made, as though the gown itself had feelings and was expressing its gratification over the fitting use to which it was being put. Then came the hose, which were of such finely spun white wool that she was able to mold them closely and neatly to her legs. Last of all came the shoes, and she marveled at the comfort of them in spite of the snugness of the fit.

There was a hat as well, a breath-taking hat of yellow velvet with an edging of the green. She held it up on one finger and knew it to be perfect.

Her mind was racing excitedly. "Who can I be," she asked herself, "that he thinks me worthy of such costly things?"

The tall stone building was coming to life. Valerie could hear footsteps in the halls and voices raised sharply in admonition and instruction. She went out on the landing of the narrow inside stairway and stared down. There was evidence of considerable activity below and curiosity took possession of her. Here was a chance to see at close range the inside of this fabulous shop. She began to descend.

She was conscious at once of strange and beguiling odors, heavy, rich, mysterious. Spices from the East! She glimpsed through an open door a long room with metal bins extending along both sides and, as the odors were almost overpowering here, she concluded this was the spice storeroom. Through other doors she caught glimpses of rare things—beautiful furniture and shining armor and, most interesting of all to her, the sheen of colored materials draped over tall frames. A clerk, with a sheet of paper in his hand, passed her on the stairs at a running gait. She heard him hesitate and then stop; and she knew that he had turned and was watching her, and wondering, no doubt, who she could be.

On each floor she encountered oldish men and women, all of them attired in gray with a red heart on one arm, who were plying brooms and otherwise setting the place in order for the day's trading. One of the women, a sharp-faced crone, stopped sweeping as she passed and stared at her with eyes sunk far back in her wrinkled mask of a face.

"I saw you last e'en when you came," whispered the woman. "You wore a ragged chammer cloak then, my girl."

Valerie tried to brush by but the crone gripped her by the elbow. "What a pretty little *garce* you are! I could tell you things to your profit if you were of a mind to listen to old Dame Trix." The woman glanced about her furtively and then made a gesture with one finger crooked above the rest. "Do you know the meaning of that? It's the sign of the Coquille. You know what *that* is!"

"No," said Valerie, who was becoming frightened. "I'm from the country and I know nothing of Paris."

"You've brought yourself to the right market, my small one. I've been able to set many girls from the country in the way of neat profits." The hoarse voice of the old woman dropped still lower. "Now don't try to tell me you've never heard of the King of the Coquillards."

"I know of one king only," faltered Valerie. She had heard a great deal, as had everyone, about this organization which extended all over France. It was particularly strong in Paris where, she knew, the head of the order lived in hidden splendor. At the moment, however, she had one thought in her head only: to get away from this evil old creature.

"Ha!" grunted the crone. "*This* king rules the best subjects in Paris. Bold rufflers, with gold in their *pilles* and ready to spend it all on pretty girls like you. Vendenguns and mercerots and king-davids, who know how to please the ladies as well as pick locks." She nodded her head on its palsied stalk of neck. "If you want a man like that, my lively sprig, you come to me. Ask for Dame Trix. That's all, just Dame Trix. And"—leering with sudden malice—"if you have any regard for your baby face, you'll keep a still mouth about what I've said."

Valerie pulled herself free of the clutching fingers and ran blindly down a dark passage. The desire to get away filled her mind so completely that when she came to a door at one end of the hall, she opened it without thinking. The room in which she found herself seemed familiar to her at once. It had whitewashed walls and many windows through which the light of the early morning sun was beginning to shine. A low oak screen closed off the section in which she stood and beyond it she saw a man hard at work before a table. He looked up at the sound of the closing door and she saw it was Jacques Coeur.

"Good morning, my child," he said, smiling. "I seem to have been successful in the selection of clothes for you. And how pleasant it is to find that you're an early riser! I didn't expect to see you as soon as this. But here you are and there isn't anyone about yet to disturb us. This will be the best time for us to have our talk."

2

The Moneyman had discarded his outer tunic for greater comfort and facility in working and had turned down the collar of his smock. This gave a full view of his neck, which was brown and muscular, an entirely adequate pedestal for his impressive head. His leggings were scarlet on one half and green on the other, as she could see now that he had risen. He had kicked off his shoes and they lay on the floor beside his chair. They looked surprisingly small for a man of his robust proportions. The gold tassels on their upturned green tips would have appeared foppish to anyone not accustomed to the supreme elegance of the day.

"Come!" said Coeur to the girl who was so abashed at the mistake which had brought her into his presence that she had not ventured beyond the door. "Come over here and sit down. I have a hundred questions to ask you."

When she took a chair beside his table, he subjected her to a close scrutiny. Then he nodded his head in approval. "If I had entertained any doubts before, they would now be swept away. You look so much like—— But that I must leave until later."

It had been no exaggeration when he said he had a hundred questions to ask. He drew out the story of her life, eliciting more information than D'Arlay had secured in his talks with her. He was like a lawyer with a witness on the stand before him. Leaning forward so that no expression of hers escaped him, he shot his questions at her so rapidly that she was in much the same position as a French soldier when arrows from the English archers rained about him; and, if the truth must be told, with some of the same need to be wary.

When he had satisfied himself about her history, he began on questions of a more general nature.

"If I gave you a royal d'or, what would you do with it?"

"A royal d'or!" It was clear she was startled by the mere mention of such a princely coin. "I've never even seen one, my lord."

"All the better. What would you do with so much wealth?"

Valerie gave serious thought to the point. "I would have it changed into the smallest coins, even *rouges liards,* my lord. I would make sure the reckoning was in *Parisis* and not *Tournois* so that I wouldn't be cheated. Then I would put the coins away in many places, never more than two in one place. I would never show more than one liard at a time and no one would suspect me of having so much."

Coeur nodded his head approvingly before going on to the next question. "Suppose you had a choice to make. Let us say, between a Bible, a gold chain, and a bolt of the best camelot cloth. Which would you take?"

"The bolt of camelot cloth, my lord," she said without hesitation.

"I didn't expect you to say that. Can you tell me what guided you in making your selection?"

The girl said to herself with a trace of inner alarm, "Have I given the wrong answer?" After further thought she began on her explanation. "I would treasure a Bible above everything. But, my lord, I can't read and never expect to be able to. Would it be right, then, for me to have a Bible? There are so very few of them and it would be sinful to waste one on me. It would do so much more good in the hands of people who could read it."

"That," said Coeur, nodding, "is sound reasoning. You would be wrong to choose the Bible."

"If I had a gold chain," she went on, "they would say I had stolen it and I would be put in prison. When people like us are put in prison, even if we're innocent, we're put to the torture. And after that, my lord, we are never again of much use."

"And what of the bolt of camelot cloth?"

"It could be traded for many bolts of plainer material and perhaps even a band of fur and some good beads. There could be a little money over into the bargain; but not enough to get me into any trouble. So you see, my lord, the cloth would be the practical choice."

"You've convinced me, Mademoiselle, that your choice was the right one."

His next question was projected with a suddenness that suggested he hoped to catch her off guard. "Tell me about Damian Maret. Was he a mirliton player? Did he carry the gay-horse on the stage?"

Valerie looked up indignantly. "He was a fine actor, my lord. A very fine actor. He was a musician also, of course; all actors must be able to play in case of need. But"—drawing away and raising her head proudly—"they always gave him fine parts."

"If he was a fine actor, why did you live so poorly? I'm told he didn't treat you well."

The girl found it hard to keep her indignation from showing in her voice. "He did as well for us as he could."

"Come, Mademoiselle, you're shielding him. You know full well that he was a lazy rascal. I am told also that he drank to excess. Did he beat you when he was in his cups?"

Valerie sprang to her feet. Angry tears filled her eyes. "You've been kind to me, my lord, but you've no right to speak of him in this way."

"Come, my child," said Coeur, in a placating voice. "You must not take amiss what I have said."

"If he drank," she explained, "it was because he had such bad fortune! Now that I know what you think of us, I am sure there is no need for us to talk further."

Coeur indulged in an approving laugh. It was clear that he was well pleased with the way she had responded. "Sit down, Mademoiselle. For all I know, Monsieur Maret was the greatest actor in the world and a man of rare and goodly disposition. I was testing your mettle." He nodded his head and beamed at her. "I'm glad to find you so loyal. It would have disappointed me very much had I found you meek and unready to speak up.

"Mademoiselle," he went on after a moment, "I have one more question to ask. It refers to something that happened twenty-five years ago."

Valerie's head came up with sharpened interest. "Twenty-five years ago? That was when the Maid——"

"Yes." Coeur's voice carried a reverent note. "The most important date in all the long history of France, Mademoiselle."

They looked at each other intently for several moments and then the Moneyman smiled. "You're getting a hint of my purpose, I think," he said. "Yes, my child, we now come to the point of this questioning which you have so patiently endured. You've wondered why I asked so many things which seemingly lacked all reason. It was because I had to be sure in my mind first that you had spirit and intelligence, and some common sense as well, before I went any further.

"My doubts have been resolved," he continued, nodding his head. "And now tell me what happened twenty-five years ago."

"It was then the Voices began to speak to the Maid."

"Yes, the Voices spoke in the ear of a peasant girl and told her what must be done to save France. Many in high positions in the state knew already what must be done but they lacked the power to make the King see the truth. God selected His instrument well. He chose a girl of the common people. But, unfortunately for France, Jeanne D'Arc did not live long enough to finish the work to which she was called." He paused to allow his words to have the desired effect. "Valerie, if you had lived then, and the choice had fallen on you, would you have obeyed the Voices?"

"I trust I would have had the courage to obey as the Maid did," she answered in a low voice.

"I'm sure you would. I'm sure you would have that same great faith if—if a second summons came now."

"I think, my lord, that every girl in France dreams of the chance to follow in the footsteps of the Maid."

"Would you be prepared to face the consequences, whatever they might be? Think well, Valerie Maret, before you answer. It may be that the time has come for another summons. Not a summons to ride into battle in shining armor. The miracle of Jeanne D'Arc can never be repeated. It would take a far different form, my child. There would be no glory in it, and perhaps not more than half-a-dozen people would ever know the truth. Shame and not glory might be the reward you would find." He paused before asking, "Do you want me to tell you anything more?"

The girl looked into his eyes without any hint of reservation in her own. "Yes, my lord."

"There is a long explanation I must make first. I must take you deeply into my confidence and I must have your solemn promise that nothing I tell you will ever be repeated."

"You have my promise."

He began to speak, lowering his voice instinctively as he explained the purpose which had entered his mind when he first saw her.

3

When the Moneyman completed his explanation with no more than one sentence to tell what was expected of her, "Someone must take the place of Agnes Sorel, someone with the good of France at heart, and you, Mademoiselle, are my choice," her reaction was instant and instinctive. She cried out: "No, no, my lord Coeur! You can't mean it!"

"But I do mean it."

Her face had become scarlet. "I—I'm not suited. How could I pass myself as a lady at court?"

"You could be taught. I don't think it would be very difficult to fit you for the role. You've good blood in your veins, unless all the signs are at fault. You're bright and quick. Yes, my small one, you would soon learn all the tricks and wiles of a great lady."

"But, my lord, don't you see that—that I shrink from the thought of such a life!"

"The Maid didn't shrink from the kind of life she knew was ahead of her."

"But that was different! It was glorious! She rode in white mail at the head of the armies of France. There was nothing shameful about it."

"She died a shameful death, a cruel death. She knew from the first what would come of it but she didn't draw back. But, my child, it's not my intent to urge this on you. You must think it over and decide for yourself. All I want to say is this: I have no doubts whatever that you could carry on the part Agnes Sorel has played."

Valerie turned her head away so that he could not see her face. She fixed her eyes on the nearest window through which sunlight was now pouring generously. "My lord Coeur, does it not seem strange to you that it's the Lady Agnes I resemble?"

"When we have time to investigate thoroughly we may find some blood relationship to account for it."

She kept her head lowered as though unwilling to meet his eyes while talking of such matters. "What," she asked, "would I have to do to fit myself for life at court?"

"You would need an education. It would be necessary to read and write and even cipher with figures. Just the beginnings of such things, fortunately. A lady is not supposed to read like a scholar or write like an *écrivain;* her gentility would be suspect if she did. I'm sure, my child, that everything else would come easily enough to you. Down inside yourself you are more of a lady now than many I know who were born to great estate."

"How long would it take?"

"Six months perhaps."

"And after that? I mean, if—if the plan should succeed?"

The Moneyman's eyes narrowed in calculation. "The war will be finished in less than a year. I'm ready to stake my official head that it will be short and decisive. We'll clear France of the enemy before another winter. . . . The rudder must not fall into weak hands for five years after peace comes. . . . Your age is sixteen at a guess. You could give us six years and still have all the best of your life before you."

Valerie said in a low tone, "Would there be enough years left to—to make my peace?"

Jacques Coeur's face sobered at once. Reaching out, he took possession of both her hands. "Do you believe that what I have asked you to do is a sin in the eyes of God?" he asked. "I've never taken my God out of a book nor fashioned Him in my mind from priestly words. He may be stern but He is just. He knows how much France needs peace and honest rule, how terribly her people will suffer if these are denied them any longer. Can it be sinful to help bring this about?" He pressed her hands reassuringly. "The God I know is a very wise God, understanding and human, and He would not weigh a small transgression against a great accomplishment!"

Nothing more was said for several moments. She was turning over in her mind the things he had told her, sitting meanwhile in a rigid position, hands clasped tightly in her lap, eyes on the floor.

He was distressed to see that there had been a distinct change in her appearance. Her cheeks had become pale and there was a trace of violet shadow under her eyes. The resemblance had become more pronounced.

Finally she began to speak. "I must have time, my lord. I know that everything you've said must be true. And yet—and yet I can't be reconciled to what it would mean."

"You must take all the time you want."

"Must you know today?"

"No, my child. Not today. Nor tomorrow. Nor the day after that."

She sighed deeply. "Then I will think about it. I will try to conquer my feelings, but I must tell you that I don't think I shall succeed."

He reached out a hand and raised her face so that he could look into her eyes. "Take all the time you need," he repeated slowly. "You must come to your decision only after thinking it out with the greatest care—and with your heart as well as your mind. I want you to know this: if the answer is Yes, it must be reached willingly. You must be entirely sure of your readiness to make this sacrifice. Otherwise, I want your answer to be No."

She turned and walked to the door. Here she stopped and hesitated. Finally, with a suggestion of color once more in her cheeks, she came back to him.

"Does—does the Sire d'Arlay know of this?"

"I told him yesterday what I had in mind."

"Is it—is it permissible to ask what he thought of it?"

Coeur looked at her shrewdly, suspecting that this might prove a crucial point with her. He answered, however, with complete frankness, "He was against it, my child."

"May I ask why?"

"The Sire d'Arlay is a man of high ideals and great generosity. But he's not logical. When a ship is on the point of foundering, it becomes necessary to throw the cargo overboard, no matter how valuable it may be. D'Arlay knows that the ship of state is in danger of being wrecked but he would rather go down with all hands than part, for instance, with his belief that the honorable and proper thing should always be done. That is fine for him but what of the poor crew?" The Moneyman paused and smiled. "I'm fond of Robin and you mustn't think I speak of him in anger. There is this also, Mademoiselle, to account for his attitude. He likes you, and wants to spare you."

Valerie bowed. "Thank you, my lord. It was kind of you to explain."

4

On the third day, having received no word from Valerie, Jacques Coeur went to the factor's wife. She was a talkative woman, with a tendency to dramatize everything: by intonation, by gesture, by expression, most of all with a flow of detail she employed to flesh the bare framework of fact.

"This girl I don't understand," she admitted. "She's interested in nothing. I talk to her; she doesn't listen. I cook for her the best; she doesn't eat. I make for her rye bread, fresh from the oven, and all women know it's good to preserve the beauty. Lentil soup by my own mother's recipe. And sambocades! Ah, such richness of curds and whey, baked in a coffin of crust and flavored as it should be with elder flowers. But will she eat? No, my lord, she takes a few bites and then she says, 'I have no more appetite.' But that cat, it eats enough for her! It eats everything I give it and then it goes back to my kitchen and steals the fish heads, and then it goes downstairs and eats the food of Old Benedisto who tends the rear gate and who brings his meals wrapped up in cabbage leaves."

"What does she do with her time?" asked the Moneyman.

"That, my lord, is hard to answer. She sits and stares out of windows and, if you ask her questions—which I have done a hundred times—she doesn't answer. She goes to the oratory and prays. Once only she seems to come to life. She laughs and talks about Mysteries and about her mules and about the time when the rope and the hook which lifted an actor off the stage broke and dropped him on his fat Guillaume. It was this morning, my lord. She even takes my children down to the grass bailey and plays with them there. She teaches them a game called Tat-and-Spat. And she imitates for them."

"Imitates?"

"Yes, my lord. She makes herself like people she has seen about the shop. Eduard, the little old bachelor who sells in Eastern Silks and who has to put his thumb in his mouth when he reckons. And Dame Trix who is a sweeper and who drinks. And Philbert the High Stepper who cleans out the stables. But it was for a short time only, my lord. She has the cockroach again as soon as she gets back, and not another word does she say."

Father François was even more disturbed about her. "Monseigneur, she prays by the hour," he reported. "I've tried to be of help to her but she says there is nothing she can tell me. I said to her, 'Daughter, what great sin have you committed which cannot be told to a man of God?' Her answer was that it was about the future she prayed and not the past. I've questioned her at length, Monseigneur, but she gives me no slightest hint of what she has on her mind."

Coeur said to himself, "She's not the tattling kind to run to neighbors or the priest with everything. That is good."

Father François seemed to feel that he was proving neglectful. "What more can I do, Monseigneur? Must I stand by and see this poor child struggle alone with her troubles?"

"This much I know about it, Father: there's nothing you can do to help her."

The Moneyman encountered Valerie that afternoon. It happened to be in the Armory and she was standing in one of the windows, gazing out in the mood of complete preoccupation which had so disturbed the factor's wife. The sun was pouring through, making her hair glisten warmly and striking on the well-polished surfaces of a suit of mail by which she was standing. Coeur said to himself, "If an artist put that on canvas, people would think it a picture of the Maid."

She turned at the sound of his steps. When she came forward to meet him, she had shaken off the mood of abstraction entirely. He knew at once that she had made up her mind and, also, what her decision had been.

"I shall do as you wish in the matter, my lord."

Coeur studied her face with a gravity which matched her own. "Are you quite sure? Have all the fears and reservations left you?"

She nodded slowly. "Yes, my lord."

"And you're entirely willing to make the sacrifice?"

She answered in a low tone. "I've come to see that it's not only my duty but my privilege. Yes, my lord, I am willing. Sometimes even I find that I'm glad. I'm so sure about it now that I wonder why I didn't see it clearly at first. How slow and stupid I have been! Taking three days to make up my mind!"

"I'm glad you took the time, Valerie. Now your mind is made up so firmly that it won't change with every twirl of the weather vane. This won't be easy for you, my child. There will be plenty of ups and downs; there will be days when everything will seem wrong. There will be times when you will weary of the hard work and the uncertainty and the—the danger. You understand, of course, that there will be danger?"

"Yes, my lord. But at no time have I been concerned about *that.*" She wore a worried frown, nevertheless, when she asked, "When do I begin?"

"I've a plan which I hope to get settled this evening. If all goes well, your education will start tomorrow."

Valerie tried to face this fact cheerfully but he noticed that her chin trembled a little. "I fear, my lord," she whispered, "that I will be a *very* poor scholar."

The Moneyman continued to study her face with an absorption which kept him silent for some moments. "Today you remind me of the young Agnes so much that I am carried back," he said at last. "I can almost believe myself at the King's court on the day when she first came. Ah, she was so young, so lovely, so very grave! She won all our hearts—and some of them she kept. You look exactly as she did the first time I saw her. She was in a green gown; and I think that memory must have prompted me in selecting this dress for you, my child. Her cheeks lacked the tan of yours and her hair was done in a different way. But otherwise you are the young Agnes I remember so well. . . . I think, my child, that the resemblance goes deeper than looks. You seem to have the same spirit, the courage, the sweet good temper I've always loved in her!"

Chapter VIII

I

JACQUES COEUR took a pride in having systems for everything. In the room he used at the Louvre—all the other ministers had suites, with chapels, refectories, pantries, even cellars of their own and stables for their horses and armories and formal gardens—there was a long table with an equally long bench behind it. Each day when he arrived, he would find piles of letters and documents at intervals along the table. When he had gone through one pile, he moved along on the bench to the next; and facing him would be the official with whom he was to discuss the matters contained therein. When he reached the end of the bench, his duties as Moneyman were over for the time being.

On the day Valerie reached her decision, he completed his tasks at a relatively late hour. Walking to one of the windows, he looked down into a busy courtyard of the palace. Men, looking dwarfed at the distance, were coming and going in the jingling harness of war. With a sudden sense of satisfaction he said to himself, "That's one thing they'll never be able to take away from me, that I persuaded Charles to the need of finishing the struggle."

Nicolas came stumbling through the dusk of the room, saying in an aggrieved tone: "And why didn't you light the candles, master? Do you think yourself above such ordinary needs as light or do you fancy yourself a cat to see in the dark? The Sire d'Antenne is waiting outside. I would like to slam the door in his face!"

There was a hint of jocularity in Coeur's voice as he said, "Show the splendid fellow in, Nicolas."

The "splendid fellow" proved to be a foppishly dressed young man with a black patch over one eye. Any observer who caught the slyness and greed in the other would have been forgiven for thinking that the accident, if accident it had been, would have been much more of a boon had it resulted in closing both.

Coeur waited for Nicolas to withdraw and then addressed his visitor.

"Come and sit beside me, my honest Georges, so that we can talk in low tones. In no other way can we discuss the kind of business which always brings you here, my perfect paragon of honesty."

The visitor, whose skin seemingly was thick enough to absorb any amount of verbal pricking or bludgeoning, seated himself at the table with no suggestion of umbrage. He said in an even tone, "What I have for you today is worth double the usual fee."

"I'll judge of that," declared Coeur sharply, "after I have heard what it is."

The young man with the black patch was watching the Moneyman closely with his one eye. "It's the most vital piece of information I've ever had for sale. I've some hesitation about telling it, as you will understand, my lord Coeur. There is danger in passing it on."

"Speak up!" said Coeur impatiently. "We both know that the skin of an informer is always in some danger. Isn't it rather that the odor this time is so strong that even your well-seasoned nostrils can feel a distaste?"

The Sire d'Antenne proceeded to tell his story. He had called to see his sister, who was married to Guillaume Gouffier and was in ill-health because of the imminence of her fourteenth child. By some error of calculation (he smiled as he gave this information, as though proud of what he had done) he had found himself not in his sister's quarters but in a small room which opened into a larger apartment where Gouffier conducted his affairs. He had become aware at once that his sister's husband had important visitors. There was a murmur of voices from the larger room, many of which he had no difficulty at all in identifying. With a skill in such matters which he regarded clearly as an accomplishment, he had succeeded in opening the door slightly and in spying out the land. There were seven men in the room. He had recognized all of them.

The talk going on inside had reached his ears in snatches only but he had heard enough to realize that the gathering was not a chance one, that it had been called by Gouffier for a specific purpose. He paused at this point and waited.

"And what was the purpose, my expert at keyholes, my agile gatherer of gossip?"

"To discuss ways and means of persuading the King to dispense with the services of his Moneyman."

Coeur smiled as though he took a certain sardonic satisfaction in the situation. "They will find they are too early. I've not yet paid the whole cost of the war."

"They're not looking at the immediate future, my lord Coeur. They won't make any kind of move until after Rouen has been taken. Then, my not-too-generous employer, watch yourself! The pack will be upon you!"

"My ill-wishers grow more daring, it seems. They're no longer content to snap at my heels like a pack of jackals. What form will the attack take, when it comes?"

There had been talk, explained the informer, of getting together evidence to lay before the King. The management of the mint at Bourges, which Coeur had controlled in the earliest days of the reign, had come in for much discussion (Coeur smiled at this, for Charles had lived at Bourges then and had been so poor that he had needed to clip the coinage in order to have meat on his table), and there had been some talk about the supplying of bombards to the Turks to assist them in their war against Christian states.

While the bearer of tales was telling what he had seen and heard, Jacques Coeur was piling up coins on the table in front of him in the form of a pyramid. He had seemed completely absorbed in this occupation but in reality he had missed nothing. He looked up the instant the story came to an end.

"And you'll tell me the names of the seven men?"

"If the fee is to be doubled."

"The fee will be doubled, my spotless paladin, my cavalier of clean conscience. See! It's ready for you here."

The man with the black patch named the conspirators, counting on his fingers as he did so.

At the end Coeur nodded his head with a return of his sardonic mood. "I could have named them myself, I think," he said. "They would all profit personally by my removal. It happens that six of the seven are in my debt at the moment." He raised both hands and then dropped them inertly on the table. "These brave and honorable knights should be grateful to me. I'm paying for a war in which they will have a chance to display their gallantry and win renown for themselves. Instead they plot my ruin."

The Sire d'Antenne counted the coins with great care. Then he nodded and rose to his feet. He seemed well pleased with himself.

"That patch on your eye is the sign of a war pledge no doubt," said Coeur.

"Yes, my lord Moneyman-for-the-time-being. I've sworn not to discard it until I've performed some noble deed in the fighting with the Engloys."

Coeur laughed mirthlessly. "I've heard of half-a-dozen other great knights who are wearing patches for the same reason. I could give you the names of three who have forsworn a certain pleasurable rite, in which their ladies would play a part, until the enemy has been driven from the country. How unfortunate it would be for them if the war dragged on for another twenty years! I know of one who has declared himself not to bathe until his doughty arm has brought him just acclaim. Not that the oath will make any particular difference in his habits." His voice rose. "I would like to propose a more useful and logical oath for the lot of you to swear. That you will obey the orders of your leader when it comes to the fighting. That you won't charge when you see fit yourselves—as you did at Azincourt and so lost the battle—but wait until the order is given. That you won't scorn to protect your archers, because the poor fellows are of low degree, nor allow the enemy to cut them to pieces while his own bowmen rain deadly arrows on the army of France! In other words, that you will behave like real soldiers and not like sulky and overbearing fools!"

"You seem to have little respect for chivalry, my lord Coeur."

"So little, Sire d'Antenne, that I—— But let that go for the moment. I'm a buyer of secrets and so only a degree better than you, a seller. I don't need to tell you, my model of rectitude, that all ministers of the King employ spies to know what is going on! You sell to all of them, I don't doubt. But under the circumstances I'm not in a position to suggest that another oath you might take would be not to sell information about your friends."

The wearer of the patch smiled without a trace of rancor. "I need the money," he said. He waved a hand jauntily as he was leaving the room. "I'll continue to serve you, Jaquet the Fox, as long as you have gold to pay me."

Coeur called out in a sudden burst of anger: "Nicolas, Nicolas! Get a window open in there! That splendid fellow has polluted the air!"

2

Jacques Coeur was late in reaching the Grand Salon. The long tables were already filled and at *dressoirs* along the walls the court carvers were basting the roast meats with orange juice and rose water and sprinkling them with salt and sugar and spices. At first glance it was impossible to see much more of the company than the towering headdresses of the ladies. Some of these rose as much as three feet above the heads of their wearers and no two were alike. There were some which resembled windmills with broad surfaces of shimmering satin, a few which sported horns as widespread as a stag's, others which were heart-shaped with armorial bearings picked out in precious stones, and many which were further complicated by bands of velvet looped around the head and falling to the floor. The general effect was much the same as that produced by a company of standard-bearers in a victory processional or a saint's day parade.

Coeur perceived at once that the company had taken advantage of the fact that the royal family were enjoying their meal in the privacy of the Queen's own salon by relaxing ceremonial to the extent of supping *à deux*. Each gentleman was sharing his plate and cup with a lady, and already a certain boisterous levity had developed. There was one vacant chair and into this the Moneyman slipped quietly.

"I begged the privilege of your company tonight, my lord Coeur," said the lady who was to share his plate. "For a long time I've desired a chance to talk with you."

She was a mature beauty of thirty or perhaps even a few years in excess of that turning point in the lives of the women of the day. Her warm brown eyes smiled at him from under a comparatively inconspicuous hennin of velvet.

Coeur was surprised that the much-sought-after Comtesse de Burey should have expressed a preference for his company, and his manner showed it. "I'm most deeply honored, Comtesse," he said, with a bow. "This is doubly fortunate, as I've desired a talk with you. We have an interest in common."

"Yes," she agreed. "You refer, of course, to my brother-in-law. I had a note from him last night but I haven't seen him yet since his return." Isabeau de Burey allowed the furred edge of her fan to brush her companion's shoulder with the slightest suggestion of coquetry. "I make no secret of the fact that I'm interested in everything he does. But you need not look so disturbed, my lord Coeur. I was in accord with the purpose which kept him away so long."

The Moneyman studied her face with a steady eye. "I'm indeed happy to know that, Comtesse," he said. "We still need every adherent, particularly one whose charm can be of service to us."

"I've been such a loyal supporter of your policy that some on the other side have treated me coldly," whispered the Comtesse. "Even my husband had been won over to our way of thinking. Not"—with a sudden hardening of her very lovely eyes—"that Regnault's support would ever be of much help to you. He has shown such a capacity for making enemies!"

Despite his deep interest in the topic, Coeur had already begun to dip his spoon into the soup before them. "The royal cook is doing us special honor tonight," he said. "This *soupe dorée* was the great Taillevent's most conspicuous triumph. I can never resist it."

The rich potage clearly was a dish that none of the company could resist. It was made of slices of brown toast fried in yolks of egg and white wine and then floated in rose water, sprinkled with saffron and sugar. The ladies and gentlemen alike were spooning it up voraciously.

The Comtesse shook her head sadly. "It's too rich for me. I am no longer young"—she paused as though willing to have him enter a denial—"and there is no longer any doubt that I can take on weight too readily. It's a great trial."

He was well aware, nevertheless, that her throat and shoulders, generously exposed in the mode of the moment, displayed a dazzling white roundness of contour. "It seems to me that you grow lovelier every day," he said.

A *squire de gobelet* poured wine into the cup they were to share. Coeur raised it with an appreciative hand and offered it to his companion. "Saint-Pourcain!" he said. "We are indeed being honored. The very best of all wines. Will you condescend to take the first drink?"

The Comtesse took a sip and then handed the cup back to him. "Robin has been most secretive on one score," she said, returning to the subject which interested her most. "He has never let me know the exact nature of the relationship between you. Is it such a very great secret, then? I confess to being an inquisitive person, my lord."

Coeur took a deep swallow of the wine. "I see no reason why it should be a secret at all. D'Arlay has never shown any reluctance to having it known that he has an interest in my enterprises. In fact, I've every reason to believe he is proud his fingers have dabbled in—in what the rest of our company here tonight would call 'vulgar trade.' What is it you want to know?"

"Well," she said, "how it began, for instance."

"I can understand why he has never told you that. I saw him for the first time on an occasion when his spirits were very low. Someone he thought a great deal of, Comtesse, was being married. I advised him to go away and even took the liberty of suggesting he sail on one of my ships. He acted on the suggestion and it did him much good. We have been friends ever since."

As he spoke Coeur was watching the profile of his companion. It was well worth studying: a good brow, a delicately arched nose with proudly chiseled nostrils, full eyelids, and lashes of unusual length. "No wonder Robin was so unhappy when she threw him aside," he said to himself. "She must have been irresistible then." Now she had a reputation for ambition and selfishness, but he was not entirely inclined to accept this estimate. Court beauties were always the targets for envy and malicious tittle-tattle. He went over in his mind the stories circulated about Isabeau de Burey: She had tried hard but without success to succeed Agnes Sorel in the affections of the King; she thought of little else but her looks and even went to such extremes as bathing in strawberry juice and drinking vinegar instead of wine to retain the milky whiteness of her skin; she paid visits to a learned doctor at the University who was said to dabble in magic and who was even rumored to be on the point of discovering the Philosopher's Stone; she cared for her husband's brother much more than she did for the Comte and made it clear to the latter that she had married him for his title alone. Coeur was sure of one item only in this indictment, the last named.

"Quite a few years ago," went on the Moneyman, "I found myself needing funds rather badly. I was adding to my fleet of ships and I had, perhaps, rushed into construction more boldly than was wise. I was so hard pressed that it was a great help when D'Arlay made me a loan. I've always considered that he did me a great service."

"I *did* know of the loan."

"It was bold of him as well as generous. His share of the estates, into which he had just come, was badly stretched in the process. In fact, he found it necessary to put a mortgage on his lands."

"I didn't know of the mortgage. Regnault would have been furiously opposed if *he* had heard of it."

"I am telling you this in confidence, Madame. The loan was well protected. I did better for him than a bottomry bond by which he would have had for security a certain ship and could lose everything if that ship went down; I gave him his security, in fact, on the goods in my shops and so he couldn't lose. The loan was repaid quickly enough but I felt that his trust had placed me under a never-ending obligation. Ever since I have considered him a silent partner and he shares in certain of the profits. He will always do so."

The Comtesse continued to watch him with a speculative eye. "It's within the bounds of possibility then that my sweet Robin may become a very rich man?"

Their plate had been filled with gobbeted trout. The Comtesse refrained from eating but Jacques Coeur began to ply an enthusiastic knife. "Will you forgive me if I indulge in a boast?" he asked between mouthfuls. "He's a rich man now as a result of this share in my enterprises. He should become very much richer as time goes on."

"I'm very happy to hear it," whispered the Comtesse.

"You see, Madame," went on the Moneyman, not averse to fanning the regrets she might be harboring over her matrimonial mistake, "my enterprises are different from anything the world has ever seen before. There is no limit to the growth I foresee. Actually I've made no more than a start. Your brother-in-law continues to help me in many ways. He will continue a partner, a silent one it is true, in the—the empire of trade I am building."

The trout had been succeeded by venison and furmenty, a combination invented two generations before by Taillevent, the famous royal cook of that day. The wheaten flour of the furmenty was boiled in milk with melted sugar and cardamom seeds and the result was a piquant accompaniment to the strong flavor of the meat. It was a favorite dish of Coeur's but the Comtesse did not touch it, contenting herself with a small mound of *marrois* which one of the helpers placed on her side of the plate. Into this well-spiced combination of hashed fish and cod's liver she dipped a sparing knife at intervals.

"I'm the richest man in the world today," declared the Moneyman proudly. His eyes were glowing with enthusiasm but he was taking good care to pitch his voice so low that he could not be heard by anyone else at the table. "What will I do with my wealth if it continues to grow? I don't know. In fact, I never give that a thought. I'm not doing this for the sake of money. I like power but I'm not thinking of that either. I lack words to tell you the vision that prompts me to go on and yet I can see the future clearly enough. The world will be a different place, a better place, when commerce becomes man's chief interest and"—he paused significantly—"when soldiers are considered of small account. Comtesse, that's what I am striving to bring about: to make the rules of the countinghouse of more moment than the Code of Chivalry, to provide a greater degree of comfort and happiness for all people. It's coming. Nothing can hold it back. I want to bring that welcome day closer."

"I find it hard to believe in the possibility of such a future," said the Comtesse. "But—you are a most ardent advocate, my lord Coeur."

The royal cook had provided a special Warner, the dish which served as an intimation that the course had been finished and another was to begin. It consisted of two figures, almost life size, representing a shepherd and shepherdess made of various kinds of edibles. There was an artist in the kitchen, a potential Phidias born to waste his talents among pots and pans and to work in lard and pastry instead of enduring stone. The figures were startlingly real. The faces had been faithfully contrived out of browned dough and they smirked at each other in bucolic fidelity. Each carried a small basket. When the lid of one was lifted, a pair of canaries began to sing inside. Doves flew out from the other, a half dozen or more. They flapped confidently about the room and even perched on the shoulders of the company in expectation of being fed.

Jacques Coeur joined in the applause by clapping his hands briefly. He then plunged back into conversation without any delay.

"You've known D'Arlay a long time, Comtesse?"

"Yes, Monsieur. All my life. The estates of our families adjoined in Anjou, although the De Burey lands were much more extensive than my father's holdings. We were much of an age, Robin and I. You perceive, my lord, that my honesty is great enough for even such a damaging admission as that. We played together as children and I saw him every day as we grew up. Robin was a kind and gentle boy and a very good companion. I was always fond of him."

"But you married his older brother."

"Yes, I married his brother."

There was a pause. "You are an ambitious woman, I think, Comtesse," said Coeur.

Isabeau de Burey nodded in agreement. "That is true. I see no reason for not acknowledging that I would like to have more influence at court. I have some beauty and I'm sure I have more intelligence than most of these"—she lowered her voice cautiously—"these very stupid people about us."

"It was to better your chances, then, that you married the Comte de Burey? You wanted the title?"

The brown eyes of the Comtesse narrowed slightly before she nodded a second time. "You have asked me a direct question and I feel disposed to give you a frank answer. Yes, my lord Coeur, I married Regnault for his title and the position it would give me at court. He has been a great disappointment to me and I feel no need to conceal the truth on his behalf."

"Did D'Arlay understand the reason for your preference?"

"Not entirely. He charged me with it at the time but I—I denied it. He was even more modest then and so he found it easy to believe I could prefer his brother." She dipped her hands in a ewer of hot water offered by one of the servitors and dried them carefully on the linen towel draped on the handle. "I don't know why I am telling you this. I'm making admissions, in fact, which will give you a very bad opinion of me."

Coeur took a final drink of wine and shoved the goblet aside as a signal it was not to be refilled. He turned to study his companion more closely. "It is in your mind perhaps that you could be of use to me?"

The Comtesse returned his gaze steadily. "It has seemed to me possible. You need friends at court."

"Yes, Comtesse, it's possible I may need friends in the unpredictable days ahead of us. A lady of your position, and with your charm, could be useful to me." He asked, after a moment, "Are you in need of funds?"

"Always," she sighed. "My selfish spouse has been very extravagant. Our debts are heavy—so heavy that we are forced to the most trying expedients to pay his creditors and still keep up appearances."

"Have you ever applied to D'Arlay for assistance?"

She hesitated before answering. "I've been so frank with you already that I might as well tell you everything. Even if it gives you a still worse opinion of me. Yes, my lord, I have sought his help when—when things became particularly difficult."

"And has he been willing to help?"

"Of course. My dear Robin is the most generous of men. He has never needed more than a word from me."

"In return for what you may be able to do for me, you might prefer to come to me when the necessity arises."

The Comtesse did not withdraw her eyes. "That possibility has occurred to me."

A born bargainer, Coeur liked nothing better than to have the lead come from the other party to a transaction. He said to himself with satisfaction, "This is a fortunate coincidence. I'm in a position now to make arrangements to suit myself."

"It happens, Comtesse, that you could be of direct aid to me now," he said aloud. "There's a rather delicate undertaking which I think could be put safely in your hands. It would be a profitable venture for you."

The lady had an instinct for bargaining also. She said nothing.

"Before I explain the nature of it," Coeur continued, "I must touch on a delicate point without any bearing on the undertaking itself. I must make a stipulation. You won't like what I'm going to say but I'm always forthright in my dealings and I believe in speaking openly and to the point."

The lady's eyebrows raised slightly and involuntarily but she answered in even tones, "I'm ready to listen to anything you have to say, my lord Coeur."

"I'm very fond of Robin," said Coeur, after a moment. "It's a matter of deep regret to me to realize that he's not happy. I don't mean that he is actively unhappy. He enjoys such work as I entrust to him. He has his books and he dabbles a little in philosophy and science. But here he is, a man of thirty or so and still unmarried. He should have half-a-dozen children around his house by this time. Books are a poor substitute for a family, Comtesse. I'm beginning to fear he will never marry now; and that is a bleak prospect for a man of his disposition. I'm quite disturbed about him."

"I've never stood in the way of his marrying," said Isabeau.

"Not directly, or openly, perhaps. But I wonder if he's likely to think of any other women as long as a certain bond remains unbroken? If that bond were snapped or permitted to fray, I think he would soon find someone to suit him. I'm certain of one thing, Comtesse: you, and you only, are in a position to break that bond."

A long silence developed, each waiting for the other to break it. Coeur won.

"Am I to understand this is your stipulation?" she asked.

Coeur nodded. "Make me a promise to do everything you can to break that bond, Comtesse, and I'll be so generous with you in the other matter that you will never know any financial embarrassment again."

For the first time a touch of color showed in her usually cool white cheeks. Watching her closely, Coeur realized that she was finding it difficult to control her resentment. He waited anxiously, not sure that her need for security would get the upper hand.

She asked finally, "Must I give you this—this extraordinary pledge before you tell me the nature of the undertaking?"

The Moneyman said to himself triumphantly, "She's going to agree." Through force of habit he waited before answering. "I may tell you this much, that it would involve taking a young girl under your tutelage and care for a period. Before saying anything more, I must ask you a question. I must be sure that certain information I have received is correct."

"As you wish."

Convinced in his mind now of the outcome, he asked, "You had an uncle named Gilles de Voudrai with estates in the southern part of Berri?"

"Yes. My uncle Gilles died about ten years ago."

"He had many children, I believe, most of them illegitimate."

The Comtesse permitted herself to smile. "A great many."

"What did he do to provide for those born out of wedlock?"

"Nothing that I know of. My uncle was not a rich man. He had squandered his resources and his estate was in a sad condition when he died."

"Have his heirs concerned themselves over the plight of his illegitimate issue?"

"Knowing my cousins as I do, I'm quite sure they've done nothing at all.

Do you wish to imply that they've been negligent or unnatural in the matter?"

Coeur shook his head. "I'm not concerned with the ethics of the situation. I want to be sure of one thing. Have your cousins kept track of them?"

Isabeau indulged in an easy laugh. "If you had known my uncle Gilles, you wouldn't require an answer. There were too many of them, Monsieur. I'm not sure that even he knew how many he had. There is nothing unusual about that."

Supper was over. There was a loud scraping of chairs on the stone floor as the company rose to leave. Most of them paused by the door where servitors offered them the spiced *boute-hors* which brought each meal to a close. There was a loud clatter of talk.

"I'm satisfied now to tell you what I have in mind, Comtesse," said Coeur. "Do you feel disposed to give me more of your time when we reach the apartments of the Queen?"

Isabeau kept her eyes lowered. "I—I must think of what you have said first."

Coeur smiled at her. "By all means. Whatever the decision, permit me to say this has been a most pleasant and profitable supper. I've enjoyed your company very much."

Chapter IX

I

A GALE took possession of Paris that night. It came from the northwest and roared down the river and over the rooftops. It was not the mischievous kind, snatching at hats and making clotheslines dance, but a baleful storm with fingers of ice and lungs of steel. It brawled fiercely about the spires of churches and forced its way through faults in the glazing to mutter in the aisles like the whisper of heresy. It swirled down the streets and caused tavern signs to swing like bells in a steeple.

By morning the river was rolling in yellow turbulence. Masses were being sung in empty churches and the shutters of most shops remained up. D'Arlay had intended to make several visits but a single glance from the window of his bedroom on one of the top floors of the house in the

Rue Grenier sur L'Eau was sufficient to dissuade him from that purpose. He decided to stay indoors.

Leaving the window, he paused beside an unfinished object made of clay which occupied a small table against one of the walls. It consisted of a round cylinder about two feet in length protruding from a cradle of crossbars. It was not hard to recognize, for it was an excellent model of a bombard, the new kind of cannon which was to be used against the English. He and Pregent Kennedy had filled in time by making it but had not yet finished the equipment for breech-loading and firing. And now it would remain unfinished, for Pregent Kennedy had left.

He had returned the previous noon after a visit to the headquarters of Jacques Coeur and had proceeded immediately to pack his saddlebags with his meager belongings. As usual he had volunteered no information at all.

"You are going away?" D'Arlay asked, standing over him as he meticulously folded in his one change of underclothes.

"Aye. I am grateful to you for your kindness in letting me fill a humble bed in your handsome house but I'll have no further use for it. I leave at once."

"May I ask what brought about this sudden change of plan?"

The Scot straightened up and gave frowning consideration to the advisability of answering. "I go," he said finally, "at the behest of the Moneyman."

"Does your mission concern Valerie Maret?"

Another long pause. "Aye. I go to Berri to make inquiries about her. I'll be gone for several weeks at the least reckoning."

D'Arlay nodded his head approvingly. He was glad an effort was to be made to trace the girl's parentage, and convinced that no better agent could have been selected.

By further questioning he learned that Kennedy knew nothing more, except that Valerie still lived with the family of the factor and was not to be seen by visitors. He, Kennedy, had been denied the opportunity of talking with her before leaving.

When the Scot had tossed the saddlebags over his shoulder and departed, D'Arlay realized that he could no longer keep up his pretense of indifference by staying away. It had required the exercise of all his strength of will to keep from rushing to Coeur to protest still more urgently than he already had done and to the girl herself to prevent her from making such a serious mistake. Each day he had paced up and down, wondering what had happened between Coeur and Valerie, even his anxiety about the forthcoming duel relegated to the back of his mind.

Having decided against the idea of venturing out into the rain-swept streets himself, he was surprised when a step on the stairs announced a visitor. It was Gaspard, the arms master. He came in with water dripping from his clothes and trickling down his cheeks and nose.

"I didn't expect you in weather like this," said D'Arlay.

"A man must live," declared the arms master cheerfully. "If I didn't come here, my lord, I would have nothing to do today and the state of my purse makes idleness a luxury I can't afford."

D'Arlay took down his sword from a metal fastener on the wall. He gave it a preliminary cut with the feeling of satisfaction he always enjoyed when it was in his hand.

"I'm disposed to think, Gaspard," he said, "that you will come off second best today. Very much second best. I feel in the mood for swordplay. This good blade of mine fairly tugs at my hand."

The arms master contented himself with saying, "I will do my best," as he threw off his sodden cloak and rolled up the sleeves of his tunic. He was a stockily built fellow with muscles which rippled under the brown skin of his arm. His movements were deliberate, but when he took a step forward it was easily to be seen that his whole body was like a beautifully adjusted machine.

D'Arlay advanced, treading on his toes in eagerness to begin, his blade extended in front of him. "On guard!" he cried.

The swords touched and held for the customary moment. Then D'Arlay drew back and lunged vigorously. There was a grind of steel as the arms master parried the thrust. The bout was on; and an exultant power coursed through D'Arlay's arm as he went seriously to work.

This mood did not last, however. Facing him, as he countered his opponent's steel, was a stained-glass window representing Samson with jawbone in hand. D'Arlay had never been pleased with the subject. Now, as he advanced and retreated and lunged and parried, he was less pleased than ever. The uplifted arm of the strong man seemed to him to represent the might of Jacques de Lalain and he fancied he could see a slight resemblance to himself in the cringing Philistine on whom the jawbone was descending.

Isabeau had been responsible for nearly everything about this house in the Rue Grenier sur L'Eau. As soon as he had acquired it, she had descended on him with a builder and a glassmaker in tow and had taken over the direction of the improvements. It was a house of the type known as foreland, with masonry foundations and a succession of frame upper stories, each of which reached farther out into the street until the roof seemed in imminent danger of toppling over; a picturesque structure in its original guise, with N-shaped beams and thatch of red and yellow plaster and an infinity of quaint design in the woodwork both inside and out. There were moments now when he did not like his Paris home at all. Isabeau had succeeded in converting it into an imitation of the pretentious hotels of the great families; but, he thought, a not particularly successful one, despite the fact that the windows blazed with all the hues known to the glassmakers and the ceiling of the ground floor had been ripped out to give him an imposing and thoroughly uncomfortable Great Hall.

Despite the parallel he had read into the subject of the glass window, he was quite pleased with himself when the bout came to an end. Wiping his streaming brow on the maroon velvet of his sleeve, he said to his opponent, "You didn't touch me once, Gaspard."

The arms master grunted. "That's true, my lord. I didn't get by your guard once. You have great skill with the sword."

Removing the cork from the tip of his weapon, D'Arlay added with an air of satisfaction, "On the other hand, I got through your guard quite often."

"Four times, my lord."

"Well," demanded D'Arlay, dropping on a bench and spreading out his long legs with the feeling of comfort that follows any physical effort, "what do you think of my chance?"

Gaspard did not answer at once. He was rolling down the sleeve of his tunic. Then he reached for his leather jerkin and struggled into it. It was a full minute before he ventured an opinion. "You will have no chance at all, my lord."

D'Arlay was puzzled as well as disturbed. "But why?" he asked. "What more can you expect of me?"

The arms master shook his head gloomily. "I've seen Jacques de Lalain in the lists. There has never been anyone to equal him. His strength passes belief and he fights with the fury of a gored bull. In addition he has great skill with all weapons."

"With the sword it's skill only which counts. The answer to his greater strength is in the lightness of the foot. I can keep out of his reach until I see an opening for a thrust of my own."

The man did not seem convinced. "But your legs lose their nimbleness when encased in grevières and with iron shoes on the feet."

"We're to fight without armor of any kind."

Gaspard looked his surprise. "Has the Burgundian agreed to that? It will make a great difference. You'll have a chance to spit him before his greater strength can have any effect. But," with a return of his doubts, "it will be wise not to depend too much on that. You must fit yourself for a long bout and that will mean much hard work."

"I'm prepared to do whatever you think necessary."

The arms master nodded his head approvingly. "If you are serious, I can promise to make a different man of you. It will mean"—Gaspard gave a quick glance to convince himself that the drastic advice he must offer would be accepted in the right spirit—"the greatest discomfort for you. You must eat nothing but the foods I select. There must be exercises twice a day and a long run to improve your wind. Our bout today was a short one, my lord, and yet you are still panting and covered with perspiration. When you have followed my advice for a long enough time, you will come through a little dancing lesson such as this without a damp hair on your head. I must be honest with you, my lord. You are soft and short of wind and you have muscles like a chitterling."

"As I said before, Gaspard, I'm ready to place myself in your hands."

The arms master reached for his cloak and hat. "May I ask how old you are?"

"I've turned thirty."

"You look younger than that. It's a late age to begin on the heavy work I must give you. I can say this much for you, my lord, you haven't got yourself a monstrous weasand like most men of your years." After a critical survey he went on, "There's a little extra fat here and there on your bones which we must get rid of at once. Eat sparingly. Soups and meat only. No bread, no pastry, not more than one drink of wine at each meal."

"A miserable kind of life you are plotting for me, Gaspard."

"But a longer life," ventured the arms master, "than you are like to have if you don't do everything I say."

D'Arlay had been reduced to a thoroughly unhappy frame of mind. "I thought he would be well impressed," he said to himself. "Well, I must set myself humbly to doing everything he says. I must forget I have a brain and a heart and remember only that I have muscles to be developed. I must strive to make myself into the kind of honorable knight who thinks only of killing other knights."

2

He was still engaged in these gloomy speculations when another visitor arrived. It proved to be the last person in the world he could have expected on such a day, his brother. The Comte de Burey slouched in on flat feet, leaning forward as he walked and peering ahead of him with the anxious pucker of shortsightedness. He had become paunchy and bald and his long face had the sallowness of bad health; but in spite of all this he still exerted some small vestige of what had once been a debonair charm. Dropping his wet cloak from his shoulders and allowing it to fall behind him on the floor, he revealed the fact that he was attired in the extreme of fashion. A ruffled tunic fell almost to his knees, his thinning shanks were covered by parti-colored hose, and the sleeves of his tunic were like the trunks of full-grown trees. He stopped and looked about him, teetering uncertainly. It was clear that he was at least partially drunk.

"Ha!" he said, squinting at his brother. "What have you been trying to do, make yourself a rival of Marco Polo? You've been away for six months and I've been needing you desperately. I heard last night you had condescended to return—and here I am, in all this rain, with an ache in my bones as though I had been put on the rack. *That* is how badly I need to see you!" He walked farther into the room, laying his feet down with the greatest care and balancing himself with difficulty. "There are times when I suspect the gout has laid its foul hand on me."

"Your sins are catching up with you, Naulty," said D'Arlay. Then he smiled and extended his hand. "I'm glad to see you."

"Ha!" snorted the Comte. "It's Isabeau you'll be glad to see. How could you stay away from her so long? By'r Lady of Marmoutier, I must have an eye to my health now that you're back. If I should die, you would strip the shoes off my feet before they were stiff in your haste to get into them."

"A jest in very bad taste, Naulty. And I doubt very much if you'll leave as much as a pair of shoes, the way things are going with you."

"It's bad taste to let the whole world know you're in love with your brother's wife, my Robin. Oh, I concede it's partly my fault. You wanted her and I took her away from you. I might have expected, knowing what a determined, unchanging young dog you are, that you would go on mooning after her. But now I confess to a growing distaste for your undying devotion, as I suppose you call it." He dropped limply into a chair. "Can't you see that I shall perish if you don't produce a hot posset at once to revive me? And do you call this feeble pindle of flame a fire? Is it by mean economies such as this that you keep yourself so affluent, my closefisted brother?"

D'Arlay called to his servant. "Helion! Mulled wine at once. And then another log for the fire."

"The days of your devotion to Isabeau are over," asserted Regnault de Burey when a flagon of wine had been brought him and the fire had been stirred up to a hot blaze. "That's what I've come to discuss with you. You must marry at once. I may tell you without more ado that I've found the wife for you."

"Has it occurred to you that I might prefer to find my own wife?"

The Comte glared over the rim of his flagon. "Has it occurred to you that we might have all the family estates taken away from us if we don't find a way at once of paying off my debts?"

D'Arlay's mood sobered. "Is it as bad as that, Naulty?"

"Things couldn't be worse. They hang over me like a flock of vultures, these bloodsucking leeches from Lombardy. They give me no peace. I can no longer pay the interest on my debts and at the same time keep up any pretense of living like a gentleman. Do you want to see the lands of your ancestors in the hands of filthy moneylenders?"

"No!" said D'Arlay. "I'm as concerned about that as you are, Naulty. The debts must be paid in some way."

"Are you in a position to pay them?"

"I've benefited through my association with Jacques Coeur, but not to that extent. It would take a very rich man to repair the damage you've done to the family fortunes, brother."

"It comes down to this. You can't dandle around fancy free any longer, my fine Robin. You must take a wife with a large enough fortune to save the lands of De Burey from going out of the family." He supped at his wine before adding in a tone of voice faintly apologetic: "There is also the matter of a male heir to succeed and carry on the name. That will be your responsibility also. I'm not likely to supply the deficiency. Make no mistake, it's not *my* fault. I've cast a dozen laggen-girds[1] around the countryside."

D'Arlay seated himself beside his brother. After several moments of intense and unhappy thought he began to speak. "I've always known, Naulty, that it would come to this sooner or later, that I would have to marry with an eye to both these considerations. My duty has always been clear to me but I've put off marrying as I haven't seen anyone I felt I could endure living with. Now it seems I must face the problem. It's unfortunate from my standpoint that the crisis should come at the very moment when I suspect I've fallen in love—and with someone with no name and no prospects. In fact, I couldn't have made a worse choice, as you would emphatically agree if you knew anything about the lady in question."

[1]A reference to illegitimacy.

The Comte was so taken aback by this piece of news that he stared fixedly at his brother, the whites of his eyes showing (or what would have been the whites if they had not become a bilious brown) and his mouth open to display a prominent front tooth. "What Isabeau will think of *this,*" he said, "will add to my discomfort for longer than I care to contemplate. By'r Lady of Marmoutier, she will take it ill!" He crossed one leg over the other and groaned with the pain. "But we have no difficulty here at all. If the wench is as lacking in prospects as you say, no one will want to marry *her* and you can keep her for yourself after you're married."

"You are wrong. In the first place, she has no idea that I've fallen in love with her. When I marry someone else—and it seems that I must—I shall never see her again."

"You would be well rid of one as uncomfortably virtuous as that."

They sat in silence for several moments and then D'Arlay asked, "Who is the lady on whom you've fixed your eye?"

The Comte answered with cheerful readiness. "A perfect choice, a flawless diamond among women, or at least nearly flawless. Listen to her perfections. A widow, well under thirty, one child only—a girl, quite sickly and not likely to survive—fair to look upon, lively, and so much property in her own name, mostly in the way of estates in Angoulême, that our debts could be paid off and still there would be enough to muffle up the whole family of De Burey against the winds of adversity."

"Who is this paragon?"

Regnault watched his brother with a slightly furtive air as he pronounced the name. "Clothilde de Trepant, widow of the Sire de Trepant who was killed in a lance-running at Bordeaux some six months back. He was killed, in fact, just as you began your endless travels and I've been watching for you ever since." Satisfied that D'Arlay had never heard of the lady who might become his wife, the Comte proceeded to an explanation. "There is one small circumstance which will bear telling. A few months after the sire's death, her page, standing behind her chair with company in the room, was observed to reach down and give her a sly pinch. It was assumed from this that she had been allowing the boy certain privileges."

In a tone of voice which seemed to say, "If I must marry for wealth does anything matter?" D'Arlay asked, "What of her looks?"

"Ha!" cried his brother. "There we are on the firmest ground. She has hair which tends to red, eyes on the order of green, a pert nose, and a figure that is most pleasantly slender. I can promise you this: by day, she will amuse you with her wit; by night, she will battle it out with you in the briskest and sweetest of dalliance." Regnault de Burey nodded his head like a lawyer at his summing up. "I have looked over the field with a thoroughness bred of desperation. This one is the pick. She will be both wife and mistress, she will be like a beautifully embroidered purse which will never empty no matter how often you reach into it for gold. Of all who possess the necessary property, she has the most virtues and the fewest faults. My advice to you, brother, is this: take her at once."

"You will allow me, I trust, to—to look about me first?"

"There's no time to waste." The Comte went on in a grumbling tone. "Touching this matter, I put little trust in you. There was the case of the Lady Alys de Guiraut a few weeks ago. Oh, I've heard all about it. You were riding north with the household of the Comte. The daughter, a pretty chick, was inclined to like you—for reasons which I fail to understand. And what did you do? You took sides against her with some half-wild creature, some greasy hobgoblin; and now the Lady Alys can't think of you without wishing the wind would set in another direction." He began to enumerate the holdings of the Comte de Guiraut. "A tract of eight hundred acres within a dozen miles of Tours. Sixteen sweet vineyards in the very heart of the wine country. Three châteaux, one on the Loire. A house in Paris. A castle on the Garonne large enough to hold an army. And you, my wise brother, offended her on behalf of this verminous trollop with the head of a turnip——"

D'Arlay said shortly, "I promise to waste no time in reaching a decision."

The Comte got slowly to his feet. He was on the point of leaving but then changed his mind and turned back. "Have you been sending money to Isabeau?" he demanded.

"No. I've neither seen nor been in communication with her for six months."

"Then where does the gold come from which has been in my house for the last two days? The servants have been paid. Isabeau, pretty creature, has been buying materials for dresses. Can it have anything to do with Jaquet the Fox paying her visits?"

D'Arlay sprang to his feet. A preposterous notion had entered his head—one which became less preposterous, but still completely unwelcome on second consideration. "Are you telling me that Jacques Coeur has been seeing Isabeau?"

"Twice in the last few days. Whispering together like a pair of conspirators. When I ask her what it's all about, she just stares at me—that cold stare my wife reserves for me alone. And now this cousin is coming. Not a full cousin, mind you. Some little chit, a bastard no less of my wife's rampaging bull of an Uncle Gilles. Why is this child being brought into my household?"

D'Arlay understood the whole story now. He walked over to a corner where clothes were hanging on pegs and took down a heavy cloak. He was thinking: "He's going too far. I won't permit it!"

"When I asked Isabeau the reason, she said the child was in need of a home. Ha, no doubt! But Uncle Gilles has his get scattered all over Berri, and all of them are in need of homes. Why this sudden solicitude over one of them? You know as well as I do that this wife of——" He stopped, clearing his throat, and erupted noisily in the general direction of the fire. "I almost said this wife of *ours*. That will show you how I feel about the way you patter after her and jump at her beck. Well, this wife of *mine* is a beautiful woman, as you will agree, a woman of intelligence and charm. We both admire her very much. But we both know that her heart is not the kind to swell up suddenly to the bursting point over the plight of a distant connection, one she has never seen, moreover. Why is she so concerned over this ill-begotten brat?" Another phase of the matter, one which seemed to cause him the most acute annoyance, occurred to the Comte. "If my house is to be filled with sniveling children, why is none of the money given to me?"

"Because, no doubt, they realize that giving money to you would be as sensible as feeding gold pieces to the fish in the Seine."

The head of the family continued to grumble. "I might be brought to see reason if they would give me a share of the fruits of this—this back-stairs conspiracy, this underhanded foisting of bastards on me."

D'Arlay started to walk in the direction of the stairs. He was so filled with resentment that he found it hard to speak. "Come! I'm going with you! We must see about this at once!"

Chapter X

I

COEUR, who could be cheerful in most circumstances, looked about him as they mounted their horses and said, "The storm will surely moderate before we get there."

"It will become worse!" declared Nicolas tartly. "The Grant Oberie is washed out. A drunken fuller was drowned this morning in a pool near Saint-Gervais."

"In spite of that we must be on our way."

They rode out with their horses' hoofs splashing loudly in the water which swept down the street. Valerie was beside the Moneyman while Nicolas, grumbling audibly, brought up the rear. It became evident at once that the servant's estimate had been the correct one. The rain was coming down with all the fury and volume of that downpour which covered the earth after forty days and forty nights. They kept their heads down and made no attempt to talk except once when the wind ceased to howl and Valerie took advantage of the chance to ask, "What is she like, my lord Coeur?"

The Moneyman ruminated for a moment. "The Comtesse is very lovely," he said. "She has intelligence and charm, and a very great deal of determination. How you will find her when she first gets up in the morning, or if you stumble on her when her hair is down, I can't say."

The Hôtel de Burey, which they reached in due course, towered high above the street. The carved inscription and the family arms on the arched masonry shield over the postern gate were proof of the antiquity of the building as well as of the importance of the family, but nothing could offset the impression of dilapidation the house created. The copper gutters under the roof were full of holes and the water dripped from them in dreary persistence. The pointed sentinel towers, bulging out on each corner, had been so long in disrepair that they seemed ready to tumble down. The iron balconies were rusted. The only sign of habitation was a smudge of smoke from one chimney which the wind pounced upon and forced downward in wisps about the eaves and windows.

But to Valerie it was most grand and impressive. "It must be a very great family, my lord," she said, in a far from happy tone.

Coeur helped her down from her horse. "An old family," he whispered. "But because of the Comte's fondness for dicing and women, and his father before him whose fancy ran to lawsuits, they are as poor today as a beggar's cloak. My friend D'Arlay, though the younger brother, is in better case than the Comte."

The Comtesse met them at the head of the stairs. "My lord Coeur!" she cried. "I had given up all hope that you would come on such a day."

She might have given up hope but that had not prevented her from being well prepared for the unexpected. Her flowing kirtle was of a diamond-shaped pattern of brown and yellow and was overwhelmingly becoming. Her sleeves, puffed generously at shoulder and elbow, were laced with straps of gold thread. Contrary to custom she wore nothing on her head. There was design in this, undoubtedly, for her hair had a crisp natural wave. Her fine wide brow showed no trace of the passage of the years; her eyes were as warmly responsive as a girl's; her generously exposed neck and shoulders were white and enticing. Following nervously in the rear of her escort, Valerie looked at the Comtesse and thought, "She must be the loveliest woman in the world, lovelier even than Agnes Sorel." Frightened though she was, the girl noticed that the kerchief of this beautiful lady was tucked under her waist and wondered if this was the custom at court. She saw also that there were no rings on the fingers of the Comtesse but that she wore one on a chain about her neck. "She thinks her hands look better without them," thought Valerie, "but she wears that one on a chain as proof of her regard for the person who gave it to her."

"You are drenched," said the Comtesse to Coeur, solicitously. She turned and looked at Valerie. "And this is the girl?"

"Yes, this is Mademoiselle Maret."

The Comtesse nodded. "You are welcome, my child."

The girl dropped a rather forlorn curtsy. She was feeling more awe with her surroundings each moment and in addition was acutely conscious of the condition to which the storm had reduced her. Rivulets of water were trickling down her cheeks and her hair was hanging in damp wisps.

The Comtesse looked her over critically and indulged in a puzzled shake of the head. "Well," she said, "there must be a reason for all this. Have I been told everything? The resemblance eludes me, my lord Coeur."

"Under better conditions it's unmistakable."

"Then I shall have to wait."

Valerie thought, "They talk about me as though I were not here. Is that one of the habits I must learn?" She was beginning to have doubts. "I think she's hard in spite of her beauty. She isn't going to like me at all."

The Comtesse continued to study her new charge. "Collect your wits, my child," she said. "You're supposed to be a cousin of mine, and the servants will wonder if you face them with so little assurance."

"Yes, my lady," quavered Valerie.

"You must accustom yourself to calling me 'cousin.' And your name from now on is Valerie de Voudrai. You must be very careful. A single slip might undo everything."

"Yes, Cousin."

"That is better." The Comtesse then called, "Guillaumette!" in a peremptory tone.

A middle-aged servant appeared promptly in the doorway, bowing and saying, "Yes, my lady?"

"This is my cousin, Mademoiselle de Voudrai, of whom I have spoken. As you see, Guillaumette, she's wet through. Show her to her rooms at once and see that she has everything she needs." Smiling at Valerie for the benefit of the maid, the Comtesse added in an affectionate tone: "I'm so happy you have come at last, my child. You must have a hot bath at once or you will be ill. I shall drop in for a talk a little later, dear Valerie."

"Come, Mademoiselle," said the maid. Under the deference of her voice there was a suggestion of the polite scorn felt by the servants of the great for lowly family relations.

Coeur had not failed to observe the evidence of panic in Valerie's manner. He walked over and said in a whisper: "You'll soon get accustomed to everything, even though it's strange to you now. You mustn't be frightened."

"I *am* frightened," she whispered back. He could not be sure whether the dampness of her cheeks was due entirely to the storm. "The Comtesse doesn't like me. I can tell by the way she looks at me."

"You're imagining it. She will soon be very fond of you."

"My dear Valerie," said Isabeau, with the slightest trace of impatience, "you will get a cold if you stay in those wet clothes any longer. Go with Guillaumette."

When they were alone, the Comtesse raised her fine dark eyebrows and smiled at her visitor. "Well!" she exclaimed. "All I can say to you is that I'll do my best."

"That is all I ask." Coeur smiled back at her. "During the few days we have been in partnership, I have conceived a great respect for my—my fellow conspirator. I'm sure this task is well within your powers." He bowed. "I must leave now. I'll return soon, tomorrow perhaps, to talk matters over with you further."

2

Coeur had been gone a few minutes only when the master of the house returned. The Comte was puffing by the time he reached the top of the stairs and, when he appeared in the doorway, he was so bedraggled in appearance that Isabeau could not help laughing. Then she noticed that his brother accompanied him and she cried out gaily, "Robin!" She ran to meet D'Arlay, saying, "How glad I am to see you! But I should be severe with you instead, for truly you've been most rude. Why have you been so tardy in coming to see us?"

"I'm happy now that I'm here," said D'Arlay. "As to my tardiness, which I humbly admit, there have been countless things to keep me at work."

She placed her hands on his shoulders and stretched up on tiptoe to give him a sisterly kiss on the cheek. Then, suddenly, her fingers tightened. In a whisper so low that her husband could not hear, she said, "Robin, my dear Robin!"

D'Arlay stepped back rather hurriedly and turned to his brother. "You've made no secret, Naulty, of your feeling that my visits here are in the nature of intrusions. In spite of that, I must ask the privilege of a few minutes alone with Isabeau."

"Very well," said the Comte. "I'm depending on you to get to the bottom of this mystery. And"—wagging an admonitory finger—"you will be firm and let my sweet spouse know what we've decided between us."

Isabeau frowned when her husband had withdrawn. "Mystery? Be firm with me! What, pray, is all this?"

"By mystery he refers to the arrangement you've entered into with Jacques Coeur. It's no mystery to me." D'Arlay frowned. "I'm disappointed, Isabeau, that you've been weak enough to let yourself be persuaded into playing a part in it. It's not only the danger, which is serious enough in itself. Your reputation would be tarnished if this became public. As Regnault doesn't know about it, I'm taking it on myself to insist that you give the thing up."

The Comtesse placed a hand on his arm and by exerting a faint but unmistakable pressure directed him into a chair beside the hearth. She sat for a moment on an arm of it and allowed her head to rest against his shoulder. Then she got quickly to her feet.

"That," she said, in a whisper, "to let you know that I still love you as much as ever. I wanted you to know before—before we get very angry with each other. Which may happen in a few minutes." She lifted an arm with a graceful gesture to pat her bronze curls back into order above one ear. "If you had existed as we have for years in this dreadful, hateful poverty, you wouldn't be so quick, my dear Robin, to insist that I refuse the benefit of—of this regular supply of golden eggs which has been offered me."

"You mean, then, that Jacques Coeur has tempted you beyond the point where you can resist?"

There was still a trace of disbelief in the way she nodded her head. "He's being so generous that sometimes I believe I am living in a dream, a beautiful golden dream. Robin, Robin, you can have no conception of the difference it has made already! Some of the most pressing debts can be met. There is gold in the house. Gold, Robin, gold! The servants have received their wages. The candles in this room are made of wax. Real wax! Can you imagine such extravagance?" She smiled then and lifted her skirt a few inches, giving him a glimpse of a slender ankle. "Satin hose, and embroidered with gold thread! Robin, you must try to understand. I am free in my mind for the first time in years. Would you take this blessed relief away from me?"

D'Arlay studied her in silence for several moments. "It's not necessary for you to accept these fees from Jacques Coeur," he said finally. "Regnault and I have been discussing the future and we've decided there is only one solution to the tangle in which he has involved himself. I must find a rich wife for myself. He, in fact, has already found one."

Isabeau dropped her eyes so that he could not see the expression in them. "He has talked to me about this for years. It never entered his head that he might ease our troubles by economy on his part. No, he was determined to wait until you could be persuaded to a wealthy marriage. Now that *you* tell me this, I know it must be so, that you are going to marry—and that I'm going to be very unhappy about it." She looked up then. One of the candles only had been lighted and the room was dark in consequence. "You have been so faithful, my Robin. For so many, many years! We mustn't calculate how many; I am sure I shouldn't risk having the passage of time charted too closely. . . . I think you should know, Robin, that it was to save you from this that I agreed to what the Moneyman asked."

He may not have believed this. At any rate, he brushed it aside quickly. "No matter how generous he may prove with you, it wouldn't suffice to clear up the debts. And"—after a moment's pause—"there's the matter of an heir."

Isabeau had not won back his allegiance after her marriage, and held it all the years since, without the exercise of infinite tact and the employment of her full charm. She understood him thoroughly. One thing she realized about him was that to dispute a point was the surest way to confirm him in his determination but that he would yield quickly before any hint of ridicule.

She permitted a silence to fall after his reference to the need for an heir to the title and lands of De Burey. This, she knew in any case, was the point to which there was no answer. An heir must be forthcoming and it was now manifest that she would never present one to the present holder of the title. She permitted the silence to continue until she saw the first suggestion of uneasiness in his face. Then she hurried into the breach with a question.

"Who is she, this woman Naulty brings forward as his choice?"

"Someone I don't know. She's a widow and her name is Clothilde de Trepant."

Isabeau cried in a strained voice, "Oh no! Oh no!" After this first, and effective, reaction to the suggestion, she paused before going any further. "I might have expected it!" she said then, shaking her head hopelessly. "Naulty has no sense in such matters, none at all. This woman"—she pronounced the two words with a verbal reflection of the distaste a good housewife would display on finding a soiled undergarment folded away with the best linen—"might do as a mistress for your brother but never as a wife for you. Give the idea no further thought, Robin. I promise to convince him that he's wrong." Then, with calculation, she began to laugh. "*What* an idea! Really, my husband is an absurd creature! I'm sure we must disregard him from now on and settle these matters between ourselves."

Isabeau walked over to one of the windows. The rain was turning to hail and lashing against the glass with the uneven spatter of a drumming boy. Drawing the curtain back, she looked out into the storm. "You mustn't think of venturing out tonight. We have no other guests and so we shall sup *en famille*. I'm afraid we won't be very cheerful company. Our difficulties will weigh on our spirits. And, of course, the presence of this hedge brat will be a very great nuisance."

D'Arlay joined her at the window, where he looked out with an air of deep depression at the blur of roofs and chimney pots. She studied him openly, realizing, as she always did, that the quality of fineness about his features was more desirable than mere good looks and that there was both strength and sweetness in the habitual gravity of his expression. "I won't give him up! I won't give him up!" she said to herself. She had promised Jacques Coeur that she would, but without any serious intention of living up to her bargain. She had been on the point of making a reference to this absurd condition but she now felt an inner warning in time. It would be like her brother-in-law to decide, if he knew of it, that he shared with her the responsibility of carrying out her promise.

She turned and placed a hand on his arm. "I'm a selfish woman, Robin," she whispered. "Such a selfish creature, indeed! You have good reason to know that, haven't you? I married someone else and yet never since have I been able to bear the thought of losing you." She shook her head slowly back and forth. Then she smiled with a resigned gravity. "And now we face the situation which has been hanging over us for so long. You must at least grant me this: enough time to see if I can't turn my alliance with the Moneyman into a source of sufficient revenue to remove the—the grim urgency about it."

D'Arlay's response to this was so abrupt and bitter that she realized at once she must withdraw quickly and find a stronger position. "I came today to tell you," he said, "that under no circumstances must you go on with this. If you go against my wishes and the dictates of your own good sense and finer feelings, then you must accept——" He did not finish but she knew he had meant to say that she would never see him again.

She answered in a hurt voice, as though he had prevented her from making her meaning clear by breaking in prematurely. "My dear Robin! Will you allow me to go on? I was going to say that the arrangement with Jacques Coeur is a small matter, after all, one that can be broken at a moment's notice if needs be. But your agreement with Regnault that the time has come for you to marry is quite different. Your whole future life, your happiness, depends on *this*. I wanted to say that you mustn't move as quickly as your attitude threatened. You must be *very* sure. Feeling about you as I do, I can't sit quietly by and see you rushed into an absurd marriage with one of these lusty creatures your brother thinks will make suitable wives. My selfishness now has become a determination to see that you suffer as little unhappiness as possible." She leaned forward and looked up at him with her brows raised in a suggestion that, after all, they were perhaps being unnecessarily concerned. "And finally, my severe Robin, I wanted to say that no matter what you must do and no matter how much I may be called upon to endure, you can at least"—a smile crinkled up the corners of her eyes—"forget it all for one evening and stay for supper, can't you?"

3

When the Comtesse entered the bedroom, Valerie was bundled up from ears to toes in a woolen houppelande, the most practical article of feminine attire. Her hair had been thoroughly dried and then combed and brushed until its usual golden glow had returned. The discreet use of strawberry foam had put a trace of color in her cheeks. The Comtesse looked at her in silence for a moment and then ordered Guillaumette to withdraw.

"I begin to understand," she said. "You are rather lovely, child. I can see the resemblance now. When you are properly dressed, it will probably be most striking."

"Thank you, my lady."

"Cousin. You must get into the habit of calling me that."

The Comtesse seated herself in a chair close to Valerie and studied her closely in silence. It was a bare room—the interior of the house reflected, as well as the exterior, the poverty which had hung over the family so long—with only two chairs, a chest against one wall, a small and somewhat decrepit *prie-dieu,* and a bed in one corner. It was a single bed, with plain coverings and the merest imitation of a canopy.

"And now it begins," said the Comtesse. "It's not going to be easy for you, child, nor for me either. Do you understand that you must be prepared to do whatever I say and to work very hard?"

"I shall at least be a willing pupil, my lady—my cousin."

"What a lady must know," continued Isabeau, "could probably be told in a few words. It comes easily and naturally when you are born a lady and grow up as one. But for you to acquire it now will not be easy. You must start by realizing that everything you have done and thought and believed is wrong."

"Yes, Cousin. That much I know."

"And it won't be enough to make a lady of you. If a certain pair of eyes are to be attracted, you must have some of the grace and sprightliness of the Lady Agnes. The sprightliness, at least, will be a real difficulty."

"Please don't judge me by today, Cousin," said Valerie. "I am a—a little abashed."

"Naturally, child. I didn't mean to be critical. I am trying to make you see that the change in you must be as complete as the improvements we will make in your wardrobe." Isabeau continued to study her charge with a discerning eye. "I must contrive to let you see the Lady Agnes. You must watch her closely and note every movement. She has certain mannerisms all her own, a little studied, perhaps, but undeniably effective. The happiest result would be if you could catch a suggestion of them but not enough to look deliberate. And now you must be dressed. You will sup with us tonight."

She summoned Guillaumette back to the room and issued detailed instructions in the matter of the clothes Valerie was to wear. "There will be no time for an aromatic bath," she added. "Use my best perfume, Guillaumette. And a touch, just a touch, of melilot on her face. Her hair suits me as it is."

Guillaumette was back in a very short time with a billowing armful of clothes. She proceeded then to remove the houppelande and the kirtle that Valerie wore under it. Accustomed to dressing in her own cramped corner behind a curtain in the Maret tent, the girl looked distressed at being thus publicly disrobed, particularly when the removal of the kirtle revealed that she wore a third garment under it, a pair of woolen leggings which fitted her snugly from waist to knees. The maid looked surprised at this discovery and turned to her mistress in a mute demand for instructions.

"What is that peculiar thing you are wearing?" asked the Comtesse.

"A winter garment, Cousin," faltered the girl. "Is it—is it not customary?"

"I have never seen one before," laughed Isabeau. "What a very ugly thing it is."

"But it's very warm."

"Comfort is the last thing a lady must consider. Do you think we enjoy wearing these high headdresses? I get a headache whenever I use a heavy hennin. It's quite as bad with sleeves. The very latest are long enough to touch the floor. They are a great nuisance and a great absurdity; but as they are the mode, they must be worn."

"Mademoiselle has perhaps never heard of the *toute-autour?"* ventured the maid. "It keeps one warm without the need for garments such as these."

Mademoiselle had never heard of the toute-autour but the promise of such a substitute brought her no comfort when Guillaumette proceeded to remove the leggings. She blushed when robbed of this last cloak to her modesty. There was no reason, however, for her to feel any shame. The Comtesse studied her nakedness and said to herself: "The little slut has a lovely figure as well. What pretty thighs!"

Fortunately for the girl's peace of mind, the maid quickly dropped a *robe-lingue* over her shoulders. It was long enough to reach below her ankles and was made of warm woolen material except for the sleeves and a band about two feet deep at the hem. These were of the finest linen, daintily embroidered in forget-me-not blue. A surcote of a darker shade of blue was then draped over the chemise. Valerie's nervousness left her at once and was replaced by an excited interest, for this was much the handsomest dress she had ever seen. It had a train at least a yard long, and open pointed sleeves with edges embroidered in gold. The skirt had V-shaped slashes on each side, crisscrossed with gold bands. The reason for the linen attachments to the chemise was now apparent. They showed through the slashes and under the sleeves with each movement of the arms.

Valerie looked at herself in a mirror that the maid held up in front of her and for one amazed second could not believe that the fine lady reflected there was herself. A touch of natural color appeared in her cheeks, growing to a rosy flush. She gave a short and excited laugh.

"I—I look quite different, I think."

She had a moment's worry over the low cut of the surcote, which revealed all of her neck and much more than a suggestion of the youthful line of her breasts, but she dismissed it at once, thinking, "I'm to be a lady and so it doesn't matter."

"And now, Mademoiselle, you will see what a toute-autour is," said Guillaumette, producing a long velvet band. This she passed through loops on the robe-lingue a foot above the ankles. The ends were then drawn together tightly and tied in a bow.

"It holds your chemise close to you, Mademoiselle, and so keeps you from getting cold," she explained, taking advantage of the fact that her mistress was looking elsewhere to give the girl's hand an encouraging pat. "There are loops also on the inside of the surcote. When the weather is windy, the toute-autour can be drawn through them as well. That holds all the skirts together snugly."

"It serves a double purpose," pointed out the Comtesse. "You can't take a long step. You had better practice, child, or you will stumble when you go down with me to supper."

Valerie found some difficulty in accustoming herself to the close confinement of the velvet band but, after pacing the length of the room several times, she was able to adjust her steps to it. The test was still in progress when a loud rap sounded on the door. Guillaumette answered it and they saw the long and solemn face of the Comte de Burey staring into the room over her shoulder.

"How dare you intrude yourself on us, Monsieur!" demanded his wife in a tone of the deepest annoyance.

The Comte pushed his way into the room, giving the maid a surreptitious pinch on the hip as he passed her. He was still feeling the effect of his libations, for he carried himself stiffly and essayed each step with all the care of a ropedancer. When he reached the center he stopped and bowed.

"I heard that the little cousin had arrived, Madame," he said. "It seemed to me fitting to wait on you at once and extend her my welcome."

"As you wish," said Isabeau carelessly. "This is Valerie, Monsieur. She will sup with us. If you had cared to contain yourself a few minutes longer, we would have joined you below."

The Comte found it necessary to take several steps nearer to see the new arrival closely. As soon as his nearsighted eyes had succeeded in taking her in, he reached enthusiastically for her hand and planted a kiss on it.

"Madame, my congratulations," he said. "Your cousin is charming. Having full recollection of your uncle Gilles, who bore a close resemblance to a heron or some member of the bird family, I am surprised and pleased. I am doubly happy to welcome her to our—our contented family circle. My respects, Cousin Valerie."

"Thank you, my lord," said Valerie.

"You resemble your mother, no doubt," added the Comte, peering at her closely. "Could I have seen her? There is a certain familiarity about your face, child, which makes me think I must have known her at some time."

Noting the animated beam in her spouse's eye, the Comtesse said impatiently: "If you'll favor us by withdrawing, Monsieur, Guillaumette will complete Valerie's toilet. The shoes remain to be put on."

"I have no intention of withdrawing," declared the Comte. "After all, she's my cousin, if only by marriage. Proceed with your pleasant task, Guillaumette. Ah, a neat foot, most commendably small. You will pardon me for saying, Cousin, that I was laboring under a misapprehension. I thought the girls of Berri ran to heavy hoofs like their horses."

"Your arm, Monsieur," said Isabeau, rising. "We are ready to accompany you to supper."

Even with the support he was able to get by leaning on his wife, the Comte found it hard to negotiate the stairs. He paused after each step, his breathing audible and labored.

"Madame," he whispered between wheezes, "are you prepared yet to tell me what this is all about?"

"I'm prepared to tell you nothing," answered Isabeau shortly.

"I squeezed a little out of that close-mouthed brother of mine. He's staying, no doubt? I need not ask. I note, Madame, that you are dressed with most particular care."

"Robin is staying, of course."

"Now, Madame, about this girl. You know the proverb, 'She shames her mother who does not resemble her father'? Your little Valerie does not resemble in any way that old bloated gander of an Uncle Gilles. If he sired this dainty little dabchick, I've lost all sense of blood lines."

"Have more care," demanded Isabeau. "The girl will hear you."

"Some conspiracy is afoot here, Madame. I must have a personal share in the prosperity which has visited our house so unexpectedly. Now that I've seen the cousin, my ideas as to the size of my share are going up. Going up, Madame, up, up, up!"

4

If there had been any doubts as to his feelings in D'Arlay's own mind, if he had felt that he still hovered on the brink of complete devotion, his first glimpse of Valerie descending the stairs in her new guise dismissed all such mental miswending by sending him headlong over the edge. He went down, down, down, his head in a whirl, his senses swimming in a new delight with her. It was with difficulty that he regained control of himself when he heard Isabeau say in an indifferent voice, "This is my cousin Valerie," adding immediately, "We'll go right in, as supper is ready."

The Comte dropped inertly into the master's chair on the dais, with his wife on his right and Valerie on his left. D'Arlay sat in a muse on the other side of the Comtesse.

The master of the household seemed to have a liking for proverbs. He said in a wheezy voice, "'A short mass and a long dinner.' I trust, Madame, that the unwonted prosperity of the De Bureys will be reflected in the supper you have provided for us."

Valerie looked about her with astonishment, never having seen such a large and grand apartment before. The fact that it was also bare and shabby made no impression on her. The table below the dais was large enough to accommodate several score although not more than a dozen servants were seated there. The hall was so long, in fact, that she could not make out the subjects of the tapestries hanging on the walls at the far end. The candles lighting the dais were elevated in massive silver candelabra of such height that they spluttered in the drafts far above her head. Two pages in azure livery were engaged in serving the meal, though they found plenty of time to idle about the *dressoirs* and to whisper cautiously. The dishes on which the food arrived were of silver, embossed with the De Burey tree. A sense of excitement began to stir in her. "I had no idea," she said to herself, "that life could be as grand as this."

"Well, little cousin," said the Comte, leaning toward her and giving her arm a cautious nip, "you're a quiet kitten although I seem to read the promise of a lively spirit whenever you raise your eyes long enough to allow me a glimpse of them. It's clear you owe nothing to Gilles save the bare fact of paternity. You will bear me out that he always loved the sound of his own voice." His tone had been rising. "There are many douse stories I could tell about him——"

"I am sure, Monsieur, that our cousin has no desire to hear such memories of her father as have been retained in *your* mind," said Isabeau. She regarded her husband with a look of steady animosity. "As you've already imbibed rather generously, my Regnault, I've given orders that only one wine is to be served tonight."

The Comte was too deep in his cups to offer any defense. He blinked shortsightedly and fumbled at the front of his parti-colored tunic, producing with some effort an *oculus berellinus,* a pair of round crystal discs bound together by a bar of silver. These he fitted on the inflamed bridge of his nose and then proceeded to stare intently at his wife.

Valerie had heard there were magic instruments which people in derision were beginning to call "spectacles" but which were reputed to restore seeing power to weak eyes. Her own eyes grew round as she looked at him.

"Am I no longer master in my own house?" muttered the Comte. "Madame, you go too far."

Conversation lapsed after that. The Comte munched resentfully and cautiously, as though his teeth were giving him trouble. Isabeau and D'Arlay talked together in low tones. Valerie was too busily engaged in noting all that was done to have anything to say. Her curiosity banished appetite also.

She was realizing how much she had to learn. Beside her plate she found a knife and a strange instrument with two straight prongs. Her first thought was that the latter might be used in conveying food to the mouth, but a tentative effort in that direction was a failure. The prongs refused to take a proper grip on the food and she hastily desisted, deciding that she must do nothing until she had seen how the others went about it. She noted then that they were using their forks (she was to learn the name later) to hold the meat while cutting it into slices for eating. The slices were lifted to the mouth on the circular ends of the knives which were indented to keep the food from slipping off. Spoons, circular in shape and quite large, were used for the pastries. When it came to fish, however, her companions threw nicety to the winds and went vigorously to work with their fingers. Valerie noticed the fastidious way in which her hostess dabbled her fingers at intervals in a ewer of water and was very careful to do the same.

To observe all this closely she found it necessary to lean forward slightly and this brought D'Arlay within her range of vision. She was pleased to see that, although his conversation with the Comtesse ran along without a break, he looked continuously in her direction. The Comtesse became aware of the fixed way in which he was regarding her charge. She glanced at Valerie with a hint of a frown and then, turning back to D'Arlay, said something which caused him to lower his eyes. He did not keep them averted, but it was only at intervals afterward that he allowed them to stray to the other end of the table.

The one glance that the Comtesse had directed at Valerie had been sharp, direct, and suspicious. It convinced the girl on one point. "She's not going to like me." This thought lodged itself so firmly in her mind that she began to indulge in rather dismal reflections on the kind of existence she might expect while she remained a member of the De Burey household.

To escape from these uneasy speculations she resolutely turned her thoughts to Jacques Coeur. How different he was from these people of noble birth! He had been so kind, so quick to understand her, so willing to accept her as an equal. In the short span of time since she had first seen him she had become convinced that he was the greatest man in the world. She was ready to follow his guidance in everything, being certain that whatever he said and did would be right. "Even," she said to herself, "if he tells me I must never disobey this cold Lady Isabeau."

To the great discontent of the Comte, supper consisted of a few dishes only. He partook of them all with a snuffling absorption and his fingers toyed impatiently with his empty wine cup. At intervals he addressed himself in aggrieved undertones to his wife. "Madame, you remain your frugal self in spite of everything," and, "A reasty supper, Madame, with which to welcome the pretty little cousin." His annoyance reached a still higher point over the fact that the fire on the hearth at one side of the long room, above which the azure band and the three silver stars of De Burey were almost regally blazoned, was not throwing out enough heat to make tenancy of the dais comfortable.

"I'm of a mind, Madame," he announced, pushing aside his plate on which he had heaped up a *blanc dessore* of minced pheasant mixed with milk of almonds, "to exile myself to the comforts of country life. There I will be warm at least."

The Comtesse roused herself to a sense of her own discomfort. She clapped her hands and called to the pages, "Alain, Froy, have them bring in more logs." Then she turned to the Comte. "An excellent idea," she said. "I'll put no obstacles in the way of your departure, Monsieur."

Regnault de Burey considered the point for several moments, then he adjusted his spectacles and squinted through them at Valerie. "On second thoughts, no," he said. "I have a conviction, Madame, that life here, in spite of the pestilential cold of this gloomy prison, will prove much more interesting."

Chapter XI

I

LIFE for Valerie fell into a pattern the next day which was repeated more or less closely each day thereafter.

The bedroom was dark when Guillaumette awakened her. "Five o'clock, Mademoiselle, by God's good grace," said the maid. She was carrying a taper. Her face, shining moistly above a shapeless red garment, looked no more than half awake in the uncertain light. Valerie's mind was filled with uneasy speculation. She had no idea of what lay ahead of her but was sure that this would prove the most difficult day of her life. It was reluctance to begin the ordeal and not a desire for more sleep which caused her to shrink back under the bedcoverings.

"Come, it's time to rise," said Guillaumette, giving the girl's bare shoulder a shake. "You'll want to go to the *Chambre Basse?*"

Valerie guessed at the nature of the suggestion and said, "Yes, Guillaumette."

The maid wrapped her in a warm robe and put woolen slippers on her feet. "It is a distance," she said.

It was indeed a distance. They descended a flight of stairs which were still as dark as in the middle of night, traversed a gloomy hall where the cold of the stone floor could be felt through the slippers, found their way down another staircase even darker than the first, passed a series of open doors through which servants could be seen preparing food, and finally arrived at a door with curtains draped on each side.

The maid drew the curtains together after them. "That's to warn anyone who comes," she explained, "that the room's in use."

The bareness of the great house had left Valerie unprepared for the luxurious nature of the Chambre Basse. The floor was carpeted and warm to the feet. A charcoal-filled brazier, standing beside the Bishop's Throne, was emitting a comfortable glow of warmth. The Throne itself, which seemed to the girl to stand up rather absurdly high, had arms padded with velvet and panels of needlepoint on both back and sides. The pavilion above it, to be let down when extra warmth was required or to pamper the modesty of the user, was of rich camelot cloth. There was a table containing a variety of bottles of perfume, rose water, and spirits of lavender.

After leaving here, they traversed halls in a different direction and came in time to a smaller room where another chair with a pavilion above it awaited the girl's occupancy. It was shaped somewhat like a jack-in-the-pulpit and turned out to be a bath in which she had to sit with her knees in close proximity to her chin. It was a pleasant experience, however, for Guillaumette poured into the warm water a succession of scented liquids, powder of eucalyptus, elder blossoms, mint, thyme, and dried lime blossoms, filling the whole room with their intoxicating odors.

Breakfast followed in Valerie's own room, consisting of a plate of lampreys, a chop, a single slice of rye bread ("Madame insists on it because it does not make one fat," explained Guillaumette), and a glass of a fiery substance called *eau de vin*[1] instead of wine. All the ladies of the court had taken to drinking it, explained the maid, because the King's physician had recently given it out to be the most healthful of all drinks.

Guillaumette shook her head over the meal. "It is clear," she said, "that things have taken a turn for the better with us. Not that there was any improvement in *my* breakfast: It must be desired that Mademoiselle become most rosy and plump."

One swallow of the eau de vin caused Valerie to choke and refuse more of it, healthful or not. She shook her head at the chop but proceeded to make a good breakfast on the lampreys. Guillaumette watched her for a moment and then, having reached the conclusion that her charge was to be trusted, began to make talk.

"Is Mademoiselle going to like it here?"

Valerie answered, "Yes." Then, as though her question had a bearing on the one the maid had asked, "Is Madame the Comtesse as good as she is beautiful?"

Guillaumette answered with a wry smile. "Good? It's a word to be given many meanings. She's a good mistress, even though she has a sharp tongue and a swift hand for a box on the ears. She has a temper, the mistress.

[1]Brandy, the making of which had just commenced.

Watch out when the color of her eye changes to red! And she's a close one! She questions the *squire de gobelet* every day, and how she watches the food supplies in the kitchen! If a rat nibbles a corner of cheese, the mistress knows about it. She sees everything. I promise you she never misses a thing that Monsieur the Comte does."

"Even when he gives someone a pinch?"

"Mademoiselle also has a quick eye," said the maid. "Mademoiselle will find that Monsieur is a great one for pinching bottoms."

Valerie continued her meal in silence for several minutes. Then the maid said, "Madame should be in a better mood now that the Comte's brother has returned."

"Why should that make a difference, Guillaumette?"

The servant threw back her head and gave forth with a loud cackle. "What difference does it make? Mademoiselle! Madame the Comtesse has been in love with the Sire d'Arlay for years and years and years! Everyone knows it, even Monsieur the Comte."

After a moment Valerie asked, "And does he love the Comtesse?"

"Naturally. There was a time, when they were both younger, when he loved her to distraction. Ah, it was very sad!"

Valerie sat back from the table. She felt both uneasy and dispirited. The Sire d'Arlay had seemed to her the kindest of friends, one to whom she could always turn for help and support. That he was in love with the Comtesse should make no change in his relationship with her but she was realizing that it did. She felt that something had been lost which had been of the greatest importance to her.

Guillaumette began to tell everything she knew about the matter with much shaking of her head and winking to lend extra point to the narrative. D'Arlay had been in the East after the marriage but immediately on his return he had begun to visit his brother's house regularly. At first he always occupied a chair at the far end of the dais and from there he had watched the beautiful chatelaine with worshipful eyes. Gradually she had promoted him along the board until finally, one night, he was granted the supreme happiness of sitting beside her. From that time on he sat nowhere else and the talk between them had been of the kind which excluded all others, being conducted with heads bowed close together and in the lowest of tones.

That had been, the maid explained, when the Sire d'Arlay was young and so much in love that he had not been able to hide his feelings. As he grew older, he had become more guarded and had paid fewer calls. Nevertheless, there had been much talk on the outside and particularly at court.

Some courtier had written a couplet about it to the effect that when the Comte had a sore throat it was *mal de rougegorge* (a play on the word for robin) and all the beautiful ladies and great noblemen had gone about quoting it and even singing it to a popular air. The Comte had been very angry that time and had raised a scene when he came home.

"But," said the maid, giving her head an emphatic nod, "it's my opinion, Mademoiselle, that now the rose has begun to wither on the vine. If it were not that Madame the Comtesse is such a one to hold on! . . . And now, of course, he must marry a rich wife and *that* will be the end of it."

"He must marry?" Valerie found it hard to keep from showing the dismay she felt at this further development.

Guillaumette raised her shoulders. "Certainly, Mademoiselle. He must marry to save the estates. The master has debts"—she made a circle of her arms to indicate that the debts were of mountainous proportions—"and they can never be paid unless the Sire d'Arlay brings a fortune into the family. We have all known this for years. It is clear, is it not?"

"Yes, it is clear," said Valerie unhappily. "Is it also known who he is to marry?"

The maid laughed again. "It hasn't gone that far. But when it does, Madame the Comtesse will try again to put porret in the syrup—to spoil the dish, you understand. This much I know. The Sire d'Arlay is now most unhappy about everything. I think he would like to run away to the far ends of the earth."

Valerie had other questions to ask but the chance for further conversation was ended at this point by the arrival of Madame Barquet. Guillaumette retired at once into the background to await such orders as might be given her.

Madame Barquet was reputed to know all the beauty secrets of the East, whence all such secrets came, and her services were much in demand among the great ladies of Paris; and even, it was whispered, among the wives of wealthy merchants who defied the sumptuary laws by insisting on dressing as well as the aristocracy. She came sweeping into the room with dry clothes, a sign that the storm had stopped at last, but bringing in on the end of her long train enough mud to prove that the effects of it were still to be encountered on the streets. She was an elderly woman with a succession of chins and a body like a tun of wine. Valerie looked at her with dismay and thought, "What can she know about beauty when she is so ugly and dirty herself?"

Madame Barquet had many curious habits which manifested themselves quickly enough but the most curious of all was apparent at once. She addressed many of her remarks to herself.

"Madame Barquet," she said, surveying the girl with a calculating eye, "you will have your hands full with this one. You will indeed, Madame Barquet." She bobbed her head so emphatically that the hennin she was wearing flailed about like a windmill in a storm. "Mademoiselle is from the country?"

"Yes, Madame," answered Valerie, feeling even more humble than ever.

"That is good. Mademoiselle knows nothing. She won't dispute with Madame Barquet who knows everything. Saints and sinners! When before, Madame Barquet, have you seen such fingernails! Is it possible the girl has been grooming horses?"

A long dissertation followed on the care of fingers and toes. Valerie, who had never thought of them as anything but adjuncts to her daily labors, was amazed when the woman proceeded to clip the nails almost to the quick. Her surprise mounted when they were dipped into a mixture she had always believed to be a deadly poison and then vigorously polished. The final step was the real surprise of all—the application of a stain which left them a warm and lustrous pink.

"Always," said Madame Barquet, when the operation had been completed, "I leave the nails until the last. But Mademoiselle's were in such a state that something had to be done about them at once."

She stood up then and considered the girl's figure with a speculative eye. Pleased, apparently, with what she saw, she proceeded to confirm her impression by running her hands over the bosom, arms, and hips. Her touch was quick and expert.

"The daily rubbing will be light," she said. "There is a little of the surplus weight of youth to be lost—it's always in the worst possible places, Mademoiselle—but mostly the rubbing will be needed to make you graceful. Ah, Madame Barquet, these middle-aged mountains of flesh who come to you to regain the bloom they have lost through stuffing their stomachs and bringing brats into the world every ten months or so, how much they would pay for such firm breasts, such a sweet roundness of limb!" After a moment's consideration she announced: "There will be no need to wear wrappings around the hips. The lightest of bands around the breasts will do."

A minute inspection of the face followed. "Saints and sinners!" she cried, in a reproachful tone. "A freckle on the point of the nose! Has she been so careless, so foolish, so unmindful of her advantages, as to expose herself to the hateful effects of the sun? Avoid the sun, Mademoiselle, it is the enemy of feminine beauty! The moon—ah, that is different. Every evening, if possible, you must expose yourself for at least an hour to the beneficent rays of the moon. It will make you lily white; and it's white flesh which makes desire grow in the eyes of men." Addressing herself to the maid: "Now for this treacherous freckle. Oatmeal paste and lemon juice must be applied to the nose every night before going to bed."

Madame Barquet, her labors for the time being completed, deposited her bulging form in a chair. "Guillaumette, the wine!" she said. While waiting for the order to be obeyed, she opened her mouth and proceeded to rub her almost toothless gums with a brown spice. At the same time she kept a sharp eye on her new charge.

"You've been told, Madame Barquet," she muttered, "that you are to see nothing and to say nothing. If the pay is steady enough, you will say nothing. But what you see would make a dainty little morsel to tell your ladies. Your ladies expect you to fill their silly ears with gossip while you pummel and rub and salve their fat bodies." She continued to mutter. "Is it really the fair Lady Isabeau she is cousin to? Now *that* is something to think about, Madame Barquet."

She departed after swallowing her wine. It was then the turn of the physician. He was small and sharp of eye and very restless and chipper of movement. "Like a squirrel," Valerie thought. The physician lacked the courage of Robert de Poitevin, for he had trussed himself up in one of the chemical-soaked tunics and his breath was lethal with garlic.

He found nothing wrong with Valerie. In fact, as a physician, he seemed to resent that she was so safely removed from the need of his ministrations. "It goes against all the laws of nature for one to be so healthy," he complained, in his chirping voice. Then he nodded his head in the maid's direction. "Calomel once a month. It will purge the poisons which are concealed somewhere inside her. See that she never drinks cow's milk. Half a cup of mare's milk a day if she craves it, but no more; it's dangerous stuff to take into the human stomach. We must guard against every kind of chance. Above everything see that her bed has red hangings. She'll never catch the smallpox if you do."

After the little man had departed, Guillaumette said, "The good father from the University is here to give you a first lesson in reading and writing."

Valerie felt a cold chill take possession of her. "They say," she whispered in an awed tone, "that one must have a very clever mind to learn letters. I am tempted to run away."

As it happened, the ordeal did not begin that morning after all. Before the priest from the University put in an appearance, a summons was received for Valerie to go at once to the apartments of the Comtesse.

2

The bare aspect of the old house was not reflected in the rooms dedicated to the comfort of the chatelaine. The main chamber of the Comtesse was fully and warmly furnished. There was a *secrétaire* under a canopy of brown velvet, a long table which obviously was many centuries old, a beautifully carved crucifix on one wall. The window hangings were of fine linen and most cheerfully blue. The Comtesse was sitting at one end of the table with a vanilla stick burning beside her.

It was clear that she had not been up long. Her hair, which showed reddish tints through the brown, was bound in braids on the back of her head, and the tip of a yellow bed slipper protruded under the hem of her skirt. She had a goblet of eau de vin in front of her.

"Good morning, Cousin," said Valerie.

"Good morning. I've just had a note from Monsieur Coeur, asking us to pay him a visit this afternoon at his largest shop in the city. He'll have an assortment of things to show us which may be useful for your wardrobe. We'll leave here at three o'clock and I suggest that you be ready before the hour."

"Yes, Cousin, of course." Valerie spoke eagerly. "It's a wonderful shop. I saw enough of it to know that it contains the most beautiful things."

Some of the severity went out of the voice of the Comtesse. "I'm looking forward to the visit. My own wardrobe needs replenishing. . . . I want to tell you, child, that you behaved yourself well at supper last night. You made no mistakes and you—you looked quite presentable."

"Thank you, Cousin. I watched you and I didn't do anything until I had seen you do it first."

"But," said Isabeau, with sudden sharpness, "you show a tendency to copy me in ways that I don't relish. After supper I went to your room to bid you good night and from the door I saw you walking in front of your mirror in what I suspect was an imitation of my manners and walk. I went away without letting you know I had been there. I want you to understand that I was deeply offended."

Valerie's cheeks flushed guiltily. "I'm sorry, Cousin. It's a habit I have and I see now that it's a very bad one. Need I say that it won't happen again?"

"I trust not." Isabeau hesitated before going on. She was deeply annoyed, it was clear. "I'm not in a position to judge of the excellence or otherwise of your aping of me. But this I must say: you're mistaken in thinking I swing my hips when I walk. The way you exaggerated the motions was—was vulgar in the extreme. I was very angry and very hurt."

"I'm sure it was a stupid attempt on my part, Cousin."

The Comtesse gave a cold nod of forgiveness. "We'll say no more about it then. I suggest that you return now to your lessons and that you be ready promptly this afternoon."

Valerie was thoroughly ashamed of herself for making such a mistake on her first day. As she left the room, however, she was thinking that the Comtesse did not look so lovely in the mornings and that she was undoubtedly older than she, Valerie, had at first supposed. "And," she added to herself, "she *does* swing her hips a little when she walks."

3

The shop of Jacques Coeur stood in a cluster of buildings back of the Louvre and within sight of the Hôtel d'Alençon and the Petit-Bourbon. It had been the city house of some great personage in its earlier periods. Planned both for show and security, its walls towered up in gloomy grandeur above the street to end in a confusion of stone turrets and flying buttresses.

The two ladies arrived promptly at half-past four and were escorted to a large apartment where a busy official asked them the nature of their needs. The mention of the name of De Burey had a magical effect. He drew himself up and said in an important voice: "Yes, my lady. You are expected. You are respectfully requested to visit the floor above."

They stepped out into a confusion as great as the daily hubbub of the streets. Torches blazed at all corners of the court, for the walls shut it in so closely that a blanket, seemingly, could have covered the square of sky visible above. Customers were passing to and fro. Porters with bundles on their backs were everywhere.

The walls were lined with open galleries, one above the other. Valerie began to count them but lost track in the upper reaches where the stone tracery of the railings merged into confusion. There were outside stairs at each end, one marked *Up* and one *Down,* and the clatter of heels on their stone steps added to the din. Their guide led the way to the upward-bound stair and from there to the white-plastered bureau of the master of this humming beehive.

Jacques Coeur greeted them in a jubilant mood. "In three more days," he told them, "this main bazaar of mine will be gnawed as clean as a rind in a cupboard. Did you know the building is to be used for war purposes?

Some of the goods are being moved to other shops but the largest part of the stock is being purchased by the good people of Paris. Did you meet any of my heralds on the streets, crying the bargains to be found here?" His eyes were snapping with enthusiasm. "You must forgive me, Comtesse. I'm a merchant first and last, and at times like these I tread on light toes. I'm as excited and happy as a captain who has won a great victory. But you needn't fear that the cupboard is empty. I've seen to it that some of the very best things are left for you."

Valerie had arrived in a depressed mood to which a number of things had contributed: the information she had been given about D'Arlay, the reprimand from the Comtesse and, back of everything, the uncertainty and fear she felt whenever her mind cast on into the future.

Her spirits lifted, however, when the Moneyman led the way to an adjoining room which was well lighted by a score of candles. She paused on the threshold with a gasp of astonishment and pleasure. The place was filled with fabrics in all the rich colors of the East. There were frames along the walls hung with lengths of the rarest silks and the very choicest of satins while in the center a vermeil table was heaped with velvets and shimmering brocades. Smaller tables had assortments of camisoles and *baignoires* and chemises of Flemish linen, embroidered surcotes, flowered jupons, and lacy gorgets for the neck. One was given over entirely to purses and the gipsers which ladies wore at their waists, to hold the small coins their husbands trusted them with, and leather cases for prayer books. Another displayed hoods of velvet and hennins of all kinds.

Coeur said proudly, "The Queen of Sheba never had the likes of this to choose from."

He reached into one of the wall frames and held up a bolt of silk for their inspection. Both ladies exclaimed with involuntary delight and reached out simultaneously to feel its tempting texture. It was a cream color like the subdued glow of the setting sun. "From Cathay," he said reverently. "It's the finest silk to be found in the world today. They call this shade by a word that means kiss me. A good name for it. Not only does it hold the kiss of the sun but it promises that the wearer will create that desire in every male beholder."

The Comtesse took an end of the silk and held it against her cheek and hair. "I must have it," she said. "It's better suited to me. I shall have the bodice cut so tight that it won't matter where the line of the neck comes. It will drop low over the hips, still very snug, and then flare out into a fifteen-fluted skirt. The sleeves will widen at the shoulders and taper tightly to the tips of the fingers, and must be tufted, I think, with dull gold buttons."

Coeur was completely the merchant now. He studied her with an expert eye and agreed that this particular shade was better suited to her. He then turned to Valerie and considered the color of her hair before reaching down a bolt of velvet. "And this for Mademoiselle," he said.

It was blue with a hint of peacock green, a perfect shade for corn-colored hair. "It is called Angel's-Eye," he said. He draped a fold over her shoulder. "The East keeps the secret of this shade. We have fine blue dyes here in France but nothing to equal this. For trimming, I think it needs gold ornaments of the kind we call *orfrays* in the trade. Fortunately there's a wide assortment of them still."

He brought out many more materials, each one seeming, if possible, more desirable than the earlier ones. A table had been cleared for the purpose and it was soon piled high with them. There were lengths of rich camocas (which was sometimes called Beyond-the-Sea), camelot cloth, cendal and satanin for linings, Alexandrine velvet, Turkey cloth dyed a deep red, satins in shades of pansy, canary, rye flower, summer gray, and amorous desire. The two visitors paid most attention to one called Lively Ghost, which derived its name from a tendency to change color. Sometimes it was gray, sometimes blue, occasionally it deceived the eye with suggestions of green, and at all times it seemed to shimmer and flash like a hint of distant lightning in a rain-washed sky.

If any piece of material did not seem suitable for Valerie, it was irresistible to Isabeau, and so not one of the beautiful specimens was allowed to be set aside. "You must have this," the merchant would say. The mound of accepted stuffs grew to a pyramid like a miniature Tower of Babel. "Surely," thought Valerie, her eyes glowing with excitement, "this would do for the trousseau of a princess!"

The Comtesse showed a trace of worry. "How are we to explain such fine things? Everyone knows how thin our purse is, and Valerie is to pass as a dependent relative."

"It can be said that she's a special pet of Jacques Coeur's." He gave the girl's cheek an affectionate pinch. "She *is* that already."

He began then to bring out accessories which caused Valerie's head to swim with delight. There were gold-mesh cornettes and bourselets for the head in lieu of the extravagant hennins; kerchiefs so finely wrought as to be almost transparent; gorgets of a shade called *ynde* which was a vivid blue; stiffened panels of embroidered Turkish velvet to be worn over the chemise; stockings of turquoise and gray-pearl and flamelet of sulphur.

The excitement mounted when he came to the question of shoes. Both ladies, it seemed, had an especial interest in this important adjunct of feminine apparel. Valerie was transported when he produced a pair *à la poulaine* which were of green Cordovan leather and curled up at the toe with a gold tassel. They were so small and delicately contrived that they looked like early spring buds. She continued to exclaim as he removed the ones she was wearing and put them on instead. They fitted perfectly.

"Never have I seen anything more lovely!" she said ecstatically.

She was equally pleased, however, with a second pair which he brought out. They were known as *fauves botes* and made of very softest leather, with coral velvet lining and spirals of gold thread in place of buttons in which seed pearls nestled like drops of dew.

"These," he explained, "can be used for a special purpose. When you wear them with the sides turned down like this, it means you have made a pledge. A love pledge, Mademoiselle."

He had left something for the last, considering it, quite clearly, to be the prize item of all. There was a trace of excitement in his fingers as he spread before them a bolt of cherry-colored cloth. "There is a story about this," he said. "It comes from a monastery in the southern part of China. The priests have magic powers and many secrets, the making of this cloth being one of them." He smoothed the surface with a careful touch. "It is much like camelot but finer and infinitely more durable. They spin it from the hair of newborn kids. It is as soft to the touch as silk and yet it will wear like a suit of Milan mail. They say it has a magic power to change its shade just enough to suit anyone who wears it; provided, however, that the wearer has a heart without envy or malice. It will lend our little Mademoiselle a vivid quality. She will look in this like an autumn wood sprite or a princess from the high mountains where it was made." He turned to the Comtesse and beamed happily. "When our Galatea is clothed in this, she will be fairer than Helen and Cleopatra and Balkis combined!"

They were breathless when the time came to go. "Have you calculated the cost?" asked Isabeau, in a weak voice.

"The cost? It doesn't matter. That is my responsibility, dear lady. If we beat the English, we will all walk in paths of glory, and such small matters will be forgotten. If we lose? In that event, the victors will have less to pick from my bones."

Chapter XII

I

TUDDUAL THE HERALD wiped his hands on the front of his emblazoned tabard and winked across the table at Guillaumette. "By Gis! They're a glum lot tonight," he said.

Guillaumette looked up at the three silent figures on the dais. There had been little conversation since the meal began. "Madame's not happy. When Madame has the cockroach, the others are unhappy too. It's very simple."

The herald demanded, "And why does Madame have the cockroach?"

"You're a stupid mome if you lack the answer to that, my Tuddual," said the maid, with a scornful sniff. "The Sire d'Arlay has not been here for"—she paused to make an accurate count—"for a month and three days. Is it not enough to put an edge to her temper? She has been boxing ears right and left. It's very hard for those who cannot keep themselves at a safe distance."

The herald gawped up at the figure of his mistress, sitting very straight and staring ahead of her. "What keeps the sire away?" he asked.

"It may be that he's ill. It may be that some other lady is filling his eye. It may be the Comte has told him to stay away. Who am I to know? Truly, Tuddual, I wonder sometimes that you have enough wit to sound your horn." The maid indulged in a reminiscent giggle. "You should see the getling's imitation of you!"

"Mademoiselle?"

"Who else could I mean? Mademoiselle, of course. She's a rare one to mimic. She takes you off to a white—you and your look of an ox and your silly questions. I tell her she takes you off better than any of the others."

The herald's slow gaze turned toward Valerie. All he could see of her was her head and shoulders, for the table on the dais was several feet higher than the one at which the retainers were eating. He could tell, however, that she was more handsomely attired than usual. Her headdress was of the finest velvet and of a rich blue shade to match her ermine-trimmed tunic. She was lifting slices of preserved ginger to her mouth with a fastidious motion of her fingers which would have passed scrutiny at the court itself.

"Mademoiselle imitates *me?*" The idea seemed to please him. His eyes, which resembled partly poached eggs both in shape and color, seemed almost to achieve animation. "I would like to see it, Guillaumette. When can I see her imitate me, Guillaumette?"

"She's a clever one!" said the maid pridefully. "Ah, what a mimic! You should hear her when she does Master Alain whose voice is beginning to crack. It's enough to make you split your sides. And she does old Gracien, with his nose which always runs and his bumbling and his lameness in the one leg. But she's best when she does you, my Tuddual."

"Does she do the mistress? Or Monsieur the Comte?"

Guillaumette snapped at him. "You great mome! Most certainly she does not."

The Comte de Burey was not comfortable. He shifted uneasily in his chair and grunted. One of his feet had swelled and was causing him much pain.

He crunched an *échande* in his mouth and mumbled a question to his wife, "Have you quarreled with that brother of mine?"

Isabeau raised her brown eyes in an admirable simulation of surprise. "Have I quarreled with Robin? Of course not. What put that idea in your head?"

"My amiable spouse," said the Comte, dropping his voice, "it's the only conclusion open to me. I've missed his earnest face. The only thing that would keep him away would be a disagreement with you. So—unless this damnable pain in all my muscles has destroyed my reasoning powers, there has been a rift."

The Comte began to munch another of the small pastries, making a wry face when he discovered there was a fig in it. His bodily discomfort was so great that he was getting little satisfaction from wearing new clothes. He had on a parti-colored velvet jacket, brown on the right half and yellow on the left, which was as new as a chicken just out of the shell. Ordinarily the luxurious feel of the fresh finery would have put him in a preening mood.

Valerie was watching them as closely as she dared. She knew that the prolonged absence of the Sire d'Arlay had been the cause of the many spells of nervous anger in which the Comtesse had been indulging. So far the servants had been the victims of her upset state of mind but Valerie had been expecting that the winds of displeasure would begin to blow in her direction. She leaned forward sufficiently to see her mentor, saying to herself, "She looks so cool and white and unruffled and yet underneath,

I'm sure, she's burning with vexation." Isabeau, certainly, had never looked more charming. She was wearing a gown fashioned from one of Coeur's materials, a warm brown silk with bands and trimmings of gold. Only the possessor of real beauty of shoulder and breast could wear a bodice so tightly fitted.

"I was at court this morning," said the Comte, breaking the silence again. "I bring news which you will like as little as I do."

Isabeau looked up quickly. "Indeed?"

"The King walked in the gardens this morning with—— Who do you suppose shared the royal saunter, my heart?"

"Antoinette de Maignelais, of course."

"Yes, it was the De Maignelais vixen. She minced along beside him and looked up into his face and trilled with delight at every word that fell from his lips." The Comte gave an apprehensive glance at Valerie and then dropped his voice to a whisper. "Are you not likely to be too late?"

Isabeau looked up quickly. "What do you mean?"

"There's no need to explain. We understand each other, my sweet one. When I saw her garcing along beside him, I felt quite disturbed and sure the—*the new entry*—would be too late in the field."

Isabeau answered coolly, "I think not, Monsieur."

"Why are you so confident? I tell you the lusty little creature was taking full advantage of her opportunity this morning."

"She's trying too hard—and too soon."

The Comte shook his head with a lack of conviction. "I'm not at all sure you're right."

"Agnes Sorel is not dead." Isabeau spoke in such a low tone that only her husband could hear. "She knows of her cousin's behavior and at the proper time she will take steps. Someday she will appear at the King's side again. She will be pale and wan; but make no mistake, she will still be lovely, as lovely as ever, if in a different way. The King will fall under her spell again. It has never failed, Monsieur. The vulgar little Antoinette will be forgotten immediately."

The Comte chafed the bridge of his nose and squinted down into the composed face of his wife. "I'm told the Lady Agnes is too ill to make an appearance."

"She won't be too ill to show her power for the benefit of the over-anxious cousin. She'll never be too ill to wind Charles of France around her finger."

The Comte hesitated. His manner indicated that he was deeply concerned over the news which he now had to tell. Leaning toward his wife, he asked, "Has it come to your ears that Jacques de Lalain is back in Paris?"

Isabeau shook her head. "I've never taken any interest in the exploits of that great ox."

"It's clear then," said her husband, "that my brother has not told you that there is a duel pending between them."

The shock Isabeau felt at hearing this was so great that she did not notice something which her eyes would have been quick to detect under any other circumstances, that Valerie was as distressed as she was.

"It can't be true! Robin wouldn't have been so foolhardy——" The coolness of the Comtesse had deserted her. Her cheeks had taken on a flush. "Regnault, do you mean it?"

"Unfortunately, it's true. It seems they met the first night of Robin's return, and quarreled. The story I had today was that the Burgundian insisted on enough time to acquaint himself with the use of the new type of sword. They're to fight, it seems, with the sword. There's a slight satisfaction there. Robin has skill with the weapon." The Comte shifted uneasily in his chair. "I asked you about him a moment ago because I was hoping the stubborn fellow had confided something to you which would serve to allay my fears."

"Have you forgotten," asked Isabeau, with a desperate suggestion of hopefulness in her voice, "that the King has issued an edict against dueling?"

"That won't prevent them from meeting. All Paris has gone mad over the prospect of seeing the Burgundian in action, particularly in view of the unusual conditions. It has gone too far for the will of the King to stop it." The Comte remained sunk in uneasy speculation for several moments. Then he blinked solemnly and turned to look at his wife. "This is what I hear. The duel will be fought somewhere outside the city. The place won't be given out but the word will be circulated quietly at the last moment to a limited number. That will throw the officers of the Crown off the scent—or such is the hope. In any event, I doubt if the King will try to stop it. It would be a most unpopular move and our liege lord is tender toward the feelings of his subjects."

Isabeau was looking down at her plate. After several moments of silence she asked in a strained voice, "Will he have any chance?"

"Little enough. The Burgundian is the greatest fighter in the annals of chivalry."

"This duel mustn't be fought!" Her voice rose with a suggestion of hysteria. "I shall go to the King and demand that his edict be enforced!"

Her husband responded gloomily, "It would do no good, my heart." He shook his head slowly. "Everyone wants the fight to go on. Even if our liege lord strove to prevent it, some way would be found to set his authority at naught."

"Where is Robin?" demanded Isabeau. She was showing signs of panic. "Why can't he be placed under arrest in advance? That has often been done to prevent duels. Why can't Jacques de Lalain be ordered to leave Paris now? Has the King no power at all?"

"Neither Robin nor Jacques de Lalain can be found." The Comte sighed hopelessly and fumbled with his aids to vision. "It's clear they've gone into hiding to prevent any such steps being taken. They won't be seen until they appear in the lists tomorrow at whatever place is decided on."

"Why has Robin kept this to himself? Was he afraid he might be put under arrest?"

The Comte nodded his head. "That was his reason quite clearly. Even the Moneyman knew nothing of it until today. He was at court and heard it the same time I did. I talked to him afterward and he seemed stunned by the news. It was his intention to urge action on the King but he had little hope of succeeding."

Isabeau burst out suddenly. "Has he gone mad? Is he determined to throw his life away? Regnault, there must be something we can do!"

"Have you ever heard, my spouse, of the Code of Chivalry? There's nothing we can do."

Well down below the salt Guillaumette said to those around her: "Why are they so silent up there? I'm sure they haven't said a word for at least ten minutes."

Chapter XIII

I

AS JACQUES COEUR GALLOPED across the Petit-Pont, causing the wooden planking to rock and creak, he was conscious that never before had he seen the ill-fated old bridge (it was continually falling or being washed out in the floods) so crowded. A continuous stream of horsemen were crossing with as much tendency to haste as he was showing himself.

Foot travelers were striding ahead and spitting their resentment like gibbed cats when forced to step aside for the more fortunate wayfarers who rode. An occasional carriage rumbled along in the single-minded procession.

The Moneyman was in no doubt as to the meaning of this activity. "The secret, which was to be so closely held," he said over his shoulder to Nicolas, "is known, quite apparently, to all Paris."

"Did you expect anything else, master?"

They pulled in to a more circumspect pace on leaving the bridge. As they rode through the dark arch of the Petit-Châtelet, Coeur looked up at the windowless walls of that grim old prison. "It would be in the power of our liege lord to throw everyone who attends this duel into jail," he said to Nicolas. "Yet all Paris is going—laughing and joking and looking for chances to gamble on the outcome. There's less respect for law here, I believe, than anywhere else on earth."

Emerging into the light, they pulled up in front of a house with a single window set in its beamed and plastered front like the one eye of Cyclops, and Coeur whistled a bar from "The Old Man of the Mountain." In a very few minutes D'Arlay came out, pulling the brim of his roundlet well down over his eyes to escape recognition. He swung a leg over a horse hitched at the mounting post and rode off with them. Coeur's critical appraisal of him netted the conviction that he was cool and composed in spite of what lay ahead of him.

"You've had your pains for nothing," said Coeur. "You could have remained comfortably at home and the law wouldn't have raised a hand to interfere with you. Last night I laid the papers for your arrest before the King and begged him to sign them. He shook his head and said you were a bad subject—everyone is a bad subject who doesn't please him at the moment—but that he would take no steps. I offered to tell him the place selected for the encounter and he smiled and asked if I thought him less informed than the poorest citizen of Paris. I suggested that, as a state of war will soon exist, Jacques de Lalain be treated as an alien and sent immediately on his way back to Burgundy. It did no good. Our liege lord seems perfectly content to have his law broken."

D'Arlay indulged in a wry smile. "It's possible, Jacques, he would like to be rid of such a bad subject."

"If he were rid of everyone to whom he has applied that term," declared the Moneyman, "he would be left with a thinly populated country to rule."

D'Arlay did not seem aware of the reason for the hurrying crowds.

"What is happening?" he asked. "Is it another Exodus? Have English armies been reported up the river?"

"Doesn't it occur to you that these crowds are on their way to see you fight the Burgundian?"

D'Arlay gave his friend an incredulous stare. "But it was given out we were to meet on the other bank, in the fields a mile beyond the Grange-Bâtelière. It was expected that anyone curious enough to want to attend would be thrown off the scent and go there instead."

"You are to fight," said Coeur testily, "in a secluded dip of land to the right of the Chartreuse Monastery and every idle mother's son in Paris is on his way there. The original twoscore who were to share the secret has grown to a mere twenty thousand. Well, what can you expect? This is Paris."

"I've made a new will," said D'Arlay, taking advantage of the fact that the pressure of the crowds had forced them so close that he could speak in a low tone. "With the exception of one bequest, everything is to be applied to paying off the debts. I've taken the liberty again of naming you as executor."

"Do you wish to tell me anything about the one bequest?"

"No, not now, Jacques. It's to someone for whom I have a—a great affection."

Coeur said in a grave tone, "God grant there will be no need to apply its provisions."

Despite the ever-present evidence of the milling crowds, they found it hard to credit what they saw when they reached the place selected for the encounter. It was a flat stretch of land with a slope at one side which became wooded after a rise of perhaps twenty feet. An enclosure had been marked out, using the slope as one side, and pavilions had been erected at each end. The enclosure was two hundred yards long and a third of that in width but already the space around it was tightly packed with people, except the slope, which was being reserved for spectators of noble birth. The waiting crowds were at least fifty feet deep, and still farther back they were using the stumps of trees, overturned carts, and any convenient rise of ground to obtain a view of the enclosure. Entertainers were plying their trades: magicians, jugglers, ropedancers, and mountebanks of all kinds. One enterprising butcher had dug a long ditch and built a fire in it, over which the carcasses of three oxen were turning on spits; he would reap a rich harvest later, when the duel was over and the spectators could give a thought to bodily appetites. Paris, in short, was turning the occasion into a holiday.

They reined in their horses on a hillock overlooking the scene. D'Arlay's eyes rested for several moments on the pavilion at the far end of the enclosure. It was of spectacular size, purple and rust in color, and with the flag of Burgundy flapping insolently on a tall shaft in front. Signs of activity about it indicated that Jacques de Lalain and his party had already arrived. D'Arlay's own pavilion was a much smaller one, of plain gray with the azure band and silver stars of De Burey on the shield suspended at the entrance. It was so small, in fact, that he could barely see it over the heads of the mob. A single squire and Helion awaited him there, and he could not help contrasting the modesty of his preparations with the evidences of pomp and splendor at the other end.

For the first time his composure showed signs of deserting him. He turned a disturbed face to his companion. "I expected to fight before a handful of people," he said. "I've never had to face a crowd like this before, Jacques. I confess to you that I find the prospect nothing short of appalling."

Coeur dropped a hand on his shoulder. "It will stir you up to your very best efforts."

A knight riding by shouted to an acquaintance, "Five of the biggest coins in my purse on the Burgundian!" The answer came back in a scornful tone: "I'll offer you the same wager. The Burgundian should win with a single thrust."

Coeur found himself sharing the nervousness of his companion. "What condition are you in?" he asked.

Some of D'Arlay's confidence returned. "I'm in better physical shape than ever before. I've been training faithfully for weeks. My sword arm is as hard as iron and I can step through a lively bout without feeling any fatigue. The Burgundian won't win with a single thrust, Jacques. That much I promise you."

2

Jacques Coeur scowled at the knot of admiring friends and respectful squires and heralds crowding the interior of the purple-and-rust pavilion. He scowled with even more feeling at Jacques de Lalain himself. The great champion, in a state of complete nakedness, was stalking up and down, glad of the chance to show off the power of his mighty shoulders and the bulging muscles of his legs. The expression on his arrogant face said as plain as any words, "Have you ever seen the like of me, you puny, ordinary mortals?"

"The point must be decided at once," said Coeur impatiently.

"The point has already been decided," declared the Burgundian. He stopped in front of Coeur and gestured regally. "I've nothing further to add to what I've already said. We will wear breastplates and helmets but with the condition I have named. There's no manner of sense in contesting the point longer, Sir Merchant."

"I'll inform the Sire d'Arlay that your overweening pride prevents you from listening to the voice of reason. I'll tell him you have closed your mind to all considerations of fair play."

Coeur brushed aside the silken flap and stalked out of the pavilion. The only hope left was that the storm, which had been threatening for days, would break and so make the meeting impossible. He glanced up at the sky and, to his dismay, saw that an aisle had opened in the clouds through which the sun was making a half-hearted effort to shine. There would be no help from the elements.

His appearance brought a roar of disapproval from the spectators. Twice already he had gone from one pavilion to the other in his efforts to convince the Burgundian that he must abide by the original agreement. Not knowing the real reason for the delay, the crowd made it clear that the blame was being laid at the door of D'Arlay. "Is this a meeting between two honorable knights in mortal combat," demanded a voice, "or is it a matching of wits, a contest in diplomacy?" The rabble in the front rows had reached the point where nothing but immediate action would suit. "Fight, fight, fight!" rose the cry from all around the enclosure. "Bring out your man, Jaquet—if he's not afraid to face the Burgundian!" The tension was increased by fear that officers of the Crown would arrive to stop the duel before the fighting began.

The Moneyman called as he walked down the enclosure, "The Burgundian wants to change the rules to his own advantage!" The spectators, however, had passed the stage where they were open to reason. The only response he got was further chanting of, "Fight, fight, fight!"

He found D'Arlay pacing nervously up and down inside his pavilion. The latter turned and asked in a strained voice, "Well, was an agreement reached?"

"I could do nothing with him," answered Coeur, his eyes full of smoldering anger. "He still contends that in yielding the choice of weapon he gave up his right and that he's entitled now to make these demands."

"He didn't yield the choice. I won it by the toss of a coin."

"I've dinned that into his ears a dozen times. All he says in reply is that he won't enter the lists unless you both wear breastplates. To that he has now added another condition. A hole over the heart must be cut from each plate. They must be heart-shaped and, of course, of equal size. He demands this as proof that his insistence on the use of armor is due to a sense of fitness and not to fear of your blade."

D'Arlay frowned. "A curious stipulation," he said.

"There's no doubt in my mind that he sees some advantage in it," declared Coeur. "My advice to you is to refuse his conditions."

D'Arlay was silent for several moments. "We're in no position to dispute with him any longer," he said then. "Listen to them out there! They're sure I'm the one who's holding back. Jacques, I must give in and fight him in the manner he demands. Accept his stipulations, in God's name, and let us have it over."

Coeur said, "It's for you to decide." To himself he added, "He's going to his death, but my hands are tied and there's nothing more I can do."

D'Arlay got to his feet. "What arrangements were suggested for the cutting of the plates?"

"An armorer will attend to that immediately. It will be done in the lists so all may see what is afoot." Coeur paused and then broke out with sudden vehemence: "Think well, Robin, before you agree. I tell you this man who is called the greatest fighter and most honorable knight in all Christendom is as sly as a fox and ready to take advantage of you in every way."

D'Arlay smiled without any hint of mirth and dropped a hand on the Moneyman's shoulder. "Don't lose heart, old friend. Come, take the word back to him that I have agreed." He turned to the servant. "I must wear all my best clothes today. Like a bridegroom, my Helion."

Coeur decided to make one more effort. "Robin," he said, "you and I have always agreed in our opinion of the Code of Chivalry."

D'Arlay, who had begun to disrobe, looked up and nodded in assent. "Yes, Jacques. My opinions haven't changed in any respect."

"And yet here you are," declared Coeur, in a bitter tone, "preparing to fight to the death with a knight much stronger and more skilled than you are. If you come out of this alive, it will be by the grace of Almighty God. And what is the reason? A dispute into which the pair of you fell over the wine cups. You're prepared to throw your life away in a futile quarrel."

A brazier of charcoal was burning behind them but there was still enough chill in the air inside the tent to make D'Arlay's teeth chatter. He began to dress with an urgency which rendered conversation difficult. "I can't deny," he said, "that the quarrel between us was a futile one."

"Then be wise enough now to refuse to go on with it. The conditions the Burgundian insists upon are a sufficient reason."

D'Arlay shook his head. "No, Jacques, my friend. The issue can now be settled only in the lists. And yet I assure you that I feel about such matters as I've always done."

"Is there nothing I can say or do to stop you from throwing your life away?"

Helion was slipping the gambeson over his master's shoulders. D'Arlay did not reply until the operation had been completed. "Do you think," he asked, "that I could live out my life with a charge of cowardice hanging over me?"

Coeur threw up his arms in a despairing gesture. "Chivalry," he declared, with intense bitterness, "flourishes on fear quite as much as on honest courage. Most knights abide by the Code because they're afraid of what others will think and say. Let me tell you this, Robin: This is a time when you should be above such fears. France needs every stout heart and strong arm today. Where does your real duty lie? Should you preserve your life to fight the English or risk it today against this Burgundian coxcomb who has no intention of taking any part in the war?"

"But don't you see," asked D'Arlay, with a resigned shake of his head, "that under the Code I would not be allowed to fight the English tomorrow if I didn't fight Jacques de Lalain today?"

3

The space on the slope, which had been reserved for the nobility, was rapidly filling up when Jacques Coeur stationed himself among the spectators there. He was in a mood of such preoccupation that he was barely conscious of the fact that close at hand a party of pikemen, who wore no insignia of any kind nor any distinguishing colors, were keeping clear a place capable of accommodating a score or more and from which a most favorable view of the enclosure was obtainable. He concluded that some great nobleman was taking this method of assuring an advantage to himself and his immediate retinue.

A herald entered the lists and stationed himself in front of the favored section to make an announcement of the conditions under which the duel was to be fought. Raising his voice, he laid special stress on the cutting of the heart-shaped holes in the breastplates of the contestants. As he spoke an armorer was at work in the lists, in full view of everyone, and the clang of his hammer and chisel on the steel provided a fitting punctuation to the words of the herald as he proclaimed, "This is done, brave gentlemen and fair ladies, to provide vulnerability, to place the two champions in constant jeopardy from the play of the blades." The crowds stirred and a hum of talk arose from all quarters. This was something new, something novel. It would make this gladiatorial encounter one long to be discussed and savored.

Jacques Coeur said to himself with deep inner disgust, "If they knew how much trickery goes on beneath the surface at all tournaments and all knightly meetings they would think less of this precious chivalry!"

If he had not been so bitterly concerned over the outcome, he might have found some relief in the beauty of the setting. No period in history has ever exceeded this one in its understanding and appreciation, and its use, of color. The spectators, massed solidly about the enclosure, presented a remarkable spread of contrasting hues. It was not only on the slope where the nobility clustered that this was to be found. There, the towering hennins of the ladies and their rich cloaks of so many delightful shades of red and green and blue (the wonderful blues of the Middle Ages!) and the costly plumes which bobbed on the heads of the men and the tufted magnificence of their enormously padded shoulders combined to create a man-made spectrum which was nothing short of breath-taking. The common people, who noisily filled the other side and swarmed about the pavilions so insistently that the bare points of pikes had to be offered to hold them back, were almost equally gay and diverse, with this exception, that the finery of the nobles was new and the colors on that side were sharp and untarnished and as spectacular as an aviary of tropical birds, while the clothes of the commonality, having been much worn and continuously exposed to wind and rain, had mellowed to shades of amethyst and topaz and rich blues and browns and warm greens and gray and common mulberry, the whole blending so miraculously that the rabble were even more rewarding to the eye than the aristocracy.

The voice of the herald sounded from the other side of the enclosure where he was making the same announcement for the benefit of the common people. Coeur heard the words repeated, "to provide vulnerability" and an admonition to the "good people, citizens and varlets of all degree," to remain orderly in "the face of whatever befall." A commotion to his right drew his attention and he saw that a party of men and women, all wearing masks, were filing into the space which had been kept free. The fact that they considered themselves under the necessity of concealing their identities, together with the richness of their attire, made it evident that they were from the court. The Moneyman studied them closely, thinking it should be easy for him to discover who they were. He was still engaged on this quest when he heard his name pronounced in a feminine voice behind him.

"My lord Coeur."

It was Valerie, accompanied by one of the De Burey pages, a somewhat gangling youth in a cloak which obviously had once belonged to a more mature member of the household, for it was lapped about him and the sleeves hung down over his fingers. Valerie herself was handsomely attired in a brocaded cloak with a collar of brown fur which framed her face effectively. On her head she wore a trim hennin of the same fur.

"I had to come!" There was a look of acute distress on her face. "My lord Coeur, is it true that—that he's in such great danger?"

"Yes, my child. He's in the very greatest danger. And there's nothing to be done to help him." The Moneyman regarded her with an air of sternness. "How is it that you are here? Did you have the consent of the Comtesse to coming?"

"No, my lord. They, my cousin and Monsieur the Comte, left many hours ago to come, and I—I persuaded Godefroy to bring me. I couldn't stay away while he was in such peril! He has been so kind to me, my lord Coeur, so considerate always!"

"I haven't seen the Comte and Comtesse de Burey here."

A brief smile lighted up her face. "It seems, my lord, that they had been told a different place. On the other bank. I very much fear they are there now. It was Froy who knew there had been a change of plan and that it was to be here." The smile had vanished as quickly as it came. "Is there nothing, nothing at all, to be done, my lord?"

"Nothing." Coeur shook his head with an air of depression which equaled hers. "All we can do, child, is stand here and watch—and pray that God and his patron saint will watch over him and bring him safely through."

While he talked, he had been keeping the newly arrived party within his vision, and he now saw something which made him gasp with surprise. A gust of wind had swept across the enclosure and, finding the mask of one of the ladies insecurely attached, had carried it away. Instinctively she clasped her face with both hands, crying, "Good St. Agnes!" And then, realizing that the mask could not be retrieved, laughed rather ruefully and said in a voice which reached Coeur's ears, "Sire, as the wind has played me this trick, I must either make myself absurd by hiding my face in my hands or withdraw from your presence."

Jacques Coeur addressed Valerie in an urgent tone. "My child! Move over here in front of me. Look to your right. At the lady who is unmasked. Look long and well, Valerie. It's important." He leaned down and whispered in her ear: "That is Agnes Sorel!"

She followed his instructions and remained for several minutes in a fixed and silent contemplation of the pale and beautiful lady who ruled the heart of the man who ruled the kingdom. She noted that the face of the King's favorite was not only pale but very thin and that her eyes, despite the smile with which she strove to make light of the mishap, had an unhappy look. She noticed also that the hand Agnes Sorel was holding near her face was thin almost to the point of transparency. More than anything else, however, she noticed how successfully the unfortunate lady strove to maintain a fiction of good spirits and how infinitely becoming to her fragile beauty was the dark blue-and-gray cloak which wrapped her about.

Valerie remained in silent regard so long that the Moneyman leaned over her and whispered, "Well, my child?"

"She has the loveliest and sweetest face I've ever seen," said Valerie, in a rapt tone. "I'm thinking, my lord, how mistaken you have been in seeing a resemblance in me. Truly, that is impossible! She's not only beautiful, my lord, she has an expression, a light in her eyes, which will never be found in any other face."

"I was not mistaken." Coeur was speaking in a tone just above a whisper. "You are her fleshly counterpart, my child. After you've lived as long as she has, and perhaps suffered as she has, you may acquire that expression, that light in the eyes, which comes from the sweet and stanch spirit within her."

"My cousin was right about her. I heard her tell the Comte that someday soon Agnes Sorel would reappear at court, pale and ill but as lovely as ever; and that, when she did, she would sweep all opposition away with the greatest ease."

Coeur did not reply at once. "My brave lady!" he said finally, blinking his eyes as though to conceal a suggestion of moisture. "Yes, my child, she's as lovely as ever. And she has swept all opposition before her! Ah, if I could only count on her support always! There would be no problem then. There would be no danger for France!"

One of the other ladies, whose face was not familiar to Jacques Coeur, had found a remedy for the situation by removing her own mask and covering Agnes Sorel's face with it. The favorite thanked her in a laughing voice and then said something to the King, who was wearing a domino which covered his face completely. He nodded his head and laughed in turn. By this time the rumor had spread that Charles of France was among the spectators and the masked party was usurping all attention.

Valerie had returned to her former position where she could no longer see the court group. "Did you spare a glance for the King?" asked Coeur, in a whisper.

She shook her head instantly and emphatically. "No, my lord. I thought the man nearest her must be the King, but I—I didn't dare look at him!"

A hand tugged at Coeur's sleeve and he faced about to find a youth beside him, dressed in the unrelieved black of the bombardiers. This was enough to capture his attention and interest at once. The newcomer was a pleasant-looking boy with dark blue eyes, and obviously he was in a much disturbed state of mind.

"I am Alain de Kersai," said the boy. "I respectfully request a word with you."

The name won all of the Moneyman's interest at once. "Alain de Kersai," he repeated. "You are cousin to Jacques de Lalain."

The boy nodded. "Yes, my lord Coeur."

"He objects to having you serve with the guns."

"Yes, my lord." Alain de Kersai looked about him apprehensively and then lowered his voice. "Jacques is a great knight-errant and I am proud of him. And yet I'm compelled to say that he's both blind and stubborn. It's because of his attitude to my serving with the guns that this duel is being fought."

"I understood so." Coeur was studying the boy's face with close interest, realizing that some conflict of mind had brought him. "You have something to tell me, I think."

"Yes, my lord. I've a confession to make." His voice sank still lower. *"I know something.* Something which would be of use to the Sire d'Arlay. I thought of telling him, but—but, my lord, I couldn't make up my mind. The Sire d'Arlay is championing my cause, and yet to tell might be a betrayal. I didn't know what I should do. And so—I did nothing."

Coeur placed an arm on the youth's shoulder. "Do you feel free to tell me what it is?"

Alain de Kersai hesitated. Then he began to speak in so low a tone that Coeur had difficulty hearing him. "Perhaps I should tell you so you can judge better. Jacques has a weakness of the eye which makes it hard for him to face the sun. Always he finds it necessary to maneuver so that he can be free of it. If his opponent knew that, he might contrive to keep Jacques in the sun as much as possible. It would perhaps balance the scales better—for we know, of course, that my cousin is stronger and more skilled than the Sire d'Arlay."

Coeur's eyes narrowed slightly as he considered the value of what he had been told. "I have small knowledge of such matters but it seems to me that this would be of service. It seems to me also that the Sire d'Arlay should be told.

"This also I should tell you. My cousin will carry a bitter enmity into the lists. Nothing will satisfy him short of the killing of his opponent. If his blade finds the vital spot, he will drive it home. And—and, my lord, he'll have no difficulty finding the heart! What I'm telling you now reflects on the honor of the family and yet I feel it must be told. My lord Coeur, he has been preparing himself for this duel with an eye solely to the final condition on which he insisted—the hole in the breastplate over the heart. He selected an arms master of the exact height and weight of the Sire d'Arlay and practiced with him every day. On the man's armor there was a red cross painted over the heart. For two months Jacques has been training himself to reach that mark."

"I knew there was something of the kind back of the condition!" exclaimed Coeur.

A flush of anger had taken possession of Alain de Kersai's face. "Day after day it has gone on! There has never been any deviation, always the same thing! He has become uncannily expert in that one respect."

"And in addition he has insisted they wear body armor and helmets so that D'Arlay's point may reach him a hundred times and do him no harm! And this is chivalry!" Coeur suddenly seized the youth by the arm. "Alain, I must go to my friend at once and tell him. Jacques de Lalain had enough advantage before, with his weight and great strength and skill. Now D'Arlay will have no more chance than a ewe led to the shambles! Are you willing to have me tell him?"

The boy nodded eagerly. "Yes, my lord!" he whispered. "I should have had the courage to go to him myself. If you can reach him in time, it may perhaps save him from the consequences of my—my weakness and indecision!"

But it was too late. Before the Moneyman could reach the foot of the slope the guards had spread their pikes out point to point to prevent any invasion of the enclosure. A fanfare of trumpets sounded, announcing that the contestants were coming into the lists.

4

The wind was causing the Burgundian flag to twist and fold and unfold with a loud cracking sound as Jacques de Lalain emerged from his pavilion, preceded by two heralds sounding a note of defiance on their trumpets. He had reached his station in the center by the time the

Moneyman had returned to his place on the slope, and was acknowledging the cheers of the spectators with a regal lift of his steel-clad hand.

The great champion was attired in white from the tossing plume in his helmet to the bleached leather leggings which he wore under the faude or iron petticoat suspended from his waist. Even the steel of his body armor had been burnished so diligently that it completed the effect. He looked enormous.

The sympathy of the spectators was with D'Arlay, but this did not prevent them from greeting the Burgundian with loud cheers. He was the living symbol of the principle of force which dominated the life of the day. He had never been beaten in the lists. The spectators, antagonistic to everything Burgundian, had nevertheless such respect for his prowess that they watched him with craning necks and loud whistles of awe. Rather than miss seeing him in action, they were content to have the insignificant Frenchman he was to face go down to defeat and perhaps death. The spectacle was the thing.

Trumpets sounded from the other end of the lists. The note produced by D'Arlay's heralds seemed thin and meek, as though to emphasize still further the all-too-obvious contrast between the two antagonists. It could not be denied that the comparatively unknown knight from Anjou looked unimpressive when he emerged. He walked down the slope to the lists with his usual hurried step, like a burgher making for his place of business rather than a champion stepping out to battle. There was no suggestion of the martial about him save that he was clothed in armor, and even in that respect there was something lacking. Armor was made to satisfy the vanity of the wearer as well as to protect his body, but D'Arlay's was as plain as the flapping robe of a hedge priest. Whereas the plumes of the Burgundian stood up above his helmet in snowy arrogance, his were gray and inclining to droop. His squire, carrying the sword, had forgotten to don his tabard with the De Burey arms and he was so embarrassed that he stumbled twice in following his master to the battle station.

The spectators, who were French almost to a man, watched the entrance of their champion in a dead silence.

Coeur looked down at Valerie whose face was pale. "God be merciful," he said, "and show him the way to prevail over this bloodthirsty Goliath as David did in the Valley of Elah!"

The same comparison had occurred to others. One of the royal party, after a glance at the figure of D'Arlay, said aloud in a resigned tone of voice, "All he needs is a slingshot in his hands."

It was D'Arlay, nevertheless, who opened the attack and he did so with such unexpected vigor that the Burgundian was put on the defensive at once. De Lalain abandoned the colossus-like pose he had struck and seemed in danger even of losing his balance as he struggled to pull himself together. A roar of approval went up from the closely packed ranks of spectators. The fight, it was clear, was going to be better than they had expected.

They were seeing something new, something completely novel in the bloody calendar of conflict. There was a frenzied jostling of shoulders and elbows as the spectators fought for better positions, a better chance to watch the streak of slender steel in the hands of D'Arlay as it wove about the seemingly inert blade of Jacques de Lalain, hissing and striking with the suddenness of an adder. They were accustomed only to the heavy two-edged sword and the cut and slash of cumbersome stroking like the swing of a blacksmith's hammer. This new weapon, about which there had been much skeptical talk in the town the last few days, had a magic quality. The Burgundian seemed almost as much at sea as the watchers. He was stumbling about like a bear in the first dazed and angry moments of a baiting.

A suddenly exultant Jacques Coeur held up a finger every time the leaping serpent's tongue ended with a grind of steel on armor. In a few minutes he had both hands in the air, fingers extended. "If it had not been for Burgundian guile and unknightly trickery," he cried, "the great Jacques de Lalain would be a dead man now!"

But in spite of the fact that long weeks of application had failed to supply him with skill to equal that of his opponent, the Burgundian had suffered no more than scratches on the surface of his breast armor. Alain de Kersai touched Coeur on the arm and said, "It's such a small mark, my lord, I fear it will take luck as well as skill to reach it."

The interest of the crowd, trained by much watching of gladiators in the lists to a technical expertness in all points concerning the use of weapons, was centering on this new method of swordplay. Someone in the group surrounding Charles of France said in an approving tone: "There's an undeniable gentility about the thing. It has the sharp bite of an epigram." Coeur heard the remark and nodded his head in agreement. D'Arlay, he recalled, had always contended that someday the sword would be the recognized weapon of gentlemen.

After several minutes had passed, Alain de Kersai glanced at Coeur and asked, "How do you think it goes, my lord?"

The Moneyman answered with a confident nod. "Robin has touched him nearly a dozen times. As far as I have been able to see, De Lalain has been inside his guard once only."

The young knight didn't seem happy in spite of this. He was silent for a moment and then he shook his head. "But, my lord Coeur," he said, "that single touch was no more than an inch from the unprotected heart."

"Robin also has been close."

"That's true. But I have been watching carefully and I've seen this: My cousin makes few thrusts but each time he seems to fail by very little. He's holding himself in reserve. I've a very great fear that soon he is certain to strike home."

Coeur did not answer immediately. Alarmed by what the young knight had said, he watched both contestants with an aroused intentness, noting that Alain had been right as far as the Burgundian was concerned. Jacques de Lalain gave no hint of anxiety over the dangerously facile attack that D'Arlay continued to press against him, depending clearly on the protection of his body armor. His return thrusts never varied: a straight drive down from the shoulder with all of his great strength back of it.

"Robin must end it soon."

"Yes, my lord Coeur. If he doesn't, it won't finish the way we hope."

Neither of them had made any mention of it but both had noticed that Jacques de Lalain's back was turned to the sun and that D'Arlay had been continuously under the necessity of fighting with the blaze of it in his eyes. The struggle continued under these conditions, the slender figure in somber mail still doing all the pressing. The Burgundian had set himself firmly on his massive legs and seldom moved except to retreat a step when the intensity of the attack put his defense at fault. There was still a suggestion of unruffled confidence in the figure under the tall white plumes, a hint that he was biding his time.

Coeur's early confidence began to wane. He realized that the weight of the armor must be exhausting D'Arlay's strength. How much longer could he remain on the offensive? "God and St. Martin direct his aim!" whispered the Moneyman under his breath with a sudden feeling of the most intense fear. "If he doesn't strike home soon, he's lost!"

He looked at Alain de Kersai and saw tears in the boy's eyes. "I like his chances very little," said the young knight. "Only a lucky thrust will save him now."

The chance for a lucky thrust clearly was small. The Burgundian, careless of all other attack, never failed to parry any stroke which came dangerously close to the exposed point.

A moment later the young knight cried out sharply, "Look!" D'Arlay had circled to his opponent's right and the Burgundian, forced to pivot about to face him, had shown unmistakable signs of discomfort at being thus exposed to the rays of the sun. Whether D'Arlay was aware of this or not, he continued to so maneuver that De Lalain had no opportunity of getting back to his former comfortable position. The result was at once apparent. The confidence of the great champion seemed to have been shaken. He was defending himself with a certain clumsiness and there was again a suggestion about him of a bear at the baiting post.

Alain de Kersai said in a tense voice, "The Sire d'Arlay has discovered the weakness for himself!"

"And he's making the most of it!"

"From now on"—there was a jubilant note in the boy's voice—"Jacques will know what it is to fight at a disadvantage!"

"God grant it's not too late!"

They had eyes only for D'Arlay's blade after that and so they saw each move which led to the finish. They saw D'Arlay pause and then circle swiftly around his opponent's right. They saw him feint and then drive his sword straight up in the direction of De Lalain's heart. The latter, for once, was not ready. There was no grinding of steel in contact. The thrust went home.

They saw the great champion stagger, and knew that the point of the sword had reached the unprotected portion of his breast.

Both were incapable of speech in this final moment of the long and doubtful battle. They stood in silence while a roar of almost incredulous delight rose from the closely packed rows of spectators. Coeur crossed himself reverently and thankfully when he saw that his friend's sword did not come away.

But they had reckoned without the reserves of strength in the great frame of the Burgundian. The latter's sword arm still had the power to strike. Seriously wounded, he managed to raise his weapon and thrust out at his opponent. Coeur and his companion had been praying for a lucky thrust. They saw it achieved now but not in the way they had hoped; they saw a blind stroke which sent the point of De Lalain's sword straight to the open space in D'Arlay's armor.

Chapter XIV

I

TUDDUAL arrived with a message from the Comte de Burey while D'Arlay was watching the fall of the snow from his windows in the Rue Grenier sur L'Eau, delighting in the way the whole world was turning white. The snow had been coming down heavily and soddenly for hours. It had piled up over the doorsteps, it covered the roofs, it filled the leads and gutters; and every window sill, every cornice, every turret and buttress was trimmed with ermine like the robe of a court lady.

The message took the form of a slip of paper on which the information had been painfully and almost illegibly scrawled that the Comte had something urgent to tell his brother and, being confined to his own fireside by a severe attack of some pestilential malady, was under the necessity of insisting that D'Arlay pay him a visit. The latter nodded to the herald and said he would accompany him back, although he knew that Robert de Poitevin, who had been attending him, would seethe with indignation when he heard.

As soon as D'Arlay reached the street there was a great commotion. People of all ages and conditions poured out of the other houses and stood knee-deep in the snow to watch him pass. A boy struggled through the drifts and with triumphant pride touched his sword as he went by.

The Hôtel de Burey was dark and cold when D'Arlay arrived. Servants scuttled through the drafty halls with blue faces and hands sunk deep in their sleeves. The wind could be heard in the upper reaches, battering at doors and causing pennons on the walls to rustle and flap and flutter. Candles guttered and a cross-grained fire in the entrance hall emitted clouds of smoke instead of heat.

D'Arlay found his brother ensconced in a small room at the head of a short flight of stone steps. He was wrapped voluminously in a hooded red robe. His bulbous nose, which was somewhere between brown and purple in color, suggested a worm coiled in a geranium bloom. Not content with the heat given off by the fire on the hearth, he had seen to it that some of the coals had been scraped out on to the stone floor and had both feet stretched over them in a sling. As the sling was looped over the top of a chair, there was an alarming lack of security about the arrangement. He blinked at his visitor and motioned to a chair.

"Ha, the hero of Paris!" grunted the Comte. "Nay, of all France. You are aware, no doubt, that your sword has become legendary and will be classed with the Cloak of Invisibility?" His voice dwindled away into a mumble. "You will go down in history, my stout brother. And I, Regnault de Burey, the head of the family, the head of one of the oldest and greatest families, moreover, am of no more moment in the minds of men than"—drawing on the argot of Paris—"the last echo of a fiddler's full dinner. I should be grateful to you, brother Robin. I've been smiled upon by people who have always disliked me. I've been singled out by Dunois to be tossed a greeting like a bone to a dog. I've been taken aside and congratulated. And all because I'm the brother of the Sire d'Arlay. Does it seem to you also that there is a tinge of irony about all this?"

D'Arlay sat down beside the muffled figure. "If this sling should break or slip," he said, "you might achieve a more lasting fame than mine as the accidental discoverer of a new cure for the gout."

The Comte paid no attention to this warning. He twirled one end of his mustache which was limp from lack of waxing. "Since you are a national hero," he said, "the question of your marriage assumes so much importance that our liege lord is taking it in hand. I've been informed that he has a wife for you and will summon you shortly to let you know the royal pleasure."

This accomplished the purpose of arousing D'Arlay's interest most thoroughly. The latter swung around and surveyed his brother with an air of intense alarm and dismay.

"It seems strange," he remarked, "that our liege lord, who has never before shown any signs of being aware of my existence, should suddenly decide to take such an interest in my affairs."

"It became certain that he would at the moment when the point of your sword wounded the Burgundian. If you had succeeded in killing him, your importance would have doubled. You are now in the nature of an asset. . . . It would be a good match for you, Robin. The girl is a royal ward and just turning thirteen. The marriage would take place at once but, naturally, it couldn't be consummated for a year or so. She has been a favorite of the King's—a nice little thing, with brown hair and eyes and a neat figure. You always get a modest answer from her, 'Yes, perhaps, thanks, maybe, please.' She'll make an obedient wife. It would be easy for you to become fond of her."

"Perhaps you'll condescend now to tell me her name."

"Her name is Amorette de L'Anguinais."

"I've never heard of her."

"She's a rich plum. Her father left her a sweet domain, on the eastern rim of Armagnac, and our liege lord has seen to it that no greedy fingers have been dipping into it. Your friend, the Moneyman, has looked after it with an even more jealous eye. I'm convinced her dowry would be ample for all our needs."

The Comte suddenly leaned forward and regarded his brother with an air of dramatic urgency. "In spite of all this," he said, wagging a forefinger at D'Arlay, "I've brought you here to warn you against this match. It would be a mistake. You must get away before any summons from the King can reach you. Do you understand? You must leave at once. Today."

D'Arlay was thoroughly mystified. "For years you've dinned into my ears the need to marry a rich wife. Here we have what seems to be a perfect arrangement, of the King's planning, moreover. And now you say I must avoid it by running away. Are you serious?"

"Robin! Attend closely to what I'm going to say. I'm the head of the family and I insist you obey me in this matter." The Comte's manner became even more urgent. "Don't you see that we have the chance now to make the family of De Burey the most powerful in all France?"

"On what do you base that sweeping assertion?"

"It's a matter of three months since you saw the little cousin. In a few minutes I shall take you up to renew your acquaintance with her." The Comte indulged himself in a smile with an edge of slyness to it. "You'll see a remarkable change in her. What doubts you may have had about the success of the scheme will vanish at once. . . . If she wins the degree of approval we expect, it may be deemed expedient to marry her off at once. A husband in the background is the best kind of cloak. . . . Well, why shouldn't you be the lucky man? If you married her, you could control the state through her influence with the King."

D'Arlay was so startled that for a moment he made no response. Then he began to laugh. "I suppose you are serious about this but I intend to treat it as a joke—as a joke in the very worst of taste. Understand this at once: I refuse to become the King's cuckold. And now, with your permission, I'll pay my respects to the ladies and return to the couch I should never have left."

The Comte did not seem disturbed. He nodded his head. "I didn't expect you to say yes at first. I expected you, in fact, to rear and snort and puff fire and fill the air with pious protestations. Your mind has always been like an uncured cheese with a fermentation of high-and-mighty notions going on inside it. All I ask, Robin, is that you think it over. The more you think about it, the more sensible it will seem. And in the meantime you must keep out of the royal clutches. My advice would be to get yourself to Arlay as fast as this pestilential weather will permit."

"All the thinking I could do in a hundred years wouldn't change my mind. The family will never become wealthy and powerful by the backstairs—not, at least, if it depends on me. As for the King, I can say no to him if I desire as easily here as at Arlay. I have no intention of running away."

"Isabeau is in attendance on the Queen and the little cousin is about to begin her dancing lesson with Old Ricciardo. I suggest," said the Comte, giving his brother a calculating side glance, "that we go up together and watch the lesson. Jacques Coeur is with her now, as it happens."

The Comte removed his feet from the sling and cautiously touched the ground with them. "The pain's gone!" he exclaimed, nodding his head with satisfaction. "There's been some kind of miracle here. I shall be able to walk or even cut a caper or two during the dancing lesson, if I feel like it."

2

The room to which he led his brother was being used for the drying of clothes. Two lines were stretched along the walls, from one end to the other, on which dangled garments, some of an intimate nature. It was a large room and quite obviously had been used once for less menial purposes although the nature of its former employment was hard to determine. There had been a chantry at one end but the enclosing screens had been removed, thus exposing to view the altar, or what was left of it. A family as poverty-stricken as the De Bureys could not afford to keep a chantry echoing with prayers for the souls of long-dead ancestors.

Valerie was standing in conversation with Jacques Coeur when they entered. She was facing the door and so she saw D'Arlay at once. She came forward to meet him, smiling in welcome and with hands outstretched. She did not say any of the things which might have been expected under the circumstances, no expression of her pleasure in seeing him again, no reference to the pride she had felt in his exploit in the lists, or her relief that he had recovered so quickly from his wound. In fact, she said nothing at all. But her eyes conveyed all this to him, and much more; they told him that his unexpected arrival was the greatest boon she could have asked on this stormy day, that his long absence had been for her an unhappy deprivation, that he remained her most highly prized friend.

He was finding it hard to speak himself, for the Comte had been well within the bounds of truth when he said there had been a remarkable change in her. She looked older and her manner had a suggestion of gravity about it. Also she was thinner, as though she had found the process of change a trying one; there was the hint of a hollow in her cheeks and the merest suggestion of a violet shadow about her eyes. In spite of this, perhaps in some degree because of it, she was lovelier than she had been when he first saw her. She had poise now and she walked with ease. There was grace in every move she made, in the carriage of her head, in the way she raised her arms, in the use she made of her hands. Her hair was dressed with restraint but it had lost none of its molten beauty, and it seemed to say, I am contributing to this portrait of a lady but at any time I could let myself go again most joyously in unruly curls.

As he watched her come toward him he knew that he could never marry the King's ward. He was saying to himself: "This is the second time I've fallen in love and once again the lady of my choice is placed by force of circumstances beyond my reach. This time I'm in love for all eternity and so I must reconcile myself to a lonely life."

It was D'Arlay who broke the silence. "It's a long time since I've seen you, Mademoiselle. A matter of many months."

"But I've been much luckier, my lord," she answered. "I saw you—just a month ago."

D'Arlay was so startled that he looked to Jacques Coeur for confirmation. The latter smiled and nodded his head. "It's true. She was at the duel. One of the pages knew where it was to be held and she talked him into accompanying her. In fact, she stood beside me and watched what was going on with an anxiety which at least equaled my own."

"I hope never again in all my life to feel so much anxiety, my lord," said Valerie.

"Old Ricciardo is waiting," said the Comte. He was shifting about from foot to foot and beating his hands together. "Perhaps we should all take a dancing lesson in order to keep warm."

The master was an Italian and he was so enormously fat that his stomach quivered like a bodge of oats as he came forward from the corner of the room where he had been waiting. In spite of his bulk he stepped lightly and with easy balance.

"What is it to be today, my lord and Mademoiselle?" he asked in a voice as high-pitched and thin as a bird's. "Will Mademoiselle go through the steps of the *pavane?* It is a dance of great dignity."

The Comte grunted in dissent. "The pavane? It's for giddy-gaddy dowagers of fifty or more and rheumatic old bucks who can't step to a faster air than a dirge. I suggest, Dancing Master, that you have her show us something of all measures. The pavane, if you must, but certainly the *Lège-de-moy* and the Calf's Feet and the *tricotet* and the *courante.* The courante above everything. I may tell you that I was the best dancer of the courante in all Anjou in my day. Ha, you should have seen when I swung my partner. Her skirts flew up so high——"

He broke off and began to hum the words of the chorus to which the courante was performed, *Sy vous ne savez dire, Yo!* His memories getting the better of him, he raised himself on his toes with both arms extended above his head. Giving his body a twirl, he brought his heels down and shouted with zest, "Yo, yo! Yo, yo!"

Coeur asked Old Ricciardo, "How is your pupil progressing?"

The huge round face lighted up with enthusiasm. "Ah, my lord, perhaps I shouldn't say so while she is here but, truly, Mademoiselle is in a way to become a very fine dancer. She has every quality. Such *diversità di cose!* Never have I had a better pupil!"

"Come, no more delay!" The Comte took Old Ricciardo by the arm and started him in the direction of the center of the room. "Get out your pipes and begin. Get the pavane over and done with first."

Coeur drew D'Arlay to a bench at one side of the room. As they watched the preparations for the lesson, finding it necessary to twist their heads about to see through the well-filled clothesline, the Moneyman began to speak in a low tone. "You were in an abstracted mood when you came in and from that I judged your brother had been telling you of the King's choice of a husband for his favorite ward."

"Yes, and I find myself in a serious predicament. I must run contrary to the royal will. I've no intention of marrying this girl who is, I understand, a mere child."

"She's the catch of the year, Robin. Make no mistake, there are a round score of eligible courtiers who would give anything to be in your shoes." Coeur was watching his friend closely. "Do you mind telling me your objections to the match?"

D'Arlay decided the real reason was a secret he could not share. Instead he said: "A disinclination to matrimony at the moment. Perhaps it's a disinclination also to having anyone, even our liege lord, select my wife for me."

"Don't you intend to marry in time?"

D'Arlay hesitated before answering. "There's nothing more certain than that I should marry. You know how deeply in debt my brother has managed to get himself. There seems no other way of saving the family lands. And yet—when it comes to the point I always find that I can't take a wife for no other reason than because she is rich enough to pay off the debts."

"Well." The Moneyman made no effort to urge him to a different decision. "It's your own life which is concerned and so you must make the decision yourself. Fortunately you are in a position at the moment to stand out against the King. You've become a national hero and our liege lord would hardly dare rouse public wrath by meting out any punishment."

As they talked, Valerie had been dancing as directed by Old Ricciardo. She had gone through the dignified steps of the pavane, holding her head high and swaying very little as she turned and curtseyed. Then he had sent her to the farthest extreme and she had danced the Lège-de-moy, with hands on her hips and her heels beating a furious rataplan on the floor in time to the fast tooting of the master's horn. After that she had gone to the tricotet, which happened to be her favorite. Holding her blue skirts no more than a modest inch off the floor, she had swayed and pirouetted, moving her feet all the time as fast as knitting needles in the hands of an industrious housewife. By the time she was through, her cheeks were flushed and her eyes were sparkling.

Jacques Coeur watched Valerie as she drew a fan from her sleeve and began to swing it back and forth.

"Well," he whispered, "what do you think of her now?"

"I've been sitting here in a state of wonder, not daring to believe my eyes," answered D'Arlay. "She has been most completely made over. It's nothing short of a miracle."

"Yes, it's a miracle. Even her voice has changed. Have you noticed that it's lower and more self-possessed? Your charming sister-in-law must be given the credit. She has brought about these improvements in our little Puss-from-the-provinces. We had many arguments but I always gave in and in the end I always acknowledged I had been wrong. She's a very clever woman." He gave D'Arlay a quick look out of the corner of one eye. "Could a better candidate be found?"

D'Arlay shook his head reluctantly. "I'm compelled to say that a better candidate could not have been found."

As Valerie danced, the Comte had hovered on the edge of things, humming loudly, skipping about and improvising dance steps of his own (the pain had left his feet apparently), and offering a great deal of advice. Now he clapped his hands together as a signal that he had something to say.

"We have come to the courante," he announced.

"But, my lord," protested Old Ricciardo, "one can't dance the courante alone."

"Didn't you hear me say 'we'? I shall dance with Mademoiselle. And I promise you, Master Ricciardo, you will say at the finish that never before has the courante been executed with more skill and zest. We will give to it as well just the right amount of"—he turned and winked at Valerie—"just the merest hint of naughtiness. Come, little cousin, take your position opposite me."

The courante can be danced by any number of couples. One participant sings a verse of the song while the gentlemen advance boldly toward the ladies who retreat before them with a simulation of coyness. All then join in the chorus and each man seizes his partner and gives her a vigorous twirl. Then they bow and separate, the gentlemen returning to their positions.

"It will be better with just the two of us," said the Comte. "I shall never have to change partners and, by'r Lady of Marmoutier, that suits me perfectly. Cousin, sing the first verse."

Valerie began in a gay voice:

"Penotte se vieult marier
On ne scet à qui la donner."

Then she clapped her hands and the Comte joined in with the chorus:

"Sy vous ne savez dire, Yo!
Yo! Yo! Compère, commère.
Sy vous ne savez dire, Yo!"

He pranced forward with goatlike abandon as he sang, kicking his heels backward and tossing his arms about, his face wreathed in a toothy grin. Seizing Valerie in his arms, he swung her high in the air. Then he released her, bowed with an exaggerated sweep of his arm, and danced backward to his station.

"Brava! Yo! Yo!" he cried. "Now I'll give you a verse. A fanciful little

thing I wrote myself. It's a trifle on the—the unconventional side, I'm afraid. It's a good thing Madame the Comtesse isn't here as I'm sure she would find fault with my sentiments."

The verse he proceeded to sing was rather more than unconventional. It was much better suited to a romp in a tavern, with greasy rufflers and blowsy women dancing to it. The Comte bawled it out at the top of his voice and then skipped forward with arms outstretched. This time he swung Valerie so far in the air that her skirts twirled about her ankles and threatened worse indiscretions. Releasing her, he raised himself on his toes and executed an elaborate pirouette, shouting for good measure, *"Yo, yo! Yo, yo!—— Yo!—— Yo!"*

"What's going on here?" demanded an angry voice from the doorway.

Silence fell on the room as Isabeau swept into it. The Comte's arms remained stretched above his head and he watched her with obvious uneasiness. Old Ricciardo stopped tooting on the horn and his mouth fell open with dismay.

Coeur leaned over to D'Arlay. "In public esteem you are the bravest man in all France. Have you the courage to stay and face this situation? Or would you rather withdraw before the fair Isabeau sees us?"

"I'm in favor of withdrawing," whispered D'Arlay.

Coeur motioned to Valerie to follow them. Then the two men got cautiously to their feet and tiptoed from the room.

BOOK TWO

Chapter I

I

A SENTRY called "Halt!" and swung a lantern over his head to inspect the party. When he recognized Jacques Coeur, he said: "I know *you,* my lord Moneyman. Many's the measure of wine I've had at the Grant Bande within seeing of your shop. Are these your people?"

"Yes. Direct us, if you please, to the headquarters of my lord Dunois."

The word that Jacques Coeur had arrived spread quickly through the camp. Men poured out of houses and tents to give him a welcoming cheer as he passed. They left bivouac fires in the fields and the shelter of hayricks. He found himself ringed about by faces which looked wild and dirty in the light of the torches. The soldiers were friendly, however, and he heard one phrase repeated over and over again, "The good Jaquet sees to it that we're well paid and fed." He had to acknowledge greetings so continuously that his right hand seemed to be rising and falling in perpetual motion.

The commander of the army occupied a large tent, through the open flap of which men passed in and out in a steady stream. Dunois sat on a stool with a stalk of wheat in his mouth and a tame pigeon on his shoulder. There were maps everywhere: on the ground, attached to the sides of the tent, on the backs of chairs.

"Well, Jaquet!" said the commander, nodding to the new arrival. "Have you come to witness the great victory my knights are gabbling about?"

Coeur took possession of a stool opposite him. His face had assumed an air of gravity. "I came, Bastard, because I heard things which disturbed me. I had reports of large bodies of our troops at Elbeuf, at Amfreville, even as far south as Beaumesnil. I heard of scattered operations north of the river, as far away as Pontoise and Gisors."

Dunois turned his head so carefully that the pigeon did not take alarm. He picked up a map and handed it to the Moneyman. "The crosses marked in red indicate where detachments of troops still linger." He smiled to himself and asked, "What conclusions have you drawn from these reports?"

"That the concentration you ordered before Rouen has not been carried out."

Dunois gave a nod. "Are you a master of military wisdom as well as everything else?"

"My servant Nicolas allows me no chance to feel any pride in myself; I wear him, in fact, like a hair shirt. He says I believe myself to have the boldness of Alexander the Great, the military sagacity of Belisarius, the leadership of Caesar, the personal courage of Bertrand du Guesclin." Coeur had been speaking in a light tone but at this point his expression changed to one of complete gravity. "I make no such claims. I'm a merchant, a man of peace. But this much I have no hesitation in saying: I have some knowledge of strategy, enough to know when things are going wrong. . . . Do you expect to get the concentration completed in time?"

Dunois answered in a quiet voice. "They have affairs of their own to attend to, my fine knights. There are personal estates to be redeemed. Castles to be retaken. Ladyloves who beg not to be deserted. They are brave, but of what use is courage if no sense of discipline goes with it? They had their orders to join me here at once but they'll arrive in their own good time." He shook his head with sudden rancor. "We promised the King, you and I, that Rouen would be in his hands before the first snows fell. We have swept across Normandy without a single check. It has been one victory after another. But now I have little hope of making good our solemn assurance to our liege lord."

"Are the English in strength in the city?"

"Somerset and Talbot are both there. They're bitter hard fighters. Their forces are small but I can't risk defeat by attacking them with the strength now at my disposal."

Jacques Coeur did not put into words the angry thoughts which filled his mind. Was the triumphant march of the lilies of France to be interrupted by a nobility which held itself above obedience to orders? Riding through the camp a few minutes before he had seen the bodies of soldiers dangling from trees, some with willicoats wrapped around them as a sign that they had been hanged for rape, others with the entrails of sheep to show that their offence had been the pillage of the countryside. The thought ran through his mind, "If Dunois would hang a few nobles for disobedience, we would soon win this war."

Dunois asked a question. "And now, my master of strategy, what would you do if you were in my place?"

Coeur accepted the challenge promptly. "Many times I've stood at the Beauvoisine Gate in Rouen and looked at the walls of Le Petit-Appui against the skyline. If I were you I would treat Somerset and Talbot to a demonstration. I would concentrate the power of our cannon against the castle and blow it to pieces before their eyes. I would demolish it so thoroughly that the Englishmen would realize the fate awaiting Rouen if they were foolhardy enough to hold out."

The commander leaned over and gave him a pat on the shoulder. "Jean Bureau left me not more than an hour ago. I made that suggestion to him. We discussed it at some length and—we decided it would be impossible. You see, Moneyman, we lack cannon at the moment and we're short of bombardiers to handle them."

The Moneyman looked aghast at this information. "I was of the opinion that Jean Bureau was well equipped and organized for the whole campaign. What has gone wrong?"

"The smiths who cast the cannon have been at fault. The barrels show a tendency to crack and explode. Bureau has lost forty of them in the last month. Each time this happens half-a-dozen gunners are killed. The result? There is now a scarcity of trained handlers and the few who remain alive are becoming wary. They've no appetite left for serving in the pits. . . . I've little hope, Jacques Coeur, that Bureau could accomplish the reduction of Le Petit-Appui if I gave him orders to try."

The Moneyman gnawed his underlip in concentrated thought. Finally he asked a question. "Tell me, Bastard, is there no way of discovering when the bore of a gun is flawed?"

"Yes. When a gun has been fired and smoke is seen issuing from a crack in the barrel, it can be taken for granted that the next time it is discharged it will blow itself to pieces. But often when there is a crack all the smoke escapes through the muzzle and the touchhole and so no warning is given; and it is fired again, and it explodes, and the souls are freed from the bodies of many gunners."

"But," said Coeur, frowning thoughtfully, "if some way could be found to close the muzzle and the touchhole, then the smoke would find its way to any crack, and due warning would be given."

"Quite true. But how, Moneyman, would you go about closing them?"

"It would have to be done by hand. A man would be stationed at each end with cloths ready to wad into the hole as soon as the gun had been fired. There's no other way in which it could be done."

"And these unfortunate men would have to stay beside the cannon when it was fired instead of running for shelter. It would be sure death for them. Could you hope to find men who would volunteer for this suicidal part?"

After a moment's further consideration Coeur asked, "Are you content to have me see what I can arrange in this matter?"

"You have my full consent."

Coeur got to his feet. He had been in the saddle since sunrise and he was stiff and weary. In spite of his desperate need for rest, he delayed to ask another question. "When the King rides into Rouen in triumph, will the bombardiers have positions of special honor in the procession in recognition of the great part they've played?"

"I'm not sure," answered Dunois, "that the nobles will consent to the bombardiers riding in the procession. In the first place the good knights are still against the use of cannon. They refuse to see that all our victories have been won by blowing the walls down around the ears of Godon garrisons. In the second place, they abide by rules. There is no rule to say what position in a victory procession should be assigned to men who demean themselves by winning battles in new ways; hence the real victors will find themselves excluded."

The Moneyman began to speak in low and impassioned tones. "I'm the son of a merchant. You are the illegitimate son of a prince. Both of us have suffered from certain hardships and limitations because of this and I think we may open our hearts to each other in full confidence. Bastard, has it ever occurred to you that this is an absurd and topsy-turvy world? For a hundred years France has been beaten by a much weaker country. Have you thought that the Code of Chivalry is to blame? And consider how much trouble is caused because all honors and responsibilities are given to men without any consideration of their qualifications! They may be stupid and treacherous and corrupt but they are their fathers' sons. That is the only point to be considered, and so these oxheads, these vain peacocks, are given the power to govern and control justice and fight wars. These knights who are delaying you now wouldn't be in command of troops if it depended on their fitness to command."

When Dunois smiled at his vehemence but did not volunteer any comment, the Moneyman concluded, "We live in a wrong-headed world, Bastard, which worships blood and respects brawn but sees something vulgar in brains."

"You are uttering rank heresy, Moneyman," said the commander. "In fact, there's a smack of treason in what you've just said. I should refuse to listen to you. But," indulging himself in a smile, "as we are speaking in confidence, I may tell you that sometimes I think what a pleasure it would be to sell all my knights on the hoof. They should bring a good price in the market."

2

Jacques Coeur was given an old mill on the edge of the encampment for the use of himself and his party. In addition to Nicolas and two other servants, there was a scrivener and a neat little individual with a beard trimmed to a point who looked exactly what he was, a learned man from the University. It was to the latter that the Moneyman addressed himself as he glanced up through an opening in the ceiling into the black cavern of the mill above.

"My good Ferrand, this is a dusty hole and full of drafts. But it offers us shelter and we must make the best of it."

The room in which they found themselves was small and filled with spare querns. An opening in the floor led to a subterranean region through which water was rushing. Ferrand de Cordule said with a suggestion of a shudder: "I've a great fear of drowning and so it would be impossible for me to sleep down here. I will be almost equally uncomfortable above. There are, I think, bats. I've always had an aversion to bats and owls."

His suspicions were confirmed by a sound of rustling and a sudden trill from far up in the blackness. The scholar shuddered as he began to climb the ladder.

"If those who say you've made a compact with the Prince of Evil were to hear that," commented Coeur, with a laugh, "they would declare it was no earthly sound. Don't let it disturb your slumbers for tomorrow I expect much work from you."

Ferrand de Cordule stopped climbing and looked down over his shoulder. "I must confess, my lord Coeur," he said, "that I don't understand your desire to have these plans completed so rapidly." He had a packet of papers under one arm and he held them out as he spoke. "The war has just begun. It may be years before you can build the shops for which I'm drawing plans with such feverish haste."

"You're wrong, my friend. The war will soon be over. But even if it were to last for years, there would still be little enough time for all the things I want to do." He crossed the floor and looked up at the man of science. "War destroys old wealth and creates new. When peace finally comes to France, men will have gold in their purses and a desire in their minds to spend it on the blessings of peace and ease. We must be ready to take advantage of that when the time comes."

"But I fail to see——"

"You are a scholar. You know how to make steel. You know how to erect large buildings. But, my good Ferrand, you know nothing whatever about commerce and money. Less than nothing; because you have notions in your head which are wrong. Now I, I am a man of trade. When I look over those papers of yours, I know that a triangle means fire, a cross and arrow iron, a circle and dot gold—but otherwise they are a mystery to me. I can't make head or tail of your charts and plans. But—I know as much about money and its curious habits as you do of Vases and Philosophic Eggs and Athanors and Puffers. And I am telling you this out of the knowledge I have: For a year at least, after peace comes, France will be drunk with prosperity."

"It is true," said the scientist, "that I'm not familiar with the ways of commerce. But it would seem to me that the time to take advantage of prosperity is when prosperity is upon us."

"You will be startled at what I am going to say," declared Coeur. "I'm preparing to double the number of my shops. I must see that they are stocked with a wider assortment of goods. I must add at least two ships to my eastern fleet. I must build a new fleet to sail the northern seas and trade with the Hanseatic ports. In addition to that, Ferrand de Cordule, I must start to make goods myself, to have forges running and fires blazing and workmen by the thousands wearing the heart-and-shell device on their sleeves. And that is the part which concerns you. I look to you to build me the shops and forges I shall need."

"All this will take a great deal of gold," suggested Ferrand de Cordule.

"And I have little gold left at the moment. It's a strange position for me to find myself in—I, Jacques Coeur, whose coffers have always bulged with it. The war is proving more costly than I estimated. But—it matters not at all. My credit, with victory in sight, is so good that I can raise any amount I need."

The Moneyman had taken to pacing up and down the dusty room. "Draw me the plans!" he exclaimed. "You still seem to doubt if it can be done. *A Vaillants Coeurs Rien Impossible!* Because men have labored singly over little forges to make bars of steel no thicker than the blade of a sword, must we always be content to work that way? I want workshops so long that from one end you won't be able to see the tilt hammers at the other. I want forges so large the fires in them will blaze like the pit itself. I have the mines and the ore now. Here in Normandy and in Bretagne and in Berri and Le Nivernais."

"Must I finish them tonight?" asked De Cordule mildly. "Or will you permit me to point out that we have been in the saddle all day and are sadly in need of rest?"

Coeur laughed. "I don't think I'm ever unreasonable in my demands. All I ask you to do is to finish the plans for me in half the time it would take anyone else."

"I can only say that I'll do my best." Ferrand de Cordule disappeared into the blackness above.

Dunois had ordered that sentries be placed about the mill. They could hear the one in front singing as he paced up and down. He had a deep voice which he was raising in a hunting song:

"Of St. Hubert I sing, and the blaze and the brach hound,
Red drips the blood from the tusks of the boar . . ."

He was interrupted at that point and they could hear him asking questions of a new arrival. A moment later the door swung open and Pregent Kennedy entered, dressed in the black uniform of the bombardiers. He remained in the doorway, blinking his eyes in the light of the torches.

"Welcome, Sir Scot," said Coeur, who had stretched himself out on the top stone of a quern for lack of a chair. "I've waited a long time for your report."

"You compel me to an admission, my lord Coeur," said Kennedy, in a tone which indicated reluctance on his part. "I've never mastered the art of writing. Is it a matter for shame? I will tell you that few men of high rank in my own Scotland can do anything with letters. They make their cross and that is all."

"It's equally true of France. No apologies are called for, Sir Scot."

"Not being able to write you, I was on the point of seeking you out when I heard that the bombardiers were being organized and trained. It was clear to me that it was more necessary to give my services there. I threw in with them at once and it was a good thing, my lord, that I did. They were a poor lot when I joined. I said to them, 'It's cannoneers I will make of you or may Master Clootie catch me on the prongs of his fork.' But I couldn't train bombardiers and seek out my lord Coeur at the same time; and so my report to you had to wait."

"Your decision was sound. Nothing has been lost through the delay." Coeur motioned to the servants to withdraw, which they did by climbing the ladder, and then he nodded his head at the Scot. "I'm all ears for what you have found in this matter."

"I went straight to the village you named. There was little to be learned there beyond what you already knew. When survivors began to creep back to the village, there was left only blackened walls and burned fields. They hid themselves in the ruins like rats and all they had to eat was the bark of trees and the frozen stalks of cabbages. Few of them lived through it. In the village today there are no more than five people who have any memory of the raid; and of these five none has any suspicion of the existence of our little mademoiselle."

"Up to this point," declared Coeur, "I find your report completely satisfactory."

The Scot nodded slowly. "Even had they an inkling of the truth," he said, "it is clear, my lord Coeur, they would never connect this mysterious survivor with—with a certain Mademoiselle de Voudrai."

Coeur frowned at him. "Have you seen fit," he demanded, "to carry your investigations beyond the instructions I gave you?"

"I have ears to hear."

"Is it in your mind to emulate the thirty young men of Timnath and plow with my heifer?"

The Scot did not seem in any sense disturbed by the harshness of the Moneyman's tone. He proceeded, as usual, to give an upward twirl to the ends of his mustache. "Scotland is a grand country in all respects save one," he said. "It is poor. A man may be born with a single shilling and die with the same shilling in his pouch—and not a second one to keep it company. If I'm to fatten my purse, I must do it before returning to my native heath."

"I intend to employ you in other matters and to pay you what you are worth."

The Scot indulged in a bleak smile. "If you do that, my lord, you will pay me a great deal of siller." He nodded his head slowly several times. "That's all I need to know. If you intend to continue the pleasant little gratuities, I shall serve you faithfully and—with the utmost discretion."

"Go on with your story, if you please."

Kennedy proceeded to tell in full detail of his search. It had been necessary for him to act with unusual caution but he had uncovered one fact which in his opinion pointed to the solution without any doubt. The oldest of the survivors, a baker whose oven had escaped the fire, recalled that a young wife in the village had been serving as foster mother to an infant from outside at the time of the raid. This young woman was described by the baker as "a roomy heifer who brought her own calves into the world once a year without fail and lost them all."

The foster child, however, had displayed more vitality, surviving the perils of its first year and dying by violence (as the baker confidently asserted) with the woman when the Free Companies burned the village.

"Does the baker know who the real parents were?" asked Coeur.

Kennedy gave a negative shake of the head. "On the contrary, my lord, he's sure that no one in the village knew, not even the foster parents. The woman, who was a wanton glaverer about most things, never had a word to say about the child; which seems proof that she knew nothing herself. It was certain that the couple were being paid well. The husband bought a cider press and a brood sow and the woman wore a new tunic of fine green Flemish cloth about the village. The real parents must have been people of substance, my lord."

"I've never had any doubts on that score. The girl herself is the proof." Coeur looked sharply at his companion. "You have more to tell me, I think."

Kennedy indulged in a slow wink. "Aye, that I have. What would you say if I told you that about the time the child was delivered to the foster mother, a young gentleman who lived in that district fought a duel with a nobleman from the south over the attentions of the latter to his sister?"

"My interest would be aroused but I would wait for more details."

"Quite properly, my lord Coeur. I never myself make the mistake of jumping to conclusions on scanty evidence. But listen to this! The sister had given birth to a child out of wedlock. As her lover was a married man, her shame could not be covered by marriage. The brother was killed in the duel and the lover was never seen in those parts afterward."

"It might be a coincidence," said Coeur thoughtfully. "But most certainly it's an interesting one."

"Aye, it is interesting." Kennedy gave his head a wag. "It's more than a coincidence, my lord. The duel was fought in a town less than a dozen miles from the village. It occurred a month after the birth of the child which in the meantime had vanished, though it was known in the town that a foster mother had been found for it. Everything fits together."

"What of the poor mother?"

"She felt her disgrace as much as might be expected. She died soon afterward. The circumstances of her death were—quite distressing, my lord Coeur."

"I am inclined to think," declared Coeur, after some moments of reflection, "that you have probed to the root of the matter. But there are important details still to be explained. You have mentioned no names."

"The mother's name was Céleste de Lansanne. The family was noble but poor. There were a dozen brothers and sisters at one time but only one has survived, a brother who has the estates, such as they are. I found him less communicative than a gravestone, my lord; for on a stone, after all, you find names and dates and sometimes indications of the character of the deceased. He told me nothing. He had mean little eyes, set close together, and his mouth jerked so much as he listened to me that I wondered at first if he had critters in his beard. He heard what I had to say and then motioned to the door."

"You got no confirmation from him?"

"Not a thing, my lord. I wasn't surprised. He had to consider that I might be seeking to make claims on the estate. He looked frightened when I demanded to know the name of the father. I'm disposed to think the father was a man of some consequence."

"Is it your opinion, then, that no one will ever make any move in the matter?"

"That is my opinion."

"And you've told me everything?"

"Everything, my lord."

Coeur seemed reluctant to accept this assurance. "I know you for a goundry rogue, Pregent Kennedy," he said. "How can I be sure you aren't holding something back?"

Kennedy drew himself up with an air of injured pride. "You have my word. Is that not enough? Then let me tell you that I am fond of the lass. I would do nothing to hurt her."

Coeur looked at him curiously. "I believe you mean it. I had to be sure because I also am fond of her and I want nothing to stand in the way of ascertaining the truth. When the war is over we'll go into the matter again. There will be ways of persuading this brother to tell us what he knows. In the meantime, Monsieur Kennedy, I depend on you to keep a still mouth."

3

The knights who had joined the bombards were making their headquarters in a small inn on the outskirts of the town around which the army was encamped. Escorted there by Pregent Kennedy, the Moneyman found the place filled with young men, some of them so very young that their cheeks had never known the scrape of a razor. They had discarded armor and were sitting around in the ease of loose tunics. As befitted men who fought in the stife of the guns, they were dressed in black from head to foot and, at first glance, seemed a somber company, an impression quickly dispelled by the eagerness of their eyes and the steady clack of their tongues.

"Look at them!" said the Scot pridefully. "Have you ever seen the equal of them, my lord?" He laid a hand on Coeur's arm. "Listen to them. Can you make head or tail of it?"

The words being bandied back and forth had no meaning at all for Jacques Coeur. He heard references to *tampions* and *fireballs* and *munions* and such expressions as *easing the orgues* and *sighting with the dispart*. The general discussion seemed to be concerned with the advantages of bronze over iron.

"My lords," said Kennedy, raising his voice until it could be heard over the din, "I bring you company tonight. This, my brave young men, is Jacques Coeur."

All conversation stopped and every head in the room came around on the instant. Alert eyes fixed themselves on the man who had made the resumption of hostilities possible. For a single second there was silence in the low-raftered room, and then an unexpected thing happened. With one accord the young knights got to their feet and cheered. They cheered so loudly that it sounded almost like a salute from one of their guns. They waved their goblets above their heads and shouted eager greetings to the Moneyman. The nearest thumped him heartily on the back, crying, "Here is our good Jacques!" A voice from the rear of the room shouted, "Buy us bronze barrels and plenty of good corned powder, and we'll blow the Godons back across the Channel."

Coeur waved to them. "When France is freed, we will have the bombardiers to thank for it!"

"The bombardiers and Jacques Coeur! The winning combination for France—the purse of Coeur and the guns of Bureau!"

Looking about him, Coeur saw that the common room of the inn had taken on the color of the company. Instead of lances and battle-axes on the walls, it had elevation bolts and missel rings and wooden fids. Hanging from a rafter was a copper hinge with a placard attached on which was lettered, "All that was left of the gates of Ourges after a direct hit." Another placard read, "Our pledges are not to fair ladies but to our country," and beside it, to lend significance, dangled one of the black patches which knights wore to denote vows.

Finding that the attention of the company had transferred itself elsewhere, the Moneyman took a seat with the Scot at a table near the end of the room. From there he watched what was happening with a lively interest. Plenty of drinking was being done but a certain ritual was invariably observed. The Knights of the Guns (as they called themselves) would stand up in line with arms linked in such a way that each man could drink from the goblet of his neighbor on the right. One would cry, *"Nous y voici!"* and the rest would say, *"En aval!"* as they emptied the goblets at one draught. Anyone who paused for breath was compelled to pay for the next round.

To add to the confusion in the crowded room, they had attached a hangman's noose above the main door of the inn and one of their number, keeping hold of the end, would let it drop around the shoulders of each new arrival. A quick pull on the rope would draw it tightly around the neck, and the shouts of laughter which greeted each successful operation were loud enough to drown out the scream of surprise and pain from the victim. When no victims presented themselves, two of the knights would sally out into the street, seize a passer-by, and propel him within by force.

D'Arlay came down the stairs soon after Coeur's arrival. He also was in black but he had succeeded in giving himself an air of elegance by a black plume in his cap and the use of onyx buttons on his doublet and in the tufts of his sleeves.

When he saw Coeur he waved a hand in greeting and walked over to the table where the latter was sitting.

"I was told a moment ago that you had arrived in camp," he said. "I'm more than happy to see you because you may know a way out of the difficulty in which we find ourselves."

"I know all about it," answered Coeur. "I've already seen Dunois. We hit upon a plan which may solve the matter."

He began to explain his belief that the loss of life could be prevented by packing the ends of the cannon after each discharge. D'Arlay listened intently and agreed at once that it was worth trying. He would see Jean Bureau in the morning, he said, and discuss the plan with him.

He added, however, that some very special inducement would have to be found to get the men into the mood to try anything so risky. Their courage had not been equal to the severe tests of the past few weeks.

After the matter had been thoroughly debated, D'Arlay looked at the Moneyman with an air of some reluctance and asked a question, "What word have you of Valerie?"

"Nothing for weeks. In the last letter from the Comtesse she said they were both well." Coeur studied D'Arlay with so much intentness that the latter began to wonder as to the reason. "Are you as much against me in this as ever?"

D'Arlay answered emphatically: "I am. My feeling, in fact, has increased."

"Then you'll understand my reluctance to answer your question. How do I know to what lengths you may permit this antagonism of yours to go, my dear Robin? You have a touch of the zealot in you, of the fanatic even. You might—— Well, it isn't necessary to speculate as to what you might do. Tell me this: when you saw the Comtesse last, did she give you any information?"

"She said nothing."

"There you are. She is a woman of discretion. Much as she likes you, she saw good reason for leaving you in the dark."

"She was right—and you also," said D'Arlay. "As I'm against you, I can't expect to be taken into your confidence."

Coeur asked suddenly, "You are very fond of the little cousin?"

After some hesitation D'Arlay nodded his head. "Yes. I am—I am very fond of her."

"Your fondness perhaps had something to do with your refusal of the King's ward?"

"I'm afraid so." A sigh accompanied the answer. "I saw the choice of our liege lord and she was—quite a nice child and rather pretty. I think she would have proven dull and prim; but that, after all, wouldn't have weighed much in the balance. I should have agreed to the match. But every time I tried to bring myself to the point of expressing my willingness, I would think of Valerie—and my resolution would weaken and disappear. I realize how foolish and wrong-headed I was about it. I've lost the best match in the proffer of the King. I've gained the royal dislike. And the great folly of it is that I know I must marry a fortune sooner or later."

"You've no idea that someday you may marry the little cousin?"

D'Arlay shook his head sadly. "No, Jacques, I've known from the start the impossibility of that."

Then, quite abruptly, Coeur began to laugh. He reached out and gave his companion's arm a vigorous shove. "My good friend, I've no fear of your attitude in the matter. I was—do you know how the Coquillards put it?—I was *tozing your ribs*. I would gladly tell you everything, knowing that you would never betray my confidence, if there was anything to tell. As a matter of fact, Robin, I may"—he leaned forward to add in a dramatic whisper—*"I may not go any further with it!"*

D'Arlay was too startled to make any comment immediately although the look on his face showed that he was delighted beyond measure. After a moment the Moneyman proceeded with an explanation.

"It's not that I've suffered a sentimental weakening. I have a streak of sentiment in me, as you've probably noticed, but I hold it sharply under control when it comes to matters of importance. The truth is that I may not need her. The war is being won and I seem to be getting my full share of the credit—in some quarters at least. The King has never been more cordial or more dependent on me. I always had a great reluctance to the idea, which was not mine as you will recall." He paused and then proceeded to sum up briskly: "It comes to this, then, that I'm not sure it will be necessary to proceed to the point of carrying out the plan. I may be content to—to consider that I have a weapon in reserve, for use if the need becomes great enough. I'll see to it, of course, that no one will suffer in the meantime. Our little Valerie can remain in the De Burey household and I will continue generous in my support."

"Have you told them of this?"

Coeur shook his head. "No, no! I haven't committed myself. I must always maintain a safe line of retreat. How can I tell what the future may bring?"

D'Arlay said in a fervent tone: "Jacques, my friend! I'm so happy I can't find words to tell you how deep my feelings go."

Alain de Kersai joined them when a supper of roasted boar's head and cold fish was served. "If my lord Coeur cares to listen to the talk one hears where Knights of the Guns assemble," he said, with an earnest air, "he may find cause for surprise."

"What is the nature of the talk?"

"It is new. In fact, my lord, we sometimes speak of ourselves as the New Men. It began when the Sire d'Arlay fought with my cousin, Jacques de Lalain, and got the better of him. Everyone started to speak then about the new weapon, the light sword. We didn't stop at that. We thought that times were changing and we were all in favor of the things we saw coming. We realized, my lord, that my cousin Jacques belonged to the past."

"That is true." Coeur nodded his head gravely.

"We're all rather amused over the follies of the past. Chivalry? It has been the absurdity of the ages."

The Moneyman, who had been finding it hard not to smile, became suddenly quite serious. "I'm very much interested, Alain," he said. "You see, I've felt that way about things for a long time. I've made no secret of it. You and the New Men will live perhaps to see great changes."

"To us, my lord Coeur, you are a symbol of the new age. You are a man of the people and yet you've risen to a place in the councils of the King. *You* don't believe the world so perfect now that any thought of altering it is wicked. That is what Jacques de Lalain and his sort think."

"No," affirmed Coeur seriously, "I don't believe the world to be perfect as it is. I'm doing what I can to change it."

"We've often said that," declared the boy excitedly. "In this very room we've talked about you and we've agreed that what you are doing is right. We are revolutionary in our ideas, my lord. Even you might be shocked at some of the things we believe."

"I doubt it, Alain de Kersai," said Coeur, with a smile. "You see, I am revolutionary in my ideas also."

Chapter II

I

THE WHITE ANTELOPE and red roses floated over the keep of Le Petit-Appui and so Coeur knew that the English were still holding out. He stood up in his stirrups and gazed down into the enclosure where the guns were voicing their demands for the capitulation of the garrison. Smoke belched up over the wattled wall.

There were half-a-dozen large bombards in action, raising their snouts from the great frames of oak, in which they were bedded, like the heads of serpents protruding from a pit. They were being fired in turn, and the work of reloading began almost as soon as the smoke ceased to erupt from the muzzles. That the unloading was slow was owing to the cumbersome nature of the machines and not to any lack of energy on the part of the men serving them. The latter moved with furious speed, darting about on the gravel floor like devil's attendants skipping on the edge of the Pit—an effect heightened by their close-fitting black jerkins and hoods. They had to place powder in iron chambers separate from the bombards, carry these to the lower end of the tubes and clamp them tight with iron stirrups, and then set trains of the explosive to burning on the tops of the barrels. When the flames began to travel with a loud crackle like fire spreading across stubble, all work was suspended. The men in black, with the exception of two of their number, ran to places of safety behind a tall barrier. The pair who remained at their posts went into furious action as soon as the explosion was over, one rushing to the cannon's mouth, the other to the touchhole, to wrap the apertures with thick folds of felt.

The Moneyman smiled with pride. His plan had been put into practice and had solved the difficulty which a few days before had threatened to silence the guns. As a result, a large breach had already been opened in the outer wall of the castle and the bombards were now pouring their shot against the massive gray barbican. The English would have to give in soon.

He rode up to a young knight who sat his horse outside the entrance to the enclosure. "How long is the bombardment to last?"

"One more round, my lord," answered the knight. Then he stood up in his stirrups and waved his arms, cheering wildly. "A hit!" he cried. "A hit! A clean hit! Saw you ever a shot to equal it, my lord?"

A bombardier had raised his gun to the limit of its elevation (it had seemed, in fact, to be pointing at the sky), and the resulting shot had soared over the castle walls. By pure accident it had cut the pole which carried the flag of the defenders. The antelope and roses fell out of sight.

Other knights had been posted on horseback at intervals along the rise of ground. They now came riding up excitedly. The black flag with green lilies, which waved above the enclosure while the guns were being used, came sliding down; and men with blackened faces climbed over the top of the wattled wall and rushed up the grade to see the results of this miraculous shot. They jumped and danced and exchanged ecstatic slaps on the back. They began a song, "Poor Harry Sixt'" (for Henry of England was already showing signs of mental instability), which French soldiers liked to throw in the faces of the invaders.

Coeur took the first knight by the arm and drew him to one side. "Where is the Sire d'Arlay?" he asked.

"There," pointing down into the pit. "The one removing the wadding from the muzzle of the first gun. He'll be up in a few minutes. The guns will need half an hour to cool off."

When D'Arlay appeared, the Moneyman found it hard to recognize him. His friend's face was as black as a smith's, his hands were burned and covered with powder stains, his clothes were scorched and ragged. He raised his arms in front of him as though in self-defense. "No lecture, if you please," he said. "I weary of explaining my reasons for this."

"I've had the explanation already. None of the men were ready to risk their lives and so you thought it necessary to set an example. After which enough of them came forward to keep the guns well manned again. I heard all about it last night."

"Did you hear that the Scot, Pregent Kennedy, was the next man to offer himself? The pair of us still work together, a belted knight and a former captain of Free Companions doing the work of common men. A matter for much scandalized comment. I confess that my opinion of the Scot has climbed sky high."

"Do you know that at court your action is considered proof of madness rather than courage?"

"I'm aware that they laugh at me and say I'm a dangerous crackpot," said D'Arlay, his blackened face widening in a smile. "It doesn't matter. I don't care what they think."

"What brought me here today," Coeur said, "was to convince you that you needn't go on with this. You've shown the way and the guns are booming again. You've had more than your share of risks."

D'Arlay shook his head. "I'm not a bellwether. What would they say, the brave fellows who take as much risk as I do, if I left them now? No, I offered to tend one of the guns and I must go on. It may not be much longer. I predict that Le Petit-Appui will capitulate tomorrow and after that the English may decide it's useless to hold out any longer in Rouen. The war will be over if they do."

"It's true," said Coeur, "that the English leaders were showing a desire to discuss terms with us. But when some of the citizens of Rouen tried to let us in at a weak point in the walls, old Talbot came roaring up with a handful of men and gave our scaling party a warm welcome. We took a costly beating. Since then the English haven't talked about terms. Old Talbot is a seasoned fighter and he boasts that he has never laid down his arms. It's quite likely he may decide to fight it out here to the last man."

From where they stood they could see the French forces camping along an undulating ridge. Fires had been built at intervals for warmth as the wind was from the north and the air had turned raw. The sound of bugles reached them, thin in the distance but full, nevertheless, of the urgency of war. From the look of things a great army lay there, waiting the order to strike; but Coeur knew this was because of the craft

Dunois had shown in his dispositions. Many needed companies were still missing.

Coeur laid a hand on his companion's arm. "Listen closely, Robin," he whispered. "The concentration isn't yet complete. If the English get an inkling of how weak we are, they'll decide to fight. . . . We aren't as close to the end as you think. You've done more than enough here. Wash that black off your face, have the surgeon attend to the burns on your hands, and be ready to ride on with me to see Dunois. I've talked to him and he wants to use you in more fitting ways than this."

D'Arlay shook his head. "You've convinced me I should stay here. We must reduce Le Petit-Appui quickly. That's the one way to make Talbot see reason, and the sooner we start the guns talking again, the better our chances will be. Until the castle falls, Jacques, I must remain at my post."

Pregent Kennedy joined them, walking with a limp, one hand going through the motions of curling a mustache end which had been burned away long before. He seemed blacker and more ragged even than D'Arlay. "You find us at our worst," he said. "In another hour or so—provided, of course, we—er, continued to survive—we would have succeeded in removing some of this filth. You have observed, no doubt, that none of the usual trappings of heroism go with serving the guns. Could you tell us from a pair of overworked chimney sweeps, my lord Coeur, or scarecrows left out for the winter in a cropped field?"

Coeur could not refrain from smiling as he inspected the grotesque figure of the Scot. "This is the first time I've seen you without a tartan somewhere on your person."

"Aye," agreed Kennedy in a gloomy tone. "I assure you that I feel undressed without my colors; but truly it would be a sorry thing to subject them to the devil's stife in which we spend our days. I lay this injunction on you, my lord: that if I'm killed, no matter where or when, and even if it's hard to find much that remains of the mortal guise of Pregent Kennedy, you will see to it that I'm buried in a proper and honorable grave—and that my tartan is draped about me."

"I will consider it a sacred obligation to do as you wish."

"Thank you, my lord. And also I thank you for the grateful and costly wine which you keep on our table. We toast your health in it every night."

As they talked, Coeur's eyes had been busy, darting along the French line and from there to the road which ran on to Rouen. It was clear that he was not pleased with what he saw.

"Does it seem to you," he asked his two companions, "that our line is thinly held hereabouts? Even more thin than at any other part?"

The Scot nodded his head. "Aye, my lord. It seems as thin to me as kilts in a wintry blast. And I'll tell you the reason. They still have it in their heads that it's devil's work we're doing here, sorcery or witchcraft or any evil name you care to put to it. They prefer to keep well to the wind of us."

"Do your neighbors ever visit you? Do they come over to watch the guns in action?"

"Not a mother's son of them has been near us. They jeer at us and call us imps of Satan and powderpolls. They cross themselves or hold their noses when we pass."

"Who are in command of the troops on each side of you?"

D'Arlay answered. "Jehan de Mottes on the right. Enguerrard de Tencon on the left."

Coeur received this information with a rueful look. "Two gallant knights," he said. "If it had been a matter of deliberate intent, we couldn't have picked two commanders more certain to fight in accordance with the dictates of chivalry—nor more certain to lose the day for France! Kind Father in Heaven, save me from the likes of Jehan de Mottes and Enguerrard de Tencon!" He shook his head back and forth in a mood of deep apprehension. "I'm not sure you could count on those two stiff-necked fools to lend a hand if the English attacked the guns!"

He continued to study the French position with growing discontent. "This isn't the planning of Dunois. He has to make the most of spare numbers but he would never leave his guns exposed so openly. Where is Jean Bureau?"

"At the headquarters of my lord Dunois," answered D'Arlay.

The Moneyman took a turn or two along the slope of the ridge. Then he pointed to the Rouen road. "Look!" he commanded. "Tell me what you see."

"Very little," said D'Arlay. "The air lacks clearness this afternoon. With a good light we can sometimes see the outline of the Beauvoisine Gate. But not today."

"We can see no more than half the distance today. Suppose that an English force suddenly appeared from the side road to the right? Suppose it headed at full speed in this direction? Would there be time for Jehan de Mottes and Enguerrard de Tencon to get their men to horse? Would there be time even to convince those two valiant blockheads of their duty? Or to get word to my lord Dunois of your plight?"

D'Arlay measured the distance with his eye. "No," he said, "there would be no time for anything except to rally to our own defense. It might prove a serious disaster for the arms of France."

"Go at once," urged Coeur, "to the man in command during the absence of Bureau. Point out the danger to him. Make him see we must take steps at once, that messengers must be sent to Jehan de Mottes and Enguerrard de Tencon. They must be told you have reason to expect an attack in force and that they will be needed—promptly and in full strength! Arrange a signal with them. You are higher here and would see the English first. A red flag flying on that knoll ahead of us will tell them the foe has been sighted." He kept his eye fixed on the Rouen road as he talked. "Never have I been more sure of anything than about this. Talbot is too good a soldier to give in without making one effort to silence our guns. Conditions at the moment are perfect for an attack." His voice raised to a high note of urgency. "Make haste, D'Arlay! There's no time to be lost!"

2

Jehan de Mottes had answered the messenger sent to him earlier by saying in a gruff voice, "A knight doesn't carry pig's feathers!" which was a common saying at the moment and meant that he considered it beneath him to take any part in operations which involved common men, in this case the bombardiers. Enguerrard de Tencon had made no response at all.

When the guns started the *danse macabre* again—a term often applied to bombardments, referring to the strange rites once practiced in the cemeteries of Paris—and a first suggestion of crumbling began to show in the gray walls of the barbican, Coeur realized that for a matter of at least half an hour he had given no thought to the danger of attack which had seemed to him so imminent before. He forced his mind back to the realities of the situation, knowing that the danger was greater than ever. The responses of the two neighboring commanders made it unlikely that much help, if any, could be expected from them.

He walked to the edge of the mound and shaded his eyes with one hand, the better to see the Rouen road stretching on into the north. There was a haziness in the air which made it impossible to see far. He strained his eyes to study the shadows into which the highway dissolved, and at first he was sure it was imagination which made him fancy he detected movement and changing color. Gradually his conviction veered the other way. There *was* movement. He became certain of it.

Imagination could not supply the flashes of light which he saw regularly and which might be made by the sun striking on armor or on the polished steel of weapons.

His worst fears had been confirmed. An armed party was moving down the road. He could see now the toss of horses' heads and a standard floating in the van. He knew that no French patrols would have ventured that far into enemy territory and so he was certain it was the English.

He began to shout: "To arms! Engloys! To arms!"

A squire sprang into action and planted the red flag as a signal that the enemy had been sighted. Two others started off to warn the neighboring companies, running as fast as their steel-encased legs would carry them. A fourth went forward to the slope where the New Men were waiting the word.

The young knights were already fully accoutered for action and were standing in rows along the top of the ridge, leaning on their upright lances. Their horses, held by squires, pawed the ground in front of them. Behind them were a half-dozen of the mounting platforms which knights used in getting to saddle when weighted down with armor. These consisted of wooden stands. For the heavier knights, however, there was an additional contrivance, a long wooden arm attached to the platform and curved like the ancient slings which had been called trebuckets. At the end of the arm was a steel torret and a hook. When the difficulty of mounting could be overcome in no other way, this hook would be attached to the belt of the weighty knight and the arm would swing him around into his saddle like a crane.

The mounting platforms would not be used. The New Men were light of frame and would need no more than the shoulder of a squire when the signal to mount came.

Jacques Coeur walked along the line until he came to Alain de Kersai. He looked into the face of the young Burgundian and was surprised to see the color in his cheeks and the sparkle of anticipation in his eyes.

"It will be sharp, Alain," he said. "I fear you can't count on any help. Your neighbors are so steeped in the gall of their sacred traditions that they may refuse to aid you."

"All the better," said the boy eagerly. "We want to do this by ourselves, my lord Coeur. If they come over to help, they will claim all the credit for beating the enemy off."

"But the odds will be heavy against you."

Alain de Kersai studied the approaching English for several moments.

They were in clear sight now, a raiding force of considerable size. That they were lightly armed was apparent from the speed at which they rode. Coeur had already concluded from this that their purpose was to make a quick thrust and then get away; but there was no comfort in that, for they could wipe out the bombardiers in the short time they would allow themselves.

"They are no worse than five to one," said Alain. His manner was confident and cheerful.

The Moneyman looked along the line of young faces and saw everywhere the same exultant light, the same eagerness for the conflict. A sense of pity took possession of him. They were all so very young—some of them still looked like pages—so full of high spirits and the joy of living. It was an intolerable thought that they would soon be engaged in a fight to the death with the trained horsemen of the invading troop, that many of them would die under the blows of alien swords or be cut to pieces by the hoofs of maddened horses. He had always considered war a wasteful interruption to life, a cruel and senseless obsession of man. Now he began to realize in fuller measure the stupidity and cruelty of it. He felt a sense of responsibility for what would happen, knowing that but for his urging and his offer of finances the fighting would not have been resumed. "But it had to be!" he said to himself, in a mood which demanded justification. "France was bleeding to death. For each of these boys who die now, thousands of lives will be saved in the future."

"Alain," he said, "I would gladly give everything I possess to spare you this!"

"Would you rob us of our chance?" exclaimed the young knight. "My lord Coeur, this is the duty for which we've been trained—to guard the guns. So far we've had nothing to do, except to ride as escort when the batteries were on the move and stand to arms when a bombardment was on." He pointed excitedly at the English column which had come within a thousand yards or less. "They'll be on us in a few minutes, my lord! This is what we've longed for all these months." He raised his lance and gave it an exultant shake. "We'll show them now that the New Men can fight!"

Coeur glanced desperately to the right and then to the left. There was no sign of preparation on either side. It was certain that the brunt of the attack would be borne unassisted by a small company of green young men. In deep bitterness he realized that the commanders who thus refused to lend their aid would not be accounted cowardly or remiss, that no punishment would be meted out for the deaths of these gallant youths as there had been none for the slaughter of French archers in the lost battles of the war. "They will not carry pig's feathers!" he said aloud. "God grant a way to make them carry for all time the burden of the shame they have earned today!"

"Out of the way!" cried an urgent voice behind him.

The Moneyman hurried out through the ranks. His back was turned when the order was given for the charge. He did not look when the thunder of the action filled his ears, and he saw nothing until the impact of steel on steel drowned out the shouts of the contestants and even the wild screaming of wounded horses. Swinging about, he discovered with a sense of almost guilty relief that he could see from where he chanced to be only a small segment of the battleground. A clump of trees and an outward jutting of rocks closed off the rest. Within his vision, however, were rows of embattled figures on plunging horses. He saw the rise and fall of battle-axes at close range, the tossing of plumes in shiny helmets. He heard sounds which made him wish he could get far enough away to be out of hearing.

Someone ran by him shouting, "Out of the pit, everyone, they'll be here in a minute!" The Moneyman had no idea where he had left his own mount but it did not matter; he had no intention of riding off to safety while the frightful carnage went on below. He heard excited cries from close at hand but otherwise was not aware of company on the ridge until a hand touched his shoulder and a hoarse voice, which he thought was that of Nicolas, said in his ear, "Come, master, while there's yet time!" A horse, with blood streaming down one flank and nostrils flaring wide with fear and pain, came galloping up the slope. A loose piece of harness caught in the branches and the runaway animal was thrown to the ground, crushing someone (it did not seem to matter who) under it. Through it all Coeur was aware that the guns went on firing steadily. "That is D'Arlay's doing," he said to himself. "He's determined to fire as many rounds as possible before the guns are lost."

The sound of battle lessened, then waxed and grew, and lessened again. Then the sound seemed to be coming from farther to the right. Coeur ran forward, tripping over a body and getting to his feet quickly without pausing to identify the victim. He found himself at the edge and looking over at the lower ground held by the troops of Jehan de Mottes. The English had changed their course and were riding hard and fast in that direction.

A few, a very few, of the New Men came riding back up the slope. More came on foot, climbing slowly and with obvious effort. The number returning seemed to Jacques Coeur pitifully small.

3

The talk in and around the large pavilion of Dunois that evening was all of the surrender of Le Petit-Appui, which had taken place at nightfall, and the death of Jehan de Mottes. Out of this rose speculation as to how long Rouen would hold out now that the English leaders knew the full power of the French cannon. It was whispered that already the English had authorized the burgesses of the city to open negotiations. There was a note of jubilation under all the talk and even Dunois was seen to smile.

The Moneyman had gathered the news by the time D'Arlay, well scrubbed and arrayed in his best black clothes, joined him there.

"The story that all these geese are telling and believing," said Coeur, a smoldering fire in his eyes, "is that Jehan de Mottes saved the guns and lost his life. That great ox, who allowed our fine boys to go to their deaths, is being made into a hero! I've tried to tell the real story but no one will listen to me. Here is the way they look at it: The English attacked and were repulsed. Jehan de Mottes was killed in the fighting. He was a knight. *Ergo,* he was responsible for the victory. I've had a dozen quarrels about it already!"

"What did happen?" asked D'Arlay. His hands were bound in black and they seemed to be causing him a great deal of discomfort. He was unable to keep them still.

"My belief is that the English leader didn't think it possible the rest would stand by while he attacked the guns. He suspected a trap and didn't want to drive any farther into our lines. When the young men checked his advance—he could have come on again, of course, after the first few minutes of fighting—he changed his plan. He swung around to his left and paid his respects to Jehan de Mottes in passing. Then, glad to have escaped the trap, he ordered his troop to return. And now we come to the part played by that gallant and honorable paladin, Jehan de Mottes. It seems he didn't have time to get all his armor on. He was fitting his *bavière* into place over his face when an English lance pierced above it. The point, by some queer trick of fate, found the tiny area where his brain was located. And now he will go down in the annals of this war as a hero!"

"Many others died today whose heroism will never be mentioned."

Coeur nodded his head soberly. Then he asked, in a hesitant tone as though he feared the answer, "What was the cost of our victory?"

"A heavy one. I find it hard to speak of it, Jacques. Alain de Kersai didn't come back. Nearly half of those fine lads were killed in three minutes of the most bloody fighting since the start of the Hundred Years' War!"

Chapter III

I

THE MEMBERS of the King's immediate train were eating a fine supper in a sour state of mind. In the center of the table was a roast swan with its body silvered and resting on green-colored pastry. Dunois sat in front of this elaborate but rather inedible dish and winked across its gilded beak at Jacques Coeur who sat on the other side.

Shortly before the company sat down, an English spy had been caught in the courtyard of the castle. His neck being committed to the rope in any event, the islander had boastingly asserted that his purpose had been to kill the three men who were most dangerous to England, whose removal, in fact, would make victory possible again for the invaders. He had named Dunois first, of course; but then he had amazed and chagrined the military leaders and the great knights by passing them over and asserting in a bold and confident voice that the other two were Jacques Coeur and Jean Bureau.

In spite of their mortified feelings, the knights were feasting mightily on three main dishes: roast beef, stewed kid, and chined salmon, and helping themselves to great handfuls of the roast train. All, that is, but Dunois himself. The commander was taking advantage of the fact that they were in Normandy to sup lightly on the rich angelot cheese for which that province was famous, contenting himself otherwise with a thin slab of white bread and a flagon of Malmsley wine diluted with water.

"The spy has been hanged," announced the commander, in a loud enough voice for everyone at table to hear. "It seemed a pity—a man of such rare and sound judgment."

This sally was received in glum silence. The general looked up and down the board with something of the expression of a cat which finds itself surrounded by mice, and reached a hand to the dish containing the feathered quills.

"Is it possible that the English," he began, picking his teeth fastidiously, "who are losing because of the guns are better aware of the importance of them than the French who are winning with them? And touching his thought of my good friend and gossip, the Moneyman——"

A hand touched the shoulder of Jacques Coeur and a respectful voice said in his ear, "His King's Grace desires the presence of my lord Coeur." He rose reluctantly and bowed first to Dunois and then to the rest of the company. He wanted very much to hear what the commander was going to say about his selection by the Englishman whose neck had been stretched. Well, he would hear about it later and so all he would lose was the opportunity to watch the glumly supercilious faces of the knights who were not going to find it to their liking.

The capture of the spy had created an atmosphere of unusual caution in the castle. The corridors, which ordinarily would have been dark and full of shadows, were now so well lighted by torches on the walls that no one could pass through them without being seen by many wary eyes. One captain of guards went to the length of halting the Moneyman and looking him over carefully, muttering in half-apology that one had to remember the uncanny skill spies had at disguise.

The chamber occupied by Charles of France was approached by a steep flight of stone steps at the head of which stood two guards with drawn swords. It was a small tower apartment and so brilliantly lighted that nothing could be concealed within it. On a table in front of the monarch were articles of clothing in a high but orderly pile. Coeur's quick survey told him that there were scarlet hoods and pointed hats of miniver and round beaver hats lined with velvet, not to mention a variety of rich cloaks and tunics. His master, he realized, had been immersed in the task of selecting a costume for his triumphal entry into Rouen.

"Ha, my good Jacques," said Charles, in a contented tone of voice, "I've made up my mind. By St. Martin of Tours, it wasn't easy! I had to be sure my decision was the right one. I shall wear"—the royal eyes lighted up as he reached into the pile and drew out a beaver hat—"this one. It is handsome and it will provide the best base for the crown. I shall change the lining to crimson and have the brim turned up all around."

"I'm sure you've made the right choice, sire."

"The King of Sicily will be on my right hand and my brother of Maine on the other. Behind us will ride"—the King sighed, for he had little liking for any of the trio he proceeded to name—"the three Comtes, St. Pol, De Clermont, and De Nevers. The order in which all my gentlemen ride has been settled to my satisfaction. The Comte de Dunois will head a party to greet me at the Beauvoisine Gate and I am naming you, my friend and counselor, to be at his right."

A sense of sardonic amusement took possession of the mind of the Moneyman. "Can it be that our liege lord doesn't want us in his train because my father was a merchant and the brave Dunois wears the bar sinister? Or does he consider in all honesty of mind that it will be an equal honor to welcome him into the captured city? I have a strong suspicion it's the first."

Charles was addicted to detail. His eyes beamed with satisfaction as he proceeded to enumerate some of the arrangements he had made. "You are to wear crimson. I suggest velvet although you can choose baudekin if your liking runs to that material strongly. Velvet is to be the note of the day—well, make your own selection. The hat, crimson. I advise a sugar-bag shape and I must limit your ornamentation of the brim to seed pearls. Under no circumstances, diamonds; I consider them too ostentatious and, in fact, vulgar. I am trying to prevent the wearing of ostrich feathers but some of my gentlemen have an almost fanatical liking for them which I may find hard to control."

For a quarter of an hour longer he talked about the various arrangements for the great day. Coeur listened without making many comments. Whenever he did drop an amending suggestion his advice was so sound that Charles immediately adopted it. An old seneschal in a green-and-white tabard came in to stir up the fire on the hearth and to replenish the flagon of wine at the King's elbow. It was clear that he was a favored servant for he took it on himself to say, "Your King's Grace, the hour is growing late."

"There are two matters on which I desire your advice, good Jacques," said Charles, motioning impatiently to the seneschal to withdraw. "The first concerns the Lady Agnes. I may tell you, Moneyman, that she's to have another child and her health is not good. I don't accept the opinion of Robert de Poitevin who dins his gloomy predictions into my ears, but I'm forced to believe that she requires the most particular care. In spite of her condition, which makes travel hard for her, I'm ill content to have her far from my person. Now here is the difficulty. My duty will keep me in the field for the winter months. The child will be born in February and I am loth to see nothing of her in the meantime. What do you advise under the circumstances?"

Coeur gave the matter careful thought. He was delighted that the King desired Agnes Sorel near him, for it meant that he also would have the opportunity of seeing her and even of consulting her. He could tell her of the steps he had taken to meet her wishes in the matter of a successor and of the doubts he now entertained as to the need of doing anything more about it. So far he had told her nothing. In fact, he had not had a chance to speak to her for months. He had seen her, of course, on the few occasions when she had appeared at court, but all that had passed between them each time had been a bow from him and a smile from her, with a slight gesture of her thin hand to express her regret that anything more was impossible.

After several moments' thought he raised his head. "Sire," he said, "the terms of the capitulation will clear the English out of much of the province north and west of Rouen. I suggest, therefore, that the lady in question be directed to take up her residence at the Abbey of Jumièges and that she go at once before the winter sets in and—and before her condition will make travel impossible for her. There is a manor house a few miles away at Mesnil-sous-Jumièges which belongs to the abbey and which would provide her with ample room for her attendants. By giving her the manor house, the guest wing at the abbey would be available in case it became advisable for the court to pass any time at Jumièges. As you know, sire, the good fathers of Jumièges are well endowed and have added to their wealth by centuries of industry and thrift. They're in a position to entertain visitors well, even lavishly."

The King nodded his head with instant approval. "An excellent arrangement, my good Jacques. The idea of Jumièges had occurred to me but I wasn't aware of the existence of the manor house. I was afraid that the guest wing, which I have never seen, of course, would be restricted in size and hardly suitable for any—any duality of arrangements. You have removed my doubts and I shall act on the idea at once."

The royal attention then turned itself in another direction. It was apparent that the King was somewhat perturbed. He looked down at his lap and frowned. Finally he said in a hesitant voice: "I sent you, Moneyman, a list of appointments I proposed to make—governors and minor officials for the sections of Normandy which we have succeeded in winning back. You've returned it and I find, to my surprise, that you're suggesting an entirely different list. Is my judgment so faulty? I confess to being irked at your attitude and I'm demanding to know what reasons you can have had for this—this flouting of my wishes and my carefully considered judgments."

Coeur did not indulge in any of the protestations of loyalty and humility which constitute the usual approach to debates with royalty. His relationship with Charles had always been surprisingly direct. As a man of business he would lay the facts before his master and state his views with few reservations. When necessary he would dispute a point as man to man without any attempt to soften the effect of the facts. There had even been a camaraderie of sorts between them, dating back to the days when Charles lived in Bourges and depended on Jacques Coeur for the alleviation of his poverty. The King sometimes called his minister in affectionate tones "My old Jacques!" and the Moneyman would, on occasion, indulge in a facetious salutation which consisted of an oriental bow from the waist and an "Oh, King, live forever!" uttered in exaggerated tones.

The Moneyman lost no time, therefore, in voicing excuses for what he had done. He launched into a justification of his list. "Sire," he said, "I wish to point out first that it will take a great deal of energy and ability on the part of your new officers to set this country to rights. Think, liege lord: many sections have been harried and burned, they have been fought over several times, and the people who are flocking back to claim their lands and houses will be without food. Ways must be found at once to get food in for them, to bring it over roads that are almost impassable. Families have been broken up, and one of the first duties of your officers must be to assist parents in finding lost children and in getting homes for the poor little waifs who live like wild creatures in hedges and the slums of the towns. There will be bitter conflicts over the possession of lands and so there must be cool heads to settle disputes. In short, sire, the men into whose hands you give the reconquered provinces must be capable of restoring order out of chaos in the shortest possible time.

"And now, sire," went on the Moneyman, "look over this list of the men you have selected. I concede they would do certain things very well. They would bring dignity to their posts, they would preside at official banquets with a fine air, and they would see to it that their guests were properly seated. They would conduct tournaments and settle points of dispute between knightly contestants. Some of them might prove capable at collecting taxes and crown revenue. But, sire, none of them would turn a finger to bring in food for the starving people. They would think it of small concern to make fair settlement of disputes about the possession of houses and lands. Parents would never find their lost children." In his earnestness he placed both hands on the edge of the table and leaned forward toward the King. "The men I respectfully suggest as better fitted for these posts may not have the same prestige. But, liege lord, they are the kind of men who will labor day and night to get food into their towns and villages, to help the people in their misery and want, to let the humble and downtrodden sup at once on the sweet wine of restoration. I beg of you to consider these points well. It is important, as you have said so often yourself, sire, that the people who are being reclaimed from alien rule be helped to content and loyalty."

The feelings with which Charles followed this argument were reflected clearly on his face. At first he was resentful, then his rather gloomy countenance took on the aggrieved look of one who sees himself being thwarted of a pet desire, and finally he came around to an expression of reluctant agreement. He riffled through some papers in front of him until he found the documents in question. After glancing them over, he dropped them back on the table and called in a peremptory tone:

"Ulysse!"

The seneschal came in at a senile trot, his face showing a scandalized regret that his royal master should have an unanticipated want.

"Your King's Grace?"

"Ulysse!" The voice of Charles was sharp and reproachful. "My *bon morceau!* Has it been forgotten? Is the King of France of no consequence to his servants? Must his selection of officials be criticized, changed, torn to pieces, derided, laughed at? Are his few and simple wants always to be forgotten? Must he demand his bon morceau before it is produced for him?"

Leaving the room in a frenzy of self-reproach, the ancient seneschal gave Jacques Coeur a glance, nevertheless, which said he was convinced that the outburst was in some way the fault of the Moneyman. He returned in less than a minute with a silver platter on which reposed a glass bowl of a most beautiful garnet shade containing a mixture which defied quick classification. From long experience Coeur knew what the mixture was: a frothed-up bed of cream flavored with sugar, cinnamon, and a dash of verjuice. Beside the bowl was a small heap of cracked walnuts.

He proceeded to dip the nuts into the contents of the bowl and then to crunch them with relish—a reluctant relish because of his unhappiness in his servants.

After a half dozen or more had vanished down the royal throat, Charles progressed to a smile. "You are right!" he said to Jacques Coeur. "I had promised posts to many of these people and it seemed a convenient way of getting them settled in office. Why must the men about me be so lacking in the needed qualities? Yes, my good Jacques, you are right. I concede the wisdom of what you have said. We must have men capable of restoring order quickly."

The King got to his feet and dropped a hand on the shoulder of his Moneyman. "You are always right. What would I do without you, Jacques Coeur? I would be lost! I've always known it; and now, when there is so much talk and idle tattle, I acknowledge it to you openly. We must stand together, my old Jacques!"

The Moneyman was on his way out, glowing with the words of praise he had heard from his sovereign, when the King called him back.

"Jacques Coeur!"

"Yes, sire."

The mood of the monarch had changed. He had seated himself again and his attitude suggested deep gloom. His shoulders sagged, his arms rested limply on the table. Even a large emerald which he wore on a gold chain around his neck seemed to lack its rich glow.

"Jacques Coeur, Jacques Coeur! There are times when I feel I am losing everything worth while. Why, at this time when I am winning back all of France, must I lose those who mean the most to me? She is going to die! I speak sharply to Robert de Poitevin, I tell him he's a croaking beldame, I say he knows nothing. But down in my heart I'm sure he knows. Yes, Jacques Coeur, she's going to die!"

2

D'Arlay found the New Men squatting in groups on the earthen floor, engaged in a game called *honchet* which required the use of boards and men. One of them looked up and asked, "Will the procession be starting soon?"

D'Arlay peered through a crack in the oiled paper which covered the one window. "The sun is under and it's hard to tell the time," he said. "But I think it will start in a very few minutes now."

The players pushed aside the men and scrambled to their feet. There was a casual air about them as they strolled outside but D'Arlay knew that it was assumed. The yard of the inn was completely deserted. Everyone who could get away, even the stablehands, had gone to Rouen to see the King of France take possession of the city after all the years it had been in enemy hands. The young men grouped themselves about the entrance, their heads turning of one accord to the south.

A loud trumpet blast reached their ears, the work clearly of a whole company of heralds blowing lustily in chorus. It was possible, even at the distance, to detect the note of triumph in the concerted voice of the trumpets: the King of France had made his entrance into the ancient city through the Beauvoisine Gate.

"It will be a rare sight," said one of the New Men with a sigh. "They say the King will glitter with jewels from head to foot. My lord Dunois wears a sword set with diamonds which Jacques Coeur has given him."

"I've never seen the King," said another. His tone was wistful. "I suppose all the beautiful ladies of the court will be there."

After a pause the first speaker asked: "Do you suppose our comrades who died will be watching—and wondering why we're not in the procession?"

A third voice broke in, rough and scornful of such weakness, "The souls of our dead comrades will have better things to do than to watch a lot of elderly knights and fat dowagers dressed up in their finest clothes. I thought processions were great when I was a boy of five but now—I propose we choose sides and have a game of *La Soule*."

There was a long pause and then the first speaker nodded in agreement. "Maxime is right about it. If our comrades *are* watching, they won't want to see us mooning around. Why should we let anyone know our feelings have been hurt? Get out the ball!"

A large round globe, made of straw with a thin covering of leather, was produced and a game of La Soule begun. At first there was a listlessness to the struggle for possession of the ball. No signs of energy or enthusiasm were displayed. Gradually, however, the players became more interested, the action grew in warmth. In time the struggle was waging furiously and the loud shouts of the contestants made it clear that, for the time being at least, they had forgotten the slight which had cut them so deeply.

When D'Arlay returned to the inn he found that a letter had been delivered there for him. His name on the outside flap was inscribed in a hand he recognized at once, the hasty but well-formed writing of Jacques Coeur. It was a short note.

This is to tell you, my good friend, that I have reached a decision you will approve. I am now convinced it is not necessary to adopt *extreme means.* I am going to drop the plan and I propose to see the Comte at once and let him know. I send the word to you in this way because it seemed to me likely you would be low in mind today and it might serve to raise your spirits.

D'Arlay threw the sheet of paper into the fire and watched it burn. Then he turned and gave vent to his good spirits by a twirl of one foot as he started for the door.

"The highest of the bars has been taken away!" he said to himself.

3

The Comte de Burey had followed the campaign in the train of Charles of France. There had been little for him to do, beyond donning his armor (which chafed him painfully) in the mornings and keeping it on all day. After the entry into Rouen, however, things were changed in that respect. He became one of the busiest men about the King.

The duty assigned him had something to do with supplies of horses from the west (he was a little hazy about the matter himself), but it was not this which set him into such a lather of activity that the skirts of his shortened houppelande flapped about his shanks and his bag sleeves were constantly in motion. Some days, in fact, he could transact his official business in fifteen minutes. Even when things were at a point of seemingly high tension, he was never engaged at it for more than an hour.

The demands on his time and attention came from participation in matters of a far from official nature. In the first place he was an active member of an exclusive court clique which indulged in orgies of competition in that fascinating new form of entertainment, cards. As the King was known to frown on all such pastimes, particularly now that he had girded himself to the duty of finishing the war and expected all his immediate attendants to take things as seriously as he did, the games had to be played as privately as possible. A tower room had been found for the purpose. It was so high and so difficult of access that it was unlikely the King would ever make his way to it; and here at all hours of the day and night the zealous players gathered. There were ladies (for the lure of cards was strong enough to induce bright-eyed young matrons as well as fat dowagers to essay the weary climb) as well as gentlemen competing for the possession of Tib and Tom and Tiddy, as the high cards were called. The stakes were steep, and so cardplaying proved profitable for the Comte de Burey. He was a good player, although none of his opponents realized it. Holding his cards tightly cupped in his unsteady hands and quite close to his eyes, he kept track of every piece of cardboard which fell on the table and noticed every expression on the faces of his opponents. As he mumbled to himself a great deal and had a tendency to fumble when playing his cards, they were disposed to laugh at him and treat him as of little account; but the fact stood that he almost always won.

But an even more profitable pursuit than cardplaying occupied a large part of his waking hours. As usual, when a victorious army has engulfed a large slice of territory, a busy traffic had developed in what was offhandedly called *lettres de marque*—that is, letters of safe-conduct, of identification, of leave of absence, of admission to military areas, of right to trade with the troops and the liberated inhabitants. Some were obtained properly and legally, after much running from one department to another, but the King's ministers were not prepared to issue such papers in unlimited quantities and so the demand had to be met by forged copies. Handsome prices were paid for both kinds and in short order an organization, working *sub rosa* and made up largely of crown officers, had sprung up to supply the ever-growing demand. The Comte's part in the transactions consisted in obtaining the signatures, real or forged. He spent hours each day waiting in anterooms for chances to get a minister's name down on the sheaf of documents he carried under his arm. The officers of the Crown were scattered throughout the huge rectangular palace the English had built on the river and which Charles had selected as his own headquarters while in Rouen (he had no option in the matter, for the city was a shambles of razed public buildings, of burned wooden houses, and of trade centers which the invaders had used as cannon foundries), some of them being located even in the oratories and the pantries and in temporary sheds erected on the mall and tennis grounds and in stuffy cubbyholes in stables and cattle sheds.

Frequently his pursuit of signatures took him to the office of the Moneyman which was located in the courtyard in what apparently had been a menagerie at one time, for there was a strong animal odor about it. Jacques Coeur invariably was busy but he would attend to the Comte's requests without making him wait. They were, needless to state perhaps, legal signatures the Comte sought when he went near the keeper of the King's purse. If Coeur knew that his visitor was engaged in the preparation of spurious documents as well, and it is inconceivable that he would not know, he said nothing about it.

One day, however, he looked at Regnault de Burey with a suggestion of annoyance in the pucker of his brow. "You must have a great number of friends, Naulty. And you must have a heart as big as a great spreading oak to go to so much trouble for them. I'm assuming, of course, that you wouldn't—shall we say, demean yourself?—by doing this for any kind of a reward."

The Comte did not relish the tone in which the words had been spoken. "You know quite well, Moneyman," he grumbled, "that I have need for every little round coin, silver as well as gold, which I can entice into the yawning maw that I call, somewhat inaccurately, a purse."

On two occasions Jacques Coeur said: "There's something we must talk about, Comte, as soon as I have half an hour to spare. As you know, they give me no peace here."

He did not find the needed half hour, however, until one day about a week after the French court moved into the palace vacated by the leaders of the English Army. He met the Comte outside the door leading into the crowded anteroom of the King and drew him down the corridor to his own quarters.

"Comte, I've come to a decision," said the Moneyman, digging his hands deep into the pockets of his cloak and frowning thoughtfully. "I may tell you in confidence that I no longer doubt the King will want me to remain in his service. He has given me the most positive assurances of his cordiality. For some time I have been skeptical as to the need for any special measure."

Sensing what was coming, the Comte frowned at his companion. "Do you mean," he demanded, "that the toads of doubt are hopping in your head as to the need of carrying out the plan?"

"That is what I mean. I mean much more than that, gossip Regnault. I have, in fact, made up my mind. I'm dropping the plan."

Seeing the end of all the good things he had been enjoying, the steady jingle of gold in his pockets, the secure future, the Comte protested energetically. Did he, Jacques Coeur, understand the risk he was taking? Was he not underestimating the amount of opposition which had developed at court? Could he be sure the cordial mood of the King would continue?

The Moneyman brushed such arguments aside. He contented himself with an assured nod and a final word. "My mind is made up, Comte. You understand, of course, that this will not mean a loss for you and the Comtesse. The payments will be continued to cover the cost of the girl's maintenance. There will be compensation for you also."

The Comte put little trust in promises, perhaps because he used the ones he made himself as a basis of valuation. He departed, therefore, in a thoroughly depressed mood, his mind occupied with schemes to repair this damaging blow to his prospects. Coeur called after him: "There's no need for repining, gossip Regnault. A great prosperity lies ahead of

France in which all of us will share. You will pay off your debts and still have enough left to dine on golden plate. I promise it."

The Comte proceeded to the King's anteroom. Ordinarily his spirits lifted as soon as he breathed the atmosphere of the court, finding stimulation in the pervading sense of competition, the undercurrent of intrigue, the continuous battle of wits. Today, however, he remained sunk deep in gloom. He walked slowly into the long and drafty room, his eyes fixed on the floor, muttering indignantly to himself. He did not respond to greetings.

"This passes belief!" he thought, with an aggrieved shake of his head.

And then an idea occurred to him, a sure way out of this impending difficulty. It was such a brilliant idea that he stood still in the exact center of the room for several moments to consider it and to savor the gorgeous prospect it opened up. He slapped a hand against his thigh and said aloud, "Of course!"

"Of course what?" demanded a voice at his shoulder. "Is it new sap in your veins which is making you dream dreams? Or are you just sampling the visions of a withered old age?"

The Comte did not turn to identify the speaker. He walked triumphantly from the room, his head held high, his fingers itching for the pen which would put this dream or vision, whichever it was, into the process of consummation. "Does he think me some countinghouse varlet to jump at his beck and call?" he demanded of himself. "I have no need of the great Moneyman in this. I, Regnault de Burey, will take the reins into my own hands and there will be resolution and skill and craft in the driving!"

He made his way briskly to his own quarters. Two rooms had been assigned him in a tower on the river side, a small room for himself and an even smaller one for the three servants he had brought with him. "A pen, Hugan!" he shouted, when he reached the apartment. "Ink and paper, knave! And quickly."

It took some time to supply these most unusual needs, for the Comte was not a scholar and had little use for writing materials. Finally, however, his demands were filled and he set himself to the task of inditing a long letter to his wife in Paris. He labored over it a considerable time, his nose close to the paper, his lips repeating the words as he put them down. He deleted and rewrote and made an infinity of blots, saying to himself finally, "By'r Lady of Marmoutier, it is clear that neither my head nor my hands have a clerkly inclination!"

When the epistle was completed, he picked up the final sheet and read over the last paragraph with a sense of satisfaction in a task well done.

And so, my heart, I am sure you will agree with me that we must go on ourselves from where he has left off. This chance is too great to lose because some last-minute scruples fill the head of this puffed-up furrier. We must arrange it so our liege lord sees the little cousin before his liking for the De Maignelais vixen gets too strong a hold on him. If he likes the copy of his beloved original, the Moneyman will be in no position to call a halt.

Join me at once, sweet spouse, bringing our candidate with you. Need I point out she must be kept in the dark? Come in state. Bring all the best clothes the Moneyman provided for her—all her most charming gowns and hats and cloaks, the silkiest willicoats and all the laciest whimwhams. Our liege lord must see her at her best.

Set out immediately on receipt of this and spare not the horses in the coming!

Chapter IV

I

ISABEAU read the letter from her husband with varying emotions. She was upset over this disruption of a program which had been proceeding so smoothly and profitably. She felt also some hesitation about going on with it. This was not because of scruples on her part but rather to an instinctive suspicion of any scheme hatched in the mind of her spouse. More than anything else, however, she experienced a deep anger with the Moneyman for the decision he had reached.

"It's always the way!" she said to herself bitterly. "When it comes to the point, men shy away and raise objections. They cannot do this, they must not do that! They prate of honor. Honor! It's no more than a mask they carry about, these self-appointed masters of ours, to hide themselves behind when they need an excuse for some weakness. . . . Men are made to be obeyed but not respected."

She reluctantly left the comfort of her own warm hearth and ventured out into the halls which the chill of winter had already claimed. Although she had thrown over her shoulders a cloak with a fur hood, she shivered and began to run, and it was with great unwillingness that she stopped on encountering the same physician who had been summoned to see Valerie on her first arrival.

"Messire," she asked, drawing the cloak about her more closely, "will Mademoiselle be well enough to undertake a long journey at once?"

The physician's eyes opened wide with surprise. "A long journey? Did I hear you aright, my lady? Did you mean a journey *now,* in this cold and bitter weather?"

"You heard me aright. Yes, Messire, a journey *now.*"

"My lady! She's so ill she would die of shock if we were so ill-advised as to move her as much as from one room to another."

The Comtesse said to herself, "It's indeed aggravating that the little slut chose this time to become ill!" Aloud, she asked, "From what malady is it that she suffers?"

The physician lapsed at once into the vagueness in which medical advice was almost invariably cloaked. "A fever, my lady. There are many fevers but I haven't yet determined the exact nature of the one from which she suffers. The source of the disease? I do not know. If I did, I would become famous and rich. Of such matters, Aetius says—— But I must not distress you with opinions. This much I have done: I have bled her copiously, I have given her a clyster of herbs and scammony, I have had her bathed with hot water and distillations of oak leaf. I have even"—his eyes became filled with a zealous glow—"I have even tried something new. I am administering drinks to her of aniseed and polypody. To thin her, my lady, to remove the noxious matters from her body by reducing the flesh."

The Comtesse, who had shown a disposition to cut his explanations short by brushing past him, stopped suddenly. "To thin her!" she said indignantly. "Don't you realize, Messire, that she is already thin? Is it your idea to save her life by reducing her to such a paucity of flesh that her beauty will be lost? You will cease these new treatments at once, Messire! Polypody, indeed! Of what use is life to a woman without beauty?"

The physician was so discomfited that he stammered in replying. "But —but, my lady, I was acting in her best interests as I—as I conceived them."

The Comtesse completed the act of brushing by him, saying as she proceeded down the hall: "I will have no more of this stupidity, Messire. I order you to do nothing further until I have seen her myself."

She was disturbed, when she entered Valerie's bedroom, by the flushed condition of the patient's cheeks and brow. It was clear at once that her charge was quite ill, certainly more ill than she had supposed. The room was so warm that even Guillaumette, who was warming a sheet in front of the fire, had acquired a flushed look also.

Tossing feverishly from one side to the other, Valerie said in a weak voice, "I am so ill, Cousin, that I am like to burn up."

The Comtesse walked briskly into the room. Her first step was to whisk up the black-and-white cat which was ensconced on the foot of the bed and carry it to the door. Anatole-Raymonet arched his back and protested his ejection by a vain effort to rake the arms of his captor with his hind claws.

"Please!" protested Valerie. "When I am ill, my old cat always stays close beside me. He seems to know."

"This time," declared Isabeau, returning to the bedside, "he will be kept out of the room. I don't know why I tolerate the creature anyway. He's always in trouble. This morning he stole a fillet of fish in the kitchen. . . . Cousin, I have received word that we must proceed north at once. It's a matter of the greatest importance."

Valerie raised her head to look at her mentor but lacked the strength to sustain that position. She fell back on the pillow, saying in a tone of self-reproach: "How unfortunate that I should be ill! What are we to do, Cousin? Is it possible that I could be left behind?"

"It is *not!* You must get well as quickly as possible. You must exert your will to the utmost."

Valerie nodded her head feebly in agreement. "Yes, Cousin, I'll do my best."

"Is it necessary to tell you what is back of this summons?"

"No, I think not. I will—I will try hard to get well."

The Comtesse said in a bitter voice, "That physician is a fool! There's nothing to be done about it because all the others are just as bad." She turned to Guillaumette. "The air in here is very close. Light a vanilla stick at once."

She closed the door behind her emphatically but not quickly enough to prevent a black-and-white shape from bounding in and flying to its previous post on the foot of the bed.

Guillaumette walked over and patted Valerie's hand. "A lot of sympathy you had from her! Get well quickly, indeed! Does she think all you have to do is to say, I am better, and then step right out of bed?" The maid nodded her head and winked mysteriously. "I know what's wrong with her, Mademoiselle. She had a letter from *him.*"

Valerie remained still for several moments, a sign that her interest had been roused. "From the Comte?" she asked.

"One came from the master today but the one I meant arrived several days ago. It was from the other."

Valerie did not need to ask any questions. She knew that the letter had been from the Sire d'Arlay.

"She wasn't pleased with it, Mademoiselle," said Guillaumette, leaning over the bed and whispering. "She stayed in her room for hours. When she came out—— Ah, was she in a temper!" The maid nodded her head eagerly. "I wish I knew what was in it. Perhaps he has flipped his tail feathers at her and said good-by. Perhaps he was telling her——"

"You mustn't talk about such things to me, Guillaumette."

"I know, Mademoiselle. But, truly, she has been in a mood for such a long time!"

This was not an exaggeration as Valerie knew only too well. The Comtesse *had* been in a mood, almost from the time the Comte and D'Arlay had left to join the army. She had vented some of her ill temper on her charge. She had been extremely hard to please, never letting a day pass without pointing out faults. Valerie laughed too much ("A lady must not show much sense of humor, Cousin, the men don't like it and consider it vulgar"); she was impulsive, she said and did things as the mood seized her, which was wrong because ladies must always be cool and dignified; she was continually in a hurry, which was very wrong because haste must be left to servants. But the main fault, which she pointed out on innumerable occasions, was Valerie's failure to think like a lady.

"Inside yourself," the Comtesse had said on one occasion, "you are still a waif, the daughter of a wandering actor. Perhaps you *were* their child. If that is the case, nothing can be done to change you. But if it's in you to alter your way of thinking, I want you to understand that you must do so quickly. You'll never act like a lady until you're sure in your own mind that you are one."

Valerie had been honest enough to acknowledge that her mental attitude had not changed completely. "But more and more," she had added in her own defense, "I find myself doing the things you've taught me to do without conscious effort. I feel sure of myself most of the time."

"You must be sure of yourself all the time," Isabeau had said sharply. "I can't help you. It's something which must be felt and which can't be explained."

On every occasion thereafter, when Valerie did something which displeased her, she would say, "*There!* That is what I mean." Valerie would

"Until tomorrow, my lady."

Isabeau laughed. "One da[illegible] [illegible]most that no one will notice if she en[illegible] [illegible]o bedrooms, which is the very least we ca[illegible]

"The Widow Barbier," said the Sc[illegible] [illegible]ead, "won't stir from that room until the full time is up. [illegible] [illegible]ost rigid, my lady. She stayed in bed for the first nine days as required, and now she has been sitting on the black sheet on the floor for a month and no one, saving her maid, has been inside the door in that time. My friend and I have been in the house for a month and we haven't laid eyes on her. Well, there was one occasion when the maid took us into the yard where we could see into the room. She"—the Scot's eyes began to beam—"is a buxom woman with a fine eye in her head and she won't remain a widow long."

"I'm not interested in the woman." Isabeau considered the situation and finally gave her head a reluctant nod. "If we can't have anything better, I suppose we must accept with good grace. Will you take us there at once, Messire?"

"It will be for one night only. I advise you to start for the abbey in the morning as the Comte will be waiting anxiously. And I assure you, my lady, we can't get back to the house too fast to suit me. You see, I don't trust this friend of mine."

Isabeau looked dismayed at this statement. "Are you afraid he will steal your things? Messire, what kind of place is this you are taking us to?"

"No, no, my lady. Lockie Bell is a fellow countryman of mine and I vouch for his honesty, even though he comes from Edinburgh. I meant in regard to the widow. I've been away from the house for three hours now, and how do I know what he has been doing in my absence? Has he forced the door and introduced himself to the notice of the lady?"

"I assure you," said the Comtesse, in a tone of angry reproof, "that I'm not interested in this rivalry for the favor of a shoemaker's widow. All I ask is that you take us to the house at once as we are sorely in need of food and rest and warm baths."

The Scot turned and winked for Valerie's sole benefit. "You should see the stock of shoes ready for sale and the great mounds of leather in the cellar! How he kept such a stock in wartime is a mystery. The yearly profits will be truly handsome—and the widow won't be able to manage it alone." He directed the rest of his remarks to the Comtesse. "It's my belief, my lady, that the time to catch a widow is when she emerges from her vigil on the black sheet. She's so hungry for companionship then that the first male face she sees seems to her to shine like that of an archangel —even if it's the lean visage of a middle-aged Scot."

Isabeau was amused in spite of herself. "I hope, for the poor lady's sake," she said, "that your companion has more to offer her than you have."

"Lockie Bell? My lady, he's a sour little fellow with bilious eyes and hair the color of a carrot which has been left too long in the ground. It's said of Lockie that the only prodigal thing about him is the number of yellow freckles on his face. He's small and thin and mean. But in spite of everything, my lady, I'm afraid of him. He has a way with women."

The house looked far from pleasing from the street and the first glimpse of the interior set the nostrils of the Comtesse into twitches of disapproval. The room to which they were shown, however, was large and had two beds which was, perhaps, better than they might have expected. Isabeau glanced about her, at the undraped walls and the ancient bench in a corner and the beds, one of which was large and the other quite small.

"Where will the servants go?" she demanded of the Scot who lingered in the doorway.

"The widow's maid has a room back of this. Your women can go in with her for one night. The men will have to do the best they can in the cellar. I've slept in my time on worse couches than a pile of leather."

The Comtesse dismissed him with a wave of the hand and then turned to Valerie. "I must have the large bed," she remarked. "The least discomfort makes it impossible for me to sleep. You will have to be very quiet, Cousin."

The maid who had been selected to accompany the Comtesse and whose name was Bona went below to make demands for fresh linen and hot water. It was some time before she returned, and she brought nothing but a very small wooden tub and a bucket half filled with steaming water. "They don't seem to know much about bathing here, my lady," she said.

The Comtesse looked at the meager supply. "There's barely enough for me. Fortunately, Bona, we will be having supper here and so Mademoiselle will not require a bath. I'm very tired. You must undress me and bathe me at once."

Valerie had been looking forward to the luxury of hot water but there was no appeal from this decision. She stretched herself out on her small and lumpy bed, keeping her eyes studiously away from the center of the room where Isabeau, not averse to showing that she was still slender and white of skin, was standing naked in the tub while Bona bathed her.

When this was finished, the Comtesse walked to the bed and lay down with a sigh of content. The maid began to pat and knead the flesh of her legs and stomach with quick and unsparing strokes of her strong hands. This was a matter of daily routine but Valerie had never been present when it occurred. A disinclination to watch so personal a ministration kept her eyes turned in another direction.

A second deep sigh of content and the rustling of a silk sheet gave notice that the rubbing had been finished. The maid left the room and in a few minutes the Comtesse stirred and called, "Cousin!"

The girl looked across the room. The Comtesse was lying under the sheet and her reddish hair was spread out artfully on the pillow.

"My child," said Isabeau, in a voice from which all trace of critical authority had vanished, "you must have thought me unfair and even cruel to you. I realize that I've been a hard taskmaster. But now that the time is drawing near for the test, I think you will say I was justified in being so severe. You see, Cousin, I had to be sure there were no flaws, no shortcomings in you. The risk in what we're trying is so great that we have to be very, very sure. . . . I've made life hard for you and there must have been times when you hated me. But as a result you're ready."

Valerie was completely disarmed by this speech. "There have been times," she said, after a moment, "when I thought you unreasonable. I was convinced you disliked me. After what you've just said, I can see how needful it was to be strict and exacting with me."

The brown eyes of the Comtesse, which could be so hard and unrelenting, smiled at her over the top of the sheet.

"I think you're going to succeed," she said. There was a pause and then she added, watching the girl intently as she did so, "We must all be on our guard from now on. A careless word might start talk and upset everything. You must suspect everyone, my child. Never discuss this matter and, if questions are asked, pretend you know nothing. This applies to my far-from-discreet husband, to the Scot, to the Sire d'Arlay. You must be careful even about what you say to Jacques Coeur." She laughed lightly. "You must be careful what you say to *me!*"

Valerie nodded her head gravely. "I'll be careful, Cousin."

"That's all I wanted to say. I hope now that there will be no more misunderstandings and no hard feelings between us." Isabeau closed her eyes. "I think I shall have a rest before supper. This continuous traveling has taken most of my strength."

Valerie brought herself to making a request which had filled her mind from the moment she saw the Scot. "Cousin," she said, "I ask your permission to go below and see Messire Kennedy. I'm sure you knew he was sent by my lord Coeur to find out what he could about my parentage. I'm burning to know what he has to tell. I—I'll be most careful, Cousin."

The eyes of the Comtesse opened and she studied her charge carefully for several moments. "Very well," she said. "He would think it strange if you didn't speak about it."

Valerie found Kennedy in the front storeroom below. He smiled when he saw her and said: "I've been expecting a visit from you. Here, sit down beside me. It's the best seat this place has to offer." He looked sharply at one of the apprentices who was busying himself in a corner of the room. "Out of here, Galbert!" he called. "Find some other task for yourself for the next half hour.

"And now, my little lady," he said, when the boy had left, "we may speak freely. It's plain to be seen that many things have been happening, and all of them for the best. The clothes on your back must have cost" —pausing a moment for a rapid calculation—"a round dozen nobles. I was not unprepared for the change as I have been hearing things. I've a well-trained ear for such matters, I assure you."

He got to his feet and began to pace about the room, flailing his arms to keep warm. He watched her out of one corner of his eye as he did so. "She's innocent of guile," he said to himself finally. "She holds up her head and there's a glow in her eye. She believes herself another Maid or—which she thinks the same thing—another Agnes Sorel. I must show care in what I say to her."

He said aloud, "There are questions you would like to ask?"

The girl responded to this invitation eagerly. "There are indeed, Monsieur. My mind is full of them. I want to know everything you learned when you—when you went to Berri at my lord Coeur's behest. I've heard so very little. Monsieur, I want to know about my mother and father, my real parents. I can't tell you how I've longed for this chance to see you alone and ask the questions which are never out of my mind."

"There are things I could tell you," admitted the Scot. "There are things I didn't tell the merchant, believing them to be for your ears alone."

"Can you tell me who I am?" she demanded, with a suggestion of breathlessness in her voice. "Can you tell me my rightful name?"

"Your mother's name was Céleste de Lansanne. Who your father was I don't know. To find out his name will require further inquiries, leading into a different part of the country. All that, my lady, must come later; perhaps when the war is over and Pregent Kennedy can undertake tasks in which there will be," he winked slowly, "a little profit for himself."

"Tell me everything you know," said Valerie eagerly.

"You will want to hear first what little I can tell you about your father. He was a grand handsome man, of goodly proportions and with hair as yellow as a Norseman."

Valerie's eyes were beginning to glow. "Was my father tall?"

"Aye, he was tall and as sturdy as a fine young oak. I heard stories of his skill with weapons."

The Scot proceeded to tell her the story of the duel which her father had fought with her mother's brother. The girl listened with absorbed interest and, when he came to an end, assailed him with an eager flood of questions. What part of the country had her father hailed from? Was he married at the time? Did he have a family? Did he see her mother after the duel was fought? She received little in the way of answers save negative shakes of the head. Finally she gave it up and turned instead to questions about her mother. On this score he proved much more communicative.

"She was of a good family, one of the best in those parts though not one of much wealth. For generations the heads of the family had shown a most deplorable tendency to let money slip through their fingers. On the other hand, they were, without exception, men of stout loins. Your mother, Mademoiselle, was the fourteenth to arrive, although, naturally, most of the earlier ones had died in infancy. All this had so reduced the family resources that there was no silver cup to present to the child at her christening."

"My poor mother!" Valerie sighed. "If I had thirteen uncles and aunts, some of them must still be alive."

"One only, an uncle. His name is Eduard and he lives on the family holdings today. A hard cullion, I found him, as grasping as a lowland lawyer. It was little I could get out of *him!*"

"Does he, my mother's brother, know that I'm alive?"

Kennedy shook his head emphatically. "On the contrary, he's sure you died before you were a year old and he's well content it should be so. It would do you no manner of good to ask him for help."

Valerie drew her head up proudly. "I would never ask him for help under any circumstances. From the little you tell me about him, I am sure he was not kind to my mother when—when she needed kindness so much." There was silence for several moments. "Monsieur Kennedy, tell me about my mother. That's what I long to know above everything else."

"She was a small person, small and dark of face. It seems that she had a liveliness of spirit for in the family she was called Flammèche. Even though she was the youngest and a little slip of a thing, she it was who ran the household. She would talk back fiercely to the lawyers when they said there was no more money and she made the servants do their work well. She sewed and she schemed and she saved." The Scot nodded his head in high approval. "A rare fine lady she must have been."

"How long did she live after I was born?"

"Not long. The tight-lipped brother would tell me nothing but I cuitered myself to an old harridan of a servant, with a face as sour as the last cucumber in the vat, and I had it from her that as soon as your mother was strong enough she left the house. Weeks later she was found with the family of a freeholder of land some distance away. She was earning her keep by working in the fields. But"—with a shake of the head—"there was more spirit than good sense in what she had done. The work was too hard for one of her gentle upbringing." He crossed himself. "Inside the month she was dead."

Valerie continued to ply him with questions. From the meager responses she received, she was able to piece together a picture of the mother she had never seen: proud, sensitive, brave, unwilling to face her shame in dependence but lacking the strength to break through the bars. Now that she knew this much, she realized there could be no happiness for her in the story. "But it's better to know the truth," she said to herself. "It's better to know something of my mother as she was, and to understand her and love her, even though there's pain in the knowing."

"There's one other thing I was told," said Kennedy after it seemed he had repeated everything he knew. "She was a good singer and she had a gift for mimicry. As a small girl she was often punished for imitating her parents and her brothers and sisters, as well as guests who came to the house."

Valerie smiled gravely. "That's the final proof," she said. "Now I'm quite sure this unfortunate lady was my mother."

A small man, easily recognizable as Lockie Bell from the description Kennedy had given of him, put his head in through a door at the rear. Behind him Valerie could see the face of Godefroy, the page who had accompanied them from Paris. Godefroy was a tall youth with the intense dark eyes of his native Provence and he had fallen in love with her as violently and hopelessly as is possible only with boys of his age.

"The widow," announced Lockie Bell, in a voice so resonant it seemed to be issuing from a vacuum, "has risen and dressed herself as she considers it only fitting for the Comtesse to have a room to herself. It's a very proper gesture on her part and adds to the high opinion I've conceived of her."

The maid of the household pushed in after him with supplementary information. "She's put on her new black dress. It's all silk, Messires, and has jet buttons as big as my ears. And she's going to prepare the supper herself. She's *such* a good cook!"

"Your mistress," declared Lockie Bell, "is an exceptionally fine woman in many ways and I'm prepared to have you give her that as my opinion."

Kennedy, who should have been pleased at the turn of events, was staring at his fellow Scot with an air which combined displeasure and suspicion. "How is it," he demanded, "that you seem to know so much about the lady of the house?"

The little man boomed out with laughter. "I've stolen a march on you, Pregent Kennedy," he said. "I've got the better of you. As usual. I've seen the widow and talked with her. I think I may claim, Pregent Kennedy, to be on a friendly footing with her already."

Kennedy scowled at him and avoided the necessity of making a rejoinder by drawing Valerie to one side and whispering to her, "You had better go now or that pretty Jezebel upstairs will think we're up to some mischief."

3

They arrived in due course at the Abbey of Jumièges which they found already filled to overflowing. Not only was Charles of France there with all his special train to occupy the guest dormitory, but the nobility of France had come flocking north over the snow-packed roads to bask in the light of the royal countenance. They were distributed over the countryside, in manor houses and castles and in taverns. The Comte de Burey greeted his wife on their arrival with the welcome intelligence that he had secured the exclusive use of a manor house about three miles east of the abbey.

"It isn't large," he said, eying her as though he feared her opinion of the place. "There's a sunny room for you, my spouse. I have to sleep in a dark, damp hole like a sepulcher." He had moles' feet attached to his garters but this remedy for the gout, which was believed to be infallible, did not seem to be doing him any good. He hobbled painfully. "The little cousin is looking well again, I'm *very* glad to see. Your letters frightened me about her. I expected to find her a lank-cheeked skeleton, wabbling along on broomstick legs." He took advantage of his wife's inattention to give Valerie's thigh a quick pinch. "And here I find her rosy and sparkling and well plumped out again with the sweet cushioning of youth."

They had not been in possession of their new quarters half an hour when Godefroy announced that the Sire d'Arlay had arrived and was dismounting in the courtyard. The Comte had already disposed of a flagon of wine in great gulping intakes and had retired to his dark, damp hole for a nap. The Comtesse flew from the room to make herself more presentable, leaving Valerie to greet the visitor alone.

When D'Arlay came into the room and saw her, he found himself swept away on a tide of emotion. He wanted to rush across to her and gather her up in his arms. He wanted to hold her tight, to bury his face in her hair, to feel her cheek against his own. A voice inside him was saying with a vehemence he had never felt before, *I love her, I love her, I love her!* Why, the same voice was demanding, should he continue to regard the obstacles which circumstances had erected between them? Why should he not forget everything else and declare his love in the tempestuous words which filled his mind?

Valerie was feeling something of the same emotion. She had been aware that a fondness for him was growing in her but certainly she was not prepared for the warmth of the feeling she experienced at the sight of his grave, dark face. She said to herself in alarm: "This is wrong. I must put him out of my mind. I—I must be sensible."

"I was surprised to hear at the abbey that you had arrived," he said. "My brother had told me Isabeau was coming to join him but it was most pleasant to hear that she was accompanied by a cousin who could be no one, of course, but you."

Valerie thought, "Why is he surprised?" Was it not to be expected, under the circumstances, that she would come? She looked up into his face but found no answer there. It was not capable of expressing anything else at the moment but the emotion which filled him.

"If you had arrived an hour later," he went on, "I would have missed you. Jean Bureau had sent me here to consult with my lord Dunois. I saw him last night and I had a foot in the stirrup to return to camp when the word reached my ears that the Comtesse de Burey had arrived and—and a cousin who has become of such importance to me——"

Isabeau swept into the room at this moment, crying, "Robin! How happy I am to see you!" and holding out both hands to him in welcome. Good use had been made of the few minutes she had allowed herself. All trace of the fatigue of travel had vanished from her face under the hurried ministration of Bona's expert fingers. Her hair was piled high on her head and she had donned a gown which was striped green and yellow and blue and had a train which twisted and shimmered behind her with the unmistakable susurrus of the richest oriental silk. Her ermine-trimmed sleeves had fallen back, revealing to the elbow the whiteness of her arms.

D'Arlay said, "I'm happy to see you, Isabeau." He raised his hands to take hers and then drew back, holding them out in front of him with an apologetic air. They were still heavily bandaged in black.

"What's wrong, Robin?" asked his sister-in-law. She looked at him reproachfully. "Have you been wounded? And I was not told!"

"It's just the usual thing. Powder burns. It's not serious, of course, but I confess to finding the condition of my hands not only a great inconvenience but quite painful as well."

Valerie had retired to a chair at some distance, intending to take no further part in the talk. At this, however, she rose and joined them.

"It may be more serious than you think," she said, in an anxious tone. "Do they pain you continuously?"

D'Arlay nodded. "The master surgeon said the burns would heal quickly but it's clear now he hadn't calculated correctly. The pain seems to grow worse each day."

Valerie turned to the Comtesse. "Will you permit me, Cousin, to look at them? I know something of the care of hands. Those who live on the road, as we did, must understand how to cure them when they become poisoned or burned."

The Comtesse made a gesture which meant that she would not stand in the way if Valerie thought she could do any good. "But," she said, immediately after, "I think it would be wise if Robin went to his surgeon again as soon as possible."

Valerie seated herself in front of D'Arlay. He held his bandaged hands out for her inspection.

"How long is it, my lord, since you got these burns?"

"It was ten days ago."

She made a clucking noise to convey her sense of dismay. "Ten days! That is bad, my lord D'Arlay. They shouldn't have taken so long to heal. It's clear your surgeon didn't know much of burns." She glanced at Isabeau, who had seated herself close at hand and was watching what went on attentively. "I shall need hot water, Cousin. May I ask Guillaumette to get some? And I'll need linen for the fresh bandages."

"Of course."

While the water was being heated, Isabeau talked to D'Arlay in low tones. Realizing that this was designed to exclude her from the conversation, Valerie busied herself by clearing a table. As she did so, she cast an occasional glance at them, acutely aware of the proximity of the attractive brown hair of the Comtesse to D'Arlay's shoulder. The regularity with which they laughed or indulged in a mutual shake of head made her conscious of the close intertwining of their pasts.

When the water was ready, she had D'Arlay move to a chair at the table and seated herself beside him. Isabeau moved also, taking a position so close at hand that she could see everything.

Valerie found herself reluctant to begin. "I'll betray myself when I touch his hands," she thought. "She'll see how fond I am of him." D'Arlay was in the same dilemma. The first contact of her hand on his had sent a tremor through him. He watched the Comtesse apprehensively out of the corner of his eye. She was sitting close beside him and her gaily-striped skirt, which she had spread out like a fan, covered one of his feet with a deliberately proprietorial suggestion.

Valerie set to work finally. She soaked the bandages in the water and then peeled them from his hands with so much care and skill that he felt very little pain. As she went along, she gained more confidence and was no longer disturbed by the watchfulness of the Comtesse.

"What I know of medicines comes from the Egyptians [gypsies]," she said. "They use the very hottest applications for burns. But physicians have different ideas. They say the treatment should be cold and dry. Could anything be more wrong? See, my lord, he bound your hands so tightly that the blood can't reach the injured parts. Ah, the wicked, ignorant man, he has even covered them with potter's clay! At first the clay is well enough, for it relieves the pain. But to leave it on after is truly a most serious matter. In a few days, perhaps even sooner, your hands would have begun to mortify."

She worked swiftly. First she cut the blisters and separated the scars, removing the dead layers of skin and flesh with hot water, and with a sureness of touch which amazed him. Then she prepared a defensive to be applied to the inflamed parts and a hot emulsion in which the fresh bandage was to be soaked. It was clear that she put much reliance in the effect the emulsion would have. "I always carry the ingredients with me," she said. "It has seed of quince in it and fenegreeke and other things which I must not tell you because it's a very great secret. The Egyptians, with whom we traveled often, made me swear never to tell the whole recipe. But it's both soothing and healing in its effect, my lord. How much better your hands will feel!"

Then she applied an ointment. It was a basilicon unguent (she explained), made of white lilies and sweet almond and even with a little wax mixed in to give it body. As soon as it touched any part of his hands the pain stopped there at once; but D'Arlay could not be sure that this magic effect had anything to do with the ointment itself, for he was very certain that the touch of her fingers was enough to cure him of any ill.

When the bandaging had been completed, she nodded and got to her feet. "There!" she said. "I hope, my lord D'Arlay, you'll have less discomfort now."

D'Arlay smiled gratefully. "The pain has gone. You have wrought a miracle and I'm comfortable for the first time in a week. I'm deeply in your debt, Mademoiselle."

The Comtesse nodded to Valerie in dismissal and then engaged D'Arlay in conversation for some time. She found that he was uncertain as to Coeur's plans, having been actively in the field for months and out of touch with the Moneyman, but inclined to believe that the plan was to be abandoned. Isabeau, pretending to be in the same position, told him she had brought her charge to Jumièges to be in readiness for any decision Coeur might make. D'Arlay looked relieved and said, "I'm convinced, Isabeau, that you will have had your long journey for nothing."

When she complained of his neglect, he answered simply, "France is at war." To her plaintive suggestion that he might at least have written her, he held out his bandaged hands and said that he had been suffering from burns so continuously that the use of a pen was impossible.

"I think you've been mad!" she said. "There's no glory for a man of gentle blood in serving as you've done, even though people speak of your courage. Didn't you realize the mistake you had made when you weren't invited to ride in the victory procession?"

D'Arlay smiled and answered simply, "No."

It was, in fact, a very unsatisfactory talk for Isabeau. She dared not make any outward display of affection. Her husband, in spite of his afflictions, walked with a light foot and had a habit of entering rooms unexpectedly. D'Arlay was in a detached mood, uncommunicative and aloof. When he rose to go, saying that duty demanded his early return to camp, she felt that her efforts to win him back to the old footing had been without result.

The Comte popped into the room with the abruptness of a jack-in-the-box almost immediately thereafter. His eyes were still partly closed with sleep and his scant hair was standing up in ludicrous wisps.

"I feel," he grumbled, "as though I could spew up sick eels at the least provocation."

"Robin was here," said his wife. "He has just left."

The Comte gathered his scattering wits together at once. "You were properly discreet?" he asked.

"I told him nothing. The Moneyman gave him some hint of a change of heart but, luckily, they haven't seen each other for months."

The Comte stretched himself out in a chair and suppressed a yawn. "Everything seems to be working out to our advantage, my heart. Coeur is in Paris and isn't expected to return for some time. Agnes Sorel has given birth to her child, another girl. She had a difficult time and is now in such a state that no one is allowed to see her. She occupies a manor house close to the abbey."

Isabeau asked quickly, "Will she live?"

Her husband shook his head. "She's not expected to survive much longer. I asked the little medicine fellow about her and he gave me a gloomy shake of the head. The King still hangs on to a shred of hope, I'm told." He looked at his wife and smiled. "The portents are favorable. We have everything in our hands, my sweet spouse."

"Then," said Isabeau, with an air of satisfaction, "we must see that she's brought to the notice of the King at once. It must be done before Jacques Coeur returns."

"Of course." There was self-satisfaction even in the way he placed one knee over the other and swung his swollen foot back and forth. "I have a plan. It's not original, for I confess I took it, in its bare outline, from a book, but I think I shall improve on the original conception. The book, my lovely Isabeau, is one into which you have seldom dipped and from which you have derived less, perhaps, in the way of precept than you should. I refer to the Bible."

Chapter V

I

THE Comte and Comtesse de Burey were going to be late for the King's levee this cold morning of February seventh. Despite the fact that it was his own tardiness in getting out of bed which was responsible, the Comte proceeded to raise his voice in complaint as they jogged along the snow-packed road.

"We shall miss seeing him emerge with his face moist from sleep and his hair standing out like the bristles of a wild boar. It will be a great deprivation."

Snow had covered the vineyards which surrounded the abbey in all directions. More had fallen during the night and the branches of the trees drooped with the weight of it. The tall abbey towers had been turned into glistening columns of white against the dull gray of the winter sky. To anyone seeing them for the first time, these magnificent spires could have been nothing less than breath-taking; they were so high, so perfect, so symbolic of a faith which reached up from a rude and wretched earth for benediction from the skies. But the Comte and Comtesse de Burey had seen the twin towers on too many cold mornings to have any feeling about them at all. They did not even look up.

"It was along this road," said the Comte, "that the wicked wolf carried the weekly wash of the monks of Jumièges."

"What nonsense are you talking now?"

"Not nonsense at all, sweet spouse. I refer to the favorite legend of the abbey: How a wolf, which killed the faithful abbey mule, was cowed by the stern abbess of a nearby nunnery, where the wash was taken, into doing the work of the mule thereafter. A highly moral tale, my heart, even though I lack the piety to accept it literally." He gave his head a shake. "And what a sad fate for the old wolf! No more light-hearted killings, no chases in the moonlight, no frolics with lively little she-wolves! Instead he spends his declining years carrying the soiled copes of fat priors and the befouled frocusses and the greasy drawers of monks." He glanced sideways at his wife who was staring straight ahead of her. "Can it be you are not interested in the moral of this tale?"

They turned in through the arched gateway of the Church of Notre Dame and proceeded on foot across the cloister garth. Their heels made a crunching sound on the packed snow. A young monk, crossing from the other side, dropped his eyes when he saw Isabeau and increased the speed of his footsteps. From the choir of St. Pierre came the sound of monkish voices raised in melodious plainsong.

They were the only ones late this morning. The anteroom in the palatially large guesthouse was empty and the royal seneschal, standing at the refectory door, raised a green-and-white striped arm with a gesture like St. Peter forbidding the Gate to eagerly flocking souls. "You know the rule, my lord Comte and my lady," he said smugly. "This door must remain closed until the levee is over."

They sat themselves down in outer space. The anteroom was dark and cold and the prospect of a long wait was not pleasant. Isabeau let her face sink into the folds of her fur gorget and said plaintively, "I think my feet may be frozen and I *know* I have taken a cold."

But waiting in all this discomfort was to have its reward. They had not been seated more than ten minutes when the outer door opened and an oddly assorted group came in with all the order and pomp of a procession. In the lead was a tall individual with a face as round and expressionless as a loaf of bread and a gait of exaggerated dignity. He was carrying a wand with a crook to which a white silk bow had been tied. This he tapped down sharply with each step he took. Behind him came a manservant carrying on outstretched arms a large velvet cushion on which reposed a wooden cradle. Third in line was a bulging female whose arms were filled with every conceivable object a baby might need, including a doll with painted cheeks and agates for eyes. Bringing up the rear was a young lady in a fur-lined cloak who stopped just inside the door and looked about her with the most complete self-possession.

"Jeanne de Vendôme!" exclaimed Isabeau. "I hadn't heard you were here."

The young woman shook back her hood, revealing a shock of reddish hair which frizzed out in all directions. There was an aggressive hook to her nose and an equally aggressive look in her gray-green eyes. She nodded to them and curtsied.

"It's a week since I came, Comtesse," she said. "But this is my first visit to the abbey."

Isabeau looked inquiringly at the file of servants and then at the cradle from which a thin and scarcely human wail was issuing. "You are married, my good Jeanne?" she asked.

Jeanne de Vendôme nodded her head and laughed. It was a strident laugh and without a trace of mirth. She had a habit, as was demonstrated later, of laughing at the most unexpected times, particularly when she was talking. "I have a husband," she said. "But the child is not mine. No, no *indeed*. I mustn't linger here, but if Madame the Comtesse cares to accompany me, I shall be happy to explain."

2

Isabeau followed the procession down a hall with high-barred windows to a room at the far end in which an adequate fire was blazing. Jeanne de Vendôme saw to it that the cradle was placed close to the hearth and then turned to the Comtesse.

"It's the child of the Lady Agnes Sorel," she whispered. "I've been engaged to take charge of it."

"You're fortunate to have such a good appointment."

The young woman tossed her head with a suggestion of protest. "It's not what I had hoped for. I desired a place in the household of the Queen. Still"—with one of her pointless laughs—"it's better than staying at home with my husband's mother and the three selfish pigs of brothers he keeps about the place."

"You're not likely to see the Queen now," said Isabeau. "But you're certain to see the King quite often."

Jeanne de Vendôme shook her head. "If the Lady Agnes lives, you mean, and I think very little of her chances. We're staying at the Manoir de Mesnil which belongs to the abbey, and so far His King's Grace hasn't deigned to visit us." The young woman handed her cloak to the maid and took up a position in front of the fire. She waved at the servants in dismissal. "Get along now, all of you. You'll attend to the tasks I set for you, if you please, and at once! Blanchette, the child will need another warm blanket."

When the servants had withdrawn, she nodded her head and laughed triumphantly. "At home my husband's mother has encouraged the servants to be insolent to me. I'm making sure that it's different *here!* They jump to obey when I speak to them." She dropped her voice to a confidential level. "The King is to see his child for the first time this morning. For him to visit *us* would have been an open acknowledgment of paternity, and *that* would not have done by any means. But he couldn't wait to see her any longer so out we had to come in all this cold. No one is supposed to know we're here so I must ask you to leave in a few minutes, dear Comtesse. We're to go back while dinner is being served." She indulged in a laugh, somewhat louder than any that had gone before. "I've been instructed in the need for the most complete secrecy. It's all very absurd!"

Isabeau looked down at the small white face in the cradle. "It doesn't seem a healthy child."

"What can you expect? The mother was very weak before the accouchement and it was a wonder either of them survived."

Jeanne de Vendôme joined Isabeau and looked down at her charge. The child was bound up in rollers and bands and was so tightly strapped to the swaddling board that it seemed a miracle the poor little creature could breathe at all.

"I'm doing everything to keep it alive," said the young woman. "My appointment will end if it dies. But it's a puny thing, Comtesse."

"She would be a pretty child if she were not so very thin. How is the mother?"

"She hasn't long to live. Understand me, Comtesse; I speak from hearsay only. I've been a full week in the house and as yet I haven't laid an eye on my lovely and famed lady. It's given out that she's too ill to be seen and only her physician and her maid are allowed in her room. But I know the real reason for all the secrecy and the darkened rooms, Comtesse. It's her vanity. She can't bear to be seen."

"I can understand that," said Isabeau. "When I'm ill, I allow no one to enter my room except the physician."

The child's custodian tossed her head as though to say, "And you think I can't understand because I am not a beauty like you." She made no open response until the spell of resentment had passed. Then she said in a somewhat sulky voice: "Truly, my poor lady carries things to an extreme that's hard to believe. She allows no light in her room. None at all. Even the shutters are kept tightly closed. When her physician comes, he's received in darkness. She eats nothing and only occasionally does she take a sip of wine."

"She must be wasting away fast."

Jeanne de Vendôme nodded in avid agreement. "They say she's no larger now than a girl of eight or nine. I'm sure it would be a shock to see her. Even her head has become smaller. Her arms are no bigger around than my wrists." To demonstrate the last point, she drew back one sleeve and revealed a coarse wrist, covered with reddish hair. She nodded with assurance. "Make no mistake, Comtesse. She'll soon be a dead woman."

Isabeau looked at her companion attentively. The abnormal width between the eyes gave a suggestion of oddity to her face. There was, Isabeau saw now, an undoubted air of slyness about this Jeanne de Vendôme, and she made a mental note to the effect that the young woman could not be trusted far but might prove useful in spite of that.

Jeanne de Vendôme indulged in another of her pointless laughs. "Once, when a door opened to let someone in, I heard the Lady Agnes say, 'God forgive me for the life I have lived!' She pretends to be very pious now that the end is near. The chaplain has instructions to say whenever he has occasion to address any of us, 'Be good, be unselfish, be *virtuous*.' We're told not to discuss the child with anyone on the outside. Is it not absurd?"

The baby whimpered faintly. Isabeau looked down at its small creased face with both awe and dread. Never having been brought to childbed herself, she knew nothing of motherhood and did not dare approach the cradle closely for fear of doing something wrong. It was perhaps because she had no knowledge of the care of children that she found herself wondering if it were necessary to keep the infant strapped down to the board and swathed in so many tight coverings.

The custodian broke in on her reflections with a question. "Have you heard that another note was found pinned to the King's pillow?"

The Comtesse looked at her with instantly aroused interest. "I didn't know. How strange that word of it could reach you and not get around at court. I've heard no whisper of it."

The girl nodded with self-satisfaction. "We hear things, even though we're this far away. It was three nights ago. One of the Grooms of the Chamber drew back the curtains—and there it was! It was in verse and *quite* amusing. It warned the King that Jaquet the Fox was gobbling up all France and that someday he would gobble up the King just like one of those turkeys he has brought in from the East."

"How did the King take it?"

"He was very angry at first and said nothing. Then he began to laugh and said, 'He's a generous fox, at any rate, for he has bought back Normandy for me.'"

The Comtesse plied her with questions about the incident in an effort to find out everything possible. She was particularly insistent in probing for information as to what the King had said and done.

Jeanne de Vendôme was willing to tell all she knew. "I heard it said," she whispered, "that later, when the King was in bed and sipping his nightly posset, he suddenly became thoughtful and said, 'A man must be very clever to become as rich as Jacques Coeur.' When someone answered, 'Or very unscrupulous, my liege lord,' the King made no comment. But he put the posset aside as though he found no further pleasure in it. It was strange, wouldn't you say, that he made no answer at all?"

Isabeau did not reply but to herself she said, "It was not strange. I know what was passing through the royal mind."

In the exhilaration of finding herself on such intimate terms with one of the great ladies of the court, Jeanne de Vendôme inclined her head closer and proceeded to tell of another incident. "Did you hear that a letter to my lord Coeur was addressed to our house? It carried the seal of the Dauphin and had come from his place of exile. I was told it was given to the King who had it opened. The Dauphin was proposing that the Moneyman help *him* to take his father's place on the throne. My lord Coeur laughed when the King handed him the letter and pointed out many reasons why it was a forgery. It was not only a forgery, he said, but a very clumsy one. The King listened to him with a face as white as chalk and said never a word. The enemies of my lord Coeur took much comfort out of the incident."

"My dear Jeanne," said the Comtesse, "let us make a compact between us. If you'll engage to tell me such information as you hear that may be worth passing on, I will, for my part, pay you a substantial reward."

"Dear Comtesse," answered the young woman, "I am very greatly in need of money."

3

On her return Isabeau found the anteroom in the sole possession of her husband. The Comte had taken advantage of her absence to acquire a tankard of wine and was in the act of imbibing from it when she entered. He stared at her over the rim with a fixed and expressionless eye.

The Comtesse hovered above him accusingly. "Are you too drunk," she demanded, "to understand something I must tell you? Something of the greatest importance?"

He lowered the tankard and wiped his lips fastidiously. "These are not ideal conditions, my spouse, to set a mind such as mine to skipping lightly down the path of understanding. I don't try to conceal from you that I'm slightly bosked. Nevertheless, I'm still capable of following a direct and intelligent statement of fact."

His wife frowned at him impatiently. "Listen to me carefully," she said. "Things have happened which I find most disturbing. The opposition to the Moneyman is growing stronger all the time. And bolder, much bolder. Regnault, we must act at once. Do you hear me, at once!"

The Comte placed the tankard on the floor beside him. He took the ends of his mustache between the thumbs and forefingers of both hands and strove, unsuccessfully, to give them a twist. "I shall arrange everything, my beautiful spouse," he declared.

Chapter VI

I

LOOKING out over the top of the highest dunghill ever raised as a monument to French husbandry, Valerie had watched from her bedroom the round beaver hat of the Comte and the fluttering green hennin of the Comtesse disappear down the road. She shivered and thought how fortunate she was that she did not have to go out.

Guillaumette had placed a copper basin filled with water in front of the fire and now was engaged in warming the clothes her mistress would wear. "Hurry, Mademoiselle!" she called. "You'll freeze if you stay at that window any longer."

Valerie crossed the room at a run and, when she reached the fire, stepped forth with considerable reluctance from the bed blankets she had wrapped about her. The maid quickly dropped a woolen tunic over her head. "You had better wash before I put anything else on you," she said. "You shouldn't have gone to the window—you're blue with cold."

Valerie rolled her sleeves above the elbows, gave her hair a twist with one hand and attached it at the back of her head with a comb, then proceeded to wash herself with the ice-cold water. She whistled as she did so, happy in the knowledge that the Comtesse was not there to tell her that whistling was unladylike.

A rap came on the door and Godefroy put his head in to announce, "My lord Coeur has arrived."

Valerie looked up from the basin. "Are you sure? We were told he was in Paris and wouldn't come back for a long time."

"He's here," said the page. "And asking for you, Mademoiselle."

The dressing was finished in quick order and it was no more than five minutes later that Valerie made her way downstairs. The Moneyman was pacing up and down the long room which occupied most of the ground floor of the house. He was reading letters and, as he finished one, he stuffed it into a pouch at the right of his belt and brought out another from a pouch on the other side.

He stopped his pacing when he saw Valerie and gave her a warm, if somewhat preoccupied, smile. "Ah, my little minikin," he said. "You look completely recovered. That is good. I'm taking you with me on an important errand this morning."

Valerie said, "Yes, my lord?" in an interrogative tone which carried a distinct note of alarm. She was thinking, "Am I to be shown to *him?*"

"To see the Lady Agnes Sorel. I was unexpectedly summoned back from Paris by the King and found a note from her on my arrival, asking me to see her and to bring you with me." The Moneyman looked down at her with the undiminished amazement he always felt. "You grow more like her all the time. My sweet lady will have a surprise when she sees you. I'm afraid it's going to be a day of surprises for her, for I have something to tell her which she won't like. I had intended to tell you also, my child, but now I think it better to leave all discussion until after we've seen the Lady Agnes."

"What does she know about me?"

"Nothing except that you are the one I selected in accordance with the agreement between us. She doesn't know who you are nor what you look like."

Valerie was apprehensive of the results of the meeting. "It's certain, my lord," she said, "that she won't approve of me."

He smiled and gave her arm a reassuring pat. "Have no fears on that score. It's not going to be as much of an ordeal as you seem to think. I doubt if there will be any talk between you. She has been failing fast and I question if her strength will allow of that. She wants to see you, and that's all. I'm not sure of the wisdom of taking you; but her wish in the matter was stated most unmistakably."

"Will I do as I am?"

After a moment's inspection the Moneyman nodded his head. "There's no need to change but I suggest that you don your best cloak as well as something attractive for your head." His hand had strayed in the direction of the pouch containing the unread letters. He checked the motion halfway, however, and stared down at her with renewed interest. "It's indeed strange," he remarked, "that none of my spies have picked up any hint of your existence, my child. They never miss anything."

Valerie frowned with surprise. "Spies! I don't understand, my lord."

Coeur laughed ruefully. "Did you think a man could become a minister of the King and wield as much power as I have had without taking steps to know what's going on? Unfortunately it's necessary to fall into the system that everyone uses who aspires to position and influence at court. Yes, I pay spies, many of them—the most expert listeners at keyholes, the most assiduous practitioners of the art of snooping and sneaking and tattling. During the time I've been Moneyman to the King I've employed no fewer than thirty-four of these admirable characters to keep me in touch with the spirit and the talk of the court. It makes my gorge rise to depend on such a scurvy lot—liars and cheats, all of them, and some with the best blood of France in their veins!"

Valerie left the room to dress for the journey. While waiting for her, Coeur paced up and down, thinking bitterly of the information these spies of his had poured into his ears immediately on his arrival. It had been made abundantly clear to him that the success of the French armies had not served to check the machinations of his enemies. The air of the court was filled with whispers. It was being said that Ferrand de Cordule was preparing poisons and spells for the elimination of all who opposed the Moneyman, even of the King himself! It was furthermore declared that De Cordule had succeeded in more concrete aims, such as the making of a copy of the King's seal with which Jacques Coeur would now be able to issue orders and proclamations without his liege lord's knowledge or consent. Most of the stories being circulated were trivial and absurd but they added up to a volume of calumny which might have the desired effect in the mind of the one man who counted, Charles of France.

He stopped his pacing and shook his head angrily as though to clear his mind of such unpleasant reflections. "What does it matter?" he asked himself. "Let them talk! I'm higher than ever in the favor of the King and the malicious tattle of these drones can have no effect at all!"

2

There were peasants standing knee-deep in snow about the Manoir de Mesnil where the Lady Agnes was reported to be dying. One of them gaped up at Jacques Coeur and asked, "Can you tell us how the great lady fares, lord?"

The Moneyman helped Valerie to alight. "She fares ill," he said.

The peasant crossed himself. "'Tis a bad thing, lord," he muttered. "A bad thing for the poor people of Francc. She has been our friend."

The manor house was a severe structure of dark gray stone with a single hint of graciousness in the carving of the pointed arches above the main door. It had a chapel which formed the base of a low rounded tower and a sloping roof from which small windows jutted unexpectedly.

As they approached the entrance, Valerie looked up at Jacques Coeur and said in an anxious whisper, "I'm so frightened that my knees are starting to tremble."

They were greeted inside by a manservant with a forefinger pressed ostentatiously to his lips. "Not a sound, my lord," whispered the man.

"Is your mistress worse, then?"

The servant was so close to the point of blubbering that the only answer he could give was a nod of the head. He clamped a hand over his mouth and glided away through a door in the rear.

Coeur became aware that a young woman was standing above them on the landing of the stone stairs. There was no light where she stood and all he could make out at first was the intentness of her eyes and the bold curve of her nose. He decided she must be the one who had been appointed to take care of the child. Jeanne de Vendôme was looking at Valerie, her eyes wide with surprise. "She sees the resemblance," thought Coeur.

The manservant returned with tears streaming down his face. "My lady will see you," he said, brushing an arm across his cheeks. "Her voice was so weak I could scarce make out a word. And, my lord, her old hound has started to bay again. It is a sign."

The man led the way through a door opening off the right of the hall. The room they entered was so dark that Coeur walked slowly and kept both arms extended in front of him. The fetid air gave him a strangling sensation in the throat. By the light of a single candle burning at the end of the room he made out a small grating in the far wall.

A voice from behind the grating said, "Ah, Jacques Coeur, to what a sorry state I have been brought!"

The Moneyman took a few steps nearer. His heart was pounding and he found it difficult to keep his voice steady.

"Dear Lady Agnes!" he said. "The thought of what you've been suffering has never left my mind."

"It won't be long now, Jacques Coeur. A few days, a few hours even. So little time to make my peace, and so much to repent!"

She had been propped up to a position where she could see him without being seen herself, for he could barely detect the outline of her head behind the grating.

"No one ever had less to repent, dear lady," he said. "It was my hope that today I would find you easier in body as well as mind. Is it possible your despondency is because of lying here in such unnecessary discomfort? You need fresh air and light. I would like to see all the shutters thrown wide open."

There was a pause and then she sighed deeply. "Allow me my final vanity. I want to be remembered as I was, not as I am. I shrink from the thought of any eyes resting on me. I have—I have changed so dreadfully! There is little more of me now than the skin on my bones—I, who was once so fairly endowed!" Her voice rose. "This hateful sick body in which I'm chained! It can't be mine! I was always well and people said I was fair to look at. My life was like a dream of loveliness. It was the touch of silk on the skin, the warmth of the sun in a garden. Eyes turned to me and they always smiled. Ah, Jacques Coeur, why must so sweet a dream end in this way—in suffering and ugliness?"

"You must believe, sweet lady," said Coeur earnestly, "that those who have admired and loved you can never think of you as anything but lovely still."

"If you saw me now, you would turn your eyes away quickly." He heard her move as she said this. It was evident from the slightness of the sound that her body had little substance left. Nothing more was said for several moments. "My good friend Jacques, have you brought the girl?"

"Yes. She's waiting in the hall."

"I find myself very curious about this lady who may inherit some of the dream in which I've lived. Is she lovely?"

"Yes, dear lady. Quite lovely. How could we have hoped to put her in your place if she were not?"

"I know of her, no doubt?"

"No, she doesn't belong to the court. She's young, no more than seventeen years."

A pause ensued. "So very young? Was that necessary?" There was the merest hint of dissent in Agnes Sorel's voice. "I'm glad your choice didn't fall on anyone I knew. It makes the thought of a successor a little less difficult."

Coeur waited for a moment and then began to speak in hurried tones. "I brought her here because you asked me to do so. But, my lady, I've made up my mind to go no further. I don't think it necessary; but, even if it were necessary, I would withdraw." He leaned closer to the grating in his desire to convince her. "I became the King's Moneyman at the invitation of our liege lord and not through any conniving and scheming of my own. I've filled the post honestly and loyally. If I must fight to hold my place now, I prefer to do so with my own weapons."

"What weapons, my lord Coeur?"

The Moneyman indulged in a sweeping gesture. "I possess a power all my own. It's something new and yet so potent that I feel disposed to put all my faith in it. The power of money, Lady Agnes. My finger is in every dish. There's scarce a man in the King's train who's not in my debt. As a last resort I could buy their support by the remission of obligations."

The voice behind the grating said wearily, "There are other ways of wiping out debts than by paying them. Dead men make poor collectors."

A door opened somewhere in the rear of the house and then closed again quickly, but not before a sound of unrestrained weeping had reached his ears. He thought, "It's a sign that the mistress has lived a good life when servants weep at her passing."

Agnes Sorel spoke now in a tone which showed how little strength she had left. "I didn't think it would be necessary this late to convince you of the need of proceeding. Don't put too much faith in this money power you speak of. The King is your largest debtor and you must know how he will feel. He hates to owe money but he has an equal aversion to paying off his debts." Her voice changed. She continued in low but excited tones: "I am dying, Jacques Coeur! Make no mistake about that. And when you stand on the brink of eternity, you see by a blinding white light. I can see everything so clearly! . . . Jacques Coeur, Jacques Coeur, you are in great danger! You must listen to me. You must do as I say. Don't let your pride stand in the way."

"It isn't pride, Lady Agnes."

She seemed almost out of breath when she spoke again. "Let me see the girl now. I won't have the strength to question her. Have more candles brought so I shall be able to see her well. My eyes grow poorer with each hour which brings me closer to the time when—when they will close forever."

"Are you certain you want to do this?"

"Quite certain. Perhaps I'll feel easier in my mind if I can approve your choice." She demanded with sudden impatience: "Is what I have done of such small importance that no effort need be made to carry on my work?"

The Moneyman returned to the hall where he found Valerie sitting on a bench against the wall. The candle had guttered so low by this time that she was little more than a shadow.

"You're to come now," he said. "Don't be disturbed. You won't have to see her or speak to her, and it won't take more than a few minutes."

She pressed close to him in the darkness and laid a hand nervously on his arm. "This place frightens me, my lord. It's like a house of the dead."

Coeur called an order to the manservant who answered it by bringing two candles. The Moneyman took them from him and led the way back. He seated Valerie close to the grating and placed both candles on a table beside her. Her nervousness was apparent in the tensity with which she twined the fingers of both hands in her lap. She kept her head up, however, and even ventured a look at the grating behind which her invisible judge sat.

Coeur drew up a chair beside her. "I've seen you so seldom of late," he said, "that I feel entirely in the dark about you. I assume that coming north has interrupted your studies."

"Not entirely, my lord." Her voice was steady enough. "I have a few books with me and I try to read in them each evening. It's hard because some of the books are not meant for—for beginners. I go very slowly, my lord Coeur." After a moment's pause she continued in a more animated tone: "Cousin Regnault has promised to get permission for me to see the books and manuscripts in the abbey library. He tells me there are wonderful things there. The Holy Word itself and many books with rich embellishments and even"—she looked doubtful of the propriety of going on—"even many of the old fabliaux, written out fairly and most easy to read. I'm looking forward to my visit."

"It's clear," said Coeur, nodding and smiling by way of encouragement, "that you're becoming quite a scholar."

No sound had come from behind the grating but there was a tension in the air which could be felt as surely as though the watcher herself could be seen. Coeur led Valerie on to talk of many things: her instructors, the advances she had made in other lessons, the people she had encountered during the long ride to Jumièges.

The girl soon lost all trace of self-consciousness and spoke with ease, even laughing when the things she spoke of roused her sense of humor.

A finger tapped on the grating. Coeur walked over and lowered his head to whisper, "Yes, my lady?"

"Send her away now, please. But we must have a talk, my lord Coeur, while I still have strength. I am—I am completely bemused! I can hardly believe what I've seen. I think this must be a—a fancy, a vision!"

Silence greeted him when he returned to his station at the grating after seeing Valerie back to the hall. It continued so long that he began to think Agnes Sorel had lapsed into unconsciousness. Then he heard a low sob, followed by others at irregular intervals.

"Jacques Coeur, Jacques Coeur!" she said, when the sobs had begun to subside. "What is this you've done? She's so much like me that—for a moment—I wondered if I had died and it was my own body that I saw." There was a long pause. "Who is this girl? Where did you find her?"

Coeur told the story as briefly as he could. Agnes Sorel made no comment until he began on the results of Pregent Kennedy's investigation of the girl's past. He could hear her stir then on her couch.

"But the names, the names!" she demanded, with a hint of excitement in her voice. "Who was her father?"

"That mystery has not yet been solved," said Coeur.

"Where was the village in which she was found?"

"In the south of Berri."

"I knew it!" The voice of the sick woman was pitched high and it was clear that she was much excited. "I was sure this close resemblance could not be accidental. Jacques Coeur, the father of this girl was my brother, my favorite brother who died three years ago. He told me of a romance he had had with a young woman of Berri and of her death after giving birth to a daughter. His wife was of a jealous turn and so he made no attempt to claim the child." She paused and he could hear her breathing. "There can be no doubt about it! None, Jacques Coeur! My brother and I were so much alike we were often mistaken for twins when we were young. It's not surprising the girl resembles me. I had a warning of the truth the instant she came into the room."

Jacques Coeur found himself willing to accept this conclusion without any question. After several moments of consideration he said: "You'll want me to investigate further, no doubt. It should be an easy matter to arrive at the facts now."

"Take whatever steps you think necessary. But for my part I need no further proof. I know, Jacques Coeur, that she's my brother's daughter; my mind is completely free of doubt."

The Moneyman seemed to have lost concern over what she was saying. He leaned closer to the grating, so close, in fact, that he caught a glimpse of her on the other side of it.

"My lady," he said, "I've a little knowledge of many things. I'm not a physician but I know enough of medicine and the human body to be sure that you've talked overlong. I beg you to excuse me now, with the understanding that I am to return later, after you have rested. Perhaps you'll care to see me later in the day. If not, I must wait until tomorrow."

"No, I must finish what I have to say. If you go now, I may never see you again. Jacques Coeur, my best of friends, I confide my new-found niece to your care. She is sweet and intelligent and, I think, of fine and resolute character. I'm sure I can trust you to look after her well. It's my last earthly wish that she have a better life, a kinder one, than I have had." She was silent for several moments and then she began to speak again with an insistence which left her breathless after very few words. "You must find someone else. You must select a girl capable of accomplishing what we had in mind. As for my niece, see to it—see to it, Jacques Coeur, that she——"

The voice died away. Coeur did not wait for her to continue. Seizing one of the candles with urgent haste, he hurried in to her through a curtained arch in the wall beside the grating.

3

The room was so dark that at first he could make out nothing except that the small squares of light, which entered by way of the grating, cast a checkered pattern on the opposite wall. Then he saw that there was a window and made his way to it cautiously to open the shutters. This he accomplished with some difficulty, finding it necessary first to break the parchment which took the place of glass in the aperture. The shutters had not been opened in some time and it took all the strength he possessed to loosen the locks. When the wooden frames finally swung outward with a creaking of reluctant bolts, he filled his lungs with the fresh air which rushed in.

The room, he now saw, was so tiny that it was hard to determine the purpose it served in the household routine. It contained two pieces of furniture only, the couch under the grating, on which the dying woman lay, and a small table with medicines, a flask of wine, and a shallow glass.

Coeur turned his eyes toward the couch. He was so shocked by what he saw that with the utmost difficulty he compelled himself to draw closer. Agnes Sorel had lost consciousness. Her head was turned away from him on the soiled pillow but he could make out that her cheekbones protruded sharply and that the skin had sunk into deep blue hollows on each side of her brow. Of the beauty which had made a legend of Agnes Sorel not a vestige was left; she was a wraith, robbed of all semblance of her former self, no longer even a caricature of the famed Lady of Beauty.

He stood over her, the same thoughts running through his mind which she had given expression to a few minutes before—that it was doubly sad to see a life which had been lived in beauty and splendor come to such an ending. Then a more urgent consideration drove all other thought from his mind. He knew much more about medicine than he had taken credit for; and, looking down at the gaunt face of the patient, he realized that something must be done without any delay if she was to be summoned back to life.

He glanced at the medicines on the table and shook his head in instant and emphatic rejection. Then he poured a little wine into the glass and diluted it with water. Placing a hand under her head to raise it from the pillow, he held the glass to her lips and forced down her throat a few swallows of the liquid. "Come back, sweet lady," he said. "You must not leave us yet. Can you hear me?"

He was so intent on his efforts to revive her that he did not know he was being watched until an unfriendly voice broke the silence of the room.

"What has happened, my lord?"

He glanced up and saw that Jeanne de Vendôme was standing in the doorway, her eyes fixed on him intently. Still holding the glass to the lips of the dying woman, he studied the face in the doorway, and a conviction grew in him that something hostile and even malignant had entered the room with her. He was sure that this strange-looking young woman was to play an important part in his life.

"The Lady Agnes became unconscious as I talked with her," he explained. "She was scarce breathing when I reached her. Now she shows signs of coming around. See, she's breathing more naturally. I think she'll regain consciousness any moment."

"Am I to summon the physician, my lord?"

"Yes, at once." Coeur lowered the sick woman's head to the pillow and replaced the glass on the table before looking up. Jeanne de Vendôme had not moved. She was leaning against the frame of the door, her gray-green eyes watching him with a disturbing closeness.

"Your mistress needs immediate attention," he said sharply. "Go for the physician at once."

The young woman still did not obey. "How does it happen that the window is open?" she asked. "It's against all orders. My lady has most particularly instructed us that no light is to be allowed in."

"I opened the window. If I had not done so, it's quite possible your mistress would be dead now. That's a matter I intend to discuss with the physician. Is it Robert de Poitevin who is here today?"

"Yes, my lord. He has had instructions from the King to stay here and give my lady all his attention."

"That is good."

The girl still did not go. "You have broken so many rules," she said impudently, "that I'm not sure it's safe to leave you alone with her."

"You will go at once or I shall see to it that someone else is found for your post!"

Jeanne de Vendôme went then but with a swishing of skirts and a toss of the head which suggested both unwillingness and displeasure. In little more than a minute Robert de Poitevin came hurrying into the room, breathing indignation. Agnes Sorel had recovered some degree of consciousness by this time. Her eyes had opened and she was breathing easily. The little physician gave her one appraising glance and then shook his head protestingly in the direction of the open window.

"My lord Coeur, my lord Coeur!" he said in an outraged tone of voice. "This is a fault, a very grave fault indeed. My lady's orders are that no light or fresh air is to be allowed in any part of the house. What will she think of this?"

"The air in this house is more deadly than any disease," declared the Moneyman. "You would be well advised, good friend Robert, to use your own good judgment in such matters as this."

"My own judgment—and I think it good—is against the admission of the raw air from outside. It carries disease with it, my lord Coeur. It chills the body and lowers its powers of resistance. Air, my lord Coeur, is one of man's most deadly enemies."

The sick woman stirred slightly. The physician hurried over to the couch and regarded her with anxious solicitude. He touched a finger to her forehead and to her lips, frowned doubtfully, and then gave a quick nod of the head. "She has suffered no ill effects so far from this unseemly exposure to the—the elements," he declared. "But she must be removed at once to her bedroom. I say it to your face, my lord Coeur, I opposed her will to see you. I gave in to her most reluctantly. I know you too well. You're not a soothing person. You talk, you demand, you give orders. You're not made for sickrooms."

He broke off to clap his hands twice with an emphatic clack. When the manservant answered the summons, he instructed him to have the couch carried back to the bedroom at once.

Coeur looked down at the dying woman and was amazed to see that a change had come over her. The lines of her face had softened and some of her beauty had come back. It was clear that she had regained some measure of peace for there was the suggestion of a smile on her lips.

"My sweet Lady Agnes," he said in a low voice. "Have you anything else to say to me? Have you any further commands?"

If she heard him, she made no sign. Her eyes, perhaps resenting the light, remained closed. The physician took him by the arm and led him to a corner of the room.

"It will be a miracle," he whispered, "a veritable miracle, my lord Coeur, if our poor lady lives through the night."

One of the shutters had blown shut and the other was flapping back and forth. Coeur walked over and bolted it tight. He remained there in the dark for several minutes, his mind full of the past. He thought of Agnes Sorel as she had been when she came to the court, young and zestful for life, her beauty so startling in its flawlessness that men became speechless on first seeing her. "I pledged her my allegiance then," he said to himself. No one could say he had not kept his pledge. He had helped her, consulted her, considered her interests in all things. Between them they had kept Charles of France on the right path. It had been a perfect partnership, understanding, unselfish, complete in the confidence they gave each other. "No one has ever guessed how deep my allegiance has been," he said to himself. "And now this is the end."

The couch was being carried out. He waited until the sound of the servants' steps could no longer be heard. Then he said to the physician in a low tone, "It will be hard to reconcile myself to living in a world which Agnes Sorel has left."

4

When they emerged into the open air the noon sun had turned the countryside into a blaze of beauty. With the persistence of withwind, the snow had settled everywhere, leaving few traces of other color in tree or bush. The fields crisped and sparkled in this moment of supreme combination of winter sun and winter snow.

Nicolas stepped up and announced that a messenger had arrived from the abbey with word that Jacques Coeur was to return there at once. The Moneyman gave a nod of recognition to the horseman who had brought the word.

"The order is from the King?"

"Yes, my lord."

Coeur turned to Valerie. He was thinking, "How excited she will be when I tell her that the mystery of her birth has been solved at last!" He smiled affectionately as he raised her gloved hand to his lips. "I've something important to tell you, my child," he said. "But as I must leave you now, it will have to wait until I can find the time to see you again. By good St. Martin, it's the best of news! Your pretty eyes will sparkle with delight when I tell you what I've learned today—and what I have decided!"

"Then come soon, my lord."

As he struck off on the direct road to the abbey, with Nicolas in the rear protesting the headlong gait at which he rode, Jacques Coeur gave serious consideration to his future course. What Agnes had said about the attitude of the King had shaken his confidence to some extent but not entirely. "The life of the court is the only one she has ever known," he thought. "She judges everything by court standards. She hasn't any conception of the power I've acquired. She doesn't think it possible for anyone to fight his enemies with the weapons he has forged himself. I have influence and wide connections of which she knows nothing—and I have my sharp wits and the power of my great wealth."

He cried aloud, much to the alarm of Nicolas, "They'll find that Jaquet the Fox can fight, when pressed to it, like a wolf at bay or a lion on the prowl!"

Chapter VII

I

THE ABBOT OF JUMIÈGES had decided on this particular day to partake of dinner in the refectory where the monks had their meals. Wearing his bishop's ring with the smallest trace of ostentation (for, after all, the right to wear it was the most prized privilege of the abbots of Jumièges), he sat in the center of the dais with a guest from the court on each side of him and watched the monks below in a silence which seemed almost to smolder. The guests dined sumptuously on gramose soup, a sided haddock, a roast of venison, and at the finish a *setewale,* which was the name given to an uncommonly rich pastry with ginger flavoring. They washed these fine dishes down with the very best of wines the cellars could provide and seemed to be enjoying themselves to the utmost. The good Abbot, however, contented himself with the three dishes being served to the members of the order: dried beans, cheese, and bread; and he ate of these with the sparse appetite of dissatisfaction.

"I'm deeply distressed, Messires," he said toward the close of the meal. "The honor paid us by the King in coming here is a great one, to be recorded in our annals and remembered with pride for all time. But it must be said that all this is upsetting to the discipline of my people."

One of the guests, sipping his wine with indolent enjoyment, remarked that "it should be refreshing for the members of the order to catch again a glimpse of the life of the outside world."

As though crushing an undesirable insect with a downward swoop of a sandaled foot, the Abbot gave this heresy the immediate dispatch it deserved. "It is to escape all contacts with earthly prides and pomps that these gentle fellows of mine have joined the order," he stated. His voice achieved an oratorical ardor. "They have put the temptations of life and the lusts of the flesh behind them. And yet they cannot fail, no matter how circumspectly they walk nor how resolutely they keep their eyes lowered, to see something of what is going on about them. And this must be said, Messires: You bring inside our doors the life of the outside world in its most beguiling and dangerous form." He shoved his wine cup away from him with an impatient gesture, as though it too belonged to the world which must be kept at a distance. "Observe, if you please, the monk at the end of the hall, the one who stands without movement and with his arms folded on his breast. It is Brother Pellion and he was discovered in laughing converse with a maid belonging to one of your ladies." The Abbot's voice grew deep with indignation. "She was a forward creature with a disrespectful tongue and a willingness to animal lust in her eye. Brother Pellion has been standing on that spot for the better part of two days and he hasn't had a morsel of food in that time. There he will stand, in full sight of the food, until I grant him remission of his punishment or until he drops from exhaustion. It's more likely to be the latter, Messires."

One of the guests ventured a mild protest. "Is it not a severe sentence, considering the nature of the offense?"

The Abbot swallowed a crust of bread with a wry face as though he found it as bitter as chestnut husks. "The nature of the offense?" he exclaimed. He had intended to expatiate on the point but held himself in control and, after a moment of silence, went on with an explanation of the steps he had found it necessary to take. "I've imposed new rules to continue in force as long as we have courtly visitors. The brothers are not to be blamed, poor, bewildered fellows; but they must be saved the contamination of earthly contacts. Each must submit in turn to the *minuto* as fast as the infirmary can take them; an extra bloodletting will stifle bodily inclinations inside them. They are no longer to be allowed the freedom of the grounds. All their spare time must be spent in the carrells, improving their minds with the written word. They have always been allowed a half hour during dinner for conversation with their fellows. This privilege has been withdrawn. They must eat in silence."

The two guests had been wondering at the unwonted stillness throughout the hall. The members of the order had partaken of their frugal fare with no sound other than the clatter of spoons and cups on the table and the shuffle of the servants' feet. Their wants had been indicated in the sign language of the monastic world. The thumbs and first fingers of both hands bent in a circle meant, I desire bread. The tip of the first finger held to the first joint of the thumb was to be interpreted as, Pass the beans. Both hands joined obliquely together was a signal for an additional slice of cheese. Early in the meal a brother who sat just under the dais had in a forgetful moment raised his voice in speech. At the first syllable the bitter eye of the Abbot had fastened itself on him and the speech had broken off with the jarring suddenness of a note of music when a string snaps. For a full minute, while the long rows of cowled heads had remained bent over their platters, the accusing eye had transfixed the culprit, and not so much as the scrape of an imprudent heel had been heard in the hall.

"Brother Pellion was in charge of the bath," continued the Abbot. "I had foreseen difficulties when it became evident that the members of the King's train, who could not be received here, would look to us for bathing facilities. I had issued instructions that slips of paper were to be handed to applicants with the hour named at which each might come. But Brother Pellion, who is city bred and of weak fiber, fell into the habit of speaking with the servants who came to make arrangements for their masters and"—it was evident he had intended to add the word "mistresses" but it stuck in his throat—"I've replaced him with Brother Joseph who is old and has the use of one eye only."

The arrival of a pair of royal servants in green gilets, holding well-filled platters above their heads, created a diversion at this point. The Abbot called sharply, "Come, Brother Armand, what is this?" and the cellarer, in whose province such matters lay, hurried to the dais to make an explanation.

"It's a pittance, sent from the royal table for the delectation of the brothers, holy father."

"No pittance should be served without my permission," declared the head with a frown before which even Charles of France might have trembled. "What's the nature of the dish, if I may be allowed a belated word in the matter?"

The cellarer seemed reluctant to answer. "Cheese tarts," he said finally.

"Cheese tarts! Of what avail the minuto if my charges are to stuff their bodies with the richest of foods? I count it a grievous fault in you, Brother Armand, that you did not speak of this to me."

Animation had replaced the glum silence below. The rich pastries with their brown powdering of cinnamon on top were disappearing down monkish throats with a speed which threatened to exhaust the supply in no time at all. The smacking of heavy lips told of the satisfaction the creamy tarts had brought to starved palates.

The Abbot smiled bleakly at his guests. "I shall tender due thanks to our liege lord," he said. "But my conscience compels me to say it's well the responsibility for their spiritual welfare does not rest in his overgenerous hands."

Brother Joseph, in spite of his years and the blindness in one of his eyes, had succeeded in getting an ample share of the unexpected pittance.

He was still munching with a slow and circular motion of his jaws when the signal to rise was given. As he got to his feet he winked at the fat priest who had been sitting opposite him. The latter, interpreting the wink correctly, fell into step with him at the foot of the line.

The new custodian of the bath, employing a facility for speaking with no motion of the lips which years of practice had brought him, began to talk in the lowest of whispers.

"Brother Ossiprian, it will be this afternoon. *This* afternoon. Are you sure you understand what's expected of you?"

The other nodded by way of answer.

Brother Joseph was not content to let the matter rest there. He proceeded to coach Brother Ossiprian in what he was to do. The latter, who was head carpenter and spent most of his working hours in a dark workshop below the level of the ground, listened with frowning attention.

"You're not to leave your post for an instant. According to the understanding, the King and those with him will pass through the wine cellars and into your workshop an hour from now. Even though the King is of all men the most prompt, delays are possible, and so it may be they will not arrive until some time later. Now heed me well. You're to leave the door into the bathhouse ajar and you're to find tasks to busy yourself close beside it. When the King enters the other end, you are to give three quick taps with a hammer on whatever object engages your attention at the moment. Is that clear? Mind you, Brother Ossiprian, it's not to be two taps, nor is it to be four. They are to be quick, one after the other. *Three* taps, Brother Ossiprian. You will make no mistakes?"

"No, Brother Joseph," whispered the carpenter. "Three taps of the hammer. Quick taps. There will be no mistake."

As he spoke they passed the silent figure of the culprit, Brother Pellion. Without raising his eyes from the floor, the new custodian of the bathhouse allowed one hand to brush the robe of his erring comrade and deposited in the side pocket a substantial wedge of cheese. With no motion of his lips Brother Pellion whispered, "A blessing on you, old friend."

The long double file broke up at the refectory door, the brethren going their various ways to the tasks awaiting them. The two ancient monks in the rear began to make their way across the cloister garth. Though free now of the danger of being overheard, they did not relax any of their precautions.

"You are to give the signal only if it's the King who enters," whispered

Brother Joseph. "If others come first, pay them no heed. You understand, I trust?" After a moment he added as an encouragement to good performance, "The rewards are to be generous, Brother Ossiprian."

2

Regnault de Burey had known of the King's liking for detail when he made his plans. He had dropped a hint in the royal ear that the affairs of the abbey were in a state of sad confusion. This was not, strictly speaking, any concern of the King's; the responsibilities of the Abbot included the proper control of abbey affairs as well as watching over the spiritual well-being of his charges. "But it's well known, sire," the Comte had said during the brief audience allowed him to discuss the subject, "that the worthy Abbot has not scrupled to complain about the size of the party you've brought here. He implies quite openly that the presence of so many visitors has resulted in an upsetting of daily routine. I contend, sire, that if you would make a tour of inspection you would find that the confusion has always existed and is due to laxness in supervision."

Charles had decided at once that a tour of inspection was in order and had settled on that afternoon for the purpose. Starting out at the exact moment he had set, he led a small party of his ministers through the stables, the squillerie, the spicerie, the scalding pit, the pantries, and kitchens. Everywhere he found evidence that what the Comte had said was true.

"I must have a talk with the holy Abbot," he said cheerfully as he walked down the stone steps to the cellars. "He's not to be blamed for what has happened; at least we must be sparing in our view of him. His establishment is not equipped to take care of so many. But it's not to be gainsaid that things are sadly out of hand. Yes, I must have a talk with him at once." He glanced over his shoulder at the court official who followed closest on his heels. "Did you give an eye, my lord, to the confusion in the kitchen? And the stables! Truly the services of another Hercules are needed *there!*" A titter of approval greeted the royal jest. Charles, well pleased with himself, waited until his officers had enjoyed their laugh. Then he gave his head a sober shake. "It's said the accounts are ill kept. And did you notice that last summer's vines to catch flies are still hanging here and there?"

The party walked slowly through the cellars, casting appreciative eyes at the huge tuns of ale and the seemingly endless rows of bins where the fine wines were kept, the Saint-Emilion, the Malmsley, the Muscatel.

Here was something to admire and commend without any reservations at all. The King, who liked his wine, nodded his head in approval several times and said to his attendants, "There's nothing amiss here and I must remember to speak a word for the cellarer when I have my talk with the worthy Abbot."

After the wine cellars came the workshop, where they had to step cautiously to avoid falling over saw benches and gantries and lathes. Here the aromatic scent of fresh shavings filled the nostrils instead of the acrid sweetness of the wines, but the King sniffed suspiciously and seemed intent on getting through as quickly as possible.

"What lies beyond?" he asked.

Guillaume Gouffier, who walked immediately behind, consulted a list and replied, "The bathhouse, my liege lord."

"Ha!" said the King, with deep satisfaction. "We now come to the source of the chief difficulty. I've had countless complaints of the long waits my good lords and ladies have had to endure for their turn to bathe. We must not overlook the fact that there are many of us and only one bath which might in all naturalness create an expectation of crowding. Still"—with a nod—"it's my understanding that none of the monks are due to bathe for many weeks. I think there has been bad management here."

The broad back of a solitary monk was to be seen at the far end of the workshop, bending over a lathe. He tapped briskly on an iron pipe and was so busy that he did not raise his head as the royal party passed.

The bathhouse beyond was a dark vault in which the light thrown by two forlorn cressets shone faintly. The one bath that it contained was sunk below the level of the flagged floor and it was large enough to accommodate three full-bodied monks at once. To meet the objections of the fair visitors, who preferred to bathe singly and not out in the open, the abbey carpenter had constructed screens about five feet high to be placed around the bath when desired. They were in use when the royal party appeared on the threshold and a sound of splashing came from behind them.

"It seems," said the King, pausing and frowning, "that our inspection is to be impeded by this insatiable demand for cleanliness which has suddenly taken hold of everyone."

And now it is possible to consider and perhaps admire the cunning and thoroughness which Regnault de Burey had shown in his planning. It had been necessary for him to estimate the progress of the King so accurately as to anticipate him at the bathhouse at almost this moment.

He had helped Brother Joseph manipulate his list so that the steamy vault lacked all seekers after cleanliness other than the one now in the tub. Guillaumette, thoroughly flustered, even though she had been well coached, had to be standing inside the center screen when the door opened to admit the royal party.

Everything happened exactly as planned.

Guillaumette, berating herself mentally as a Judas but clutching avidly at the silver coins (but not as many as thirty) in the pocket of her skirt, brushed against the screen and caused it to fall outward. As a result Charles of France was treated to a tableau as unexpected and unconventional as any of the tales with which professional storytellers earned their fees.

Valerie had just stepped from the tub when the mishap occurred. The fall of the screen revealed her standing on tiptoe like Venus emerging from the waves, her arms outstretched for the towel which the maid held. The resemblance to the goddess did not end with the pose. There was a suggestion of eagerness about her as though she too was in process of entering a new life. Her hair had been piled high on her head to avoid wetting, where it was held by thin bands of blue velvet; and it was a mass of curls as richly golden as the popular conception of divine beauty. There was a hint of divinity also in the slender shapeliness of her figure.

"Guillaumette!" Valerie's voice rose to a sharp and very human treble. "What have you done!"

"Mademoiselle!" wailed Guillaumette, scrambling frantically to raise the screen. "Oh, Mademoiselle! What have I done indeed!"

After the first moment of shocked inertia, Valerie moved swiftly. She did not, however, make the mistake that instinct urged on her of plunging back into the water, thus ending the episode with a loud splash, and on a note of farce. Nor did she rush with agitated leaps for the shelter of the side screen which was still standing. Instead she whisked the towel from the grasp of Guillaumette and wrapped it about her until nothing was to be seen but her head and the pleasantly sloped contour of her white shoulders. Then she moved so swiftly that the spectators, standing in frozen attention on the threshold, were hardly aware of motion on her part until the screen hid her from view.

"Oh, Guillaumette!" she gasped as she cowered in the dark corner, still holding the towel about her with a frantic insistence. "What a dreadful thing! I think I shall die of shame!"

"Can you ever forgive me?" sobbed the maid.

"How *could* you have been so careless! What will they think? Everyone will hear! Guillaumette, do you think we can get away before anyone finds who we are?"

The maid slipped the linen undergarment over the shoulders of her mistress with fingers which strove to make amends with haste for what she had done. "We'll get away as soon as we dare, Mademoiselle," she whispered. "I'll go first to make sure that no one is watching."

"Hurry, then, hurry!" said Valerie, with almost breathless urgency. She held up her arms so the warm winter tunic could be dropped over her head. "Guillaumette, you've had many chances to see the people here. Did you recognize any of those men?"

Candor forced Guillaumette to make an admission. "I'm very much afraid, Mademoiselle, that one was the King himself!"

Charles of France stumbled once or twice as he led the way back through the gloom of the carpenter shop. "Gouffier," he said, "it will be necessary to delay the inspection of the bathhouse until a more suitable time."

"Yes, sire," agreed Gouffier, with a smirk in his voice.

"I was informed," went on the ruler, "that we would find the place empty. It was so stated to me." He paused and, when he went on, a note of eagerness was permitted to show in his tone. "What an extraordinary thing! By'r Lady, I'm still unwilling to believe what I saw!"

The deep-set eyes of Guillaume Gouffier squinted up in surprise at his master. "If my liege lord will permit me to say so, I saw nothing extraordinary. We stumbled, most unexpectedly, on a very pretty girl in the act of stepping from her bath. It has happened before. I could quote several episodes in support of my statement, drawing them from history, both sacred and profane."

They passed from the carpenter shop into the long, cold crypt of the wine cellars where their footsteps echoed hollowly. The King sniffed the pungent winey odor and said: "On my honor, I feel the need for a stoup of the very strongest wine these bins can produce. It was like seeing——" The ruler paused and gave his head a bewildered shake. "Gouffier, I swear I saw a ghost back there."

"A ghost?" Gouffier presumed on the high standing he had in his master's regard to make light of the matter. "It was not a ghost I saw, sire. What I saw was a young woman fairly glowing with life and health. If there was anything ghostly about those warm, rounded limbs of hers, then, liege lord, I renounce forever the fear I have had of the supernatural."

"What I meant," amended the King testily, "was that she resembled someone so very much that she seemed like a ghost from the past."

The expression on his counselor's face showed such complete lack of understanding that Charles added, "Do you mean you failed to see the resemblance?"

"What resemblance, sire?"

Charles of France seemed reluctant to go any deeper into the matter. "Well, Gouffier, since you failed to see it, we'll let it rest there. But I must tell you that I was quite dazed by what I thought I saw in her."

Gouffier's face, which had a simian quality of slyness and malevolence about it, wrinkled up into a grin. "Sire, the young lady vouchsafed us no more than a fleeting glimpse of her charms. I am forced to an admission. My eyes were too busy elsewhere to reach any impression of her—her facial aspect."

The King offered no comment. He was making a mental note of the exact time when the episode had occurred so that it would be possible to discover from the monk in charge the name of the fair occupant whose turn in the sunken tub had been so rudely interrupted.

3

Valerie knew a journey was contemplated as soon as she returned to the manor house. Half-a-dozen saddles were warming on the hearth and there was a rope strung in front of the fire on which as many cloaks were suspended. She looked inquiringly at the Comtesse who was writing a letter in a corner of the room.

"Are we leaving, Cousin?" she asked.

The Comtesse frowned. She was such an indifferent scholar that the composing of a letter entailed the utmost effort and concentration. Valerie was convinced it was intended for the Sire d'Arlay and she said to herself, "She's sending him a message of farewell." Then she indulged in a second thought which left her with a guilty feeling of triumph. "It will do her small good." That D'Arlay had not been to see his sister-in-law since his visit on the first day of their arrival had been gleefully discussed and interpreted in the De Burey retinue, as Valerie had learned from Guillaumette. "He has given her up for good," was the way the maid summed up the situation. The reaction to this among the staff had been one of complete approval, as the popularity of the Comte's brother had grown with the fame he had won. "It's time he rode a new saddle," they said. Guillaumette's opinion, which she had expressed many times, was, "You ought to marry him, Mademoiselle, but if you do, watch out for Madame."

Valerie found it necessary to repeat the question, "Are we leaving today?"

"Yes." Isabeau sanded the letter and folded it with a frown. "We start for Paris as soon as the horses are ready."

"But, Cousin——"

"But, Cousin!" repeated Isabeau impatiently. Her eyes matched her hair in color and so it was clear that writing the letter had stirred her emotions. "Do you question the wisdom of leaving? I was sure you would be delighted. For my part, I can't get home soon enough."

"But——" Valerie felt a growing conviction that there was something back of this hurried exit she did not know about but which undoubtedly concerned her. "But, Cousin Isabeau, does my lord Coeur concur in this?"

The Comtesse drew her brows together. "Are we so beholden to my lord Coeur that we needs must consult him about all our plans and movements?"

Valerie was thinking: "Has it been decided I'm not suitable after all? Did that dreadful mistake this afternoon have anything to do with it?"

The Comtesse stood up, letter in hand. "Since you have had the bad grace to ask such a question, I'll tell you this: He knows of our leaving. It was settled between us."

"What has happened to change everything this way?"

"Nothing has happened. It's only that we think it better to return at once. Agnes Sorel will be dead before morning and the King will then depart without any delay."

"Am I to see my lord Coeur before we start?"

The Comtesse answered in a sharp voice: "No, Cousin, you will not see him. Didn't you hear me say we leave as soon as the horses are ready?"

The Comte entered the room at this point. He was cloaked and hatted for the journey and looked so much like a bear with a red nose that Valerie wanted to laugh. No fewer than three coats had been wrapped about him and his beaver hat had been pulled down over his ears where it was held in place by a woolen band wound many times around his head. He cut an absurd figure most certainly, and yet there was an air about him which suggested an expansion of his self-esteem.

He squinted at the girl and then asked his wife in an anxious whisper, "Has she any suspicions?"

Isabeau gave her head the merest shake and then said in a complaining voice: "My cousin has been questioning the wisdom of leaving this afternoon. She isn't sure yet we have the sanction of Jacques Coeur."

"Then your little cousin, Madame, shows less than her usual good sense. Does she think I would start at as late an hour as this on an impulse, a whim? I wouldn't stick my nose outside the door of this malodorous hole if I didn't have the best of reasons for it."

Godefroy entered and began to gather up the saddles. "We'll be ready to leave in another five minutes, my lord," he said.

The Comte groaned. "My bones will ache unbearably before we are through. I must have another glass of warm wine before I offer my protesting limbs to this torture."

"You've had enough wine already," declared his wife.

The Comte treated her to a steady look. "I'll have another drink, Madame, and you will order it for me without another word."

When Isabeau gave the order at once, Valerie said to herself in wonder: "This is indeed strange. What can have happened to bring this change between them?"

Chapter VIII

I

AT THE western boundary of the Hôtel Saint-Pol, where the King had taken up his residence on returning to Paris following the death of Agnes Sorel, there stood three houses. How they came to be there was a mystery. They backed against the meandering palace wall, which happened to be straight at this point, and so might well be a cause of worry to a nervous monarch who feared assassins. From the upper windows of these intruding houses it was possible to look down into the palace gardens, another disadvantage. Charles would have cleared them out long ago but for the fact that the indemnities to the owners were certain to be heavy; and so there they stayed like three burs in the tail of an otherwise sleek stallion.

The first of the three had once belonged to a family of some distinction and wealth but for the better part of a generation it had been used for commercial purposes. Men were seen to issue at all hours of the day from the ground floor which had been cut up into an infinity of tiny dark cubicles for the transaction of business, and bales of goods were constantly being craned in and out of the upper windows.

The third was equally large and had once been of corresponding importance; but the owners, less farsighted than the proprietors of the first, had given up when the roof began to disintegrate and the walls to crumble. It had been untenanted for many years, and people now took other routes to avoid passing it, because of their belief that it was haunted by evil spirits.

Between these two disreputable reminders of greatness long since departed was a house of a distinctly different type. It was much smaller, it was comparatively new, and it was as neat as a burgher's house in one of the suburbs which were stretching out far beyond the walls of the city. Its stone front had recently been scraped, the copper hinges on the door shone cheerfully, and over the entrance was a lantern enclosed in a new iron frame with the head of a griffon on top which must have come not long before from the forge of the smith. In spite of its immaculate appearance, there was something furtive about the little house. It seemed to shrink within the shelter of its gone-to-seed neighbors as though anxious to avoid notice. Its cleanliness did not succeed in achieving for it an air of virtue. It was like a strumpet who went about her ancient trade unobtrusively instead of romping and brawling in taverns and who preferred quiet attire to the vulgar finery of her competitors.

One afternoon in early March the Comte de Burey halted his retinue at the corner of the Logis de la Reine, which was still some distance from the neighborhood of the three houses, and instructed them to await his return there. He then proceeded on foot with Valerie, who had accompanied him. Guillaumette clumped along in the rear, her arms filled with bundles. It was a lovely day. Spring had put in an early appearance and a friendly sun shone on the dirty old city in an effort to coax out thin edgings of green along the banks of the river and in unexpected nooks here and there. The beauty, however, was lost on Valerie. She had been told nothing except that she was to make one of the party; but the purpose of this trip into the Marais, that part of the town where the great palaces clustered, was not hard to divine.

There was no one in sight when they stopped in front of the little house, but the Comte had no sooner raised the knocker on the front door than two men put in an appearance and ranged themselves beside him. They were armed with bills and short swords and they were prepared, quite obviously, to take things in hand if it developed that the newcomers had no right to be there. That contingency did not arise. The Comte said something in a low tone to the man who opened the door and they were admitted immediately.

Valerie looked about her with apprehensive eyes but was forced to the conclusion almost immediately that the interior was far from what she had expected. Nothing she had seen at the Hôtel de Burey or on her recent travels had prepared her for the richness and warmth of this unusual house. The walls were not bare and discolored with dampness but were covered with tapestries and hangings in cheerful colors. The floors were not wet and slippery but were hidden under carpets of the kind provided by the *tapissiers sarrasinois,* the latest Parisian guild, for the great and the wealthy of the city. Her feet sank into them as she walked diffidently behind Regnault de Burey. She had never seen anything like the furniture but she sensed that all of it was costly and rare.

A woman came from an inner room to greet them, saying in a stiff and precise voice, "And is this Mademoiselle de Voudrai, my lord Comte?"

The Comte stopped dead still and looked at the newcomer with unbelieving eyes. She was absurdly tall and thin with a neck which was swanlike in length if not in grace. A small head protruded forward from the end of it and a shovel nose, somewhat meaty in color, jutted out in turn from the head. It seemed almost inevitable that the weight of the nose would be too much, that it would bring about her collapse as the last small block will cause a child-built tower to fall. She would have been a completely comic figure had it not been for her eyes, which were sharp and hard.

"Can it be possible?" he whispered to Valerie. "What vision of beauty is this to banish the memories of all other fair women: Helen receiving the apple, Eleanor whose lusty charms won her two kings as husbands, Flora, Fredegonde, Héloïse?"

He knew who she was, however, even though he had not been prepared for her eccentricities of appearance. "Yes, Damoiselle Henriette," he said aloud, with a deep bow. "It's my understanding that she's to be left in your care."

The lean form of Damoiselle Henriette arched itself in a bow to Valerie. "I'm happy to welcome you, my lady," she said. "We have striven to anticipate every wish in the hope that you will be happy here. May I offer you refreshments before you leave, my lord?"

The Comte declined on the ground that he had left his escort some distance away and did not want to attract notice to them by too long a wait. He then kissed Valerie's hand. "It begins, my little pet," he said to her, in a cautious undertone. "You have nothing to fear. The staff has no other purpose but to see that you're comfortable. As for this drooping beanstalk, this disjointed old passionflower, I hardly know what advice to give. I would dub her harmless but for that eye of hers. Well, treat her almost as an equal—but never confide in her."

"I will try to be most careful in everything," the girl whispered back nervously.

The Comte drew himself up and bowed ceremoniously to each of them in turn. Then he said, "Farewell, Cousin," and departed through the front door.

"Would my lady like to go to her bedroom now?" asked Damoiselle Henriette, her head teetering on her grotesque neck as she turned in the direction of an inner door.

Valerie did not reply at once. She was wondering for the thousandth time if the sudden departure from Jumièges had been at the wish of Jacques Coeur. If he had known, and approved, why had she not heard from him since? Always before she had received notes at fairly regular intervals, and his long silence made her suspect that he did not know where she was. What disturbed her most was her uncertainty about the step just taken. Had she come to this house with the Moneyman's knowledge and consent? Isabeau had said that he knew, even going into details of the discussions there had been on the subject. And yet—the doubts she had felt at first still lingered in her mind. They had been augmented since arriving at this outwardly prim but aloof habitation situated so suspiciously on the edge of the King's greatest palace.

The tall woman repeated her question. Valerie collected her wits and replied in the affirmative. She then followed the Damoiselle up a flight of stairs to a large room on the floor above. She had no time to study the unusual pieces of furniture they passed on the way but her fears had not wholly vanquished her curiosity and so she marked each in her mind as worthy of examination later. Among them was a clock (she had seen clocks on the walls of great buildings and still thought of them as belonging in the realm of magic), surmounted with a gold globe and which ticked with an unbelievable regularity. She saw an esperver and did not know what it was (later generations would call it a hammock), even though it was suspended between stands as ornately carved as a chancel rail. It seemed to her suggestive that a chair at the end of the main room was built like a throne, with flying buttresses and napkin panels on the side decorated in quatrefoil. Through an archway leading into a room at the rear her eye picked out a monster buffet—an amazingly tall buffet even for an age which liked them tall and imposing—and she noticed it had castles elaborately carved on its top points and that gold and silver and enamel broke out all over it like a rash of adolescence.

She had passed all these marvels without pausing but she stopped when she came to the doorway of the bedroom. Inside was a bed which looked at first glance like a throne. It was unusual in having a full tester, the beds of the period being content, for the most part, with an overhang at the head. The posts were as big around as the barrel of a cannon and the curtains were of samite interwoven with gold, hanging in graceful folds like an emperor's robe. It was so high that the carvings above each corner of the tester touched the ceiling. The effect of this great height was to make the bed itself seem at first glance both short and narrow; but on stepping closer she found this to be a delusion, as it was capable of holding four tall men without any difficulty at all.

"It's called Pepin the Short," explained Damoiselle Henriette, in the tone of awe one might use on viewing the sacred relics in the Sainte-Chapelle.

Although she was familiar with the custom of giving names to pieces of furniture and decorations, particularly beds and standing cups, Valerie could not prevent herself from laughing. "Don't you think, Damoiselle Henriette," she suggested, "that it would have been more fitting to name this one after the giant Nemrod who was so tall his head touched the clouds?"

"Pepin was a great king," declared the other severely, "and the father of Charlemagne. It's the greatest of honors for one's bed to be named after a king."

Valerie's inner comment was that the bed should have been named Charles, for she had no doubts that he had slept in it. This conviction grew that night after Guillaumette had disrobed her and had tucked the covers up around her neck and had left her alone in the immense expanse of counterpane which, very clearly, had never been meant for one. She could not get to sleep, for the curtains had been drawn on all four sides and it seemed to her that she was looking up into a long tunnel of shimmering material with a quivering light in a lantern suspended from the top. The candle in the lantern was small and the only purpose it served was to distort the folds of the hangings and the floral designs into which the satin covering of the tester had been drawn; and, as she passed into the first stages of sleepiness, she fancied that she saw heads up there, some of them wearing crowns, and all of them staring down at her intently, as though wondering what a girl of the people was doing in a bed which had been built for a king. She would have sprung out of this closely muffled niche to seek a bed where darkness would close her away from these grinning, wicked faces but the languor which accompanies the near approach of slumber held her a prisoner, and in the end the faces faded away and the light of the candle seemed of no more significance than any star seen through a window at night. She fell off to sleep.

2

Valerie said little at dinner next day but Damoiselle Henriette, who sat at table with her, talked continuously as she pecked with the small appetite of ill-health at a salad of plums and Roman lettuce. Her conversation never deviated: the great but unacknowledged part women had played as nurses in all the great wars, the debt that France owed to Jeanne d'Arc, the ease with which a young woman known as Mademoiselle Margot had succeeded some twenty years before in beating all the men of France at tennis. "There's a lesson in this," she concluded. "Men haven't taken it to heart but to a few women the meaning is clear. Man's superiority is a sham, a self-fostered delusion!"

On rising to leave the table, she bowed to Valerie and said, "It's my earnest wish, my lady, that you'll always have a place for me in your household."

Left to herself, the girl strolled into a small room at the rear of the house where she had seen a few manuscripts and books. She picked up one of the books, a beautifully illuminated copy of an early part of the *Imitatio Christi,* but even the inspired text of that favorite book of the age failed to hold her. After a few minutes of laborious progress she let it fall into her lap.

She had been disturbed by Damoiselle Henriette's last remark. "That woman," she said to herself, "knows about everything. Or why should she think I'm to have a household of my own? Yes, she knows why I'm here and I am sure she regards me with contempt." Nothing but honeyed words had been spoken and yet she was certain she had seen in the sharp eyes of the tall woman an aloofness, a suggestion of sardonic acceptance of the situation. "If I am a success," so ran her thoughts, "all the ladies of the court will hate me, and plot against me, and, I suppose, envy me. I'll have no peace as long as I live. If I fail—everyone will consider it a great joke, I will be laughed at and my lord Coeur also." She was convinced, suddenly, that she would not succeed, that the idea had been doomed to failure from the start; that, in fact, the best thing she could do was to leave this house at once and run so far away that no one concerned would ever find her again.

But could she run away? Guillaumette had come to her that morning with a disturbed look on her face. "Mademoiselle!" she had whispered. *"We are prisoners!"*

"No, Guillaumette. You're imagining things."

"But, mistress, I'm not imagining things. Just a few minutes ago I was of a mind to step out for a breath of fresh air. But no sooner had I shown my face outside the door—there's only one door, for the house is built flat against the palace wall—than one of those two men we saw yesterday appeared from nowhere and grins at me. 'Where do you think you're going, my fair one?' he asks. I told him that was no concern of his and that it was clear to me he had been turned in at a pork-due.[1] He grins all the more and says to me, 'If you think you're going out, minikin, just think again. No one goes out, not even your mistress.' I said to him I would leave the marks of my fingers on his stupid face, but he said, 'It's orders, my old beauty.' And when I went to the Madame—— Do you know what the servants call her? Old Here-Comes-My-Nose-My-Ass-Is-Away-Behind. Well, it was the same. She jiggled that head of hers about and told me I must stay in the house and put my curiosity to bed."

Valerie had been warned that every possible precaution would be taken and so she was not particularly exercised over the fact that they were not to be allowed to show themselves on the streets at any time they desired. Now, however, she began to ponder seriously the position in which she found herself, and the knowledge that she was to all intents and purposes a prisoner added to her desire to be free of the chains they were forging for her.

She was deeply immersed in such thoughts when a sound behind her made her stiffen with alarm. She was alone in the room, and the noise, moreover, came from the part where no one could possiby be hidden, the rear wall which, if Guillaumette's information was correct, was against the high stone barricade of the Hôtel Saint-Pol. It was repeated. She sprang to her feet and turned about in time to see a section swing open in what she had assumed to be a wall paneled solidly in dark oak. A man stepped through the opening thus provided and closed the door after him. The panel sank back into place, and once more the wall presented an appearance of unbroken surface.

The intruder bowed to her and smiled, the smile having some trace of diffidence about it, as though he also was finding the situation a difficult one. He was of middle height and was wearing a handsome glaudkin of

[1]On the Nativity of the Virgin the peasants of France were required to give one pig in eight to the nobleman on whose land they belonged. This was known as the pork-due.

green velvet which covered him from head to foot. His face could not be called handsome but there was a rather amiable quality about his long nose and heavily lidded eyes. A gold chain was looped three times around his neck and his right hand toyed with it nervously as he took a few steps toward her.

"I must ask your indulgence for appearing so suddenly and so—so mysteriously, my child," he said. He smiled again and asked, "Do you know who I am?"

Valerie had dropped to her knees. Keeping her eyes on the floor, she answered, "Yes, sire."

"Come," said the King, reaching out a hand and helping her to her feet. "There is no need for further ceremony. I come today, not as the King of France but as a man who has seen you and who finds himself very much interested in you."

Valerie found enough courage to raise her head and meet his eyes; but, after the first quick exchange of glances, she allowed her lids to drop again. That he had shown some embarrassment on entering was proof of his human qualities, but he was, after all, the greatest and richest king in the world and she found it impossible to summon immediately any of the assurance needed to meet the situation.

"It's extraordinary!" The King was staring at her fixedly, and it was clear that he was both puzzled and excited at what he saw. "A favor, Mademoiselle. Will you indulge me by looking me full in the face?" Valerie obeyed by raising her eyes. He studied her intently. "Extraordinary indeed! And now the profile, Mademoiselle." Valerie turned her head and kept it in that position for several moments. She heard him draw in his breath. "It's even more apparent that way. And now, sweet child, will you raise your head a little higher?" Before she could obey, he reached out and placed his hands on her shoulders. He drew her around until they were facing each other again. She could feel a slight tremor in his hands. "Would you close your eyes for a moment so that the lashes rest on the cheeks? And now, if you please, a smile. Thank you, that is the final proof! Truly it passes all belief! It is a miracle!"

He had thrown back the glaudkin, revealing under it a tunic of plum-colored velvet with bands of ermine about the neck and sleeves. Since her elevation to this new life, Valerie had seen much in the way of rich clothes, but she had never encountered anything to equal the costume Charles of France had donned for the occasion. Over the tunic, and extending from neck to waist, was a panel of silk as tawny as an orange skin and embroidered with gold thread in an intricate pattern designed around scarlet roses with diamonds in their hearts. There was a sapphire dangling from the gold chain and a spatter of precious stones in the front of his belt.

The King motioned her to sit down and then drew up a chair for himself, placing it directly in front of her. "I saw you a week ago," he said, leaning forward, and never taking his eyes from her face. "It was at the street fete to celebrate our victories. In the afternoon I went against the advice of all my officers—I put on a domino and sallied out to watch the merrymaking in the streets. I had a rich reward for my pains: I saw *you,* sweet child, sitting on horseback with the Comte de Burey watching the procession. I was not more than six feet from you but, of course, you didn't see me. I watched you for a long time, I saw everything that happened, I heard every word you said! I was concerned for a moment when one of the maskers stopped and tickled your cheeks with feathers at the end of a wand."

Valerie nodded and smiled. "He was a tall man and he was dressed like a clown."

"He said to you, 'I am the prince of fools, the monarch of hulverheads, the perfect product of the world of doddypolls.' And you said, 'That's a rash claim to make in a field where there's so much competition.' And then you laughed—a merry laugh, a charming laugh. I was entranced by it. As I stood there and watched and listened, I knew that I—I had become enamored of you."

Whatever composure Valerie had succeeded in gaining deserted her promptly. "Sire," she said, "I—I am overwhelmed! I don't know what to say."

The King took possession of one of her hands. "I have a confession to make to you. It wasn't an accident. It wasn't chance which led me to the spot where I saw you. It had all been arranged. I had seen you once before and I asked the Comte to contrive some way by which that very great pleasure could be repeated. It was planned with the utmost care, my sweet Valerie. And now I am happy—— Ah, how happy I am that I went to such efforts!"

The trace of embarrassment which had shown in his manner when he entered the room had vanished. He was completely in command of himself and of the situation. His eyes glowed with ardor as he captured her other hand and drew her forward toward him. "And now I have planned something else. I have planned *this.* This house is yours, with every comfort I could find for you, with servants to tend you and guards to give you security. I'm hoping to pay you many visits here. I desire you near my person."

Her confusion had increased as his had diminished. Lowering her eyes, she answered, "That will be as my liege lord wishes."

"No, no! That won't suffice me. I am seeking to ascertain your wishes. I shall come only as often as you desire to see me."

He broke off abruptly and began to ask her questions. Had she ever been in love? Was she prepared to cut herself away from her past life and all its relationships and act as though it had never been? Was she prepared to place herself unreservedly in his hands? Did she like children? Was she willing to bear them?

Her answers seemed to please him, particularly when she used a speech which Isabeau had prepared, "This is more honor than I can ever merit and greater happiness than I had ever dared to expect."

He kissed her hands impulsively. "Ah, my child, my pretty Valerie!" he exclaimed. "The resemblance, which still amazes me, goes deeper than the surface. How fortunate that this heritage of beauty and grace and sweet understanding has been given you! That it has come to you unimpaired!"

A moment later he released her hands and settled back in his chair. "And now let us talk," he said. "We must become acquainted with each other. You know nothing of me except that I'm the King of France. I know nothing of you save that you bear an amazing likeness to the loveliest of all ladies, and that everything about you pleases me. I've taken great care in the selection of the furniture, thinking to make this little nest a pleasant and beguiling habitation for you. Everything comes from one of the royal palaces or from estates which are in our hands. The buffet was used by the Englishman"—he was referring, quite apparently, to Henry V—"when he was in Paris. It's the only piece of its kind in France and that may balance the odium of its former ownership. The bed was in the Tournelles and I've slept in it many times." He paused over the last words as though to prevent any overlooking of the natural implication, that he expected to sleep in it many times more. "Do you like what I've done?"

"Everything is beautiful beyond belief, sire. I wish I could find the words to express how deeply honored I am."

The King brushed aside the need for further amenities with a wave of his hand. A thought had occurred to him which he hurried to put into words. "The Comte tells me you have a gift for mimicry. Show me what you can do. It will be an amusing step toward our—our better acquaintance."

"But, sire"—Valerie was reluctant to follow this suggestion, being convinced that what seemed to her a very modest gift would fail to amuse so great a personage as the King of France—"you would find it dull and—and trifling. I've imitated only the servants of my cousin and some low characters I had seen before. I'm certain, sire, they would interest you not at all."

The King smiled. "What of our good servant, the Comte de Burey himself?"

Valerie's brows puckered with uncertainty. Then, after a moment's thought, she smiled. "The Comte? Well—perhaps. He wouldn't be hard, as he has many odd traits, as you must have seen, sire. But—would it be proper to make light of him in this way?"

The King swung his chair around so that he could command a good view of the whole room. "From this moment on, my pretty one, the wishes of your king should weigh more with you than the feelings of Regnault de Burey. In any event, I swear myself to secrecy. He will never know that you have copied his ways for the amusement of Charles of France."

Valerie walked to the end of the room where she remained for several minutes with her back turned. When she swung around and faced him, the change in her appearance was so great that he gasped with surprise. "By good St. Martin," he cried, "you really look like him!"

She had drawn in her cheeks and thus given a suggestion of length and lankness to her face. One lock of hair had been pulled over her brows, and by some device, which had more to do with the spirit than the flesh, her expression had been changed to one of biliousness and misanthropy. She peered about her with shortsighted intentness as she came across the room with a shuffling gait. It was in the matter of the walk, however, that she proceeded to achieve her best effect. She moved as though her joints were stiff, placing her feet down cautiously and tenderly; with so much caution, in fact, that any stranger would have believed her to be suffering from a combination of gout and broken arches.

When she spoke, the King started in surprise, for the voice was so much like Regnault de Burey's that it was hard to believe it had been produced by anyone else. "The devil has his pincers on me today," she said, snuffling and grunting between words. "I think my flesh is being given a tweeze for every innocent little slip I've made in my whole life."

Charles of France threw back his head. "If all his misdeeds are remembered, our poor Comte will suffer torments through eternity," he said, laughing loudly.

Valerie proceeded with other imitations of the Comte, drawing on her memory of things she had heard him say. She gave a version of his meeting with Damoiselle Henriette which made the King laugh still more loudly. Finally she raised the small purse attached to her belt and gave it a shake. "That," she said, "is the sweetest sound ever to fill the ears of human beings. Don't tell me of the twittering of birds in bosky thickets or the chanting of heavenly choirs or the blast of a trumpet sounding the advance. No, by'r Lady of Marmoutier, nothing can compare with the clink, the jingle, the rasp, the sweet cuddling together of gold coins in a pocket which has been empty for years!"

Charles rose to his feet and walked over to where she was standing. He placed his hands on her shoulders and gave her an appreciative shake. "You are a clever little vixen!" he said. "And I love you for it. How much I shall enjoy seeing you imitate my ministers and the people closest about me! Of course that must needs wait on your opportunity to see them and know them. I intend, dear child, to make that chance come soon."

She allowed the lines of her face to resume their normal aspect and brushed the hair back from her forehead. The King nodded his approval without releasing her. "Even while I laughed, I was regretting the absence, if only for a few moments, of my lovely little charmer," he whispered. "Now you are again the perfect image of everything I most admire and love. Let me look at you closely before I go."

Suddenly he swept her into his arms and began to kiss her hungrily, on the mouth, the eyes, the ears, the cheeks, and brow. "I shall come back soon, my small one," he exclaimed. "I know that I am going to love you very much."

Chapter IX

I

FRESH from the confusion in which they had existed at the Abbey of Jumièges, the members of the King's court were luxuriating in the magnificent accommodations of the Hôtel Saint-Pol. This great sprawling palace was capable of housing the whole train and with all the dependents they cared to bring. Even Jacques Coeur, who had always been allotted whatever space was left after the other ministers had been satisfied, had a large suite to himself in one of the most recent additions, a neighboring palace which had been acquired during the time of the King's grandfather and which was now incorporated within the rambling wall. True, it was a dark and granite-like structure in which even the rooms that the sun could reach were cold and dreary. The Moneyman found it necessary to keep candles burning beside him at all hours.

He had finished his day's work when the clomp of a spurred boot sounded in the anteroom and Nicolas put his head in to announce, "My lord Dunois to see you, master."

The commander of the French armies came into the room, nodding and smiling to the only one of the King's ministers for whom he had any respect. "Moneyman," he said, taking a chair, "I've come to give you a word of warning."

Coeur sighed. The air was full of rumors and hostile signs. Many friends had nervously taken advantage of favorable opportunities to whisper warnings in his ear. He had not needed these friendly words of advice, being capable of reading the portents himself. It had been clear to him for some time that the tide had turned and was running against him.

"What have you heard?" he asked.

"I've just come from the King." Dunois spoke in a tone which conveyed a suggestion of the dislike he felt for everything that had to do with courts and courtiers. "It's his intention to move quickly against the English in the west and south now that Normandy has been regained with such ease. Did you know of this?"

"No." Coeur almost choked over the word. It was inconceivable that Charles would make this decision without consulting him. It had been his arguments which had led to the breaking of the truce and the reconquest of Normandy. His money had made the campaign possible. He realized suddenly that the peril of his position was much greater than he had been prepared to believe. If Charles would go this far, he could be expected to go to still greater extremes.

"I knew the matter had to be decided soon," he said, after a short spell of bitter thought during which he had tried unsuccessfully to find some acceptable explanation for the affront. "After you, Bastard, I had more right than anyone to share my King's confidence, and to advise him in the making of war plans. I confess to a retching of the spirit at the injustice." His eyes had a strained look as he turned to face the army commander directly. "Is there no gratitude in kings?"

Dunois indulged in a gesture of resignation. "Kingship," he said, "is the hardest of all trades. There's little difference in being King of France and King of the Coquille. In each case you have selfish, cruel men around you, ready to go to any lengths for the favors and the preferment they demand

—and prepared to sacrifice king and throne and country to that end. A successful king is tougher and more selfish and cruel than the men he employs. Look at poor Harry Sixt' of England—a gentle, unselfish, devout man. His country is drifting into civil war and he's losing all his dominions in France. He's a failure. I think we could have saved the Maid if we had thrown aside all dictates of strategy and expediency and marched to the rescue. We took what seemed the sensible course, the tough course, if you prefer: we left her to die." He sighed. "I'm a seasoned soldier and I've seen men perish by the thousands. But, Moneyman, the crew around the King are too tough for me."

After a moment's silence Coeur asked, "What did you hear?"

"The discussion was all of funds. The King is in a panic over what it would cost to drive the Godons out of Bordeaux and at the same time pay you for the cost of Normandy. The idea wasn't put into words exactly but the suggestion hung suspended in the air in full understanding of all that the expense of the western campaign could be blithely assumed if some way were found to escape settling with you."

"If I went to him and said, 'Sire, consider the debts paid,' what would he do?"

"I very much fear," answered Dunois, "that the pride of our liege lord is a complex thing. He might hesitate to put himself under an everlasting obligation to you. You would acquire thereby more stature than any subject should have. And I don't believe he would want the credit for Normandy to repose so exclusively and permanently in your hands. He would much prefer to accomplish the cancellation of the debts by other means."

Coeur had turned his head and was staring out of the window. There was nothing to see, for the room was high up and night was beginning to fall. He would have seen nothing in any event, his mind being too occupied with the unpalatable truths the old soldier was stating.

"The war," said the Moneyman finally, "has cost double what we figured at the outset. I've found it necessary to go back and back to the moneylenders. My estates have been put up one by one as security, even some of the goods in the shops as well. I could survive the loss of the original amount, but if it became known that none of the debt was to be paid, the Lombardy merchants would be about my ears in a moment. They would take everything away from me. They might even compel me to wear the green hat of bankruptcy."

"If I didn't know you to be as hard a fighter as any of them," commented the soldier, "I would feel very much concerned about you, Jacques Coeur."

The Moneyman achieved a mirthless smile. "Yes, I'm a fighter. I can be as tough as they can. But with this difference, Bastard, I am not selfish. My toughness has always been applied to different ends." He lapsed into silence and it was several moments before he resumed the discussion. "What you've told me caps the things I've been hearing for the past two weeks. A crisis has been reached. Need I say that I'm grateful, eternally grateful to you, old friend?"

The soldier got to his feet. His hand dropped to the jeweled hilt of his sword. "You made me a present of this, Jacques Coeur," he said, "and all Rouen was agog when I rode in with it at my side. You're too resourceful to reach such a stage, but if it should ever happen that you are in need of aid or of money, I shall be very unhappy if you don't come to me."

Silence prevailed in the room after Dunois had left. The pair of candles beside Coeur did little to combat the gloom which settled down with the passing of day. They had guttered to a low point when Nicolas came grumbling into the room.

"It's late, master," he said. "The Sire d'Antenne is out there but I'm going to tell him to take himself off."

Coeur straightened up in his chair. "Send him in!" he said sharply.

"But, master," protested the servant in sulky tones, "what he has to tell will keep until tomorrow surely."

The Moneyman half rose to his feet, his hands gripping the edge of the table. He was more angry with Nicolas than he had ever been before. "I told you to send him in!"

Nicolas knew when to submit. He vanished with alacrity and a few moments later the Sire d'Antenne appeared in the door.

Coeur was too disturbed over the situation in which he found himself to greet the informer in the usual facetious vein. He asked in a matter-of-fact voice, "Well, what is it this time?"

"As usual I've been fishing diligently in the sea of information and I've brought up a pearl," said D'Antenne. "You will be very much interested in my find, my lord Coeur. It has to do"—he was watching the Moneyman closely in spite of the lightness of his tone—"with the King's new mistress."

"The court is full of rumors about the wavering fancy of our liege lord," said Coeur indifferently. He turned away and resumed his staring out into the night. "You must bring me a better catch than that, splendid fellow, if you expect to rouse my interest."

"But this is a fact, not a rumor. The King has fallen in love. Madly, it's said. Who the lady is or where she comes from are mysteries to which no answers have been found. The King is so enamored of her that even the enemies of Jacques Coeur find it hard at times to reach his ear." He grinned maliciously. "That should be proof of the depth of his interest! Do you want to hear more?"

"Yes. At the usual rate."

The informer crossed one elegantly clad leg over the other. He was handsomely attired in sky-blue velvet with white trimmings and there was even the sparkle of a ring on one of his fingers. Coeur, noticing these signs of prosperity, said to himself, "This slimy purveyor of secrets has been taking his wares to profitable markets."

"The King has seen the lady in question three times and has spoken to her once only. Nevertheless, his surrender is so complete and overwhelming that she has already been established in a house with a train of servants to look after her. It's whispered he has ordered the letter S and the emblem of the surelle tree taken off all the silver he gave the Lady Agnes so that it can be presented a second time. The most curious thing about this is that the lucky lady is said to be as much like the Lady Agnes as though they were sisters——"

Coeur's features were too well schooled to give any inkling of the shock he had experienced. He sat quite still for several moments while the informer went on with other details. His mind was filled with alarmed speculations but, when he looked around at his visitor, his face gave no hint of this.

"Where did you hear this story?"

"From a close source. I prefer not to tell you the name of my informant. I wouldn't dare, in fact."

"Is the story likely to get into circulation?"

The Sire d'Antenne shook his head emphatically. "For the best of reasons the few who know about it are not telling. I question if more than three people have shared the secret."

"Why are you so certain of its truth?"

The informer raised one hand from his knee and gestured with it by way of answer.

"Where is the house?" asked Coeur.

"I could make myself a rich man if I knew."

"Can you prove the truth of this story by finding out about the house?"

D'Antenne gave some deep thought to this. "I'm not sure. Certainly it would be difficult, and it would be necessary to cross a few palms. With gold, not silver, and plenty of it."

Coeur named a sum. A covetous flush came into the cheeks of the informer and he answered without further hesitation: "I'll do your bidding even if I have to slit a throat or two and bestow the boon of my attentions on the fat wife of some court official."

"I must have it tonight."

D'Antenne indulged in further thought. Then he nodded his head. "If I get it at all, I shall have the information for you in a few hours."

2

Jacques Coeur started out to find his way to the apartments of the King. The route he followed took him through a gate leading into a tilting ground, at the far end of which he passed through another gate, high and ivy-clad, into a maze of formal gardens. After that it was a case of one gate after another, and then doors and staircases and dark passages without number. The Hôtel Saint-Pol was like a walled city.

In the course of his wanderings he had encountered people at every turn. Most of them he recognized, and all of them knew him, but for the first time since he had been summoned to court to become the King's Moneyman, he found himself ignored. Men and women turned away at his approach or acknowledged his greetings with a hasty word or reluctant nod. Even the servants and the guards (the palace swarmed with the latter), quick to sense a turn of sentiment or a dip in fortune, stared insolently through him as he passed. Nothing could be more indicative than this. Jacques Coeur read the signs aright but he was not prepared for what happened when he reached the double doors, with the lilies of France in gold leaf on the panels, behind which were the anterooms of the King.

A captain of guards was stationed there who looked at him and said in a voice which carried an undertone of regret, "I have orders not to admit you, Monseigneur."

Coeur was too stunned to speak at first. He had not expected a deliberate and public rebuff. It had never entered his mind, in fact, that he would be refused a chance to discuss the situation with his royal master. He studied the face of the captain for a moment, wondering if this was a ruse on the part of his enemies to prevent him from reaching the King.

"Are your orders from the King himself?"

"Yes, Monseigneur." The officer looked about him hastily. Convinced that he could not be overheard, he added in a whisper, "The people of France will always remember that you brought them peace at last, my lord Coeur."

"It's unfortunate that the voice of the people doesn't penetrate within official cabinets." Coeur turned on his heel. "This is probably the last time we will see each other. Farewell, my good captain, and thanks for the kindliness with which you have carried out your orders."

He started slowly on the return trip, his head lowered in thought, thus saving those he passed the necessity of refusing to meet his eye or to acknowledge a greeting. There was no longer any doubt as to what the future held. Charles had closed his mind as well as his door. As Dunois had hinted, the King would now find some other means of avoiding the payment of the war bills than by accepting a voluntary cancellation.

He was passing through a passage even more lacking in illumination than the rest when he heard his name called in a feminine voice. He stopped and looked about him. The woman who had accosted him was standing in the shadow of a high-windowed alcove which in daylight would command a view of the tennis grounds. She placed a finger on her lips and beckoned him with her other hand to join her.

"My lord, I have something for you," she whispered. "It's from the Sire d'Antenne."

Coeur said, "He has lost no time if your message is what I think."

She was a young woman, small and dark and rather attractive. The Moneyman did not recognize her as one of the ladies of the court but it was clear she was above the station of a servant. He decided she must be the wife or daughter of some minor official. It was obvious that she was too nice to be concerned in any of the devious transactions of the Sire d'Antenne.

"I've a note," the girl whispered. "But I'm not to hand it to you until you give me the money."

"But, my dear lady," protested Coeur, "I don't carry that much gold on my person."

She looked troubled. "He said it was most important. That he had found what you wanted. I don't know what's in the note, my lord, but the importance of it was such that the Sire d'Antenne didn't dare take it to you himself."

Coeur's hand had been searching in a pouch he carried under his tunic. Having a fondness for unset precious jewels, he was in the habit of carrying some of his special favorites with him. When he extended his hand for her attention, an emerald of good size lay on the palm.

"This," he said, "is worth considerably more than the sum agreed upon. If you know anything of jewels, you will accept this without any question at all."

"I know very little." She was disturbed at the need to make a decision. She studied the emerald and then looked up into the face of the Moneyman. "I—I don't know what to do. It seems a very fine stone but I've no idea of its value. It has never been my luck to possess anything as costly as this."

"Please believe that I wouldn't deceive you. I assure you, my girl, that you may accept this with an easy mind."

She said in the tone of one who has decided to make a plunge, "Give it to me, my lord Coeur." She produced a small slip of paper which was doubled over and sealed tightly. The exchange was effected.

A kindly impulse caused him to ask a question, "How does it come that you are acting as go-between in this matter?"

She looked at him defiantly. "The Sire d'Antenne and I are friends."

"No, my dear." Coeur gave his head a shake. "No attractive woman can ever be a friend of the Sire d'Antenne."

She favored him with an angry look but then she threw her head back and laughed rather bitterly. "You are right, my lord. We began as friends but that didn't last long. I am his mistress. He has others, of course. I've always known it but I am so much in love with him that I—I try to forget." Her tone had become unfriendly. "Is there anything else you want to know?"

Coeur had been watching her compassionately, knowing that a liaison with the Sire d'Antenne could bring her nothing but grief and pain.

He broke the seal and convinced himself that the note contained the information he required. "I'm content," he said. "As content as your lover will be when he sees what you take him in payment." Then, in a kindly tone, he added, "I'm very sorry for you, my child."

The conversation had been carried on in guarded tones, but at this the girl began to laugh without any effort at restraint. "You are sorry for me? Then we are even. I, my lord Coeur, am sorry for you!"

This transaction with the emissary of D'Antenne, for the few minutes that it lasted, had succeeded in diverting the Moneyman's mind from the perils gathering about him. He was brought back to reality with a severe jolt when he reached the landing outside his suite of rooms. Nicolas was there, his arms filled with clothes which clearly had been hastily assembled. Behind the servant, a royal servitor with a pike in his hands leaned against the door.

Coeur knew what this meant and he asked one question only. "When did it happen, Nicolas?"

"A few minutes after you left, master. There are three of them in there now, going over your papers. They're strewing everything on the floor and quarreling among themselves. My lord Gouffier is one of them."

"That was to be expected." Coeur gave vent to a brief and mirthless laugh. "They must think me very careless if they hope to find anything of value within such easy reach of their fingers. They're wasting their time on household accounts."

"They've put seals on all the windows, master."

"But the enormity of what they do they can never seal up. It will go down in history as the greatest injustice of this age."

Now that the blow had fallen, Jacques Coeur felt a deep sadness but no anger. His mind went back to the past. He thought of his first shop at Bourges, of his first visits to the East, and of the series of inspirations which had led to his dominance. That he had become the richest man in the world and had paid for a war out of his own purse were no longer important. What he was thinking of, as he stood there outside his locked door, a discarded minister of the Crown, was his vision of a different and better world which he had hoped to see in his own lifetime.

"If they tear down what I have done," he said, aloud, "men will soon forget what I've taught them."

Coming back to the present he said to his man, "An abrupt and bitter ending, Nicolas, to twelve years of devoted service."

The critical tongue of his servant could find no other answer for once than, "Yes, master."

The Moneyman turned to the guard who had been watching them with open curiosity. "Where do you hail from, my friend?"

"From your own country, lord. From Berri."

"Will they believe in Berri that Jacques Coeur has deserved this? Will they think he has been a bad servant to the King?"

The man shook his head stoutly. "No, lord, no! They will never think ill of Jacques Coeur."

"Adversity is sometimes a friend. It shakes a man out of his complacency and sets him to the doing of better things." He drew a gold coin from his pouch and handed it to the guard. "Consider this, my good friend, a token that you saw the Moneyman of France at one of the supreme moments of his life."

Nicolas, who was scarcely able to see over the bundles he was carrying, did not seem to agree with this. "Adversity has never been a friend to me," he declared. "Where are we to go now, master?"

"We are going to the house of an acquaintance whose name had better not be mentioned here. Come, Nicolas. I have a disinclination to stay within these walls. Let's start at once, even though I lack a hat."

"They," said Nicolas, tilting his head back in the direction of the rooms, "think they are going to present you with a hat. A green hat."

3

The house in the Rue Grenier sur L'Eau was lighted up as though for a ball when they arrived. D'Arlay, however, was supping alone in the hall and showing a good appetite over a dish of mutton chops and a *salade* of the crests and livers of chicken. He raised a flagon of wine when he saw Coeur enter and called to him in a cheerful voice, "You're just in time to drink a pledge with me."

"You seem in a mood for celebration," said Coeur, advancing into the long room until he stood beside the chair of his friend.

"I am. I accomplished something today which made me very happy. I sold this house at a figure more than double what it cost me."

"Then you drove a good bargain."

"I had no idea of selling until a man who reeked of newly acquired wealth called two days ago and asked if I wanted a buyer. He told me there had been no building done in Paris since we took the city back from the English, or very little. The city is filled with homeless people and prices have gone to the skies."

"It always happens during a war. Money changes hands. Those who had it before sell their houses and estates to those who made fortunes during the fighting. Jacques Coeur was the richest man in the world a year ago but what do you think he's worth today? The man you sold to was an army contractor, no doubt?"

D'Arlay nodded. "He made the carriages for the cannon." Then he smiled. "The man has a marriageable daughter who will have a very large dowry. Perhaps I should have married her and kept the house."

Coeur looked at him with an increased interest. "Do you mean that the sale was for that purpose?"

"Naturally. I intend to apply the money I receive to the debts on the family estates. It will reduce them sufficiently to keep the creditors content. Having done that much, I shall consider myself no longer under obligation to marry a rich wife. I shall be free to—to marry the one I want."

Coeur seated himself at the table. He looked at his friend with an air which expressed both reluctance and self-reproach. "It seems," he said, "that I've been responsible for raising another obstacle in your path. Two things happened today which leave us, you and I, in unenviable positions."

He proceeded to tell of the steps the King had taken and of the information D'Antenne had given him about Valerie. D'Arlay's face, as he listened, displayed a wide range of emotion: incredulity, anger, dismay, and, at the finish, a gloom which seemed all the deeper because of his earlier exhilaration. The only comment he made was that Valerie's plight was the work of his brother and Isabeau. They had been very secretive and had refused to tell him anything, even keeping her whereabouts from him. He added that he was sure she did not know they were acting now on their own initiative.

Coeur was inclined to agree with him on the last point but he said that he wanted to be convinced. They must find some way of getting in touch with her and acquainting her with the facts. If self-interest had not prompted her to willing participation, they must then arrange her escape. It was to discuss these points that he had come.

"I've been in a glow of satisfaction for hours!" said D'Arlay, with a sudden display of bitterness. "Ever since the sale was completed, I've been making plans for the future. I was sure that things at last were shaping themselves in the right direction." A pause ensued and then he continued in a lower tone, "Has it occurred to you, Jacques, that my bad fortune may offset yours? That—that you have the game in your bandon?"[1]

"You mean that I can now rely on assistance from Valerie?"

"Yes." D'Arlay nodded his head somberly. After a moment he said, "Yes," again. He had placed his hands on the edge of the table and had, apparently, found something about them worth a prolonged study.

"That thought occurred to me as soon as I heard what they had done. I want you to know that I dismissed it without any hesitation or regret. I've no intention of profiting by it. I came here tonight to discuss plans with you for getting her out of their hands while there's still time."

D'Arlay looked up at that. "From what you've told me, it's quite clear that nothing else will restore you to the King's favor."

"I know that. You're thinking me inconsistent, no doubt. It's not inconsistency and it's not any sudden surrender to a chivalrous instinct. I wish I could honestly claim that my present attitude springs from the highest motives. But, now that the crisis has been reached which I foresaw, I realize that I would never have been capable of carrying through the plan I made to meet it. For a reason, my dear Robin, that I didn't know existed before; and not one in which I can take any satisfaction. My pride!"

"Your pride?" D'Arlay's tone made it clear that he did not understand.

"You will have to bear with me while I indulge in a long explanation." Coeur said this in a tone from which he could not exclude a suggestion of

[1]In his own hands.

the readiness he always displayed to discussing himself. No subject interested him more. He was prepared to talk about his own motives and mental reactions as though they belonged to someone else. He had even developed a habit of referring to himself in the third person. "This Jacques Coeur," he would say, or, "This unusual figure who has risen from the ranks of the people," or even, "I sometimes find it hard to understand Jacques Coeur myself."

"I realize," he began, "that I'm unfortunate enough to have been born ahead of my time. The men of two hundred years hence will be doing the things I do today. They will be thinking then as I think now. My spirit is imprisoned in this strutting, bloody, foolish age. Pity me, Robin; I am a man of hard business sense and vision and here I am, living in the age of Chivalry!

"I know that I'm regarded as mad and dangerous," he went on. "What do I care what they think? Does an eagle listen to the jackdaws chittering among themselves about him? But I do care what the men of my own kind, the men of the future, will think—and what they will say about me. I would trade some of the years that are left me for a look into the future and a glimpse at what the history books will record about me."

He had risen and was pacing up and down the room. "Jacques Coeur is always willing to say when he has been wrong. He now avows that you were right at the start and he was wrong. He doesn't want it recorded in history that he regained his post with the King through petticoat influence. He wants to be remembered as Jacques Coeur the pioneer and not Jacques Coeur the pander." He continued his pacing, gesturing freely. "I've led the world along new paths. I've changed the whole face of commerce. I've seen visions of the future and have tried to let the people of this mad age benefit by them. If an ungrateful King destroys all that I've done, I'll find a way to start over again. And I'll build a new empire of trade which will cover, if not France, the rest of the world!"

When he stopped at the table he had regained his composure. "I leave in the morning for Bourges, Robin. I must prepare to meet the storm. I'm going to see to it that no gold is left in any of my shops and that all my ships keep out of French ports. If they break me, I must be ready to make a new start.

"In the meantime," he added, "I've learned where the girl is. I shall leave it to you to take whatever steps seem necessary. But before you do anything, make sure she hasn't been carried away by visions of power and wealth and ease. She is human, Robin, and mustn't be blamed too harshly if she feels disposed to follow the path of opportunity."

"I'm sure she hasn't yielded to selfish motives."

Coeur smiled. "You're a man of stanch faith, Robinet de Burey, but you haven't been at court as much as I have! Still, I too have a great fondness for the child. And so I hope you are right."

D'Arlay had risen to his feet in a fever of impatience. "Where is she?" he demanded. "Tell me so I can start to work at once!"

Coeur drew out the paper and handed it to him. D'Arlay unfolded it with eager fingers. He read aloud:

"The middle house of the three which back on the western wall."

"Do you know the house?" asked Coeur.

D'Arlay nodded his head. "There are three houses built against the wall of the Hôtel Saint-Pol. They're so conspicuous that everyone has wondered why they haven't been torn down. This couldn't refer to anything else."

"Can you get into the middle house?"

It was D'Arlay's turn to surrender to a theatrical impulse. "I will not only get in," he declared, "but I will get her out of there, even if it has to be done over the prostrate body of Charles of France!"

"The less we have of heroics," said Coeur, in a dry tone, "the better it will be for all concerned. Get her out of the place by all means but not over the body of the King. Not over any bodies at all, in fact. We're in a sufficiently dangerous position as it is. I commend to you, Robin, the exercise of complete discretion."

Chapter X

I

AFTER three hours of the most exacting preparation, Valerie's toilet was completed. Isabeau, satisfied with her finally, had departed. Looking from the rear window of her bedroom, the girl could see the gardens of the palace over the high stone wall and the maze of turrets and spires and bell towers with their multiplicity of whirling girouettes and flying buttresses which gave a suggestion of a child's fairyland to the Hôtel Saint-Pol. This, then, she said to herself, was the beginning. This was the start of a life of ease and luxury, perhaps also of power and responsibility; certainly a life of trouble and worry and humiliation, and always of pain.

She left the window and began to pace slowly about the room. It was necessary to walk with deliberation for she had a very long train. To turn so that the train followed as easily and gracefully as the tail of a mermaid, and without any agitation or careening or doubling over of the material, called for the utmost skill. There had to be a discreet reaching back of one foot, not attaining quite the proportions of a kick (which would have been highly vulgar), to guide the stately and shimmering flow into its appointed course. She found herself perfect in this most difficult feat of ladyship and felt a natural glow of satisfaction. If one has a task to do, there is always a sense of pride in doing it well.

The three hours had wrought a miracle in her appearance. In the first place a new way had been evolved of doing her hair which had seemed excitingly successful. It was allowed to curl closely and naturally on her forehead and was then drawn back from her ears (which were permitted to show—a most daring innovation) in a series of loose waves. It was piled rather high on the back of her head where it was held in place by a comb with the letter V picked out in diamonds, which had arrived the day before without any note or identification of the giver—not that any was needed. She wore no hennin at all, and this was a deliberate and rather frightening innovation in an age when the outward hallmark of feminine gentility was extravagance of headgear. It was hard to decide whether the resulting effect was one of naïveté or sophistication. It had been the hope of Isabeau, in fact, that it would partake of both qualities. Seeing herself in the mirrors which servants had held up around her, Valerie's eyes had lighted and a tinge of natural pink had appeared in her cheeks; for neither inner mood nor outside circumstance counts at such a moment.

Words are poor instruments to convey an adequate conception of her gown. It was like a phenomenon of nature, such as a blending of colors in the sky at sunset. As words are the only available medium, it must be stated that the costume consisted of an undergown of the cherry-colored material Jacques Coeur had selected for her with such discrimination. Breath-taking in the bolt, it took on a new magic when seen close-fitted to the neck and shoulders and tapering to a tight V on the back of the hand, and falling to the floor in the voluptuous abundance which has already been noted. There was a strange quality to this sun-ripened red material; for although it shimmered with the impeccability of newness, it suggested age also, as though patient yellow hands had worked on it endlessly, their labor culminating in this brief beauty like the bloom of a century plant.

Above this was draped an overgown of deep ivory velvet which seemed to catch and reflect some of the warmth of her skin and hair. It was high-waisted almost to an effect of pertness, resting with daring insecurity on the extreme tips of her shoulders and coming to a very low V in front. It then cut away sharply below the waist to give full play to the beauty of the cherry skirt. The oversleeves were of the velvet. They fitted the roundness of her arm most snugly at the shoulder but then fanned out until they achieved a fullness to match that of the skirt. The relaxing of an arm allowed the hem of the sleeve to touch the floor!

This ivory overgown, with its gay and impertinent originality of design, was diapered in a pattern of gold thread which twined about tiny rosebuds of the cherry material. Sewn along the edges was narrow ivory lace, so old and fragile it seemed like cobwebs enjoying a last moment of beauty before crumbling into dust.

Her pacing took a three-sided course, for the giant bed, Pepin the Short, jutted out so far from the wall that it cut the room into that shape. She was still awed by this majestic piece of furniture. That morning she and Guillaumette had measured it, using a folded sheet for the purpose. Valerie herself had scrambled up one of the massive posts and had taken a tumble on getting down, so that the accuracy of the measurement was open to some question. It showed, and was probably not far wrong, that the bed from floor to top of tester was fourteen and a half feet high. The lantern suspended from its ceiling had been removed at Valerie's insistence, for it had gone on causing curious shadows which generally took the form of heads adorned with crowns.

Doubts multiplied in her mind as the light of day diminished. It was growing dark quickly and she seated herself at the rear window to look out at the palace which was dissolving into sharply etched masses of black. Lights began to show in windows, winking on in such numbers that it looked as though the stars had come down from their high station and were clustering close to earth. As she watched, her doubts rose to a peak and she found herself several times on the point of rising as the instinctive first stage of flight. "I can't! I can't!" she repeated over and over again.

To add to her uncertainty and bewilderment there was the continued silence of Jacques Coeur. She had received no message of any kind from him. Did he know of the turn things had taken? Was he in the confidence of the King? During the weeks which had followed their sudden departure from the neighborhood of the abbey she had been reassured on this point many times by the Comtesse. But doubts still persisted in her mind. Did the Moneyman know that Charles of France was coming to share supper with her this night?

She was beginning to feel a repugnance for the queenly magnificence in which she was attired. Looking down at the rich folds of the cherry gown, she had a desire to take it between her fingers and tear it to shreds. The perfume, which Isabeau had artfully sprayed on every layer of clothing, made itself so evident with each move that she felt cheapened. It was a very special perfume, a combination of Hungary Water, which was innocently concocted from tips of rosemary distilled with aqua vitae, and a distillation from much farther east which was not innocent at all—an exotic scent with a base of musk. The result of this blending was perfect for the purpose; and, because of that, Valerie hated it.

The room was becoming dark. Guillaumette was in the next room but her mistress made no move to summon her and have the candles lighted. Valerie was welcoming the gloom as a friend, because she had no desire to be seen in this suspicious finery. She continued to watch the lights in the windows of the palace, wondering what the people there, the disdainful ladies and the ambitious gentlemen, would think if they knew. They would hate her, of course, and fear her because of the power she might attain, and they would do everything to make her lot difficult. "What are they talking about now?" she asked herself. "About me, perhaps. Are they planning all the things they will do against me?"

For several minutes she had been conscious of sounds. First there had been a rustling in the vines which covered in dark green the wall outside her window, but she had paid no heed to this, believing it was caused by birds. Now she heard a hint of cautious footsteps, first on the roof above her and then on the landing outside her door. Suddenly she began to feel an acute alarm. She was on the point of calling out to Guillaumette when a familiar voice spoke to her.

"Don't be alarmed, Valerie. Make no sound, I beg of you. I'm in enough danger of being discovered as it is."

It was D'Arlay. He had opened the door just sufficiently to make sure that she was alone in the room. He came in now and closed it softly behind him. Pausing beside a table to deposit a bundle he had carried attached to his belt, he remained there in a listening attitude for several moments.

"It seems reasonable to believe now that no one observed my somewhat irregular method of getting in. I climbed a vine on the side of the wall from a low section of the roof of the next house. There was danger I might be seen from the street."

So much emotion had been stirred in Valerie that for a moment she said nothing at all. Then, in a low tone, she asked, "What brings you here?"

"I came because Jacques Coeur was able finally to trace you. Both of us had been striving to learn your whereabouts since you left Jumièges so unexpectedly; but without any success at all until yesterday."

Her emotions had narrowed down to one, a sense of indignation. "Do you mean," she asked in a tense voice, "that my lord Coeur doesn't know what has happened since we left?"

"He has known nothing. My brother and his wife refused to tell us about you. It has been a maddening situation."

"I thought it strange I never heard from him. Then—he doesn't know I have seen the King?"

"He heard it yesterday for the first time."

"But," she asked, "why have they done this? I don't understand at all."

D'Arlay suggested that they seat themselves. "You see," he said, "Jacques Coeur had changed his mind. He decided not to go on. My sister-in-law and my brother didn't agree with him. It's quite clear now that they made up their minds at once to proceed without him and that they arranged the sudden departure from Jumièges so he wouldn't be able to communicate with you."

"Did my lord Coeur think I was acting with them willingly?" she asked, after a pause during which they had looked into each other's eyes with the utmost gravity.

He shook his head. "No. But he wanted me to make sure on that point first of all."

"And you?"

"Valerie," said D'Arlay, finding it impossible to give expression to the intensity of his feeling, "I knew from the first that you had been deceived."

Indignation was now giving way in her mind to a faint stirring of hope. Perhaps it would not be necessary for her to go on. Perhaps it would not be incumbent on her to see again that constrained man with his possessive eyes and greedy long nose. Then, as she remembered how far the arrangements had been carried, she gave up in despair.

"The King," she said, in a whisper, "will be here in half an hour."

D'Arlay sprang to his feet at once. "Then we have no time to lose. Can we be sure of the half hour? If so, I think it can be managed." Then he paused and looked down at her earnestly. "It's only fair to tell you that—that your success is assured if you go on. It's quite clear that he, the King, has capitulated. Everything that Agnes Sorel had is within your reach."

Valerie answered with lowered head: "Never from the first have I had any desire for that kind of life."

"No one could blame you if you decided to accept this—this glittering opportunity."

She looked up at that. "Wouldn't you blame me?"

There was a long pause. "My feelings are too much engaged to take an impersonal view," he said finally.

What she thought of this was not apparent for another idea had occurred to her, causing her to ask in an anxious voice, "But what of my lord Coeur? Will his interests suffer?"

"He insisted you were not to give that any consideration. He has been dismissed from his post at court. He's now on his way to Bourges to raise his defenses against them. It's probably too late to do anything for him. But—he would refuse, in any case, to benefit himself by sacrificing you. He wants me to take you to Bourges where plans can be made for the future."

She had been holding her feelings in close check but at this point she lost control of them. "Please, help me to get away!" she said, looking up at him beseechingly. "I can't stay here now. The thought of it sickens me!"

"I came prepared to help you."

"But how?" Now that it was possible for her to give up, she was frantic with anxiety to leave. "This house is closely guarded. Do you think I could climb down the vines?"

"I'm afraid not. They were so loosened by my weight in climbing up that I was sure near the end I wouldn't get the whole distance. But there's a chance to reach the roof of a low wing next door. If—if you're ready to take a certain risk."

"Yes, yes! I'm ready for any risk."

"Then," he said, nodding in the direction of the bundle on the table, "you will find clothes there. You must be dressed as a man to take this way of escaping."

"I don't care! I would do anything to get away now."

She took the bundle and retired to a small room adjoining the one they were in. Anxiety put speed in her fingers and she was back in a much shorter time than he had expected. It was so dark that he could barely see her. This was just as well, for she said in a constrained tone, "They are a very poor fit."

"They'll serve to get you out of here. Come. We've little time left."

Valerie's courage showed signs of deserting her when they climbed out of a window in the roof and found themselves on a slate surface which sloped sharply. In front of them the wall of the deserted house stood straight up, shutting off all view in that direction. To the left they could see the twinkling lights of the palace, to the right the city, with no lights showing at all. Peculiarly enough no sounds reached them from the palace, but out of the darkness that was Paris came the beat of horses' hoofs and the grind of carriage wheels and the voices of men raised in song and laughter and blasphemy.

She shivered and said, "I'm certain I shall never be able to climb down from here."

D'Arlay reached out a hand to her. "It always looks harder than it is. We must work our way along until we come to a flat projection near the back of the house. From there we can jump to a lower roof of the next house."

"Is it a long jump?" she asked in a sudden panic.

He did not answer at once. "It may seem long at first glance. But it's quite easy once you make up your mind to it. When I was a boy I used to play with the son of one of the servants who was about my own age. He was called Philbert the Climber and he wasn't afraid of anything. I often saw him climb the wall of a building and he would take jumps so long that I would be afraid to watch. He said it was easy. All he did was close his eyes and say, 'Here goes poor Philbert—O Lord, guide his feet!'—and then leap."

"And did the Lord guide his feet?" she asked nervously.

"Always. I never knew him to be hurt."

"If we—survive the jump, what do we do then?"

"Helion has horses at a tavern around the corner. We must leave Paris tonight, of course."

He could detect a note of dismay in her voice. "Must I go in these clothes?"

"Yes. There will be barely enough time for us to get out before the gates are closed for the night."

Valerie sighed and said, "Then we had better start before my resolution fails me."

The flat space, from which they would find it necessary to launch themselves, proved to be so small that there was barely room for both of them to occupy it at once. Another building, on the palace side of the wall, made it impossible for them to see anything beyond. "That," said D'Arlay, "was a foundry for the repair of armor. Lately it hasn't been used, and it's occupied only by a large family of rats. I went all through it while investigating the chances of getting in and out of this house and I found the entrance through the wall which the King uses. It has been most cleverly devised." He paused to calculate the time. "Being the most punctual of men, I judge that our liege lord is in the act of reaching at this very moment for the spring which releases it."

Valerie was not listening. Holding tightly to his arm, she peered down into the darkness.

"It seems a long way. Is it as much as—twenty-five feet?"

"No, it's fifteen at the most. The darkness makes it seem more."

They stood side by side for several moments and then D'Arlay said, "It would be wrong if I told you there was no danger in this."

"I know there is."

"But it's our only chance. If there had been any other way, I would have taken it instead of this." He stopped and looked down at her as though anxious to watch how she would receive what he was going to tell her. Her face was almost completely in shadow. "There's something I must say to you first. I love you very much."

Apparently she had been taken by surprise, for he could see her head turn up quickly toward him. They were standing so close together that he felt a tremor in her arm. When she spoke it was in a hesitant voice. "I—I thought you did, my lord Robin. But I wasn't sure."

"It began the first time I saw you. I kept it to myself and tried not to let you see how I felt because of the obstacles which stood in the way. They seemed insurmountable then. The main obstacle was removed when you told me back there that you would come with me."

She said nothing but he knew there was a question in her mind. "There was another which I'm sure you knew about. I was under the necessity of marrying a rich wife in order to save the family estates. I've provided for payment of the most pressing debts and I consider myself relieved of any further obligation. Even if I hadn't sold the Paris house, I doubt if I would have been in a position after tonight to help my brother. It may be necessary for both of us to leave the country. If that should prove to be the case, you and I will be starting life all over again. There will be no obstacles left. Unless—unless the state of your feeling for me should be one."

There was a long moment of silence and then she said in a whisper, "I know of no obstacle."

D'Arlay took her hand and raised it to his lips. "There is no time," he said rapturously, "to tell you how happy I am. Are you ready?"

"Yes. I'm ready."

"Then close your eyes for a moment and say, 'Here go poor Valerie Maret and Robinet de Burey. O Lord, guide their feet!' "

2

The quarterly wage payments were being distributed to the domestic staff at the Hôtel de Burey. The seneschal had arranged the money in tiny piles of silver with slips of paper under each on which the name of the recipient and the amount were written. This was for the convenience of the Comtesse, who insisted on presiding but had such scant facility with figures that everything had to be ready for her.

The servants stood in a long line (with expectations pathetically high in contrast with the smallness of the sums to be received), and the mistress called out each name in turn. The receipt was acknowledged in every case with a stock phrase, "God and Our Lady bless you, sweet mistress." Isabeau usually had something to say to each, a morsel of praise, a sharp demand for better service during the next quarter, an admonition of a personal nature. Today, however, she had nothing to say. Her mind was elsewhere, for her hands fumbled with the coins as she absentmindedly turned them over.

Her thoughts ran in one direction entirely. "He has been to see me three times only in the past year. Has he stopped loving me? Does he think the past can be dismissed so lightly? Does he consider me like the willing wife of a hatmaker or a woman of the streets that he treats me this way?" She moistened her lips and looked straight ahead of her with unseeing eyes. "I'll never let him go! I'll not permit anything or anyone to come between us! Has he any idea of the lengths I'm prepared to go to hold him?"

She had a few coins only to distribute when the Comte entered and crossed the room slowly, motioning to the seneschal to withdraw.

"Will Madame be kind enough to finish at another time?" he asked.

Isabeau needed no more than one glance at his face to realize that something was wrong. She said in a sharp voice, "You will all leave the room." When the last of them had gone, she looked up at him apprehensively.

"Well?"

"She has run away!"

"Do you mean——"

"I mean your so-called cousin who might be a real daughter to your rascally Uncle Gilles from the evidence we now have of her baseness and ingratitude! She ran away a few minutes before the King put in his appearance. Never in all history has a golden opportunity been lost on such a narrow margin of time." He hawked viciously. "I have just come from court. Need I inform you that our liege lord was in a silent mood, staring down the length of his nose and saying not a word? Once his gaze met mine and I read there such an intensity of dislike that I knew the fortunes of the house of De Burey were due to experience the greatest decline in its history."

The hand of the Comtesse was trembling with a fury she was unable to control. "How did the ungrateful creature get away?" she demanded.

The Comte threw back his head and neighed unmirthfully. "She had assistance," he said. "I had the whole story from the mouth of the Damoiselle Henriette herself. A most romantic tale, my spouse! A vine-covered wall was scaled by her rescuer as though for an elopement. There followed a change of attire and the girl went away with him, her chastely slender legs encased in masculine hose."

"And who," asked Isabeau, in a whisper so low he could barely catch the words, "assisted her in getting away?"

"Who? Must I humiliate myself by naming him? Madame, it was my brother. He was seen getting to horse with her a block away. It was your one-time admirer who seems to have transferred his vagrant affections to this yellow-haired wench."

His wife's hands were busying themselves with the silver coins which remained in front of her, spreading them with restless fingers, building them up into new piles and immediately leveling them again. He was shocked at the change which had come about in her appearance. There was a heavy flush on her cheeks. Leaning forward to observe her more closely, he perceived that the tip of her nose was covered with fine red lines.

"What will the King do?" she asked, after a long pause.

"I wish I knew what is in his mind," answered the Comte gloomily. "The story will be hushed up in order to spare his feelings and on that account he will be limited in the punishments he can administer. The girl will vanish from sight and never be heard of again. They—Robin and the Moneyman—will see to that. As for Robin, I doubt if our liege lord will be able to touch him. He's a popular hero since he poked his sword into the ribs of the Burgundian and he couldn't be shoved into the Bastille without stirring up talk all over the country. The facts would come out then and our liege lord would cut a ridiculous figure. I don't believe he would fancy the role of jilted lover." The Comte paused for a moment of gloomy thought. "If the whole story reaches his ears, the brunt of his displeasure will be kept for Jacques Coeur. The layer of the golden eggs will be killed and plucked—and not so much as a feather will come our way, sweet spouse."

"The whole story will reach the King's ears!" promised Isabeau.

The Comte was wearing a new cloak of plum-colored velvet, one of extreme cut with yellow and vermilion sleeves so huge that they increased his width twofold, and so richly embroidered and embellished and overlaid with buttons and links of chain that he resembled an eastern potentate. This magnificent garment he slipped off his shoulders and dropped on the edge of the table. "How will I be able to pay for this absurd vanity," he asked, "if no more golden eggs are found in the nest?"

His wife did not seem to have heard him. "The girl must be punished!" she said in a low tone, as though talking to herself. "She must be made to suffer in every possible way! I shall have to think of means of hurting her." She paused and then went on in a voice which contained a small shred of satisfaction: "She is fond of Godefroy. It would cut her deeply if we sent him home on the ground of cowardly conduct."

The Comte would not agree to this. "The boy has just reached the stage where he'll be useful to me," he said. "In any case it's Robin who deserves to be punished most. It will be to the point if you find ways of paying him back for the ill turn he has done us."

Isabeau answered quietly, "I had no thought of letting him escape easily!"

The Comte sank into a chair and scowled at the wall. "As he is my own brother, I'm forbidden to wish his death by hanging or to see him stripped of all his goods and turned out to beg. I can't curse those who begot him because they begot me also; though it's now my belief they were giving less attention to results when they brought him into the world. But it would suit me well if the King's torturer could acquaint him with the fine frenzy caused by hot eggs under the armpits or a leg bone crushed in the brodequins. Is it too much to ask that he itch eternally with the emerods and suffer all his days with a running of the reins?" His imagination continuing to work, he went on to name such other satisfactions as occurred to him. "I hope he will have to dine all his days on flyblown forcemeat and have nothing but viscous wine to sup. May St. Gatien, the patron saint of innocents, turn the other way when the good Robin walks in Paris of nights. May his slumbers be an endless nightmare. May——"

"I," said Isabeau, "am not content to indulge in idle words. I'm interested only in punishments we can inflict ourselves." Even her voice had changed and become deep, uneven, unnatural. "That much satisfaction at least is left to us. I'm going to see to it that they are all treated as they deserve!"

The Comte was too unhappy to continue the conversation. He got to his feet, snuffling loudly, and left the room. His wife remained at the table for several minutes, staring down at her hands which lay motionless among the broken mounds of silver. Then she rose also and procured ink and a quill pen. She began to write.

She wrote three letters, inditing them with painstaking effort in the uneducated round hand of a child. Each note was identical: an invitation to the recipient to wait upon her at once to discuss a matter of the utmost importance. She then addressed them to Guillaume Gouffier, Pregent Kennedy, and Jeanne de Vendôme. At the top of each she wrote the word *Urgent* and underlined it three times.

"I think I see the way," she said aloud. "I shall make them suffer as no one has ever suffered before!"

Chapter XI

I

THERE was a time when it was believed, particularly in the preparation of pieces for the theater, that the most romantic of situations had been achieved when a pretty woman was compelled by circumstances to don male attire. This is a delusion which disappears rapidly whenever put to the test. As a matter of fact nothing is more certain to dispel romance than the troubles and vexations which immediately arise.

The first hint of difficulty on this occasion came when the trio, after a brisk canter through dark streets, came to the Porte Saint-Michel at the exact moment the lieutenant in charge signaled with an uplifted hand for the gates to be closed. D'Arlay called to him in an urgent voice, "One moment, if you please, Monsieur Lieutenant!" while he fumbled in his pocket for the necessary credentials.

The officer was a little fellow, wearing a cloak with enormously puffed-out sleeves which made him look like a monkey in a lion's skin. Most fortunately he recognized this late-comer. "Sire d'Arlay!" he said, bowing low. "You're just in time. One second more and"—gesturing eloquently—"it wouldn't have been in my power to help you." He bowed again so that the plumes in his hat touched the ground. "I saw you fight the Burgundian and it would have gone against the grain to do you a discourtesy. Is the sword at your belt the one you used on that glorious occasion?"

D'Arlay nodded affirmatively. "I own no other, Monsieur."

"These are your servants?" After a perfunctory glance at the papers, the officer let his eyes pass quickly over the two figures behind D'Arlay. Then, with what seemed almost a jerk, he brought them back to rest speculatively on Valerie. He raised his eyebrows and sidled over beside D'Arlay.

"When one stands guard at the gates of Paris," he whispered, "one sees things, my lord D'Arlay. How many times have I perceived bright eyes staring out from behind the closed curtains of carriages which were supposed to be empty! And the apple-cheeked little creatures who come in on the tail end of carts, looking for chances to better themselves! And the muffled-up ladies going out who prove to have beards when you take a look! But—*tcha, tcha,* Sire d'Arlay! Why do you think it necessary to put this one into leggings? No one can mistake her for what she is—at least no one as observant as I am of the—of the differences."

As they heard the gates clang to behind them, D'Arlay leaned back and spoke to Valerie. "He saw through your disguise at once. I'm afraid we're going to run into plenty of difficulty. Not even these ugly clothes Helion got for you—I left the selection to him as I was busy reconnoitering the ground, and I crave your pardon for the shoddiness of his choice—can conceal the fact that your face is lovely and that your legs, instead of being muscular, are undeniably pretty."

"My cloak comes to my ankles when I'm standing. I could wear a patch over one eye and put some stain on my face. But—will there be need for it? Surely I'm to wear proper clothes now that we're safely out of Paris!"

D'Arlay shook his head. "The King may decide to have you followed. It would be an absurd thing for him to do under the circumstances, but a wound to the pride is a great incitement to folly. We must ride hard and fast until we are well out of reach. Certainly it won't be safe for three or four days to stop long enough to find clothes for you. And can you think of any surer way of giving them a clue to our direction than a tailor who has supplied an outfit for a lady disguised as a man?"

It was clear that Valerie was unhappy over the situation but she said nothing more at the time. They rode until one o'clock through a light drizzle and then decided to spend what was left of the night at a roadside inn. She insisted on helping Helion with the horses and took the precaution of using a back door on entering. The late roisterers in the common room at the front thus had no chance to make the same discovery as the lieutenant of guards.

Fearing a hue and cry, D'Arlay had decided they must be up at dawn. As he and Helion were dressing hurriedly by the light of a very small candle, a tap came on the door between the two rooms. In response to his invitation to enter, Valerie opened the door a few inches.

"I am sorry to disturb but I—I find myself in a most distressing position."

D'Arlay buttoned his outer tunic at the neck, made sure that his servant was equally well along with his toilet, and then said, "Come in and tell us about it."

"I cannot, my lord. I am—only partly dressed. When I put on these clothes yesterday I found there were things I didn't understand about men's attire. There was no time then to ask questions and so I did the best I could. But I knew, as soon as I stepped out to join you, that there were things I had failed to do."

"I think I know what the difficulty is," said D'Arlay, in a completely serious voice. "The solution will be found in a belt of the strongest linen which you are supposed to wear next your skin or over the shirt if you prefer it that way. You have such a belt?"

"Yes, my lord. I have the belt in my hand."

"Have you noticed that there are a dozen or more holes along the bottom of the belt?"

"Yes, I noticed that."

"You will find a corresponding number of holes in the top of your leggings. Now, all you have to do is to take the short thongs of leather, which are usually kept in a small bag attached to the belt, and draw each one through a hole in the belt and then through the nearest hole in the leggings, and knot it. The leather thongs are called 'points,' as perhaps you know."

"But, my lord, there were no points in the bundle you gave me yesterday!"

"It's no wonder then," said D'Arlay gravely, "that you suffered from lack of that most necessary sense of security." He looked accusingly at Helion, whose expression was an acknowledgment of guilt. "It seems that Helion forgot to put any points with the bundle. I'm tempted to punish him by giving all his points to you and letting him spend the day in the expectation of disaster from which you suffered yesterday. Still, we must be sensible and so I'll divide my points and his into three equal shares and we'll all have to do the best we can until a more adequate supply can be secured. As you will be short on points, it will be advisable to draw them up as far as they'll go and then knot them tightly. Only in that way will your hose fit the legs snugly and without wrinkles."

"Thank you, my lord. I'm sorry to be so much trouble."

All the difficulties had not been solved, however. It developed a few minutes later that the belt could not be taken in enough to fit her waist comfortably. It was handed through the partly opened door and additional holes were punched in it. Then, in a most apologetic voice, she acknowledged that her shoes were too large and were threatening to drop off her feet with each step. The solution decided upon after some discussion was to sew bands of felt inside the heel and instep, and Helion was dispatched to the kitchen to obtain the necessary supplies.

When she finally emerged from her room, she looked so trim that D'Arlay's worries of the previous evening returned. "You're bound to attract too much attention," he said. "We must take other precautions before we risk showing ourselves again at an inn."

Valerie was in a subdued mood when they started out. She said very little and gave a strained smile when he rallied her on her lack of spirits. "I had a dream last night," she said. "It was a very cruel dream and I'm still depressed by it."

"Tell me what it was," he urged. "I'll expound it for you as Joseph did the dreams of Pharaoh."

She shook her head. "I don't want to talk about it yet. I'll tell you later."

The weather had cleared. They took to the road as the sun forced its way above the horizon. The gray of the sky turned to blue and there was a pleasant promise of warmth in the air. It was such a perfect morning, in fact, that her spirits began to lift. When they had been an hour on the road, she surprised herself by singing a few bars from a popular song.

For the sake of appearances D'Arlay was riding in the lead. Because in her improved mood she desired companionship, she set her horse to a gallop and came caracoling up beside him.

"This is the loveliest day I've ever known," she called.

D'Arlay had been thinking the same thing, although his sentiments were not inspired by the weather. He noted with approval the ease of her carriage and the lightness of her hand on the reins. The pressure of the air on her cheeks had brought color to them and her eyes were bright. She had gone abruptly to the other extreme in mood. She laughed and chattered and indulged in snatches of song and even gave him an imitation of Charles, rubbing a finger slowly down her nose and saying, "I come, not as King of France, but as a man——"

They were riding together now, their horses tossing manes in close accord. She looked across at him and smiled in sheer good spirits.

"You seem quite gay and happy this morning," he said.

"And haven't I the best of reasons?"

"Perhaps. I would be more disposed to feel as you do if I could read the future."

"I've forced myself to forget the future. I'm living in the present." She raised her free arm and gestured about her. "It's a lovely day. I can feel the breath of the south already. There are no signs of pursuit. Most of all I'm beginning to realize that it's true."

"What is true?"

"That—that I'm free of a shadow under which I've lived for more than a year."

He waited to see if she had anything to add and then asked her, "Have you no other reason for being happy today?"

Her eyes had become fixed on the road ahead. "Well—I ride in good company."

"That's better. But—it isn't the answer I had hoped for."

They were approaching a turn from which the road swung sharply downward and for a few minutes it was necessary for both to keep a careful watch ahead.

D'Arlay took up the conversation then. "It's only with the greatest difficulty," he said, "that I keep my arms to their regular tasks. Every moment since we started they've been demanding that I allow them to reach out and drag you over here into this saddle with me. There has been a madness of delight in me which has grown with each second. I'm filled with such a tumult that I—that I don't know how I control the impulse to shout aloud. Valerie, I'm so happy that if Charles of France were here with us I would slap his face with my glove in sheer exuberance!"

He sobered abruptly. "I'm weak at dissembling," he added. "If I allow myself to continue thinking like this, it will show in my eyes, in my manner. Everyone we meet will know you are a lady and that I love you. I must discipline myself, and I must begin now. We are three men riding together. Helion is unmistakably my servant. Because of the clothes he chose for you, people will think you a servant also. I must treat you as one when people are around, and so I must avoid slips by maintaining the same fiction when we are alone. You see the good sense of this, I trust?"

Valerie watched him as he went through this difficult explanation. Smiling to herself and lowering her eyes, she answered in a respectful voice, "Yes, master."

"Of course," he said, "there's no one within miles of us at the moment and so it might be we could postpone the start of this—this most unpleasant pretense."

"Is it, then, no longer necessary for me to drop back at once and spend the rest of the day in the company of the sprightly Helion?"

"No," answered D'Arlay with a smile. "But it might be easier for me if you did."

Darkness caught them that night far from any roadside inn. They were lucky enough to sight almost at once a small farmhouse close to the road. To their dismay, however, D'Arlay's vigorous knock on the door was without results. No lights appeared and they could hear the loud clang resounding hollowly through empty rooms.

"The place seems to be deserted," said D'Arlay in a disgusted tone, after a last angry effort with the knocker.

"There's a barn behind it, master," said Helion, who had been investigating.

D'Arlay decided in favor of the barn. "It will be easier to break into," he said, "and it will have straw or hay for us to sleep on instead of bare floors."

The barn proved to be a ramshackle affair, with moonlight showing through gaps in the roof and the clay floor covered with a low mound of musty hay. Helion busied himself with the horses, tethering them in a corner and producing fodder for them from the feed-bags. Valerie and D'Arlay seated themselves together in the center. There had already been suspicious rustlings in the hay and, having no liking for rats, she wrapped her cloak carefully about her feet and ankles.

"And now," she said, "I can't postpone any longer the telling of my dream."

"Was it an unpleasant one?"

"It was about the Comtesse." Valerie was speaking in a repressed tone. "She came to me and told me something. I could read both hate and triumph in her face. What it was she told me I can't remember but of this I'm sure—it had to do with the future and it frightened me so much that I wakened up in terror and found that I was crying out, 'No, no!'"

"If you remember the rest so clearly, you must surely have some recollection of what she said."

Valerie shook her head. "My mind is blank on that point. It must be that she's planning some—some form of revenge for what we have done."

"That I can believe. But, Valerie, you mustn't worry about it. After all, what can she do? Neither of us, I most sincerely hope and trust, will ever see her again. But tell me more about the dream. Where did it take place?"

"In a very large room with a high ceiling and, it seemed, hundreds and hundreds of candles. There was a tapestry on one wall, representing the death of Absalom in the tree——"

"Was there," he asked, in an excited tone, "a drinking horn on a table under the tapestry?"

"Yes." Valerie nodded slowly. "I seem to remember that it had a silver eagle on top and that it stood on the feet of a bird."

D'Arlay was quite excited now. "That is the *Chambre de Charlemagne* at the Hôtel Saint-Pol. Have you ever seen it?"

She shook her head. "No. But it was very clear in my dream. There were many people about but they weren't close enough for me to see their faces."

"And Isabeau came to you in the *Chambre de Charlemagne* and gave you this message you can't remember?" He paused in thought. "It may be she's planning some sort of revenge which has to do with the King. Why otherwise would you see her in his chamber of which you have no waking knowledge at all?"

Valerie asked in a low voice, "Will she, Isabeau, be angry enough to go to such lengths?"

"I am sure"—nodding his head gravely—"that she'll be angry enough to do anything against us. She'll do anything that lies in her power."

They sat in an unhappy silence for several minutes. Then Valerie asked suddenly, "Did you love her very much?"

He nodded his head reluctantly. "I loved her so much when I was young that nothing else counted. Then she married my brother; and after that it was a sharp passion I felt, an angry passion, a determination to hold something of what I had lost. Gradually it cooled and then"—he smiled grimly—"then she had become a—an obligation from which I couldn't escape. I can tell you in all honesty, Valerie, that for many years my only desire was to break the bond." He paused and turned to face her anxiously. "I am ready to swear a solemn oath that at no time, not even when I was a boy and believed her the sun and the moon and the stars of my existence, did I feel for her the love that I have for you!"

2

There was still no sign of pursuit the next morning but, taking no chances, they rode long and hard. Valerie wore a patch over one eye and she never mounted or dismounted when there were spectators, for fear a lack of masculine ease would show or the feminine turn of a leg. She kept her cloak wrapped about her, which proved uncomfortable as the temperature rose with each league they rode southward.

This went on for two days more. The same discomforts had to be borne; but now a new one, and a harder to endure, made itself apparent —the lack of water. The inns at which they stayed were for the most part primitive, particularly in respect to bathing facilities. It was an accepted rule of the road, in fact, that travelers waited for baths and for the washing of their clothes until they reached their destinations. Argue and cajole as they might, they obtained no better than small basins of lukewarm water for the first nights of their southward flight.

On the fifth day Valerie could not resist the chance offered by a shaded bend in a stream close by the road. She reined in her horse.

"There are none about," she said. "Would it delay us too much if I took a bath there?"

D'Arlay looked doubtfully at the stream which flowed swiftly by. "I fear it's deep. Can you swim?"

Valerie smiled. "You seem to forget that nearly all my life has been spent on the road. I never bathed in a tub until I was sent to live with the Comtesse. In fact, my lord, I have some recollection of bathing at this very spot a few years ago when we were on our way to Tours. I—I swim with some skill."

D'Arlay stood guard on the road above the pool and Helion took up his station below. They knew when she plunged into the water by the loud gasp with which she proclaimed its unexpected coldness. It must have been very cold, in fact, for she returned fully dressed within a few minutes, looking refreshed but a little blue.

The bath had not been a complete success. "I found it very distasteful to dress again," she said, looking down at her muddy tunic and hose with a shudder. "I can't abide such dirtiness any longer. I must find a way to wash them tonight or my flesh will shrink from the need to get into them again tomorrow." She went on with some haste to explain herself. "You'll think this strange from one who lived so long on the road. It's because of what I had to endure then, my lord, that I have this feeling now. To be wet and unclean makes me think I am back once more in that kind of life, that the past has—has overtaken me. Something happens inside me. I have such distaste for these clothes that I feel I am imprisoned, body and soul." She looked up at him in an appeal for understanding. "I hope I don't sound ungrateful and hard to please."

"Tonight you shall have hot water to wash your clothes," vowed D'Arlay.

And water she had, a large and ancient tub filled to the top with it. It was steaming hot. Only the proffer of a heavy silver coin had reconciled the landlord to such an unheard-of luxury.

When D'Arlay made his way late in the evening to the one bedroom the inn boasted for the accommodation of guests, he found that Valerie had been making good use of the hot water. A line was strung across the space from corner to corner and on it her whole wardrobe was hanging limply like a file of scarecrows on a windless day. She had donned their common spare cloak in the meantime but, as the evening was unseasonably warm, had allowed it to drop about her waist. He caught the merest glimpse of a white shoulder as she hurriedly struggled into the cloak on the opening of the door.

"I regret profoundly that it has been necessary to turn the room into a washhouse," she said.

He sat down on one side of the bed and regarded her with a serious air. Valerie looked up at him and smiled, at the same time giving her head a shake.

"You are so very serious-minded, my lord Robin," she said.

He acknowledged that this was true.

"You allow yourself to worry about things when it isn't necessary."

"Yes. That also is true."

"And now tell me, what are you so concerned about at the moment that you haven't smiled since you came into the room?"

"I'm concerned about what we're to do tonight." He turned and indicated the bed, which was a truly enormous one. "Do you know that this is the only bed in the inn?"

"I heard the landlord say so." She did not seem disturbed. In fact, she was making no effort to hide the twinkle of amusement in her eyes.

"We must stay in this room, the three of us. Helion and I would gladly sleep outside the door but to do so would be to let everyone know you don't dress your sex."

"But *I* could sleep outside the door while you and Helion occupy the bed. As I'm the younger servant, it wouldn't seem amiss. Or unusual."

"Do you think I could sleep at ease, knowing you had the hard floor for your portion?"

"But what other course is open? Are you willing to agree that we all share the bed?"

D'Arlay shook his head emphatically. "No! No! Do you think I would ruin the reputation of the woman I love?"

"Who would know?"

"Stories of the kind get out somehow. No, Valerie, any other course but that."

Valerie indulged in a puzzled frown. "We must get through the night. If we don't do the one, we must do the other."

D'Arlay was sure he had the solution. "You shall occupy the bed while Helion and I sleep on the floor beside it."

Valerie gave her head another shake. "If it became known that we had spent the night together in one room, would anyone believe we had been so—so extremely conventional? Is honor satisfied when you sleep five feet from me instead of two? Is there innocence in bare boards and sin in a mattress?"

D'Arlay looked more worried than ever. "Then," he said, "I see no answer to this riddle at all."

What decision they would have reached if left to themselves can only be conjectured for at this moment a knock came on the door. D'Arlay opened it to find the landlord on the threshold with two dusty travelers beside him. The keeper of the inn bobbed his head in an excess of apology.

"There are more guests," he said. "It is a difficulty, lord. I must not turn them away; and this is the only bed I have. It is intended for five, lord." He lowered his voice for D'Arlay's ear alone. "They are worthy merchants who are going to the spring fairs in the south. They will be humble. They know their place and won't intrude on you more than is necessary."

"Can a man intrude further than to share your bed?" demanded D'Arlay.

He looked at the new arrivals without any effort to conceal his feelings. They were an oddly assorted pair. One was in his middle years and had succeeded in growing fat without achieving any of the benevolence of appearance or the jollity of manner which can mitigate avoirdupois. He looked vicious and grasping and inexpressibly vulgar.

The other was small and thin and as active as a monkey. He had close-set eyes and black hair sprouting from ears and nostrils and on the back of his hands. There was a certain similarity about their clothes which had been gaudy and pretentious when new but now were soiled and sadly out of shape.

"I am a poor man, lord," insinuated the landlord. "I can't afford to turn away guests with money in their pockets."

D'Arlay darted a quick glance in Valerie's direction. She was keeping her back turned and he believed that he saw her shake as though with distress or inner laughter. After watching her for several moments he became convinced that it was the latter. "If that is how she feels," he thought with a sense of resentment, "why should I strive to find a way out of this dilemma?" It had not yet occurred to him that the arrival of these two unprepossessing guests had provided them with the solution of their problem, that the addition of two strange bedfellows would preserve her reputation.

He said to the landlord: "We rise at daylight. Otherwise I would insist that these new guests of yours leave before us. To save time, it's our intention to sleep in our clothes. They must be content to do the same."

The fat man said in a hearty voice: "That's entirely to my liking. I haven't been out of my clothes for ten days."

His point won, the landlord made a discreetly hasty exit. The smaller of the two stalked into the room with complete self-confidence. He grinned like a monkey and pointed a finger at the clothesline.

"You should feel at home here, Old Guts," he said to his companion. "Do you care to give a free exhibition of your skill? Or does it seem to you the rope is a trifle thin for a dancer of your weight?"

The fat man emitted a snort of dissent. "It's true enough, King Zoser, that I've taken on a pound or two. But when I step on a rope, I still have no more heft than a soul winging its way to paradise. I could take this rope, flimsy as a woman's virtue though it seems, and do a trick pavane or a back handspring or even a quarter-time mince. With or without music."

He laid a hand on one end of the line as though prepared to demonstrate the truth of what he had said. D'Arlay interposed hastily, "There will be no ropedancing here, if you please."

The fat man desisted at once with complete good nature but his companion was not so amenable. He scowled at D'Arlay and then turned his attention again to the articles of clothing strung on the line.

"You couldn't fit your long legs into these," he said. "They must belong to that small measure of ale over there in the corner. What's wrong with him that he has to be so particular about what he wears?"

"If we are to begin with questions," said D'Arlay shortly, "I have some to ask which you might find embarrassing to answer."

His realization that the newcomers were merchants, as the landlord had said, but that they purveyed entertainment and not goods, made D'Arlay think of demanding after all that they be sent away. When he whispered to Valerie what he proposed to do, however, she shook her head.

"No," she whispered, still finding it hard to control her amusement, "I think they may belong to the Coquille. They could do us a lot of harm."

"This is no laughing matter."

In the meantime the corpulent ropedancer had started to take off his shoes, sitting on the floor to do so. As he removed each he beat the mud from it on the side of the bed. Then he stretched himself out at full length on the mattress and gave vent to a contented snuffle.

The small one swung a bundle from his back to the floor and sat himself down beside it. It contained his stock in trade and he proceeded to take each article out in turn: a selection of wands, half-a-dozen balls, a leather cone marked with cabalistic signs, several knives, a cloth serpent with spring joints, a black silk cloak. After giving each the most careful examination he returned it to the bag, making sure it went back into its appointed place. By doing this he succeeded in putting himself into a complacent humor again.

"I'm young at my trade, Old Guts," he said, "but no one can say that I'm not good. Do you know a juggler as skilled as I am? Have you ever seen a saltimbanco with as many tricks?"

The ropedancer flexed his huge legs luxuriantly. "Can you keep six knives in the air at once?" he demanded.

There was a moment of silence. "I can keep four."

"I knew a man in the Low Countries who could do six, and never make a mistake."

The small man's temper flared up like a dry bulrush when thrust into coals. His beady black eyes snapped.

"So! You dribbling mooncalf, you great gobbet of *lard de carême!* You knew a man who could keep six in the air? It's a lie! You want to buy flutes, do you? I know a man who's going to feel my knife in his gizzards."

In an instant they were at it hammer and tongs. The little conjurer danced up and down in fury, screaming foul epithets. The fat man sat up in bed and bawled insults back at him.

D'Arlay took the juggler in hand and gave him a vigorous shake. "There's a limit to our patience," he said angrily. "Get to bed without more ado."

King Zoser subsided at once and gave D'Arlay an impudent grin. "Just as you say, Lord High-Sniffer. But I've got to do my flex first."

He walked to a spot in front of the one window (which was clamped down tight) and proceeded to contort his body in various ways. He held out each hand in turn and exercised the fingers for minutes at a time. He rolled his arms, twisted his neck, thrust his chest in and out with loud expulsions of breath, and cracked his joints with a sound like branches breaking in a storm.

The ropedancer shook his head at D'Arlay when the latter showed an intention of stopping this performance. "He has to go through it twice a day, lord. It keeps his muscles supple so he can do his tricks."

"It's true," whispered Valerie. "I know it because we often traveled in the company of such as these."

The juggler, his exercising finished, stretched himself out on the bed beside the ropedancer. Helion took his place on the other side of the fat man and seemed to fall asleep immediately. D'Arlay looked down at the small amount of space left and whispered to Valerie, "This will be like consorting with thieves or sleeping in a pig wallow. And yet it must be done. I'll sleep facing them and you take the outside."

After all five had settled into their places there were several minutes of silence, broken only by the loud breathing of Helion. Then the fat man began to snicker. "I'm reminded of a tale I heard once," he said. "It seems there were three people met at an inn, a hatter, a high toby, and a harlot. The hatter was on his way to a fair, just as we are. The high toby had slit the throat of a lagbelly merchant in Paris and was on a safety sweat. The harlot—— Well, I need not go into *her* reasons. The inn, as it happened, had one bed only, even as this one——"

"Spare our ears!" said D'Arlay. "I don't want to hear another word out of you, rogue, or I shall be compelled to wind this rope around your neck and teach you a new kind of dance."

The fat man said sulkily, "I thought only to speed your lapse into sleep with a merry tale, one to be repeated profitably to friends or whispered into the ear of a mistress like grace before meat." He twisted his bulk over on the other side, making the bed creak, and in a few minutes had forgotten his pique in slumber.

Realizing that it would be unwise on many counts to fall asleep himself, D'Arlay summoned up a train of reflection well calculated to keep him awake. He began for the hundredth time to speculate on what would happen as a result of Valerie's flight. He had no doubt that his own part in it would become known. He would have to leave the country. That would lose him his well-loved domain of Arlay but he would not be left destitute. There was plenty of gold to provide a start in some other part of the world. He went over in his mind the countries where sanctuary might be sought: Navarre, Spain, Portugal, Italy, Scotland, the Low Countries. When he reached the strip of Baltic country which housed the Hanseatic League he paused, for he had heard that fortunes were to be made there. In that far northern land he might still act in concert with Jacques Coeur.

An hour passed. The snoring of the three sleepers had merged into a steady antiphonal chorus. D'Arlay, who had not changed position, was inclined to believe that Valerie was still awake but he could not be sure until she said in a hesitant whisper, "My lord Robin?"

"Yes."

"Do you think he—King Zoser, the small, dark one—suspected?"

"He looked at you closely but I don't believe he saw anything wrong."

"I'm not sure. I could feel those eyes of his on me and it made me most uncomfortable. Do you think we should rouse Helion and get away while they're sleeping?"

"No, we would give ourselves away if we did."

There was a long pause. Then she whispered again, "My lord Robin?"

"Yes."

"Was ever lady in such a position before?"

"I—I think it unlikely."

"Is it proof that I'm not a lady, after all, that I can feel amused over my plight? I'm so well accustomed to men like—like this King Zoser and the fat one that I don't seem to mind them very much."

He felt her shake as though she found it hard to keep from laughing. He was seized suddenly with the same desire and checked it with the greatest difficulty. "We must be careful," he whispered, "or we'll waken the others."

"Just imagine," she whispered back, "what the Comtesse would think and say if she knew!"

Her mood changed then with the unexpectedness he had already observed in her and which would always keep him, as she put it herself later, "trying to jump through hoops." He heard her give a deep and unhappy sigh.

"I've brought so much trouble to you and to my lord Coeur also."

"You must remember that it was he who began this." He stopped to make sure that all three of their bedfellows were still contributing to the chorus. "Try to get some sleep now as we shall have to get away earlier than we first planned."

"It will be much better if I stay awake."

In spite of her good intentions she fell asleep after all. His first intimation of it was when she ceased to toss and turn. Then he detected a broken rhythm to her breathing which turned gradually into an even volume of pleasant sound not unlike the purring of a kitten. He smiled to himself in the dark. "Now I must stay awake without fail."

A wave of happiness passed over him as he became conscious of the pressure of her shoulder against his. "It will soon be my right," he thought, "to hold her in my arms, to hear every night this sweet purring of content close to my ear!"

A more rosy note injected itself into his consideration of the future. The gold that he possessed, all of it safely stowed away, would be sufficient to assure them comfort wherever they went. His thoughts reached at last a land of everlasting enchantment where he and Valerie lived together, counting what they had lost as small. He pictured a white house on the side of a hill, from which perhaps the spires of the Eternal City could be seen, a road dead white in the sun winding down from it; the sound of children's voices in an olive grove back of the house. It might be, he said to himself drowsily, that adversity had been the prod needed to set his feet in the direction of happiness. . . .

The first light of dawn was showing through the window when he wakened. Valerie was lying in his arms, her head pressed against his cheek. The night had been warm and the cloak she wore had slipped off. He knew this because the shoulder resting on his right arm was bare and his other hand touched her elbow. He reached out cautiously with his left hand and found the cloak at the level of their knees. Drawing it up with the greatest care, he draped it over her. Then he sat up in bed and gave her shoulder a tug.

Valerie stirred at once. She drew a hand across her eyes and then looked quickly in the direction of the window. He heard her say in a horrified whisper, "I've been asleep!" It was not until she had raised herself to a sitting position that she discovered he was also awake.

They stared at each other, her eyes full of self-reproach. "I'm sorry, my lord Robin!" she whispered. "My only excuse is that we were long hours in the saddle yesterday. I was more tired than I realized."

"I hope you slept well."

She nodded. "I must have slept soundly and well, for I find myself completely rested."

"Then," thought D'Arlay exultantly, "her head did not find my arm an alien resting place! She came to me in her sleep as naturally as though she knew she belonged there!"

He was amazed to find how fresh she looked. Enough light came through the window for him to see that her eyes were wide open and that there was even a slight tinge of pink in her cheeks.

Valerie drew the cloak tightly about her and then put a foot to the floor. "If my lord Robin will be good enough to turn his head," she whispered, "I shall dress myself at once."

3

The morning of the seventh day found D'Arlay convinced that it would now be safe to change their traveling arrangements. They had spent the night at a large and pretentious inn where they had been allowed the use of three rooms. D'Arlay's was a large room with a hearth of its own and a towering armoire carved with the arms of a noble family (he could not be sure which family it was) and with ochre daubed on for background.

He was breakfasting there most substantially on a grilled fish and choice white bread, Helion acting as go-between with the kitchen, and Valerie standing behind his chair to anticipate his wants. The sun had climbed well above a ridge of hills in the east and was pouring cheerfully into the room. The fish was excellent, the wine cool. When Helion left the room, he took advantage of the chance to give her a more personal greeting.

"It's going to be a pleasant day for riding, my loved one."

She did not answer immediately. It was in a low tone that she finally said, "Yes, my lord Robin."

Laying down his knife but not turning in her direction at once, he allowed himself to say some of the things which he had been suppressing with great difficulty.

"You must have realized that I've been existing under an almost unbearable strain. To see you, to have you near me, and to be unable to tell you how much I love you!" To his own surprise he found himself giving voice to a rush of words which actually verged on the poetic. "I swear by God above me, and all the saints on the calendar, and all the shining angels with silver wings in heaven, that I love you more than any man has ever loved a woman since Adam's eviction! Even in those ill-fitting clothes that my dull, unfeeling clod of a servant selected for you, even with a patch over your eye and a deliberate dab of mud on your chin, you are the loveliest creature in the whole world."

"Aren't you breaking your own rule, my lord Robin?"

"I am!" He spoke with emphasis, even a trace of violence. "It was a foul rule, one that could be justified only by the peculiar circumstances in which we found ourselves. But now, by good St. Martin, it's no longer necessary! It's certain we're not being followed. I wanted to be sure in my mind, and now there can no longer be any doubts. And that means we have no further need for such rules. It means we can set about getting you proper clothes at once. It means——"

He turned in his chair then, expecting to find her as pleased as he was himself. Instead he found that she was wearing an artificial smile in the hope, obviously, of hiding her real feelings.

"Valerie!" He got to his feet and reached out to capture her hands. "You're not well? Has anything happened?"

"I had the same dream last night," she said, forcing herself to speak. "She came to me again, the Comtesse, and said the same things to me. She was wearing the same dress. I still can't remember what she told me but I know I was left with as much fear as before—fear for you and my lord Coeur as well."

"Could you see any of the others in the room this time?" he asked, after an uncomfortable pause.

She shook her head. "No. They were all as vague as the first time."

"You don't believe that it's Isabeau who wants to warn you of some danger?"

"No, no!" There was an almost fierce emphasis in her voice. "She comes to threaten me. She makes it clear how much she hates me. If the dream is a warning, it comes from—from another source."

"Is there anything more you can tell me about it?"

She wrinkled her brow in concentration. "One figure began to step forward. I was waiting anxiously to see who it was—and then the dream ended!" She said nothing more for a moment and then she began again in urgent tones: "We mustn't delay a moment! Much as I would like to get rid of these clothes, I can't stand the thought of waiting that long. We must get to Bourges and warn my lord Coeur. And then we must get away ourselves, far away—as far and as fast as we can!"

D'Arlay said, "It shall be as you wish, my heart." As Helion entered the room at that moment, he gave instructions that the horses were to be brought out at once and the landlord paid. Helion, looking surprised and not too pleased at this prospect of more hard riding, left the room. His master turned back to Valerie who had not succeeded in reaching a calmer state in the meantime.

"Where do you want to go after we leave Bourges?" he asked.

"To Spain, to the Indies, to Cathay! Anywhere, my lord Robin, if it's far enough away from *her* and the evil she's plotting against us!"

"And you're ready to go with me?"

She started to speak but changed her mind. Her eyes dropped and she frowned thoughtfully. Finally she looked up at him again. "If you want an answer to that, I think you should word the question differently."

It was his turn to frown. "I don't understand."

"I couldn't go with you except as your wife. So far I haven't heard you mention the word marriage."

"But"—he was both surprised and startled—"I've made it clear that I'm deeply in love with you."

"But isn't it true, my lord Robin, that the great gentleman who seduces a village maid lets her think that he loves her?"

D'Arlay looked seriously disturbed. "The point is well taken. I've been at fault. But it seemed to me that you couldn't fail to know what I meant."

"Robin," she said, addressing him thus for the first time, "you're a member of a very old family. You're a landowner in your own right and a great knight. As for me—no one knows who I am. I'm still no better in point of fact than the daughter of a strolling actor. When there is this difference in our stations, things can't be taken for granted as between equals. Not, at least, by me. I must always wait until you are ready to tell me what is in your mind."

"What is in my mind now," he declared, "is that I never want to be parted from you. I count all time lost until I can take you to a priest and have the marriage vows pronounced over us."

"We can't spare the time," said Valerie sadly. "Not even for that!"

Helion put his head in at the door to announce that the horses were ready.

No time thereafter was lost. Valerie would remain in the saddle so determinedly that she would have to be helped down at night. Even though they were now riding through the valley of the Loire, they did not linger to enjoy the beauties of that fabulous country. They paid no heed to the great winding river and the hills on the skyline; to the magic castles (which were even more beautiful in their reflection in the water); or the windmills turning as though ashamed of any form of hurry in a land of such enchanting peace; of the mule trains and the boats on the river in which men sang as they pulled at the oars; of the knights in armor who rode the river paths with cavalcades behind them.

To Valerie there was something about the valley of the Loire of much more importance than its serenity and charm. Another girl had ridden here in the garb of a man and had made an immortal name for herself. She knew the story of the Maid from beginning to end and was amazed to find that D'Arlay was almost completely ignorant of it. She would have liked to correct this serious flaw (which all members of the aristocracy shared at this time) by pointing out the places where Jeanne D'Arc had been and by recounting what happened in full detail. But the time could not be spared. Once she reined in her horse in front of an inn long enough to say: "She slept one night under that chestnut tree and when they asked in the morning if the rain had disturbed her she said, No, she had been listening to voices which drowned out the thunder." Another time, but without drawing rein: "When she crossed the river here the ends of a rainbow rested on each bank and heavenly music could be heard for miles hereabouts." It was then she asked, "Don't you feel, my lord Robin, that a benediction will always rest on this land because it was here the Maid led the armies of France?"

In spite of this determination to reach Bourges before the consequences she read in the dream could overtake them, she sometimes lapsed into a more normal mood. Once she asked him which country he would prefer if he were forced to go into exile. After some thought, he expressed himself in favor of Portugal. Her own choice was Italy. She explained it by saying that it was the home of great poets and painters and builders. "I know so little," she said. "It would be wonderful to live in a country where all the learning of the ages is being put into use."

D'Arlay fell into a mood of deep unhappiness at this point. "There's only one country where Frenchmen may live with any content," he said, "and that is France. And in all France there's no place to equal the domain of Arlay. Have I ever told you about it? Ah, my love, it passes all description! It stands on the slope of a green valley, and there's a stream below which is just like a beautiful woman because it's capricious and sometimes even quarrelsome and it winds about so much that it takes five miles to do one, and sometimes it's shallow and sometimes, most unexpectedly, it's very deep, and at all times it's the loveliest sight on which the eye can rest. The hills stretch away for many miles in all directions. The woods are dense and of the darkest green, and the trees about the house are like old friends. The winds which blow down the valley seem to sing rather than roar. In fact, the peasants have a song which they say comes from the sound of the March winds."

Valerie, listening to him attentively, caught some of his enthusiasm. "It seems perfect," she said.

D'Arlay sighed. "No, it has never been perfect. It has lacked a chatelaine. If you were there, it would be the most perfect place in the world. And now"—he gave an even deeper sigh—"that chance has been lost. You will never see Arlay."

4

D'Arlay was standing at the window of his room, looking down into the yard of the inn with some uneasiness. Steaming horses were being unharnessed there and rubbed down by a crew of vociferous servants.

When a knock sounded on the door, he answered in a preoccupied voice, "Come in!"

It was Valerie who obeyed the summons, and he needed no more than a glance to know that she was the bearer of serious news. She remained in the doorway.

"We must get away! At once!" she said, in a tense whisper.

D'Arlay left the window and walked to the door. They faced each other for several moments in silence.

And then something happened which no one, least of all the two participants, could have anticipated. He reached out, suddenly and with a touch of violence, and gathered her into his embrace, saying in a smothered voice, "My poor Valerie, my sweet Valerie, you are frightened!" She responded with the same spontaneity. Her arms went up around his neck and she buried her face in the soft brown velvet of his shoulder. They stood thus for some time. Then, taking her face in his hands, he kissed her. It was a long kiss and it expressed everything he felt for her: love, devotion, passion, a tenderness beyond words. It was their first kiss and it had required the realization of imminent danger to bring it about.

He touched her hair and said, "My dear one, I must get you away from here at once." Then the flood engulfed him again and it was fully a minute before he was able to think of anything save the wonderful fact of her presence in his arms. When he finally stepped back, it was like awakening from a dream.

"What is it that has happened?" he asked.

Conscious of the time which had been lost, she began to explain in a hurried whisper. "When the new party arrived, I went into the hall and looked down the staircase, thinking it would be wise to see what manner of men they were. I recognized one of them at once. He was in charge and I knew he was of the court because I saw him when we were at the abbey. He has a face one doesn't easily forget."

"Do you know his name?"

"I heard the Comtesse speak of him at the time." She paused, her brow puckered in thought. "I seem to remember his name as Gouffier."

"Then I need to know nothing more! He may be following us, but it seems more likely he's bound for Bourges on some errand connected with Jacques Coeur." D'Arlay nodded his head emphatically. "In any event we must see that warning reaches Coeur at once. That means an all-night ride."

"You can't leave me here, so go with you I must." She gave him a confident smile. "I'm young and strong. There were many times when I had to drive or ride all through the night. I can do it again."

"I looked the place over before coming up. There's a gate behind the stables, so we can get away without being seen." He gave her grave face the most solicitous study. "We'll be eight hours in the saddle and riding hard the whole time. Are you sure you can stand it?"

"Quite sure." Then the gravity of her expression deepened. "Do you think my dreams were meant to warn us of this?"

"It's possible. I know this, that the presence of Gouffier with the party is an ill omen." Then his face took on a happy smile. "Tomorrow will be an eventful day in Bourges." His arms reached out for her again. "We will be married as soon as we arrive."

Chapter XII

I

WHEN the clock struck one, Nicolas put his head in at the door of his master's room to ask, "Did you hear that?" At two he repeated the performance, speaking in a more urgent tone. Jacques Coeur paid no heed. He was seated at a long table, which quite apparently had been brought from the East for it was of fine red wood and built of a curious design. The top of the table was covered with papers on which he had written in his rapid flowing hand (quite different from the precise script of the period) and to which he was adding at a furious rate. He did not raise his head.

At three Nicolas decided to make himself heard. He began to speak in such a loud tone that his master looked up at once from the sheet on which he was engaged.

"Is it your wish to hasten the time," demanded the servant, "when you will take that post you think yourself so well fitted for, Moneyman in the Kingdom of Heaven?"

Coeur answered in an impatient tone, "I must finish what I'm doing while the matters are fresh in my mind." Then he looked up at his man and smiled. "You're thinking of your own need for rest as well as mine, Nicolas. Go to bed, then, in God's good name, so that I won't be interrupted any more by that ugly head of yours peering in at me. I weary of your solicitude, my dear Nicolas, and I weary of the complaining look you wear on your ill-natured face."

"Have I ever gone to bed before you, master?" Nicolas spoke in an aggrieved tone. "Never, as you know full well. Why should I start now after all these years of dancing attendance on you, and watching you, and waiting on you, and dandling round like a dog after the huntsman? No, master, I go to bed when you do and not a moment before."

He returned to the anteroom in which he spent nearly all his time. "Three hours' sleep we've had in two days," he muttered. "What new devil is eating at his vitals that he can't stop work? Not that I care about myself——"

When he roused himself from the slumber into which he had fallen, the first rays of the sun were lighting the windows of the room. Sounds of industry reached him from below—the clang of hammers and the screech of saws (for the architects still had possession of the house and their workmen swarmed all over it), and, less evident but quite unmistakable, a hum of voices which indicated that the members of his organization summoned by Coeur to Bourges were also up and about. Nicolas stretched himself, after a guilty glance at the door leading into his master's room which fortunately was closed, and walked to a window. He could see all of one wing, on which a roof of high-slanting angles was being built. A man of some authority, carrying a roll of papers under one arm, was swinging himself up among the rafters and calling out orders as he did so. Nicolas had watched him climb on a score of mornings, expecting to see him fall and kill himself, but so far had not been rewarded by so much as a stumble.

In the courtyard, which the servant could see by leaning far out of the window, groups of men were standing about. He could hear one voice above the rest, a voice trained to make itself heard over the roaring of sea and wind.

"Ha!" said Nicolas with a smile. "It's clear Jean de Village wasn't drinking last night or he wouldn't be up so early." He leaned out still farther and called: "Jean! Jean de Village! Come up, the master will be asking for you in a minute."

In answer to this summons there appeared in the doorway a few moments later a man whose stature lent credence to the stories of giants which were used currently to frighten disobedient children. Coeur's great sea captain was not only inches taller than anyone else, he was even wider in proportion, with shoulders as massive as gun platforms and legs like the gnarled trunks of trees. Increasing the effect, he wore a grotesquely padded jacket of yellow cloth, tufted with black buttons and laced about with bands of sky-blue silk and so many chains that they clanked as he walked, and sleeves extravagantly puffed which made him lose all semblance to humanity. He seemed, in fact, like some gigantic animal straight out of the legends. His face was a leathery melon with a sickle mouth and eyes of bland and washed-out blue.

"Is the great man awake already?" Jean de Village demanded, stalking into the room.

"Awake already!" repeated Nicolas with a proper indignation. "The great man has been up all night, with his nose in his papers, while lesser men wallowed in slumber like swine. He hasn't slept a wink. Nor have I."

"You lie!" said the sea captain, with good-natured finality. "I can see by your eyes, you ugly old toad, that you've just roused yourself. And I'll tell you this: I'm no droil and I don't wallow in slumber like swine, I sleep with the thoroughness of a hibernating bear, but when I wake—I'll have you know, Master Nicolas, that I wake growling and that I'm likely to tear interfering servants like you to pieces."

Before Nicolas could make any move to prevent him, the sailor opened the inside door. He walked in, closing it after him with a resounding bang.

The Moneyman looked up and nodded. "Good morning, Jean."

"That rubber of salt in raw wounds," said Jean de Village, "that whining bergherst, that saw-toothed oracle of ill news—in other words, your servant Nicolas whose ungainliness of mood you suffer for some reason unknown to anyone else—tells me you have been standing every watch. This is not wise, good master and uncle-in-law. How can you keep a clear head for the problems which face you if you deny yourself the benefit of sleep?"

The Moneyman wrote the final words on a sheet and then, with a frown of abstraction, began to gather all the papers together. "My brave Jean," he said, "I have set down full instructions as to what must be done in all eventualities." He leaned back in his chair and passed a hand over his eyes with a gesture of the greatest weariness. He was pale and there were deep shadows under his eyes. "As soon as things are in order, I shall meet their charges and then, if necessary, leave the country. I am prepared"—he paused and sighed unhappily—"to abandon my shops and my factories in France, to see the work of a lifetime fall into ruins. But there's another side to the picture, my brave Jean, a brighter side. I'm going to start over again. I shall go to Rome—where His Holiness has a good opinion of me and will extend a welcome, of that I am assured—and from there I'll begin to build another empire."

He paused for several moments and then smiled at his companion with easy confidence. "Jacques Coeur," he said, "is greater than the business he has created in France. The business may die but if Jacques Coeur lives, he can build it all over again. That is what he will do now, either here or in Rome."

He began to gather the papers up and to seal them. "No other hand must touch them yet," he said, "not even that of my critical conscience, Nicolas the Unconvinced." As he sealed each note, he added it to a pile at his elbow which grew until it threatened to topple over. "I must save what I can before the blow falls. I've prepared notes to the number of twenty-two. Here, for instance"—holding up the last one of the lot—"are instructions to get your ships out of harbor as soon as the blow falls. If the time comes to open this one, you'll find I provide for a rendezvous off Marseilles and for one of the fastest in the line to patrol the coast and warn those coming in from the East not to put in at any French port. I have thought of every possibility and provided the answer for it.

"In the absence of D'Arlay, on whom I counted in this emergency," went on the Moneyman, "I'm confiding these to you. You must keep them with you always so that they can be produced as each need arises.

Everything will depend on how quickly my plans are put into operation. All my factors will stand by me but every foot of the journey must be charted for them." He looked up at the sea captain and indulged in a somewhat uncertain smile. *"A Vaillants Coeurs Rien Impossible!* We shall have to demonstrate now the truth of the Coeur motto, Jean!"

The captain gathered up the notes and stowed them away in a capacious inside pocket. "Your desires will be obeyed," he said. "I assume from what you have said that I'm to turn everything over to D'Arlay if he arrives in time. That I'll do gladly."

Nicolas knocked at the door and, without waiting to be summoned, came into the room. "The Sire d'Arlay has just arrived."

"That takes a weight from my mind!" exclaimed Coeur, springing to his feet. "Bring him up at once. We'll breakfast here together, the three of us, Jean."

"He has a lady with him," announced Nicolas, with the same air of unconcern. *"The* lady, master. They both seem—in a state of mind. The Sire d'Arlay says he must see you at once."

A change had come over the Moneyman. The lines of fatigue seemed to have left his face, his color had improved, his eyes had lighted up. He gave the sailor's wide shoulder a reassuring tug.

"Truly, my Jean, this is good news. Go down and greet them for me. Bring them up in ten minutes. By that time I'll have finished all this."

2

D'Arlay had been waiting in the courtyard in a state of impatience which can readily be understood. As soon as he had helped Valerie out of the saddle, she had curled up on an outside bench and had fallen asleep at once. He looked down at her now and said to himself, "She rode like a veteran of the wars, my pretty bride-to-be." He was on the point of summoning a domestic and having her taken to a bed when he was joined by the man who had been seen earlier by Nicolas in the act of climbing the roof.

"Good morning, Sire d'Arlay."

D'Arlay recognized him as the architect from Paris who was building this amazing house for Jacques Coeur. "Good morning, Monsieur Pelle. You are at work early."

"I would hazard the opinion," said the architect, glancing at the recumbent form of the girl, "that you and Mademoiselle were in the saddle all night."

"We were. My companion rode with me stirrup to stirrup and it's no wonder she's now completely exhausted." D'Arlay glanced up at the unfinished walls hedging them in. "You seem to be making progress here."

The architect nodded morosely. "Is this your first view of it?" he asked.

"I was here when the walls were beginning to rise. I haven't been back since."

Monsieur Pelle burst suddenly into a flood of words. "This"—motioning about him—"could be the greatest monument in the world to the art of the builder. I, the most advanced thinker among architects, found at last a man who wanted a house along new lines, who had ideas of his own which were good. We worked together well at the start. We planned a house which was practical as well as beautiful. It doesn't consist of one huge Great Hall like a cathedral to reflect the glory of the owner—and grouped around it a huddle of rooms like ratholes in which he and his family and his dependents live and sleep in squalor. Instead, we have a well-balanced structure in which all rooms are of a comfortable size, with ample fireplaces and plenty of light. We built it as strong as any castle. This was to be a house at least a century ahead of its time, and yet a perfect one. Only for a man with the vision and genius of Jacques Coeur could such a house be raised."

The architect stopped and shook his head despondently. "And then what happens? The weak sides of the man begin to show themselves, his pride, his vainglory, his buffoonery. He needs must have the house original in matters where originality is out of place. Observe the designs in the stained glass of the windows! Nothing classical, nothing dignified! They must show ships, *his* ships, or the shops from which his wealth comes. Have you seen what he has carved over the doors and windows? Mottoes! *Trade* mottoes, Sire d'Arlay! Have you observed the carved groups in bas-relief? Comic subjects instead of proper scenes from the Scripture, jokes at the expense of knights and the nobility. Over each door he must have a scene to designate the purpose of the room. A scullion with a ladle in his hand to show the kitchen, a head peering through sleeping curtains for a bedroom! Sire d'Arlay, the man has a touch of madness in him."

In spite of the impatience which possessed him, D'Arlay had already visited the ground floor and had observed some of the curious samples of Coeur's originality. He had counted a dozen mottoes, trite and threadbare for the most part, some of them repeated over and over in the carvings. He had smiled at a group in bas-relief showing two jesters on mules, tilting in imitation of brave knights in the lists, with broomsticks for lances and market baskets for shields, and had thought, "Jacques is paying his respects to chivalry." He had seen the figure of the Moneyman in various groups on the walls and had been puzzled as to the meaning behind the scenes. After taking it all in, he had realized that the house was a monument to the man himself; as, indeed, it was, a tribute to a daring spirit born centuries too soon, a man who sensed the ignorance of the dark age in which he was chained but who was not above flaunting his success openly before the fellow mortals he despised. It was, d'Arlay had concluded, a house to defy description or classification, a lovely, enduring, vainglorious, daring, amusing, sometimes vulgar house.

"Jacques Coeur has been an enigma to the world," he said to the architect. "Now he ceases to be that. Everything about him is revealed here. This house *is* Jacques Coeur."

"Yes," said the architect, in a grumbling tone. "It started to be Coeur *and* Pelle. Now it's all Coeur."

D'Arlay's mind went back to his urgent need for a talk with the master of this extraordinary structure. "Where is he?" he demanded. "I must see him at once! I have news of the gravest kind!"

"Where is he?" Monsieur Pelle made a despairing gesture, using both hands for the purpose. "That is what I ask myself a dozen times a day. He shuts himself up and no one is allowed to see him. I have had a hundred bitter arguments with that mule in human form who sits in his anteroom."

D'Arlay resumed his pacing, saying to himself: "I'll break in his door if he doesn't send for me soon! What possesses the man? Does he put no trust in me that he disregards my arrival in this way?"

It was with a sense of deep relief that he spied Jean de Village emerge from the main section of the house and come striding across the yard.

"Welcome, Jean!" he cried.

"Welcome, Robin!" boomed the giant, his face beaming like the ruddy sun of evening which it resembled in every respect. "My ears have been filled with the tales of your great deeds but my eyes have been empty of any sight of you. I would have given two years of my own life—and by St. Christophe whom I'm said to resemble, I value every minute of the life I am allowed!—to see you gobbon the ribs of the Burgundian with that lath of yours."

They shook hands with the warmth of old friendship but the smile which accompanied the act remained on D'Arlay's face no more than a moment. "Jean!" he cried. "There's danger ahead of us! Officers of the King are on their way here and will arrive soon. Jacques must know at once! Why does he hide himself away?"

Jean de Village smiled. "How long have you been waiting?"

"Half an hour. An hour. It has seemed longer than that—it has seemed an eternity!"

"You have waited," declared the sea captain, "exactly nine minutes. The great man was finishing some work on which he had been engaged all night when he heard of your arrival and he craved your indulgence for that much longer. I'm to take you in now."

The eyes of the huge man settled on the form of the sleeping girl. He stared at her for several moments with every evidence of interest and then he turned back to D'Arlay and winked.

"Is this the one?" he asked. "I've heard whispers about her. By St. Christophe, she's a pretty thing though I'm compelled to say she's a trifle on the small and meager side. I like my women large and lively and with something to swing when they walk."

D'Arlay resented the limited nature of this praise. "I am wedding her today," he announced stiffly.

Jean de Village swung around to face him, wearing a look of complete incredulity. "You are wedding her! Come, Robin, I've always known that someday you would marry the richest heiress in France. This girl, if the stories I hear are true, hasn't a name of her own or two whites to jingle in her purse."

"Do you think," demanded D'Arlay fiercely, "that any of us will be left with fortunes or lands in France? Have you no conception of the danger in which we stand? We'll all be driven into exile—if we have the good fortune to get away. I never expect to see Arlay again."

He reached down and gathered Valerie into his arms. When she stirred drowsily but did not waken, he looked at the giant sea captain and said, "She's been nearly twenty-four hours in the saddle, Jean. She may not be an heiress but I count myself the luckiest man in the world."

D'Arlay carried Valerie into the main hall. She wakened then and asked, "Where are we?" in a puzzled tone. She was so weary that, when her feet touched the floor, she could barely stand and found it advisable to cling to his arm for support. They ascended a marble stairway of most imposing proportions and entered the anteroom where Nicolas sat, clothed in gloomy authority.

The latter consulted a clock on the wall behind him. "Ten seconds early," he said accusingly. Then he motioned over his shoulder in the direction of an inner door. "But you may go in. He's expecting you."

D'Arlay stood no longer on ceremony but rushed headlong through the door. He called to Coeur, who was standing at a window: "Jacques, there's not a moment to lose! Gouffier is on his way here with a party of officers. It may mean he carries a warrant for your arrest."

Jacques Coeur did not seem disturbed at this announcement. He smiled at Valerie who had entered the room behind D'Arlay. "I have no words, Mademoiselle, to express the pleasure I take in seeing you," he said. "You've ridden all night, I judge, to bring a warning to Jacques Coeur. That was brave of you and I thank you with all my heart. But"—he spread out his arms in a gesture of resignation—"what is there for us to do?"

D'Arlay laid an urgent hand on his arm. "Get away at once, Jacques! We must all go. To Spain, to Italy, anywhere! We'll not get justice here."

Coeur's brows drew together in a frown. "Run away?" He shook his head. "I've been expecting this. It won't be hard to blow into thin air the shabbily trumped-up charges they may bring against me."

"It will do you no good to prove them false."

Coeur indulged in a laugh which had no trace of mirth in it. "This much good, Robin: My good name will be vindicated in the pages of history. This is not a situation, my friend, from which one may run away. It must be faced sooner or later. If I showed them my heels as you advise, it would be accepted as a confession of guilt; and Jacques Coeur would be remembered as a traitor and a thief."

The room in which they stood was large and handsomely appointed. There were tapestries on the walls and carpets on the floor. The chimney, heaped with six-foot logs ready for use, had columns and fluted pilasters of marble and panels patterned in gold overlay. The Moneyman walked to one wall which was covered by an oriental hanging. This he drew aside, revealing a high panel of overlapping steel plates confined in a thick metal frame. The purpose this served was apparent only when he ran one hand gropingly over the surface. A crack appeared at the edge of the frame and the panel began to turn inward.

Coeur said to Jean de Village, "Will you excuse me if I take my two friends inside for a talk? It will be for a few minutes only." He bowed to Valerie. "Will you be good enough to enter?"

The room into which they stepped was a small one, containing no furniture save two chairs and a plain table. There was a chimney with tiny windows on each side which admitted very little light. The Moneyman let the metal frame close after them. "No one else, not even Nicolas, has the secret of the spring," he said. "You'll see nothing here to excite you but someday it will be better worth a visit. Learned doctors and historians and scribes will strive to get their fingers on the papers I shall leave here. There will be plenty to make the search worth while then."

He ensconced his guests in the chairs and seated himself on a corner of the table. "So, our friend Robin found you and brought you away," he said to Valerie. "That's good. Before I hear how it all came about, I have this to say to you. You must both stay in France. Exile is a sad thing for a Frenchman. He knows that no other corner of earth will reward him for the effort of living. His thoughts turn backward to the sunny land he has left. He accepts exile as a last resort."

"But you——" began D'Arlay.

"Jacques Coeur is not to be measured by ordinary standards. He will be too busy with the tasks ahead of him to have time for repining or—or memories." The Moneyman nodded his head reassuringly. "The King is not in a position to bring charges against you. What have you done? No, you must stay and face it out." He paused and smiled first at one and then at the other. "You are to be wed?"

"As soon as we can find a priest."

"I knew it! It was written all over you, Robin. Although you are tired and dusty, your eyes shine with triumph, there is a hint of the conqueror in your stride." He reached out and shook D'Arlay's hand. Then he turned to Valerie and gave her cheek an affectionate pat. "I am glad, my children, and I wish you everlasting happiness."

"And now the story!" he exclaimed, after a moment. He nodded to Valerie. "You tell it. I count on your feminine sense of dramatic fitness to adorn the story properly. D'Arlay would recite it in a few precise words which would be good for nothing but a ledger."

She did his bidding, telling in full detail of the abrupt departure from the north, her translation to the little house against the palace wall, her meeting with the King (she skimmed over this part briefly), and her flight with D'Arlay. The Moneyman listened attentively and at the finish made one comment only. "I was right," he said. "I chose my candidate well. Men's preferences run in well-defined grooves."

Then he sat up straight and said, "And now I have something to tell you, my child. Your name."

Valerie straightened up in turn, all trace of drowsiness leaving her at once. She stared at him, her lips parted with eagerness.

"My name!" she repeated.

"Your father was Enguerrard Alphonse Charles Sorel. He was the favorite brother of the Lady Agnes. And so, my child, your name is Valerie Sorel."

The girl cried, "My lord Coeur!" She was so taken aback that for several moments she could say nothing more. She continued to watch him with eyes round with the excitement of this amazing announcement.

"The Lady Agnes recognized you as soon as she saw you that morning," he went on. "When I returned after taking you away, she told me her reasons for knowing that you were her brother's child, apart from the close resemblance you bore her. She had no doubts at all; as I had none when she was through."

Valerie had recovered enough of her composure to ask a question. "Did she know the circumstances of my birth?"

Coeur shook his head. "She was aware that her brother had an illegitimate child in Berri, a daughter, of whom all trace had been lost. Beyond that she knew nothing."

"Nothing of—of my mother?"

"I think not. We had little chance to talk about it, for the poor lady was drawing close to her end, as you know. She expressed one wish concerning you: that you would have a happier and fuller life than hers had been."

Valerie looked up quickly. "And that was the reason you changed your mind?"

"It was the final reason. Before that I had been aware of a great disinclination to proceed." He remained silent for a time, his head sunk in thought. When he resumed speaking, it was in a reflective mood. "Her word was always law with me. Even had I felt I must use every means in my power to hold the favor of the King, I would have bowed to her wish in this. Yes, she had only to speak and I—I did her bidding."

He walked across the floor and drew back a piece of tapestry which covered the upper part of one wall. This exposed a sculptured bas-relief, rather awkwardly executed but with fidelity to its main characters. These were three in number. The first was Coeur himself, for there was no mistaking the turban-shaped headdress, the furred cloak, and the chain at the neck. He stood before a lady who was reclining under a tree. On the head of the lady was a plain circlet and her hand was raised toward it in a gesture which suggested a doubt. Of the third figure only the head was seen, staring from the foliage of another tree. It was the King, for on his head was a crown; and on the regal countenance there was an expression of consternation.

D'Arlay walked over and studied the group with a puzzled frown. "What does it mean?" he asked finally.

Coeur laughed. "What does it mean? I provide the riddle but not the answer. When they find the way into this room, after I'm gone, they'll puzzle their wits just as you are doing now over the enigma I've left for their confounding. There's a hint in it of a certain truth—but no more."

They were interrupted by a sound of tapping on the wall which contained the secret door. A pause ensued and then Jacques Coeur said: "Nicolas, no doubt. He thinks it's time we stopped talking."

The tapping ended abruptly. "He shows less than his usual persistence," declared Coeur, with a frown. "Has something happened to stop him? I think we had better see what it's about." With his hand on the inner spring, however, he turned back and faced them. "There should be no talk yet of your parentage," he remarked to Valerie. "Let us keep the secret between us for the time being. There are certain legal aspects to be considered first."

"The situation we're in makes the secret safe," said D'Arlay. "We'll have no chance to talk, even if we wanted to."

The Moneyman had one more thing to say. "Never be afraid of life," he declared, in earnest tones. "The buffets of adversity are no more than tests of our spirit. I've never dreaded the future and I can look forward to what is ahead of me now with confidence that I shall always be the master of circumstances and never their servant. You are both young and I commend this philosophy to you."

He was speaking primarily for Valerie's benefit. She had become pale at the first sound, as though she sensed danger in it. Coeur had observed her reaction and he now touched her arm reassuringly. "If I have no fear of Gouffier and his errand, why should you?" he asked. "Come, we'll go out together and see what fate has in store for us."

The outer chamber proved to be empty but the hum of many voices came from the anteroom. The Moneyman opened the door and they were able to grasp at one glance what had happened while they were in seclusion. Gouffier and his party, who had traveled all night also, had arrived and taken possession. Jean de Village and Nicolas were standing together in a window embrasure and two men with drawn swords were stationed in front of them. Half-a-dozen other soldiers were in the room, lounging about insolently and talking in loud voices.

"Master!" cried Nicolas. He got no further with what he intended to say for one of the soldiers drove the handle of a sword into his side and growled an admonition to be silent if he desired to remain alive.

Valerie touched D'Arlay's arm. Looking down, he saw that her face was white and drawn. She began to whisper. "This is what the dream meant. There has been danger hanging over us ever since we ran away;

and now, my Robin, it has overtaken us! I pray God for the strength to face it!"

D'Arlay lowered his head to speak in her ear. "Courage, my love! Whatever this is about, it can't touch us."

She caught her breath. "But it can, it can! I'm beginning to remember——"

Gouffier appeared in the doorway and all eyes turned in his direction. It was evident that he had been changing into more suitable garb after spending a night in the saddle. He was dressed from head to foot in green velvet and there were three tall white feathers in his hat. On his feet were low leather shoes with toes which curled up in the extreme of fashion.

He lingered in the doorway as though willing to prolong the suspense into which the others had been thrown by his arrival. There was triumph in the upward curl of his lips as he watched Jacques Coeur.

"Master Furrier," he said, rolling the phrase on his tongue with obvious satisfaction, "I come on instructions from our royal master. I am to inform you, first, that you have been dismissed from the post you held in the King's service——"

Coeur broke in bitterly: "The war is won and so I'm needed no longer."

Gouffier's nose twitched and his eyes became even more hostile. "Acting on further orders from my royal master," he declared, "I place you under arrest. You will surrender at once all weapons on your person and go with me and the royal guards assigned to take you to prison."

Coeur's face turned white and his hands began to tremble. It was clear he had not expected this. "I had no hope of a reward for what I've done for France and for my liege lord," he said, in a constrained tone. "But I didn't believe ingratitude could be carried to this extreme."

Gouffier, who was something of a dandy, produced a handkerchief from a receptacle under his belt and rubbed his nose with it. It had been well soaked in perfume. "Need I tell you," he asked, "that what you say will be made known to those who are to sit in judgment on you?"

Coeur turned to face the man who had been from the first his most active and unrelenting enemy. "All you need tell me, Guillaume Gouffier, is the nature of the charge which has been brought against me."

"The charge?" Gouffier indulged in a wry smile. "You know what it is full well, Jacques Coeur. Your guilty conscience has already told you that the facts of your heinous crime have been brought to light." He paused, savoring the pleasure he took in the announcement he was now to make. "You are charged with causing the death of the Lady Agnes Sorel by administering poison to her."

There was a moment of shocked and bewildered silence in the room and then Jacques Coeur said in a voice no one would have recognized as his: "I am charged with poisoning Agnes Sorel! It can't be true! It's so unheard of, so cruelly false, so—so bitterly absurd! No one could think of it in any seriousness."

"It is true, nevertheless, Master Furrier," declared Gouffier. There was the suggestion of a satisfied chirp in his voice. "I have the papers with me, duly signed and sealed with the royal seal. The charge is brought by the Baronne de Mortagne, more frequently called the Damoiselle Jeanne de Vendôme."

D'Arlay felt Valerie's fingers tighten spasmodically around his arm and heard her whisper tensely: "That was the name! She, the Comtesse, used it! I remember everything now!"

Gouffier suddenly transferred his attention to her. "I have a warrant also for a maiden known as Valerie Maret who has been indulging in the fiction of calling herself Valerie de Voudrai." A look of satisfaction grew in his eyes as he studied her. "I need not ask if this is the girl. The resemblance is even more marked than I had been led to suspect. I place you under arrest also, Valerie Maret, as an accomplice in the execution of this infamous crime."

3

As they made their way slowly down the marble stairs between walls of aquamarine and under a coved ceiling of beautiful design, Coeur turned his head backward. Valerie was following immediately behind him, a guard on each side holding her arms with what seemed unnecessary tightness. Her eyes were lowered and she stumbled as though she had fallen into a daze. Behind her stalked D'Arlay, his face a battleground of conflicting emotions—anger, despair, fear. Still farther back was Jean de Village. They were taking no chances with the gigantic sailor. One of the soldiers walked behind him with sword pointed at the small of his back.

Guillaume Gouffier, in the lead, began to talk in a voice silky with confidence. "You may be certain, my good ex-minister and one-time colleague, that this charge against you has not been loosely sworn. I've read the depositions and I may tell you that the evidence is conclusive. It was a pretty plot but—the truth is out now."

He paused before a sculptured group on the wall in which the figure of the planner and owner of all this magnificence stood out prominently. "This I will say for you, Jacques Coeur. Everything you did was on a grand scale. The little I have seen of this house has amazed me. Do you also find something ironic in the thought that you won't live to see it completed?"

Two of the soldiers were bringing up the rear of the doleful procession. One of them whispered to the other, "A pretty little fawn, Pierre, to be caught in a mess like this."

The other winked delightedly. "What a story, this, for us to tell! We were in luck to be chosen, Imbert." His thoughts turned to the future. "What crowds there will be to see them cut off Jacques Coeur's head! Or do you think they're more likely to break him on the wheel?"

"I've seen both done often. Breaking on the wheel takes longer. How they screech sometimes! But what I don't want to miss is the finish of this girl. You know what they'll do to her, don't you?"

The second soldier shook his head. "I don't know . . . but nothing's too bad for women poisoners."

"They burn them at the stake. There will be a fortune in it for the executioner when he rents out windows around the Place de la Grève to see this one dance on the faggots!"

BOOK THREE

Chapter I

I

THE CELL to which Old Philippe escorted Jacques Coeur was high up in the tower of Lusignan. It was a room of some size, much the largest and most comfortable of the many he had inhabited. It had a straw pallet, a chair, and a prisoner's bucket in one corner. There was a window which, he hoped, would yield him a view of the Vonne. The air had in full measure the dank jail smell and on the walls were the usual feeble drawings and the desperate messages of earlier occupants.

Old Philippe lit a second candle and placed it on the stone floor beside the pallet. He straightened up and stared at his new charge with his sunken eyes.

"The great Lord Coeur!" he said in a whisper. "That I have lived to see him here, a number in my charge! It's a strange world, a cruel world!" He shook his head at the inscrutability of fate and then added in a brisker tone, "You have one candle a week and no more, my lord, so use a care of the utmost."

Coeur asked in an indifferent tone, "Isn't it permitted to buy additional candles?"

"Yes, my lord, it's permitted," said Old Philippe. "It's customary in all cases where prisoners have the means at their disposal. Does my lord wish me to purchase more candles for him?"

"I was examined by the warden's men on arriving," said Coeur. "They took all the gold I had with me. To be returned, it was explained, if I leave here."

The turnkey nodded his head. "It's the custom. But it's possible that my lord was able to—to get the better of the guards and secrete about his person some part of his money? It is always done, it is winked at, my lord. How else could our fine gentlemen pay for better wines, for pittances with the meals, a white bread of Chailly even, a marrow bone for feast days, or a purée of eels? Or to have pets, a pair of white mice, a friendly toad, even in cases a cat? My lord did not fail, I trust, to keep a store of money hidden for his use?"

Coeur had been successful in this respect. Concealed in the leather of an inner belt about his waist were a score of gold coins—what was left of the secret supply he had been carrying when he was placed under arrest. It did not suit his purpose, however, to let this be known. Instead, he gave a doleful shake of his head.

"There will be money for everything," he asserted, "but only when I can get in touch with certain friends on the outside. If you, Master Turnkey, can assist me in getting word to them, there will be gold aplenty: gold for extra candles and the pittances, and gold for you too, more perhaps than you have ever had."

Old Philippe did not take up the suggestion. He waggled his ancient head and said: "It is too bad. It is too bad, my lord."

Coeur looked at him shrewdly, convinced it was going to be possible to reach an understanding. He did not pursue the point any further at the moment but asked a question, "Will Mademoiselle Maret be brought here?"

He had adopted a casual tone but he was burning with anxiety and impatience inside. Not since the day when they were arrested at the great new house at Bourges and taken away, under separate escorts, had he seen Valerie or heard directly from her. She had not been confined in any of the prisons where he had been held but beyond that he had not been able to learn anything. For all he knew she already had been placed on trial. It was certain that she had been questioned continuously and exhaustively and brutally as he had been, day after day, night after night. Perhaps, and he shuddered whenever this supposition crossed his mind, she had been put to the torture to force her into some kind of confession. If this had been done—and he had no doubts at all that sooner or later she would be stretched on the rack—it was possible that false evidence obtained in this way was already in the possession of his enemies and would be brought against him when he went on trial.

The turnkey's face had taken on the deliberately vacant look with which this query had been greeted at the other prisons. He shook his head.

"There is no one here of that name, my lord."

"But there has been word of her coming? It must be that she will be sent here soon."

"I've no knowledge of such matters, my lord."

Coeur reached out and grasped him by the turned-down collar of his soiled jerkin. "I promise you solemnly, my ancient one," he said, "and by any saint you care to name, or by the beard of the Eastern prophet, that a generous reward shall be yours if you become the bearer of tidings of her. If you will come to me the first time you hear anything of her, you'll be treated with a generosity such as you've never known before."

Old Philippe shook the ring in his hand and watched the keys swing back and forth. "This reward of such lordly proportions must wait on the time when you have word from those on the outside?" When Coeur nodded in agreement, the turnkey shook his head doubtfully. "An uncertain prospect, my lord. One does not wax fat on promises. The matter must be given thought. It must be turned over most carefully in the mind."

Coeur said to himself after the old man had left and the grating of the key in the lock had announced the closing of the cell for the night, "He'll do as I wish, for I could read his purpose in his villainous old eye." The satisfaction he would have felt ordinarily at having thus managed the first step toward the carrying out of a plan of defense was lacking, nevertheless. If Valerie was not brought to Lusignan, what did they propose to do with her? Perhaps her fate had already been settled. It was well within the bounds of probability that she had been tried, convicted, burned at the stake. He knew how strongly the weight of her punishment could be used against him in that event. Seating himself in his chair, he thought the situation over and became almost convinced that this was what had happened, that Valerie was dead.

When he awakened next morning, a faint light was showing through the window. He sat up on his straw pallet with a feeling almost of gratitude. This was the first time since his incarceration that he had occupied a cell which the light of dawn could reach.

Old Philippe arrived an hour later. He seemed, by way of contrast with his usual mood, quite cheerful. With an air of pride he demonstrated that he had been able to supplement the prison breakfast with an omelet, a loaf of white bread, and a bottle of wine.

"Saint-Emilion, my lord," he said, pointing to the wine. "The best in the cellars."

The prisoner looked at the iron tray containing these concessions without manifesting any great degree of satisfaction. "You have decided, then," he said, "to take me on faith."

The turnkey nodded briskly and emphatically. "We have talked it over, the others and I," he answered. "All of us feel that there is little risk in waiting."

"You've decided wisely." Coeur reached down into a corner of one pocket and drew out a coin. He tossed it to the old man whose ancient claws caught it neatly. "Something the Governor's men overlooked. I found it this morning."

The turnkey pocketed the coin and winked familiarly. "It's always so," he said. "It never fails that the clumsy fingers of the Governor's men overlook a few coins in the corners of pockets. Is it not odd, my lord, that prisoners always have such convenient pockets? They have corners into which coins creep, knowing they will be safe there. It is curious also, my lord, that the owner never discovers at first that he has been lucky. It is a day, two days, three, a full week, before the money is discovered."

Each day after that Coeur asked the turnkey, "Have my friends been located in the town yet?"

"No, my lord," was the invariable response.

"Are you sure," he demanded one morning, "that those you are depending on to find them are persons of diligence? Have they sufficient intelligence for the task?"

"It is my own brother-in-law and my good gossip the blacksmith I am using, my lord. I can assure you they would do anything short of strangling their wives or selling their immortal souls to the devil for the reward you offer. Also, my lord, they are acting with a man of the very best mind, a seller of books who came here from Paris."

"It's very strange. My friends must have traced me here by this time. There will be no mistaking them, Master Turnkey. Jean de Village will be the biggest man ever to show himself in the valley of the Vonne. When he puts his foot down, the very floors quiver. As for the Sire d'Arlay, he is prone to walk or ride with head bent forward and the sword he carries is longer than those of other men. They may be going under different names, Old Philippe. Have you cautioned your dawdling bloodhounds on that score?"

The turnkey bobbed his head. "A dozen times, my lord, I have said to them, Ask no names but watch for a sailor of mighty frame like the hull of his own ship. Be at ease, my lord; if your friends come, the word of it will run through the town like the pox."

Each day also the prisoner would ask, "Has there been any report of Mademoiselle Maret?" and each day the answer would be the same, "No, my lord, we've heard nothing concerning her."

2

The chill of fall was in the air and a damp wind blew along the ramparts overlooking the Vonne. D'Arlay looked up at the towers of the prison, beneath which the town seemed to cower and hide, and said to his companion, "They've caged the lion securely this time, Jean."

Jean de Village made no reply. He had been aware for several minutes that they were being followed. An owlish wisp of a man in gray cloak and bonnet was lingering at their heels and conducting himself with an elaborate pretense of unconcern. The sea captain stopped abruptly and bawled out a command.

"Come here!"

The little man advanced timorously, keeping his eyes on the huge sailor, and ready, quite obviously, to take to his heels at the first hint of violence.

"What do you mean by following us, you scum of the taverns, you foul breeze from the backstairs!"

The man gulped nervously and said in a thin voice, "I've been trying to get my courage up to ask if your name might be Jean de Village."

The sailor scowled down at the townsman for several moments and then said, "If you had asked me that question, I might have answered, yes."

"I thought so." The man sighed with relief. He drew closer to them and began to quote in a whisper, *"A Vaillants Coeurs . . ."*

"That's enough. Now, what business have you with me?"

"I am——" A cautious pause ensued. "My name is not important, my lord. Suffice it to say that I am come from Old Philippe who holds a post——" Another pause to gesture back over his shoulder in the direction of the castle.

"What word have you for us?" demanded the sailor.

"This." The townsman dropped his voice still lower. "Go to the *stationarius* at the Sign of the Silver Missal. It is on a narrow street just off the Bail Gate. Tell the stationarius who you are."

He turned and began to slink away. Jean de Village called after him, "One minute: I have questions to ask, heart of a rabbit!"

"There's nothing more I can tell you." The little man walked cautiously along the rampart and, finding himself at a safe distance from them, increased his pace with greater confidence until he took advantage of an opening off the cobbled road to disappear from sight.

They located the Sign of the Silver Missal without any difficulty although they were surprised to find it swinging in front of a tiny booth wedged in between busy and prosperous shops, a mercer on one side, a butcher on the other. The booth had a counter and a row of shelves behind that, filled with books and manuscripts and supplies of paper and ink, and that was all.

The proprietor looked up when they stepped into the booth and his eyes took in the great bulk of Jean de Village. "Your wishes, Messires?" he asked.

"We're from the East," answered D'Arlay. "Having nothing much else to do we were drawn here by curiosity, to see what manner of books might be offered for sale so far away from the University of Paris."

"You are from the East," repeated the bookseller slowly.

"It surprises us," went on D'Arlay, "to find anything in the nature of a bookshop in a town where there is no seat of learning."

"You misjudge the West, my lord. There are rich abbeys hereabouts which are glad to add to their libraries from time to time. Also there are great seaports along the coast and men who have grown inordinately wealthy in the shipping trades. They ape culture and so they pay very good prices for books of romance and the chronicles of history. They buy from me all I can get my hands on."

"But," said D'Arlay, with a puzzled air, "how can you get books to sell?"

The bookseller hesitated. Then he raised both hands and smiled. "I might as well tell you, since I suspect it's no longer a secret. I had my booth in Paris, my lord, where, as you must know, the trade in books is controlled by the University with an iron hand. I starved on the meager profits. Most of the trade is in the lending of books to the students. Can you conceive of the difficulties? They are a careless, hell-bent lot, the students of Paris. Always they were leaving the books in taverns or getting drunk and damaging them, or handing them on to others who could not pay the fee, tiny as it was. Half my time was wasted in hunting my ill-used volumes, climbing up to evil-smelling garrets, and battling with innkeepers and pimps to get my property back.

"And when a volume was brought in," he continued, his voice acquiring heat as he dwelt on former wrongs, "which the owner or the poor *écrivain,* who had written it out, wanted to sell, was I permitted to make any profit for myself? No, Messires, I was not allowed to buy it and offer it for sale at my own price. First I must offer it to the public for a month. Always it was purchased within that time and"—his voice mounted to a still higher pitch—"I was permitted by law to retain two per cent of the price for my services in selling it! Could a man with a family of his own, a mistress, and a distaste for cheap wine, live on two per cent?"

"I concede it would be difficult," said D'Arlay.

"So, my lord, I came West. When my old friends in the trade in Paris are offered a book, they say, 'What a pity to sell it for the small price obtainable here.' They say that in the West the prices are much better and then they suggest the book be sent to me. It comes. I sell it. At double Paris prices, my lord. And"—dropping his voice to a whisper—"I allow myself twenty per cent instead of two! Half of that, naturally, goes to the stationarius in Paris who sent it to me."

The bookseller then drew a letter from under the counter. "You are the Sire d'Arlay?"

"Yes. And this is Jean de Village."

"I was sure in my mind about him. Messires, I have been expecting you for a long time. I am Pierre Dupain. I was beginning to fear I would not be of any aid to those who placed this letter in my hands." He shoved it across the counter. "I earnestly advise that you refrain from opening it until you are in your rooms and free of all watchful eyes."

D'Arlay secreted the letter inside his tunic. "We will exercise the greatest care," he promised.

"Permit me to advise also that you pass here at least once a day. If I have a message for you, I shall smile and nod you a good day. If there is none, I shall be too busy to see you as you pass."

In the double room they shared in a tavern on a dark side street D'Arlay opened the note. It was in Coeur's handwriting.

I am given better treatment here but I am completely in the dark as to what is happening. A means of communication has been set up which will enable us to write. *Be discreet* but send me word of anything you hear, particularly about Valerie. I have had no news of her since the day we were taken at Bourges.

Open Number Sixteen for instructions.

D'Arlay had sewn the notes of instruction, confided to him by Jean de Village, into the lining of his cloak. Number Sixteen contained information about the nearest supply of gold. They were to go to Father Etienne at the cathedral at Poitiers "who could be depended upon in all things." The gold in the possession of this friendly priest was to be held at his, Jacques Coeur's, disposal.

"It's ten leagues to Poitiers," said the sailor. "We can get there by nightfall if we set out at once."

3

Old Philippe wore a satisfied look and the tray he carried was loaded with fare other than that provided by the Governor of Lusignan. A well-tuned ear might have detected the faintest jingle of coins in his pocket.

"My lord," he said, depositing the tray on the floor beside the bed where Jacques Coeur was reclining, "I have news for you of the best."

Coeur looked up quickly. "It concerns Mademoiselle Maret?"

"It does indeed, my lord. She is here at last."

Coeur got to his feet and pumped the turnkey's arm up and down. "My friend!" he cried. "My ancient graybeard, my trusty one! The reward I promised shall be yours. When did she arrive?"

Old Philippe displayed some caution. "As to that, my lord, I am not fully informed. A few days back, I believe."

"And what of her health? What of her spirits? Her bearing?"

"I have not seen her, my lord. The reports I hear are that she has eaten very little since she arrived. A morsel of food, a sup of wine. Never more, my lord."

"Is she ill then? Is her lack of appetite due to the treatment she has received?"

"She is thin. Quite thin and pale."

"Has she"—Coeur forced himself to ask the question which had weighed so heavily on his mind—"has she been put to the torture?"

Old Philippe shook his head with a comforting positiveness. "I am told she hasn't, my lord. I am told her lack of appetite is due to lack of ease in her mind. She asks one question of everyone who has seen her. She asks it over and over again."

"What manner of question?"

"She seems concerned about being burned at the stake. It has been told her it is the law for women convicted of poisoning to be put to death in that way. She is right, my lord, it is customary. It seems to fill her mind. She talks of nothing else. She seems to have a great dread of the stake, my lord."

Coeur turned away. With lagging steps he walked to the window and stood there, staring out at the small square of sky which could be seen. "Yes," he said, in a repressed voice. "I'm not surprised. It's easy to understand that her mind would dwell on that. My poor child!"

When Valerie appeared in the door, Coeur's first impression was that she had become blind. She advanced slowly, giving no sign of seeing him.

She was dressed in clothes which had been supplied her in prison. The skirt dragged, the sleeves were badly soiled, there were rents in many places. Pieces of straw clung to all parts of her attire and to her hair. She was thin and there were deep shadows under her eyes. It was plain to be seen that long before she had abandoned all hope.

"How cruelly they have treated the poor child!" thought Coeur.

She remained standing just inside the door, her face turned toward the window, one hand held over her eyes to protect them from the unaccustomed light.

"Valerie!" he said.

She turned quickly at the sound of his voice. The look of wonder on her face changed at once to joy. She stumbled toward him with both arms outstretched.

"They didn't tell me I was to see you!" she cried. "I thought I was being taken to another cell. Oh, my lord Coeur, how I have longed to see you, to know how you fared!" Her eyes were becoming accustomed to the light and she peered up into his face intently. "Have they treated you well?" She paused and then burst out again: "Where is Robin, my lord? Have you any word of him?"

Coeur nodded slowly. "He's here in Lusignan. I've found a means of communicating with him."

"Will you send word to him, my lord, that I—that I love him so much he has seldom been out of my mind even—even when I've been gripped with the worst fears?"

"Yes, I'll send him your message at once."

He placed both hands on her shoulders and studied her with a troubled frown. "You mustn't let your confidence desert you," he said. "Everything is going to turn out well; be assured of that."

The girl allowed her head to droop. "I've given up all hope, my lord," she said. "At first I was certain you would find a way to save me. I waited, expecting each day the door would open and I would be told I was free. But nothing ever happened, and so I had to accustom myself to the truth, that you were a prisoner also and unable to do anything for me. I've been without hope for a very long time; how long I can't say, because I've lost all track of time. I've been in the dark so much that my only way of telling night from day is when meals are brought me."

"You mean they've been keeping you in a windowless cell!"

She nodded her head slowly. "Yes, my lord. It was hard to endure at first but now I'm reconciled to it. You can become accustomed to any hardship, even to hearing rats creeping on the floor and toads hopping in the dark." She raised her eyes and he saw that a look of fear had taken abrupt possession of them. "No, my lord, not to everything! Not to waiting, not to hearing nothing, not to the fear of death in such dreadful forms!" She lowered her eyes again. "I'm afraid that I'm a coward, my lord!"

As he listened to her, Coeur was thinking, "If it becomes necessary, I shall make a bargain with them, my life for hers. They're so anxious to proclaim my guilt to the world that they'll pardon her willingly enough to get a confession from me in exchange." This idea had been often in his mind but always before he had thrust it aside, knowing that he would sacrifice his honor as well as his life; for a confession would be an acknowledgment that he had killed Agnes Sorel, and history would so record it.

He brought forward the chair and seated her on it, turning it so that she faced the window. "Did you ever realize before how wonderful the sun is?" he asked. "Soon you will be able to leave this dark prison and go where you wish, to some place where you will bask in light and warmth."

"Soon?" There was a faint stirring of hope in the tone of her voice. "How I wish I could believe you! But—— No, I can't believe it. I know you are saying this to make me feel better."

"You must listen to me and accept every word I say. The trial is to be held here. The date has been set although I haven't yet been told what it is. It will be soon now for I have a feeling that they are coiled to strike. This much I have learned definitely. I am to go on trial alone. If I am freed of the charge—and I can't see how they can hope to convince even the most venal of judges on such an incredible accusation—then you will be set free without appearing in court. If I am convicted, you will be tried after me as an accomplice."

The girl could not repress a shudder as she heard the last words. He hastened to reassure her. "If everything else fails, my dear one, there is a way to save you—a way I am prepared to take. Ask no questions about it but allow yourself to believe this: that you will go free in the end. I swear by my belief in God and by my hope of divine forgiveness that this is the truth."

The expression on her face had changed as she listened. The despair which had possessed her when she entered was beginning to give way. "Do you mean it?" she asked in a whisper. "Can it be true?"

"Yes, my child." He was studying her with anxious eyes. "But to gain the freedom I promise you it will be necessary to help me. It's going to be hard for you. You must be prepared for"—he paused—"for the most diabolical and cruel pressure. They will try by every means to get a confession from you to be used against me."

"How can they hope for a confession from me?" Her eyes had opened wide with a conflict of emotion showing in them: surprise, incredulity, returning fear. "There's nothing I can tell them. Do they think I would invent lies to hurt you?"

"Have you been questioned?"

"Twice. The day after our arrest I was taken before Monsieur Gouffier, who questioned me for a long time. About a month later, when I was to be removed to a second prison, I was taken to him a second time. He kept me for an hour at least, asking me the same questions over and over again. Sometimes he asked them in different ways."

"Were you threatened? When you refused to say what he wanted, did Gouffier tell you they would adopt other methods?"

Valerie shook her head. "He was disappointed. I heard him say to one of the others, 'She's sly and she sticks to her story like a leech to the arm.' He looked very angry the second time, but he made no threats."

Coeur lowered his voice. "The only possibility they have of convicting us is to get a confession from one of us. They'll try to drag one from you first, I think." He leaned down toward her, his eyes fixed intently on hers. "Your ordeal will begin soon. They'll question you, hour after hour, day after day, trying to trap you, to force you into contradictions, threatening you. You'll become so weary you'll feel like telling them anything they want, anything to be free of them, and for a chance to rest. That's where the danger lies, my child. If you give in, you'll have peace —but for a few hours only. You will have signed your own death warrant as well as mine. They'll make you promises. They'll agree to let you go free if you appear as a witness against me. Put no trust in anything they say. Their promises are worth nothing. Once you've given in, they'll make what use of you they like and then they will hurry you to—to a cruel death."

"I know it," she whispered. "I've thought it over many times and I know the consequences if I am weak enough to give in to them."

The turnkey had left the door of the cell partly open and was standing in the hall. They could see him watching them and could hear the jingling of the keys as he twirled them about on one hand.

"Old Philippe won't allow us much more time," whispered Coeur. "There are so many things I wanted to tell you, but we must talk of those which count most." He dropped on one knee beside her and took her hand in his. "They're as cunning as serpents, these men who are supposed to stand for justice and the fair administration of the law. They may come to you and say I have confessed, and that your only hope of saving your life is to do the same. They may even tell you I've made statements incriminating *you*. That is the ruse they'll depend most upon—to divide us and set us against each other. Valerie! As you value your life, believe nothing they tell you about me. I have no more thought of acknowledging a crime I didn't commit than I have of denying my Maker. No matter what torture they may subject me to, I shall stand by the truth."

"Torture!" Valerie began to sob. "I can't stand pain," she said. "I've been healthy all my life and so I know little of sickness, but I can remember every injury I've had. I suffered so much from the sting of a bee that I was sure I couldn't bear it. An ache in the ear almost drove me mad." Her voice became choked with sobs and she had to stop until the flood of weeping subsided. "Kind Father in Heaven, what am I to do? I can't swear to lies; but can I withstand the pains of torture with this weak flesh of mine?"

"Come, child! You're in no danger. You mustn't yield to your imagination."

Now that her reserves of control had been exhausted, she began to talk of the most constant of her fears. "I've been told that when the executioner has a prisoner to be burned at the stake, he strangles her first. Is it true, my lord? Can I be sure of a merciful death before the flames reach me and consume me as they did the Maid?" She covered her face with her hands. "My lord Coeur, he's supposed to draw a knot around the neck and pull it so tight against the stake that one dies quickly. But is it not possible he will forget? Will he do it only if he's given a heavy bribe? How, how can the word be got to him? These thoughts run through my head all the time. Oh, merciful God, I think of nothing else! I shall go mad, my lord!"

Old Philippe put his head in at the door. "You've talked enough," he said. "I've been generous in letting you have so much time. Now, Mademoiselle, you must come with me."

Valerie buried her face in a handkerchief. In a few moments she stood up and replaced the damp linen in her belt. Her eyes were swollen and red but otherwise she had regained control of herself.

"I'm sorry I gave way," she said. "I'm not as weak as you will think me now. I—I shall try very hard to be sensible and banish these—these weak fears."

"I know you will be brave," declared Coeur.

Chapter II

I

THE STONE STAIRS in the Tour de Mélusine, where both prisoners were lodged, seemed to curl endlessly upward. As the only light came from cressets at long intervals on the dark walls, the climbing of them was like going from one abyss of blackness into another. Two doors opened off each landing, one arched and high and with a peephole of the kind now known as a judas which could be opened only from the outside, and one low and with a small grating above it which indicated that the room beyond lacked all other means of obtaining light and air.

It was before one of the small doors that Old Philippe paused the next morning. He placed a bucket of steaming water on the floor while struggling to make the key turn in the lock. When the door creaked open, he was assailed by air of a particularly unpleasant heaviness, cold, damp, fetid.

"Mademoiselle!" he called, holding the lantern above his head and peering into the inky interior of the cell. "Mademoiselle! You are to dress and come with me. There is a hurry about it."

Receiving no response, he stepped into the room, carrying the lantern still higher and looking about him apprehensively. Was she dead that she did not answer? She had seemed the same as usual when he took her supper in the night before; but he knew from experience that strange and unexpected things happen in jails and that the most unlikely of inmates find ways of killing themselves. At first the room seemed empty. Then he caught a glimpse of her head protruding from the straw mattress on the floor.

The head moved, to his great relief; and, after a struggle, Valerie succeeded in extricating herself sufficiently to sit up. If Jacques Coeur had wondered about the straw clinging to her clothing the day before, he would have had the explanation now. To keep warm she had been compelled to slit the top of the mattress and wedge her body inside it.

"See!" said the turnkey. "I have brought you water. You are to make yourself neat and then come to the Council Room. The water," he added, "was promised to someone else who will now have to go without washing."

"This is the first hot water I've had since I came."

He had also brought a towel and, miracle of miracles, a tiny slab of hard soap. The ten minutes he allowed her, while he completed his round of cells on the same floor, proved sufficient: she was washed and dressed when he returned.

The Council Room was in the building known as the Queen's apartment. It was not large but it had many handsome Gothic windows and the furnishings were on a lavish scale. There was a massive table in the center and at the head of it sat Guillaume Gouffier, wearing the red cap and the red-and-white cloak of justice. He was flanked by two officials in similar attire.

"Valerie Maret," said Gouffier, "you have been before me twice already and you have been a very bad witness, as well you know. You have been stubborn and sly and"—he shot his head forward to look more closely at her—"and everything you have told me has been false! You've told me nothing but lies, clever lies to cover up your wicked deed and that of your partner. Today we must find nothing but truth in you." He seemed impatient to start on the task of involving her in the admissions which would cost her nothing less than her life. "If you are obdurate, it will be the worse for you!"

"I want to be a good witness, my lord," said Valerie in a supplicating voice, watching him with the frightened intentness of an animal caught in a trap. "I shall tell you the truth. I've tried always to tell you the truth, my lord, all of the truth."

"You've told me nothing but lies!" Gouffier glanced down the table at the clerk who was mending the point of a quill pen. "You must take down everything she says today, Master Herault. If she tries to evade us, we must see to it that she's trapped by her own falsehoods."

At the end of two hours the door opened and the Governor entered. He smiled and bowed to Gouffier and his associates and then looked at Valerie and raised his eyebrows in what seemingly was intended as a form of greeting. Auguste de Lenvers was an elderly man with a face like a comic mask. His eyebrows had an upward slant such as is seen in oriental idols, and his nose, not to be outdone, turned up even more abruptly. He looked, as a result, a veritable prince of good nature; an effect heightened by the fact that his stomach was round and full and his legs, as much of them as showed under his handsome velvet kirtle, were fat and grotesquely bowed.

"How have things progressed, my lord Gouffier?" he asked.

Gouffier scowled sulkily. "Badly," he muttered. "We can do nothing with her, hedge brat that she is. She stands by her story."

The Governor rubbed his hands gently and regarded Valerie with a smile which fairly oozed benevolence. "I'm disappointed," he chirped. "I expected, my lord Gouffier, that you would have the truth out of her as fast as a moneylender can coax the last coin out of a debtor's pocket."

"I give up," declared Gouffier. "She's yours now, my lord Governor. Take whatever steps you think necessary."

"I think," said the Governor, "we must now consider using—other methods."

2

Valerie spent a sleepless night. The Governor's words kept repeating themselves in her brain. "Other methods," he had said; and there could be no question as to what he had meant.

Most of the time she gave to prayer, kneeling on the edge of the rough mattress, her eyes turned fervently up to the darkness above her. "O God, Thou knowest I am innocent!" she repeated again and again. "Spare me the pain of torture. Find some way, O Lord, to soften their hearts before I'm dragged to the suffering of the rack. If this cannot be, O Lord, look down on me and lend me the strength and the stoutness of will to suffer this ordeal. Let me resist them to the end so that my tongue won't be guilty of uttering lies."

She was still praying when Old Philippe brought her breakfast in the morning. He nodded his head approvingly. "That is good," he said. Then he added: "I've brought you a fine breakfast. There are eggs as well as meat, and bread hot from the oven. And, see, a fine strong wine."

"Then I am to go below?" she asked, in a tense whisper. "Is it because of what—of what I must face that you think I need a good breakfast and the strong wine?"

Long experience had calloused Philippe's mind and it was with a sense of surprise that he now realized he was feeling sorry for her. This was due, of course, to the exceptional nature of the case. The old turnkey did not think her guilty. No one on the prison staff believed that Jacques Coeur, with her connivance and perhaps help, had poisoned Agnes Sorel.

"All I know, Mademoiselle," he said, "is that you're to go below with me. The Governor will be there, but not my lord Gouffier. It will be another questioning perhaps."

"And Gilles?" cried Valerie. "Gilles the executioner will be there! He will be ready with his hot fires and pincers!"

"Gilles will be there," conceded the old man. "But, Mademoiselle, you must not draw conclusions. There are other prisoners."

Valerie refused the food but took a drink of the wine. "No, Monsieur Philippe," she said in a voice which trembled, "it won't be for another questioning. The time for that is passed. He, the cruel fat man, said they would use 'other methods.' He meant the torture! Of course he did, Monsieur Philippe!" Her voice had lifted and it was apparent from the contorted expression of her face that she was on the verge of hysteria. "What else could he mean? What else?"

"If you aren't going to eat the fine, warm food, we might as well start."

"I can't eat anything. It would choke me. But I'm thankful to you for bringing it."

The keys began to jingle on the ring, a sign that the old man was growing impatient. "We must hurry," he said.

"Spare me a moment. I—I think I am going to my death. I must show a good front, good Monsieur Philippe, if this is to be my last day on earth."

She dipped her hands in what was left of the water he had brought the day before and laved her face, with particular care to remove all traces of weeping from about her eyes. She ran a quick hand over her hair and then adjusted her dress, brushing away the pieces of straw which adhered to it.

"Do I look better?" she asked. "I mustn't be a coward. I must seem brave and—and ready for anything they may do."

The turnkey led the way down the winding stairway. Valerie followed him with feet which had to be forced by sheer will power to do their duty. The calmness she had shown on leaving the cell was deserting her. Questions raced through her mind and she had to bite her lips to keep from crying out in panic. Would they stretch her on the rack and loosen her joints so that she would never be able to walk again? Would they suspend her on the estrapade over a blazing fire? Would they cut off the tip of her tongue as a final demand that she use what was left of it to tell the lies they required of her? Such things were done all the time, she knew, and there was no reason to hope that any leniency would be shown in her case.

They turned at the foot of the stairs into a long, dark vault with arched ceiling and no windows. Burning torches in tall iron stands supplied what light there was. Valerie was afraid to look about her for fear of what she might see. She was conscious of a heavy odor of burning.

The silence was broken by the voice of Auguste de Lenvers. "Valerie Maret, you are to come with me."

She followed him, her eyes lowered. She was able to see no more than the backs of his fat calves in parti-colored hose of red and yellow which looked ridiculously out of keeping with the occasion. He was wearing shoes of an extreme fashion, with tasseled points above the heels and toes which curled up a full foot so that he had to step with great care.

She was conscious now of others in the room, of a table at which several men were seated, of their red robes, and of the easy talk going forward among them. For one startled moment she caught a view of a huge and hairy man stripped to the waist who stood so far back that she could not make out any details of his face. She dropped her eyes again at once, knowing that this must be Gilles, Gilles the chief torturer whose cruelly expert hands would administer the instruments selected to break and tear and burn her body.

"You will sit here, Valerie Maret," said the Governor, coming to a stop and pointing to a wooden bench against the wall.

The bench was so high that only the tips of her toes touched the floor when she seated herself. She looked so small that one of the men at the table remarked on it to his companions.

"She seems a mere child," he whispered. "And, what's more, she has the appearance of being as innocent as one."

"I've never believed her anything but innocent," affirmed the man on his right. He drew his head to one side and gestured with his hands. "Innocent or guilty, it's no concern of ours, Messires. We do as we are told."

The Governor had seated himself beside Valerie with such an air of benevolence that one might have thought of him as her protector. He drew a scented handkerchief from a pocket inside his tunic and touched it daintily to his nose. If Valerie had been in a frame of mind which made observation of such detail possible, she would have seen that he was most meticulous about his dress and that his graying locks had been trimmed and curled so that they barely touched his collar, which happened to be the fashionable length at the moment.

"You must stay here," he began, "until they are through with another questioning. The prisoner has been found guilty of a most serious crime, the burning of a château in which two lives were lost, and it's believed he had accomplices. We are trying to get their names." Auguste de Lenvers gave his head a shake which indicated annoyance. "He's a stubborn fellow and we're having a great deal of trouble with him. For three days his head has been confined in the branks. It's a mask of iron, Mademoiselle, which is used for scolding women, but in this one the metal gag, which goes into the mouth and so prevents any talking, was provided with sharp spikes which cut into the tongue and the roof of the mouth with every move. We were sure he would be ready to talk. But there he is"—pointing beyond the table where the board of inquisitors sat—"and so far he hasn't uttered a word."

Valerie's eyes, much against her will, turned in the direction indicated. A man, naked save for a loincloth and with his head encased in an iron mask, was strapped in a low chair. At a command from the Governor an attendant emerged from the darkness behind Gilles and proceeded to remove the mask from the prisoner's head. Valerie shuddered. The man's face was inflamed and covered with clotted blood and the lips were so swollen that they stuck out like the jaw of an ape. His eyes were closed, his breathing labored.

"Are you ready to talk, Jean Milleteste?" called the Governor.

The unfortunate man saw the figure of Gilles, standing in readiness in the shadows. He uttered a despairing cry and sprang to his feet. The chair strapped to him hampered his movements and he had gone no more than halfway to the door when two prison attendants overtook him.

"Make ready with him," said Auguste de Lenvers.

The ropes which bound the prisoner to the chair were untied and he was then forced to a reclining position on a stone bench near the table of the questioners. With violent haste his arms and legs were strapped down securely.

"It's going to be necessary with this fellow to employ an ingenious device we have recently brought from the Low Countries." The Governor made this explanation for Valerie's benefit, speaking with a smack of the lips as though he relished the prospect. "We're informed it has never failed to bring results."

One of the red-robed men at the table leaned back to call over his shoulder, "Gilles, you black ape, what is the delay?"

A thin, piping voice answered from the other end of the vault. "The trap is ready, my lords. I am bringing it."

Valerie raised her head and saw the giant form of the torturer moving toward them. He seemed to become larger and more fearsome with each step. She saw also, with eyes which refused to linger on any one object, that the shadows from which he emerged contained the dreaded and much-whispered-about instruments used to produce unbearable pain. Not knowing what they were, but fearing them even more for that reason,

Valerie's eyes passed hurriedly over the elevated frame of the rack, the innocent-appearing water dome, the coffin-like *chambre à crucer* which was a chest lined with sharp stones and spikes in which victims were kept for days and weeks at a time. A hearth at the far end was throwing a flickering light over these fantastic shapes.

Valerie saw that Gilles was carrying in his arms a round metal container more than a foot in diameter and with an open top. When he reached the bench where his victim lay, he reversed this object and placed it on the naked stomach of the recumbent man, pressing it down carefully to make sure no space was left around the edge. It could now be seen that the exposed surface had a circular indentation the size of a small frying pan.

Gilles proceeded to build a fire in the indented top of this instrument he had called a trap. Heaping it with charcoal, he achieved a small blaze which he pumped with a bellows until the fuel crackled. The man beneath began to twitch as the heat reached him through the iron. He struggled to get free of his bonds and his breathing turned to a frenzied pant.

Valerie forgot her own plight in the pity she felt for the suffering man. She watched with strained intentness, her hands clenched in her lap. "The iron is burning into his flesh!" she gasped. "Spare him this agony, my lord!"

The Governor had risen and was watching the proceedings with a fascination which manifested itself in a continual moistening of the lips and a tendency to jerk his hands about and to open and close his fingers. He turned to look down at her for the briefest moment and to say, "This is no more than the start."

Suddenly the victim gave a loud screech. It could be seen that his whole body was straining frantically to break the bonds holding him down to the bench. The scream was followed by others until they blended into a steady stream of unearthly sound. The vaulted chamber rang with the agonized clamor.

"This is what we learned from the Dutch," said the Governor, nodding down to her with excitement in his eyes. "There are rats in the trap, three of them, great fellows with strong, sharp claws. The heat has driven them crazy. Listen to them squeal! They're scratching and burrowing into his bowels in an effort to escape!"

Valerie emitted a cry as sharp as the screams of the victim and covered her face with her hands. Auguste de Lenvers turned quickly and leaned down over her while he dragged her hands away with angry haste.

"You were brought here to watch!" he exclaimed. "You must see what it's like. Come, we must have none of this!"

But her capacity for watching was over. She had fainted. With the impatient Governor still gripping both of her hands, her body slipped down on the bench and her head fell forward limply.

The screams of the victim had ceased. Gilles had removed the trap and the rats had leaped to the floor from the raw and bleeding mid-section of the bound figure. They were scampering wildly, seeking shelter and leaving red nail marks on the stones. The prisoner had given in. He was muttering now in a voice unnatural with pain. An officer at the table was taking down what he said with flying fingers.

The Governor watched two attendants carry the form of Valerie from the chamber. He seemed well satisfied.

"I shall give her two days to think it over," he said to himself. "Then she must make up her mind to tell us the things we want to hear—or be ready to have Gilles fit the trap over her own tender little girdlestead."

3

The seller of books raised his head and smiled. D'Arlay and his sailor companion shortened their strides, paused, then turned in at the booth under the Sign of the Silver Missal. There were no other customers.

"Do you realize," asked the man behind the counter, his intelligent eyes studying them both intently, "how strong the feeling in this town runs against the King and his officers in the matter of Jacques Coeur and the girl? No one believes them guilty. On the other hand, there is a general tendency to consider the Moneyman a hero. He made it possible for the King to free our country of the invaders. He finished the work the Maid began. I'm sure a similar feeling exists all over France."

D'Arlay answered in a tone of fervent agreement. "I am as sure of that as you are. How could anyone, except the court officers who will share the spoils and the King himself, who will be free of his loans, feel any other way?"

"It seems," said the custodian of the booth, in a low voice, "that the only reward for leaders, who come up from the masses to save France, is death. First there was Marcel and then the Maid and now our great and generous and farseeing Jacques Coeur." The bookseller paused and then added in a somewhat apologetic tone of voice: "You will know from this that I had other reasons for leaving Paris than my need for bigger profits. I held views which the authorities regarded with the deepest abhorrence."

"You should be careful who hears you."

"Life is a poor thing if you have to be careful in saying what you believe." The seller of books shook his head vigorously. "I thought I could see in the changes the Moneyman was making the start of better things in the world. And this will be the end of it. . . . It's the common belief in the town that you are here in Coeur's interest. You will find a readiness to help in almost any quarter where you may seek assistance."

He lifted his hand which had been lying flat on the counter. A note had been concealed under it. He pushed it across the board.

"I was told," said the seller of books, "that it's a matter of rather considerable urgency."

When the note was opened in the seclusion of their rooms, it was found to be of even greater urgency than Pierre Dupain had made them believe.

In two days [it read] V. will be subjected to the most barbarous and horrible of torture. Her spirit is stanch but she lacks the physical strength to withstand it. I pray you, I beseech you, to take the only means of saving her. Go to the King and ask him to forbid it. No one else has the authority or will to stop these beasts who hold our fate in their hands.

D'Arlay looked at his companion. "It's fortunate that the court is at Tours. How do you estimate the distance?"

"Nearly eighty miles, Robin."

"The King must be seen as early as possible tomorrow. We have two nights and one day in which to accomplish everything. This means I must ride to Tours alone. Don't shake your head, Jean, you would founder half-a-dozen horses on a ride such as this, and hold me back to boot."

4

D'Arlay betook himself to the lobby of the royal dining hall and paced up and down impatiently while the meal within progressed from one stately course to another. An hour later he was told that the King had withdrawn by a private door to his own apartments to read and write letters and that no one would be permitted to interrupt him. He began to suspect that word of his presence had reached Charles and that the King was avoiding him. Fuming inwardly, he sought out an official of the court who came from his own native Anjou and with whom he was on the best of terms. The latter informed him that the usual afternoon hunt was to be dispensed with as the King, after his period of rest and solitude, would have a consultation with a party of Spanish envoys. He would then almost certainly go for a solitary stroll in the gardens to improve his appetite for supper. It would be a case of catching him then or abandoning all hope of an audience that day.

"And there is nothing I can do in the meantime?"

"Nothing, my dear Robin. The only hope you have now is to get a hearing in the gardens. And, a word in your ear. Let none of the court officials know what you are about. They'll thwart you by some means if you do."

Late that afternoon, acting on the suggestion of his friend, D'Arlay gained entrance to the gardens by a side portal. No one was about but he thought it wise, in view of the warning he had received, to station himself in a clump of high shrubs where he could not be seen. Here he remained a long time. The shadows of evening began to fall and the conviction grew in him that he had been sent here on a wild-goose chase. He said to himself bitterly: "There's no honesty or decency in courtiers. Even my old friend Raoul has made himself part of this conspiracy to keep me from seeing the King."

He realized the next moment that he had done his friend an injustice. Wrapped in a long cloak which covered him from head to foot and with his habitual beaver hat pulled so low over his brow that it was not easy to distinguish the royal countenance, the King had entered the gardens alone and was strolling down a path which came close to the clump of shrubs. D'Arlay stepped out from his place of concealment and waited for Charles of France to draw closer.

"Sire," he said, with a low bow, "I am the Sire d'Arlay and I beseech a brief audience with you. It's a matter of life and death or I would not have intruded myself on you in this way."

The King halted some distance off. He peered at the intruder with the care acquired by all who live their days in constant danger of attack. When he had convinced himself of the identity of his petitioner, he gave an impatient grunt.

"So it's the Sire d'Arlay!" Charles of France regarded his visitor with a cold eye. "It's a long time since I have seen the Sire d'Arlay. It has seemed to me always that unpleasant things are connected with any mention of the Sire d'Arlay. He does not come to court. He does not marry, though suitable matches are suggested which have the sanction of his King. He holds beliefs which are not in accordance with his station in life and the obligations of knighthood." The King paused and seemed on the point of turning back. "You have not been a good subject, Sire d'Arlay."

"Sire, I accepted the gage of battle when Jacques de Lalain cast aspersions on the good name of the knights of France. I fought through the whole of the Normandy campaign in the most difficult service, and I performed daily the most dangerous of functions. There has never been a disloyal thought in my mind nor a seditious word on my lips. I've never asked a favor of my liege lord. I protest, sire, that I've been a good subject."

The King's eyes had been casting about, here and there and up and down, but never meeting those of D'Arlay. Suddenly he looked squarely at the latter for several moments. D'Arlay read such a degree of animosity there that he was sure his plea would be made in vain.

"There was an occasion——" began the King. Then he stopped. "Enough. This is the day of audience. I can't deny you the privilege I allow the humblest of my subjects. What is it you wish to say?"

"Tomorrow morning, unless you order it stopped, Valerie Maret will be subjected to torture at Lusignan. She will die under it, sire, or the unbearable pain inflicted on her will force her to confess a crime of which she is innocent."

There was a long pause. That the King was reluctant to discuss the case was clear, not only from his hesitation but also from the lack of ease he displayed in his manner. "It's my belief that the usual course is being followed," he said at last.

"Then, sire, justice demands that the usual course should not be followed."

Charles regarded his petitioner somberly. "It is clear, Sire d'Arlay, that you are at odds with what we have always deemed right and just, that you disapprove of torture as a means of reaching the truth."

"Yes, sire. I gave no thought to it before, accepting it in principle as something which had always been done and which must, on that account, be right and just. But now I see it close at hand, and with knowledge of the case. I realize now, sire, that it's both wrong and cruel." The arguments he had been preparing all afternoon began to roll forth. "Torture is a survival from the very darkest ages, a weapon of oppression which should no longer be used in these enlightened days. It's a system by which insensitive criminals can go free while innocent people, who lack the stamina to withstand it, must pay the penalty of guilt."

"It was talk of this kind which led the peasants to rise in the days of the Jacquerie," declared the King. He studied D'Arlay with bitter intentness. "Does your confidence in the innocence of the girl extend also to Jacques Coeur?"

"Yes, sire. Jacques Coeur is a great patriot and a faithful servant of the Crown. It's inconceivable that he could have poisoned the Lady Agnes."

"You are ill informed, Sire d'Arlay. It is conceivable to all who have studied the evidence. It is conceivable to me."

The King looked at D'Arlay and shook his head. "It comes to this," he said, "that there is a strong case against the prisoners. A prudent and fair king does not interfere with the working of his courts. I must tell you, therefore, that I have no intent to intervene on behalf of my guilty servant, Jacques Coeur, or his lowborn accomplice."

There was a determination in his voice and manner which left no doubt that his mind was made up. Realizing this, D'Arlay decided it would be necessary to use his final and, he hoped, most effective argument.

"It's easy to believe in the innocence of Valerie Maret," he said, "when one knows she was a niece—illegitimate, it is true, but a full blood relation nevertheless—of the Lady Agnes."

The King looked up at once with a startled expression. "A niece of the Lady Agnes!" he exclaimed. "Come, Sire d'Arlay, you carry your insistence too far! I was first led to believe she was a cousin of the Comtesse de Burey. Later I learned she was in reality the daughter of a common strolling player. Now you come to me with this unbelievable claim, hoping my sympathy will be stirred."

"The proofs can be obtained readily enough. But, sire, are proofs necessary to anyone who has seen her? Could such a close resemblance be explained in any other way than by blood relationship?"

The King's resolution was shaken. He frowned, he rubbed his chin, he gave D'Arlay a dozen quick and furtive glances as though to catch him off guard and glean further enlightenment in that way. Finally he said, "And if it were true—which I do not yet allow nor entertain as a possibility—what bearing could it have on the case?"

"It's difficult for me, a subject, to answer the question my liege lord has asked."

"If you have no answer, then we may consider this discussion at an end."

"I have an answer." D'Arlay spoke without hesitation or reserve although he knew that what he now proposed to say might be construed as treasonable. "After I have given it, you may say again that I am a bad subject and worthy of punishment. But, sire, innocent lives are at stake and I must not permit any considerations of prudence to control my tongue." He paused and then plunged headlong into what he had to say.

"My liege lord, you must be aware of the feeling which exists in connection with the burning of the Maid. It's no secret that people ask why no effort was made to rescue her or to procure her release. There has never been any doubt in my mind that there were good reasons for the course followed. To attempt a rescue might have led to a military disaster. But, sire, many people don't know this and I am sure the question sometimes comes into your mind as to what the annals of the future will say about it. Sire! There can be no doubt at all that history will also record the part that Jacques Coeur has played in freeing France." He looked the King squarely in the eye as he continued: "Can you allow history to link these two events? Must it be recorded that you permitted your great servant to be convicted on evidence wrung by torture from the young and innocent niece of the Lady Agnes Sorel?"

The King was too startled to make any reply at once. He looked at D'Arlay as though he found it impossible to believe that any subject of his had dared to speak with such frankness. Finally he walked to one side and remained there for some time, his eyes fixed on the dark clouds with which the sky was overcast.

"Sire d'Arlay," he said when he returned, "you have spoken to me in words that no one has ever dared use before. That I resent them, and shall never forget nor forgive you for so speaking, must be clear to you. And yet, Sire d'Arlay, I'm compelled to admire your courage and to believe that nothing but a deep conviction could have induced you to say these things. And indeed you have probed cleverly!" he exclaimed with a sudden display of feeling. "No king can fail to think of what history will record of him and to wish his authority could run beyond his death to control the written word. I am so sensitive on this point that I have even considered you may be right. As I shall exact no punishment, I lay this command on you, Sire d'Arlay, that you never tell it that you dared to address me so, and that I listened. This must be a closed issue between us."

D'Arlay bowed. "You have my solemn promise, sire."

"The purpose of Jacques Coeur was clear," went on the King. "He intended to replace the Lady Agnes with this girl and to reap such benefit as he might through her influence. And now," he said, with sudden fury, "it becomes necessary, in order to establish his guilt, to tell the whole story in court! Things which I strove continuously to keep under cover will now be made known to the whole world!" He was breathing so hard that it was some moments before he continued. "The law must take its course. If Jacques Coeur and this girl plotted between them to remove the Lady Agnes from their path, they must pay the penalty. They will have a fair trial. One thing only must be held back. In deference to the memory of that lovely and sainted lady, the claim of this ungrateful girl to blood relationship must not be stated in court. I grant you one thing: the girl will not be put to the torture. I shall issue an order at once forbidding it." He scowled when he observed the relief which showed itself on his petitioner's face. "It's a proof of my fairness that I make this concession to a meddler who has offended me bitterly. You are a bad subject, Sire d'Arlay. It will be wise, Sire d'Arlay, if you never show your face again at court."

5

Guillaume Gouffier and Auguste de Lenvers sat in the Council Room and stared at each other bitterly. Two documents bearing the royal seal lay on the table between them.

"The King's messenger arrived half an hour after the time we had planned to begin the questioning," said Gouffier. "Thus we see, my lord Governor, that if the Sire d'Arlay had not taken it on himself to bring a copy of the order, we would now have the confession we need in our possession."

"That is true. The Sire d'Arlay is solely responsible for this upset in our plans."

Guillaume Gouffier glowered down at the two documents. He lifted one in a hand which seemed to loathe the touch of it. He allowed his eye to scan the words which had compelled them, most reluctantly, to close the torture chamber. "We must never forget," he said, in a low tone, "what the Sire d'Arlay has done for us. Never, Auguste, my friend."

A silence fell between them. The Governor had been summoned so summarily from his chambers to receive the King's commands that he had not had time for breakfast. He looked now at the tray of food which had been brought for him and which lay on the table beside the unwelcome documents. Starting to eat, he found that his appetite lacked the keen edge he usually brought to the first meal of the day. As he picked gingerly at the food, he kept an eye on the morose countenance of Guillaume Gouffier.

"I protest, my good Guillaume, that you are unduly downcast," he said finally. "Unless I'm at fault in my understanding of the King's order, it lays one prohibition on us only—we must not put her to the torture."

"And is that not enough to upset everything we had planned?"

"Not necessarily." The Governor devoted several moments to disposing of a mouthful of trousoned eel which, under ordinary circumstances, was his favorite breakfast dish. "The order enjoins us not to use torture which I take to mean the subjection of her tender limbs and fresh young body to the instruments in the torture chamber."

Gouffier commented impatiently, "Are you giving me a lesson, Auguste, in the interpretation of official language?"

The Governor smiled slyly. "Not at all, Guillaume. I am leading up to a suggestion which may enable us to achieve our purpose without going contrary in any way to the royal command. There's nothing in the order to prevent us from using other forms of persuasion which might prove just as effective."

"Be more explicit, if you please, my wise Auguste."

"There is," said the Governor, beginning to attack his food with some of his habitual zest, "the matter of cells. A cell can be so uncomfortable, so wearing on all the senses, that it has the same effect as torture. It is, naturally, a slower method but—— Ah, my still wiser Guillaume, it is very, very sure!"

Gouffier proceeded to give the problem some thought. "You have a cage?" he asked finally.

"Naturally. I was on the point of mentioning that possibility."

Valerie was led to a cell on the ground floor of the Tour de Mélusine. It was large and airy and light. More than that, it was furnished in a manner bordering on the elegant. There was a bed with a canopy and pillows with white linen covers and steps at one side with embroidered panels. There was a chair, large and padded and with rests for the feet as well as the arms, a cabinet for bedroom utensils, a crucifix on the wall, a row of pots containing flowers in one window. It was, clearly, destined for the occupancy of prisoners of the very highest order.

She came in with a white face and hands which trembled visibly (for, of course, they had not told her that the will of Charles of France now stood between her and the torture chamber), but the sight of all this luxury brought her some degree of reassurance. She looked about her and said, "It's a beautiful room."

The head turnkey, who was in charge of the arrangements, shook his head at her. "Wait, Mademoiselle, until I show you what is behind that curtain."

For the first time she became aware of the significance of a heavy brown tapestry which cut off one wall of the apartment. She grew pale again and asked in a frightened voice, "What is it, good master?"

The turnkey drew the curtain back and Valerie's hand went to her lips to suppress a cry of alarm. The space behind it was taken up by a cage with wide black iron bars. It was a grim-looking thing, with a huge lock on the door and panels of metal attached at each side. One panel carried the words, "Avow All or Suffer Herein," and the other, "The Eye of the Lord Is Turned Away from Ye." The proportions of the cage were of a sinister peculiarity. It was not high enough, clearly, to allow an occupant to stand upright nor long enough to permit of lying down. It was so designed that any unhappy individual compelled to remain inside it would perforce sit with knees drawn up or lie on the floor in the trying position known as the Jackknife.

The turnkey unlocked the door of the cage and said, "Mademoiselle is to go inside."

She looked about her at the comfort of the room and then at this grim receptacle, and shook her head. "I should have known," she whispered. "There is no kindness or justice in them."

Guillaume Gouffier and the Governor entered soon thereafter and found her ensconced behind the bars with her chin resting on her knees and a look of bewilderment and horror on her face. Dusting his nose with his handkerchief, Auguste de Lenvers approached the cage and looked down at her.

"Mademoiselle," he said, "it has been decided that the limits of your obduracy are to be tested in ways other than those used in the chamber you visited the other day."

"Yes, my lord," said Valerie, beginning to tremble afresh.

"But we haven't given up our intention of getting the truth out of you. You will stay where you are without being allowed out for any reason whatever, not even for illness or bodily disability, until you are prepared to talk. Do you understand that?"

"Yes, my lord."

"I would advise an early surrender to reason. Long tenancy of the cage has invariably an adverse effect on the health."

Guillaume Gouffier had been looking about him with a satisfied air. He now volunteered a suggestion.

"I think, my good Auguste, it would be wise not to draw the curtain. We must allow Mademoiselle, while she sits there in such obvious discomfort, to enjoy a view of the soft bed, the luxurious chair, the cool water in the basin and the other utensils needed for bodily uses, which will be hers as soon as she makes up her mind to be sensible."

Chapter III

I

JACQUES COEUR had completed his breakfast when the door of his cell opened with a scraping and squealing of hinges to admit the Governor.

Auguste de Lenvers was attired in festive garb, a white cloak over a blue tunic, a tall feather in his hat. With fingers tucked in his belt he looked about him, taking in the generous light pouring through the window and the neatness of the cell.

"You live in considerable comfort," he said, in a tone which implied that such had not been intended. "Well, it won't be for long. I've come to tell you, Jacques Coeur, that your trial begins today. The court will open in half an hour. It will be your wish, no doubt, to take some pains with your attire before going down."

The prisoner looked at him with disbelief. "The trial begins today!" he cried. "Surely you don't mean what you say, my lord Governor."

"I mean what I say, as you will discover immediately."

"Are you aware, are the judges aware, that I've had no notice?"

"I am giving you notice now, Jacques Coeur."

The prisoner indulged in an angry laugh. "You deign to jest at my expense. What can I do in half an hour? I haven't yet been told the nature of the evidence on which this infamous charge is based. How, then, can I be expected to meet it and offer my defense? Are the judges aware also that I've been given no opportunity to summon witnesses on my behalf?"

"You raise two points and I shall answer them in the order you have propounded them," said the Governor. He raised a finger. "First, the Bed of Justice, before which you are to appear, decided you were not to know the nature of the evidence. If you did, you would come before them with devious reasoning on your tongue and carefully contrived testimony to offer in defense. The course of justice would be delayed." Another finger went up. "Second, it's not intended to permit the calling of witnesses for the defense. It will be clear to you, therefore, that the decision to open proceedings today is in no sense a hardship. Further waiting would have been of no service to you."

Coeur had listened with growing consternation. "My lord Governor, this is contrary to all established rules!" he cried. "Have I heard you aright, that I'm not to be allowed to call my own witnesses? How can I be expected to prove my innocence if only the perjured evidence of this woman, and those who support her, is to be heard?"

Auguste de Lenvers smiled. "You should realize by this time, Jacques Coeur, that there is no expectation that you will prove your innocence. The case against you is strong and conclusive." He glanced about the cell a second time. "Is there anything you require before going below? Did they bring you hot water this morning? I gave orders you were to be well supplied. Has your razor a good edge? I like my prisoners to be presentable when they're led in for trial."

Coeur looked him steadily in the eye. "Truly I am being highly favored," he said. "I'm forbidden to defend myself. I'll go into court as completely silenced as though my mouth had been gagged. But at least I am allowed hot water and a sharp razor. Could I ask for more?" He gave vent to a short laugh. "You are most kind. I shall strive to repay your very great kindness by not bringing any discredit on you."

2

The Bed of Justice had been set up in the main hall. It took the form of a square surrounded by a frame partition not more than ten feet high over which black hangings had been draped. One corner of the square had been left open to serve as an entrance and opposite it was a dais with five chairs and a table. Here the judges sat in all the dignity and austerity of long robes trimmed with ermine and black hoods bearing the fleur-de-lys. A raised tier of seats ran along all four sides. Here were seated the distinguished guests (as he learned later, there had been a mad scramble to obtain places), ladies as well as men, and all in a high state of expectation. A second and lower row was occupied by officers of the court and lawyers. Out in the center, where every pair of eyes could rest on it, was a low-backed chair. This was for the prisoner.

All seats, including those of the five judges, were occupied when Jacques Coeur was led in. He had recovered his composure. There was even the suggestion of a cold smile in his eyes as he walked to the chair in the center. Here he paused and glanced around the line of closely packed seats, at the fine ladies and gentlemen rustling in silks and satins in the top row, and the lawyers below with paper on their knees and pens that were already scratching busily.

"This is indeed a great honor," he said. "For months I've dwelt in solitary confinement but at least I'm to be tried in the full light of day and even with much pomp and ceremony. I perceive that we have a goodly and distinguished company. All my acknowledged enemies are here, all who have reason to anticipate benefits from my downfall, all my debtors. But my most august judges, and you also, my ladies and gentlemen, I'm compelled to note one omission. None of my friends are here."

There was a moment's silence and then someone, probably one of the less favored who stood outside the wall of the Bed and could hear but not see, began to laugh. A titter ran along the tiers of seats in which even some of the lawyers, usually the most guarded and obsequious of men, joined.

"Strange as it may seem, I have friends," went on Coeur. "I didn't expect to find them here. I think, my lords and ladies, they could be found at this moment in the streets leading to this prison where Jacques Coeur goes on trial. I'm sure they fill the square in front of the cathedral and that they are taking a more sincere interest in the outcome than those who sit within these walls. I'm sure that all over France the eyes of millions who are my friends will be turned in this direction and that in their hearts will be prayers for the man of common birth who rose to be the King's Moneyman and who played a rather unusual part in freeing the land from the hated invaders."

Guillaume Gouffier, who sat at the center of the judges' table, said sharply, "The accused will take his seat so that the proceedings may start."

Coeur squared around to face his judges. He looked at each in turn and there was no longer any suggestion of a smile in his eyes. They had become hard, combative, doubly alert.

"In the performance of my duties as a minister of the King," he said, "I have always been fully conscious of the fact that I have enemies. I've been especially aware of the enmity of three men. Permit me to name them: Guillaume Gouffier, Antoine de Chabannes, Otto de Castellane. Is it a coincidence, or is it an indication of the nature of the justice which can be expected here, that these three men are seated among my judges? But even the presence of my most active ill-wishers among the five who are to judge me is not the greatest of the many shocks I have experienced today. Am I to believe my eyes when I see that the other two judges are—

Jean Dauvet, the King's Attorney General, and Jean Barbin, King's Advocate! These two learned men will first try the case. Then, having completed their efforts to prove me guilty, they will take their seats with the three other judges—that most impartial and benevolent trio—and help to reach a verdict on their own efforts! Truly"—his voice rose until it resounded through the hall—"this is the most glaring mockery of justice! After this we may expect to see students at the universities mounting the platform to award themselves degrees and sinners deciding on their right to pass the gates of Paradise! After this we may accept it as truth that honesty has fled our courts of justice and innocent men are at the mercy of liars and cheats!"

The hall was in a tumult. From beyond the partitions, where the late arrivals stood, came the sound of much loud comment and even of scuffling, as proof that the words of the accused had aroused dispute. In the tier of seats where the favored ones sat ladies whispered behind fans and gentlemen in beaver hats expostulated over the effrontery of the prisoner. Guillaume Gouffier was pounding angrily on the table for order. "There will be no making of speeches!" he shouted repeatedly.

Coeur waited for several moments and then took advantage of a lull to continue with what he had to say.

"My words are not intended for the ears of the court," he declared. "I can't hope to win leniency from my judges nor need I fear that what I have said will deepen the enmity with which they approach their tasks. I'm hoping that a whisper of what I've said will reach those men and women who crowd the streets before my prison and fill the cathedral square and, in time, the people of France. I want my friends to know the odds I face. I want my countrymen to go on respecting Jacques Coeur and knowing him innocent, in spite of any verdict which may be rendered here. I want them to go on believing me innocent of this unthinkable and absurd and utterly revolting charge!"

He stopped speaking, glanced slowly about the room, and then sat down in the chair. Crossing one leg over the other, he raised a hand and then dropped it as a signal that the hearing should start.

3

The first witness was Agnes Sorel's maid, a small woman overcome with her grief. She was weeping when she came forward to testify and the fount had not dried up when she left. Sometimes it was no more than a gentle irrigation of the cheeks but, whenever the nature of the evidence warranted, she would puff and catch her breath and sometimes burst out into loud blubbering.

Guillaume Gouffier questioned her himself, establishing first her identity and the post she filled.

"Did you see the Lady Agnes constantly during her long illness?"

"Yes, my lord. I was always with her. I slept beside her bed—when I was able to sleep, my lord, which was seldom on account of the worrying. I took her to the *chaise percée*. I washed her in scented water twice a day——"

"I'm sure you were faithful, but——"

Nothing could stop the witness on this point. With swimming eyes she expatiated on the daily ritual of the sickroom. She was full of details about sponging and scrubbing and dosing. Gouffier gave up the effort to stem the tide and turned her over to Dauvet, the Attorney General, with a gesture of despair. The latter, skilled in the control of loquacity, brought her promptly to heel.

"You say your mistress allowed no eyes but yours to rest on her. Does that apply to her physician?"

There was a sternness in his voice which robbed her of the desire to wander.

"Yes, my lord. It was always dark in the room when he came."

"But there would be candles?"

"Not always."

Jacques Coeur heard this with satisfaction. "When I question this woman," he said to himself, "it won't be hard to make her admit how little there was to be done, that Agnes Sorel was dying and they all knew it. Later I shall get the same admissions from the physician himself." Now that the action had begun, he felt his interest quickening and even a small measure of optimism as to the outcome. He knew as much of law as though he had been a lawyer himself and he was sure it would prove easy to pick holes in the case they had built up against him.

Dauvet was proceeding with his questioning of the witness. "But you were not with your mistress the morning of February eight when she talked to Jacques Coeur?"

"No, my lord." The maid's manner and tone suggested that her absence on that occasion had been a calamity, a mistake of earth-shaking magnitude, and that all the dire things which had happened since could be traced back to it. "I didn't want her to see him. I told her she was not strong enough and that it would be better to send him away."

The Attorney began to lead the witness through a full recital of the events of the morning when Coeur had seen Agnes Sorel. Her mistress had spent a restless night and had shown symptoms of weakness during the morning. Nevertheless, she had said at once that she would see the Moneyman. The witness had assisted in moving her to her station in the darkness back of the grating and had then returned to the bedroom. She had proceeded to take advantage of the chance thus offered to introduce some light into the room (by candle and not by opening the window) and to do some necessary cleaning. She was engaged in this task when she discovered the Damoiselle de Vendôme looking at her from the doorway. "He brought a lady with him," the latter said, meaning Jacques Coeur. "A girl who looks so much like our mistress it would be hard to tell them apart." The witness had answered, "That is impossible, for our mistress is the most beautiful woman in the world and no one could look like her." The custodian of the recently born child had given her head a toss and said: "Then go and see for yourself. She's sitting in the hall, waiting for him, and looking frightened." When the witness went on with her task, Jeanne de Vendôme had said, "I'm going to see what this man is doing." She had vanished, and in a few minutes the witness had gone out to the hall to see the girl who resembled Agnes Sorel so much. The hall was empty. She had said to herself, "This Jeanne de Vendôme may be of gentle birth but she's a mischief-maker and a great flutterhead."

When Jeanne de Vendôme had come back to the kitchen in a state of great excitement and had announced that Jacques Coeur had dared to open the window of the room where her mistress lay and that she, Jeanne de Vendôme, had seen him administering some liquid to her, the witness had wanted to go at once to the assistance of her mistress. The physician had forbidden this, saying he would go and would summon her when she was needed. She had tried to tell him she was needed at once but he had said sharply: "Get her room ready for her. It's filthy and the air is vile. Set lemon sticks burning."

"How did you find your mistress when she was brought back?" asked Dauvet.

"She was conscious, my lord, but so weak I was afraid she was dying. I said, 'Oh, sweet lady, what has been done to you!' She opened her eyes but didn't seem to recognize me. I said to the physician, 'Is she dying?' and he said in an angry voice—but he wasn't angry, my lord, he's the kindest of men—'Of course she's dying.'"

"Did he take measures to revive her?"

"Yes, my lord. He burnt some feathers under her nose. She opened her eyes again and said in such a weak voice I could barely hear her, 'Am I still alive, then?' She seemed disappointed, my lord, that it should be so."

"Did you remain in the bedroom after she had been taken back?"

"Of course, my lord. Did you think I would leave my poor sick lady? I didn't leave, not for a single moment, until the next morning when Monsieur de Poitevin told me my mistress was dead."

"You hadn't realized she was dead until he discovered the fact and told you?"

The grief of the witness led to a prolonged outburst. "No, my lord," she said finally, blowing her nose on a big handkerchief. "She had been lying still for so many hours! I thought a dozen times the end had come but when I asked him he said, No, she was still breathing. And then at last he said, 'She is gone, Bénédicte.' It seemed to me he was saying the end of the world had come."

Gouffier made a motion to his fellow judges and the five heads drew together. For several minutes they conferred in whispers.

The delay in the proceedings had lessened the tension in the courtroom. People began to talk. Beyond the partition someone laughed.

The judges shifted apart and Dauvet resumed his questioning.

"Did you know what the prisoner gave to your mistress when he was alone with her?"

"No, my lord."

"Did Jeanne de Vendôme speak of it to you later?"

"No, my lord. As soon as my mistress died, the Damoiselle left and took the child with her. I didn't see her again."

"Did Monsieur de Poitevin speak of it?"

An incredulous look spread across the woman's face. "To me, my lord? Oh no, my lord. He never spoke of such matters to us. And none of us dared ask him questions. He would have flayed us if we had. But"—hastily, as though fearing she had given a wrong impression—"he was always kind to us, my lord."

"From the moment it was known that Jacques Coeur had given your mistress a drink was there doubt in the minds of anyone in the house that the Lady Agnes was dying?"

There was so much malice and unfairness in the wording of this that Coeur controlled himself with difficulty from shouting a protest. The witness seemed puzzled at the form of the question and hesitated, frowned, and then said: "No, my lord. We knew there was no hope for her."

"That's all. The witness may retire."

Jacques Coeur got to his feet. "There are questions I desire to ask the witness, my lords," he said. He looked at the maid and smiled reassuringly. She resumed her seat and waited.

Gouffier turned in his chair and stared hard at the prisoner. The expression on his face showed such a degree of malice that Coeur, who had become reconciled to anything in that quarter, was surprised and uneasy. The presiding judge said, "It's not the privilege of the accused to question the witnesses. The prisoner will resume his seat."

Coeur was unable to speak for a moment. That he was not to be allowed witnesses of his own had made it evident they were prepared to go to any lengths, but it had not entered his mind that he would be refused the right to question his accusers. He was so dumfounded that all he could do at first was to stare up at the satirically smiling countenance of his archenemy. Then he burst into a torrent of protest.

"It's always the privilege of the accused to ask questions of those who testify. How else can the truth be sifted from the evidence given? This is a right, my lords, that is accorded the lowest malefactor——"

"It's not a right accorded to you, Jacques Coeur."

"Does this mean I'm not to be allowed to make any defense?"

Gouffier's eye ran along the row of court officials seated on a bench beneath the dais. It came to rest on one who held a bundle of cloth on his knee. He made a motion and this officer rose to his feet.

"When the evidence has all been heard," said Gouffier, "the accused will be allowed time to make a statement. Until then he's to remain seated and he must be silent."

"Must I be silent while my fate is decided by judges who refuse me the ordinary rights granted without question to thieves and footpads?"

"The prisoner must be aware there are methods of compelling obedience. I hope it won't be necessary to resort to them. If, however, he persists——"

"I promise you, Guillaume Gouffier, that I have no intention of accepting this base injustice in silence."

"So be it," said Gouffier. He motioned again to the officer. "You will obey the instructions given you."

The officer walked across the court until he stood beside the prisoner. He was holding the cloth, which took the form of a hood in both hands.

"If the accused attempts to speak at any time without the permission of his judges, you will wrap that hood securely over his head. Keep a close eye on him, Usher, and nip in the bud any effort to utter as much as a single word aloud. We must have no scenes or interruptions; nor must we permit the utterance of seditious ideas in a court the King has set up for dispensing justice." Gouffier turned and spoke to the bench where a dozen lawyers sat, their hands full of documents. "Is the next witness ready?"

Chapter IV

I

JEANNE DE VENDÔME took the stand on the second day. There was a loud outburst of comment when she came into the main hall. The people who filled the space outside the frame partitions shouted and shoved and struggled furiously for a look at her and were with the greatest difficulty compelled to form a lane by which she could reach the Bed of Justice.

She had dressed herself for the occasion with an obvious desire to appear at her best but the result was not happy. Her dress was green, the shade of green which suggests poison, and there was too much of everything: too many loops of fur and embroidery; too much lace around the edges and too much of it standing up aggressively at the neck; too much padding about the hips. Her sleeves were so extravagantly long that only one hand could be seen (devoutly clutching a rosary with taut freckled knuckles) and the skirts were much too full and of such length that they swept the floor a full yard behind her with a swishing sound.

She walked with her head lowered and seemed subdued by the responsibility which rested on her. This was a pose; for, passing the chair where the accused sat, she raised her eyes for a single moment and stared straight at him.

Jacques Coeur said to himself, "She makes it very clear that she hopes to be the instrument of my ruin."

Jean Dauvet took the witness in hand. He left his seat at the table and escorted her to a chair just below it and a little to one side.

"Damoiselle de Vendôme," said Dauvet, taking up a position in front of her, "you have given us in preliminary hearings the information we needed about yourself and how you came to accept the post in the household of the Lady Agnes Sorel. In the interests of brevity, we don't propose to go over that again. The facts are duly noted down and we are content.

Today we shall begin with your story of what happened on the occasion of the prisoner's visit to the Lady Agnes."

The witness bowed with an affected gravity, keeping her eyes determinedly lowered and drawing back her sleeves so that all could see the rosary clasped in one hand.

"What time on the morning of February eight did you first see Jacques Coeur?"

"It was between nine and ten. My charge—the child, I mean"—she indulged in her habit of speaking in a laughing tone, as though there was cause for amusement in the distinction—"had not been well. I had ordered a special posset and was on my way down the stairs to watch its preparation when the door in the front of the manor was opened. Jacques Coeur entered, accompanied by a lady."

"Did you recognize the lady?"

"No, my lord. I had never seen her before. But I was impressed instantly by the resemblance she bore to my—my mistress."

"You mean the Lady Agnes Sorel?"

"Yes, my lord. It was quite astonishing. I stood on the stairs and watched. I watched the girl and not Jacques Coeur because I was fascinated by her appearance. It was"—her voice raised in another outburst of meaningless laughter—"as though the Lady Agnes, fully restored to health and a little younger, had entered through the door."

"Did they see you?"

"Not at first. They stood in the hall for several moments without doing anything because it was in darkness like the rest of the house."

"But it was not too dark for you to catch the resemblance that the woman with the accused bore to your mistress."

"The house had been shuttered for weeks, my lord. My eyes had become accustomed to the gloom. And, of course, there was one candle in the hall. The resemblance"—the tendency to laugh was becoming more pronounced with each sentence she spoke—"was so very great, my lord, that it could not be missed, even in a dark hall and with a single candle."

"Did they make any move as they stood in the darkness of the hall?"

"Not at first."

"Did they speak to each other?"

"Yes, my lord. Jacques Coeur whispered something to the girl. I couldn't hear what it was he said."

"Did the girl answer him?"

"I don't remember that she did. I think she nodded only."

"But a little later they made a move? After their own eyes became accustomed to the gloom, perhaps?"

"Yes, my lord. Jacques Coeur spoke to her and she nodded again. Then she reached under her cloak—it was a long cloak with fur, for it was very cold that day—and brought out a small bottle. She handed this to him."

Jacques Coeur forgot everything else in the indignation inspired by this fabrication to connect Valerie directly with the alleged crime. He sprang to his feet.

"It's a lie!" he cried. "I declare——"

Blackness blotted out everything. Two powerful arms were clasped about him and were forcing him back into his chair. The hood had been wrapped around his head with such violent effectiveness that he could see nothing and found it almost impossible to breathe. He struggled to get free but had no success at all for the arms of the officer seemed like the folds of a python. He tried to cry out but the thickness of the cloth muffled his voice.

He could hear the officer swearing under his breath. "So, you didn't believe it, buzzard of Bourges! . . . You had to stand up and raise your voice to the noble judges, you maker of stinking furs! . . . One more such move and Antoine will smother you black in the face!"

When his head was released from the folds of the cloak he fell back in his chair and lay there limply while his lungs battled to resume their function. When his breathing became normal again, he sat up and wiped the perspiration from his face with an arm that trembled perceptibly.

"The accused now realizes," he heard Guillaume Gouffier saying, "that when he was forbidden to speak except in answer to direct questions, it was intended that the order should be obeyed. And now the questioning may continue."

Dauvet commenced at the point where he had left off. "Did they know you were on the stairs and so had seen the transfer?"

"No, my lord."

"Can you tell us anything about the bottle?"

"It was filled with poison."

"How did you know that?"

"Because, my lord, the physicians see to it that all bottles filled with poison have a special top. There is an arrow on it, painted red."

"Everyone knows that, of course. I wanted to bring out the fact that this particular bottle bore the distinguishing mark. It had the red arrow?"

"Yes, my lord. I was startled when I saw what it was the girl had handed to him and wondered what use they were going to make of it."

"It was natural for you to be surprised. Poisons are supposed to be carried only by physicians and, with the necessary permission, by medical students. As the accused and this mysterious lady were neither of them physicians nor students of medicine, it was to be expected that possession of a bottle of poison would be a matter of considerable surprise and even—alarm."

"Yes, my lord. I was frightened. It was like watching a Mystery."

Dauvet paused and looked meaningly at his fellow judges. "And what did the accused do with this lethal instrument that his accomplice had given him?"

"He nodded to her and hid it under his belt."

"He said nothing at all?"

"Nothing, my lord. It seemed to me they both understood and that no discussion was necessary."

"It's clear, at any rate, that there was none. You say you felt fear. Do you mean that you had a sense of impending tragedy?"

Jeanne de Vendôme paused. Then she allowed her voice to drop. "I was certain they were plotting some kind of mischief."

There was about this a suggestion of preparation in advance, even of rehearsal. At any rate an effect favorable to the prosecution had been achieved. The spectators within the enclosure were sitting forward on their seats watching the young woman in green. From outside the partitions there was a sound of much scuffling of feet and of unrestrained talk.

Coeur had recovered sufficiently to follow the evidence and at this point he felt a tug of real alarm. The story being told by the witness was not only completely false but clumsily conceived; but he would not be allowed to question her after she had finished and so it would stand unchallenged. Would it be accepted as truth? Looking with an almost feverish haste about the chamber, at the tense faces of the spectators, he realized that the story had produced the desired effect.

Jean Dauvet, satisfied with the impression that had been made, resumed his questioning.

"What happened after that?"

"He looked up and saw me on the stairs."

"What did he do then?"

"Nothing. But he looked startled, my lord. At that moment one of the menservants came into the hall and said that the Lady Agnes would see him. He followed the servant out."

"And the girl remained?"

"Yes, my lord. She seated herself on a bench in the hall and waited."

"How did she act while waiting?"

"It seemed to me, my lord, that she was nervous. She was listening closely and staring in the direction he had taken. At every sound she gave a start."

"How long did you watch her?"

"A few minutes only. Then I walked back up the stairs. The child was still restless and so I went to the kitchen by the backstairs to get what was needed for her myself. There I found Bénédicte, the personal maid of the mistress, and I told her that Jacques Coeur had brought a girl with him who resembled the mistress very much."

"How long did you talk to Bénédicte?"

"Not very long. I was busy getting the posset for the child."

"While you were attending to your duties, did you wonder what Jacques Coeur was doing?"

"Indeed, yes, my lord. I thought of nothing else. I was certain he had some ill purpose in mind. When the posset was ready, I gave it to a maid and told her to feed the baby. I would have attended to this myself except that I felt I should see what he was doing. I told Bénédicte so."

"The girl Bénédicte has already given us her story which confirms what you are telling us. What did you do next?"

"I went, my lord, to the small room with the grating where the Lady Agnes saw visitors."

"And what did you find?"

There was another long pause. Jeanne de Vendôme raised her eyes and stared hard at the prisoner before replying. The almost hysterical suggestion of laughter was no longer noticeable in her voice. It had become tight with feeling.

"I found—— My lord, I could scarce believe my eyes! He, Jacques Coeur, had opened a window. The room was so light I could see everything plainly. He was bending over my mistress with one hand under her head and with the other was administering a drink to her. I thought—— My lord, conceive of the situation! I had suspected his purpose on first seeing him and what was I to think when I found him thus?"

"What construction did you put on his actions?"

"I was afraid he was making her drink the contents of the bottle the girl had given him. I cried out to him to stop."

"What happened then?"

"He looked up. He seemed startled and, I think, afraid. He allowed the head of the Lady Agnes to fall on the pillow. He said my mistress had become unconscious while they talked and that he was trying to restore her."

"Did he say what he had given her?"

"I asked him and he said it was wine and water. He put the glass down on the table then."

Jean Dauvet paused with an air of deliberation. He looked along the tiers of seats with an air which said, "I know what you are thinking and that there is a doubt in the minds of all of you—a doubt which I shall now proceed to dispel." Then he turned back abruptly to the witness.

"You have told us you suspected the accused was in the house for the purpose of poisoning someone, your mistress almost certainly, as it was to see her that he had come. Then you saw him holding a potion to her lips. Why didn't you raise the alarm at once?"

Coeur, watching every move they made and striving to catch each intonation of voice, was convinced that this again had been carefully planned in advance. The raising of a doubt by the King's lawyer would be accepted as proof of the desire of the judges for a fair inquiry and it would make the answer of the witness more telling in its effects.

Jeanne de Vendôme hesitated most convincingly. "What could I have done, my lord?" she asked. "I had, after all, no more than a suspicion to act upon. If I had cried out for help and accused him of trying to poison my mistress, and it had been found that it was only wine and water he had given her, what situation would I have been in? He was powerful, the King's Moneyman, the friend and confidant of the Lady Agnes. I was the custodian of her child, an unimportant figure in the household. There are grievous penalties when one such as I brings false charges against one such as he. I was afraid, my lord. I didn't want to be put in prison."

Dauvet nodded encouragingly. "Mademoiselle, it's not hard to understand why you acted with some degree of caution. The penalties for false accusation are, as you have said, grievous. I think you've answered the doubt which had risen in my mind and, in all probability, in the minds of the other judges."

Dauvet proceeded with his examination. "The girl, Valerie Maret, was not in the room at the time?"

The witness shook her unruly shock of hair. "No, my lord. It has been told that she was in the room a short time before and saw the Lady Agnes. But she had gone when I came in."

"We have fixed the time that she left the room, after a few moments with the Lady Agnes, at ten minutes before you appeared. In the meantime"—he paused for effect—"things had happened."

He looked about the room as though appraising the effect this was having on the spectators. Satisfied, apparently, with what he saw, he turned back to the witness.

"And now go on with your story, if you please."

"I asked Jacques Coeur if I should summon the physician and he said yes. But instead of letting me go, he kept me in the room by asking questions."

"Did the thought occur to you that he was anxious to keep you longer so that the drink he had given the Lady Agnes would have its full effect?"

"Yes, my lord."

"But you did go for the physician?"

"Yes, my lord. I went to the kitchen and told Monsieur de Poitevin he should go in at once. He was very angry when I told him Jacques Coeur was in the room and had given her something to drink. He said, 'I shall have a quarrel with Jacques Coeur. He's a dangerous fellow.' Then he left."

"Did you go with him?"

The large green bows on the hennin worn by the witness shook negatively. She answered in a voice pitched small to suggest timidity and weakness. "No, my lord, I'm ashamed to tell you that I—I fainted."

Dauvet's voice took on a sympathetic tone. "To what do you attribute the fainting spell?"

"I think it was due to what I had seen and the strain of not knowing what I should do."

Only the presence beside him of the watchful officer with the cloak prevented Jacques Coeur from interrupting again. He wanted to say: "The maid did not speak of this fainting spell. There is a discrepancy here."

If Jean Dauvet was conscious of the discrepancy, he did not deem it necessary to clear the point up. He went on to another question.

"How long was it before you recovered?"

"They told me it was ten minutes before I became conscious again." She was still speaking in a small, hurt voice. "In falling my head had struck against the pail in which water was brought from the well. I felt quite sick and dizzy. I didn't have the strength to do anything until one of the menservants came in. Then I asked him what had happened to the Lady Agnes. He said she was so weak she might die at any moment. I asked him where the physician was and he told me that he had been summoned by the King."

"Was the serious condition of the Lady Agnes known to the rest of the household?"

"Yes, my lord. Everyone expected she would not last another day. They were sure nothing could be done to save her."

"Why did they think that?"

"Monsieur de Poitevin had said so before leaving for the abbey. He told Bénédicte that there was nothing to be done but—to wait."

"Where was your mistress?"

"She had been taken back to her bedroom. She was barely conscious."

"Did you see her?"

"No, my lord. It was Bénédicte who told me. I didn't see my mistress again."

"Did you tell Bénédicte what you had seen and what you suspected?"

Jeanne de Vendôme shook her head. "I did not. I knew that Bénédicte liked my lord Coeur and that she would make trouble for me if I told her. I spoke about it to the maid who helped me with the child. She became more frightened than I and said I mustn't speak of it again. She began to cry and say that the great Moneyman would have us put in prison if we said anything against him and that we would be whipped and even put to the torture. So, my lord, I said nothing more about it then."

"But after the Lady Agnes died, you decided you must speak, did you not?"

The mass of green ribbon which made up the hennin was agitated again by a vigorous nod of the head. She answered in a voice which had become surprisingly strident. "I couldn't keep silent any longer! It preyed on my mind, my lord, and I couldn't sleep. I used to dream about it and I would waken up crying. Finally I knew I would go mad if I didn't do something."

"And what did you do?"

"I went to my lord Gouffier and told him everything. I felt relief at once, my lord, even though I didn't know what might happen to me as a result of what I had done. I could sleep once more."

"And it was after you spoke to him that my lord Coeur was placed under arrest and charged with the poisoning of your mistress?"

"Yes, my lord."

Dauvet suspended comment for several moments. The sun was high by this time and was pouring through the windows near the top of the stone walls and lighting up the glum tapestries and the heavy black furnishings. For the first time since the trial began the chamber seemed warm and even cheerful. This, combined with the excitement of the evidence, had stirred the spectators to a high pitch. A hum of talk was rising from all quarters. Heads were nodding and hands waving in violent gesticulation as the story of the woman in green was discussed.

The Attorney looked at Gouffier and the latter responded by giving the table a sharp rap with a mallet.

"Silence!" he intoned. "If this talk doesn't stop at once, it will be necessary to clear the chamber and proceed without spectators."

This threat had the desired result. Silence settled down over the crowded court. Dauvet strode across the floor until he stood close by the chair where the prisoner sat. The balance of the examination was conducted from here.

"In my opinion," he said, in a louder voice than he had yet used, "it was most fortunate that you did as your conscience bade you. Since you brought to us these facts, which you have now stated openly before this Bed of Justice, other evidence has been found which bears you out. This new evidence, which vindicates you completely, will be introduced as soon as your testimony is complete." He glanced along the tiers of spectators with a triumphant smile before bringing his eyes back to the face of the prisoner. "There is one more point I must discuss with the witness. So much depends on the answer that I beg for complete silence in the chamber."

He raised a hand in the direction of the witness. "You have told us of seeing the girl hand to the prisoner a bottle which you recognized as a container of poison. Do you know what has happened to it?"

"Yes, my lord."

"Will you tell the judges what you know?"

The witness sat up straight at this, realizing that the crucial point of her evidence had been reached. Her eyes turned to the prisoner with the same satisfaction that could be read in those of the prosecutor.

"After I had recovered from the fainting spell," she began, "I went to the room behind the grating. The shutters had been closed again and it was so dark I could see nothing. There was a strange odor in the room. I had to light a candle. And then I—I found——"

"Speak louder, if you please. It's desirable that everyone should hear."

"I found the bottle on the table beside the couch. The stopper was out and was lying on the table beside the bottle."

"Did that account for the strange odor in the room?"

"Yes, my lord. I raised it to my nose and found that the strong smell came from it."

"Did you recognize the smell?"

"I can't tell you what it was, my lord. But I recognized it as an odor I've always associated with poison."

"Did you observe anything else?"

"I saw, my lord, that it was half empty."

"What did you do with the bottle?"

"I may have done something very wrong, my lord. I took the bottle with me and, when I told my story, I gave it to my lord Gouffier."

Dauvet motioned to a court official and the latter carried a bottle over to the witness.

"Is this the same one?"

"Yes, my lord."

"You are quite sure?"

"I am positive it's the same one. I recognize it by a scratch on the side of the glass."

"Smell what is in it and tell me if it is the same as what you noticed that day."

Jeanne de Vendôme took out the stopper and raised the bottle to her nose. Then she nodded her head. "It's the same, my lord."

Jacques Coeur had been following this evidence with an incredulous air. He now said to himself, "Is there no end to these shameless lies they have invented against me?"

The end had been reached for the time being. Dauvet smiled at the witness and said: "Thank you. That's all we need to hear. You are free to leave the court."

Chapter V

I

PREGENT KENNEDY had dressed himself for the occasion with the utmost care. The tartan around his neck had been mended, his cloak had been cleaned and pressed, his riding boots shone with the polish rubbed into them. This should have given him confidence, but there was, in spite of it, an air of wariness about him when he appeared in the open corner of the Bed of Justice. He glanced about him, bowed jerkily in the general direction of the judges' table, and said in an audible voice, "Here he is, Messires, Pregent Kennedy at your service."

One of the court officers urged him forward with a compelling forefinger on his elbow. Kennedy shook him off with a muttered, "Leave be, fellow, I beg to tell you that I'm a gentleman of Scotland and a soldier of France." He strode forward slowly and came to a stop beside the chair of the prisoner.

"My lord Moneyman," he said, in a low tone, "it's my intention to tell the truth touching such matters as may be brought up but I want you to know that I'm not here of my own free will."

"The witness," said Guillaume Gouffier, staring at him angrily, "will take his proper station at once. He will speak only in answer to questions from the judges."

The Scot obeyed to the extent of taking up his position in front of the table. "My tongue," he said, "may obey the order of the court but I'm making no promises for it. It's an unruly tongue and very likely to say what it pleases."

"Unruly tongues," declared Gouffier, "are often made obedient by the simple process of cutting them out. The witness will do well to bear this in mind."

Having thus, as he thought, reduced the Scot to the state of mental trepidation in which witnesses are supposed to exist, the King's minister said brusquely to the court official accompanying Kennedy, "Take this fellow to one side." Then he leaned forward in his chair and stared about the room.

It was clear that he had something of importance to say and was consciously trying to prepare the ground for it, to raise expectations. He looked first along the row of lawyers (who seemed to become more down-at-heel in appearance and more obsequious in attitude with each session), then his eyes lifted and traveled the crowded tiers where the nobility, male and female, sat in their satins and velvets and their arrogance. Finally he gazed out through the entrance of the walled Bed at the crowded areas where the common people scuffled and clamored among themselves.

"I think," he said, turning to his brother judges for their approval, "that the time has come."

It was not necessary, apparently, for him to explain further. The heads of the other four waggled in agreement. Raising a hand, he signaled to the officer standing guard on the door leading to the tower.

A few moments later this door swung open with an abrupt clang which had something of the effect of a blast of trumpets. All heads turned abruptly in that direction and, for the moment, all other sounds ceased.

First through the door came the Governor, Auguste de Lenvers. He had attired himself in peach-colored velvet (rather faded and napless, it must be stated, and not entirely above a suspicion of grease spots) and he walked with such a consciousness of drama on his puffy and perked-up features that he would have been a comic figure under any other circumstances. After him came the head turnkey, carrying a large iron ring on which the prison keys jingled. As there was nothing in prison procedure to make his presence essential, it must be assumed that the shambling figure with the keys was included in the procession to satisfy a desire on the part of the judges for a touch of symbolism. Behind the turnkey walked a slender figure in white with guards on each side holding her by the arms. To say that she walked is not strictly correct. She had been released from the cage (and hastily bathed and clothed and given strong stimulants) not more than an hour before and her legs were still too stiff and cramped to function normally. She progressed, in fact, with short and hesitant steps and was in constant need, obviously, of the support of the two guards.

Auguste de Lenvers stepped aside after entering the legal enclosure and waved a hand to the turnkey to do likewise. In a thin voice he instructed the guards to lead their charge to the center.

The entrance of Valerie Maret produced all the effect the judges may have hoped to achieve. She was extremely thin and pale but these results of her incarceration tended to increase rather than diminish her resemblance to the deceased Agnes Sorel. Those among the nobility present who had been often in court gasped with surprise. It was not hard for them to believe that the well-loved mistress of the King had risen from the grave to appear at this inquiry into the manner of her death.

A complete silence had fallen on the courtroom. Valerie, believing that her turn had come to stand trial (which meant to her that Jacques Coeur had already been convicted), was in a state of physical collapse and experiencing a degree of fear which can only be compared to the feelings of a rabbit in a snake pit. She had not raised her eyes as she was escorted across the room, and she continued to keep them down as she stood tremblingly in front of the judges.

Gouffier said in a sharp tone to the guards, "Turn her about so that all may have a chance to see her."

In obeying this order the pair had to hold her up by force as they pivoted on their heels, for she was no longer capable of any effort at locomotion. As the turning progressed, more gasps came from people who had not been able up to that time to get a good view of her face. If the judges had expected her appearance to be a sensation in court they were being amply justified.

"That will do," said Gouffier. He turned to his fellow judges. "I contend, my lords, that an important point in the case against the prisoner has been demonstrated."

At this moment Valerie fainted. The arms of the guards, linked through hers, kept her from falling, but her head slumped forward and her body went as limp as a doll's from which the sawdust has been lost. The puzzled faces which the guards turned to the judicial bench said as plainly as words, What do we do about this?

"Carry her out," instructed Gouffier in a tone of complete indifference.

The pair, uncertain of the method they should use, elected to walk out as they were, with the result that she dangled on their arms (and this was a grim piece of symbolism which had neither been planned nor expected) like a figure hanging at the end of a rope.

"And now," said Gouffier, "the Scot will step forward."

2

If he expected to find Pregent Kennedy in a chastened mood, the presiding judge was promptly disillusioned. That hardy exile from his native land had watched the scene just finished with a degree of emotion which manifested itself in a heightened color and a nervous twitching of the fingers as though they yearned for the cool feel of his sword handle. Whether or not this had hardened his resolution to oppose the desires of the court, it became at once apparent that he was not going to be an amenable witness.

Dauvet began on his interrogation, drawing from the witness, with some difficulty, the details of his meeting with Valerie Maret and of the trip to Paris where she had fallen under the eye of Jacques Coeur. Kennedy answered each question briefly, pausing to consider his reply with the greatest care and volunteering no information beyond what was asked.

"When did you learn that the prisoner had foisted the girl on a noble family under a name which implied a distant relationship to them?"

The Scot paused to consider. "I heard she was known as Valerie de Voudrai some time after she had been taken into the household of the noble family in question. And, my lord judge, if there was any foisting done, it was with the full knowledge and connivance of the family in question."

"We will tolerate no more comments of that kind. But, as you have made this statement, you will tell us what grounds you have for it."

"My grounds?" The Scot laughed. "Pure hearsay, my lord. Put it down that I repeated gossip, rumor, idle chatter, whatever you will. But put this down also. It was hearsay which I'm convinced is true."

Dauvet looked as though he would like to apply some disciplinary measures. Thinking better of it, however, he proceeded with his interrogation.

"Did the prisoner hire you to pay a visit to the southern part of Berri in the hope of getting more definite information about the parentage of the girl?"

"That is true."

"Was it as a result of this investigation you made that she assumed the name of Valerie de Voudrai?"

"No, my lord. Jacques Coeur had learned something of her parentage from other sources. I was sent to secure what information I could to clear up the point more definitely."

"And what did you learn?"

"Very little. I found proof of what was already known, that she was not the daughter of the deceased actor. Such facts as I was able to learn seemed to point to the accuracy of the information which had come previously to my lord Coeur."

Coeur had felt the same emotions as Kennedy when Valerie was led into court but in an intensified form. Back of the pity and anger he experienced had been a sense of guilt because it was through his scheming that she now stood in peril of her life. If anyone had dared to look at him while she was in the courtroom (it is doubtful if any did) it would have been seen that dejection had gained a stronger hold on him and that he slumped down in his chair with the air, for the first time, of a beaten man.

The examination was continuing:

"Did you discover positive proof that her real father was a member of the family of De Voudrai?"

"No, my lord. But I found evidence to convince me she was of illegitimate birth and that her father could have been of that name."

The King's Attorney frowned. He also sensed that this witness, from whom so much had been expected, was not disposed to give evidence unfavorable to the prisoner.

"Did the prisoner tell you," he demanded, "his reason for his anxiety about the parentage of the girl?"

"He did not."

"You knew he was spending large sums of money to educate the girl, to see that she acquired all the graces and niceties of deportment. You knew also, I'm certain, that a veritable fortune had been expended on her wardrobe. What did this suggest to you?"

"It suggested to me that he had gone"—the witness hesitated and then concluded with a word from his native tongue—"that he had gone *daft!* In Scotland, my lord, we would not spend as much money on the wardrobe of a queen."

"You must have guessed his reason for such liberality. Or did he take you into his confidence?"

The Scot shook his head. "He said nothing to me. It's true I indulged in a guess."

"And what did you guess?"

"I guessed," said Kennedy dryly, "that he was spending his good money on the girl because he wanted her for himself."

A ripple of laughter spread through the court. Gouffier frowned angrily and pounded on the table with the gavel of authority. Dauvet consulted with his fellow judges before resuming the examination. He left his seat and descended to the floor where he took up his station directly in front of the witness.

"It has been made clear to everyone in this court," he stated, "that the girl Valerie Maret bore a close resemblance to Agnes Sorel. That was the purpose in producing her at this stage. That the resemblance transcends anything in the probabilities of nature has been shown by the effect she produced when she entered this room."

The Attorney looked about him before proceeding. "This startling resemblance is the key to everything that has happened. It is my contention that it supplies the reason for the poisoning of the unfortunate lady." He swung around abruptly on the witness. "Did you realize the truth, Monsieur Scot? Did you know it was because of this resemblance that Coeur had picked her out, that he had spent a fortune to bedeck her like a princess of the blood, and that he had her taught to act and speak like a lady?"

Kennedy waited for a moment before replying. Then he contented himself with one word.

"No."

Dauvet was nonplused, not having expected such a flat lack of co-operation. "It's said you are the shrewdest member of a very shrewd race. How could you have failed to grasp the point of the masquerade being prepared under your eyes?"

"I failed to grasp the point for two reasons."

"State them."

"First," said Kennedy, "the masquerade, as you call it, was not being prepared under my eyes. I was with the Army. I may say that I was training men to handle the cannon and so playing an important part in preparing for the victory of France. Second, I didn't know the girl resembled the King's lady."

His questioner indulged in a scornful laugh. "You failed to see what everyone in this room grasped in one amazed second of time?"

"Aye," answered the Scot calmly. "I had never seen Agnes Sorel."

A tendency to titter on the part of the ladies in court was checked by an angry tap of the mallet. Dauvet studied the witness as though in doubt of the wisdom of continuing his examination. He decided to try once more.

"We're sure you are as anxious as the court that the full truth should be arrived at. Tell the judges if you can recall any time that the prisoner, Jacques Coeur, gave you any intimation, any hint, of his purpose in educating the girl Valerie Maret."

Kennedy snorted scornfully. "Does it seem to you likely, my lord, that if he plotted the murder of the Lady Agnes Sorel he would drop any hints of his purpose before a mercenary with the reputation, as you stated yourself, of being 'the shrewdest member of a very shrewd race'?"

Dauvet threw his arms in the air. "The witness," he said to his fellow judges, "is deliberately obstructive and hostile. There is no use wasting more time on him.

"The point is established in the minds of all who have studied this case," he went on, "that the accused saw some advantage to be gained out of the resemblance Valerie Maret bore to the Lady Agnes Sorel. What was it that he planned to do? The girl had beauty, vivacity, youth. It's not our function to inquire if he proposed to establish through her an influence at court. This Bed of Justice was not set up to probe into the political aspects of the case. Whatever the motive of the accused may have been, we are sure of one thing: that he could not hope to reap any advantage until the Lady Agnes had been removed from his path. That certainty raises many startling speculations. How can we tell how many other victims might have suffered the same fate if the facts in connection with the death of Agnes Sorel had not been brought to light so soon? His boundless ambition had created a feeling among all who shared the confidence of the King that he had become a menace to the state. He knew this full well. Was it in his mind to free himself of all opposition?" The speaker paused and gestured in the direction of the witness. "It was our hope that this man who had played some part in the beginning of the conspiracy would be in a position to throw light on the motives of the accused and the scope of his plans. It seems that he's not able to do so. Or"—frowning bitterly—"he has no intention of telling us what he knows. So be it! Fortunately we have enough evidence on the factual side to prove the prisoner's guilt. That will suffice. The ends of justice will be met even if we're not able to go further and draw aside the curtain which now screens the workings of a blood-guilty mind." He turned to Kennedy and said sharply, "You may retire."

The Scot drew himself up proudly and bowed to the judges. Then he tossed the tartan of the Kennedys across his shoulder and began to retrace his steps to the entrance. He gave no further sign of recognition as he passed the prisoner but their glances crossed for a brief moment. It was as though each had said to the other, "Greetings, friend."

3

On the morning of the third day the clerk found it necessary to repeat his summons for the first witness before any attention was paid. Then a florid little man entered the enclosure. He had a neatly trimmed beard and there was something about the hang of his tunic and the set of his hat which smacked of the scholastic. Dauvet greeted him with a cordial, "Good morning, Doctor," which not only confirmed the hint of his garb but established the fact at once that there would be no difficulty with this witness.

"Your name?"

"I am Olivier de Bousse, regent at the Bons Enfans St. Honoré."

"You are of the University. You have come a long way, my good doctor, to lend your testimony in a case you must find particularly distasteful. However, no one else could serve as well and we were under compunction to bring you all the way from Paris. I desire, my worthy doctor, to extend to you the thanks of the judges who make up this Bed of Justice. And now, were you ever in attendance on the Lady Agnes Sorel?"

"Yes, my lord." The witness spoke in rich, full tones as though addressing a classroom. "I was summoned to see her, with a number of other doctors from the University, at the request of Robert de Poitevin. This was at the time when it was first realized she was with child."

"It was in Paris?"

"Yes, my lord."

"What did you think of her condition then?"

Before committing himself to a reply, the witness ran his fingers through his beard—a favorite gesture. "She was in a condition of great physical weakness. That much must be allowed. She felt ill in the extreme and she talked as though she expected to die. In spite of that, my lord, I was convinced she was not in a dangerous condition. I studied her with the utmost care before reaching the conclusion that all the symptoms were the result of—of her expectations."

"You expressed this opinion at the time? To the other physicians in attendance?"

The witness nodded his head emphatically. "Assuredly, my lord. I am always outspoken in my opinions and I voiced my optimistic view to all of them. There were five of us, including Robert de Poitevin. Our opinions were not hastily reached, my lord. We gave long and prayerful consideration to her condition, realizing how great our responsibility was. We could not allow ourselves to err through a leaning to the bright side. We considered every possibility."

"Did any of the physicians disagree with you?"

"One. Robert de Poitevin. He felt her condition was somewhat dangerous. But permit me to say"—the witness smiled with a suggestion of unctuousness—"that our good Master Robert, having attended her for many years, had a deep personal interest which inclined him to alarms. Also permit me, my lord, to voice my own opinion which is that in temperament he rides a gloomy horse. He is prone to take the least favorable view of things. . . . However, after the last of our several consultations, he was more disposed to agree with the rest of us."

"Do you still consider you were right?"

"Yes, my lord. Her death has not changed my view of the case. Nor has it changed the opinions of the other doctors from the University who were with me then."

"Unfortunately we can't summon all to give their testimony here. I feel certain that the judges will agree with me that you, as the acknowledged authority on cases of this nature, are in a position to speak for the rest. Did you have occasion to see the Lady Agnes later?"

"Yes, my lord. It was when she was in Paris on her way to the Abbey of Jumièges. I was asked to see her and did so on two occasions. She was close to her time, my lord, and all her symptoms were aggravated, both in body and mind. She was more certain than ever that she would not survive the ordeal."

"And you?"

The great man from the University smiled knowingly. "My lord, it has been my experience that all ladies as they approach the period of accouchement are prone to have the same fear. It is an almost inevitable phase at some time during the long wait. Perhaps"—he raised his shoulders and hands in a gesture of acceptance—"it's a part of the punishment of Eve. It means nothing—nothing at all. I laugh at my poor little ladies when they tell me their fears. I will allow, however, that the Lady Agnes had this tendency in a somewhat exaggerated form. My opinion is that she could not be considered in actual danger. I left her with every hope and expectation that she would regain her health after bringing her child into the world."

"Were the other physicians in attendance at the same time?"

"Yes, my lord. All of them had been summoned. Again they were in agreement with me."

"What of Robert de Poitevin?"

"Well, my lord, he would be a very poor physician indeed if he had not entertained fears for the lovely lady who had confided herself to his care. I recall that he considered her too weak to be altogether certain of surviving the ordeal."

The feelings with which Jacques Coeur listened were influenced by his knowledge of the witness. When Olivier de Bousse had come into the enclosure, he had said to himself, "That great windbag!" The doctor, in his opinion, represented the least worthy element at the University. He was pedantic and opinionated and yet at the same time servile to all forms of authority; a coddler of the great ladies who came to him for medical attention, a theorist who covered up his lack of experience and judgment with a smother of learned words. The prisoner said to himself now, "It's very clear why this toady has been brought as a witness."

The reason became clearer with each question asked. The doctor seemed determined to convince the judges (if they needed to be convinced) that Agnes Sorel would have lived if nature had been permitted to take its course.

"Did you see her after the child was born?"

"Unfortunately, no. But I received reports from various sources which kept me advised of her condition. This was done"—proudly—"on orders from the King, who desired that I should know."

"Did you still hold to your view that she would regain her strength and, in time, her full health?"

"I did. Nothing that I heard had any effect on my opinion. Permit me to say this, my lord: I have known scores of cases where ladies lapsed into a condition as weak as that of the Lady Agnes and yet recovered in due course. My lord, it happens all the time."

"And do you then believe that she died of poisoning?"

"I am certain in my mind that she was poisoned."

"Can you define that further by telling us on what your opinion is based?"

"On the brief space that elapsed after the time when the poison is said to have been given her. Consider, my lord, she had been lingering for weeks without any visible, or actual, change for the worse. Suddenly she is dead! It happened within a few hours from the time the visit of the prisoner was paid to her."

It was now Dauvet's turn to hesitate and the reason again was a desire to phrase what he had to say with special care.

"There are some who have declared that no one could be guilty of administering poison to her because it was so apparent that she was on the point of death. You don't agree with that?"

The witness responded with indignant emphasis. "I do not, my lord."

"You think she would have overcome the weakness which kept her abed if someone hadn't wanted her out of the way?"

"It's not for me to say what God might have done. Death comes at strange times and in strange ways. But without Divine intervention to claim her soul, Agnes Sorel would have lived."

The royal questioner bowed and smiled as though putting a period at the end of a well-rounded and thoroughly satisfactory passage. "And now, my good doctor, I must ask you to enlighten us on certain matters which also have an important bearing on this case. Did you know at the University of Paris a man who went by the name of Ferrand de Cordule?"

"Yes, my lord. A doctor of science and, so I have been assured, a man of ability."

"Do you subscribe to that opinion?"

"I had respect for his knowledge. I had none for the man."

"Will you explain why you had no respect for the man?"

"If it's your wish. But I shall answer with some unwillingness, my lord. It's not fitting to criticize another scholar, even one whose field is science."

"It's important to have your opinion and I must ask you to overcome your scruples."

"So be it, my lord. I had no regard for Ferrand de Cordule because he dabbled in what we sometimes call the wicked sister of science. Black magic it is more often called, my lord. Let me explain what it is. The study of science leads men of weak fiber to experiments of a forbidden nature: the making of gold, my lord, the secret of perpetual life, the concocting of charms and spells and love potions."

"And the making of poisons?"

"The making of poisons above everything else. It's my opinion that this is the worst of all the evil practices which have grown out of these experiments in forbidden paths, in the shaking of fruit from the Tree of Knowledge. By so doing science becomes the servant of crime and violence."

"And did Ferrand de Cordule turn his hand to experiments in black magic?"

"It was well known at the University that he did."

"Was he known to have had success?"

The eyes of the witness widened. "A degree of success, my lord, that baffles the understanding. It was the general belief that he had succeeded in piercing the veil which God has drawn over what He has forbidden man to know. I had this from so many sources, and with so much convincing detail, that I never questioned its truth."

"And this dealer in black magic left the University some years ago?"

"Yes, my lord. He left to enter the service of Jacques Coeur."

"In what way could he be of service to Jacques Coeur?"

"This much I may state as a fact. He sailed to the East on one of Jacques Coeur's ships and spent much time in Egypt and the lands of the Turk and even farther east, in Arabia and Persia. He brought back many of the secrets of the East."

"What manner of secrets?"

"They were of many kinds. But most particularly they were concerned with the poisons of the East."

Dauvet held up a hand to the occupants of the dais, saying, "Let me have the confession, if you please." When a document was given to him he carried it to the witness.

"Do you recognize this handwriting?"

Olivier de Bousse took the paper and studied it carefully. Then he gave it back with an affirmative nod.

"Assuredly, my lord. It's the handwriting of Ferrand de Cordule."

The word "confession" had stirred up fresh apprehensions in the mind of the prisoner. Ferrand de Cordule had nothing to confess. The work he had done had been confined to the planning of workshops and the improvement of methods of forging and smelting. His journey to the East had been for the sole purpose of studying the making of steel in Damascus, and such secrets as he had brought back with him had dealt with that distinctly practical subject. If he had signed a paper containing accusations against his master he had done so undoubtedly under extreme pressure of some kind.

"Why are you sure it's his handwriting?" Dauvet was asking.

"I saw letters from him many times and also manuscripts he had prepared. There is no mistaking it. He had what you would call an individual style, my lord."

Dauvet walked to the dais and, when he returned to his station beside the witness, he carried the bottle of poison in his hand.

"Do you know what this is?"

"It's a poison."

"Can you identify it for us?"

The doctor took the bottle and examined it closely. He removed the stopper and smelled the contents. Finally he handed it back with a confident nod.

"It's an Eastern poison, my lord. It is rare and a most powerful one."

"It's the wish of the court that you read the description on the third page of the confession of Ferrand de Cordule and then tell us if the poison described there is the same as that contained in the bottle."

Olivier de Bousse read with great care the section of the letter pointed out to him. He then took up the bottle again and looked it over with even more attention than he had shown the first time. It was several minutes before he expressed an opinion.

"Undoubtedly, my lord, the reference in the confession is to this very poison."

Dauvet's voice had a triumphant ring as he dismissed the witness with a wave of the hand. "That will be sufficient, my worthy doctor. You have been instrumental in throwing much light on the problems before us. You have the thanks of the court."

When the man from the University had withdrawn from the enclosure, Dauvet picked up the document and said, "With the permission of the other judges, I shall now read the confession which Ferrand de Cordule has made. It is of the utmost importance and I must demand that the spectators remain absolutely quiet."

The first paragraph convinced Jacques Coeur that the letter was a forgery. Ferrand de Cordule's style had always been crisp and compact and straight to the point. This was written in a rambling, and in places almost incoherent, fashion. It was not only full of obscure allusions and references of a supposedly scientific nature (a practice that had been anathema to the precise scientist) but it contained gross errors which the prisoner detected at once and which, he knew, could not have been committed by the meticulous De Cordule.

That the officers of the King had gone to the extreme of forging a document to strengthen their case was the final proof that they would stop at nothing. Jacques Coeur felt an icy sensation at the heart. For the first time he saw his position as hopeless. "I am doomed," he thought. "Someday it will be known that this so-called confession is all lies, that every scrap of evidence brought against me is false. But there will be no satisfaction in that for me. I will be moldering headless in a criminal's grave when the truth is revealed."

His depression grew as another consideration crossed his mind. "If I am to save Valerie, it will mean that I shall be compelled to affirm all these lies that have been told—and then the truth will never be known!"

While these thoughts filled the back of his mind, he had been listening to the reading. It was an astounding document. The testator alleged that he had been lured from his post at the University by the promises of "much wealth and greatness in keeping" made by Jacques Coeur. There had been an understanding between them that he, Ferrand de Cordule, would devote himself to delving into the secrets of nature and that the Moneyman would provide him with everything he needed for the purpose. The tasks to which he had set himself had included the turning of other metals into gold (no claims of success were made on that score), the evolving of better mining methods, the concocting of perfumes and, above everything else, the making of poisons "of such rare subtlety that death follows soon on its use and no one can perceive the reason therefor." There had been an urgency in Jacques Coeur's instructions in the matter of poisons and the testator confessed that he had brought back from the East a poison which gave his master the power he craved.

Dauvet held up the bottle for all to see. "Here," he declared, "is the poison that Ferrand de Cordule brought back with him from the East. This is the poison that was given to Agnes Sorel and which caused her death. Had Jacques Coeur made any use of it before he gave it to her? A question, truly, for disturbing conjecture! Would it have claimed other victims later? That is a speculation God alone can answer now."

Dauvet folded the document and replaced it on the table. He then turned and faced the eager listeners.

"It was the purpose of the Bed of Justice," he declared, "to summon Ferrand de Cordule before it and, by process of examination, supplement his statement with the details which would have made the guilt of the accused still more clear. Unfortunately this is impossible."

He paused for effect and then continued in a low voice: "Ferrand de Cordule has gone to seek the leniency he needs. Two days after this confession was signed he was waylaid by thieves while returning by night to his house in Bourges. His body was found by the side of the road the next morning. And so this remarkable but guilty man was removed from the possibility of earthly punishments for the sins he had committed against nature and against his God."

Jacques Coeur gasped audibly. Then he glanced about the room, expecting to find traces on the faces there of the incredulity and horror he felt himself. He was disappointed in this. Everyone seemed to have accepted without reserve this announcement of the death of an important witness. There was some whispering and nodding of heads but not a suggestion of protest or of unwillingness to believe the explanation given.

"My old friend was foully murdered!" he said to himself, wishing passionately that he dared stand up and proclaim his belief for all the world to hear. "He was put out of the way so they could prepare this false confession without fear of complication or contradiction. And there's nothing I can do! I must sit here in silence, knowing that my friend's death brings my own closer."

4

The judges supped that night in the dining salon of what was known as the Queen's apartment. They were in high spirits. Confident that their task had been accomplished, that Jacques Coeur's guilt had been established, their talk ran largely on the division of spoils.

It was understood that the Crown would have to be satisfied before any other hands could be dipped into the dish. Charles would get the gold, the ships, the ex-Moneyman's share in the ransoms (there was a profitable traffic in captured English noblemen), and the buildings in which the shops were located. But the prisoner's many estates were a different matter, and the eyes about the board were filled with greed and contentiousness as they discussed what would be done with them. It was assumed that each would receive at least one of the estates and they fenced bitterly over the disposition of the richest plums.

Antoine de Chabannes, who like most old soldiers had a ravenous liking for sweets, kept reaching for the well-spiced gobbets royal and saying at intervals, "Saint-Fargeau must be mine." The château of Saint-Fargeau in Puisaye had been purchased by Jacques Coeur from the Marquis de Montferrat and it was the rarest prize of all.

Gouffier was taking no part in the discussion, from which it might have been inferred that he had already arranged for his own share of the spoils and had nothing to gain by bickering with his fellow judges. He was eating little.

Gouffier rose to his feet when Auguste de Lenvers appeared in the doorway and motioned in his direction.

"He wishes to see you," whispered the Governor, when Gouffier joined him.

"Jacques Coeur?"

"Yes. I was with him a few minutes ago and I can tell you that he's in a desperate mood. He looked at me as though he was already dead and was seeing me from the—the other side."

When Gouffier faced Coeur in his cell, after closing the door in the Governor's face, he realized that the description given by the latter had an aptness to it. The ex-Moneyman was sitting on the side of his bed. He looked up for a moment only, and in that brief crossing of eyes Gouffier was convinced of his resignation to the inevitable.

"I've selected you," said the prisoner, "in preference to any of the others to listen to a suggestion I am going to make. There's a forthrightness about your villainy which makes it possible to deal with you and avoid all preambles."

Gouffier smiled and nodded his head. "I'm gratified by your good opinion."

There was a pause and then Coeur spoke in a low and hopeless tone of voice. "I'll make a bargain with our royal master."

"What offer do you wish to make our liege lord?"

"A confession. Although I'm as innocent of the death of Agnes Sorel as the mother who bore her, I'm willing to sign a paper that I poisoned her as charged. In return Valerie Maret must be cleared of the charge of complicity and released at once."

Gouffier found it hard to keep the elation he felt from showing in his face. More than anyone he knew how much the King desired a confession from the servant he was treating with such treachery. Charles had been sensitive to the public clamor against the arrest of Jacques Coeur and he knew that no one was likely to believe any verdict the five judges might bring in. But a confession! That would ease the royal conscience and justify Charles to his subjects.

Gouffier prided himself on driving a hard bargain. He looked down at the prisoner and shook his head.

"We're proving our case right up to the hilt," he declared. "We don't need a confession from you."

Coeur roused himself sufficiently from his apathetic mood to say with a suggestion of impatience, "I know as well as you know yourself, Gouffier, that the King would give much to have me clear him in this way."

"But the price you ask is too high."

"It is my price."

The judge shuffled his feet in the intensity of his thought. "Are you aware," he asked finally, "that in certain high circles there is a desire to see the girl share your punishment?"

"I've told you my terms." Coeur's voice now displayed a note of resolution. "Do you think I would put my head in the noose and besmirch my own reputation for all time for any other reason than to save this girl I have involved in my ruin?"

"I tell you that you ask too much," repeated Gouffier. "It's possible the

King would agree to dealing leniently with her but his goodness of heart would not go beyond a promise to save her life."

"Let me tell you, then, the least I will agree to. She's not to be brought to trial. She's to be publicly exonerated and released unconditionally before I put my signature to the paper in question."

"It couldn't be done that way!" cried Gouffier in emphatic dissent. "The girl could not be released until she had appeared to answer the charge. You would have our promise. Isn't that enough?" He paused and then demanded, "Don't you put any trust in our word?"

Coeur looked up and met his visitor's eye squarely for the first time. "None," he said. "I would refuse to believe any promise you made me. I would refuse to believe any promise the King made."

Gouffier frowned. "You've grossly insulted the King of France!" he cried. "You, a common furrier, have expressed a doubt of the honor of our liege lord."

"Yes," said Coeur calmly. "When you take my proposition to Charles of France, tell him that I refuse to accept his word. Tell him he must fulfill his part of the agreement before I carry out mine."

"That means we must be ready to believe your word!"

"You can do so without any hesitation or doubt. I'm not a king, Guillaume Gouffier, or a king's judge."

The visitor shrugged his shoulders. "Very well," he said. "I will take your message to the King. I may even advise him to accept." Then, abruptly, he began to laugh. "There's no one to hear me say this. Moneyman, I don't blame you. Where you are concerned, we're not to be trusted, any of us."

Chapter VI

I

IT WAS LATE in the afternoon of the third day when Guillaume Gouffier, in his capacity of presiding judge, consulted a list lying in front of him and said: "We now come to the last witness. The ushers will summon Monsieur Robert de Poitevin."

The physician came in with a quick step and a frown. He did not look in the prisoner's direction and Jacques Coeur said to himself, "The good Robert is in a mood."

Without any explanation, Gouffier elected to conduct the examination himself. He stared down at the witness with a suggestion of wariness in his eyes and said, "You were in the manor on the morning Jacques Coeur came to see the Lady Agnes?"

"I was in the manor every morning for several weeks. I remained in constant attendance until her illness terminated in death."

"We are interested only in the morning when she saw him. Did you see him yourself when he arrived?"

"No, my lord. I heard of his arrival and went at once to my lady, urging her to refuse to see him. I was certain she lacked the strength to see visitors, even as close a friend as Jacques Coeur."

Gouffier assumed a smile which he endeavored to make ingratiating. "You tell us she lacked strength. That was natural, as she had been ill for a long time and she had just passed through the—the trying ordeal of motherhood. But after hearing the evidence of the learned doctor from the University, I'm sure you're not disposed to think that her condition at the time was serious."

The frown on the physician's brow seemed to deepen. "It was so serious," he declared, "that any strain could have brought about the end."

The presiding judge scowled. "We believed from what you said at the preliminary hearing that you thought she would recover."

The physician's breath exploded in an indignant snort. "Impossible, my lord judge! I made it clear that I entertained no hopes for her at all."

"Then you failed to express yourself properly."

"Or"—with growing heat—"you failed to grasp the meaning of what I said."

Gouffier leaned forward the better to glare at this witness who dared answer him back. "I shall tolerate no more of this insolence," he declared. "It's your opinion only and of no importance whatever. We will go on, if you please. . . . You told the Lady Agnes that it would be a mistake to see him?"

"I did indeed. My opinion had no effect on her. She said it was her last chance because her end was near——"

"Master de Bousse has explained about her fears on that score," interrupted the judge.

"She decided she must see him then or not at all. She insisted he was to be sent in."

"Have you any idea why she felt it incumbent on her to see him?"

"It was most natural," declared De Poitevin. "They had been close friends for many years. She had made him an executor of her estate, to act with me and one other. It's conceivable that they had many things to talk over before she died."

The insistence of the witness on the imminence of her death brought an angry flush to the cheeks of the judge. Gouffier paused and swallowed hard before continuing with the examination.

"Let us come, then, to the episode with which we are chiefly concerned. Do you recall that some time after the prisoner was admitted to his audience, the Damoiselle de Vendôme came to you?"

"Yes, my lord judge."

"Was she in an excited state?"

"She was very angry. I didn't pay much attention to that at first because she was always in a temper over something. She quarreled with the servants, she criticized her mistress, she told me I knew nothing of medicine, she spoke sharply of the King and all his ministers. She saw no merit in anyone. A very disagreeable person, in short."

"You say you paid no attention to her at first. Does that mean you saw reasons for doing so later?"

"Yes, my lord. When she told me Jacques Coeur had walked into the room beyond the grating. This made me very angry. I could hardly believe my ears when she said he had given the Lady Agnes something to drink."

"You went to the room at once?"

"I ran there! To my surprise the room was light. Coeur had dared to open the shutters."

"A suspicious circumstance in itself."

The witness had been ready to continue with his evidence. At this remark, however, he paused. He looked up at the judge.

"A suspicious circumstance, my lord? I don't understand you."

"It's clear," said Gouffier, "that the prisoner would not have gone so contrary to the wishes of the mistress of the house if he had not felt he needed light to accomplish his purpose quickly."

"On the other hand, my lord judge, would he not have desired darkness to cloak his misdoing if he had gone into the room with criminal purpose? Would he have made the room light so that anyone who happened to come near, as the Damoiselle did, could see what he was about?"

The flush deepened on the cheeks of the presiding judge. "Are you here as an advocate for the prisoner?" he demanded in a furious tone. "I wish you to understand that you're not permitted to express opinions before this Bed of Justice. You're here to answer questions and you must limit yourself in your responses to matters of fact and personal observation."

The witness drew himself up to his not-too-considerable height. "You invited discussion of the point, my lord judge. Perhaps it's to be regretted that I couldn't agree with your opinion as to the significance of the opening of the shutters. But, at any rate, I gave you my honest view of it."

Jacques Coeur was following the evidence closely for the first time in three days. With a faint stirring of hope he said to himself: "My old friend Robert is testifying like the honest man I know him to be. They had better have a care or he'll tear such holes in their fabric of lies that all the perjury in the world won't serve to mend it!"

It was clear to him now that the judges had taken the witness for granted, to the extent, at any rate, of assuming he would not prove hostile. It was inconceivable to them that a man of humble station, dependent on the favor of those above him, could do other than support the ministers of his master, the King.

A light was beginning to grow in the eyes of the prisoner. "They're a stupid lot!" he said to himself. "They thought all they had to do was to silence me. The case has been prepared so carelessly that they have no control over their own witnesses."

Perhaps Gouffier had also reached the conclusion that greater care would have to be shown. He was beginning to phrase his questions so that the witness would have no further chances to express unwelcome opinions.

"What did you do on finding the prisoner beside the couch of the Lady Agnes?"

"I stated my disapproval most sharply."

"What explanation did he give?"

"He said she had fainted while talking to him and he had hurried to her side to give her a restorative."

"Was there any evidence that he had done so?"

"Yes, my lord. There was a cup on the table beside the couch. It was half filled."

"Did you assume that he had given her the rest?"

"I had already been told so."

"That's true. By the Damoiselle de Vendôme. What condition did you find her in?"

"She was not yet fully conscious. I saw at once that his visit had been harmful."

"Did you think her condition due to the dose he had given her?"

"I was certain it had done her no good. He had no knowledge of medicine. How could he tell what was needed?"

With each moment the prisoner was gaining a clearer insight into the situation which existed. The judges knew that the responses they would get from the witness on many points would not suit them. Nevertheless, it had been necessary to call him to testify. They were making the best of it by ignoring all the important aspects. There were a dozen questions he should be asked, vital questions. Did the witness see the bottle of poison on the table? Did he discover that the cup contained poison from the bottle? Did the Lady Agnes show symptoms of poisoning? Did he administer antidotes?

Jacques Coeur was certain that none of them would be asked.

It became apparent at once that he was right. Dauvet took up the burden and proceeded to examine the witness with minute care about the evidence he had already given. He refrained from asking anything on these important points. His questions were so cleverly phrased that the concurrence of the witness in the evidence given by others with reference to the poison could be assumed. After nearly an hour of this adroit maneuvering no one in the room, except the prisoner and the witness himself, could have believed otherwise.

Finally Dauvet looked up at his colleagues and received a nod from Guillaume Gouffier. He nodded in response and turned back to the witness.

"I have one more question to ask you, and one only. After Jacques Coeur had given the drink to Agnes Sorel and had left the manor house, were you certain she was dying?"

"It was clear she was sinking fast. But——"

"Thank you, Master Physician. That will do." A peremptory wave of the hand accompanied the verbal dismissal.

The hearing of evidence was completed.

2

Although Jacques Coeur had reconciled himself to the certainty that he would be declared guilty, it was with a sense of shock that he realized there was no longer any opportunity to combat the testimony offered against him. The small measure of renewed hope he had felt when Robert de Poitevin entered the court guttered down like a dying candle. His eyes had been fixed on the narrow window above the dais through which the last rays of the afternoon sun had made their way into the room and it seemed to him symbolic that the patch of sky turned dark as he watched. "It's all over," he said to himself. "There's no way of undoing what they have done with their lies."

Then he noticed that De Poitevin had not left his station in front of the judges' table. The expression on the face of the physician showed the amazement he felt that he had not been asked any of the questions he also knew to be vital. Gouffier said sharply, "The witness is not required any longer." The little man, with the greatest reluctance, turned to withdraw.

To the surprise of everyone Antoine de Chabannes elected to speak at this moment. An old soldier, who had grown stiff of movement and heavy in build and face with the passing of the years, he had seemed out of place among the more alert ministers of the Crown who made up the board of judges with him. He had said nothing at all. Sitting impassively beside the presiding officer, he had seemed to take little interest in the proceedings. Perhaps his mind had been occupied with visions of the fine round towers of Saint-Fargeau hidden away in the forests of Auxerrois and the rolling land he hoped someday soon to claim as his own. Perhaps also the desire to make these dreams come true influenced him. Raising himself in his chair, he said in a rumbling voice, "I desire to ask the witness a question."

The physician returned with willing briskness to his place. Guillaume Gouffier stared at his soldier colleague as though apprehensive of the nature of the question to be asked.

"It's late," said the presiding judge. "The hearing has been most thorough."

"It is a small matter, perhaps, but bear with me in this." The old soldier smiled and nodded his square shaggy head. "I've noticed a gap in the evidence. Did you," to the witness, "see the bottle of poison on the table as well as the cup?"

For the second time that day Jacques Coeur sat up straight in his chair. A glow came into his eyes that told of awakened interest, even that his mind had resumed its normal briskness. He sensed that of all the questions left unasked this had been the one the other judges feared the most. The angry flush, which came so easily to the cheeks of Guillaume Gouffier, spread up beyond the narrow line of his temples. He scowled at his inept neighbor as though he wished him many leagues away, even in a far country where the climate would be much warmer than the overheated atmosphere of the Bed of Justice.

The spectators, sensitive to the currents of feeling among the chief actors in the drama, seemed aware already that matters had taken an unexpected turn. Silence suddenly fell on the room.

"No, my lord judge," said Robert de Poitevin in a loud voice, "I did not see the bottle of poison on the table. It was *not* on the table, my lord judge."

"But," said the old soldier, his dull eyes framed in a puzzled frown, and disregarding the impatient tug that Gouffier gave his elbow, "I'm sure the girl said it was there all the time and that she returned to the room later and got it."

"She was mistaken, my lord. It was not there."

Speaking in a voice he strove to keep composed but with very little success, Guillaume Gouffier addressed the witness. "It's clear that you were so disturbed over what had happened that you overlooked the bottle."

"No, my lord. That is not clear at all. You must know that the form of container in which all poisons are kept was designed so that it could never be overlooked. It's inconceivable that a man of medicine could fail to see a bottle of poison with its arrow beside a patient in whose welfare he took the absorbed interest I felt in the Lady Agnes Sorel!"

"It must be, then," said Gouffier, "that the accused made the grave error of returning to the room later and leaving the bottle on the table then."

"No, no, my lord! That could not be! The accused left the room before I did and he had no opportunity of returning to it."

Antoine de Chabannes did not seem aware even yet of the enormity of the blunder he had committed. He blinked his eyes and said to the witness: "I can't make head or tail of this. At any rate, Master Physician, you knew it was poison in the cup?"

Gouffier waved a peremptory hand at the witness to forbid an immediate reply. Glancing sideways at the old soldier, he said: "Since you raise the point, my lord, I must declare your question one to which the witness cannot give a proper reply. There's nothing on record to show that he tested the contents of the cup. I'm sure our colleagues agree with me that there's no object in pursuing your query further."

The witness was not to be shoved aside in that manner. In a loud voice he proclaimed, "I tested the contents of the cup!"

It must have been clear to Robert de Poitevin that he was daring the wrath of the King's ministers and, presumably, of the King himself. Nevertheless, he showed no hesitation, no disinclination to go on. He stood up straight, his round stomach stuck out in front of him, his eyes full of righteous zeal.

The court was in an uproar now. The spectators were chattering excitedly, the lawyers were scraping nervous heels and whispering. From beyond the partition came loud and unrestrained talk. Gouffier brought down his gavel and declared in an angry voice, "The hearing is over and the guards will clear the court at once!"

This evoked shouts of protest from the people on the other side of the partition. Cries of "Let him speak!" "The truth is coming out at last!" and "Brava, Robert de Poitevin!" filled the air. The pikes of the guards rang unavailingly on the stone floor.

The physician took advantage of a momentary lull to cry in a high-pitched voice which everyone could hear, "I tested what was in the cup! It was wine and water!"

Gouffier had the gavel raised but at this he lowered it silently and placed it beside him on the table. He motioned to the guards and ushers to restore quiet in the court. When this had been done, he began to speak in reluctant tones.

"In view of the statements of the physician who tended the Lady Agnes in her last illness," he declared, "it will be necessary to continue the hearing. Too much has been said—or perchance not enough. Either the Damoiselle de Vendôme has given false evidence before this court or Robert de Poitevin has been guilty of negligence in the care of an illustrious patient and of the further offense of endeavoring to obstruct justice." He glared down at the witness. "We must now ascertain which it is."

Jacques Coeur had been watching the scene with a deep sense of relief and deliverance. The break had come exactly as he had known it would—if it came at all. A single one of the forbidden questions had been asked and had received an honest answer; and doubts had been raised as to the validity of the whole case against him. Each additional question now would lead inevitably to others, until the effect perhaps would be like a landslide which begins with the dislodgment of a few stones. If the more astute of the judges did not succeed in getting matters under control (and this would be hard without giving the appearance of deliberately throttling the truth), the case which had been so maliciously constructed against him would be wafted out the windows of the Bed of Justice.

The prisoner looked up at the four bitter faces on the dais and the bewildered and uncomfortable countenance of the one who had started this upheaval. He had heard whispers of the designs Antoine de Chabannes entertained on his much-prized château and it seemed especially fitting that the bungling had been his. "What is your chance now to look over the vineyards and the woods of my fair domain and call them your own?" he said to himself.

Gouffier, whose face had not lost its suggestion of white fury, rapped for silence again. This time he was obeyed instantly.

"The remarks of this witness," he said, "have qualified the case against the accused to this extent: that we must now inquire more fully into the movements of our main witnesses at the time in question." He turned to Dauvet. "I'm out of patience with the turn things have taken. I leave the examination to you."

Dauvet rose to resume the role of questioner. He seemed wary of the witness and began with the greatest circumspection.

"Why do you say the accused had no opportunity to visit the room behind the grating after you both left?"

"I sent a servant at once to clear the room. Jacques Coeur left the house before this was completed."

"You are not speaking from direct observation of what happened. The servant in question will be recalled and then we shall see"—scowling at the witness—"if what you have stated is a mere assumption."

"You will find I'm right."

"We know this to be true: that Jacques Coeur and the girl smuggled the poison in. Agnes Sorel died quickly and unexpectedly thereafter and the bottle was found later by the Damoiselle de Vendôme in the room where the victim had been. Any discrepancy in detail will be cleared up later."

There was a pause and then the witness spoke in a voice which could be heard clearly in all parts of the court: "Agnes Sorel did not die quickly and unexpectedly. She had been on the point of death for many days."

"The court has heard the evidence of the learned doctor from the University who is quite certain she would have recovered. An opinion"—Dauvet glanced about the court and paused to lend additional emphasis—"in which all his colleagues share."

Coeur found it hard to restrain himself from shouting, "Olivier de Bousse is a quack and a liar!"

"This poison," said Dauvet, "was brought from the East and, as we have learned, it acts slowly and leaves no trace. You have"—with an ironic rise of voice—"no fault to find with that statement?"

"I have. I challenge the statement, my lord."

"Are you going to set yourself up against the combined wisdom of the practitioners of medicine at the University?"

De Poitevin did not give a direct answer. "I'm an authority on poisons, my lord judge," he said. "I've given a good part of my life to them. I've read of such magic potions but I've never seen them. Nor has any man of medicine of my acquaintance. In my opinion they are a myth like—like the fire-spitting dragon and the furnace which changes other metals into gold."

"Are you denying that De Cordule brought this poison back from the Orient? A poison which leaves no trace after death?"

The witness shook his head. "I doubt it but I'm in no position to deny it." Suddenly his voice gained in volume until it had an oratorical ring to it. "But I am denying, my lord judge, that this bottle contains such a poison!"

Dauvet was so completely taken aback that for several moments he said nothing. Then he asked, "Did you hear Olivier de Bousse identify it as the one described in the confession?"

"Olivier de Bousse knows nothing of poisons. If you'll bring him back and allow me to question him, I'll convince you of that in a very few minutes." Before he could be stopped, the witness reached up to the table and took the bottle in his hands. He gave it a vigorous shake. "Smell it, my lord judge. Is the odor a familiar one?"

Dauvet put the bottle to his nose briefly and then returned it to its place. "I fail to recognize it," he said.

"What did the odor remind you of?"

"I think it gave a suggestion of bitter almonds."

"Exactly!" cried the witness triumphantly. He sniffed loudly and then looked about him. "Everyone within a radius of ten feet," he declared, "must have recognized the odor given off. Twenty—nay, thirty, witnesses to it, my lord judge! . . . And now let me tell you what this poison is. It's not a rare poison from the East. It isn't even one of the rare varieties we use here, such as briony or turpeth or sea-hare or leopard's gall. It's one you hear of constantly because it's used a great deal." He turned to face the spectators on the seats nearest him. "I'm sure some of you who recognized the odor can tell the court what it is."

Gouffier's gavel hovered in the air but before it could descend a chorus of voices called, "Laurel!"

Robert de Poitevin cried, "You are right, it is laurel!" Then he swung back to Dauvet. "Yes, it's laurel, my lord judge. As many of you will know, it's made from the leaves of the laurel bush and it's potent enough to cause death quickly."

Jacques Coeur's heart was racing with new hope. He was thinking,

"They were so confident they became careless. They didn't see to it that the poison put in the bottle was one from the East. They filled it with the first they laid hands on!"

Dauvet glowered. "The contents of the bottle will be examined again. You are very positive, Master Pill Maker. But let me tell you this: the point is of small moment. Olivier de Bousse says it came from the East. You say it didn't. It does not matter which of you is right. The poison in that bottle was given to Agnes Sorel and brought about her death. *That* is the point which counts."

"It was sixteen hours after Jacques Coeur left her that Agnes Sorel died," said the witness. "Laurel kills quickly. This is fortunate, for the victim suffers great agony. But it loses its power to kill after a certain time has elapsed. If it so happens that the victim survives an hour, he is almost certain to live. A longer period than an hour is a guarantee of survival. The fact that the Lady Agnes lived for sixteen hours is the most conclusive proof that her death was not due to a dose from this bottle."

The silence in the room was more dramatic than any tumult could have been. For the first time since the hearings began, not a single pair of eyes rested on the prisoner. The attention had been transferred to the pudgy figure of the physician.

"After Agnes Sorel died," the witness went on, in a reverent tone of voice, "we took out her heart to be embalmed. Three other physicians were present, all men of recognized worth. Call them and they will confirm what I am going to tell you. The blood of those who die from laurel poisoning is dark, their skin is livid. We found nothing of the kind. . . . My lords, when laurel kills, the face of the victim carries an indelible mark of the throes of death. The Lady Agnes Sorel died slowly and in peace. She drew her last breath with a smile on her lovely face, a smile as sweet and gentle as she herself had always been in life. The smile remained there after death. . . . My lords, she was not poisoned!"

The stillness which followed this speech was broken by a sound as though all the spectators had sighed in unison. It was a sigh of complete conviction, perhaps also of relief.

From the start of the proceedings Jacques Coeur had carried in his pocket an important letter. It was one of several which had not been taken from him at any of the prisons where he had been incarcerated because they dealt with business detail and had been deemed of no importance. This particular missive was one of the few weapons he possessed for his defense.

He looked cautiously at the upright figure of the usher standing as usual beside his chair. The man's mouth had fallen open and he was so absorbed in what he saw and heard that, clearly, everything else had been forgotten. The prisoner leaned out quickly and gave the motionless figure a vigorous shove. The usher gave a grunt of surprise and went over in a heap on the floor.

Coeur sprang to his feet and waved the letter in the direction of the judges' table. "Here," he cried, "is the final proof. A letter from Ferrand de Cordule. I can produce a dozen more like it. Compare the handwriting in this letter with that in the confession he's alleged to have written and you'll find that document nothing but a clumsy forgery. It's a pack of lies and absurdities!"

Coeur resumed his seat as the usher picked himself up from the floor. The spectators had listened to what he said with every evidence of excited interest, but the judges had paid him no attention at all. Four of them, all very solemn of face, had their heads close together in serious discussion. Antoine de Chabannes was taking no part in the talk. He sat apart and looked dismal and thoroughly penitent.

Suddenly Jacques Coeur began to laugh. It was a high-pitched burst of mirth to which he gave vent and it drowned out all other sounds in the court. He laughed so long and with such heartiness that his body shook. The usher made no move to stop him.

"Guillaume Gouffier!" Coeur called. "A certain agreement reached between us may now be regarded as null and void."

It was significant of the turn things had taken that the usher still made no move to control him.

One of the guards approached the prisoner and said in a tone of voice which carried a new note of respect, "You are to return to your cell, my lord Coeur."

3

Old Philippe had said that morning, as he took in Valerie's breakfast, "It will end today." He had then looked about the cell and added in a pessimistic voice, "Enjoy this comfort while you may, Mademoiselle."

Valerie spent the day in such a ferment of spirit that she could not remain still. She went at frequent intervals to prostrate herself before the crucifix and to pray fervently that the Lord would cause truth to prevail in the solemn room below where her fate as well as that of the Moneyman was being decided. She left her food untouched.

She had little real hope of the outcome. The reports Old Philippe had given her of the progress of the case had always been filled with gloom.

The evening before he had said with many glum shakes of the head: "There's the confession, Mademoiselle. The Moneyman won't be able to answer *that!*" Her prayers, therefore, had a desperate note, as though she feared that nothing short of direct intervention from above would be of any avail.

When the light coming through the window began to fail, she knew that the hearing would soon be over if it had not ended already. From that moment on she kept listening for approaching footsteps. She was sure she would be able to tell what the verdict had been by the sound they made.

An hour passed, and then another. Valerie gave up listening. Her worst fears had been confirmed. The prison attendants had come to have a certain gruff affection for her. If the decision of the court had been in Jacques Coeur's favor, they would have come quickly to give her the glad tidings. They delayed their coming because the news was bad and they disliked the necessity of telling her.

The cell was in darkness when she finally heard footsteps approaching along the stone corridor. It was Old Philippe, for there was no mistaking the rheumatic hitch of his stride. He was walking slowly.

"My lord Coeur has been condemned!" she cried aloud. "God in heaven, what are we to do? It will be my turn next. And then—and then——"

Old Philippe came through the door holding a lantern in his hand. "You haven't lighted your candle," he said in a complaining tone.

"No," she answered, speaking from a far corner of the room. "It seemed—it seemed more fitting to wait in the dark."

Old Philippe lighted the candle with fingers that trembled from age. "It has been the same way often before," he said, grinning to himself. "They seem to think the dark hides them when it comes to the final word."

Valerie came forward out of the shadows and faced him. She was composed in manner, although her cheeks were pale and she kept her eyes averted. There was strain in her voice when she spoke.

"You have word for me. Is it—is it bad?" And then, without waiting for him to answer, she went on: "There's no need for you to tell me, Philippe. I know what the decision was. My lord Coeur was found guilty. Oh, it was certain from the first! I knew it when I was taken into court that day. I didn't look up but I saw them. I saw my lord Gouffier. He was like a great, cruel cat, stretching his claws and ready to pounce on the poor mice trapped below!"

She had come close enough for him to see her face clearly. To his great amazement he discovered that she had in some way succeeded in changing her expression. Her lips were drawn back in an imitation of Guillaume Gouffier and there was the same deep indentation between her eyes. Although it was certain that she was near the point of a hysterical outburst, she began to speak with a perfect rendition of his voice.

"That will do!" She nodded and looked about her, one hand smoothing the other, a familiar habit of Gouffier's. "I contend, my lords, that an important point in the case against the prisoner has been demonstrated."

Then she drew herself up as though pronouncing the verdict. "You are declared guilty, Jacques Coeur, and sentence will now be passed upon you. Later we shall have before us this woman of low degree, this impostor, who acted as the accomplice——"

She began to laugh, a high-pitched outburst which changed quickly into a flood of tears. "You need not tell me, Philippe," she sobbed. "I know that he was found guilty and that now—that now—there is no hope for us!"

"But, Mademoiselle"—the old man spoke in a puzzled manner—"what is all this—this carrying-on? I didn't say the prisoner was found guilty. I didn't say the news was bad. I would say on the whole the news was good."

There was a moment of tense silence. The sobbing stopped. She repeated the word, "Good?" in a toneless voice. Then she reached out with a frantic urgency and seized his arm. "Good! Did you say good? Do you mean—do you mean he was acquitted?"

The turnkey slipped the ring back over one wrist and gestured with his free hand. "The charge of poisoning has been admitted to be false."

Valerie's knees gave way and she sank to the floor. She began to cry again, slowly at first and then with mounting volume and intensity.

"Is it true? You are not deceiving me? He has—he has really been acquitted? God, I thank Thee, humbly and earnestly, for saving him from them!"

"You will be free in a day or so, Mademoiselle. No charge is to be brought against you. But"—he gave vent to a sudden cackle—"the lady who told all the lies is in trouble now. It's said she'll have to do public penance for bringing false charges. I was glad to hear *that,* Mademoiselle. The lying, green-eyed vixen!"

"And what of my lord Coeur? Does he go free also?"

The turnkey shook his head. "No, Mademoiselle. The word is that he will be held and tried later on other charges. I saw the list—treason, robbing the royal purse, helping black heathen Turks. It's a fearsome list, Mademoiselle."

Valerie's sense of elation deserted her suddenly and completely. She asked in a stricken voice, "Does he know?"

"Yes, Mademoiselle. I've come from his cell just this minute. He was eating a good warm supper—some roast venison I begged from the kitchen for him—and talking with good cheer. He said to me that now you were free he could face them with a clear conscience and fight them claw and fang. He said he had beaten them once and would do it again. He was in a very good mood, Mademoiselle."

"But, Philippe, what does it mean? Why are they holding him and letting me go?"

The turnkey shook his head gloomily. "It's like a fork, Mademoiselle. If they don't catch him on one prong, they will on another. But you have no more worries. They won't put you back in the cage. Tomorrow perhaps the papers will be signed and then you will be free of them."

Chapter VII

I

D'ARLAY had two horses saddled and ready at the entrance to the Lusignan prison when Valerie was released next morning. Unfortunately it had become known in the town at what hour she would be set free and the space in front of the grim stone pile was so crowded that he was compelled to remain on the edge of things. The clang of the gate swinging open brought cries of "Here she is!" as the eager townspeople fought to get closer to the foot of the paved ramp. D'Arlay caught no more than a glimpse of her face before she was engulfed. She was wearing a hood well down over her brow but he had seen enough to know that she was thoroughly frightened and bewildered.

By the time he reached her, the cloak she was wearing had been torn from her shoulders and was being divided into small pieces as souvenirs. One old woman, using a knife which she had carried in the palm of her hand, had succeeded in cutting off a lock of hair. Valerie gave a gasp of relief and joy when he reached her side after several minutes of battling.

"Robin! I'm nearly suffocated!" she cried, as she surrendered herself into the shelter of one arm. "Please, get me away from these people!"

He had to draw his sword finally and threaten to cut a path through the crowd in order to reach the horses. They mounted in haste and turned in the direction of a street which wound up to the higher reaches of the town. But they were not yet free. A gaunt figure, in a jerkin stained grotesquely with a jumble of colors, dashed out in front of them, raising one arm and shaking it excitedly.

"One moment!" cried this apparition. "You must hear what I have to say! If you refuse me your ears, you'll lose the chance to waken a blind world to the recognition of genius."

D'Arlay cried impatiently, "Out of the way, scarecrow!"

"Yes, I'm a scarecrow," said the man. "But also I'm an artist. I'm a great artist. So far the world has refused to see the genius which inspires my canvases. I am overlooked, brushed aside, sneered at. I starve in a cold garret. I can't afford to buy the colors I need. Monseigneur, if I were allowed the honor of painting Mademoiselle Maret, if I had the chance to capture the beauty she shared with the dead woman, it would be a different story. Everyone would want to see the picture. They would ask who this great artist is."

D'Arlay said, "We're leaving town as fast as our horses will carry us and so we can't help you to your deserved fame." He drew out a royal d'or and tossed it to the artist. "That, at least, will get you food and fuel and some of the colors you need."

The interruption had given Valerie a chance to look about her. She drew in her breath in surprise when she saw that all the windows in the tall and narrow houses fronting on the prison square were filled with heads. There were watchers even on the sharply sloping roofs. Children were being held up by chattering mothers so they would catch a glimpse of her and have something to remember when they grew up.

"It would have been just like this," she said to herself, "if I had been tried and found guilty and they had dragged me out to burn at the stake. I think people like this would enjoy it more to see me die in the flames!"

This train of reflection brought her close again to a state of panic and she cried beseechingly to her companion, "Please, we must get out of here quickly!"

By the time they had followed the course of the winding street to a wider thoroughfare above from which it was possible to catch a view of the river, she had recovered from her fear. She looked up at the sky where a September sun shone brightly, and cried out with pleasure.

"It seems a lifetime since I saw the sun last," she said. Then she began to feel a realization of what this meant. "Robin, I'm free! I'm not to go back to prison! They can't touch me now. I'm free!"

"Yes, you are free and they can't touch you again. Your patron saint must have pleaded your case well and so persuaded the Heavenly Father to reach down a protecting hand. Nothing else could have saved you."

"I'm so happy now." Abruptly her mood changed back. Her eyes had fallen on her skirt and had become conscious of a new disaster. "Robin! They've cut my skirt to tatters! There's hardly anything left of it."

D'Arlay laughed. "You're lucky, my sweet one, to have any clothes left at all."

In a moment she began to laugh with him. "What does it matter? I'm free and that's all I need care about." She looked down at the bright blue waters of the Vonne and exclaimed in wonder at the beauty of it. "How lovely the world is! And now I belong to it again, I'm a part of it and not a number in a dark cell."

For the next few minutes she rode beside him in a perfect transport of happiness. She kept turning her head from side to side for fear of missing something. She found beauty in the dirty streets and charm in the glum old houses. She looked at a tavern sign painted the green of bile and eagerly spelled out the name, *Le Dur-bec* (the hawfinch). She chattered with more abandon than was ever displayed by that shy species of bird, asking her companion an infinity of questions about himself. She hardly waited for his answers before going on to something else. The miracle of having someone to talk with seemed to have gone to her head.

Suddenly she stopped. She turned in the saddle and looked at him questioningly. "Robin, where are you taking me? I've been so full of the joy of finding myself alive again that I've not thought about it before."

D'Arlay leaned over and took possession of her nearest hand. "We go first to a sleepy little village about six miles south of here. Word has been sent ahead to the priest, Father Eligius, that we are coming and that we want him to marry us. Pierre Dupain says he's a right-thinking little man and so we may assume that he'll be ready with book and bell and candle to—to make the journey we are about to take together a much more proper proceeding than the last one we made in each other's company."

Valerie reined in her horse and gazed at D'Arlay with unbelieving eyes. "You are still willing to marry me?" She spoke in a tense whisper. "After all that's happened? Dearest Robin, I—I am a notorious woman! Only by a great miracle have I escaped the flames they light for women poisoners. You saw what happened back there. I'm afraid it will always be the same. People will go out of their way to see me, they'll whisper behind my back.

My name will be coupled with Gilles de Retz who murdered all those babies. *Valerie Maret the poisoner!*"

"In Arlay," he said, still keeping possession of her hand, "we'll live in a world of our own. There are no close neighbors and no town within a dozen miles. Let the outside world talk about you if it has nothing better to do. The murmur of our own stream and the wind in the trees will keep us from hearing."

Her eyes had filled with tears. Keeping them lowered, she said in a whisper: "You would sacrifice everything for me, Robin? Is it through a sense of pity that you're ready to do it?"

"My reason for wanting to marry you is sheer selfishness," he answered. "I take the most intense pleasure in seeing you, in having you near me. I can conceive of no joy to equal the knowledge that you belong to me. I want you to sit beside me at meals, to lie beside me in bed, to ride with me, to share all my thoughts. I don't want to talk to anyone else as long as I live. If I can't have you, life will be a complete desolation. So you see," he added, after a pause during which he tried vainly to catch her eye, "there's nothing fine or self-sacrificing, nothing noble at all, about my attitude. I'm an intensely selfish fellow who insists on getting what he wants."

Valerie looked up then. Her eyes were still slightly misted but this did not obscure in any degree the happiness which showed in them. "I won't be able to resist such selfishness as that," she said.

They had been riding through streets which showed few signs of life. A man standing in front of a tavern had sprung into action suddenly as they passed and had run after them for a few yards, crying, "I know you, you're that woman!" but this had been the extent of the interest they had created since leaving the neighborhood of the prison. Now, however, they reached a small square sleeping in front of an old church of green stone. A smiling man with a basket under his arm confronted them.

It was Pierre Dupain. He waved a hand to them, saying, "You escaped the crowds more quickly than I thought possible. Nonetheless I came on time."

"This," said D'Arlay to his companion, "is a very brave man to whom you owe your life. If he hadn't shown the courage to establish a system of communication between us and Jacques Coeur in prison, we would never have been able to save you from the torture."

"Then you must be Pierre Dupain," said Valerie, extending her hand to him. "I heard about you from my lord Coeur. I shall be grateful to you, Monsieur Dupain, as long as I live."

The bookseller took her hand and kissed it. "A small risk to take in such a cause," he said. "As for saving your life, Mademoiselle, I think the credit for that goes to the one who made the midnight ride to Poitiers and convinced a certain great man that you should be spared."

Valerie turned quickly to D'Arlay. "What is this? I've heard nothing of a ride to Poitiers."

He brushed it aside. "It's a story I may tell you some time."

Pierre Dupain held up his basket, from which the neck of a bottle protruded. "A wedding breakfast," he explained. Then he added with a twinkle, "They say the efforts of a good cook are wasted on a bride and groom; but my wife is a *very* good cook, as you will perhaps discover."

"Was the word sent to the priest?" asked D'Arlay.

The bookseller nodded. "The messenger is back already and reports that the arrangements have been made."

"Au revoir, Pierre Dupain!" said D'Arlay, kicking his heel gently into the ribs of his horse. "Two people will always remember you with gratitude."

2

The priest in the nearby village was right-thinking, as had been reported, but he was much more: he was a gentle old man with a love for all mankind showing in his deep-sunken eyes and with an infinity of the wrinkles of kindly humor clustering at the wicks of his mouth. When the ceremony had been performed in his little church—it must have been one of the very smallest in all France and its tower was shaped absurdly like a salt shaker—he walked between them down the aisle with an arm over the shoulders of each.

"I count this an honor," he said. "You are brave young people. You, my daughter, have been through a terrible ordeal but you are very young and I don't believe you'll carry the scars of it long. You, my son, have assumed a responsibility which will not be easy. You will be much criticized and perhaps persecuted. The expression you wear tells me you'll count such difficulties a small price for the joy you'll know in this union. Keep the belief in your hearts that Our Lord will be lenient to you both and show you the way to real happiness."

His house was joined to the church by a covered walk over which vines clustered like a solid wall. They realized immediately how fortunate this was. A curious knot of people had already gathered in front of the edifice.

"Word has reached the village that you headed from Lusignan in this direction," whispered the old priest. "You must stay with me tonight and resume your journey at dawn. It will save you inconvenience; and I will be selfish enough to find much pleasure in your company."

Accordingly they had their wedding breakfast in a small walled garden back of the house. It was so small and the walls were so high that little sun reached it, no more actually than a splash of light on one side of the ivy-covered brick. However, it was pleasantly tangled with late flowers and there was a pear tree on which the fruit had turned a ruddy color.

They seated themselves together under the pear tree and Valerie spread a handkerchief on the ground to serve as cloth. Pierre Dupain had not overpraised his wife's cooking, for the breakfast she had prepared passed all commendation. There were hard-boiled eggs colored with saffron and flavored with cloves; a cheese of Montreuil, made from fresh cream and generously sprinkled with sugar; a bread of two colors, white and brown, the result of alternating layers of wheat and rye; and a pair of custards baked in flaky crust called darioles over which the hand of the good housewife had not been niggardly in shaking the cinnamon. The wine was light-bodied and it left the tongue and throat refreshed. Both of them were hungry and they finished the contents of the basket to the last crumb and drop.

"I had hoped," said Valerie, tidily clearing up all traces of the meal, "that there would be a chance today for me to get new clothes. The memory of the prison, and the taint of it as well, will always cling to what I'm wearing. These are things they found for me when they took me out of the cage. As you see, my lord Robin, they're very dull and also a very bad fit."

"I've lived this morning in such a glow of content that I've hardly noticed what you have on," he answered. He cast a belatedly appraising eye over her attire. "You're right, my heart. That dress doesn't sufficiently become you."

"Bice!" said Valerie bitterly, holding out her sleeve which was of the dull gray known by that term. "All my life I've had to wear it and all my life I've hated it! Once, when I was a very small girl, it was promised me I was to have a new dress for my birthday. I said to my mother—to Madame Maret—'Please, *Maman,* anything but bice!' She was a kind woman and she promised me it would be either pink or blue, the colors I craved most. I especially wanted pink. When I got the dress, which color do you think it was?"

"Pink, I hope."

She shook her head with the sadness of the memory she had brought back. "No, my Robin. It was bice. They hadn't been able to afford anything better. Now you will understand why I dislike this color so much."

After he had settled his wife comfortably in a corner of the wall with his cloak as a cushion, D'Arlay sought the old priest to see what could be done about the problem of clothes.

"I find it necessary to ride over to a somewhat larger place this afternoon," said the priest. "Perhaps I could get something for my lady there and bring it back in my bundle. What articles do you want, Monseigneur?"

D'Arlay began to indulge in expansive instructions. "Everything, Father Eligius. You may tell the tailor that I want the best he has. The materials must be rich. The fashioning must be becoming and with a degree of art."

The priest let fall a diffident hint. "It's a small town, my lord. You must not expect too much of it."

"As for the color," went on D'Arlay, "I want pink, if you can get it. Otherwise blue."

"But—but, my lord! Have you a long ride ahead of you?"

"Yes. A continuous journey of perhaps two weeks."

"Then permit me to make a suggestion, my lord. The colors you name would not be practical for such a long journey. Nor would it be wise to select rich materials. I would most strongly advise a good wearing material. The color should be gray."

"Not gray!" cried D'Arlay. "Father Eligius, there are reasons, the very best of reasons, for this dress to be frivolous and gay and in no sense practical or sensible. It must be rewarding to the eye and the heart of my wife. I want a plume in the hat, an ostrich plume——"

"Monseigneur! We are not in Paris or Tours or Lyons!" protested the priest. "There will be no ostrich plumes in the town to which I ride. It will be a matter of very great luck if I'm able to get your lady as much as a colored ribbon for her hat."

Valerie was sleeping when D'Arlay returned to the garden but she wakened almost immediately and sat up against the wall. She had lost the happy mood of the morning.

"I'm realizing how selfish we've been!" she said, looking at him with guilty eyes. "My lord Coeur is still in prison and we haven't mentioned him all these hours. I confess, my Robin, that I've been selfish enough to want nothing but happiness today."

D'Arlay began to talk in optimistic terms. He was convinced that his friend had weathered the worst of the storm in escaping conviction on the poisoning charge and that he would be able to meet successfully any new charges they might bring against him. "He has been an honest and capable minister to the King," he pointed out. "They won't find a shred of real evidence against him. He has on many occasions made up deficits in the royal purse from his own funds and said nothing about it. The proof of this will be in the household books."

"But will they allow the books to be brought into court?"

"Perhaps not. But how can they expect to make a case against a man who has been as honest and disinterested as that? Any charges they make will be trivial and as false as the heart of Judas. The truth can't be kept from showing itself."

Valerie was far from ready to believe this. "It was a miracle which saved us!" she whispered tensely. "Can we be sure it will happen again? Can the truth prevail if they refuse to let him speak in his own defense or to call witnesses? Will they let him consult his own records?"

D'Arlay was not to be robbed of his optimism. "The odds against him can never be as great again as they were this time. Yet he won. If there isn't another miracle, there will always be the Coeur genius to find a way out—and the Coeur luck." He walked over and seated himself beside her. "Come, my love, this is not the day for doubts. We're entitled to happiness for a few hours and it isn't selfishness to want that much. I have many things to tell you and so I must begin at once. The good priest will be back before the afternoon is over and that is little enough time to tell you how much I love you."

3

They had supper with Father Eligius in a stone cubicle off the kitchen. It was so small that his housekeeper could not enter to serve them. Instead she handed the dishes in to them through a circular hole in the wall, having something to say each time. Once she remarked to Valerie, "Eat well of this, my lady, for truly you're as thin as a plucked crow." It was a simple meal, consisting of a late melon, a platter of stewed goat meat, and a steaming hot mixture of vegetables.

Valerie had regained her good spirits and she chatted about the future, assuring the old priest that she intended to have a large family and that she hoped they would all be girls with the exception of the much-needed heir. "There are too many knights in the world now and too much fighting," she said, in answer to his surprised query.

Father Eligius had shown discrimination in the matter of her new clothes. The dress was blue and a good match, moreover, for her eyes. No tailor was capable of such prodigies of labor as producing a lady's gown in a few hours and so she had asked no questions, assuming that they had belonged once to someone else. The hat had been made by the nimble fingers of the tailor's wife and it had a becoming blue ribbon in it. There had been no time to change but Valerie felt perfectly satisfied, and this added to her lightness of mood.

"And now," said Father Eligius, drinking the last drop of his one glass of wine which he had diluted liberally with water, "I mustn't indulge any longer my great liking for young company. You've had a hard day and tomorrow you must start out at dawn. Come with me and I'll show you to your room."

The good-natured face of the servant appeared in the aperture in the wall and she addressed a few words to D'Arlay, wishing them much happiness. He smiled and thanked her.

"Your servant is Angevin," he said as they followed the priest up a steep flight of stone steps. "I can tell from her voice. I think she must have been born not far from Arlay."

"Yes, Micheline is from Anjou. She's a widow and a faithful servant. But there are times when she holds her tongue on a loose rein."

There was a hall above and a bedroom opening off it. Pausing at the door, Father Eligius raised two fingers above them as he pronounced a blessing.

"You've been sorely tried," he said to Valerie, giving her a smile of real affection. Then he turned to D'Arlay. "In spite of it, she is very lovely, this very young wife of yours. You must always be kind to her."

When the door had closed behind them, the happy bridegroom placed a hand on each of her shoulders and smiled down at her. "Yes, you are lovely, my very young bride," he whispered. "My Valerie! My sweet minikin, with your hair curling so distractingly about your ears! I vow no candles are necessary when your eyes shine so brightly! I swear solemnly to treat you with more than kindness all the years of your life!"

She whispered back, "It makes me happy when you say such things to me." Then she added with a nod of the head, "I'm glad we know my parents were of gentle blood, because it makes me feel less—less unworthy."

Micheline had not shared his opinion in the matter of the lighting of the room and had resorted to the usual method. A candle was burning on the table. She had gone further than that, however. There was in addition a large cluster of unlighted ones. D'Arlay smiled when he saw what she had done. "Even if she hadn't spoken, I would have known she was Angevin from this," he said. Then, realizing the number of tapers the housekeeper had provided, he burst out involuntarily with, "Does she think me the Twenty Candle Bridegroom of Nantes?"

Valerie, it was clear, did not understand what he was talking about. She came over and stood beside him at the table. "Is this some custom of your part of the country?" she asked.

D'Arlay did not answer at once. He was regarding her with a somewhat guilty air. "I thought you knew or I wouldn't have said anything about it. Yes, it's a Western custom, one of those absurd jokes people think they must play at weddings. I'm sure this is the work of the servant and that the good old priest would be angry with her if he knew."

"But what *is* the custom?"

He took her by the shoulders again and frowned down at her sternly. "You are a married woman now and I suppose there would be no harm in telling you. If you are going to be shocked, you must blame your own curiosity. Well—when a bridegroom takes his wife in his arms on their bridal night, he must blow out the candle and light another one afterward. This—this keeps on. Thus there is evidence in the morning to satisfy the curiosity of relatives and guests. Now that I've satisfied *your* curiosity, are you very much shocked and angry with me?"

A blush had taken possession of her face but she answered with a shake of the head. "No. But in the morning I may speak my mind to that old woman downstairs." Probably with a desire to change the subject, she said that she was sure Father Eligius had surrendered his own room to them. Had he noticed that part of it was devoted to the priest's memories of his boyhood days? "There's a little cap he wore once," she said, "and a hoop and a toy horse with a wisp of real horsehair stuck to its neck. And there's a plate of colored pebbles from the seashore. Somehow it makes me feel very sorry for him."

D'Arlay dropped his hands from her shoulders. It was clear that he was ill at ease. "My sweet child," he said, "it would be much easier for us if we were following the usual ritual tonight. There should be a groom of the chamber to turn down the bedclothes and to make sure they've been properly aired and to perfume the place with rose leaves. Then there should be a bevy of friends and servants to bring you in and undress you and put you to bed. After that another lot should escort me in. That's only part of it but, as I have never been through it, I don't know all the rules. I find myself uncertain as to what to do. Do you have the same feeling?"

Valerie slowly nodded her head. "Yes," she whispered.

"When Naulty was married the whole household practiced what was to be done for weeks ahead. . . . Do you think I should return to the hall and come back a little later?"

She nodded quickly. "Yes, my Robin. It's most kind of you to think of it." She took her skirt in both hands (what the curious people of Lusignan had left of it) and drew it out. "This is quite ugly, as you see, and it's such a poor fit. I—I would rather be alone when I take it off."

Then she had a sudden thought. Going to the corner of the room where the childhood mementoes were kept, she took a handful of the colored pebbles. These she transferred to one of his hands.

"Take a walk in the hall," she suggested. "Walk very slowly. And each time you make a turn, transfer one of the pebbles to the other hand. By the time they're all in the other hand, you may come back."

"I will find it difficult to walk slowly, my heart," he said.

But when he reached the landing outside the door he remained there in deep thought for some time. Finally, nodding his head in decision, he began to descend the stairs. He put each foot down carefully so she would not hear.

Father Eligius was sitting in the small room at the front of the house, straining his eyes over a book which was so heavy in its board bindings that he held it on his knees. Clearly it was his most prized possession for he was turning the leaves with a reverent hand. He looked up when D'Arlay appeared in the door and all the wrinkles on his face gathered themselves together in a smile.

"I knew you would come, my son," he said. "I've been waiting for you. Take this seat beside me. We'll talk and perhaps we'll drink a little wine. We'll talk so long that, when you go back upstairs, that gentle little wife, who has been treated so cruelly, will be soundly asleep."

They talked an hour or more. D'Arlay then returned to the bedroom with stealthy steps and was careful to make no sound in opening the door. But Valerie was not asleep, after all. She smiled at him from the bed and remarked, "How slowly you must have walked, my Robin."

A lighted candle on a table beside the bed was waiting to be blown out.

Envoy

THE story of the girl who was known as Valerie Maret until her sixteenth year, then for a brief and troubled period as Valerie de Voudrai, and after that for the balance of her days (which proved lengthy for those times and as happy as life could be in that or any age) as Valerie de Burey, has reached its climax. So far as she and the Sire d'Arlay are concerned, this long recital of events could now be considered as closed.

But the story of Jacques Coeur cannot be dismissed summarily at this point. His trial dragged on at Lusignan for nearly two years more, and on May 29, 1453 (the same day that Constantinople fell to the Turks, a very bad day for civilization), he was declared guilty on five of the twelve charges which had been brought against him. It would be waste of space to enumerate these charges, for never in all judicial history had a great political figure been arraigned on such trumpery, absurd, and baseless grounds. It had been *opéra bouffe* from the beginning, but the King of France had to be freed of his debts and the nobility could no longer abide the spectacle of great wealth and power in the hands of a furrier's son; and so Jacques Coeur was condemned to death (Charles, most magnanimous of monarchs, changed this to perpetual exile at such time as the judgments against him had been satisfied) and to the confiscation of all his property. He was compelled to make the *amende honorable* in the Palace of Justice at Poitiers, which meant appearing barefoot and carrying a ten-pound candle to confess his misdemeanors, on the same day Jeanne de Vendôme underwent the identical punishment for having sworn to false evidence against him. Anyone with the smallest grain of humor would have seen something absurd about this; but a sense of humor was the quality they lacked most of all in the brave days of chivalry, and this final phase of the judicial proceedings is recorded in history with full solemnity.

And then began a mad scramble for the spoils. First of all those gallant gentlemen, the five judges, were awarded for their fairness and skill in handling the case by a gift of estates. Even Antoine de Chabannes, that fumbling veteran, attained the goal on which he had fixed his greedy rheumy eyes, the fair domain of Saint-Fargeau. The goods in the great shops were put up at auctions, held in Paris, Tours, Bourges, Lyons, and Poitiers, and never before nor since have such bargains been known. The nobles and their eager wives bid in the jewelry and the gold and silver vessels and all the costly and curious objects from the East. The ladies competed bitterly for the silks and satins and velvets, and it is probable that the prices paid for these goods came closer to their real value. When the last fragment of candle had burned out (the auctions were conducted on the inch-of-candle method, by which the successful bidder is the last one to name a price before the light dies) the shops were closed, the shutters put up and bolted. The great enterprises of Jacques Coeur had come to an end.

To tell all this, as well as the unusual events which followed, would require more space than can be allowed. The balance of the story will be set down in the form of a few scenes; and these will be told as briefly as possible.

I

D'Arlay had been restless and unhappy since the conviction of Jacques Coeur. There was nothing he could do to help the unfortunate Moneyman (who was being kept in solitary confinement in one prison after another and was, according to rumor, being slowly poisoned) and this disturbed him so much that he could not keep still after his far-from-exacting daily duties as the master of Arlay had been finished. At such times Valerie could do nothing for him.

One day he took to horse to escape the Old Man on his shoulder and rode out to Tremblay Hill from which visitors caught their first glimpse of the manor house of Arlay. As he passed over the crest he was surprised to see a stranger coming from the other direction at a brisk trot. They had few visitors and so D'Arlay reined in his horse at once and watched this newcomer with an interest which grew almost to bursting point when he discovered it was Pregent Kennedy. He was sure the Scot would prove to be the bearer of important news.

"Greetings!" he shouted, waving a gauntleted hand. "Greetings, Sir Scot! I can tell by the light in your eyes that you have news for me which will pull me out of this fever in which I pass my days."

Kennedy answered while still some distance away: "Aye, that I have. The best of news." He raised his voice to a triumphant blast. *"We accomplished our purpose!"*

When he had reined in, the Scot proceeded with his explanation. His face, which seldom changed from its lean solemnity, was actually glowing with enthusiasm.

"Jacques Coeur is free!" he declared. "And never in the annals of Christendom has such a spectacle been seen. It was wonderfully done, my lord D'Arlay, most monstrously well done!"

"God has answered the prayers of the people of France!" said D'Arlay, crossing himself.

"Aye. There will be much rejoicing when the word is passed that the Fox is loose. But it will be a bitter day for the sour-faced King and his noble ministers!"

D'Arlay was too happy to say much at first. They had wheeled their horses, in the meantime, into the slow slope of the road which led through autumnal colored woods to the domain of Arlay.

"We had him out of there like that!" said Kennedy, snapping his fingers. "It was a"—he paused and then had recourse to his native tongue for the word he needed—"a *canny* trick we played on them. Every detail had been attended to. First, a fire broke out in the apartments of the Governor. Never have you heard such shouting, such clamor for everyone to help, and such running with buckets of water, and the Governor's lady coming out screaming in her shift. While this excitement held the attention of everyone, the Fox tied his turnkey up with ropes—there was a jingle of gold in the turnkey's pocket, you may be sure—and opened the door with the keys. The warder on the gate had been well anointed too and—he was out of the place before the Governor was through bellowing orders and his lady had borrowed a kirtle to cover her shapelessness. Ah, it was a fine bit of planning. I give the Fox due credit for it."

"The Moneyman arranged it himself?"

"Down to the last detail. All we had to do was to play our parts. The seagoing fellow was there, bellowing and ramping around and letting the weight of his hand descend on anyone who got in his way. There were other Coeur men, factors and sea captains, and all of them good fellows in a pinch. It was an inspiring sight to see how his men rallied around him in his need, my lord."

"All," said D'Arlay, with sudden bitterness, "but the one who should have been there most of all."

"You were kept in the dark by the Moneyman's orders." The Scot nodded his head sagely. "And a sensible thing it was. You had jeopardized your safety and your position as a landowner enough as it was. Your wise friend, who thinks of everything, had no intention of letting you play the scapegoat. I assure you, my lord, that none of us had any great part to play. There were half-a-dozen spry young fellows on hand to do all the little bits which might have fallen to your share." He added, after a moment's pause, "It was said also that your lady was expecting the arrival of a son and heir—another good reason for not sending you word of what was afoot."

D'Arlay was still far from satisfied. "There were good reasons for not letting me take part—that I grant you—and only one on the other side, the fact that I'll regret it as long as I live!"

They had reached a small wooden bridge spanning a stream swollen to a fair semblance of a roaring torrent by recent rains. D'Arlay led the way across. Then he turned back to his companion with an unhappy look on his face. "The hoped-for heir," he said, "proved to be a daughter. A pretty little thing who didn't manage to grasp one second of life. I think it should be possible to save more of the babies who come so hopefully into the world and depart so quickly! The physician and the midwife didn't succeed in making our poor little Anne breathe at all."

"And how is your lady now?"

"She's not strong yet. Perhaps this good news you bring will be the draught to set her on her feet again." D'Arlay's mind went back to the more pressing matter of the escape. "Do you feel free to tell me anything more of the plans? Is Jacques Coeur in a safe place?"

"The flight has been worked out as carefully as the escape. Aye, the Fox has found a safe lair for the time being." They were crossing a large glade and there was not even a vagrant bird within hearing distance; but the Scot from force of habit lowered his voice. "If it's your thought that you would like to see him before he gets out of the country, it could be arranged. I have the Moneyman's promise for you on that."

"I must see him," said D'Arlay eagerly. "I can leave at once if necessary."

The manor house boasted a long, flagged passage with an outside colonnade creating the effect of a cloister. It was here that the Scot was taken to see the chatelaine of Arlay. He found her rather wan and thin lying on a couch with covers tucked up around her neck.

After she had skillfully probed into all the important matters and had led him persistently into descriptions of everything which had occurred, Valerie raised her head slightly to get a better view of her visitor.

"And what of you, Monsieur Kennedy?" she asked. "The last time I saw you was in Paris—before all these dreadful things happened—and at the time you were contemplating matrimony. Did you marry the fair widow?"

Kennedy shook his head. "Not I!" he exclaimed. "It was the luckiest escape I've ever had in a lifetime salted and peppered and porreted with such escapes. But"—with a triumphant nod—"my friend, Lockie Bell, married her! Aye, he's a maker of shoes now, that gallant Lockie! You see, my lady, the Guild has a rule that a widow may carry on her deceased husband's trade if she remarries someone in the Guild. When the other makers of boots discovered she had taken into her bed an ugly little Scottish runt who didn't have a shilling to bless the union with and who, moreover, didn't know a last from a goloshing, there was such a storm that it looked as though the happy couple would have nothing left but the bed itself! But Lockie has a persuasive tongue and he convinced them he could become a maker of boots himself and so satisfy the requirements of the Guild.

"And now"—triumphantly—"Lockie Bell is serving his time in a basement which stinks most abominably of leather, learning to slash and clobber and cobble and sew. Every time I think of him, working away as though St. Crispin was there to jab him with an awl if he slackened in his efforts, I chuckle to myself with sardonic satisfaction."

After a long pause Valerie asked, "And so the fortune you came to France to make is still beyond your reach?"

"It's still to be made, Madame." The Scot crossed one leg over the other and gave his tartan the customary backward flick. "Now that this untimely and unmanly peace has been made and there's no profit in killing any more, I'm thinking of going on to Rome with the Moneyman. He says there will be fortunes to be picked up there now that he intends to make the city his headquarters. I hear the pious cardinals will pay well for men who can handle a sword and pink a churchly rival through the eye. I hear also that the gold and the rich goblets and the jeweled purses lie on the street for the mere stooping over. Aye, Rome is the place for one with the special talents of Pregent Kennedy."

2

It was a long ride that D'Arlay took to say farewell to his friend. After two weeks of steady journeying over the roads of the south, which were notoriously bad, he found himself one dark night on the bank of the Rhône. On the other side he could see a cluster of lights from Good King René's favorite city of Tarascon.

He waited here with Pregent Kennedy for the better part of two hours before they heard the beat of horses' hoofs. The voice of Jacques Coeur came to them out of the darkness.

"Are you there, Robin?"

D'Arlay answered eagerly, "Here I am," and ran forward. Someone slipped the hooding from a lantern and held it up cautiously so that a brief view could be had of the man who had escaped through the fingers of Charles of France. With a sinking of the heart D'Arlay saw that Jacques Coeur had become an old man. His cheeks had the prison flabbiness and they were so sunken that his nose jutted out from them like the beak of a bird of prey. His neck was scrawny and there was a stoop in his shoulders. He coughed continuously.

Only his eyes were the same. They were still alive, commanding, full of determination.

"I had hoped," said Jacques Coeur, leaning from his saddle to shake hands, "to have several days with you. But, as you know, we were detained. That leaves us a short time only until I launch myself on the last stage of my flight to freedom."

"But," demurred D'Arlay, still feeling the shock caused by his friend's appearance, "I expected to cross the river with you and share your journey through Provence."

Coeur shook his head emphatically. "King René is a kindly old dotard and he won't surrender me to his brother-in-law of France. But there will be eyes everywhere and all my movements will be reported in full. If you were with me, the fact would get to Charles quickly. You would then be in serious trouble, my good Robin. The King might think the grounds sufficient for a charge of treason. Certainly everything you possess would be confiscated." He gave his head another shake. "We mustn't allow him that satisfaction, our good friend Charles. There's a house down the road where we may rest for an hour and talk. Then I must—betake myself on the road to exile."

D'Arlay said, "It will be a hasty farewell, Jacques."

The Moneyman began to cough and it took him quite a time to control the spasm. "Don't let this habit of mine disturb you," he said breathlessly. "I didn't break out of prison to die of the lung trouble it has started in me. I'm a tough old bear, I'll have you know. If they think I'm done for, they'll get a shock when I come charging out of my lair at them! . . . I have many things to tell you and a list of instructions as long as that famous sword of yours. Come, we must get to work."

Two hours later D'Arlay watched Coeur and his party ride off on the road to the ferry. He thought, "I'll never see him again." There had been no more than a handshake between them and from the Moneyman a hearty, "Farewell, Robin. We have been good friends." D'Arlay himself had been unable to utter a word.

Now from the darkness he heard Jacques Coeur speak to Nicolas who rode beside him. He said in a tone which he did not think, clearly, could carry so far to the rear, "I'm an old man at last, Nicolas, for I find myself most uncomfortable in the saddle."

There was a sympathetic note in the voice of the servant when he answered, and this for the first time in the memory of all men, "Come, master, this won't do! You're far from being an old man."

"But I am, Nicolas. I can't be sure I shall ever set eyes on the ship that's waiting for us."

"I remember once you said you could outwork, outthink, and outwalk any man alive. I laughed at you then but I knew it was true. And you still can! I swear, master, you'll get your strength back in a day or so and outride all of us."

"You're trying to be kind; and God knows my need for sympathy must be great to make you change your tune, my old goad! But it's no use. Soft words can't patch up a weak body. I'm a broken man, Nicolas, doddering on my way to the grave!"

"Master, master! You can't mean what you're saying!"

The clatter of the hoofs on the hard road made it impossible for D'Arlay to hear anything more.

3

There had been no word from her husband for several weeks and Valerie was so worried that she was finding it hard to sleep of nights. She was wondering for the thousandth time whether the Moneyman had been recaptured and whether the Sire d'Arlay had been with him at the time. She was becoming certain as each day passed without any message that this was what had happened.

A servant appeared in the door to announce, "The Comte de Burey, mistress."

She had not seen her brother-in-law for some months and had heard nothing of him in that time. The thought leaped into her mind that he was the bearer of bad news.

"Show the Comte here, if you please."

She was startled when her brother-in-law entered the room. He had changed a great deal, being so much thinner that his face looked gaunt and long. This gave greater prominence to his eyes and nose.

In spite of everything that had happened, Valerie had kept a feeling of tolerance for Regnault de Burey and she was sorry to note how poorly he was dressed. From her first recollection of him he had been shabby, but the materials used for his clothes had been of the best and he had always looked what he was, an impoverished nobleman. Now he was attired in shoddy cloth which could not be made to fit him. His shoes were broken and patched and it was only too clear that the cracks in the leather had been painstakingly, but not successfully, clobbered.

"Ha, Little Cousin," he said, blinking his eyes at her in a manner which could be construed as affectionate. "You gain in beauty all the time, it seems; and the rest of us will soon be on the scrapheap with the broken wheels and discarded stewing pans, and the old clothes and the fish scales and the offal generally."

He grunted his disgust at the way life was treating him and it was several moments before he began to speak again. "The servants tell me that my brother is still away. What's the sly young dog up to? He must have lost his senses. If I had a wife like you, I wouldn't let her out of my sight for a minute. I said to myself when I started out, 'If she's going to yield to anyone while he's away, why shouldn't it be me?' "

Valerie was so delighted at finding that he had not come as the bearer of bad news that she smiled at him. She said, "If I ever decide to take a lover, Naulty, I promise to consult you first."

He was not taken in. "I may look forward to hearing from you, then, in a thousand years," he said. He ran a weary hand down the inflamed bridge of his nose. "I'm teetering on the brink of ruin."

"I'm sorry to hear you're in trouble." She did not add the word "again" as anyone else would have done.

"Job, sitting on his ulcers and boils and watching his wealth disappear in smoke and thunder, was rolling in content compared to the position I find myself in! Afflictions seek me out like flies to corruption. I am sick. I am poor. And Isabeau——" He paused and gave his head a lugubrious shake. "You've heard of the plight of my unfortunate spouse?"

Valerie said in an apprehensive tone, "No, we have few visitors and so we hear nothing of what goes on."

"That's strange. I thought everyone knew. Isabeau has the dead palsy."

Despite the state of her feelings toward the Comtesse, Valerie experienced a sense of shock. This grew into a closer approach to something like sympathy for the sufferer than she had thought possible when the husband of the sick woman went on into details.

"She had curious symptoms for a long time. She spoke with difficulty and sometimes used one word for another. She complained a great deal of hearing bells ringing when there was no sound at all, sometimes in the middle of the night. Then one day she fell over on the floor and lay there without moving. She hasn't moved since."

"When did this dreadful thing occur?"

"Over a month ago. The physician says she may stay like this for years. He even thinks it possible she may live out her allotted span without moving a single muscle. That's arrant nonsense, of course. He's full of nonsense, with his talk of what Paulus says and Galen thinks and his lack of ideas of what can be done for her." He went on in tones of the deepest scorn. "Jalop and scammony! Vapors of vinegar! He knows nothing, that chattering fool! He had her head shaved before I knew what he was about. My poor Isabeau! How she must have suffered as she felt him clipping off her lovely red curls—slightly sprinkled with gray if the truth must be told—and could do nothing to stop him."

"Do you mean that she can see and hear?"

The Comte nodded his head. "All her senses seem to be alive and active. She always had a great fear of being closed in. Sometimes she wouldn't sleep in a tester bed because she felt as though she would smother. She never wanted to ride in a carriage. Do you suppose"—he turned a pair of eyes on his companion which reflected a vicarious sense of horror—"that she feels that way now, being closed in and not able to move a finger to free herself? Would she scream to get out if she had the power? Truly, Little Cousin, it's a gruesome thought!"

He had succeeded in communicating some of the emotion he felt to Valerie. She wet her lips nervously and said: "This is truly awful! I—I hope some way can be found to help her—to release her!"

"The physician says that release will come only with death." The Comte sat in gloomy silence for several moments. "There's something even worse I must tell you. She can still move a part of her right cheek. I noticed it and so we began to communicate. When I ask her a question, she moves her cheek if the answer is yes. I can anticipate some of her wants. But, Valerie"—he paused again—"I've found there's something she wants to tell me. She has no way, of course, of letting me know what it is and I, so far, have been unable to guess. I haven't asked the right questions. It's truly a terrible situation!" He shuddered with so much feeling that his listener did the same. "There she sits, propped up in a chair with pillows, her eyes staring straight at me. I know that back of them is her burning desire to make me understand. I've asked a hundred questions but always her cheek remains still. But when I ask, as I do every day, if there's still something she wants me to know, the cheek quivers and shakes in eagerness."

"Do you suppose"—Valerie hesitated before putting her thought into words—"that it has to do with her wishes about her—her death? Does she desire to be released at once?"

Regnault de Burey considered the point in silence for several moments. "And if that is what she wants, what can be done to satisfy her?"

"Nothing," said Valerie hastily. "At least all you could do would be to tell the physician."

"I know what *he* would say, that brain of a cuckoo bird." The Comte snuffled with disgust. "He would accuse me of an impiety in thinking of such a thing. No, Little Cousin, that is one question I dare not ask her. Suppose the answer was yes? Then I would be in a sorry dilemma. Ever after her eyes would be fixed on me and I would know what they were saying. They would be saying, You coward, you keep me here in a misery so great that death is the only release and you do nothing for me! . . . Well, enough of this! There are worms in my flesh when I think too much about it."

They sat and looked at each other in silence for a long time. Valerie asked finally, "May I offer you some refreshment?"

"Wine, if you please, Little Cousin. One sensation does not diminish with me as the years advance. My thirst."

The Comte watched her over the rim as he imbibed eagerly from the flagon which had been brought him. "It's indeed lucky," he said, after the edge had been taken from his thirst, "that I find you here alone. That brother of mine has no sympathy for me when it comes to the troubles in which I seem always to be involved. He would sit there with a face like a graven saint and say that I deserve all this. Perhaps I do, but, by'r Lady of Marmoutier, I refuse to let my younger brother tell me so! Now you, my Valerie, have a generous share of human kindliness. The fact that I am sorely in need of money will strike home to your friendly little heart at once."

Valerie looked at him doubtfully, remembering an admonition from her husband in this connection. "Don't let Naulty wheedle you into giving him money, no matter what tale of woe he may have."

"But, brother-in-law," she said, "I have so little—a few coins of my own only and some small bits of jewelry which could be sold perhaps. If your needs are great, it will be necessary to speak to Robin when he returns."

The Comte doubled up with a sudden pain. "I have the hip gout now," he said, groaning. "Every part of my body is clamoring for ointment. . . . I think, Little Cousin, I shall content myself with what you can gather together for me. It will be given with an ungrudging smile and no lecture will go with it." He gave a wheezing sigh. "I've been lectured so much that I weary of it."

Valerie had not expected to be taken up in this way. She stammered, "But, truly, it would require such a long time——"

"I can wait. To convince you that I haven't been prodigal with my resources, I may tell you that I haven't stirred a foot from these parts for the better part of a year. Look at me! Could you tell me from a dissipated apothecary or a nip-cheese lawyer? I've just sent my last mistress away. A man can't do more than that."

4

The stricken chatelaine of Montagne-Noire, the ancestral home of the De Bureys, sat in a mound of musty cushions, her eyes motionless in a face on which the palsy had stamped for all time an expression of extreme suffering. Her hair, which the physician had so ruthlessly sacrificed, was beginning to grow again in the form of a reddish fuzz, but there was not yet enough of it to hide the curious conformation of her skull. It was well for her peace of mind (if a mind could know any peace when caught in such a prison) that there was no mirror in the room.

It was a dark room with walls damp from the last rain and with the rank smell which comes from lack of airing. It was so dark, in fact, that even the most active eyes would not have been able at first to see the two women servants who leaned on the handles of brooms in one corner. They were watching their mistress.

"Look at her!" said one of them, in a whisper. "Sitting there like an ugly idol! What wicked thoughts has she got in her mind, do you suppose, Brigitte? Do you think she sees us?"

"Of course she sees us," answered her companion. "She never misses anything, that one. She's in a rage right now because she can't order us whipped."

"She's making up for everything now. How long is it since Bona went to the trouble of bathing her?"

"I can't remember."

The second servant was an emaciated creature with arms as thin as kindling wood and the slack face of the weak in mind. Clutching her broom in her hands, she ventured out to the center of the floor. After standing in front of the motionless figure for several moments, she began to dance about the Comtesse with awkward steps and grotesque motions of her arms. Every time her gyrations brought her in front of her mistress, she would pause and then lunge out viciously with the broom, aiming it at the face of the helpless woman and drawing it back only when it had come as close as an inch of its mark. Once, cackling insanely, she ran to the wall and scraped the end of the broom on the dampness. Then she returned to her triumphant caperings, permitting the soaked straws to brush closer with each thrust at the once-beautiful features of Isabeau de Burey.

The first domestic, who had been screeching with delight over the performance, said suddenly, "Someone is coming, Brigitte!"

The Comte entered the room a few moments after the two servants had vanished in giggling haste. He advanced slowly, for his eyesight was rapidly growing more deficient and his mind was busy elsewhere. He was wondering how far the few odd coins Valerie had been able to spare him would go in meeting his most pressing needs. They rattled about forlornly in his leather purse where, as he knew only too well, they had all the space to themselves.

Slowly and somewhat absent-mindedly he seated himself in a chair facing the rigid figure of the Comtesse. The atmosphere added to his sense of acute discomfort and he sniffed as he looked about him.

"This place is as sour as a cheese vat or a public jakes!" he said aloud. "Are they keeping pigs below that such a rank odor assails my nostrils everywhere I go? I tell you, my spouse"—looking directly at the Comtesse for the first time—"it's a sorry thing when the hand of a mistress is no longer felt in an establishment like this."

He paused as though, in his absent-mindedness, he expected her to reply. Something about the figure opposite him suggested that a response was in her mind and that she was striving desperately to make him understand. The Comte was not receptive to such influences. He stretched one leg out in front of him and groaned with the pain the effort had involved. "I swallow all the nauseous messes this dolt of a physician concocts for me and yet my gout gets worse every day." Then he drew himself up in his chair by employing both his elbows and stared intently at his wife.

"My poor Isabeau!" he said. "I hardly recognize you when I see you sitting there. How much longer must you endure this?"

It became apparent then, even to one as lacking in sensitivity as he, that the helpless woman was trying by sheer force of will to tell him something. He leaned forward with his elbows on his knees and studied her face, as though the answer might be found in surface indications. The rigidity of her expression had robbed her of almost all suggestion of humanity. The eyes were wide open and staring fixedly, the lips were parted and unpleasantly moist. The physician's insistence on shaving her head had completed the picture.

Was there something different about her? It seemed to him that there had been a change but he could not have told in what it consisted, except that he fancied her breathing had become more stertorous. After several moments of uncomfortable watching, he made up his mind to the duty from which he had been holding back.

"Is there still something you want to tell me?" he asked.

The place on her cheek which functioned normally moved several times, as though to lend emphasis to the reply.

"Has it to do with your condition?"

The cheek moved again, unmistakably.

"Do you want—do you want to go on living as long as we can keep you alive?"

He was staring at her intently as he spoke, realizing the necessity of interpreting her wishes accurately. There was not as much as a quiver.

"Are you then anxious to—to die?"

There was no mistaking the meaning of the muscular answer this time. The one active part of the palsied body had for a moment fairly pulsed with life and motion.

"But the physician says you may live for a long time. For years even." The Comte was speaking slowly and with obvious reluctance. "Is—is—is it your wish that something be done to release you?"

Again the cheek moved. The Comte slumped back in his chair. He had his answer now, the one he had more than half expected to hear, the one he had dreaded. She wanted to escape from this living death, and was asking him to accomplish it, to put an end to her suffering. This was what she had been trying to tell him for so long.

Finally he began to speak in a grumbling tone. "You always preferred that brother of mine, my sweet spouse. Oh, I knew it all along. You were not hiding anything from me. It was plain to be seen you regretted your bargain. Shall I send for the gallant Robin to render you this service?" He gave vent to a short and scornful laugh. "You needn't give me any answer to that, Isabeau. It would do no good to ask him. He's too honorable, too holy, to interfere with the workings of nature and the will of God! Or, if you prefer it in plain words, he's too squeamish. But I, the despised husband, the one you've always made the butt of your ill humors, I'm not too honorable. What's more to the point, I'm not squeamish. I have the courage, inside this unknightly body of mine, to face a situation like this squarely."

He paused and changed position slowly in his chair. "Tell me, sweet spouse, shall I send for Robin?"

There was no suggestion of motion in the cheek.

The Comte laughed again and in the same tone. "I thought not. You're looking to me in your final extremity." He remained sunk in uncomfortable thought for some minutes. Then he raised his head and began to speak in sharp tones. "There's one method only. Poison. If I can obtain some—and if my present resolution doesn't desert me—are you ready to have me use it?"

The Comtesse responded with an immediacy which left him with no doubt as to her feelings and wishes. She wanted to die and was prepared for the means he suggested. He cleared his throat protestingly and writhed about in his chair.

"Do you realize what they would do to me if they found out? They wouldn't believe it was by your wish. How could you have let me know, they would ask. When I told them you had conveyed your desire by moving a muscle in your cheek, they would laugh at me. Learned physicians from the University would go on the stand and say it was impossible. My high rank would not save me. They would send me to the executioner as they did Gilles de Retz."

He got to his feet and hobbled to the door. Over his shoulder he said, "I think I must have loved you very much once, Isabeau, or I wouldn't be ready to do this for you now."

He came back some minutes later. Locking the door after him, he walked to a table which lay within the restricted area of vision of his wife. On the top of it he laid a container with the telltale red arrow.

"Yes," he said, nodding. "It's the same, the very bottle of poison they tried to say was used by Jacques Coeur to kill Agnes Sorel. For all I know it was you and that sly wench, Jeanne de Vendôme, who gave it to them in the first place. It was Guillaume Gouffier who handed it to me. As a souvenir, he said, of a laudable but unsuccessful effort."

The Comte raised the container and gave it a shake. "There's something ironic about this," he said. "One might almost believe that fate had delivered it into my hands for this particular use." He looked across at the still figure of the Comtesse. "Well? Have you the stomach for it, my poor spouse? Are you still prepared to make an end of it when this must be the means?"

There was a long pause. Then the muscle in the cheek moved.

"So be it."

And then he became aware that there had been a change in her. The breathing became less stertorous until finally he could not hear it at all. The eyes of the unfortunate woman remained open but he knew that this meant nothing. He walked over to her and felt the part of her face in which the power of motion had been left. It seemed to his exploring fingers no different from the rest. It was cold and stiff to the touch.

He realized that he was holding the container of poison in his other hand. Hastily concealing it in his purse, he ran to the door and unlocked it. He raised his voice and began to shout.

"Hugon! Tuddual! At once! I think your mistress is dead!"

5

"The Pope's fleet may be pounding at the infidels in Constantinople this very moment," said D'Arlay.

Valerie made no response. She was looking ahead and thinking, "In an hour I shall have my little Alain in my arms."

"It was a slap in the face for the King of France when the Pope made Jacques Coeur one of his captains," went on D'Arlay. "And a great feather in the Moneyman's cap. If what we heard was true, that he has been given command of a squadron, he'll have a chance to prove that his genius knows no limits!" He paused and shook his head. "But what a sacrifice he has made! He'll never start in trade again. It's very doubtful if he'll have the strength after he returns from the East to do anything as ambitious as that."

Valerie asked in a musing tone, "Will he have grown much, do you think?"

Her husband looked at her in complete puzzlement for a moment. Then he sensed the direction in which her thoughts had been running, and he smiled and reached over to squeeze her hand in its fine glove of red stamped leather.

"Our son?" he exclaimed in mock indignation. "Of course he has grown. He will have grown out of all recollection!"

"I would know him," declared Valerie, "if he had become six feet tall in our absence! But will he know *us*—his wicked parents who have been away from him for three whole months? Robin, he may think us strangers! It will break my heart if he does."

D'Arlay exclaimed suddenly, "There's the girouette above the entrance tower! See, above that clump of three trees! We're home, my love, we're home again at last!"

With one accord they began to ride faster, rising in their stirrups and staring ahead of them.

"You mustn't be disappointed," said D'Arlay, "if he doesn't remember us at all. You must allow for the fact that our Alain is only a year and three months old. Children have no capacity for remembering at that age."

"I think you're wrong, my Robin. How can we tell what's going on inside those small heads of theirs? Besides, Alain is a special kind of child, a most intelligent child." She shook her head with a sudden shift of mood. "I hoped so much we would come back with full information about his—his family on his mother's side! Three months of traveling about, and searching, and talking to everyone! And what have we to show for it?"

"I'm sure, my love, we've learned everything there is to be found. You know beyond all question of doubt that your father was a brother of Agnes Sorel. I was surprised when that old curmudgeon of an uncle in Berri finally conceded us that much. I don't believe he would have done it if he hadn't been so concerned to convince us that you were illegitimate and in no position to make any claims on his property. That, alone, was worth all the trouble we took."

Valerie sighed. "I hoped so much to learn something more about my poor mother." She lapsed into silence as they began to jog down the incline into the arm of the valley which constituted the domain of Arlay. It was several minutes before she burst out with, "I'm sure it was a mistake to hire that wet nurse for Alain!"

"She seemed a capable young woman. Isn't it a rather late hour to be having misgivings?"

"I distrusted her. She has red hair. And you know, my Robin, that women with red hair never make good nurses."

"I didn't know it."

Valerie gave him the benefit of a serious frown. "They're too much interested in their own looks. And that isn't all. I caught her in one thing before we left and it should have been a warning. Alain needed a purgative and she actually gave it to the poor little child. It's a wonder he survived!"

"And what else, pray, was she to do?" asked her husband, with a blank look.

Valerie shook her head with an air of exasperation. "I thought everyone knew. Medicine must never be given to children. Their stomachs are not strong enough to stand it. But when one is needed, the nurse must drink it herself so the child gets the benefit of it through her milk. . . . I should have been firm and insisted on someone else before we left."

They rode by a thick copse of evergreens from which a flock of migratory birds rose suddenly and wheeled off to the south with more precision than any army of men ever achieved on the march. The road twisted and dipped again and they then found themselves riding across a broad meadow at the far end of which stood the manor house. High stone walls covered with ivy gave it seclusion and protection and its profusion of windows, even in the circular surface of the entrance tower, hinted at comfort within as well as an unusual degree of light.

D'Arlay looked at his wife. "Shall we race? You won the last time and I feel a deep urge to wipe out the disgrace."

Valerie nodded eagerly but the next instant reined in and shook her head. "I'm afraid it wouldn't be wise, Robin," she said.

"You will at any rate permit me to carry you in over the threshold. We've been away so long that it seems proper again."

"And for the same reason I must say another no. I—I am at the moment somewhat heavier, fair husband."

Helion, elevated to the important post of seneschal, came out on the *tête-de-pont* to welcome them. He was dressed in multi-colored magnificence, with one leg pink and one blue and his tabard a crisscross of many shades. "Master! And my lady!" he cried, fairly dancing with excitement. "It is wondrous to see you back from your long travelings. Most fortunately the nurse is here with Master Alain. And if you had only come an hour earlier, my lady, you would have been able to greet a young knight who came seeking you."

Valerie dismounted before asking further enlightenment. "And now, Helion," she said, gathering up her skirts which were long enough to drag a full yard behind her, and unwinding the green silk gorget about her neck, "who was this guest we arrived too late to see?"

"Mistress, I am ashamed to confess that his name has left my mind," said the new seneschal, after a moment's ineffectual effort. "But he came, my lady, at the behest of Godefroy de Monglat who had bested him in a contest of arms."

"Another of them!" Valerie stopped and looked up at her husband with her nose wrinkled to express exasperation. She seemed on the point of stamping her foot. "This is too much! Robin, something must be done."

"This is the third, is it not?"

"The fourth!"

D'Arlay smiled down at her. "It's a great compliment he pays you, my love."

Valerie sighed. "But they're so much trouble! They seem to think it incumbent on them to languish and to ogle me and even to pretend devotion. It has become very tiresome."

"If I don't object, why should you?"

"When I see Froy again, I shall beg him to find someone else as the object of his devotion. I'm a married woman now—and rather unusually devoted to my lord and husband—and so there's something unseemly about these visits of defeated knights." She sighed again. "He was such a clean and honorable boy! What a pity he has had to grow up into a chivalrous knight and make a spectacle of himself in this way!"

Helion said, as though it were an afterthought: "There's someone to see you, my lord. A messenger from Bourges."

"If you'll allow me, my love," said D'Arlay, turning in haste, "I shall see this messenger at once. It will be news about Jacques Coeur."

Valerie joined him in a very few minutes in the Great Hall where he had talked with the messenger. She was carrying her son in her arms and was fairly crowing with delight.

"Robin!" she cried. "He knew me at once, the little pet, and held out his arms to me. He's well and he's fond of his nurse. I'm ashamed now of the things I said about her. Ah, my husband, this son of ours is such a fine and manly little fellow——"

She stopped, becoming aware that something was wrong. D'Arlay's face was white.

"You must be ready for a shock," he said, in a low tone. "Reports have come from the East. Jacques Coeur is dead!"

Valerie cried, "Oh no!" and then subsided into silence as he proceeded with an explanation.

"It has been confirmed that he was put in command of a part of the fleet but it's not known yet whether he got into action with it. It may be that he met a Turkish fleet and was wounded in the fighting. This much only is known for certain, that he was taken ashore on the island of Chios and died there. The island belongs to Genoa and he has been buried in the church of the Cordeliers."

For a long time there was silence and then Valerie said: "This is the end of all his great dreams!"

D'Arlay nodded somberly. "He used to talk to me and explain the things he wanted to do. He was convinced that the world would never grow out of its interest in war and killing until life itself was made more comfortable and interesting and worth while. That was what he was striving to do. . . . I very much fear that in a few years everything he accomplished will be forgotten!"

For some time they sat and looked at each other, too unhappy to put their thoughts into words. Then D'Arlay began to speak again. "The poet Homer was born on the island of Chios—or he died and was buried there. It seems to me most fitting that an epic life like that of Jacques Coeur should end in the same place."

"The King's Moneyman and the saviour of France!" said Valerie, her eyes filling with tears.

A cry of protest rose at this point from the son of the house who had been deposited on the floor. He began to crawl in his father's direction. D'Arlay lifted him in his arms.

"How he has grown, this fellow, since we went away!" he said, with an air of pride. "At this rate he will grow into a taller and stronger man than his father. I suppose"—looking at his wife with a stealthy smile—"we must expect him to become a gallant knight someday. A fine fighting man like your champion, Godefroy. Or even Jacques de Lalain."

She looked up at him indignantly. "This is an ill time for joking, my Robin."

D'Arlay continued in a more serious vein: "Perhaps nature makes a mistake in letting any living creature grow to maturity where the killing instinct develops. Why must a nice, rosy-cheeked boy become a knight with no thoughts in his head but killing other knights or outdrinking them at their wine—and smelling of leather and horse sweat and the gambesons worn too long under their armor!"

"Don't you think," Valerie cried, "that men will come to their senses in time to spare us that?"

D'Arlay shook his head. "Jacques Coeur was the only one who saw the need for change and had the courage to work for it. And now he's dead." He turned to her and smiled. "Still—it will come before long. There will be a change. Men will begin to see the folly of all this. Everything Jacques Coeur wanted—and much more—will come to pass in time. I'm sure of that, my heart."